Travis I. Sivart

# Portals:

## Omnibus: Books 1 - 3

Travis I. Sivart

Portals: Omnibus: Books 1 - 3



ISBN:

**Talk of the Tavern Publishing Group**

# Book One: Beliefs & Black Magics

# Table of Contents

Travis I. Sivart

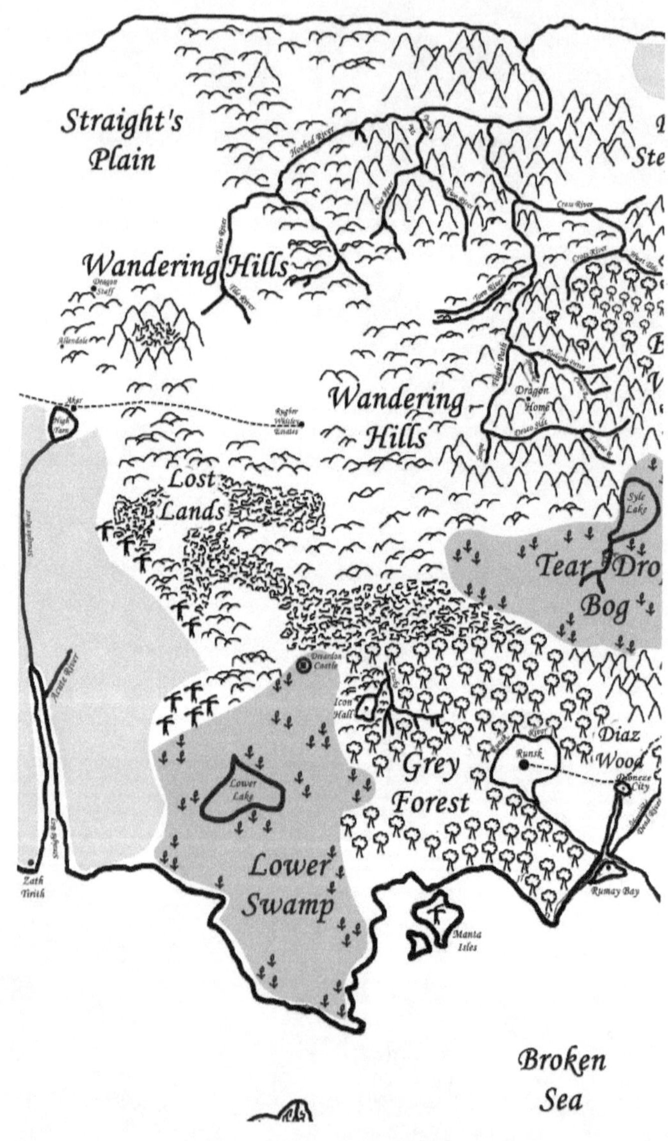
Straight's Plain
Wandering Hills
Wandering Hills
Lost Lands
Tear Drop Bog
Syle Lake
Grey Forest
Diaz Wood
Lower Lake
Lower Swamp
Manta Isles
Broken Sea
Zath Tirith
Runsk
Rumay Bay
Dragon Home
Dragon Staff
Allendale
High Tarn
Akar
Straight River
Acute River
Straight Bay
Hooked River
Craw River
Crati River
Manta Isles
Rumay Bay

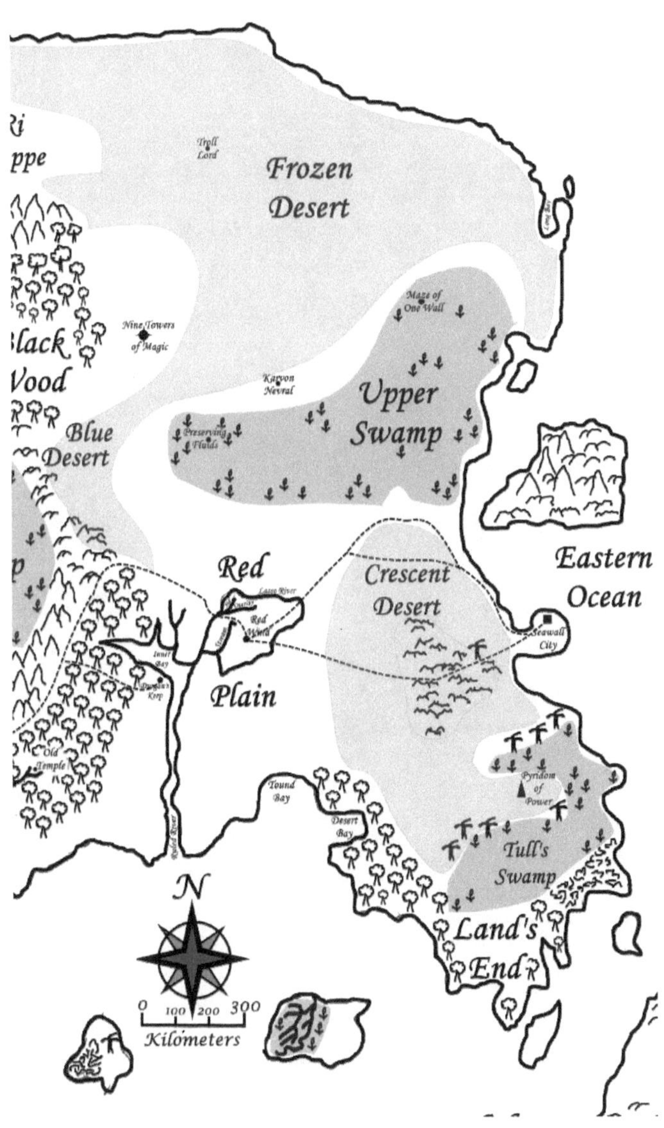

Troll Lord
Frozen Desert
Maze of One Wall
Nine Towers of Magic
Black Wood
Blue Desert
Karyon Nevral
Preserving Fluids
Upper Swamp
Eastern Ocean
Red
Lasso River
Crusta
Red World
Inner Bay
Dragon's Keep
Plain
Crescent Desert
Seawall City
Old Temple
Wald River
Tound Bay
Desert Bay
Pyridom of Power
Tull's Swamp
Land's End
N
0  100  200  300
Kilometers

Dedication

To those that seek different places and different worlds.

## Prologue

"So, you're bringing in zombies to save the world?" PepperGarten asked Jack.

"No," Jack shook his head, "I'm just bringing a few people here at the moment of their death."

"And putting them into the body of someone else who just died, right?" PepperGarten slid his goopy green smoothy closer and ran it in a figure eight on the bar top. "Sounds like necromancy."

"It's not, and you know it." Jack sighed. "It's not much different from what you went through, except it's easier to bring over their essence instead of their physical body."

"Soul, Jack, or spirit," the skinny, wrinkled old man lifted his drink, poking at something brown and withered in it with a bony finger. "You can say it. Not everything needs to be all science. You can't even explain how this hotel of yours jumps through time and dimensions—because it's impossible."

Jack looked around the Traveller's Inn, smiling softly. "I know how it does it, but don't have the words to describe it."

"It's magic!" shouted Wanderly, a diminutive man standing on a bench in a booth across the room. "I was the one who turned on the engine that allowed this entire place to become sentient!"

"Did you though?" barked the muscular man—Nomed—across from Wanderly with a laugh.

"Would you like to know what I think, sir?" asked the bartender, an automaton with a glass dome where his head belonged.

Jack turned from the two in the booth to look at Cogsley, the one being in the establishment that best understood how the inn travelled. He took in the tux and tails, the bow tie, and the top hat sitting at a jaunty angle on top of the lightbulb-like cranium of the construct and smiled.

"Cogsley," Jack said, "if I want your thoughts on something, I'll wait…and you'll tell me whether or not I want to hear them."

"Droll, sir," Cogsley drawled with the affection of an upper crust drawl, "very droll. But since you insist I share my wisdom, against my will or yours, I will merely say…the inn does this because of your silly drive to help your fellow man and the world as a whole. It has sought out, and linked up, with your own innate abilities to create the perfect storm of opportunity. It—the Inn, that is—does nothing except to take advantage of the potential happenstance triggered by your actions."

"That makes no sense, you know that, right?" PepperGarten cackled. "But, PepperGarten likes it!"

The old man leaned over the bar and slapped the golem on the upper arm, still chuckling. Wiping at the line of green goo on his upper lip, PepperGarten went on.

"So, Jack, who are you bringing over to this side this time?" the old man asked. "PepperGarten hopes they aren't like the last time. That was a disaster!"

"I don't think they will be," Jack shook his head, tapping two fingers on the bar to indicate he wanted a drink. "I've picked out three good people, all who help others without thinking…"

Jack trailed off, watching Cogsley pour two fingers of whiskey into a short, thick glass. The amber liquid washed up the sides of the vessel, leaving a receding arc. Jack lifted the glass and held it up to the people in the common room.

"One is a woman of faith, who's lost to her god." he said. "She will need to find herself before she can find the ability to help others again. She's broken in the way we break ourselves."

Jack looked across the common room, which was empty except for Nomed, Wanderly, PepperGarten, Cogsley, and himself. He hoisted his glass and tossed back the golden contents. The others followed his example.

Setting the glass down with a hard thunk, he tapped it with two fingers. Cogsley leaned over to pour another finger of whiskey.

"The second is a person who always gave to everyone but themselves." Jack raised his newly refilled drink. "They will be the heart of the trio, I think. And no matter how difficult things get, I think this will be easier than most things they've dealt with in their long life."

He raised the glass again, toasting, then drinking. Nomed eyed him over the rim of his gin, and Wanderly slurped at his ale. PepperGarten took a pull from his pint glass, thick, dark green liquid dribbling from the corners of his mouth and making its way through his wispy beard to drip from his chin.

Setting the glass on the bar, Jack covered the top to indicate he didn't want a refill. Turning back to the room, he met each person's eyes and stood up.

Cogsley tilted the bottle, pouring a triple into the glass behind Jack, the wire within his transparent dome flickering.

"The third of the triad," Jack continued, "has never known what it is to be driven by his own goals. He's probably the most challenged of the bunch, because he doesn't realize he's been missing anything. But I think he'll also be the one to have the most influence on change, but in more subtle ways than the others."

"Toast!" Wanderly cheered, raising his mug.

Jack felt a glass pushed into his hand and raised it. He threw it back, gasping and choking on the triple shot.

"Cogsley!" Jack sputtered. "I said I was done! I did the hand thing, covered the glass. You know what that means!"

"Of course, sir," Cogsley drawled. "My mistake, but if I may be so bold, perhaps you need to take a moment and unwind a bit. You are a bit…tight. And I know what it is to have a gear or spring a bit too wound. It can be a grievous thing when it releases. Best you do it among friends."

"Jack, focus!" PepperGarten grinned, his chin stained dark green like he'd been sucking face with a romantically inclined stalk of broccoli. "Why do we care about these people? You're bringing in ghosts to save the world, and that's sounds stupid."

"No," Jack breathed, waving his hand absently and watching it, "I'm giving them a second chance. Don't you get it, PepperGarten? All of you? Don't you see? I'm letting three people who are on death's door have a second chance. A chance to save themselves, and help a world where they don't feel the pressures of their self-imposed rules and expectations of what they consider the normal world?"

"I get it," Wanderly said, unusually sober, "you're letting them become more than they could in their reality by giving them a fresh start. Kinda like you did for each one of us here."

Jack stared at the small man, then nodded slowly.

## Chapter 1

Torrence fell to his knees in the snow, vomiting onto a spill of his own blood. One arm wrapped across his midsection, and the other was on the pommel of his massive two-handed blade. He supported his weight with the hand on the weapon, stopping himself from falling face first into the muck and mess between his legs.

Covered in gore, chunks of flesh and sinew decorated the blade, and a third of the sword lay embedded in the icy loam of the ground.

Around the weapon lay a half dozen bodies of gnarled men with hyena-like heads. The bodies were hacked and torn, heads crushed, and limbs twisted. More bloody weapons laid around them—broken, rusted, and chipped.

"That'll give you tetanus," Torrence said to no one, "I wouldn't want to get cut by one of those."

But one of those had cut him.

His mind deposited the information into his thoughts, like suddenly remembering where he'd put his keys, or that he had a doctor's appointment on Tuesday. Which he didn't. He'd been driving home from one when he hit the patch of ice.

"That's right," Torrence spoke again, his white fur cloak whipping around him and the wind picking up on the frozen shelf of the mountainside, "I was driving home."

Torrence pushed to his feet, using the sword to leverage himself up. Without thinking about it, he bent and wiped the blade along the still warm corpse of the creature—gnohl, his memory supplied—that he'd killed moments before. The body steamed in the air of the frozen north, and Torrence looked out across the countryside.

He was in the easternmost portion of Ri Steppe, on the western edge of the Frozen Desert. Looking to the south, he could see the Black Wood, a haunted forest contaminated by mages and wizards and sorcerers who'd once occupied the Nine Towers of Magic on its southeastern border.

"What the hell does all that mean?" Torrence asked, his memories gently blanketing him with the information.

It was like remembering a birthday party from your childhood that you didn't even know you'd forgotten. You knew it to be true, but it just hadn't been in your head at all before it was in your head. It wasn't a lost memory that makes you gasp when it showed up again. It was one of those that made you throw up your hand and exclaim, 'Oh yeah!' as you smiled.

The view in front of him, as well as the scene of carnage at his feet, conflicted with the last memory he had of what he'd been doing before thirty seconds ago.

His arm was still across his midsection, covering the vicious wound where a gnohl had almost disemboweled him. A dozen of the creatures had been in on the attack.

They'd dropped stones from above as he trudged through the knee-deep snow. The rocks had fallen around him, and he'd reacted out of instinct, bounding one way and bouncing another to avoid being hit by the makeshift avalanche.

He remembered thinking it was a pemtie idea (pemtie; the word broke his train of thought; he knew it through his body, not his own mind, as stupid or ignorant), and that their quarry—which was him—had a chance of being knocked off the side of the mountain and plummeting far down into the valley below, thus removing the chance for his attackers to loot, or eat, their target.

Then they'd attacked, swarming from hiding places, a half dozen with swords or wicked, twisted daggers. They'd charged him; one being taken out by the final melon-sized stone thrown from above.

The creature had fallen—issuing a brief scream that ended when its head was crushed at the first contact with the mountain side—and then plummeted into the mists below. Torrence had thought nothing else of that one, because it was so far down that even the sound of the body crunching as it hit the ground was lost in the fall's distance.

The others had come towards him, jabbing with their blades, but keeping a distance between them and him. He figured out why as soon as the arrows began coming down from above.

He'd charged the closest attacker—which his current thoughts wanted to call a monster—and used it as a shield. The creature had taken three arrows to the chest before it went limp and lifeless. Torrence had discarded it over the side of the mountain.

As this scene replayed in Torrence's head, he struggled with it because he also had a very different set of experiences in his recent memory.

He had gone to the doctor's, driving himself using the newly installed hand controls in the minivan. It had been nerve-racking, and his thoughts had kept going back to the fateful day where he had lost his ability to stand and walk, his father, and so much all in one car accident. An accident that people told him was no one's fault, just a patch of ice, and that he shouldn't feel guilty about what happened. These things happen, they said.

The chuz they did.

There was another word that had changed, chuz, when he had meant chuz. No, not chuz, chuz. His brain kept translating the loose meaning of his swear words to what his body knew.

His thoughts went back to where they'd been, the difference between the two words fading like a light breeze, unnoticed.

Torrence had been sixteen, and a junior in high school. He was doing well in track and field, football, and soccer, as well as being the favorite of many of the girls. He had only had his real license, as opposed to his learner's permit, for three months when it happened.

A patch of ice, loss of control, a tumbling sensation that included a sharp snapping sound from behind him, and he never heard his father's voice again after those last shouts of panic. He also never walked again.

That meant no more sports, no more girls, no more success, no more friends. He'd been broken, inside and out, completely destroyed.

He'd finished school, mostly at home, through new online courses that were offered in 'extenuating" circumstances.

But today, he'd fought those memories. He'd turned the app on his phone up, blasting music into the small minivan, donated and converted for his use. He sang along, driving and gripping the steering wheel in a white-knuckled grip, and made it safely to his physical therapy appointment.

Though he'd never walk and would be restricted to a wheelchair for the rest of his life, the doctor assured him he was doing well. It was a forty-five-minute drive, a thirty-minute wait; all for four minutes with a nurse checking his vitals, and then three minutes with a doctor that barely looked up from his notes.

The memory jumped, blending with the anger and bitterness of what he was given, what was done to him.

Shunting the thoughts away, he focused on the now, on the present, as he was taught to do when talking to his therapist.

The world lurched. It wasn't *his* world. He was on a mountainside, high above a forest in one direction and plains in another.

This wasn't right.

Where was his car? He had hit the ice, and then he was here.

He stared into the distance, his mind going blank, becoming overwhelmed. The treetops of the forest to the south were still mostly green, but just beginning to get golden, orange, and rust highlights as autumn set in. The snows in the mountains were descending, and in a month or two, it would cover the lands.

Torrence's body took over.

He looked down, moving his arm from the wound he'd received a few minutes ago that ran across his abdomen. It was a bright pink puckered scar now, like he'd visited a healer that wasn't an elder or adept, but instead was just an acolyte that did their best. He shrugged and smiled. At least he wasn't dead.

He lifted his sword, checked to make sure it was clean, swung it overhead with his right hand, caught the tip with his left, and guided it to the leather scabbard on his back. It slid into place effortlessly.

Looking down, he knelt beside the dead creatures and began scavenging whatever he thought would be useful. Rummaging through the gnohls' pouches, he pulled various items out, looked at them and either tucked them into his own pouches, or his knapsack, or tossed them to the side.

He stowed a piece of charcoal, a silver thimble, a bone carving of a bear, and a few other items. Most things were discarded, including stale chunks of bread and crumbly, moldy cheese, rust-pocked knives, and various and sundry odds and ends. The few coins, silver peks and copper fleks, were kept. He held one deep blue gemstone up to the setting sun before dropping it into the same pouch as the coins.

The waning day made him pause. He had to move. He'd been seeking shelter—and keeping an eye out for game that he could use for a meal—when he was attacked. He'd hoped to make the foothills of the mountain before it got too late. He'd seen the glint of sunlight off a stream and had been heading for that, knowing that local fauna would come to it to drink.

Reaching over to a cooling form of a gnohl, he jerked the primitive bow from its massive paw, and wrangled the quiver with a dozen and half rough arrows in it from the creature's back.

Standing, Torrence moved forward. Loping down the path in long strides, letting gravity help him along so he didn't have to put in as much effort, he quickly descended.

He knew he wouldn't reach the bottom before dark, but maybe he could get lucky and hunt on the run.

Torrence's mind picked back up, but cautiously and delicately, not wanting to interrupt the automatic actions of what seemed to be his body now.

He raised his hands, and looked at them—still leaping from the path, to the side of a hillock, to a raised knoll, bounding downward towards his destination in the distance—and saw they were different from his normal mocha-colored skin. These were a brown, but with a tinge of red mixed in. Torrence could feel his long, silky hair bouncing in its braid on his shoulders, instead of his usual tight knit curls.

He was taller than before, and wider, and the weight of it felt different. He thought about that for a moment and suddenly he was in full control of this body.

His feet stumbled under the unfamiliar balance of muscle and height, and he tripped. He went down hard, turning to one side, landing on his shoulder, and sliding two meters in a rain of gravel and sand.

Mentally, Torrence pulled his non-existent hands back from the controls.

The body stood without his help, and he heard a deep, throaty laugh come from it. The head dipped down, the hands sweeping across taut muscles, looking for injury. The knapsack shifted on his back, atop the cloak and sword, and his belt showed his two pouches still attached. The heavy grey woolen shirt had torn, but the woolen pants and leather boots were still in reasonable condition.

He moved forward again, with that easy mountain goat gait, and assured agility that came without thought.

Torrence realized he was in a body. Now, that seemed like an obvious conclusion, but it was more than that. He was in a different body, a body that had an instinctual set of skills. This body took over when he wasn't specifically trying to do anything, and a simple idea of what he wanted to accomplish was suggested, rather than pushed or forced.

He wasn't himself, in a very literal way. He was someone else. Someone who was huge, muscled, and fit. Maybe this was what his body would have been like if he hadn't been in the car accident?

Torrence searched for a mind, any thought that wasn't his own.

He found nothing.

Where was he?

Northeastern Teurone, memories answered, east of the Wandering Hills and Mountains, south of the Ri Steppes, west of the Frozen Desert, and north of the Black Wood.

Torrence fainted in his new head, but the body kept going.

## Chapter 2

The Kid picked himself up from the dust of the alley and spun to face his pursuers. His legs should have been broken from the four-story jump he'd made, and he knew he'd blacked out, at least for a moment.

He was a new man, though, and only seconds had passed since he'd jumped. It was like a dream as this new consciousness settled over him, like a new skin over his seventeen-year-old frame.

The bones of his calves knit back together, a surge of otherworldly energy filling his body. With a rush of mixed emotions—from disbelief to wonder, bitterness to hope, and acceptance of the inevitable of the elderly to the endless possibilities of youth—the Kid rose up and smiled.

He, and she, didn't have to die today.

This was the delight of a dream that doesn't feel like a dream, but instead is real. It was the moment most people always vaguely wish for, but never really expect to happen. It was that hope of winning the lottery, getting your dream promotion handed to you, or that other person saying yes to a life and future by your side.

But it was encapsulated by the Kid standing up in an alley.

Fifteen deadly assassins were after him. Rappelling down the sides of the buildings on the thin silk cords of their professions, or just dropping down from windowsill to windowsill until they reached the ground. But that didn't matter anymore. The Kid smiled, and let out a whoop that even a blind adversary could track him with.

"Talley ho, the game is afoot, Watson!" he shouted.

The Kid ran, joy in every stride, and the thrill of being alive in every action. Laughter, delight, and pure, unadulterated happiness flooded through everything the Kid did.

"Run, run, run as fast as you can," the Kid shouted, "you'll never catch me, I'm the gingerbread man. I ran from the baker and his wife, too. You'll never catch me, not any of you."

He laughed, turning the corner into the main marketplace of Durgan's Keep, skidding around a fruit cart and into the flow of foot traffic of the evening shopping crowd.

Fifteen men and women poured into the street after the Kid. They barreled into merchants and knocked over shoppers, knives gleaming as they ran after the lithe youth.

People dove out of the way, and shrill whistles of the city watch rose in the distance.

The Kid reached a city square, a three-meter-across well on a raised dais in the center, and turned to face his foes. Twin daggers appeared in his hands without him even thinking about it.

The assassins ran into the area, spreading out to cover any escape the Kid may consider. The primary streets, set at the compass points, had two people in front of each of them, and the alleys, at the secondary compass points, had one each.

"This is another fine mess I've gotten myself into, Stanley," the Kid said, laughing, and let his twin blades fly.

One assassin stumbled backwards, clutching at his bloody throat. Another fell forward, a blade protruding from her chest.

The Kid laughed again and leapt from the well into the thinning crowd towards his fallen foes.

Smiling into their fading eyes, the Kid snatched his and their weapons up, crouched and slicing their money pouches free, and dropped them into his own.

The city watch pushed into the building-made valley, cutting their way through the assassins at the edges of the square, allowing the responsible citizens a getaway route. A dozen guards replaced the assassins.

The remaining score of people that weren't involved escaped through the openings made by the patrol, and the guards—stout, tall, and broad-shouldered—formed a human barrier between the Kid and the ways out.

The Kid remembered tales, not from his own memory, but from the memory of the body he now inhabited, tales of the days before the Talisman—the comet that had dominated the sky for so long, raining down its mystical emanations and increasing the power of necromancers and summoners everywhere—of when Durgan's Keep wasn't a refuge for people attempting to get away from the demons to the southeast, or the constant trickling influx of undead from the west.

Once upon a time, Durgan's Keep was home to adventurers and merchants alike. Founded by an intrepid rokairn, Durgan, he laid out plans and sectioned off an area of wilderness to create a balanced trade town that grew into a fortified capital of the eastern part of the continent. His aeifain and other companions each put in their thoughts about what their own race would like in a section of town, and after twenty years of construction, Durgan's Keep was born.

The demon invasion of almost a hundred years ago— long before the Talisman—as maniacal beings from other dimensions flooded out of Land's End to the southeast, was the herald of change. It had started a series of events that included the now infamous necromancer, Rondarius the Foul, escaping from his multiple-century-long imprisonment.

Then, when the Talisman stopped in the sky and stayed, hanging over the land for decades, everything went to shit.

The Kid hadn't been around for that, in either form.

That thought made the person at the core of the Kid pause and consider. But then the rush of the guards and assassins allowed the Kid to stop thinking and throw himself into action.

He ran forward and leapt into the air. His feet caught nothing, but he continued to rise. The guards beneath his boots, bent suddenly as if they had been trampled over, though the Kid's boots were almost a meter above their heads.

The Kid flipped, spinning heels over head through the air and catching onto the walnut windowsill of a third-story apartment.

The surrounding architecture reminded the person inside the Kid of the Tudor era of their own world. Dark wood boxing in and slashing across walls, beige plasterwork was the dominant style. A fair amount of stonework balanced it, showing the craftsmanship of the rokairn builders of Durgan's Keep.

Pulling himself up, the Kid saw a woman's face with her mouth in a moue of surprise staring out the window at him. With a wave of his hand, he drew on the energy of his mind and touched hers.

"Hocus Pocus, baby," the Kid let out a cat-like yowl, and changed.

The woman now saw a cat, struggling outside her window, trying to pull itself up and angry people below pointed at it with raised crossbows and readied throwing blades.

The woman reached forward and shoved the window open, before scrambling backwards to avoid the flurry of daggers that struck the window frame outside and the bolts that hit the ceiling within.

She saw the cat leap inside, yowling, as the Kid ran past her, shouting a thank you to the woman.

He ran through her sitting room, threw open the door to the hall, and stopped to listen. Angry voices came up from below, and the sound of booted feet on the stairs echoed hollowly.

The Kid ran up the last flight of stairs. A square opening showed the sky outside of the stairwell. He clambered out of the window frame at the top of the stairs. His fingers grabbed unseen holds, and he pulled himself up the outside of the building. Looking down into the alley ten meters below, the Kid saw a tall, thin assassin with carrot orange hair leaning against the wall with his arms crossed, watching him climb with a dull disinterest.

It was Mezk the Damned. Well known for his pact with demons, people whispered he'd agreed to let them have his soul when he died, but he would never die of violence or injury.

*How could I know this about someone I've never seen?* The Kid thought, and his grip on the wall slipped, and he fell.

He caught himself on the window he'd climbed out of, and pulled himself upward, focusing on what he was doing, his heart pounding, rather than random thoughts about what he should and shouldn't know.

Once he gained the rooftop, he was on his way to escape. Using his magics, he pushed himself with each leap, allowing him to jump spaces two or three times wider than a normal thief could jump. With a nod and a wave, people forgot he'd just passed their window, or just didn't see him at all.

Life was grand.

Or at least it was until he settled on top of the peaked roof of a Church of Jonath. Sitting with his back to the warm chimney, his legs bent, and his butt resting on the slate shingles of the stout building, the Kid wondered about his death.

"Jonath's trident," he swore, using a phrase from the memory of his body.

He knew he'd died. He'd fallen four stories off a roof, landed on his feet, and broke both legs. Falling backwards, he'd caved in the back of his head in the cobblestone alley. But here he was, alive and well, but not the same as he was before.

He also knew that his other body, in a different world, laying in a bed, dying of stage four cancer.

He knew he had all his skills, all his knowledge, and even his memories for the most part, but he also had more. He had a second set of skills, knowledge, and memories.

These other memories were foreign, but at the same time felt more real than the roof on which he sat. They held decades of life; including a husband who'd left her; a son who died in a coma of liver failure because of alcohol poisoning when he was just a month from graduating college with a doctorate; and a plethora of skills, ranging from cooking fried foods to knitting to how to write a resume in Microsoft Word.

The Kid remembered he was once been called Jen, but that was a world away, even a lifetime away. None of that mattered anymore. He was here, and he was loving life.

*No more*, he thought, pushing any other memories to the side. He was the Kid now, and belonged here. This was his body now, and this was his world. And he would live life to the fullest this time. No more worrying about what was right or proper, or what the boss thought of her dress, or if that man in the street wanted to hurt her for the couple of dollars in her purse.

She would miss Cuddles, her Pomeranian, but the nurses would see to the dog.

He would, the Kid chided himself. He would. He would no longer be she who was, instead he would be him.

The strange thought swirled and bumped around the Kid's head. With a chuckle and shrug, he brushed the thought aside.

Standing up, he looked across the rooftops, watching twilight settle in. The low hanging cloud of smoke from wood fires cooking dinner and warming houses in the late evening filled the sky just thirty meters above the city.

He had been on a job, but it had been lost in translation.

"Que sera, sera," the Kid chuckled again, "whatever will be, will be, the future's not ours to see."

With a quick twirl, the Kid straightened up and ran for the edge of the rooftop, threw himself off, grabbed a canvas awning below to pull himself to it, bounced off it, and flipped to the street below.

Why didn't he ever think of doing things like that before tonight, he wondered as he sauntered up the street, happily whistling.

## Chapter 3

Esperanza staggered backwards, away from the crowd of strangers, reaching for her adoringly. They were all talking at once, some weeping, some screaming, and others just whispering. But all seemed grateful to her, and the words 'miracle worker' were being repeated over and over.

The dark-haired woman tripped over the hem of her long robe, her hands flying up as she fell backwards. She landed hard on her butt.

Holding her hands out in front of her, her sleeves sliding up her arms and pooling in the crook of her elbows, she stared at the blotches of grey and brown fading from her skin. Swollen and puffy flesh shrunk as she watched, veins receded to normal sizes, and capillaries healed as bruises disappeared under her gaze.

A second set of impulses, almost thoughts, flooded her mind, pushing the fear and surprise aside. They told her of the power of Latress, goddess of wind, weather, and wisdom. Mother of the twin gods, Torr and Tarra, and wife of the god of justice and earth, Jonath.

The thoughts told her of the favor of the goddess, and how it had blessed her and would shelter and protect her, and how it had guided her in healing the hundreds of sick people in this village, saving them and their children from being wiped out by the plague.

Esperanza shoved the thoughts away, pushed at that other identity, and screamed, tearing at her own hair, pulling a fistful out with each hand.

The crowd stopped. They stared at her uncertainly, not sure what to do.

One middle-aged woman stepped forward, holding out a hand, and said something in a language that Esperanza thought she should comprehend. But it wasn't English or Spanish, and though she felt she knew it, her mind blocked out any understanding because it was impossible.

The woman approached like most people approached a scared and wounded animal; cautious, slowly, speaking gently, and making comforting noises between words.

The woman came close enough to touch Esperanza and knelt as she took the younger woman's hands into her own.

Esperanza fainted.

Esperanza woke in a small room. She put a hand above her head, and it bumped a wall before she could even extend her arm all the way. She could see the wall at the foot of the bed by the faint light from the dim fire in the ceramic chiminea that stood beside the door, to her left and barely more than an arm's length away. Smoke curled from the top of it, drawn out of a hole in the mud wall. Directly across from the door was the only window in the room. Woven reeds of twisted branches created a shutter placed over the opening, then covered with a thicker blanket to keep the chill outside, and the heat inside.

Esperanza ran her fingers along the wall beside the bed, on her right. Under her hands, she could feel fibrous plants mixed into the clay to help give the wall strength. The whole place smelled faintly of must and dung, the latter from the dried horse manure that burned in the chiminea.

Rolling onto her left side on the burlap mattress filled with reeds, Esperanza saw her few possessions on a table of woven branches. It held the holy symbol of Latress, a gusting cloud with seven stars around it. Subtle etching seemed to show a face within the cloud. Beside it was her herb pouch on its thin leather belt, her neatly folded robe, a few hair combs, and a small mortar and pestle.

And a small knife in a sheath.

She picked up the blade and drew it from the holder. She stared at it.

She had been ending her life, and now she was here. This knife held her eyes as it moved along her forearm and wrist, as if of its own volition. It scratched her skin, leaving a white line in the flesh.

"Latress's Breath protect me," she muttered, wondering at the words she uttered.

That wasn't *her* God, but it felt like it was the one watching over her right now.

A rough curtain hung in the doorway and the smell of something cooking drifted from the other room. A woman's voice sang a gentle lullaby, more humming than singing, and the sound of wooden bowls and utensils clunked against each other.

The sounds stopped when Esperanza sat up, the bed creaking and rustling underneath her.

"Hello?" the woman's voice said from the other side of the curtain.

Esperanza could see a form through the opening between the wall and the hanging barrier. It looked up and to one side, giving her guest the courtesy of privacy.

"No," Esperanza muttered.

"Oh, you're awake," the woman pushed through the curtain and smiled down at her guest, "maybe you'd like to freshen up?"

The woman had a coarse clay pitcher and large bowl in her hands, and she set them on the small table beside the bed. She pulled a rough cloth, tucked into her apron strings, out and set it beside the other things.

"There's a chamber pot and scrapers under the table," the woman smiled down at her, "and just come on out when you're done."

Esperanza came out ten minutes later, looking traumatized.

The room she stepped into wasn't much bigger than the bedroom, and only had one door that presumably led to the outside.

The woman looked up from her squatting position in front of a fireplace. She was stirring some sort of stew in a ceramic pot that sat directly on the hot coals of the fire.

The rest of the room was plain. A table with two chairs sat on one side of the fire, and a low wooden bench covered with blankets was on the other side. Esperanza guessed this served as a couch, but also the woman's bed, while Esperanza was her guest.

Directly across from the small knee-high hearth, which was a brick and mud affair, was what Esperanza guessed was the kitchen. It wasn't more than a few shelves set into the mud walls with supplies neatly lining them.

"Everything come out okay?" her hostess asked, smiling and showing a mouth with missing, broken, and brown teeth.

Esperanza just stared at her as if she hadn't understood the words coming out of the woman's mouth.

"Well," the woman stood, "I'm guessing it did, otherwise you wouldn't be out here. I'm Rose, by the way. I thought you may have remembered it, but considering everything you've just gone through, it must have addled you."

Rose moved to get wooden bowls from the kitchen area, and Esperanza looked at the woman.

Rose was younger than Esperanza originally thought, at least twenty years younger, and probably in her mid-thirties, which would make the woman less than ten years older than herself. Rose must've had a hard life, and was slightly bent as she moved about the house, her grey streaked hair in a tight bun on her head held by a blue ribbon, and her knuckles swollen and red from hard work.

The decor in the house was somewhere between simple and nonexistent. Curtains of faded yellow hung over the one shuttered window, and a painted urn with a large chip from it stood on the table to hold drinking water. Wreaths and braids of dry herbs hung from the ceiling.

Rose squatted next to the hearth to spoon out some stew into two shallow bowls. She stood, groaning, and brought the bowls to the table and set them down. Taking two ceramic cups from the shelf, she set them on the table also, and filled the vessels with cloudy water from the painted urn.

"Sorry, we don't have no beer," Rose smiled sheepishly, showing her broken teeth, "or any meat with all the animals dying. Hard to make these things when so many in the village were too sick to work, or died from the plague. But that'll all be changing now that you've fixed things."

Esperanza thought that the woman would be pretty if she wasn't raised in a third-world country. Then she wondered how she'd gotten to this place, and why everyone spoke English here.

But it wasn't English, nagged some logic in the back of her head. She could understand Rose, and all the other villagers earlier, with no issue. But it wasn't any language that she knew, except her brain did know it. Like a reflex, it just caught the words, and she knew the meaning with absolute clarity.

"Come on, then," Rose waved at her, then gestured to the second chair, "you gotta eat, right? Even a priestess needs to eat, at least as far as I know."

Esperanza moved to the chair, pulled it out, and sat. It was a high ladder-back wooden chair with a woven straw seat, and surprisingly comfortable.

Rose unwrapped a loaf of dark bread, tore a hunk from it, and set it on the table in front of Esperanza's bowl. She repeated the process for herself before wrapping the bread back up and setting it aside.

The bowls were small, and the hunk of bread was about as large as your average dinner roll. Looking around, Esperanza realized that this was everything they had to eat, and it was probably more than most of the villagers had on their tables tonight.

That was when Esperanza realized she hadn't seen anyone who was overweight here. She'd seen people who were sickly thin, perhaps because of the illness the village had suffered, or perhaps because of the food shortage Rose mentioned. It could've been a combination of the two.

"Latress's rains bless this food," the words came out unbidden by her conscious thoughts, "and nourish us…"

Esperanza stopped, looking up at her hostess, who was smiling, then looked back down.

Esperanza picked up her wooden spoon, dipped it into the dark brown broth in the bowl, fished out a chunk of potato, and raised to her mouth. Sniffing without realizing she was doing it; she smelled the pungent aroma of peat moss. That was the musty smell from earlier also, she realized.

With the tip of her tongue, she tasted the stew, if you wanted to call it that. It was bland and thin, but had a faint meaty flavor of mushrooms.

Rose was watching her expectantly, smiling supportively as she ate. When the woman saw Esperanza looking back at her, Rose raised her spoon in a toast and then slurped her broth from it. Esperanza looked at the woman's shallow bowl and saw that there were no potatoes in it.

Esperanza remembered her grandmother, the woman who had raised her. The woman had only spoken Spanish, but found a way to get a job and keep food on the table, clothes on Esperanza's back, and the water and power on. And she always made sure that Esperanza had a nice dress, new shoes, and the portion of dinner that had meat.

When Esperanza questioned her grandmother why she never had any meat, her grandmother explained that it was too hard for her to chew, and she didn't want any. When Esperanza was older, years after her grandmother had died, she'd realized the truth. The woman always made sure her granddaughter had the best that she could give her, even if it meant that her grandmother went without.

Rose, sipping at her broth and watching Esperanza with her potato-laden spoon, suddenly reminded Esperanza of her grandmother.

Esperanza smiled, put the potato in her mouth with the wash of broth, chewed, made appreciative noises, and nodded at Rose.

Within minutes, the two had finished the meal. Esperanza wanted a glass of water to rinse the dirt from her teeth—the water from the urn was clouded with it—but she only showed appreciation.

Rose chatted as she cleaned up, telling her guest how everyone was doing everything she'd taught them, even boiling water before drinking it, washing things twice, and cleaning their hands before eating or sleeping.

Considering the hanging herbs, and things Rose said about teaching the villagers specific things, Esperanza had concluded that Rose must be something like the village's wise woman. And the woman did seem to care about everyone's well-being.

Something thudded against the shutter from outside, and the smell of smoldering flame rose. Through the cracks in the shutters and the front door, they could see dancing orange light. Shouts began filling the night, and within seconds screams followed them.

Rose rushed to the door and pulled it open. Over her shoulder, Esperanza could see the slow, shambling forms of the walking dead.

"Give us the damned witch," a deep voice boomed, "or I promise each and every man, woman, and child in this village will join my rotting army."

Rose looked back at Esperanza over her shoulder.

"Bring out the priestess of Latress or everyone dies," the man's voice shouted, louder and closer this time, "and then will be brought back from the dead to serve me for eternity."

## Chapter 4

Torrence crouched in the underbrush, bow held across his bent knees, with the quiver at his feet. He watched the slave train through the thicket of thorny bushes. The guards were setting up camp for the night, shouting at the chained prisoners to build campfires and other menial tasks.

The banner on a staff showed the slaver's mark and the caravan's personal symbol, a wolf head in a red circle. This was the Blood Sun Wolf slavers then, and memories of stories of their trade floated through Torrence's head. They were known for selling to anyone, for any purpose, and weren't known for their kindness or quality of stock.

Though part of him knew that slavery was common since the Downfall, he wasn't really on speaking terms with that part of him. Being in this body was like moving into someone else's house moments after they'd left it.

Things were just lying around, waiting to be used. Thoughts, memories, and innate skills honed through years of practice. Like how he'd heard the wagons, and before he realized what he was doing, he'd hidden in the underbrush. Or like last night, he'd drawn and nocked an arrow, raised the bow, fired, and killed a rabbit before he even knew he'd moved. Instincts took over if he relaxed and just knew what he wanted to do.

Slavery wasn't cool though, everyone knew that. He'd learned about it in school and heard about it all his life. Not that he'd ever known, met, or even heard of someone who'd been a slave during his lifetime; but he did know that his ancestors had been slaves.

The bottom line was that you can't own another person. He didn't even like dudes or chicks who were overly possessive of their other half, hanging all over them and blocking other people from talking or hanging out with them. He didn't like bosses that treated employees like crap, and he really didn't like bullies.

Torrence sometimes wondered if some of the kids, when he was in high school, had thought he'd been a bully. He didn't think so, though. He knew he'd picked on a few kids, but they'd practically begged for attention, and all in the wrong ways. The spazzes and freaks that liked to talk shit when they should have just shut up.

But it wasn't like he beat them up. That would've been ridiculous. Usually, they went away with a cross-armed stare, or a little verbal encouragement. And he did have that nerd friend back in the day. He'd looked out for the kid because he was okay. He didn't talk shit, even though he was smart.

After the accident, Torrence had dealt with the other side of the coin on occasion. Never directly, no one would ever pick on someone in a wheelchair where others could see. But sometimes, he heard the people laughing. Or he'd see them notice him as he was approaching a door, and they'd let it close even though he was almost to it. People ignored him more than anything, acted like they didn't see him trying to get something off a high shelf at the grocery. And the ones that did and helped him often had a look of pity.

Torrence didn't know which one bugged him more.

*Why can't people just chill the chuz out, and be cool?* He thought. *Treat others decently, without making it feel like some heroic act of kindness. Was that really so hard?*

"Work harder," a harsh voice yelled, "we don't want to get caught by the night without fires set, you dirty lazy bastards!"

"Yes, Master Dropsum." The answering voice was snarky and mocking. "We wouldn't want you to get eaten by any scary monsters, would we?"

"I'm the scary monster," shouted the first man, apparently the guy who ran the caravan, Dropsum.

The sound of a whip, followed by a ragged gasp, brought Torrence out of his thoughts.

He stood up, nocked an arrow, and fired. Just like last night with the bunny—and thank goodness this body took over when he needed to clean and cook it—he'd reacted after having nothing more than an impulse with no thought.

Seventeen men stared at the arrow sticking out of the hand of the man who had held the whip a moment before.

The fat man—who was clutching his bloody and pierced hand—widened his eyes, crouched slightly, and let out a whining shriek that started low and slow, and raised in pitch and intensity. When the sound hit its apex, he jumped up and down, screaming as much in rage as in pain. After a couple bounces, he stopped, gasping. He renewed his scream as the pain of making the arrow that stuck through his hand wobble and jiggle when he jumped, struck home.

A thin man with shaggy blonde hair and a bloody whip streak across his chest crouched in front of Dropsum and looked at Torrence with keen interest.

Master Dropsum's snapped his head to one side and made eye contact with Torrence. All heads slowly turned towards the source of the arrow.

Torrence smiled sheepishly and shrugged.

All hell broke loose.

The men, as one, drew weapons. Swords slid from scabbards, daggers from sheaths, crossbows came up, and spears were leveled at Torrence. Many of the three dozen slaves dropped to the ground, tucking their head between their knees, and covering them with their arms.

Panic flooded through Torrence, and he shook, trying to decide if he should run or hide.

His body took over.

His arms came up again, the left holding the bow, and the right pulling arrows from the quiver. One man dropped with two arrows in his chest. Another man took one to the knee, ending his career as a guard, and fell to the dew moistened dirt of the road. A third took a superb shot to the eye, and his head jerked backwards, and his body followed.

The rest rushed towards Torrence, who was frozen in fear, unsure what to do. But his body knew, and it dropped the bow.

"Jonath's trident!" Torrence shouted a war cry, but thought to himself, *Why the hell did I drop the bow? I was doing so good with the bow.*

Torrence was already moving forward, whipping his two-handed sword from the scabbard on his back, and swinging it in a wide arc. Three men had taken the lead, one in front of the other two. The sword met the man's body where the neck joins the chest, and the collarbone crumbled under the power of five kilograms of steel.

The sword twisted, and the flat of the blade hit the man in the side of the head. He crumbled underneath the blow, and Torrence spun the blade, using its own momentum, and brought it back in the other direction.

The two men that had been right behind the first skidded to a halt, holding their blades in both hands directly in front of them. The return route of the barbarian's enormous weapon, as he fell to one knee, brought the steel under the men's pommels and into their forearms.

The thing about two-handed swords is that they're not made for cutting. You can hone their blades, but more often than not, they're more of a large steel club with a flat part. They crush things as much, if not more, as they cut things.

The power of the muscle behind the blade shattered the first man's right forearm and spun him. His blade shot to his left as his arm crumbled, the point dropping and stabbing into the groin of his companion. The remaining man of the opening charge not only took his buddy's sword tip to his junk, but also had the follow through of the huge barbarian blade to contend with, and it dragged itself across the man's throat. His windpipe simultaneously crushed and torn open.

The remaining eight men—not counting the guy near the slave train trying to decide if he should pull the arrow out of his hand or not, and looking more than just a little, like he was about to cry—formed a circle around Torrence.

Torrence had a grip. It was a double-handed grip on his massive sword—and he snickered as the thought, if you know what I mean, crossed his mind—but it was also a grip on the situation. He was in it now, and he wasn't getting out of it until he'd handled it. So, he set his feet, and his mind, and readied himself for whatever came next.

Of the eight men, four had spears, three held daggers ready to throw, and the last was a gigantic man who swung a massive double-headed flail in a lazy circle at his side. Two more guards hung back, crossbows at the ready.

The spearmen stepped forward, jabbing with their two-and-a-half meter long weapons to keep the barbarian centered. The men with the daggers, in unison, drew their arms back and prepared to throw.

Torrence didn't think. Well, he didn't plan his next move, but thoughts shot through his head when he realized what was going down. The men had created a crossfire. This could be bad for him, unless he made sure that they missed him. Then they could, and likely would, hit one of the caravan guards on the other side of him.

Torrence smiled.

"You know, guys," the barbarian said, "if you run now, and pray to Chanian for speed to get away, you might live."

Torrence didn't know who Chanian was, but as he thought that, the information was there. Chanian was a god. Like a superhuman being that people prayed to for blessings in a certain area. Chanian happened to be the one who people prayed to for speed in travel, guile, agility, and stealing things.

This made Torrence think of moments earlier when he'd sworn and said, 'Jonath's trident.' Jonath was a god of Justice, and the element of earth. Guards and farmers favored him.

*Hm,* Torrence thought, *that's kinda like Mars from the Roman mythology. He was a god of war. But not many people knew he was also the god of agriculture.*

Torrence snapped back into awareness of the present moment. He apparently had ducked under a couple of flying daggers, grabbed a thrusting spear and pushed it behind him into the gut of one of the other guards. He'd also dropped his own sword, grabbed that guy's spear and spun in a circle, hitting three of the men in their heads with the thirty-centimeter blade of the appropriated weapon.

Four of the eight men in the circle were nullified in a couple of heartbeats. Three held gushing cuts on their heads, and the fourth was stumbling backwards with his friend's weapon buried in his intestines.

That left four more.

One of those didn't have his spear anymore and had two daggers stuck in him, one in the torso and another in his foot. He stumbled out of the circle, which had quickly dwindled to a triangle.

The slaves who hadn't dropped to the ground—and instead had crouched, ducked behind a wagon, or just stood stock-still to see what was happening—began shouting and charging towards any of the guards still standing. The two crossbow men went down first from their efforts, taken by surprise from behind.

Dropsum, caravan master—the fat man with the arrow through his hand—was overcome by the lithe blonde man. The slave, followed by the slaves connected to him by ankle chains, grabbed the man's hand and shoved it towards the slave master's own face. The two toppled into the dirt, rolling around as desperation for survival played out in front of the others.

The second chain gang ran to the wagon, pulling those slaves that had dropped to the ground along with them, and started grabbing anything they could use. A few grabbed water skins or food, but most had more foresight and grabbed things they could throw at their captors or use as a weapon.

A half-dozen of the people attached to the man who had attacked the caravan master joined in the activity of beating him down. The rest looked around, saw the triangle of men facing off with their rescuer, and charged in that direction.

In less than a minute, the guards were either running into the surrounding trees, injured and surrendering to the superior numbers of the slaves, or lay dead on the ground.

Torrence turned away as prisoners rejected the surrenders and offered the guards a second option of being brutally beaten to death with the slaves' chains and bare hands.

*Why does it bother me that the men were being beaten to death?* Torrence embraced the thought to keep his mind off the sounds of the murders behind him.

He'd just killed a dozen men in combat without thinking twice about it. *Was that so different? And didn't these people deserve a chance to exact some revenge for what they went through?*

This was a cruel and pitiless world, and Torrence walked away from the sounds that spoke of that in the plain language of violence.

Once out of sight, he turned back towards the caravan and wondered what else this day would bring.

"Where's my body right now?" he whispered, his stomach twisting. "Am I dying, or dead, and this is my brain dealing with me fighting for my life?"

## Chapter 5

"This's the Kid," a gruff, accented voice said as a finger jabbed into the Kid's shoulder, "and he's been doing bad things. Things like stealing, then giving it to people who didn't earn it. I have big plans for this town, and that kinda bidj ain't gonna cut it."

The Kid looked up at Jakdin, a third-rate thug for the Grey Ash gang, and focused on the man's broken nose with a scar running across it from his right cheek to his left eye.

Jakdin had been trying to make a name for himself lately and had been shaking down a lot of the street kids who actually worked for a living. The man wanted to rise within the ranks of the organization, but never seemed to get anywhere.

"Standing on the backs of people who actually do the real work again, Jakdin?" the Kid asked, smirking up at the man who stood over him.

The four toughs who always accompanied Jakdin rumbled laughter, and their leader glared around at them.

"I heard you had a run in with Mezk and some of Bokk's other men," Jakdin went on, ignoring the comment, "and that you led them into a trap set by the city watch and ran off with the score."

"Shit happens, y'all," the Kid said with a shrug, looking around the Open Door, a local dive of a pub.

It was a busy night, and the place was filled with mercenaries just returned from the Demon Front, a war zone to the southeast where people fought to keep the visitors from another plane of existence from overwhelming the last of human civilization.

Durgan's Keep, the walled city that sat on a cliff overlooking the Inner Bay, was one of the last places where men could live without fear of the constant threat of attack by demons, undead, or monsters. It had once been a thriving place; full of merchants with wares from far-off lands, travelers with tales of wonder and adventure, a mix of races that brought diversity from all over, and a solid feeling of safety from a government that worked hard to keep it all moving.

Now, it was still a pinnacle of civilization, but the events of the last few decades tainted it. A dark miasma of greed and cruelty had fallen over what was once a strong and fair place. People were as likely to slip a stiletto between your ribs as sell you the rack of lamb hanging in their shop.

The Open Door once greeted visitors, showing a taste of the city that was beyond it. Now, it was a grungy, dank place frequented by corrupt city guards who weren't much better than the criminals that they drank with.

"You gave it away," Jakdin said plainly, "you didn't even make a profit and pay your dues to the guild. You just gave it to dirty, stinking losers who live off the scraps. I don't get you, kid."

"It could be because you have a tiny brain," the Kid wasn't looking at the man anymore, instead his eyes shifted around the room because he knew the inevitable was coming, "and you can't see beyond what's right in front of your beady, little pig eyes."

Jakdin's fist smashed down on the table, cups and bowls rattling and bouncing with the blow.

The pub quieted, people looking towards the corner table where the Kid sat.

The Kid had seen Jakdin coming, had even known he was on the way. He was observant, and people on the street liked him and fed him good information, mostly. The Kid had a point to make, and swallowed a lump in his throat, wondering if it was a good idea to do this.

Sighing, the Kid leaned back and looked up at Jakdin.

"Is this worth dying over?" the Kid asked. "Do ya feel lucky, punk. Well, do you?"

"Maybe you should ask yourself that," Jakdin sneered.

Smiling, the Kid flicked a peanut shell onto the ground, and it skidded across the floor and under a table.

Jakdin and his thugs turned to watch it land.

A form, not much larger than a cat, clattered out from under the table where the shell had disappeared. It had eight legs, hair bristling on each one, an orangish carapace with razor sharp ridges, and two massive claws that clacked as it scurried towards the feet of the thugs.

"Sebastian," the Kid said confidently, "kill the boy."

The mutant crab ran at the men's ankles, one claw snapping at one thug. The man screamed as his foot was clipped from his leg.

The pub exploded into chaos.

Barmaids leaped onto tables, regulars dove behind the bar, or ran up the flight of stairs that led to the rented out rooms above, and even the burly men-at-arms from the demon front danced backwards, away from the creature.

Jakdin screamed in surprise, a high-pitched noise that caused more than one person to stop looking at the creature on the floor and stare at him.

The broken-nosed man leapt onto the Kid's table, drawing his sword—a wavy blade, like a Kris blade but three times as long.

With another gesture, the Kid unlaced the man's boots with his mind and caused the cords to intertwine with one another.

Jakdin danced around on the table, still screaming shrilly, and toppled off because his laces were tied together.

His sword skidded along the floor and disappeared into the crowd.

The Kid, now on the other side of the room and grinning, bent down and retrieved the blade.

"Thanks for the souvenirs!" the Kid said, holding up five coin pouches in one hand and saluting with the weapon in the other, as Jakdin scrambled backwards on all fours to avoid the charging creature. "I'll make sure I pass it on to some undeserving folks."

The Kid darted into the kitchen and out the open back door into the alley. Pushing with his mind, he leapt to a second-story window, pausing to deposit a half dozen gold kords—the twisted golden wires that were the local currency—that he'd taken from the coin purses of the thugs on the sill, and tapped on the window.

He pushed off again into the open air, reaching out with his mind to the opposite wall, and flew across the alley to a third-story window, and repeated the depositing of gold kords and tapping on the window.

One final leap and he pulled himself onto the rooftop.

He knew the illusion of the little monster wouldn't keep the men in the pub busy for long, especially once he'd moved a short distance away. But it was enough to embarrass the brutes publicly, and he got a sword and some loot in the deal.

Bonus!

The rooftops were the Kid's own private thoroughfare, and he moved across the city unseen and faster than if he'd taken the standard routes people traveled.

Once he was closer to the docks—his actual destination—he dropped into another back alley and casually entered the foot traffic of the street.

It was after dark, but commerce and trade were still booming here in the red-light district, even at this hour. Women and men of all sizes and shapes called out to passerby, offering pleasures of the flesh for coin.

Sweet Jewlnee called out and waved at the Kid. She was an immense woman, with a mountain of red hair coiled and piled atop her head. Her makeup was a riot of color. The rouge splashed across her cheeks, eyeliner outlining her emerald eyes, and a rainbow of eyeshadow filling out the space in between. Her silk sari of blue and gold contrasted with her kerchief skirt of a dozen different dyed silks.

The Kid smiled widely and veered through the crowd to the woman that his memory told him had taken care of him many times. Not in the romantic way, though that offer was always on the table. Sweet Jewlnee had given him a warm place to sleep on cold nights when he was just a lad, fed him buttered rolls when he had nothing else to eat, and was one of the few people that always greeted him with open arms instead of a closed fist.

"Sweet Jewlnee," the Kid said, "flower of beauty and royalty of the night mists, how are you?"

"Oh, you," Sweet Jewlnee blushed and opened her arms to take the boy into her embrace, "I'm better now that I've seen your smile. And, how're you?"

The Kid fell into her soft, warm, encircling arms, and was smothered against her ample bosom. The heavy perfumes she always wore washed over him, and even though it threatened to make him sneeze, it was a smell that brought back pleasant memories and always made him smile.

She grabbed him by the shoulders and pulled him away to arm's length, staring into his face.

"You're going away," she gasped, "you're leaving Durgan's Keep!"

"Oh, Sweet Jewlnee," the Kid's smile spread across his face without any effort, "you always could read my mind, and the minds of others. Guess that's the secret to your success?"

"That," she said coyly, "and a few of my other talents as well. But yes, the same magics I saw in you, and schooled you in, also tell me many secrets others don't need to say aloud. But, why are you leaving? Are those men being mean to you again, sugar plum?"

The Kid laughed, hugged the woman again, and then pulled away, his fingers running down her arms until they were holding hands.

A heavy pouch clinked as he transferred it from his hands to hers. Her eyes shifted towards it and then darted back to his.

"What's this?" she asked.

"A gift," the Kid's voice was tight with a fleeting moment of emotion, and he paused before going on, "for your kindness. Share it with those who need some of that kindness for themselves, but make sure you keep enough to get yourself something pretty."

She leaned back, looking at him through slitted eyes.

"You need something," she laughed.

"I didn't come here to ask you for anything," the Kid said with sincere innocence, though he blushed.

"I didn't say that you came here to ask me for anything," she smiled a gentle smile that spoke of wisdom and knowing. "You *need* something. And I can help with that."

The woman inside of the Kid felt a reaction. The kindness of this madam; this woman of the night—who had lived decades in a dark and cruel world—was offering something, not because someone asked, but because they needed it, and her heart wanted to help.

*Jen,* the Kid thought, *I was Jen, and I remember being kind, and having kindness from others who wanted nothing in return; like my first boss, or the pro-bono lawyer who handled my divorce, or Angie who was my best friend, or the nurses who answered my call bell.*

The thought fell away, like the passing memory it was. But more of Jen blossomed within the Kid, and he teared up.

"I don't know what you mean," the Kid's voice was strained and choked, "I don't want anything."

"I know, honey pie," Sweet Jewlnee said, "and you never need to ask. I know a guy at the dock, Jaimin Rabbit. He's a real prick, but he's also one of the sweetest assholes I know. He'll make your stomach turn with his annoying damned puns, but he'll help you. Go and ask for him. His ship is the Raptor Rex, it's in dock now."

The Kid leaned on the railing of the Raptor Rex, wind in his face and gusts making his dark shoulder-length hair dance. The ship moved across the midnight waters of the Inner Bay, cutting through the waves and breeze to the north, away from the Ruled River that led south to the ocean.

A young sailor, pale with a mop-top of red curls, named Jundek, was polite and offered to show him knots and when and where mess was eaten.

The rest of the crew avoided the Kid, except for an older man named Tillheim, who watched him, nodding when the Kid helped on the deck, or frowned when another sailor made a crude comment.

He didn't remember much else of the trip from the red-light district to the docks. He had a vague recollection of moving through the streets, dropping coins into beggars' cups, hats, and plates, and handing silver peks to children and anyone who looked like they'd put in a hard day's work and wouldn't earn that much in a week.

He'd lurked in the docks, searching for the ship called Raptor Rex, only to find it docked out in the harbor. He'd rented a skiff and a boatman to taxi him out to it. The man called Jaimin Rabbit had listened when the Kid told the sailor that Sweet Jewlnee had sent him. The Captain tossed down a rope and plank ladder, told him to come aboard, and shooed the taxi back to shore.

The Kid didn't know what awaited him to the north, but he did know that this world was full of adventure. He also knew this world needed a helping hand to find more than just the spoonful of misery that it normally dosed to its people.

# Chapter 6

"This can't be happening," Esperanza muttered, her hand fingering the blade on her waist, "this isn't real."

Rose's pale face reflected the torchlight of the burning brand that had hit the hut and threatened to set the moss-and-mud-covered walls ablaze.

The woman stared back at Esperanza, wide-eyed and indecisive.

Esperanza wanted to wake up. She knew she'd taken too many sleeping pills with the pint of vodka, and might never wake up, but this wasn't the heaven or hell she'd expected in death.

Could she end it right now, using the small blade she gripped? She didn't belong here. It wasn't real.

Everything felt real.

The smells filled her nose, the sounds met her ears and didn't have that thought quality of a dream that noises had when sleeping, and she felt genuine emotion instead of the impression of it when unable to wake up.

She'd only felt fear since being here. The crowd coming at her, waking in a mud hovel with no bathroom, even the dirty water that Rose had presented as if it was the finest wine, was terrifying.

Now, a man called for her head. If she was, in fact, the priestess of Latress.

She was Christian, not some unknown heathen witch of some fake religion. She'd always prayed to God in Heaven, and never even considered other faiths of people who didn't know of Christ and his works.

But here she was, watching half-rotted corpses shuffling through a village in the night. She saw one grab a man who jabbed at it with a wooden pitchfork. Its hands were fleshless and skeletal, tearing at the villager's face and throat, ripping away chunks of flesh as the man fell, screaming, under the onslaught.

Three others, what could only be called zombies, shambled to the struggle, and fell—literally fell, as in dropped face first—onto the man and began tearing out ribbons of flesh and biting into his stomach, arms, and face, choking back the bits of skin and muscle they'd torn free.

Esperanza stumbled backwards, wondering what kind of private hell God had sent her to for her sins.

A thought, a feeling, a voice in her soul pushed at her, urging her to step forward and call upon the winds, the storm, the rains, and the lightning. To call down the very forces of nature to strike down the abominations outside.

Esperanza fell to her knees, screaming and clutching her head in hysterics, her voice calling out to God, Jesus, and the angelic hosts to come save her. She sobbed the Lord's Prayer, only wanting this nightmare to end.

She clutched her knife with one hand, and the holy symbol of the Goddess Latress with the other, not realizing she'd done it.

Through tear-blurred vision she watched as Rose—who'd turned to stare at her—was grabbed from behind and dragged into the night by decaying grey arms, skeletal fingers questing for the woman's throat.

Esperanza froze.

The only person since she'd been here that had been kind to her, cared for her, and showed any understanding and patience…was now being dragged into the dark by an unearthly terror.

And Esperanza couldn't even stand up.

Something popped, like the snap of fingers deep inside her, and she was in the backseat of her own body.

Esperanza stood, rising with confidence that hadn't been there moments before. Releasing her small blade and the holy symbol, she strode forward, through the door and out of the mud dwelling, into the night.

She raised her arms, striding into the midst of chaos and horrific death, and called upon her Goddess.

"Latress," she said in a normal tone, but her voice boomed like thunder and echoed off the surrounding dwellings, "grant me the wisdom to face this foe with knowledge of their weaknesses, and your power and might, delivered upon them as holy wrath!"

Lightning arced from the dark clouds above, shooting with a blinding flash to Esperanza's outstretched hands, and then darted in a dozen directions to strike the living dead that attacked in the night.

"Latress," Esperanza intoned, turning slowly, a holy glow surrounding her, "light the night, and free these good people from the evil that threatens to consume them!"

Orbs of magical light zoomed from the priestess and flew in slow, lazy circles throughout the village. The undead creatures lurched away from the light, seeking the shadows and murk.

Esperanza saw Rose beside the hut. One of the grey creatures bent over her and four more moving towards her struggling form.

"No," Esperanza said calmly, but with an intensity that even the dead couldn't ignore.

The decaying forms turned towards her.

She took three steps forward, gripped the metal holy symbol of the clouds and stars—which she'd thought she'd left in the small bedroom, but now hung around her neck— and raised it in front of her.

Holy power, that was the only way Esperanza could later describe it, filled the area. A calm in the storm weighed on the village, and the people nearby stopped running, stopped screaming, and instead drew deep, grounding breaths. And then the pulse of energy burst forth from the symbol.

All the dead creatures that stood, walked, shambled, lurched, or moved in the path in front of her—widening as it went—slowed, turned, and faded. Their skin became translucent, and their bones within their broken bodies began to shine. The power of Latress filled them, and they hesitated for a moment, and then were pulled away as dust in the wind. Their forms dissipating like the nightmares they caused in the waking morning light.

Rose sat bolt upright. But her face didn't show fear. Instead, her eyes were ablaze with something Esperanza had never seen. She stared at Esperanza with hope. Faith. Belief. Confidence that she, Esperanza, would make all the bad things go away.

The priestess of Latress, that was Esperanza, turned away from Rose and moved to continue her personal holy crusade of eradicating the undead menace.

Rose was not offended; she saw the powerful woman who'd come into the village almost a month ago to help them with an affliction they couldn't battle alone. A woman who contracted the same diseased infection that she was saving others from. A woman who'd died last night. Then, as suddenly as her own death, had risen again, a scared and confused stranger that used a different name. But now, the priestess that had saved them all strode into the forces of darkness that had descended upon the village.

"You, witch!" the powerful male voice tore through the night, "I've come for you, and you shall die for what you did to my master, the Overlord of Death, Knight of the Darkest Night, Lord of Rot, and Regent of Revenants, Philibert the Foul. He was forever wiped from this plane of existence and banished to eternal suffering with the demons of the netherworld by your hand, and I shall return the favor upon you!"

Esperanza turned her head to glance at the ranting man. He was of average height, a bit rotund, and slightly hunched, with thinning hair. He wore a leather chemist apron, the same kind that many blacksmiths wore, but with less pizazz. It was stained with various splotches of chemical mixtures and compounds.

She stopped, cocked her head as she turned towards him, and looked at him with a mixture of bemusement and curiosity.

"This is your doing?" she asked. "This is your little army of undead?"

"It is," the paunchy man sneered, his unkempt hair whipping around his head in the wind, "you whore-slut of an impotent goddess!"

"Oh," Esperanza said with a laugh, "I remember you!"

She turned and walked towards the man, looking at him askance. With each step she took towards him, he took a half step back, and she slowly closed the distance between them.

"I also remember Philibert," her voice grew in power, and a crescendo of thunder rumbled in the air with each sentence, building each time she spoke, "he was a sad little man who intimidated others to make himself feel better about himself."

"I, Louis the necromancer, proclaim you a liar!" the man shouted.

"Really, dude?" a bit of the real Esperanza burst through for a moment. "Don't you guys have a clue about the value of a decent stage name? I mean, even J-lo would be more intimidating than Louis. Isn't that the name of the nerdy loser from Ghostbusters?"

"Ghosts!" Louis screamed, clenching his fists in front of him as he backed away from the approaching priestess, "will haunt you, devour you, and destroy your soul."

"You really don't have a clue, do you?" Esperanza asked. "Do you really think I have anything to fear from you? Don't you remember what I did to the man who taught you a third of what he knew?"

"A third?" Louis asked, his voice cracking.

"You were the one hiding behind the bunk beds when I fried your boss with lightning, bestowed upon me by my impotent goddess, weren't you? You were crying, right? That was you?"

"No," Louis mumbled, stumbling over a tree root as he backed away, and falling on his ass, "I wasn't crying. I was…"

The man hesitated.

"I was," he continued, his voice picking up strength again, "having trouble seeing because you blew up a bunch of alchemical supplies, and it burned my eyes!"

"Oh," Esperanza sighed, a gentle rumble of thunder echoing her breath, as she reached up and took hold of the holy symbol of Latress that hung between her breasts, "I see. So, the sobbing and all that snot as your master roasted to a crisp was because of some fumes that hardly bothered me, a whore-slut, at all?"

"Yeah," Louis mumbled, "I have allergies."

"Louis," she said menacingly, drawing out the vowels in the man's name like a disapproving teacher, "I think we're done here. I'm going to make it so your creations want you, but in a very different way than they did when you created them."

A burst of wind lifted the man a handful of centimeters off the ground and then dropped him unceremoniously back onto his ass.

The breath woofed out of him, and he let out a grunt of surprise.

Villagers had gathered to watch the confrontation, standing in clumps near the front doors of their huts, ready to bolt back inside at any sign that the priestess's efforts were in vain.

The dozen or so undead that had lurched into the protective darkness of the trees from Esperanza's light globes now reemerged and shambled towards their master. They were silent except for the sound of their feet sliding over the mat of dried leaves on the ground.

Louis looked up at them in surprise, a look that quickly changed to triumph. He pushed himself up to his feet, rising to his full unimpressive height, pulled his shoulders back and made his gut seem even larger, hiked up his drooping drawers, and thrust his doughy chest out.

"Yes," he breathed a throaty growl to his minions, "come to me, my children, come to your master!"

The emaciated figures limped towards him, their hands reaching for him.

He smiled and brushed his fingertips against theirs.

"Now," his victorious tone spoke of his impending victory, "go and destroy everyone so we may replenish your ranks! Then we shall travel to join Aku'ji and combine our forces with her army of the night!"

The pathetic creatures, not much more than bare skin and bones, crowded around him, grabbing his hands, his arms, and leaning into him.

"Yes, yes," he said, the confidence in his voice being replaced with confusion, "I know you love me; I know that I'm the best…"

His words disappeared in a surprised cry of pain.

"You bit me!" Louis whined, "You chuzzing bit me, you ungrateful brainless bastard!"

His voice rose with each word, and then cut off suddenly, replaced with a strangled gurgle, his body collapsing under the weight of his adoring, but eternally hungry, minions.

The creatures collapsed on top of the amateur necromancer as his life force slipped away, and the power and control he had over them dissipated. He died under their loving onslaught, and the magic he'd empowered them with left them as his last gasp left his body.

Esperanza let out a breath she'd been holding since she'd been put into the backseat of her own body. She was back in control of herself, and the instinctual drive that had led her to the actions over the last handful of minutes disappeared. Her eyes went wide when she began to understand what had just happened.

She turned to look at Rose and the other villagers, and saw they were all coming towards her, their faces unreadable.

## Chapter 7

Torrence cleaned his sword and stowed it on his back.

A few minutes later, the sounds of the fight died, as did most of the caravan guards, replaced by the sounds of chains being thrown aside, wagons being looted, and people running off into the woods by themselves or in small groups.

Torrence went back to the caravan and was stunned by how completely it had been dismantled in such a short amount of time. A few people still rummaged through the remaining rubble, stripping boots or gear from dead guards, or just standing and staring as if they didn't know what to do next.

The newly freed prisoners avoided Torrence, darting past him and giving him a wide berth. Two or three nodded or muttered thanks, but didn't stick around to see if the stranger would try to put them back into chains.

The light-haired, wiry man who'd attacked the caravan master looked up from a chest of various spices. He was stuffing a burlap sack with the smaller bags and satchels of rare herbs and seasonings. He wore the vest and boots of the man who Torrence had put an arrow through the hand of.

The man, Master Dropsum, had dragged himself away from the carnage, and Torrence could see the heels of the man's bare feet sticking out from under a bush about five meters away.

"Thank you," the smaller man stood, squared his shoulders, and looked Torrence straight in the eye, "thank you for my life, as well as the lives of all the others."

"Um, yeah," Torrence realized he wasn't speaking English, but talking in a language his body knew and understood, "no problem."

"Why, though?" the man smiled, cocking his head like a curious dog. "Why would you do something so pemtie as attack an armed slave caravan? Are you trying to get yourself killed? Or was the woman you love, one of the prisoners?"

The man looked around to see if anyone seemed to recognize his rescuer, or if the big man seemed to know anyone here. The small man shook his shaggy head.

"Um," Torrence wondered the same thing himself, "it seemed like the right thing to do?"

The smaller man laughed and shook his head again, kneeling back down to stuff more spices into his sack.

"That sounded like a question," the thin man said, "but whatever your reason, I owe you my life and I'm grateful."

Pausing, the man looked up at Torrence.

"I'm Axle," the blonde man stood, wiped his dirty hands on his thighs, and then stepped towards Torrence with one hand extended.

"Torrence," the barbarian reached to shake the man's hand.

Axle reached past the barbarian's hand and grasped Torrence's wrist, shaking it as Torrence imitated the movement.

"Torrents," Axle said, "well, it fits your fighting style, that's for sure. You were a force of nature. You didn't pause or give a second thought. You were damned impressive, my friend."

Axle released Torrence's wrist and stared up into the big man's face, smiling.

A man and woman omoved past the two, leaning on one another as they headed into the tree line. They nodded and muttered their gratitude without making eye contact, and shuffled away.

"Can I offer something in return for your heroism?" Axle asked. "You don't look like you're looking for a slave, so I guess I could offer my services if I can do anything to repay you."

"Your services?" Torrence was unsure of what that would even mean.

"Hm," Axle looked at the barbarian, "perhaps you're simple, perhaps you honestly don't expect anyone to show courtesy or kindness in this day and age."

Torrence shrugged.

Axle moved about the abandoned caravan, looking for anything the other slaves had missed before their exodus. He found a short, pocked blade in a worn leather scabbard. Pulling a belt from one of the dead men, he wrapped it around his waist and tucked the weapon into his waistband.

He stopped and looked at the barbarian again, his head cocked.

"Where you headed, Torrents?"

The big man shrugged again.

"How about this," Axle squared off in front of Torrence, "I'm going to go back to my village, Hope's Hollow. These guys caught me when I was outside of it, cutting wood. You see, I'm a woodsman and a carpenter. I make great wagons and carts, with the proper tools, if I can brag for a moment. And I'm going to go back home. My village was suffering from a plague, but a priestess of Latress showed up and helped. I expect that she's dead now, because when I was taken about a week ago, she was showing signs of the sickness herself, but she'd done a lot to help stop the spread of it while she was there. Why don't you come with me?"

"Why?" Torrence was unsure of what else to say.

"Well," Axle smiled his amiable smile again, "I'll be honest, it's for strictly selfish reasons I ask. You're a big guy, and can obviously take care of yourself, and I'd feel safer traveling with you instead of by myself. You don't seem to have anywhere in particular you're going, so Hope's Hollow is as good a place as anywhere else."

Torrence shrugged again.

"It's settled then," Axle began loading waterskins and loaves of bread into another burlap sack, "we'll travel together to my home, and see what happens from there."

"Do you think they made it?" Torrence asked.

"Who? The other people who ran off into a place called the Black Wood just as night was falling?" Axle looked at Torrence over his tin plate of beans and bread. "No, I think they were total pemties and were probably dead before sunrise. Did you notice how few corpses remained the next day? Something got those and probably got the living as well."

The two men ate in silence for a few moments.

They'd traveled together for three days, heading west along the foothills of the Wandering Mountains and the northern edge of the Black Wood. They'd spent the first night in the ruins of the caravan, building a small fire to cook over and then keep warm with the glowing coals in the night, but avoiding attention from predators.

There'd been screams, but Torrence had hoped it had been something mundane, like a screech owl or the haunting call of a fox. This was the first time he'd asked about it and regretted it immediately.

The second day was uneventful, besides a brief encounter with a territorial badger who'd hissed and gruffed at them when they came too close to its den.

Today had been different, though. The pungent smell of rotting bodies, lots of them, had reached their noses. By the time they'd decided to make camp, it was even stronger.

"What do you think that smell is?" Torrence wiped at his mouth with a small cloth.

"You know you're the tidiest damned barbarian I've ever seen?" Axle asked in return.

"Don't avoid the question," Torrence said, then turned and spat, as if to disprove Axle's observation.

Axle laughed and bent back over his plate.

"How far are we from your village?" Torrence tried to strike up conversation again.

"Probably a week from where we started," Axle said without looking up, "but it could be more if the dragons are out."

"Dragons are real?" Torrence asked.

"Well, they were," Axle answered automatically, then stopped and looked up at his traveling companion. "Was that a real question? Where have you been? Before the Downfall, the Wandering Hills were home to an entire clan of them. They kept humans the way we keep sheep."

"For food?" Torrence's eyes were wide, and his spoon had stopped centimeters from his mouth.

"Maybe," Axle shrugged, "but more likely to tend the herds of cows that have much more meat and breed quicker than people do. And to bring in more gold and stuff for their hordes."

The wind shifted, and the smell of rot came into their small campsite stronger than before. It wasn't the smell of a dead predator; carnivores had an almost earthy smell when rotting. It also wasn't the smell of an herbivore, which was rather mellow and gentle unless it baked under the hot sun for a while, and even then, it was an eruption of aroma when the body burst open from the pressure. This was different. It had a taint, not quite a chemical smell, but as if a cesspit had been covered with rotting flowers.

Torrence interrupted his own thought flow, wondering how the hell he knew all this. It's not like he'd Googled it. That meant that his body must have had enough experiences with the death of animals, mild and wild, as well as people, to know the difference between their dead smells.

Suddenly, the meaning behind that occurred to him and he sat bolt upright, his eyes wide.

"Gas?" Axle smirked.

"Dead people." Torrence's voice was much calmer than he thought it should be.

"What?" Axle spun around and looked into the shadows of the surrounding trees. "Do you see them?"

Torrence laughed at the memory of a movie from his past and again thought that sort of behavior shouldn't be normal. Did this world have zombies and vampires just moseying around and waving at folks? Was it such a common thing to see undead, like in so many movies and TV shows, that his current body didn't even react with fear, shock, or surprise?

Realizing he'd stood up, and had his huge two-handed broadsword—Torrence also realized he knew what the hell a broadsword was, it was also known as a bastard sword and was able to be used in a one- or two-handed grip—at the ready and was in a battle stance.

The weapon was held in his right hand, just above head level, and extending at an angle in front and across his body as he bent at the knees for easy movement when he needed to strike. It was a defensive stance, waiting to see the enemy's position and intention. It would allow him to swing overhead for a powerful strike, drop the weapon into a thrust, or drop his hands and the pommel to create a block, which in itself could be shifted left or right, depending where an attack came from.

A glance over his shoulder showed Axle standing behind him, across the fire; both faced outwards into the darkness, letting their eyes adjust to the shadows that the light of the fire had intensified. The smaller man held the sword he had liberated from the well-looted caravan in his right hand, and a long, thin dirk in his left.

The night moved and shifted, and pale shapes coalesced in the dark. Dozens of lumbering forms came into view, and one dark shadow, low and feral, darted forward.

# Chapter 8

The Kid had left the Raptor Rex three days ago—Captain Jaiman Rabbit had explained to him it was called disembarking—and had traveled north of the Inner Bay, crossed the road that had once brought merchants and travelers from Red Wind in the Red Plains to the east to Dioneze City and beyond to Runsk in the Diaz Woods, south of the Tear Drop Bog in the west.

He had traveled alone, staying in a small village full of suspicious people the first night, then sleeping in a hollowed-out tree the second night, and under a deadfall the third.

The fourth day had brought rain. A cold, dark storm with torrents of weather that limited vision when he entered the foothills that were bordered by the Tear Drop Bog—a salty swamp that had once connected to the ocean—on the west and the Blue Desert on the east. The desert was named because its sands had a blue tint to it from the magical runoff of mystical experiments of the Nine Towers lost in its northern reaches.

The Kid pulled his cloak tighter around himself and wished, not for the first time, that it reached to his ankles instead of ending just below his waist.

He trudged along the small path, not much more than a deer track, on the foothills between the bog and the desert.

His feet slipped, the ground crumbling underneath them, and he fell into darkness. Landing, his head hit something hard, and his vision swam.

When it cleared, he wasn't sure if he'd passed out or not. He lay amongst dozens of stone blocks in a cloud of dust that was dissipating in the moist air of the drizzle that came in through the opening five or six meters above him.

He breathed out a heavy sigh, and reached to rub the lump on the back of his skull, wincing as he touched it.

Dim grey light filtered in from above. Looking up, he could see the opening that he fell through.

"What the hell am I doing?" he asked aloud.

But that wasn't him, that was his body asking, which was a strange concept, as if he were two people, but one was all reaction and instinct, and the other was a conscious being.

"I am me," the Kid said, pushing away the other part of him that didn't seem to delight in being on an adventure.

That was the part that would've never attacked Jakdin, never left Durgan's Keep, and never wanted to explore this new and amazing world that waited for him.

*Why had I left?* he wondered.

The answer was obvious to one part of him, because there was so much more to life than one city. But the other part of him argued against it, pointing out that it was almost guaranteed to be full of unknown dangers.

"Chuz that," the Kid said aloud, standing and brusquely brushing the roots, dust, and muck from his clothes, forcing the reactive side of him deep down inside, "Life is meant to be lived, and to refuse to go out and experience it is a sort of passive-aggressive suicide."

*But to go out and experience is a direct path to death, an almost certain thing,* said the distant voice inside before it disappeared in the motion of stepping forward into the darkness.

The Kid swooned and touched the bump on his head again, his fingers coming away wet with mud and blood. He dabbed at it with his cloak and realized that wouldn't be enough.

Pulling a small canteen from the woven hemp bag over his shoulder, he poured some water on the scrape, shrugging away the thought that he was dribbling water down his back. He was already drenched from the rain anyway, what's a little more water matter?

He steadied himself on the worked stone wall with one hand, waiting for his eyes to adjust to the gloom. While he waited, he inspected his surroundings.

The hole above was three to four times his own height above him, and the fallen stones around him wouldn't be enough to stack and make his escape from… where was he, anyway?

He looked around; his eyes having adjusted.

He stood in what appeared to be a hallway, extending into the darkness in one direction. Behind him, under some stones, was a wooden bench with holes in it, each about thirty centimeters in diameter, and the musty smell of old feces hung in the air.

"I fell into the shitter?" the Kid asked out loud, and then yelled, "Shitter's full!"

The sound of his own voice echoed back to him from down the passageway.

He giggled.

"The dog peed on the sandwiches!" the Kid shouted the quote to no one, and laughed even harder.

"I decree this place," the Kid said in an official voice, "the Griswold Tunnels, and claim it for my own! I shall raid and loot, and possibly die if I don't find a way out, through this place in the name of adventure and fun!"

The Kid moved a couple meters forward to get out of the rain falling through the hole in the roof, knelt, set his satchel down, and rummaged through it. After a few moments of searching, he found an oil lantern, a metal flask of oil, and a flint and steel.

He found it fascinating to watch his own hands work of their own accord, as if on autopilot. They poured a small amount of oil into the reservoir of the lamp, capped both the lantern and the flask, pulled up some oil-soaked wick, lit it from a spark of the flint and steel, and then spooled the extra wick back down into the lantern's reservoir.

He stowed all the items in their proper places around his body.

Standing up, the Kid slung the bag back over his shoulder and neck, and moved forward and down the hall of what he thought of as catacombs. The Kid had never been in catacombs, in either life. It felt very Edgar Allan Poe and the Cask of Amontillado. Maybe something from National Treasure or one of the Boris Karloff flicks from the Kid's childhood.

The dank, sweet smell of rotting vegetation and of things that dig in dark places hung in the air. The ground was moist with dust that had settled and become a sludge over the ages, and the Kid's boots squelched with each step.

The hall turned to the right. The dark behind the Kid swallowed the light, and the dim illumination fought its way into the inky blackness ahead. The patter of rain falling into the crumbled hole faded into the distance. The thick sound of silence enveloped him, only interrupted by his own footfalls, the creak of leather, and the rustle of cloth from his own gear.

After walking a dozen meters, he came to a four-way intersection. The Kid crouched at the juncture, tilting his head one way then the other, listening for anything to break the silence.

Pushing his hand into his satchel, he pulled out a small leather pouch and drew out three stones. Tossing one to his right, he listened to the echoes of it as bounced along the floor. The moisture wasn't as thick here, and the dust wasn't muck. Instead, it was a slightly damp carpet.

The rock to the right click-thumped down the hall. The Kid closed his eyes to listen for subtle differences in its path. The echoes that came back spoke of a long hall with some openings on either side. The left hall returned almost identical results. The Kid waited, listening to see if he had disturbed anything.

In movies, the Kid remembered, catacombs and tombs always had rats or bugs in them. Which was odd, since nothing within a long abandoned and dead place could support an ecosystem of scavengers.

Nothing moved, at least nothing the Kid could detect. He laughed, the sound echoing off the surrounding stone, his mind inventing things in the dark, shuffling towards him on feet silenced by the layer of detritus of time.

He tossed the third rock forward, closing his eyes to listen. That one thumped gently across the same soft surface covering the hard floor and then clacked on less covered stone floor, the echoes speaking of a large chamber ahead.

*Yes,* the Kid thought, *come forward and free me.*

But it wasn't the Kid's thoughts. Maybe it was a thought from the body he now inhabited? But no, it didn't feel like that, either. He laughed again at the boogie man he'd made up in his head.

Standing and raising his lantern, he turned left and moved in that direction. Small alcoves appeared in the gloom to his left and his right, dust raised by his own feet dancing in the light, and he stopped to inspect the nooks.

The openings were only about an arm's length deep and were dominated by a statue in each. The figures were humanoid, but also reptilian in small ways. The one on the right seemed to have pebbled skin, and the one on the left had no hair, but a raised crest along its head and down its neck instead.

Behind each statue was a square stone, about a meter in height and width, with a plaque embedded. It was an internment chamber, as best as the Kid could tell. The writing on the plaque was not a language the Kid or his body recognized.

Each of the six alcoves in this hall was similar, though the statues each showed different reptilian mutations. Tails, claws, scales, snouts, and other features decorated the forms of ornately carved marble, and the Kid guessed that these were the heroes of some long dead species or culture.

At the end of the hall was a larger alcove, almost twice the size of the others. The statue within it was a curled dragon, its head raised as if watching the hall, and ruby eyes staring into the darkness. The Kid felt that this was a scaled—no pun intended—down version of the actual creature it represented.

He debated if he should attempt to pry the gems free. On one hand, no one had been in this tomb for a long time, he guessed, and it was unlikely that anything would object to him taking what was just lying around. On the other hand, he didn't really have any great urge to desecrate what was so obviously a work of art.

In the Kid's previous life—a memory pushed at her as who she was bubbled to the surface—she remembered visiting museums and wondering in awe at art and artifacts that were thousands of years old. She also recalled her trip to the pyramids and ruins in central Mexico, the Pyramid of the Sun, and the Pyramid of the Moon at Teotihuacán. She remembered being sad, even angry, that people had raided and looted the grand treasures that had once decorated those stone halls.

*Good,* the voice said, snapping the Kid back to the present. *You shouldn't take those. They belong here.*

The Kid shook his head, laughing at his overactive imagination. But he followed the advice, backing away from the statue before turning to explore the other hall. He moved across the intersection and found similar alcoves, statues, and burial plaques there.

Returning to the intersection once again, he turned to his right towards the chamber that had echoed in a way that spoke of open space. He moved towards it.

The room opened in front of him, and the light of the lantern spread across a space larger than the circle of illumination.

The Kid saw a double handful of wooden pews to the left and right, a second set on the other side of the room mirrored the first from across an aisle. People lined the benches, deteriorated clothes hanging from gaunt forms that had decayed in the moist air. Empty eyes stared at the center of the room.

In the middle of the chamber was a raised dais with a single step circling it. Floating in the air above it, dust motes dancing around it, was a lone, white-bladed dagger.

The Kid moved forward to inspect it, and the congregation with hollow dark stares stood as one and turned to look at him.

*Yes,* the voice said in his head, *keep coming, pay them no mind, liberate me from my prison.*

As the Kid turned to look at the dagger, it gleamed, a dull light emanating from it.

## Chapter 9

The shadow moved faster than Torrence could track, darting across the clearing and disappearing into the trees as the slower, lumbering forms shambled into the circle of firelight.

The undead that came forward were fresh, as in they weren't decayed and dried husks. Instead, they were still moist with the remnants of life and bodily fluids. They jerked and shuddered with each step, as if some remaining piece of who they'd been fought against the black magics that animated them, commanding them to seek the living, and bring them into the dark fold of a necromancer's siren call and control.

Axle didn't wait. He darted forward, bringing his weapons to bear. Knocking a groping, atrophied claw-like hand of the closest walking dead away with his thin dirk, he slashed out with his sword and cut along the belly of the tortured creature. Intestines wetly fell to the ground with a splattering noise, pouring onto the man's boots and entangling his feet as he darted to his next target. Tripping on the entrails, Axle went face down into the dirt.

The creature standing over him wailed, a breathy, pained sound that didn't come from the wounding it received.

The other dead thralls echoed the noise, and Torrence thought their suffering didn't come from fear or injury, but instead came from the horror of their remaining consciousness being forced to do things they would have never done in life.

Axle rolled to his back, stabbing upward into the thigh of another, what Torrence could only think of as, zombie. The weapon embedded itself into the bone, and the creature's step faltered as it looked down on the prone, and easy, prey at its feet.

Torrence had been watching his new friend and guide. He'd forgotten to watch for his own safety. A dozen hands grabbed at the man, pulling him to wrinkled, dehydrated lips and mouths with blackened and loose teeth.

A shadow hissed from behind the things grappling Torrence, and it almost seemed to hold a voice, and a meaning, in the noise.

Torrence raised his weapon above the arms gripping him, changed his hold on the blade, and brought the sword down and across the limbs in a swift motion.

The weakened grips broke free, throwing the things sideways with the strength of the movement.

"Aku'ji," a voice hissed from the trees.

Torrence looked towards the noise in time to see the sinewy form of the lightning-quick beast springing at him.

The thing barreled into him, knocking him backwards, and he stumbled over the small campfire and fell onto his back.

Torrence lifted his legs from the flames and rolled out of the fire. The thing from the trees still atop him, and held back from tearing into his face with pointed teeth by the sword.

The barbarian pushed upward with his weapon, one hand on the pommel, the other on the blade, at the same time as he bucked his hips and threw the thing away from him.

The creature weighed almost nothing, being barely more than bones, sinew, and skin. Its head was devoid of hair, and its face contorted in a rictus of hate and anger, as if the constant pain it felt was only held at bay by killing and feeding.

It flew off the swordsman, rolled, and leaped back into the shadows of the trees.

Buried under the impaled creature, his sword—embedded in the thing's thigh bone—ripped from Axle's grasp. His dirk flashed, once, twice, three times, and cut ligaments and tendons on the monster's neck, back, and thigh, the man moving his attacks lower along the body.

The creature still writhed, but with the puppet strings of biology severed, it had little to no control over its own body.

*It,* thought Axle, pushing the thought forcefully into his own mind. In actuality, the thing rolling off him looked like a plump, middle-aged woman that had smiled at him in his village's marketplace as he traded a few coins for a push-barrow, just three months before.

He blinked away the thought and rolled to his feet. Grabbing his pock-marked sword, he waggled it from the thing's thigh, shoved his booted foot into its gut, and pulled his weapon free.

Three more dog-piled on top of him, pushing him back into the dirt. The shadowy form of the lithe undead leaped on top of the mound of fighting forms and swiped downward with its clawed hand, hissing.

"Aku'ji," the thing rasped, clawing at Axle's eyes.

*Would an undead without eyes before it was turned be less efficient?* Axle wondered, squirming his dirk along the midsection of one creature, and pulled the weapon free, cold innards spilling across him.

Claws raked across the blonde man's forearm.

Axle plunged the blade into the bloated eye of the thing above him, pulled it free, and did the same to a second.

Torrence pulled his sword free from the body of the fifth undead creature to attack him. Body parts, still squirming and twitching, lie around the tortured torsos at his feet.

The big man spun towards his friend.

Axle struggled under three of the bloated dead; two of them clutching at their ruined eyes, and the third attempting to get to him by biting its way through the other two zombies. The ghast—Torrence's mind supplied the word—perched on top of the whole pile.

"This is some bullbidj," Torrence said, and swung his sword in a wide arc.

The blade met the rasping creature's neck, snapping it with an audible noise. Knocked three meters with the blow, the thing scampered away on all fours and into the trees, its head bouncing back and forth from its chest to its shoulder.

Torrence skewered the topmost zombie, flinging it aside, and kicked the next one from the pile.

Axle thrust the remaining creature away, rolled to his feet, slipped in the loose, wet slurry of guts, and stood, weapons at ready.

Sounds of labored breathing from the two men, sibilant gasps from the undead monsters, and the noise of the retreating ghast filled the clearing.

Axle stabbed downward, piercing one of the undead's eyes and pushing his blade into the brain. The monster went still. He chopped at the thing's neck, severing the head, and kicked it away from the body.

"Take their heads," Axle panted, "then we burn them to make sure they can't come back."

"Yeah," Torrence said, "I know that."

And he did. He knew it twice. Once from his own world and the books, movies, and TV shows that made up the mythology of the living dead, and a second time from the memories of the body he now wore.

The two made quick work of the remaining creatures, all the while keeping a watchful eye for the ghast or more of the newly made dead.

Nothing else came, though they both agreed that it felt like something was watching from nearby.

They piled the heads, after removing them from the bodies, into the fire, adding the wood they'd collected to keep the fire going.

The odd combination of wet corpses and dried extremities caused the fire to alternate between sputtering and flaring, and the two men gathered more wood as needed, always staying together.

Their clothes were wet with ichor and juices from the newly dead things, and the smell clung to them. Unlike many smells, they didn't get used to this one, and a shift in the wind often caused them to gag as the odor hit them anew.

Once they'd tossed heads, limbs, torsos, and other odd bits in the fire, the two gathered their few belongings and headed into the night.

Three days later, they arrived in the small village of Hope's Hollow. It was just after midday, the sun hidden by looming clouds that had an odd orange tint to them.

The only other encounter the men had in their journey was a two-headed bear that fought with itself as much as it snapped at them. The beast seemed to have grown it recently, they surmised by the ripped and torn flesh from which the extra head had jutted.

When arriving in the village, three men armed with mauls and pitchforks greeted them. Recognizing Axle, the men hailed him with caution.

"Axle," an older man with steel colored hair said as he nodded, "where've you been?"

"Caught by slavers outside of town, Richeal," Axle smiled at the man and rested his hand on the pommel of the sword at his waist, "got free with the help of this lug."

The three men eyed the barbarian, taking in his size and weapon.

"Torrents, this is Richeal, Frebel, and Bert," Axle said, gesturing at each man "gentlemen, this is Torrents, a swordsman of some skill, a tracker of beasts, and slayer of the undead."

"Hm," Richeal grunted, then gestured past him, "well, go on then. I think your hut is still standing, and no one's moved into it yet, but I can't guarantee that people haven't taken what they needed from it."

"Excellent," Axle bowed to the man, and then strode forward as he turned to Torrence, "at least we'll have a roof over our head tonight."

"So," Torrence followed Axle, "I want to call bullbidj on you being just a woodsman and a carpenter."

# Chapter 10

The Kid felt torn between running for the dagger hanging in mid-air before him, or turning to face the three score skeletal forms moving towards the center aisle between the rows of pews. They walked in slow, jerking steps towards him in a single file line, like parishioners moving towards the front of a church to take communion.

He ran forward, leaping into the air as he reached the first step of the dais, and felt a tingle along his skin when he entered the area surrounding the dagger.

Awareness washed over him. The feeling of being entered filled the Kid. His mind reeled as a presence intruded and layered atop his own.

He stood in an empty chamber, identical to the one he'd been in moments before. Differences lit up in vision, like how hidden objects in children's shows or that old TV series, Psyche, would reveal themselves to the characters looking for clues.

Things popped into existence, one at a time, then moved with life and motion.

The room was lit with glowing orbs of magic, casting clear white light across the immense chamber. The pews were bustling with believers; the passageway behind the Kid—that he'd just come through—was plainly visible and showed an inscription above it that said 'Hall of Heroes'. A passage to the right led to the chamber being excavated for guests, priests, and visitors on holy pilgrimages. Across from it was where the attendant priests and acolytes were housed, and showed people grouped together, laughing and talking. The two remaining halls that led to the outdoor area of worship were wreathed in fresh boughs of holly and mistletoe.

The parishioners were of many more species and races than just human. Towering people with reptilian heads prayed, short and stout rokairn mingled with lithe and graceful aeifain and dasism, and other peoples of all skin tones peppered the crowd.

A half dozen priests, resplendent in silk robes of reds, yellows, and oranges interwoven with threads of silver and gold, discussed topics, and waited in the wooden choir box for the ceremony to begin.

Then the ground shook and dust sifted down from the ceiling.

The Kid was back in the present, landing on the dais, his hand outstretched to grasp the weapon floating in the dim gloom of the chamber. His lantern had fallen from his hand in the jump, crashing to the ground and shattering. The oil, scattered on the temple floor, caught fire and small flames dotted the path the Kid had taken.

The gaunt figures were closer, and a humming rose from their forms that no longer had lungs and throats to raise such a noise.

The other vision returned.

Priests encircled the platform, hands and voices raised in prayer and supplication, as the worshipers in the room were slain by thin creatures with enormous eyes and green or grey skin. Demons ruptured through glowing orange portals, cutting down anyone within reach with swords of flame and smoke.

The Kid was again in the now, his hand closer to the blade. His fingers hit a barrier that pushed him away from the artifact.

*Don't quit now,* the voice encouraged him, *you've almost got me.*

The world spun in a swirl of colors, and the vision swelled again.

Four reptilian beings in robes stood on the dais, one at each of the cardinal points, chanting. A fifth priest lay on the altar in the center, holding a silver dagger in one hand

and a large, curved tooth, the size of his own forearm, in the other.

The room beyond was awash with blood and gore. The head of a dragon—the Kid instinctively knew that's what it was (what else could be that large and scaly?) but couldn't fathom how it had gotten inside the underground complex—lay jutting into the room from the side passage that led to the priest's quarters, its mouth bloody where a tooth had been torn free.

The voices of the four priests rose to an apex, the walls shook, and the altar crumbled. The fifth priest, on the stone table, pulled the silvered weapon and the dragon's tooth together, and stabbed them as one into his own chest.

The stone he laid on, his body, and the weapons fell into themselves, collapsing into a coalesced singularity.

The four chanting holy men's words cut off, and they screamed, but that cut off as well. A silent, unseen burst of energy rushed outward and threw the demonic and green and grey forms backwards.

Then the room was silent.

Dead forms sat in pews, and the attackers were gone, banished through the disappearing portals that had brought them here, or disintegrated to dancing motes of dust.

The Kid's hand wrapped around the handle of the dagger, and it was hot in his grip.

He was back in the present, and the dead forms were slowing, stopping, and kneeling in front of him.

Overwhelmed for a moment, he collapsed to his knees, breathing heavily like he'd just run the most frantic marathon he'd ever run.

The Kid looked at the weapon in his hand. It was a simple design, common almost, but the blade was a bone white metal with a slightly serrated edge, and the handle wrapped in blood-red, soft, leather.

Looking at the bowing corpses, he saw them begin to discorporate and fade from existence. Long dead remains appeared on the floor around the room. Pews became broken and burnt, and the few remaining items that had decorated the walls fell into ruin, returning to the state they'd been within the vision, if you added many centuries of time to them.

"What the hell is going on," the Kid muttered, running his fingers through his hair.

*Yeah, okay,* the dagger said in his head, *you aren't the best choice, and aren't really worthy, but I guess it's better than waiting another six-thousand years for someone else.*

The chamber rumbled, and a fist-sized stone fell from the ceiling a few meters from the Kid. Another clattered on a broken pew across the room. A half dozen more, in various parts of the room, followed suit.

*You might,* the voice said, *want to remove yourself from the premises immediately.*

The trail of oil fed fires doused as sand and earth drifted across them from the rapidly decaying ceiling. The light went out.

Another rumble, and the rain of stone intensified.

*Now,* the voice was whimsical, but had an edge to it, *would be better than later.*

The Kid stood, shoved his satchel behind him from where it had fallen at his side, and ran.

He ran blindly in the dark.

*Not that way,* the dagger advised, *that's the way you came. Remember, 'shitter's full'? Go the other way, through either of the passages to the north. Both lead outside, and away from certain death. Here, let me help.*

The interior of the building lit with a dim glow, the sight of the being within the magical weapon extending to its wielder.

The Kid spun, sliding to his knees in the dust coating the floor, stood up, and ran in the other direction.

A floor plan popped into his head, showing him that the way out was a few meters away. Just go through the open doorway, follow it out, and into the waiting holy grove.

More stones fell, the Kid dodging around them.

The Kid moved into the right-hand passage, sprinting, and felt a breeze and smelled fresh air.

Veering right, he followed the passage and the smell of freedom, and saw the dim light of dusk ahead of him. Interwoven branches blocked it and leaves where the holly and mistletoe had grown to cover the entrance over centuries of being unattended.

He ran straight into the tangle, slashing at the branches with the dagger, and pulling at them with his free hand.

*Ugh,* the dagger said into his mind, *this is so below me.*

"Shut up," the Kid growled.

A rumble, a cloud of dust, and a rush of air as the underground compound collapsed followed him, throwing him face first into the underbrush blocking his way.

Pushing through the vegetation, the Kid emerged into the last remnants of daylight. Stumbling forward, he collapsed to the ground and looked around, still holding the dagger.

The grove was a natural, rough semicircle of rock and bushes. Small protrusions of stone lined the natural amphitheater in semi-straight rows.

*It wasn't always like this,* the voice in his head said, sounding nostalgic, *it had beautiful carvings along the rock face, topiaries lining the edges, and stone seats for people to sit on during sermons and gatherings.*

"Who are you?" the Kid asked with exasperation, holding the dagger up to eye level.

*I am,* the dagger sighed in the Kid's mind, *I don't think you could pronounce it, but it's a bit like this.*

"I may surprise you…" the Kid started to say, but was cut off as a flood of concepts bombarded him.

Dragons, flights of hundreds of huge reptilian beings, were the beginning of what the mystical artifact showed the Kid. The color of belief, and a burst of the emotion of passion and inner drive, followed it.

*Edsumar'granoo-fisgobske-haistevan'zazott,* was the jumbled word that would be the dagger's name.

After a few moments of waiting for his head to stop spinning and his stomach to stop turning, the Kid held his hand to his head and rubbed his eyes.

"Nope," the Kid said, "you're right. I'm not even going to try to pronounce that goobly-gook. I can call you Dragon's Dagger, and that's the best you're going to get."

*How about Edsumar? That's a nickname I went by among your kind,* the voice in the Kid's head said, and it felt like it nodded. *If that's ok, that'll do. And why is it so crowded in your head? It's like you have more than just you and me in here.*

"I can handle Edsumar. And to answer your question, it's a long story," the Kid stood, "and one I'd rather not go into."

*Ah,* Edsumar said, and the feeling of understanding was in the words, *I see. Very well, that'll do.*

"Just don't add pig after 'That'll do', and we'll be okay."

*You do come from an odd place,* Edsumar said.

"Stay out of there," the Kid said and mentally clamped down.

*Oh ho,* Edsumar sounded pleased, *you do have some strength to you. Good, that'll make this easier. I think we need to go north towards the home of the dragons.*

"Oh really, do you now?" the Kid said aloud, "And why would I do that?"

*Because you have nowhere better to go?* Edsumar said. *And I have a sense of the world. You seek adventure, right? To live life to the fullest and all that stuff? Well, I can point you in the right direction.*

"Yeah, okay," the Kid turned in the direction he thought the dagger meant, "I guess I can do that. It might be a long walk, but we'll get there."

*No need,* Edsumar sounded smug in the Kid's head, *I have summoned a ride for us.*

"You have Uber here?" the Kid asked, surprised.

*What is an Uber?* the dagger asked, a gust of wind stirring up a cloud of dust.

The Kid's next words were cut off as a shape blocked out the light of the setting sun.

A gigantic form, winged with a long neck, settled onto the ridge above the Kid. Looking up with wide eyes, the Kid stumbled backwards and fell on his ass.

"Really?" he squeaked. "A mother chuzzing dragon?"

## Chapter 11

Hope's Hollow lay shrouded in a tint of orange clouds for more than a day when the Kid sauntered into it. Trinity, the human nickname of the dragon who'd flown him from the temple ruins, had dropped him off within a two-hour walk from the village.

The dragon had been a fascinating conversationalist, and apparently one of the last remaining of her kind out of the score of dragons to have survived the Downfall. The creatures were feared and despised by what were called the civilized races—humans, rokairn, aeifain, dasism, and others—and had withdrawn to the Wandering Hills many millennia ago after the Wizard Wars.

They'd built an idyllic society away from people, in what others had dubbed the wild lands. In the sprawling ridges of the mountains, they'd called to creatures to come and settle in their territory. Herds of deer and goats, and caravans of humans had answered the call. The people had settled into fertile valleys, raised herds of domesticated cattle, and harvested plentiful crops.

The dragons and people lived in a symbiotic relationship, the former providing protection and the latter providing a constant source of food with their livestock.

Trinity had talked with the Kid, exchanging stories of times gone, passing on the oral history of dragons on the continent of Teurone in this world called Aertheia to this one lone human who was a stranger to the land.

Edsumar had remained quiet most of the time, though apparently it could speak freely into the mind of its wielder and any dragon within a certain distance.

The Kid learned from Trinity that Edsumar had been a leader of their kind, and was also the dragon slain in the battle the Kid had seen in his vision in the catacombs. The dragon's essence transferred, along with the essence of the five reptilian priests, into the dagger in the ritual. The same dagger that the Kid now carried at his hip—wrapped in a rough wooden sheath he'd whittled on the trip—across from the wavy, stolen blade of Jakdin.

The orange cloud cover worried the Kid, and he walked to the village, keeping one eye on the sky and one on the trail. The winds blew warm from the west, and the birds and insects had fallen almost completely silent, only making noise when disturbed by the Kid's passing.

Hope's Hollow lay at the eastern end of a passage through the Wandering Hills. It was a cluster of hovels and huts, mostly of woven branches and mud-made clay bricks. The ground, partially covered with leaves shed by an early cold snap, showed a path winding its way through the fallen vegetation towards the settlement.

The air held that crisp feel of autumn, and the gentle scent of decaying life as the world inevitably turned towards the dying season. The scents blended with an odd partner, a tinge of rusting iron, a metallic coppery scent that reminded the Kid of blood in your mouth after biting your tongue. He glanced up at the clouds again, watching them slide and shift against one another for a few moments.

Two men and a short woman stepped away from a small, partially concealed, lean-to at the edge of the village, armed with scythes and pitchforks.

"What do you want?" A man with steel-colored hair held a pitchfork across his body and blocked the path.

"Richeal," the woman moved up next to the man, "don't be rude, he's barely more than a child."

The Kid eyed the three, sizing them up.

The man who'd spoken was broad and thick, not from overeating, but from working, and carried himself with a threatening bravado. The Kid had dealt with men like this his whole other life.

The short woman was middle-aged, but still had smooth skin even though her hair, which she'd pulled up into a bun on her head, showed thick streaks of white.

The third man was drawn and thin, flesh hanging off his jaws, with an expression that matched it.

Most men could be sorted into one of three groups, from what the Kid had seen in nearly eighty years of living in what had often been described as a man's world. The first type was bold and often bullies. The second type were meek and often walked on. The third was a balance between the two, but almost always started as one type or the other, and changed through learning and experience.

The man named Richeal seemed to be the third type, but the Kid couldn't yet pick out if he'd started out as a bully or meek. Time would show everyone's roots and true colors, eventually.

"Well, I think we've had enough strangers here recently," the other man, who was definitely the meek type, whined and leaned around Richeal to look at the newcomer, "and it doesn't bode well. The priestess was one thing, but the barbarian yesterday, and now this one, both arriving with the blood-tainted clouds hanging above us? It bodes ill, mark my words."

"Oh Shena," the woman said scornfully, turning to roll her eyes at the man, "go grow some tea leaves and find some bones in the pig pen and become a soothsayer if you want us to listen to your constant dire warnings, will you?"

She turned back to the Kid.

"I'm Eloise," the woman smiled, and gestured to each of the men in turn, "this is Shena and Richeal, and don't pay them much mind. They've been around long enough to be wary of anything and everything, but I have more sense than they do. Come on, I'll escort you in."

The woman leaned on her scythe and held her arm out for the Kid to take. He did, and they walked into the village, arm in arm.

She talked as they went, telling the Kid about what the place had been like when the first twenty people had settled here, about five years ago. Eloise had been here about five months.

She mentioned how people had come and gone—some dying, others just leaving—and how it wasn't uncommon for a half-dozen people to leave one day without warning and a wagon train to pull in the next week with twenty new people to settle. Before she had arrived, about four-hundred people lived here, and now about two hundred and fifty, but more than half of them had shown up after she had taken up residence.

The plague had taken a lot of people from them, but more were already showing up. Like the new priestess, Esperanza, that Shena had mentioned, or the Barbarian, Torrents, who'd brought with him a lost son of the village, Axle.

The Kid listened without interest when the woman began, but then thought about the law of coincidences, and how Edsumar had mentioned something about adventure in this direction. The dagger had been suspiciously quiet over the past few days, and the Kid was unsure if it was just sleeping or what was going on. Who could know the mind of a powerful dragon stuck inside a knife, anyway?

In less than ten minutes–they'd walked slowly to allow Eloise to talk–the two arrived in the village. People went about mundane tasks, but each looked at Eloise and the newcomer with mistrustful looks.

A man herded a flock of geese down the muddy road; the butcher hung sides of swine up; the baker stood next to the blacksmith—each in the apron of their profession—wiping his flour covered hands on his stained apron while discussing some topic or another with the burly, bearded man; and a dozen other common activities of small settlements everywhere were happening under the strange sky.

In the center of the cluster of buildings was a well, about two meters across, with people clustered there to trade goods and gossip.

A dark-haired woman, assisted by a smiling, craggy-faced woman, bent over a group of children, checking them over, looking into their eyes, and inspecting their hands and arms.

An enormous man, who stood almost thirty centimeters taller than everyone around him, followed by a smaller blonde man, carried two empty barrels into the crowd and set them down. The smaller man began dickering over the price of the barrels with a third man.

It was all very normal, which was odd, considering that this world wasn't very normal.

Eloise introduced the Kid around, and he earned even more apprehensive looks when he introduced himself as 'the Kid'.

Eloise told the Kid to pick an empty hut to make his own, and was kind enough to recommend one at the edge of the settlement that wasn't in too much disarray.

After meeting a few more people, purchasing a loaf of bread, bartering for a rasher of bacon with a tin box, and filling his canteen at the well, the Kid headed to the recommended dwelling.

Thunder crackled and fell into a slow rumble as the Kid pushed open the door and looked inside. It was a one-room hovel with a fire pit in one corner, a shelf over it, and a broken crate beside it. A moth-eaten blanket and a chair with three legs were the only other things in the place. The ceiling showed the eerie sky through a handful of holes that needed to be thatched.

"Well," the Kid said to the empty room, "I've slept in worse, and at least I'll have a roof, sort of, above my head tonight."

He gathered some kindling and firewood from the nearby woods, went in, and closed the door behind him. Settling onto the three-legged chair, leaning it against a wall so it would stand, he ate some of what he'd bought and a bit of cheese he had in his bag that had been wrapped in cloth. He washed it down with his water and followed that with a swig of whiskey from the flask he kept in his boot.

Pulling out his bedroll, and using his satchel as a pillow, he settled in for a nap. It took him longer than normal to doze off, his mind working at a problem that it couldn't quite figure out if it was real or just paranoia. Something was not quite kosher.

He slept.

The Kid woke, and the room was dark, except for the odd orange light emanating from the clouds. The thunder rolled, an almost constant low rumble overhead. Flashes of green heat lightning accompanied the noise.

The Kid was used to staying up most of the night, going to sleep a few hours before dawn, and then waking up just before noon.

*So was Jen,* said Edsumar in the Kid's head.

"So now you're around?" the Kid scoffed and shook his head.

Edsumar didn't answer.

The Kid went about his routine, scrubbing at his pits and bits with a wet cloth, then doing a quick wipe of the rest of him, one part at a time, undressing and dressing as he cleaned up.

He crept into the night, having decided to look around once everyone was asleep. People asked fewer questions about why you were in their house if they weren't awake. And you could find a lot more answers, a lot quicker, that way.

After checking a dozen huts, he was pretty confident there wasn't much here worth knowing, let alone stealing.

He stood in the shadows, watching the butcher creep back to his own house from the blacksmith's—a late-night, secret rendezvous, no doubt—and snickered as he thought about what the two men's wives would think.

A sudden squeak from the baker made the Kid turn back to look in that direction.

In the glow of orange clouds above, the Kid saw Eloise standing over the baker, who'd fallen to knees and then backwards to the ground, with the scythe buried in his chest.

She chanted quietly and sprinkled crushed herbs on the man. A moment later, she pulled a stoppered beaker from a pouch, and poured a viscous liquid into the throat of the dead man.

A green orb of lightning shot from the clouds above and slammed into the man's body. The corpse on the ground lurched and shuddered, then sat up.

Eloise pulled the scythe from the chest of her new minion; the Kid could see the curved blade of the reaping tool drinking in the blood that coated it.

"Rise," Eloise intoned in a smoky voice, "rise, my child, and join your brethren."

The shadows in the tree line behind the woman shifted, then moved, as dozens of undead creatures lurched, shambled, scrambled, bounced, and crept forward.

"Oh, chuz," the Kid muttered.

Eloise raised her eyes to look at him and smiled.

# Chapter 12

Eloise's hair was no longer streaked with white, or in a bun on her head. It was bright red and flared around her face and shoulders. The woman's clothing was no longer drab colors in a simple village style. Instead, it was a midnight blue robe with runes of silver thread decorating the cuffs and hem.

She took a step towards the Kid.

The Kid had dealt with powerful people—in both worlds—more times than he could count. He'd dealt with store managers, bikers, CEOs, military leaders, teenage high school students, politicians, and others in the old world. He'd dealt with assassins, murderers, thieves, angry fishwives, irate city guards, and drunken perverts in this world. Actually, that second group could have been in either world. But he'd never dealt with a necromancer backed by a hungry horde of magically animated and loyal corpses.

The Kid stumbled backwards, falling to his ass, and then crab-crawled backwards until he hit a wall. His eyes darted from her to the undead creatures moving forward into the village, and soon she was lost to his sight.

He crab-walked up the wall until he was standing. The whole time he was doing 'hfrah-frahl-hraf' sound, like when someone takes too large of a bite of steaming hot food, and was trying to cool it while it was still in their mouth. In truth, he was trying to work up the breath to scream.

That task was taken from him when the creatures behind the woman fanned out and began rushing into hovels.

At first, it just a couple surprised yells, but in less than a minute, it had become a chorus of screams and panicked shouting from dozens of different huts. Villagers poured out of their shacks and into the mud road that meandered through the center of the town. Screams were cut off in mid-breath as people were taken down in the street under the blood tint emanating from the clouds.

"By Senaria's Honor," boomed a deep shout, and a bare-chested warrior with a sword almost as long as he was tall burst from a rickety door. The rotting creatures were thrown back by twos and threes with each sweep of the man's mighty blade.

Torrence had woken to the slight sound of the hut's door opening and the shuffle of feet across the dirt floor. He'd turned to his side, his hand dropping to his sword's pommel—which had lain beside his pallet—lofted the weapon, rolled to the floor, swung his sword, disemboweled the creature.

Leaping to his feet, he ran out the door. His momentum had carried him into two more of the creatures, and they'd flown backwards when he ran through them.

Torrence had always loved good action flicks since he was a boy. Anything with Bruce Willis, Tom Cruise, or Dwayne Johnson was sure to be a favorite of his. He loved how they moved from one foe to the other without ever raising a sweat. It reminded him of his years as a high school quarterback when he'd run a sneak, weaving and spinning around the other team until he came out of the clump of boys and could sprint down the field.

But it wasn't like that in an actual fight. You got tangled in an enemy's grasp, or caught from behind, or your sweaty palms made the sword slip when you hit something.

*It just wasn't the same*, he thought, his bare foot sliding out from under him on a rock no bigger than a peach pit.

He caught himself before he fell, regaining his footing, but he was sure he now bled from the bottom of that foot.

Axle followed behind, using the massive form of the larger man as a blocker, and stabbing out with a thin sword and a similar, but unmatched, dagger. Slinking along behind Torrents, he slashed from the safety of the big man's shadow, literally and figuratively. He believed in playing it safe, and something as big as Torrents would be a waste to not use as cover.

His rapier jabbed into an eye, his dagger slicing under an armpit to cut tendons, and he moved constantly.

From the other direction, purplish lightning crashed down in the night and struck the earth. A handful of the vile things attacking Hope's Hollow flew in all directions.

A woman stood in the clearing smoke, her grey robe hung open and flapped in the night wind, revealing a plain cotton shift underneath with a symbol of Latress atop it. Her fists were balled at her sides, her face twisted, her jaw clenched with rage. Both her eyes and hands crackled and glowed with the same energy that had just obliterated the creatures in the lightning strike.

Esperanza was full of righteous fury. She'd woken to the screams of villagers in the distance, and Rose shouting from a meter away. The woman was beating some twisted form with a chair, kicking at it as it went down. The woman was also laughing between the shouts and curses.

Without thinking, Esperanza had snatched her robe, knife, and holy symbol from the peg on the wall, threw them on, and then called upon the power of Latress. A tendril of wind had snapped the thing from the floor and shot it out the door and into three others.

Esperanza stormed after it, in more ways than one.

She might be in her own personal hell, but she would not see others tortured for her sins. And she would not give up. If God wanted to test her, then she would use the tools she was given to crush this test, even if it meant using the powers of some pagan, heathen god. After all, the Bible mentioned other gods in almost two dozen different places.

A haggard woman, with a wicked smile of glee showing the few teeth left in her mouth, followed behind the priestess, kicking at the fallen creatures, or bashing them with a wooden chair leg.

Rose was committed to staying at Esperanza's side and giving whatever help she could. She'd seen this woman save the lives of more than a hundred people, die, and then rise again as a different woman. Esperanza's face even looked different, her skin a lovely almond color, her hair seemed longer, and Rose swore the priestess had been taller before her death.

When the two women's path crossed anyone in need of help, they paused to do so.

"Oh, okay," the Kid sighed, and pushed himself from the wall, drawing his stolen sword and the Dragon's Dagger in the same movement.

The Kid spun into the battle, slicing and slashing, then moving and weaving deeper into the fray. His weapons cut and bit, tearing down the undead like a well-honed machete tears through a field of weeds and saplings.

He dodged into the shadows beside a hut, crouching and waiting for one of the lumbering monstrosities to wander by so he could strike without being seen. His vision was clear, and he could see as well in the dark shadows as he could in the eerie light from above, thanks to the dagger's magics.

But the element of surprise didn't work out quite the way the Kid had hoped. Four of the rotting forms turned and looked straight at him.

"Great," he muttered, "of course the dead can see in the dark. Why wouldn't they be able to see in the dark. After all, they're dead."

The things may have been able to see him, but they weren't smart, and they bee-lined for him.

Once they were close enough, the Kid shot to his feet, his left hand holding the dagger traced a line from the first creature's groin, up its stomach and ribs. The Kid, flicking the point of the weapon upwards, pierced the bottom of the thing's chin, and slid the blade into its brain.

The sword in his right hand thrust forward, turning sideways so the flat of the blade was parallel to the ground.

When it hit a second creature's chest, the tip slid along a rib and moved between it and the next rib, and slipped into the thing's heart.

Both creatures crumpled to the ground. And the next two followed just as quickly.

The Kid stepped from the shadows into the street and looked around for the next opponent.

Torrence—surrounded by a mound of writhing, broken undead forms—shouted an unintelligible war cry and leaped over the bodies, running towards the pale line of figures in the trees that stood watching.

"Torrents!" Axle shouted. "don't go there, not yet, let's regroup first!"

The barbarian slowed, looked over his shoulder at his friend, back towards the dozens of waiting things, and then stopped.

Esperanza looked around. The village was a charnel field. Bodies of undead lay heaped among the newly dead corpses of the villagers.

Rose raised a hand and waved the few remaining villagers still alive to come to her, nodded at Torrence, and then at the Kid.

The clouds overhead growled again, causing all eyes to raise to the heavens. They split to reveal hundreds of green globes of energy spinning in orbit around a deep red, pulsing core.

A woman's voice began chanting, and the people who remained alive looked towards the sound. Eloise stood atop the largest building in the village, the blacksmith's stable and shed, her arms raised as she called upon the elements and gods to do her will.

The sickly verdant balls shot downward, each one striking and then sinking into a motionless corpse. Villagers, and some of her own minions that had been struck down.

Bodies twitched. As the survivors looked on in horror, they saw bone knit, organs drawn back into torsos, muscles come together, and skin draw back into puckered scars by some invisible force.

Then the dead began to rise. The butcher staggered into the village center, followed by the steel-haired Richeal. Shena pushed past Bert and Frebel, while leaning on the blacksmith.

The creatures struck down in the battle also rose, their recently gained wounds now just furrowed, greying flesh.

"Run!" came the shout from Axle, and he did as he commanded.

Grabbing Torrence's arm as he moved past him, he pulled the large man behind him.

Torrence resisted for a moment, before common sense overcame battle lust, and he ran as well.

The Kid was already paralleling the two paths, not wanting to be close enough to get trapped in an ambush, but not wanting to lose sight of them in a part of the country he didn't know.

Esperanza called upon the power of her goddess, but stopped when she realized Rose was tugging on her arm.

"We can't save them all, priestess," Rose said, her eyes wide and scared, "they're already dead."

She waved a hand at the hundreds of bodies staggering to their numb feet. Then jabbed a finger towards the dozen or so remaining people who were actually alive, and not just rictus puppets of dead flesh.

"But," Rose continued, still pulling on Esperanza, "we might save a few. We need to go now. We've done all we can here."

Esperanza let out her breath, seeming to deflate in defeat, and all the energy went out of her body. The light went from her eyes and hands, and she was just a woman again.

She nodded and let Rose pull her after the others, into the dark night as the orange clouds faded to a dull grey above them.

# Chapter 13

"Why would any of us listen to you?" Esperanza jabbed a finger repeatedly into Torrence's chest.

Rose tried to pull the priestess away by her shoulder.

"And you," Esperanza shrugged off Rose's hand and spun to face her, "you had us all run into the night, save the few, chuz the many. We might've been able to save more."

"Pfft," the Kid said, not even looking up from where he leaned against a tree and cleaned his nails, "girl, you would've just died with the rest of them, and probably got your friend and the remaining villagers turned into one of those things to boot."

Esperanza's face was already red, but now she was sputtering.

"Stop being such a child," the Kid said, "and face the facts; your friend is right; you have a death wish or are trying to prove something; the big guy was just doing what comes natural to him; and if we didn't get away when we did, we'd all be dead, or worse."

"Who the hell are you?" Torrence turned towards the Kid, and stood shoulder to shoulder with Esperanza, "and what the hell gives you the right to talk that way to a grown woman, punk?"

"I can fight my own battles," Esperanza spat the words at Torrence, "thank you very much. I don't need some bone head, muscle bound, creep trying to charge in and save me. Mind your own damned business, okay?"

"No," Torrence turned back to the priestess, and had to look down to look her in the eye, "as far as I can tell, this is my business. This is everyone who's here business. And I'd appreciate if you didn't just assume that I'm a pemtie because I'm big!"

"I don't assume you're a pemtie because you're big," Esperanza was jabbing him in the chest again, "I assume it because your pemtie."

"Oh," Torrence threw up his hands, mocking her and causing her to flinch back, "good come back, your mom write that for you?"

"Moms have been around," the Kid muttered, "and they know some pretty damned good come backs."

The two spun to face the Kid again.

"Did you just say," Torrence growled and took a step towards the Kid, "that my mom got around?"

"Okay, already!" Axle stepped between the big guy and the Kid, putting a hand on the barbarian's chest to halt him. Axle slid almost a meter before the man stopped. "Let's not do the job that the necromancer failed to do. Everyone just take a step back and a deep breath."

"We did a good thing," Rose said, her hands on her hips, glaring at Esperanza.

Rose hadn't ever seen the priestess like this before. As fear had taken the place of kindness, now anger had taken the place of fear.

Last night, they'd run from the village, gathering what people they could. Fourteen people were with them now, including herself, Axle, and the three that kept on arguing.

Axle had stepped into the role of a natural leader, with Rose mothering and herding the others along. The other dozen people were like lost sheep between the trauma of last night, and just who they normally were. Rose comforted and guided, Axle organized and gave out tasks.

The group had spent the night clustered together under an outcropping of rock in the foothills to the west. The orange clouds had dissipated, and the storm that had waited above, broke.

They'd returned to Hope's Hollow about noon the following day. The village had been deserted. No trace of the people or creatures from last night remained, other than remnants of the battle on the muddy road or inside huts.

After deciding they wouldn't stay here any longer, the group had gathered what little belongings they could take with them. Nothing had been looted. Apparently, Eloise, the necromancer, only took her things, and a walking dead army didn't need supplies.

A small group of new additions stood to one side, under the boughs of a large tree, and huddled in their cloaks, clutching their belongings.

Torrence turned his back to everyone, throwing a dagger into a stump. Esperanza was on the opposite side of the group, muttering angrily in a rapid language that the others didn't recognize.

"Where do we go from here, Rose?" Axle asked quietly.

The two had stepped away from the various clumps of people without planning it, and Axle had taken that moment to speak to the only other person with a level head.

"I honestly don't have a clue, Axle," Rose said, smiling up at the man, though the rest of her face showed unease.

She looked strained and tired. But they all did.

"It's gonna be okay," Axle said as he put a hand on her shoulder and rubbed it.

Rose leaned into it a little, glad for some comfort and human contact.

"I have an idea," the Kid said, making both Axle and Rose jump.

Neither had seen him there, or heard him come up.

"Where?" Axle said and realized his voice sounded angry.

"Am I interrupting?" The Kid raised his eyebrows and looked back and forth between the two with a small smile.

Axle adjusted his tone and asked, "Where do you think we can go? It has to be close enough that we can take all these people, walking, and dragging wagons and wheelbarrows. And it has to be somewhere that'll take in people who have nothing to offer except themselves. That means extra mouths to feed until they get on their feet again.

And winter'll be here soon, there's not time for them to grow crops, or even stockpile enough wood to last the snows."

The Kid nodded.

"Yeah," the Kid said casually, "I know all that. I've been around long enough to know how the world works."

"So," Rose said coaxingly, and put a hand on the Kid's forearm, "where is this place?"

"I'll tell you," the Kid said, looking down at the hand on his arm, "but you're going to think I'm crazy."

"Uh huh," Axle laughed, "Kid, I think we're all little crazy right now. Just tell us and let us decide if it's crazy."

"Okay," the Kid stepped away from the two, Rose's hand falling away.

He began pacing.

"On my way here, I met a very nice…" the Kid hesitated, his lips slipping between a smirk and a grimace, "lady on the trip. Her name is Trinity. She's very old, but doesn't act it, and very nice. She told me about a place where lots of people once lived. They're gone now. I think that happened in the Downfall."

"It sounds perfect," Rose said. "Is it far away?"

"Hold on," Axle said with suspicion and amusement in his voice, "I think there's a big 'but' coming soon. Go on, Kid, finish your story."

"Well," the Kid went on, plucking a leaf from the tree above him and tearing into small pieces, "I think they'll have left behind a lot of supplies, dry goods, maybe even grain and seeds. There's a possibility that their herds still roam the area, though they've indubitably all gone wild by now. And the place is sheltered and protected. I think it'd be a good fit."

"Uh huh," Axle said, putting a hand on Rose's arm to stall her questions, "and where is it?"

"It's called Dargaon's Hole…" the Kid began.

"And there it is!" Axle threw his hands into the air, laughing.

"What?" Rose asked, reaching for the man. "What's wrong with this place?"

"It's the ancestral home where dragons lived," Axle explained, still laughing, "and where they kept people as cattle for food."

"I don't think that matters anymore," Rose said. "It's not like there are any more dragons."

"Well," the Kid drew the word out.

Both stopped and looked at him.

The Kid now had an entire branch of leaves he was plucking at.

"Go on," Axle said, folding his arms across his chest.

"First," the Kid held up one finger, smiling, "they never ate people. The people raised livestock for them to eat. And in trade, the dragons gave them shelter and protection."

"Uh huh," Axle grunted, "what else?"

"And there might be a dragon left," the Kid's voice slowed and dropped until it was a mumble by the end of the sentence.

"But she's very nice," the Kid said, louder and emphatically, resembling an actual child trying to convince their parents to let him do something they didn't approve of, "and she didn't eat me, so she's unlikely to eat you guys, and you guys could rebuild their thing back to how it was. You know, work together."

Axle was now laughing hard, holding his sides, and sliding to his knees onto the wet grass.

Rose had seen people who needed a release after a huge stressful or traumatic event. Some cried, others laughed. Axle, apparently, was a laugher. She put a hand on his shoulder.

"Well," the Kid said, now with his arms folded across his chest, "are you guys going to go?"

"Sure." Axle patted Rose's hand as he wiped tears from his eyes. "Why not? I mean, we're all just as likely to die out here from exposure or bandits or slavers or mutant bunnies. So, why not?"

"Hold on," Rose said, looking at the Kid with slitted eyes, "what do you mean, 'you guys'? Aren't you coming also?"

"Um, no." the Kid said simply.

"And why not?" Axle asked, standing and wiping at the mud on his knees.

"I'm going after the necromancer." The Kid held up his hand to stop them before they could say anything. "I showed up here for a reason, and I didn't know what that was. Now, I'm pretty sure I know. I'm going after the necromancer."

"Okay Kid," Axle said, "you do what you need to do, it's your funeral."

"How do we get there?" Rose asked.

"Um," the Kid's brow furrowed.

*You'll draw them a map,* Edsumar said in the Kid's head. *I know the way. And I'll let Trinity know they're coming. But you might not want to tell them that part.*

"I'll draw you a map," the Kid smiled and looked around for a dry spot to do just that.

"How're we going to convince the others to go?" Rose asked Axle.

"Just tell them," the Kid shouted over his shoulder, "Come with me, if you want to live."

They watched the Kid walk away laughing.

"See?" Axle said to Rose, "we're all a little crazy here."

They turned towards the groups of frightened people to give them the news, but stopped when they saw Torrence and the priestess standing next to each other in a heated discussion.

"Uh oh," Rose said, "looks like we forgot the leave the kids with a babysitter, and they're fighting again."

Axle chuckled, and they headed for the pair.

Torrence and Esperanza looked up when they approached, both chagrinned.

"We have a place to go," Axle said. "The Kid, of all people, knows a place and it sounds pretty good. So, come with us if you want to live."

Both Torrence and Esperanza appeared startled at Axle's words.

"You two alright?" Rose asked, putting a hand on Esperanza's arm.

"Yeah," the priestess said, fingering her sheathed blade, "but I'm afraid we won't be going with you."

"We're going after that god-damned undead army," Torrence said.

Rose and Axle exchanged amused looks.

"Language," Esperanza crossed her arms, an accent creeping into her voice, "and don't take the Lord's name in vain."

Torrence's head snapped to look at her, a surprised look on his face.

She looked away, not wanting to start another fight.

"Looks like you won't be alone," Axle said. "The Kid's going that way too. Guess you can all go together."

Esperanza looked dismayed as she turned to the man, and Torrence snapped his head back to Axle, Esperanza's comment forgotten.

"No," the barbarian and priestess said together.

## Chapter 14

The Black Wood gained its name for three different reasons. The first was the shade of the trees, many of them walnut trees that had a naturally dark brown bark, but others were maple trees with a fungal growth, causing their trunks to appear almost black. This, in addition to how close and thick they grew to one another, caused most of the forest to be in constant shade.

The second reason was because this was where armies had clashed. Most recently in the Downfall, where demon armies met dragon armies. Previously, it had been mages battling priests, and before that, it was raised by wizards as a barricade from others finding the Nine Towers of Magic.

The third reason was the most recent addition to the myths, legends, and stories; that it was haunted by remnants of dark magics, the spirits of people and demons alike, and the reflections of magic from the Nine Towers to the east, now that it was uninhabited.

The three traveled eastward, following the trail of destruction and death from the necromancer's army. Wildlife had fled with the approach of the dead, leaving the forest eerily silent. Most movement was from the wind, and the occasional insect.

On the first day, they found a herd of deer laying in scattered pieces, disemboweled. Whatever had attacked them ate what they wanted and moved on. Three deer remained, but were no longer natural. Instead, standing on tottering legs, with sheaves of flesh torn away, leaving coagulated blood surrounding bare bone on their sides and flanks.

They stood over the remains of the herd, tearing at the flesh of their once protective circle of family. Hearing

Torrence, Esperanza, and the Kid approaching, they raised their twisted muzzles, bared their deformed teeth, and hissed.

One charged at the group, only to be taken down by Torrence's arrow, slicing through its eye and into its brain just meters before it reached the trio. The three agreed they couldn't leave the remaining two here in their condition, so they killed the mutant deer.

None of the three slept well that night. When they woke the next morning, rolling out of their blankets and packing their gear, they heard an odd noise from one of the animal corpses fifty meters away.

Upon approaching the thing, it burst open with a tearing noise and a swarm of insects rose into the morning sky and circled, looking for its next meal. It settled on another deer, only to have the dead animal split in half and fist-sized, beetle-like creatures lurch out and attack the flying insects in a frenzy.

"Khelikian," Esperanza muttered, "Lord of the flies and Emperor of insects. This is his domain now, and we should take our leave."

They set up a watch, with Torrence staying awake for the first handful of hours before midnight. He woke the Kid for the second watch, and the Kid woke Esperanza a few hours before dawn.

Two more days brought real animals back into the area. They heard squirrels and chipmunks scurry across dried leaves, or above in the tree branches. They saw racoons and possum moving through the underbrush, and even spotted a black bear clawing at a fallen tree, tearing away the bark to get to the grubs and bugs beneath.

The weather continued to be wet for those first few days, but as the temperature dropped, the rain dissipated, though the sky remained grey, and the clouds heavy.

It was hard to get their bearings in that weather, and with none of them being a woodsman, they did the best they could by finding moss-covered trees to help orient where north was.

When the Kid asked the barbarian why he wasn't better at this sort of thing, he answered he wasn't what he once was, and predominately knew the northern tundra and grasslands of the Frozen Desert.

On the fifth day, as they took a break around noon, sitting beside a stream to fill their canteens and waterskins, Esperanza spoke.

"I think we're being followed," the priestess said, "I haven't seen anything, but I feel something."

"Is your Spidey-sense tingling?" the Kid laughed, "Or your priestess-senses? Some disturbance in the dark side?"

"What did you just say?" Esperanza turned towards the Kid, reaching for him.

"Hush," Torrence hissed.

They twisted to look at him.

The big man crouched and crept forward on the balls of his feet, barely making a sound.

Esperanza looked back to the Kid to see him disappearing up a tree, only his calves and boots still visible as he climbed higher.

The priestess turned away to see a low, dark form darting between the trees.

Torrence skulked towards it, his left hand held in front of him, and his sword in the defensive stance he often used. The weapon was parallel to the ground, just above the height of the man's head, his elbow bent, the tip pointed in the direction the barbarian moved.

Esperanza fumbled with her holy symbol, and words of prayer to Latress filled her mind. She stopped, just as she was about to call upon the power she had access to, and forcibly dropped the medallion around her neck. Standing up straight, she thrust her hands to her sides, one gripping her knife, and the other clenched into a fist.

The Kid found a vantage point in the thick leaves above the forest floor. He watched Esperanza fidget and wondered why the woman fought with the powers she was given. Watching his companions, the Kid suspected that the three of them might have more in common than they knew.

Torrence moved forward slowly. The warrior's head pivoted, watching for movement in the trees.

"Watch out!" the Kid yelled, sitting up and straddling the branch, drawing his dagger.

Two forms slid from the shadows and leaped at Torrence.

The Kid pulled his arm back and let the weapon fly. Its course wobbled, then straightened itself, curving to hit its target.

Torrence heard the warning, but didn't look up. In the zone, his mind quieted as his senses took over. He could smell the ozone of the supernatural, mixing with the fetid aroma of rotting leaves, as his grandfather had taught him on the plains when he was just a child.

The warrior's ears picked up every sound; from the Kid above him, to Esperanza shuffling behind him, to the barely audible padding of a predator within the tree line. His eyes caught movement, his muscles loose but ready to tighten, to act in a heartbeat.

All this passed without a thought, and when the creature launched itself at Torrence, his sword moved on its own, slicing towards the leaping beast.

The thing went down; the sword passing above it. A dagger sunk into its skull where it met the neck; the beast collapsed to the ground and slid along the wet leaves until its nose reached the barbarian's feet.

The jaws moved, trying to snap at its prey, even though the body couldn't respond.

Torrence flipped his sword downward, grabbed the pommel in both hands, and thrust it into the beast's heart.

Baying sounded to the barbarian's right. In the distance, to his left, an answering cry rose. A third, fourth, and fifth joined the chorus until the only sound the three heard was the song of predators calling to their pack.

A silhouette stepped from behind a tree in the distance. Inhumanly thin and taller than a man, it drew in the dappled sunlight around it and devoured it by merely standing near it.

It pointed at Torrence.

A form tackled the barbarian from the right, knocking him to the ground, his sword flying into the underbrush. Teeth snapped at his face, huge paws pinning the man to the earth.

He rolled, throwing the beast atop him to one side.

It skidded to a halt three paces away, turning back towards Torrence. It resembled a wolf, in that it was a canine with fur, but that's where the similarities ended. It was as long as a wolf but lower to the ground, with shorter legs, and its coat wiry and coarse, as dark as the fungus-infected tree bark around them. Its snout was stubby and thick, and its long tail bristled with fur and thin spikes.

The thief dropped from above, blade piercing the skull of the animal, landing on its back. A cracking sound filled the area as the animal's back broke.

The Kid looked up and winked.

"I guess it wasn't that dog's day, was it?" the Kid smirked.

"There's more coming," Torrence scrambled to recover his sword.

"You think?" Esperanza said. "We need to get away from here!"

"They'll run us down," Torrence said. "they might not be fast, but they know how to track, and they'll move through the underbrush quicker and easier than we will."

"Into the trees, then," the Kid pulled his white-bladed dagger from the body of the first creature and moved to climb another tree.

"They'll just wait us out," Torrence shook his head, "we'll have to come down sometime, and they'll be right here."

"They'll get tired and look for easier prey," the Kid pulled himself up to the first branch and held a hand towards Esperanza, "and then we can be on our way."

"I don't think so," Torrence shook his head again, and scanned the trees, "there's something else with them. Something not natural."

"You felt that, too?" Esperanza asked.

The Kid closed his eyes and opened his mind to others, as he'd done countless times when tracking a mark in the city. His own magical abilities allowed him to find others; it was like having another set of eyes and ears, but different. Something cold and heavy washed across his mind, and a pinprick of pain shot through his skull.

"Yeah," the Kid drawled and dropped back to the ground, "he's right. This thing is dangerous, and different, and, I think the only way I can describe it is, evil."

*I could have told you that,* Edsumar said into the Kid's head.

"So," the Kid bent over to pick up Esperanza's pack, and handed it to her, "I guess we do a tactical retreat then."

## Chapter 15

The three ran, moving in the only direction that was away from the howling creatures. Forms darted along beside them, passing them and then stopping to watch them go by. Yips and growls were the pack communicating with one another, or distracting their quarry, as the chase went on.

Torrence sheathed his sword and held his bow in his left hand. He clutched his right arm across his chest, and blood welled from a bite mark on his bicep. He stumbled, shook his head, and wiped sweat from his eyes.

Esperanza ran, holding and lifting the hem of her robes. She panted from the exertion, but kept up. She looked at Torrence; seeing the wound, she noted it should be bleeding more. The skin around the entry points had puckered and was a bright scarlet. These things, pursuing them, must have some sort of bacteria in their mouths, similar to the Komodo dragons back home.

The Kid fell back, seeing Esperanza struggling to keep up, and Torrence hurt worse than he let on. He knew they were being herded; he'd done the same thing in the alleys of Durgan's Keep with his own sort of prey. They wouldn't last like this. One of the others would collapse sooner or later.

*I could abandon them*, he thought, then sighed. *No, I need them if I'm going to face off against a necromancer with an army of hundreds of undead.*

*What the hell am I thinking? Facing off against a necromancer? Someone who could actually create and control the living dead? This wasn't even some sci-fi thing where people had contracted a viral infection that did messed up things to them. This was someone who dictated their every action, like some sort of giant computer game where you could direct armies with the click of a mouse. It's insanity to go up against something like that.*

The Kid waited to see if Edsumar would offer some input on this one, but the magical dagger was silent.

The Kid needed a plan.

*The priestess is useless unless backed into a corner, and she lost her bidj. Only then did she do anything that was helpful,* he thought. *And the big guy would be face planting into the dirt sooner, rather than later.*

*Okay,* the Kid thought, *first things first. Get out of this mess, then deal with the impossible army.*

*That means finding a place they could hide, or a place these things couldn't get to. Or cleverly killing them all in one fell swoop of impossible luck. Option two was the best, but I have no idea where to find such a place.*

They'd been running for almost fifteen minutes. The trees thinned significantly, and the ground became hilly and rocky when the barbarian went down.

Esperanza ran about another ten steps before realizing it, slowing and turning back, tripping over her feet and tumbling onto the grass. She panted heavily, holding the stitch in her side as she crawled towards the man.

The forms had been pacing them for a while now, not bothering to hide from them or herd them in any direction. It had turned into a waiting game.

The Kid jogged up to the two and stood over them, his lips in a tight line, looking around to see if their position, or anything close by, was defendable at all. The answer was no to both.

The Kid sighed, drew out his sword, and loosely held the dagger in his other hand.

Esperanza rolled Torrence onto his back.

His breath came in wheezing gasps, and his eyes rolled back. He was no longer sweating, but his face was red and splotchy, and the wound in his arm had a deep purple tint to it.

"Boy, oh boy," cackled a voice, "you folks are in a bidj-ton of hurt, aren't ya?"

The Kid and Esperanza looked up, startled.

A small, thin man was sitting cross-legged on an outcropping of rock that jutted from the earth.

He wore a blend of furs and tattered cloth wrapped around his body, and his thin, wispy beard contrasted with his bald pate. He smiled, waving with one hand, and clutching a staff longer than he was tall in the other. Living vines wrapped around the wooden walking stick.

"It's that thing we felt," Esperanza gasped, "the thin man that Torrence saw!"

"No," the Kid's voice was calm, but calculating, "I don't think it is. Look at the things chasing us."

The Kid pointed to the crests of the surrounding hills. The beasts keeping pace with them crouched, hackles up, in twos and threes on top of the knolls.

"What the hell are they waiting for?" Esperanza spat, anger washing away any other emotion.

"Exactly," the Kid nodded, his eyes never leaving the small man, "I think it might be him keeping them at bay for the moment."

The man turned back and forth between the two, his head moving to look at each one as they spoke, his smile never faltering. It was like he was watching his favorite comedy routine.

"Can you help us?" the Kid gestured at the gathered beasts.

"Well," the man rubbed his white chin whiskers, "that depends how you define help. PepperGarten means PepperGarten thinks you three have bigger issues than some playful pups wanting to nibble on your toes."

One animal barked three times in quick succession, and all three-dozen leapt forward as one.

The man gave out a frustrated scream and bounded off the rock he'd been sitting on. Raising his hands, he whirled the staff above his head. Grass writhed at the edge of the small valley, and tendrils of plants burst through the soil. Vines and branches rose into the air, thickening as they grew.

The animals hit the top edge of the bramble hedge as it instantaneously grew beneath them, wrapping them in its thorny grip and tightening, expanding and blossoming.

"Doggie damn it," the withered man screeched, "PepperGarten is still talking here!"

The plant wall continued to expand and flower, though at a slower rate. Its tendril-like arms creeping around the beasts' throats and bodies, squeezing until they couldn't move. One animal let out a pained howl a moment before it exploded from the pressure of the plant's grip.

"Fine then," the man harrumphed, "if we can't have a reasonable conversation here because of these pemtie witch worgs, and their annoying hound master, then PepperGarten guesses you'll have to come for tea. Let's go."

The thin man turned and tottered towards the only opening in the wall of brambles.

He noticed the other three weren't following and turned back to them.

"Well," he put his hands on his hips, his staff jutting out in an awkward angle in front of him, "what's the matter, you don't like tea?"

"What about him?" the Kid pointed at Torrence, who lay on the ground, panting in quick breaths.

Esperanza stared, wide-eyed, between the man and the barrier that was slowly executing the animals in its grip.

"Oh, no," PepperGarten said in a mocking tone, "did someone get a wittle owie?"

The man moved forward and dropped down beside the barbarian.

"Lemme look at it," the wizened man bent over Torrence and grabbed the warrior's arm.

Torrence thrashed weakly and let out a moan of pain.

"You're hurting him." Esperanza moved next to the old man and reached to pull him away from her traveling companion.

She froze when she saw what he was doing.

The man had a handful of herbs and spat on them, then ground them into his palm, using his fist as a pestle and his hand as a mortar.

PepperGarten took a sharp, thin reed from a bag at his waist, cut a slit into the barbarian's upper arm, and then squeezed. Black ichor, mixed with thick blood and yellowish puss, oozed from the opening. The man spat into the wound and ground the herb mixture into it.

Torrence gasped and cried out, his body going rigid and lifting off the ground, though he stayed unconscious.

"Oh yeah," the old man cackled, "PepperGarten bets that hurts like hell!"

Esperanza lurched forward to pull the man away from the barbarian.

The wiry man bounced to his feet, and hopping from one foot to the other, danced back to where he'd been before.

"Ready for that tea now?" the odd little man said with a smile.

Esperanza knelt beside Torrence and inspected the injury. Small green sprouts grew from the poultice, knitting the flesh together and drawing the poison from the man.

The priestess tore a strip from the hem of her robe and lifted the man's arm to bind the healing gash.

"Don't do that," the old man said derisively. "You'll kill the cure, and you don't do that, do you?"

"How are we supposed to get him" the Kid gestured to Torrence, "to wherever we're going?"

"That's your problem," PepperGarten sniffed. "PepperGarten stopped him from dying. You don't expect PepperGarten to carry his heavy ass all the way, too, do you?"

Torrence lay on a bed of clover and grass inside the place PepperGarten called home.

It was a shelter within the root system of an enormous willow tree that leaned over a hilltop. The roots hung off the side of the hill, dug out either by man or nature, to form a hollow. Dense vines grew along the arm-thick branches that connected to the rich soil below, their leaves creating a wall to keep out the elements.

Dozens of praying mantises stood vigil on the leaves, as a handful of groundhogs nibbled at dandelions on the grass outside. A score of different breeds of birds darted in and out of the leaves above, swooping down to make a meal of fluttering moths.

A nest of squirrels, in the natural rafters of the underside of the tree, chittered in angry judgement of the guests.

A fox sat on her haunches, three kits playing at her feet with two ferrets, watching the intruders who shared her den.

PepperGarten puttered about, muttering to himself—or perhaps to the animals, it was hard to tell—dropping various berries and greens into wooden bowls. A small earthen chiminea held a ceramic teapot, heating it slowly.

"So," PepperGarten said, setting small clay cups in front of the Kid and Esperanza, "what did you pemties do to piss off a hound master so much that he brought his full contingent of witch worgs?"

Sitting on a grassy tuft, Esperanza shrugged, brushing uncomfortably at her robes to remove briars stuck there.

"I think we're just that good," the Kid smirked.

"Oh," the old man put his fists on his waist and thrust his hips forward and back, "is that so? And if that's the case, are you sure it doesn't have to do with that cranky old dagger you have on your side? How's Edsumar doing nowadays, anyway?"

The Kid jumped at the mention of the name of his magical weapon's dragon spirit.

## Chapter 16

Torrence ran. The Shadow Man was right behind him, though he never seemed to move. Each time Torrence looked behind him, the Shadow was standing there watching him.

He ran through the halls of his high school, lockers flying past him as he approached the gym. His history teacher, Mr. Stevens, stepped out of a classroom. The man gasped and turned to look at Torrence rushing past him. When he looked back, the teacher was now the Shadow Man, reaching for him with long, slender fingers made of solid smoke.

Torrence tried to scream, but couldn't catch his breath.

He ran on, stumbling around the corner, and saw the gym doors in the distance, the logo of the Battling Wolfhounds, his school's mascot, emblazoned across the two doors.

Regaining his feet, he sprinted forward; the entrance seeming to recede as he tried to reach it.

He burst through the doors that had seemed so far away just a moment ago, and into the pep rally. Painted paper banners proclaimed, 'Bash the Barbarians' and other such slogans adorned the gym walls.

Torrence slowed, panting, and bent over, hands on his knees, trying to catch his breath. The crowd howled at his entrance.

He looked into the stands, and hundreds of students had heads of the creatures that had pursued him and his companions through the Black Wood.

He stumbled backwards, turning towards the door. The Shadow Man, his mouth a thin line of pearly jagged teeth, blocked his way.

The Shadow Man reached for him.


"M-my, what?" The Kid stared at PepperGarten. "Who? I don't know what you're talking about."

"That magic dagger," the man giggled, pointing, "it's been crying and whining for someone to come get it for a long time now. PepperGarten's glad it finally found some poor sucker to take it for a walk."

"Your what?" Esperanza looked at the Kid. "You have a magic dagger? Are you bidjing me?"

"Well, it doesn't do much," the Kid put a protective hand on the dagger's red leather grip, "it's really just more pretty than anything."

"Oh ho," PepperGarten spun, picked up three of the bowls of berries and greens, carried them to the two guests, and thrust them into their hands, "and what does Edsumar have to say about that? Does it agree with you? I bet it agrees that it's pretty! Eat your grub, you're going to need the strength."

The Kid started popping berries into his mouth, so he didn't have to answer.

"Is it talking to you right now?" PepperGarten whispered conspiratorially, "Is it feeding you information the way PepperGarten feeds you grub?"

"It talks to you?" Esperanza was still staring at the Kid.

"Who you gonna believe?" the Kid mumbled around a mouthful of food, "Me, or a crazy man in the woods?"

"You're in the woods right now, mister," Esperanza snorted, "but fair point. But come on, spill it. With the things I've run across since I got here, a talking knife wouldn't even begin to be the most incredible thing I've seen."

"New here, eh?" PepperGarten cackled. "Thought so, both of you. All three of you. Too dumb to have been here the whole time."

The room grew quiet, and Esperanza and the Kid traded looks.

PepperGarten moved across the room and folded himself into a sitting position beside the fox with his legs crossed. The man began scrubbing the animal behind the ears, then down her side to get her belly.

She fell over to let the man give her belly rubs, making squeaking yips that sounded like laughter.

"You two should talk about this sometime," PepperGarten looked back at his guests, "you know?"

Neither answered, and both concentrated on eating.

"Okay then," the old man said, wiggling his arm that now had a fox kit and ferret attached to it as they grappled for his attention and their own belly rubs, "well, then just remember, and think about if you're staying or if you're leaving when the time comes."

"We can stay?" the Kid said, turning his attention to PepperGarten.

"We can leave?" Esperanza said at the same time.

"Sure," PepperGarten cackled, "we all decide that for ourselves. Just remember, you're here for a reason. And PepperGarten doesn't mean the reason you have when you're here, but the reason you don't have when you're not here."

"What's that even mean?" Esperanza snorted.

PepperGarten grew quiet and still, staring at Esperanza intently.

"That's up to you," the man said.

Cackling, PepperGarten leapt to his feet again, and moved to where Torrence lay.

"This isn't good," the wild man said. "Our third visitor isn't doing well. It seems a bit of the hound master got inside of him."

"What's that mean?" the Kid asked, "and don't say that it's up to me."

"Nope," the old man stood, plucking herbs from terracotta pots and placing them into his other hand. "This one isn't up to you. It's up to him; it's his fight, but PepperGarten will see if PepperGarten can't whip up a little something to help him out."

Ten minutes later, the Kid and Esperanza held the unconscious barbarian's thick, muscled arms as he struggled against the vile tea that PepperGarten poured down his throat.

Torrence fell through the darkness and hit the road hard, landing on his back.

The Shadow Man stood by a car, flipped over on its side in the ditch next to the asphalt. He smiled at the teenager in front of him and then turned towards the vehicle.

"You stay away from that," Torrence yelled, "my dad's in there, and he needs help!"

The figure ignored him and slowly walked around the trunk of the car, his fingers running along the bumper, his nails rasping out the sound of metal on metal.

Torrence charged, wishing he had a weapon, and closed the distance, desperate to get to the thing before it took his father from him again.

He had his sword in his hand. Torrence glanced down for a moment, and then accepted the fact that his two-handed blade was where it belonged, in his firm grip.

The scene shifted, as it often does in dreams and nightmares, with an otherworldly reality of acceptance of the impossible.

Torrence sat at a square wooden table, the sword laying across it, and the Shadow Man in a chair across from him.

"So," the smoke figure hissed, "you do fight, but only for others, and not for yourself."

The space beyond them didn't exist. It was a wall of darkness a meter away, and Torrence thought that if he reached a hand out and touched that negative space, he'd never see that limb again.

"I fight," Torrence spat the words out at the thing. "I've fought all my life. You don't have any idea what I've gone through."

"You fight, do you?" the man was fading, "then you can fight now."

The table disappeared, and the sword was in Torrence's hand. He was in his wheelchair, sitting in the middle of a dirt-floored arena.

The stands were filled with endless wolf-headed fans, howling for blood, and halogen stadium lights shone down on him, blinding him from whatever foe approached.

The morning brought frost, making the grass around the sanctuary crisp and white, gleaming and glittering in the first rays of the sun.

Esperanza stood outside, her robe wrapped tight around her and her arms folded across her breasts against the chill. Her breath misted in front of her.

She stared at the small blade clutched in her hand.

The Kid was still asleep inside, no doubt because he'd stayed up most of the night doing whatever it is he does when everyone else is sleeping.

That crazy old man, PepperGarten, wasn't anywhere to be found, but footprints crushed into the rime led away from his home.

Esperanza dreamt last night.

She'd been in the stands of an arena, a blend of something from ancient Rome and the Superbowl. Shadowy figures that she couldn't make out had surrounded her, and a scared young black man sat in a wheelchair in the center of the dirt.

She couldn't remember much more, but she had flashes of the big fight and the pain that was in it.

She wondered about her own situation, looking at the knife in her hand.

Were both of the people she was with from her world? Was everyone here from Earth? Was this place in her head, as she lay dying from the pills and alcohol, or was it more real than that? Maybe it was hell, but she no longer thought it was her own private punishment.

PepperGarten had said they'd have a chance to leave. Did they get to decide when? Or was it when they died here?

Could she end it right now, with a few simple cuts of her knife? Or was this part of the plan?

She shook her head, her dark hair moving around her face.

It was too much, and Esperanza just couldn't get her head wrapped around it.

She heard the Kid inside, talking to the squirrels and giggling as he said something about someone named Rocky and asking where Bullwinkle was, then began talking about the creature's nuts.

PepperGarten crested the hill in the distance, waved his greenery staff in her direction, and yelled something to her she couldn't hear. But she could make out his pemtie cackle.

Esperanza sighed, shook her head, turned, and went back inside.


The Shadow Man stalked towards Torrence, dragging a huge black sword as wide as a grown man's shoulders with a sloped jagged edge across the sands of the arena.

"Fight," the Shadow Man whispered in an emotionless voice.

"Look at me," Torrence shouted at his foe, "how can I fight like this?"

"Then give up," the Shadow Man said, "die, and make room for the next combatant. To live, you must fight."

Torrence pulled at his sword, dragging the tip through the sand, drawing it across his lap.

"Every day," the thing said, "you must fight. With every ounce of yourself, with every fiber of your being, you must fight."

"What kind of crap is that?" Torrence sat up in his chair. "That sounds like my old coach before a game. That sounds like every therapist I've ever seen. That sounds like complete bidj."

The crowd chanted. The sound started as a low rumble, the words blending and falling over one another.

"Life is a struggle," the Shadow Man said, "and either you rise to face what comes, or you fall to it."

The chanting of the crowd became stronger; it was only one word they were chanting, but Torrence couldn't make it out.

"You continue to fight," the Shadow Man was closer now, and raised his giant ebony weapon above his head in two hands, preparing to cleave Torrence in half, "you will fail the moment you don't fight."

The word the crowd chanted became clear, the one word it repeated over and over again came to Torrence's ears.

"Choose, choose, choose, choose," the forms in the stands intoned, "choose, choose, choose."

"Do you fight," the Shadow Man asked, his mighty weapon swinging downward towards Torrence, "or do you die?"

Torrence pulled his blade up to block the blow.


"We have to go," Torrence sat up blearily, rubbing his head, "we need to go. Now."

The Kid looked up from where he sat, playing with the kits.

Esperanza turned from stitching her robe to look at him.

"Yeah," she nodded, "I guess we do, don't we?"

PepperGarten cackled and leapt down from the root rafters above.

"Yes," the man said excitedly, "PepperGarten knew you'd make it back. You're a strong one, Torrents the Barbarian, and people shall tell tales of your steel for years to come, and not just the steel of your sword, either."

The man danced across the small room, pulling a half dozen sacks from cubby holes and crevasses.

"PepperGarten made you some things!" The man sang, holding the bags up and doing a little jig. "Meals, bandages, and maybe even some poultices in case you do something really pemtie. Again!"

He smiled; his eyes gleamed.

"Now," he said cheerfully, "get the chuz out of PepperGarten's house!"

## Chapter 17

The Nine Towers, according to information that Esperanza gave—and she seemed as surprised as the others that she knew these things—were once hidden from prying eyes by enchantments, charms, and illusions to keep the uninitiated and riffraff away.

There was a tower dedicated to each school of magic, and a secret society of knowledge protecting them. Unlike Pantageas, far in the western lands, this university of the arcane had not been open to anyone who had the gold or power to buy their way in.

The three stood on the plains to the east of the Black Wood, to the west of the Frozen Desert, and to the north of the Blue Desert. In the distance, to the northwest, a haze wavered at the base of multiple structures. Mist shifted and wavered in front of them, a thick patch of white covering the ground between them and the buildings.

Six towers reached towards the sky, five of them tall and slim, graceful in their design and architecture. The sixth was short and squat—compared to the others, though it still towered over the campus of buildings at its base—and was the pitch black of the god Onyx, one of the newer gods who'd risen to power less than a century ago. This tower sat in the center of the ruins and rubble of four other towers.

"There'll be magical wards," Esperanza warned, wrapping the thick woolen cloak PepperGarten had given her around her body, "though some may have faded without upkeep, and others may have been triggered by the necromancer and her legion as it made its way to the towers. Are you sure she came here, Torrence?"

"It's Torrents now," the big man said, "and yes, I'm very sure. She headed this direction, and my dreams showed me the towers. It's where the arena was that I told you about."

"Torrence, Torrents," the Kid said, "they sound alike."

"Which name do you go by, Kid?" Torrents asked. "Do you want us to call you the Kid, or the name you used back home? What was that name again? Oh yeah, you won't tell us. You can't even admit that you had a whole other life before this one."

Torrents had changed since he'd woke from his dream. He walked differently, and he talked differently, but the biggest difference was that he was driven. He didn't seem to wander and go with the flow anymore. He had a purpose, and nothing would stop him or come between him and his goal. He was also was a lot snarkier.

The Kid flinched.

"Okay," the Kid said, his tone nonchalant and conflicting with his body language, "you win. Torrents the Barbarian, the hero of the great white north. You and Nanook can hang out together, kick ass and take names."

"You have a smart mouth," Esperanza sneered, "for a kid."

"I might be called the Kid," the Kid said, keeping an atmosphere of cool uncaring wrapped around him, "but I've lived longer, and harder, than both you put together. Okay? Is that enough admission of my previous life? I've dealt with enough bidj, it's nice to have this little vacation of life and death. And I'm loving it, so I don't feel the need to address who I was before this."

The three fell silent, each alone with their own thoughts.

"Do you think Eloise came here to use the towers to strengthen her army?" the Kid plucked at the petals of a flower and looked down as he broke the awkward silence.

"It would make sense," Esperanza answered, staring at the towers in the distance, "if she wanted to build up her power base quickly, that would be one way to do it."

"What do you think is in there?" the Kid pulled another petal free and watched it drift away on the wind.

"Magical artifacts, like your dagger," Esperanza snuck the jab in, "and she could get a ton of them. There may be wards specifically against the undead, but then again, there may only be things to keep the living out since they might have experimented with necromancy here."

"We should go," Torrents said, "standing here isn't accomplishing anything."

He strode forward, not waiting to see if the others would follow.

They did. Esperanza quickly catching up to walk beside Torrents, and the Kid trailing after.

The trio descended into the valley of the Nine Towers, the mists parting before them. As they drew closer to the cluster of buildings, a pressure built around them. The remnants of magic, seen and felt.

Swirling fog coalesced into creatures that darted away from them, or at other times, stared at them as they passed. Whistles and hoots sounded from the tops of the halls and tenements scattered at the outskirts, perhaps belonging to owls and animals they could find anywhere, or they could've been the spirits of familiars and homunculus that once served the residents and students.

They came to an intersection, three-story barrack-like dormitories on one side, and two-story administration buildings on the other. Ahead of them stood the courtyard that the towers had once surrounded. Overgrown shrubberies—still tended by magical contraptions hovering in the air, their shears too dull to trim back the vegetation—were scattered around the open-air park.

Broken bodies of the undead littered the intersection, showing the marks of mystical energies along their withered flesh. Sooty score marks of flame marred the surrounding ground.

"I guess something reacted to the undead," the Kid said.

"She could still be here," Esperanza whispered.

"Why would she still be here?" the Kid scoffed, raising his voice a little to show he wasn't concerned. "She had a day and a half head start on us."

"Because you don't get all of the magic arsenal a place like this holds in one day." Esperanza's voice was disdainful.

"Also," Torrents said quietly, "an army moves slow, and we move fast."

"The living dead don't need rest breaks," the Kid said.

"Even though an undead army doesn't need to rest," Esperanza said, forgetting to be snarky, "the necromancer does. It takes a lot of energy to keep hundreds of these things in line and moving in the same direction. So, it makes sense that she might still be here."

"Unless she just came for one thing," Torrents interrupted, pointing at the Tower of Onyx.

The other two looked in the direction Torrents indicated.

The massive black tower dominated more than a quarter of the courtyard, the four towers from which it had seemingly grown acting as legs for its raised form. The other five towers stood tall and still beautiful behind the dark, stout fortification.

Underneath the Tower of Onyx, and all around its base, were at least three score broken forms from the necromancer's legion. An altar in the center of the shadow of the structure above it glowed with a purple aura, green lightnings arcing through it.

A single figure, shrouded in a dark mist, stood underneath it, looking straight at the trio.

Torrents drew his blade and charged in the same movement, moving across the gardens.

"No," Esperanza cried, reaching for the man, "damn fool barbarian, he'll get himself killed."

"And us with him," the Kid added, also moving forward.

The street thief darted to one side, finding cover behind bushes, and shouted over his shoulder to Esperanza, "Do you want to live forever? There can be only one!"

Esperanza huffed, and walked forward slowly, her hands working in front of her as if she were kneading an invisible ball of dough. Silver light sprung into being within the confines of her hands, growing larger as she worked it.

The barbarian reached his target, swinging his sword in an arc, only to have it pass through the figure.

The form in front of him laughed, a familiar voice behind it.

"You're a pemtie," Eloise said, "and you shall die for your pemtieity."

"Nuh uh, Eloise," the Kid said, stepping out of the shadows behind the necromancer, flinging his white-bladed dagger at her, "you are, and you will."

The blade hit the figure and slowed when it passed through her, a line of blood showing as the illusion of the necromancer wavered and shimmered.

The woman in the image screamed and clutched at the small of her back where the weapon had hit her phantasm.

"I am not Eloise, foolish child," the necromancer screamed in anger, spinning to face the Kid, "I am Aku'ji, Mistress of Death, and Wielder of Woe. And I have the scepter of Necropties, and shall have more power over the dead than any of you can imagine!"

The image hesitated, looking towards the Dragon's Dagger on the cobblestone path in front of her.

"How did you get that dagger?" she demanded. "How did you capture the spirit of a Dragon Lord? Why does Edsumar serve you?"

"Really?" said the Kid, hands on his hips, "Does everyone know about this damn thing?"

"Give it to me!" Aku'ji shouted. "It will serve me!"

"Suck my left nut, bitch," the Kid said nonchalantly and edged forward, his wavy sword held ready.

The necromancer threw both hands outward, one towards the Kid and the other towards Torrents.

A bolt of white-hot energy shot towards each.

The Kid dodged to one side, his sword taking the brunt of the blow and bending into a curled and twisted shape as it melted in his hand. He shouted, dropped the weapon, and clutched his scorched hand.

Torrents took the bolt in the center of his chest, and flew backwards, rolling heels over head and coming up on his feet. His torso smoldered, but not as much as his glare did, as he refocused on the woman.

"Wait!" Esperanza commanded, stepping beside the barbarian. Then more gently, she said, "I've got this."

The silver globe of energy was the size of a beach ball now, humming with a tinkling noise. Esperanza thrust her hands forward and the magical sphere slowly advanced, growing larger, winds and lightning exploding to life within it.

"Nobody hurts my friends," Esperanza growled.

The necromancer waved her hands and brought them together in a 'X' shape in front of her, her own magics coming to life as black swirling fog and green sparks.

The silver globe met the magics of the necromancer, and the two forces burst into a blast of silver and green.

The Kid dropped to the ground, covering his head with his arms. Torrents threw up an arm to guard his eyes, but Esperanza just watched calmly, her globe encompassing and swallowing the necromancer.

The silver sphere pulsed.

"We've got her!" the Kid shouted, leaping to his feet and pumping a fist in the air.

"Not quite," Esperonza said through clenched teeth, her face tight with concentration, "that's an illusion that she's pushing magic through."

Esperanza spoke in short, broken phrases through the effort of the magic she used.

"But I think," the priestess continued, "I might…be able…to do a little something…with it…while we…have her essence trapped."

The sphere shrank, growing smaller with each panting breath that Esperanza took.

Torrents gripped his charred chest with one hand and held his sword ready with the other.

Esperanza stood, feet spread apart, and shoulders hunched over her hands, working them around an imaginary ball, pushing it smaller and smaller. The larger globe surrounding the necromancer's illusion mirrored the effect.

The whole thing collapsed, and Esperanza's hands came together with a clapping noise.

"She got away?" Torrents growled.

"She was never here," the Kid snatched the dagger he'd thrown from the ground where it had landed, "that was an illusion."

"But I think," Esperanza stood with her hands on her knees, panting, "your dagger stopped her from escaping right away, and I got something from the magical prison I caught her in. A place, maybe. I might know where she was when she did this."

"So," Torrents said, holding his freshly blistering wound, "you know where we need to go?"

"Not quite." Esperanza moved to the big man, peeled his arm away from the injury, and inspected the area. "But I have an impression, and I think PepperGarten might know where we should go. Now, hold still, I think this is going to require one of that crazy, old man's infamous poultices before we try to travel."

"I'll keep an eye out for ghosts and goblins, while you do that, then. And what kind of name is Aku'ji anyway?" the Kid asked, "Is that supposed to be scary or something?"

"That's something coming from someone who goes by 'the Kid'" Torrents grimaced under Esperanza's ministrations.

"Yeah?" the Kid said, "Well, quiet down Torrents, because your name isn't quite a winner either."

Esperanza smirked as the two men bickered.

## Chapter 18

"So, we could've gotten a magic sword or something from that black tower?" Torrents asked as PepperGarten checked the burns on his chest.

It had been almost five days since the three had left PepperGarten's sanctuary. They'd departed the Nine Towers within the hour after bandaging Torrents's wound and had traveled until dark before setting camp and watch. That night had brought the northern lights, a dazzling display that Torrents said made him think of the equalizer on his sound software.

Esperanza had said it was God's equalizer.

The next day brought clear skies and swarms of tiny biting gnats. After much cajoling from the Kid, Esperanza reluctantly called upon the power of Latress to sweep the pests away. The rest of the day passed with no other trouble, and Torrents took a few minutes to show the Kid how to use a bow. It took over ten arrows, but the Kid brought down a hare, and the three shared a dinner of roasted coney and some tubers that PepperGarten had supplied before they'd left.

They'd arrived the following day at the odd man's domicile, just before lunchtime. PepperGarten had a simmering pot of vegetable stew brewing over a large fire outside of his home. He'd been sitting on a tree stump carved into a chair, stirring the soup with a wooden stick that still had leaves sprouting from it, when they'd arrived.

"You could have," PepperGarten answered the barbarian's question absentmindedly, "but you would've left with a lot more than a weapon. When those towers first started cropping up across all of Teurone, maybe even all of Aetheria, they gave out magical goodies to anyone who wanted one, but only one per person. But they always came with a hook in them. PepperGarten's heard too many tales about someone who accepted such a thing, and it came back to bite them in the ass, eventually."

The Kid sat cross-legged on the floor with the three fox kits playing tag on his lap and around his back, nipping at his fingers and he feinted, grabbing them.

Esperanza was leaning back on the small bed of clover that Torrents had slept in last time they were here. She was fiddling with her holy symbol of Latress, turning it over and over in her hands while staring at it.

"Okay, that should do it," the little man finished wrapping the barbarian's wound and slapped the big man in the middle of his chest and giggled.

The barbarian winced and held his hand to the area.

"Can I ask now?" Esperanza said from where she sat, not looking up from what she was doing.

"No need," PepperGarten said, "you've already asked. You don't need to repeat yourself. You said you had the feeling of green, moisture, moving in slow motion, and the smell of natural rot. But also, as if there were something, not threatening, but not helpful, watching you. Yes, PepperGarten thinks PepperGarten knows the place."

The small man hopped to his feet and twisted his hips to a rhythm in his own head as he danced across the room.

"He reminds me of Ed Grimly when he does that." The Kid said, only to receive confused looks from Esperanza and Torrents. "Never mind, before your time."

"PepperGarten remembers that," the old man said as he plucked apples from a bowl and debated which one to eat. "PepperGarten also remembers the copier guy, and the liar guy. Those were good times."

"You know our world?" the Kid stopped playing with the animals and turned to look at their host, as did the others. "Have you been there?"

"There, here," the odd fellow bit into his chosen apple, answering between chewing, "not much difference, same thing, but different."

"Great," Esperanza sighed, "more things that make no sense."

"It makes sense once you know what it means," PepperGarten said, smiling widely, "but PepperGarten thinks it's more important for you to go east and find the Preserving Fluids."

"That sounds disgusting," the Kid said, "perhaps even a little horrifying."

"Is it dangerous?" Torrents pulled a fresh shirt over his head. It was scratchy, but it covered him well enough.

"Everything is dangerous," PepperGarten answered, "if you do not know what you need to know."

Esperanza sighed again.

"What information will you give us that would be helpful in this?" the Kid said through gritted teeth. "Directions? A list of monsters?"

"PepperGarten will tell you this," the old man put his fingertips on temples, and squinted, "remember who you are, what brought you to this point, and who you want to be, and you might make it out."

"Is that a prophecy?" Torrents asked, "Is that why you put your fingers to your head? Some sort of psychic power?"

"No," the small man answered, "I just like how the colors blur when I do that!"

They'd crossed the thinnest part of the Blue Desert and entered the western reaches of the Upper Swamp without incident. It had taken two days, and they set camp a few kilometers into the bog.

Small hillocks rose from ankle deep water and tall grass. The sounds of crickets and frogs, in their final mating frenzy before winter, filled the evening air as they cooked their meal of some sort of lizard that hadn't run when they'd approached.

"I guess these things aren't used to humans around here," the Kid turned a makeshift spit over the open fire, "and didn't know to run when we showed up."

"Or it's poisonous," Torrents said blandly.

The Kid's head jerked up to look at the man.

A smile crept onto the barbarian's face.

"What?" the Kid said, leaning forward. "Is that a smile? Did the big bad barbarian make a joke?"

"Your face is the joke here," the big man said, his grin huge now.

"Lame," Esperanza chimed in, "if you guys are gonna make a bromance, please be more clever and entertaining for those of us who are forced to watch it. How long until our mutant iguana entrée is ready? The potatoes are done, and the berries will ferment if we have to wait much longer."

"It's not like back home, is it?" Torrents smiled again. "Back there, everything cooked quicker. Even over a campfire because we had metal walls, or pots, or grates to cook with."

"Oh, the good old days," the Kid sighed and turned the spit again, "before we were surrounded by all this nature and junk."

"You know," Esperanza said, leaning back against a spindly tree, "at first, I missed my phone and always having something to do. Now though, I kinda like it. It's more, peaceful without all the technology. It's like we have more time to be who we really are without worrying about the rest of the world's opinion about us and what we're doing."

"Yeah," Torrents agreed, "I definitely like watching the branches above me sway, and staring at the stars as I fall asleep. You know there was a meteor shower last night? I don't think I'd ever seen one before. I mean, I heard they were happening, on the news, online, or from someone during the day, but I never actually just went outside and looked up to see one happen.”

“I did,” the Kid said. “When I was young, my brothers would camp out in the backyard, for it seemed like half the summer when school was out. I’d go out there with them, and this was before there were streetlights everywhere, and you could really see the stars, just like we do here, now.”

“Before streetlights? How old are you?” Torrents asked, “Or were you, you know, back there?”

“Let’s just say, my mother was a war bride,” the Kid laughed.

“Which war?” Esperanza asked, “Desert Storm? Vietnam? Korean War?”

“No,” the Kid chuckled again, “World War II.”

Silence fell across the trio as the Kid watched the sun set over the mountains to the west, then glanced to the east to see the deep indigo of night advancing across the sky, stars popping into his awareness like tiny white fireflies.

Torrents and Esperanza stared at the Kid, then exchanged glances.

“Okay, yeah,” Esperanza said, “I guess you do have a little more experience than us.”

The Kid shrugged.

“Unless he’s lying about it,” Torrents said.

The Kid shrugged again.

“I don’t think it matters anymore,” the Kid turned the spit again, “not here. This is a second chance at life, no matter how much, or how little, of your old life you lived.”

Torrents and Esperanza both took a double meaning from that simple statement, though neither knew the other also felt a deep pang of regret, mixed with excitement and hope.

They ate dinner mostly in silence, occasionally pointing out something to the others. A shooting star, a raccoon in the underbrush who smelled the food, a swarm of actual fireflies dancing in the distance, and other things that they’d never taken the time to notice before. The night filled with the noise of the traffic of the wilderness. Night birds called, frogs sang the song of their people, insects chirruped, and distant predators called to one another.

The three settled down into their routine, Torrents finding a place where he could whittle some of the smaller firewood while watching the camp. The Kid bedded down, falling asleep almost immediately. Esperanza whispered prayers to her god, which seemed worlds away, and even muttered a short thanks to Latress for her protection.

The night moved, the stars spinning across the sky, and when Torrents went to stand to wake the Kid for his watch, he found a thick gelatinous layer of liquid covered his feet.

The barbarian thought he should be concerned by this, but it didn't trouble him. The viscous coating lulled him, and it felt warm and comforting.

Looking at his companions, he saw the same substance surrounding most of their bodies, even though they were atop a knoll and the water couldn't reach them.

Esperanza's eyes were still open, and she stared dreamily upward into the heavens, as if having a pleasant daydream. She was lower on the hill than the Kid, who was curled up next to the fire.

Torrents watched in dazed contentment as the clear ooze crept further up the priestess's prone form. It moved across her thighs, and then belly, in slow undulating movements, like high tide coming in on a calm lake. He watched it coat her shoulders, run across her neck, and then up her breasts. It moved across her face last, pooling in the hollows of her open eyes, then filling her nostrils, and her mouth. Soon the woman was completely cocooned in the stuff, and Torrents watched her breathing slow until it was imperceptible, and he couldn't be sure if she was breathing at all.

Slowly turning his head, disturbing the sluggish creep of the ooze working up his neck towards his own face, he saw the Kid was also being enveloped. The stuff had already made its way onto the Kid's shoulders, the highest part of the street thief who laid on his side, and was working towards the prone man's face. It slid smoothly down the shoulder into the crook of the Kid's neck, then began its leisurely journey up the side of his face to fill in his features with a thin sheen of translucent emulsion. The Kid's breathing slowed to a stop as well.

Any of this did not disturb Torrents. It didn't feel dangerous, and no part of him sensed anything that would harm them. He slowly smiled and breathed a deep sigh as the ooze made its way across his own eyes, blurring his vision, before moving to his nose and mouth. As it found its way into his final orifices, he drifted away.

# Chapter 19

Jen sat in an armchair, the kind with the little wings near the head, high arms, and that ugly, blotchy material that reminded her of colonial days. It was her favorite, having belonged to her grandmother. Handed down for generations, Jen didn't know who she'd hand it down to, because her son had died over twenty-five years ago.

She missed him terribly, even if she couldn't remember much about him anymore. Mothers were supposed to miss their children, even after they were gone and forgotten by the rest of the world. She remembered that he'd been over thirty when he died. Thirty-two? She couldn't remember, and her mind wouldn't wrap itself around the math tonight, not with the meds and the treatments.

She was just so tired. Why would the treatments be almost as bad as the cancer itself? She'd struggled all her life. Why did she have to continue straight up to her death?

Jen had started working when she was twelve, just babysitting, nothing hard. She'd gotten a job at the local diner when she was fifteen, and kept working up to two years ago, when she got too sick to keep a job.

But she had things in her life to keep her going. Things like Cuddles, her dog. She didn't know where he was right now. Maybe the in-home care nurse—what was her name? Oh yeah, it was Marjorie, or Margaret, or something like that—had taken Cuddles for a walk.

Something nagged at her though, even as sleep pulled her down. It was the thought that she wasn't old anymore. She was just a kid now. She was The Kid.

She had a new life, one that wasn't constant pain of achy joints that stabbed at her when she ran her hands under water that was too cold. One where she didn't have to stand up slowly, because her knees might give out.

She felt the gentle, warm tug of sleep pulling at her again, and she wanted to just relax and remember.

But another small voice told her that she had another life, and it was a different world.

Esperanza had nothing. She had a job, but she hated it. Hate may have been too strong of a word, but the job did nothing for her. She had no reason, other than the little bit of money it gave her to survive on, to go to that place another single day.

She had an apartment, it was in the city, and close to everything. But that didn't matter when you couldn't afford to do anything. And she didn't have any friends.

Sure, she knew people, and she called them friends. But would they answer if she called at three forty-six in the morning, she wondered, glancing at the time in the corner of her computer screen?

She didn't want to hang out with her family. Her mother or grandmother just nagged at her about things she didn't do, and disapproved of the things she did. Nothing she did was good enough for them. They told her that by now, in her late twenties, she should at least have a man, if not a couple of babies. Esperanza could barely afford her car payments and utilities. How could she afford to date, let alone raise a family?

And her sisters and brothers were living their own lives. They each had their own problems, most of them living with someone or married already, or going to college like the youngest. Esperanza's father kept asking why she hadn't gone to college, and reminded her she could still go, and even offered to help pay for it. But he was already working two jobs to put his other kids through college. Why should she burden him with more?

She looked at the bottle of antidepressants the doctor had prescribed her. It sat next to the bottle of cheap vodka. It was the same brand she'd used to drink with her friends behind the gas station when she was still in high school. It was rot gut, the cheap shit, and only good for cleaning rust out of the pipes. But it would do the trick.

A small, strange knife sat beside them. She knew it didn't belong here, but it held her gaze for a moment.

Would anyone even notice if she did this? Would anyone even miss her?

She looked out the window as the wind picked up, and it seemed to call her name.

Torrence was back in the arena, and the crowd was going wild. Dozens of Shadow Men were on their knees, clutching their heads at the noise of cheering.

Torrence turned a slow circle, looking at the crowd that kept the shadows of his past from attacking him. The shadow things shifted through faces and bodies, each one looking like someone he knew, loved, hated, argued with, fought with, cried to, or interacted with in some close and personal way at some point.

More shadowy figures were climbing over the walls of the arena, but the sound of the cheering crowd blocked them from getting in. It created a bubble of space, and the shades scrambled along the invisible dome, blacking out the open sky above the stadium.

Once all the overhead area was covered, the darkness of the shapes thickened above Torrence, and the sound of the crowd was dampened and felt slightly muted. The pressure in the air increased; a pounding in Torrence's head drummed in time with it, keeping the beat as it blocked out the encouragement of the spectators of his mind.

Jen was in court. Her husband of fifteen years sat across the table from her, smiling. He'd get his way. He'd be allowed to leave the marriage, and pay her thirty dollars a month, because she had a job and brought in enough money that he didn't need to pay alimony, just that little bit of child support.

The seventies were a decade of progressive thinking, following the free spirit roots set in the sixties. Women were equals, at least that's what they were told. But here she sat, getting screwed one last time by the man that wanted out.

Her nine-year-old son was at her sister's house, waiting for his mother and father to come home and tell him everything would okay. And his father would do that, down on one knee so he could look his son in the eye, and one hand on the kid's shoulder to let him know everything'll be alright. Daddy just needs to go away for a little while, and find himself. Find himself with the help of Linda, the blonde waitress that works in the same diner that Jen had worked in as a teenager, and who now works as the secretary in the used car lot that Jen had helped pay for when it was getting started.

She had to live life, if for no other reason than to live because her son died.

*Aw, come on, Kid,* someone said to Jen, and it felt like whoever it was had been standing right over her shoulder.

*Don't fall for this shit, Kid,* the voice urged, *you're better than this. I didn't choose you because you'd just roll over and die— and in this case, die over and over again—to feed some sort of swamp slug.*

Jen looked over her left shoulder, and then over her right one.

"Who is that?" Jen asked, but no one at the table seemed to notice the question. In fact, everyone at the table appeared to be getting a bit out of focus and growing wispy and faint, like they were dissipating.

*That's it, Kid,* the voice almost shouted into Jen's head. *Come back to me. You got this, and we got things that need to be done. Kick this thing's ass, or mind, and let's get going.*

Esperanza moved to the window and pulled on it to open it, but it wouldn't budge. Memories called to her from behind, pulling at her, begging her to come back, to nurture and care for them. But the wind called as well.

The storm rumbled, distant and fleeting, the noise almost drowned out by the fog of the pills, alcohol, and memories of her life.

Esperanza jerked on the window again, trying to tug it open. It creaked under her effort and slid up about a hand's width.

She dropped her hands down, turning them palm up, and gripped the underside of the window. She put one foot on the windowsill, and then hunched her shoulders and pulled upward. The window resisted and jerked down.

Gritting her teeth, tears coming to her eyes, Esperanza gave one last effort to open this window. The tears were frustration, anger, sadness, and all the things that called to her from the small room behind her.

The wind sang outside, singing of opportunities, freedoms, and adventure that made life so much more than the same doldrums every day, in and out.

The window lurched open, and Esperanza ducked through it and rolled out onto the fire escape. She looked back at the knife on the table for a moment before turning back to the landing.

Laughing, she grabbed the railing and ran upward, taking the steps two at a time. She doubled back when she hit the next landing and took the next flight at an even more reckless speed.

When she ran out of stairs to climb, and she realized she had made it to the roof. The wind wound around her like some giant, unseen cat, glad she'd finally came home.

The breeze pulled at clothes that hadn't been there before; the constraining clothes she's worn all her life had been replaced with flowing robes in hues of pinks, purples, and white. The sleeves, cut with lace to resemble feathers, hung down her sides when she raised her arms.

She was on a riverbed now, made of flat, rounded stones. The water trickled, rippling in the dancing wind.

Esperanza held her arms above her, raising her face to the sky; a small ball of energy forming a few meters in front of her.

It expanded, and Esperanza laughed in delight.

It grew, becoming a globe, then a large orb of shifting grays, with red and purple energy breaking through, making it look like cracks in the sphere.

She thrust her arms forward, and the wind rushed past her towards the magical, circular creation; it lifted and was flung away.

The caressing gusts lifted her into the air, swirling upward, wrapping her in its cool embrace. And then Esperanza was flying.

She sailed across the sky, looking down on the world below. All her worries, fears, and life pressures were so small and far away. She was above it all and never wanted to be stuck in that mire again.

She was free.

Torrents woke. He blinked, but there was something in his eyes. Someone's hands scraped at something on his skin, his nose, and mouth. He coughed, sputtering, and felt a thick phlegm rise from his throat and collect in a jelly-like lump in his mouth. He spat it out, leaning forward as he did.

Hands thumped his back, and voices spoke to him. They seemed to be very far away, or as if he was underwater. The sounds were muddled and muted.

"Okay, alright, stop," Torrents said hoarsely, spitting out more of the goo, holding his hands up to wave the helping hands away, "give me a second, let me catch my breath."

The hands moved away. Torrents squeegeed out his ears, one at a time, with a finger. Putting a finger to the side of his nose, he blew the gunk inside it onto the grass between his knees. He scraped the remaining ooze from his face.

Looking around, he saw Esperanza and the Kid standing in front of him, one on each side. It was full daylight, and from the position of the sun, it was almost noon.

His skin burned from the contact with the gelatinous liquid. He scraped at it, sloughing it off onto the grass.

"Here," the Kid said, holding a small cooking pot full of water towards him, "this might help. There's a rag in there, too. Take a moment to get more water if you need to."

"Thanks," Torrents stumbled to his feet, then swayed.

Esperanza's hands caught him by the elbow and armpit.

"Take it slow," the priestess smiled, "it takes a few minutes for the effects of that thing to wear off."

"You're smiling," Torrents said, confused. "Why are you smiling? You never smile."

"Don't be an asshole," Esperanza swatted Torrents's bicep with the hand that was holding his elbow. "Just go and get cleaned up. We have an undead army to track down."

# Chapter 20

The muck and mire bubbled, hundreds of dead bodies rising to their feet as one. Acres of shallow, stagnant water moved as the necromancer, Aku'ji, called upon the dark powers at her disposal. The smell of rotting flesh blended with the fetid air of the Upper Swamp.

Necromancy wasn't its own type of magic. It manipulated all five magics. It called upon elemental magics to transport the energy needed to animate the dead. It interacted with the alchemical magics, converting dead flesh to a state between what it was, and what is now is, allowing the dead to replenish themselves in ways the living could not. It conjured the cold, ethereal energies, and motes of darkness to strike the core within the dead, and give them animation. It pulled on the holy magics of the gods, drawing from their realms of faith, and bestowing the fears and beliefs of the living to give the dead the strength to walk. And lastly, it drew upon the casters own mind magics to control the things that rose to walk again after death.

A circle of over five hundred corpses, fresh and old, surrounded the rising army within the swamp. These had been gathered from caravan trains, small villages, or even lone travelers, since the Day of Phāz six years ago—the mystical day that came every four years and fell between the old year and the new.

It was pure luck that Aku'ji had come across a horde of plainsmen, warriors of the north, just a few weeks ago, and was able to catch them unaware enough to bring them into her dark fold.

But this wasn't the first time she'd gathered an army. It wasn't the second, either. She'd been dabbling in the necromantic arts for over sixty years. She felt the surge of power when the Talisman—the rogue comet that fell into orbit above the world for a decade or more—hung in the sky. She saw the other necromancers scramble for the power that the Talisman rained down upon the land.

She watched, and she waited.

The others fought each other, and all of them fought against Rondarius the Foul. The Master Necromancer had been trapped in some forgotten keep deep in Land's End. But when demons had been released upon the land, Rondarius had escaped his stone prison that hadn't been more than three paces wide. When the magical radiation of the comet fell upon the land, Rondarius rose to power, crushing heroes and decimating kingdoms with equal recklessness.

Aku'ji had found her way into the demon-infested land while war raged with armies of undead to the north and west. She found Rondarius's hidden library, and though it seemed he'd boiled most of his leather-bound tomes to survive his imprisonment, she found enough information to rise in power beyond most necromancer's dreams.

Letting the others kill one another off, she waited.

Now was the time. Humans, aeifain, rokairn, and other humanoids had repopulated after the Downfall, and were a ripe crop ready for harvesting.

She'd built her army three times over, and each time brought them here to the Upper Swamp, where a symbiotic creature fed off living creatures placed in stasis. Here, she used this non-sentient being to store her armies in a place they wouldn't attract attention and wouldn't rot while they waited.

And now she called them forth once again, the Scepter of Necropties in her upraised hand.

And they answered.

"Oh, hell naw," Esperanza said, as the three lay on their bellies, hidden by an overgrown deadfall.

They'd searched the bogs, working their way to the east, for three days before finding evidence of the dead army's passage.

The fen swallowed such signs quickly.

Now, they lay on a small hill overlooking the massive exhumation of a force that would triple the size of the necromancer's military.

The Kid had his hands cupped into twin tubes and held them to his eyes like a pair of imaginary binoculars.

Torrents stared at him, a smile quirking at the corners of his mouth.

"You know," Torrents said to the Kid, "the pemtie things you do are much more amusing now that I know you were more than three times my age."

"They work," the Kid said, pulling his hands from his eyes, and held them towards the barbarian, "wanna try?"

"Spoiler alert! It's his magic," Esperanza said, "now can we get back to discussing this suicide mission? Been there, done that, literally, don't need another t-shirt."

"So," the Kid leaned around Torrents to look at Esperanza, "you think we should just skedaddle and open up this world's first Starbucks? I thought this was why we were here."

"Well," Esperanza squirmed, "it is, but come on, how do we even begin to take something like this down?"

"Same way we eat an elephant," the Kid replied, turning back to peer through his hand binoculars again.

Esperanza looked across at the Kid, her head cocked, and her face confused.

"One bite at a time," Torrents said, and Esperanza glanced at him, "that's how you eat an elephant. One bite at a time."

"What the hell does that even mean in this situation?" Esperanza threw her hands up. "I'm not biting one of those things."

Both Torrents and the Kid were studying the raising of the army, which appeared to be almost completed, and didn't answer.

"That was a joke," Esperanza sighed, "you know, ha, ha, funny?"

"Torrents," the Kid jabbed the big guy with his elbow, and pointed, "you see that down there?"

Esperanza and Torrents both looked towards where the Kid indicated.

A group of newly raised dead had been corralled together, and four forms circled them likes wolves surrounding a foal. The thin dark figures that had wrangled the six pale figures into a tight knot launched themselves into the huddle. They tore and ripped at the recently reborn undead.

"What're they doing?" the Kid mumbled.

"They're feeding on the weak," Torrents answered, "to make themselves stronger."

"Really?" the Kid glanced towards the big man.

"Pretty much." Esperanza watched the slaughter with interest. "Necromancy only has so much energy to go around. For something to become a more powerful undead creature, they need to get the extra, for lack of a better word, nutrition from somewhere. And I assume this is how you get things like the super-fast, hissing thing Torrents told us about meeting when he was traveling with Axle, or the hound master, or other such things."

"What about vampires, banshees, or ghosts?" the Kid asked.

"No," Esperanza shook her head slowly, "I don't think so. I think those things are a different process, because they have complete free will and autonomy. Aku'ji may have some of those, but I doubt it. They take focused will to control. Most necromancers just work in tandem with them, rather than trying to dominate them."

"How the hell," Torrents asked, "do you know so much about necromancy?"

"It's this body," Esperanza shrugged. "It used to study diseases and the undead, hunting both and destroying them, and it still has all that knowledge stored inside it. Just like you and your skill with the sword, or the Kid and his illusions and backflips and all that shit. I have access to what was already here."

"So, you're like an avenging angel?" the Kid asked.

Any answer Esperanza had was lost as a sound rose from behind them, the sound of a small log snapping in half.

They turned as one.

An enormous man, or a small giant, stood over them.

He was over three meters tall, dressed in uncured furs, and his bare torso and face covered with mounds of warts and moles that grew on top of one another. The sound had been of him tearing a limb as thick as Torrents's thigh from the deadfall.

The giant swung it around and then hit it three or four times against a fallen tree to clear the loose bark. He held it up, inspecting his new club.

Torrents rolled to his feet and brought his sword up in one movement. With both hands on the hilt, he thrust forward at chest height, and the sword slid into the belly of the giant.

The behemoth looked down, squinting at the blade in his gut.

"Dead me doesn't hurt," the huge man grunted in broken language. "Magic woman make it hurt no more. But says I eat you, and I want to eat you, and make her happy. Now you can go die."

Grabbing the blade of the sword in one huge mitt, the colossus pulled it free of his midsection, slicing his hand open in the process. No blood swelled from either wound, merely a thick black ichor beaded at the openings.

With his other hand, the immense man swung his club upward, and Torrents stepped to one side to avoid it. But the blow wasn't meant for him. The tree trunk swept past, connecting with Esperanza and the dead trees above her.

The woman tumbled backwards, over the crest of the hill, and down the other side to land face down in the muck below.

The deadfall shuddered, logs falling around the two remaining men, and rolling down every side of the hill they'd been hiding on.

"Get to her," Torrents growled to the Kid, dancing around the falling timbers, "I'll keep this guy busy."

The Kid rolled to one side to avoid a shattered trunk that landed where he'd been a moment before, got to his feet and leapt on top of a rolling log, jumped to another, and threw himself into the air toward where Esperanza had flown.

Flipping, with the help of a mental push of his own magics, he landed in front of the prone form of the priestess on one knee, and one fist planted into the ground as he constructed a solid shield of mental energy.

Falling trunks crashed into it, and the physical force of the mass pushed him back, sliding his whole body along the mud and soft ground until it touched Esperanza. The shield shattered under the onslaught and the Kid took a face full of splinters.

The Kid reached down, grabbing the priestess by the collar of her cloak and pulled her face from the thick swamp water. Strings of dark vegetation hung from her.

Sticky sacks flew from the hidden recesses of the broken deadfall and landed around the two, rupturing. Hundreds of spiders the size of a man's fist poured from the broken web bags as the baby arachnids were forced into the world.

"Oh, bidj," the Kid said, looking around, "if the babies are this big, I wonder what the adults look like."

As if in response to his curiosity, three hairy eight-legged, creatures the size of ponies scurried down the hillside towards him and his unconscious companion.

"Oh," the Kid sighed and drew his dagger, "me and big mouth."

## Chapter 21

Torrents jabbed with his sword, and the hulk in front of him caught it with his sliced hand, three fingers bending backwards, bones snapping.

The goliath swung his club with a roar, and Torrents rolled to avoid the blow. The ground shuddered as the tree trunk narrowly missed the warrior.

Getting to his feet, the barbarian thrusted again, cutting into the massive thigh of his foe. Torrents shoved the weapon forward, tearing the flesh more than cutting it, and the giant fell to one knee.

The club caught the warrior in his ribs. Torrents stumbled to the side, hearing a cracking noise as the wind went out of him.

His next breath shot stabbing pain through his chest. Steadying himself, he prepared for the next strike, raising his sword overhead. The blow slammed into his weapon, blocked, but sending Torrents to one knee under the force of it.

Twisting his blade, the barbarian turned the club away, and it hit the ground beside him. Reversing the blade, he stabbed up and the sword bit into the throat of the colossus. Torrents pushed, sliding the steel through the creature's neck and out the back.

The titan jerked away, standing on his one good leg, and the sword ripped free of the barbarian's grip.

Torrents dropped to the ground, steadied himself with his hands, and kicked out. His foot met the giant's knee, and he heard a satisfying crunch.

The hulk lurched backwards, his club dropping from his hands as he fell on his butt with both legs disabled.

The sword wobbled in the fleshy sheath of the monster's neck, tearing it open further. The undead creature didn't gasp, not needing to breathe.

Torrents stood and surveyed the situation. He needed his sword to finish his foe, but the beast's flailing hands stopped him from approaching to recover it.

He clutched his side, and stooping and grunting with pain, the barbarian hefted his enemy's club. Shuffling forward, Torrents bashed at the handle of his own sword, twisting it in the thing's throat. The head lolled to one side, partially severed from its shoulders.

Torrents heaved a sigh, wincing at the deep breath, then pummeled his foe's arms and chest until it lay still, limbs broken, and ribs shattered.

The giant lay disabled, but still trying to gain its feet.

Recovering his own weapon, Torrents finished the grisly task.

Leaning heavily on the sword, the barbarian turned to look for his companions.

The Kid dragged Esperanza's unconscious form onto the solid ground of the hill where they'd watched the undead army.

A quick glance over his shoulder told the Kid that the army in question was mobilizing and moving away in ragged lines.

The small spiders scurried over the priestess's body and up the Kid's arms. The rogue dropped his friend and began swiping at the arachnids, knocking a dozen from his arms and chest.

The three adults swarmed towards him. He was unsure if they were protecting the babies, or just out for an easy meal, but he drew Edsumar and stood over his friend.

The lead spider closed on the Kid.

"Edsumar," the Kid mumbled, shaking his dagger as if to wake the dragon spirit inside of it, "if you have any awesome powers, now would be a good time to reveal them."

*You're doing great,* Edsumar said in the Kid's head. *Keep up the good work.*

The Kid slashed at the beast when it came within reach. It reared up, emitting a hiss.

The blade missed.

"Oh great," the Kid said, "they hiss. That's chuzzing terrifying. I didn't like them when they were the size of my fingernail, and I really don't like them now."

The hairy legs stroked the air, the head raised, and the monster looked for an opening. The other two caught up, and the three formed a half circle around the Kid.

"At least they don't have pack tactics," the Kid grunted, and hurled the dagger at the one lunging at him.

The blade flew with unerring accuracy and sunk deep into the head of the lead spider. The thing bucked, launching itself three meters straight up.

"And they chuzzing jump, too?" the Kid shrieked, "Oh my chuzzing god, can this get any worse?"

That's when he realized he was now weaponless, and the other two were charging towards him.

"When will I learn," the Kid dove to one side, trying to draw the giant creatures away from the unconscious priestess.

Chelicerae dug into the Kid's thigh, tearing into the flesh and withdrawing, leaving two pencil-sized holes in his leg.

The Kid screamed, flailing at the thing and wishing he had his dagger back. Then the magical weapon was back in his hand, and he was slashing wildly at the creature's exposed face.

Half the spider's head dropped to the grass, neatly severed. The Kid stabbed forward, and the blade cut a deep gash across the multifaceted eyes.

*I can always find you*, Edsumar said, *if you're close enough.*

"You think you could've mentioned this sooner?" the Kid said through gritted teeth.

*You never asked*, the dagger answered.

The Kid took a step, and the leg with the bite wound gave out, dropping him to the ground.

"In that case," he said, carefully pushing to his feet, "can you remove venom or heal that leg?"

*Don't be silly*, Edsumar said, *I'm just a dagger.*

"Right," the Kid threw the dagger again.

It sunk into the abdomen of the blinded spider and burst out the other side. The creature did a frantic dance sideways, and fell, curling its legs underneath its body and cartwheeled down the hillside.

The dagger appeared in his hand again, and he prepared to throw it at the last target, who stood a few meters away, front legs waving in the air in a striking pose and hissing.

The Kid's vision blurred, and he knew the venom was coursing through his veins. He launched the dagger again, anyway, relying on its magic to assist in the throw.

The third spider blurred in his vision and the world swam before the Kid's eyes, going watery and his head swooning.

The ground hit him, or at least that's how it seemed.

He lay on his side, panting, but at least Edsumar was back in his hand.

And everything went dark.


The Kid heard concerned voices. They weren't clear, as if he were hearing the conversation underwater.

"I think he's coming to," said a woman.

"It's about time," a deep baritone replied, "I don't believe he was pemtie enough to let those things bite him."

"It's not like we're much better," the woman sounded irritated, "you have at least three broken ribs, and I was knocked unconscious."

"How far do you think the necromancer got?" Torrents asked.

*Yes, it was the barbarian*, the Kid thought, but wished he hadn't. Thinking, and their talking, made everything spin and lurch.

The Kid rolled to his side and vomited.

"I told you to roll him to his side," Esperanza said.

The Kid felt a gentle touch on his arm, a cool cloth wipe his forehead, then his mouth.

"I'm okay," the Kid tried to say, but it came out as, "Ium oaee."

"What'd he say?" Torrents asked, his voice closer.

"I said," the Kid spoke slowly, his eyes still closed against the spinning, "shut the hell up, hearing hurts right now."

The barbarian laughed, the sound retreating.

The Kid's leg throbbed with each heartbeat, and he panted—his mouth open—wondering if he was going to be sick again.

"Can you drink?" Esperanza asked, the cool cloth still scraping across the Kid's swollen skin.

"Just let me die, dammit," the Kid mumbled into the grass poking into his cheek, and passed out again.


It was dark when the Kid woke. Pushing upright, he let the spinning subside before opening his eyes.

He didn't feel as bad as before. His stomach only lurched from the effort, threatening to let loose again.

The campfire had burned down to glowing coals, and the Kid lay a couple of meters from it.

*Probably so I don't roll over into it,* the Kid thought.

His leg still throbbed, and he probed at it with one hand. He stopped, realizing he still clutched Edsumar.

*Good morning, sleeping beauty,* the dagger said silently.

*How do you know that movie?* The Kid asked in his mind because it was easier than trying to talk with his dry throat and pounding head.

*I've had some time to poke around in your head while you were sleeping,* Edsumar said cheerfully. *You didn't have your normal defenses up when you were fighting the poison. On the bright side, that also allowed me to gift you with some of the dragon fortitude we're so famous for.*

*You went through my head?* The Kid wasn't pleased.

*Indeed,* Edsumar said, *and it's very interesting in here. Lots of stuff you keep hidden away.*

"Hey there," Esperanza knelt beside him, placing a hand on the Kid's shoulder, "how're you feeling?"

It was a testament to how he felt when he realized he hadn't heard her approaching.

"I'm okay," the Kid croaked, and looked at her, then squinted up at the sky, "and what're you doing up, this isn't your watch."

"Well," the priestess handed him an unstoppered canteen, "Torrents needed sleep, he's got a few cracked ribs and the poultice PepperGarten gave us made him sleepy after carrying you here. And you were in no condition to take a watch. In fact, I'm surprised you're awake already. It was a helluva bite, really nasty. I think most people would've died from it."

The Kid drank from the canteen. Then rinsed his mouth out and spit it to one side, then drank again.

"Yeah," the Kid lifted the dagger, "Edsumar said he helped with that."

"Handy guy," Esperanza smiled, "and easy on the water, don't want to upset your tummy again."

"Stow it," the Kid said with no real menace, "I've been taking care of sick people since before your parents were born."

"Maybe," the priestess sat back on her haunches, "and it seems the old adage is true then, doctors make the worst patients."

Meeting her eyes, the Kid searched her face. Sighing, he looked down.

"Thanks," the Kid said, "I really appreciate you guys doing this for me. You saved my life."

"Only after you saved mine," Esperanza observed her reluctant patient, "so we can just call it even and move on."

"Move on?" the Kid rubbed at his head, and realized he still held Edsumar.

He looked around for the sheath he'd carved, and noticed that they'd cut away his pants, removed his belt, and rolled him in a blanket. He waved towards his pack.

"Hand me that, would you?" the Kid said, "Please?"

"Yeah," Esperanza laughed.

Standing and grabbing the bag, she passed it to the Kid. She waited for him to settle back down before talking.

"The necromancer is gone," she said quietly, "heading south as best as we can tell. It's going to be hell catching up with her."

"Can we talk about it in the morning," growled a lump from the other side of the fire, "some of us are trying to sleep."

"So are the poultices alchemical magic?" the Kid asked.

They were walking along an animal track, moving south, through knee-high grass, following the eastern border of the Blue Desert.

Torrents led the way, picking out the easiest path while leaning on his walking staff. His ribs were still painful and healing.

"I think it might be," Esperanza said, "because these things PepperGarten gave us sure don't work like a normal one. They do a lot more. I've seen magical healing, and it can take a bunch of different forms. Some alchemists make potions, others make hot rocks, acupuncture needles, salves, creams, lotions, and once I even saw a gunpowder-like substance that exploded in a fiery flash and left the flesh healed afterwards."

The Kid grunted.

"Where do you think this witch is headed?" the Kid asked.

"You're full of questions today, aren't you?" Esperanza laughed. "And take it easy on the witch thing. You know, some folks might call me the same thing. A weather witch."

"Well, you aren't trying to kill everyone," the Kid quipped, "so I don't think we'll prepare the stake and bonfire for you quite yet."

"Good to hear," the priestess smiled sadly for a moment, then went on, "I think she's headed for the place with the largest population of people. Durgan's Keep."

"Looks like I'm going to get to show you guys my city then," the Kid said.

## Chapter 22

The three debated how to best describe the color of the sands of the Blue Desert. They all agreed that the further south they went, the more it reminded them of a blue highlighter. But further to the north, it was a deeper color, but not dark. They settled on agreeing that it was closest to a Wal-Mart blue.

What really made them wonder was the ten-meter-wide white path down the center. Calling upon the power of her goddess, Latress, Esperanza said that the blue sands held a very faint aura of magic, but the white streak was almost the antithesis of magic, and grabbed at her mystical probing and pulled it into the absence of color and magic.

"It wasn't here before," Esperanza said, "this is something new. And considering how wide it is, just about as wide as an undead army marching in rank and formation, I think our friend the necromancer may have had something to do with this."

"What's that even mean?" Torrents asked. "Did she have her undead legion bleaching the sand as they walked, in some weird Mister Miyagi, Karate Kid, lesson sort of thing?"

"I don't think so," the Kid chimed in, "but that'd be hilarious to see!"

"No," Esperanza said, "I think the necromancer was draining the magical runoff from the Nine Towers of Magic to help shore up her own magics and strengthen her army."

They traveled south for more than a week, hampered by their injuries, though they grew healthier each day. After the fourth day, they found the fresh wreckage of a caravan.

Manacles and chains, smeared with dried blood, were strung along behind one wagon, and crates of food were still among the carts.

"I know this group," Torrents said, inspecting the shattered wagons and mutilated horses, and held up a banner showing the silhouette of a wolf's head in front of a red circle. "This is the Blood Sun Wolf slavers. But I don't get it."

The barbarian fell silent, staring at the banner.

The Kid picked through the rubble, looking for a sword to replace the one he'd lost at the Nine Towers.

"Don't get what?" Esperanza toed at the torn form of a chicken.

"Slavers are very proprietary," Torrents explained, still holding the banner in his hand, "and no other slaver clan would use the banner of another. But I saw the caravan master, Dropsum, dead and laying under a bush."

"Notice something missing?" the Kid shouted from the front of the line to the back where the other two were.

Esperanza and Torrents looked around, then the priestess raised her arms in an exaggerated shrug.

"No bodies," the Kid said as he approached his companions, inspecting a saber he'd found. "There are no bodies at all, except for the animals. Who would attack a caravan, kill all the animals, and take the people?"

"Do you think the necromancer attacked these people?" Esperanza asked.

"Nope," the Kid said, rocking from his toes to his heels, "no guards, either. There wasn't a fight here. There are no bodies, no guards, no signs of struggle."

"So," Esperanza looked around, "what's that mean?"

"They were working together," Torrents said quietly. "Dropsum and his Blood Sun Wolf slaver clan were in league with Aku'ji this whole time. That would explain the bodies missing from his caravan the day after I destroyed it. And that probably means the screams in the night were the other slaves being caught and…"

Torrents went quiet, leaving the thought hanging.

"But then that must also mean Dropsum himself is some form of undead," Esperanza said, "maybe one of the higher undead, which have complete free will, free thought, and their own agendas."

"Well then," the Kid said, tossing a horseshoe side-handed and making it skip across the pale blue sands, "I guess that means all the slaves here, and the guards, and anyone who was with this caravan, have now joined Aku'ji undead legion."

"These bastards just keep getting bigger, badder, and better, don't they?" Torrents sighed and turned to the south to walk away from the caravan.

Over the remaining four-day journey south, they found more than one more caravan in the same condition, but each of these showed signs of struggle, though still didn't have any corpses except for mauled and mutilated animals.

They arrived at the small village that served as a port for the Inner Bay, the same village where Captain Jaimin had dropped the Kid off.

It took three more days to contact, then await the arrival of, the Raptor Rex via a carrier pigeon with a small enchantment from the Kid so it would seek out a moving location.

Once they'd set sail, the Captain called them to his cramped quarters. The ceiling was just under two meters high, and Torrents had to bend over to move around the cabin. The tall tables along the walls held maps, the table in the center held whiskey bottles and cups in a recess in the top. A cubby on the side of the room had the captain's bunk with drawers underneath.

The four sat around the table, after sharing a meal, and raised the ceramic cups of whiskey in a toast.

"Here's to each sunrise," Captain Jaimin intoned solemnly, "and hoping we each get a reason for something else to rise, whether it be our spirits, or our cocks!"

The rotund man laughed, and the three others stared at him, unused to such humor.

"Ladies excluded in that," the Captain corrected, still smiling, "for you I'm sure you can find something else that will rise, whether it be your nipples or your ire, and I'd say it be the latter right now."

The bearded man laughed again, looking around at the three somber faces.

"Look, kids," the Captain said, "either you learn to laugh anytime you can, or you die without laughing, because that second part is a certainty."

"Then here's to nipples and cocks," the Kid said, raising his cup again, "and may they be harder than every day we face."

The four toasted, clinking the drinking vessels and threw back their individual mouthfuls of whiskey.

"Now," the Kid said, "can we discuss a plan? Can you tell us where the undead horde is now?"

"Yeah," Jaiman said, "I can, and I will, and none of you'll like it. Those rotten rotters are at the gates of Durgan's Keep. They've been there for almost two days, from what the news that the doves bring me says."

"You talk to doves?" Esperanza leaned forward in interest.

"No, no, no, my dear," Jaimin laughed, "I have doves show up with little notes attached to their legs."

"Oh," Esperanza looked disappointed.

"Then the birds talk to me and tell me what the note says," the man said with a wide grin, "but I don't talk to them, that'd be silly!"

The priestess eyed the man, unsure if he was serious or joking.

"Durgan's Keep," the Kid reminded, "what else can you tell us?"

"Well," Jaimin continued, "Aku'ji—and she does like the sound of her own voice, doesn't she, been shouting out her name and titles every chance she gets—but as I was saying, Aku'ji has been scooping every farmer, merchant, and villager within the area around Durgan's Keep, and her forces keep growing. Even the camp followers who'd normally trail after a group like that—repairing armor and cooking pots, or even ladies of the night who sell their services to lonely men—they've all been scooped up and absorbed in one way or another, either as a meal for the more powerful undead who need such things, or as one more foot soldier damned to serve beyond death. Not to mention any of the city guard and militia that's slain in battle. It's only a matter of time before she either gets in or has made every living soul in the city into one of her minions."

"And our side?" the Kid asked. "How're they holding up? Any routes in or out? Any real resistance to speak of that might help us?"

"Wait," Jaimin held up a finger, "you want to go there?"

"Yes," Esperanza said quickly, "of course we do. Why else would we have contacted you?"

"My good looks and charm leap to mind," the Captain said with a guffaw, "but I'm glad to hear it. Looks like we have some heroes in the making. Either that, or we have three more undead warriors looking for a line to be conscripted. Let's hope it's the former, eh?"

The room grew quiet, and the three companions exchanged looks.

Torrents opened his mouth to say something, but the Captain interrupted him.

"Look, kids," Jaiman poured another round of drinks, "you got this, okay? I have faith in you, and it's better than running, right? Here's what I know that'll help: Captain Mezk has been building a resistance, shipping women and children out over the bay, and bringing in troops."

"Wait," the Kid held up a hand. "Mezk? Mezk the Damned? The one who made the deal with the demons?"

Jaimin nodded, then threw back his drink. He looked back to the Kid with a gasp from the burn of the drink and squinted.

"Don't you think he might have his own agenda attached to some things that are just as bad," the Kid continued, "if not worse than the necromancer?"

"The enemy of my enemy is my friend," the Captain said, "at least until that first enemy is gone and my once friend is back to being my enemy and stabbing my face."

Torrents tossed back his drink in response and Esperanza followed his example.

The priestess fingered her small knife, wondering if the time to use it was overdue, if she should've ended this long before now. But she had to help if she could.

"But Mezk can get you into the city," the Captain said, "which is currently surrounded by the thousands of undead. That, in itself, will be a feat of legend. And if you guys come out on top in this one, I'll buy you each a bottle of my favorite rotgut. Which is extremely cheap, so this isn't a really big kindness."

A knock on the door made them all turn and look.

"Come," Captain Jaimin shouted towards the door.

A mop top of red hair leaned in. It was Jundek, the sailor the Kid remembered from his first trip on this ship.

"Captain," Jundek, not much more than just a boy, said, "you'd better come see this, and bring them, too."

They filed onto the deck. To the south, the evening was a bright orange with a black layer above it, looking like a bad impersonation of the actual setting sun in the west.

On the shore, just a league away, Durgan's Keep was burning.

## Chapter 23

Two hours later Torrents, Esperanza, and the Kid crouched in a rowboat, a black tarp covering them, with a magical breeze from the enchanted tiller pushing them gently towards shore.

Mezk the Damned steered the boat, the two sailors—Jundek and Tillheim—ready on each side with padded oars to help if needed. A knit cap covered Mezk's carrot-orange hair, and he'd bent his lean, lanky form almost double under the canvas covering above them.

"You think you'd work a different hair color into your deal with the demons," the Kid muttered.

"Shut it," Mezk growled, "sound carries on the water, and these things around Durgan's Keep don't need much encouragement to swarm us and drag us down to the depths."

The immense wall, about fifty meters tall—which the Kid had explained earlier was about the height of a fifteen or eighteen story building, depending when it was built—rose into the darkness above them. The orange glow of fires danced across the face of buildings above, showing the city had been penetrated and the invaders were now inside.

The city had been designed for different purposes on many different levels. It had warrens underneath, dug into the bedrock behind the cliff, which had been designed and excavated by the rokairn. It had a wooded aeifain and dasism section with gardens and trees. It had a housing quarter, a marketplace and merchant quarter, an administration section, and other smaller areas, and each could be closed off from the others for defensive purposes.

There was a chance that the whole was taken, but only some contained the attackers, but they wouldn't know until they got there.

"There," Mezk pointed halfway up the rock face, "we're going through a sewer opening there. We'll need to move through the docks, and up the switchbacks until we get high enough. Then we scale the cliff side, unlock and open the bars covering the sewers, and enter them. Once inside, we can go about anywhere, depending if these damned things are in the tunnels or not."

The boat scraped something, rocking gently. They slowed, and Mezk stared at the bottom of the boat with concern.

"Did we hit something?" Esperanza whispered. "A submerged tree branch, maybe? I mean, this bay is too deep for that to be the bottom this far out, right?"

"Hush," Mezk breathed, turning his head to listen for the sound of anything touching the bottom of their craft.

Something scratched at the bottom, a long thin noise with the hiccupping pop of whatever skipping in the divots of wood on the bottom of the boat.

The craft rocked again, this time more violently.

"That's not a tree," Torrents said, pulling a long dagger from the sheath on his waist.

The two men, Jundek and Tillheim, accompanying Mezk, tensed and looked at one another, fear in their eyes. They drew dirks with soot blackened blades in one hand, and a hatchet in their other.

Mezk increased their speed, moving closer to the docks ahead. The wharf held no boats or ships, having been abandoned when the undead creatures had surrounded the city, including patrolling along the walls, around the area, and under the water.

The bay side held no lights, and no moon shone tonight, so the area was dark except for the occasional flaming brand that fell from above.

The boat thunked into something, and a grizzled hand appeared on the bow, rocking the small craft further. A second hand appeared next to the first, and then a third, a fourth, and a fifth. A withered face rose above the side, as something lifted itself from the water and tried to pull itself aboard.

Torrents slashed at the face with his blade, cutting across the thing's cheeks and the bridge of its nose. It continued to drag itself up.

"No," said Tillheim, "when the enemy is boarding, you cut his ties."

As the man said this in a whisper, he brought down his hatchet twice, once on each hand of the creature, with a ka-chunk, and severed the fingers.

The thing slid back into the water.

Jundek was duplicating the actions on the other side of the rowboat as two more of the things crested the bow.

Torrents imitated them on another undead when it rose in front of him, and the Kid joined.

The tarp that had covered them had been folded back, and now the breeze caught at it and tugged it further. The things pulling themselves up, scrambled at the tarp, using it as a line to gain access to the men inside the boat.

Mezk drew his thin blade and began slicing the rope that threaded itself through the eyelets of the tarp to hold it over the rowboat. The canvas slid away, dragged by the weight of a half dozen waterlogged creatures.

They did this as silently as possible, not wanting to draw any more attention than they already had. The loudest noise was the dull thump of a hatchet cutting through bone and sinew. Soon, they pulled away from the creatures, leaving many of them with no hands.

Within minutes, they bumped against the docks, the two sailors dropping pads over the side to soften the noise; and using their wrapped oars to guide them to the plank walkway with as little sound as possible.

Mezk tied off his craft while the others clambered onto the wharf. Then he followed, taking up the rear of the line.

Jundek led the way towards the stone walkway, as wide as three wagons, that wound its way up the cliff side, doubling back and forth and towards their destination.

When they'd reached the first switchback, wet sounds floated through the darkness from the where they'd tied off the boat. The slap of waterlogged feet sounded from below them, as the creatures from the depths followed their path.

Jundek, in the lead, moved faster, but was limited in how fast he could move because of the lack of light. If they lit a torch or lantern, it would be a beacon for the undead, and soon they would be overwhelmed.

A figure landed in front of them, crumpling to the ground with the sound of breaking bones and splattering flesh. A second followed, but this one continued to move once it had shattered on the stone, and reached up towards Esperanza with a twisted claw.

Torrents interceded between the two, and with a shove of his booted foot, the broken body flew off the side of the walkway and to the boardwalk below.

Something landed gently behind him, and claws raked down his spine, hampered by his thick cloak.

The Kid, with his vision enhanced to see in the dark from the ability bestowed upon him by Edsumar, saw the lank, dark form drop from above and land in front of him. The thing attacked Torrents, ignoring everyone else.

The Kid stabbed upward, aiming for the base of the creature's skull. His blade slid into the brain, catching slightly on a vertebra, and bumping sideways so the point jutted out of an eye socket.

Three more forms fell in quick succession, each creature dropping into a crouch and hissing, long claws flexing.

The Kid remembered these things surrounding the newly made zombies and feeding on them to increase their own resilience and power. They also matched the description that Torrents had given of the thing he'd faced in the Black Wood with Axle, before he arrived in Hope's Hollow.

Two of the things leapt at Tillheim in the middle of the group, bringing him down like wolves picking out a deer from the herd. One ripped out the man's throat in a spray of blood, and the others tore into the man's gut with both hands, disemboweling him. A quiet gurgle rose from the sailor as he tried to scream, falling under their assault.

It also cut the group in half, with the Kid and Mezk on one side of the monsters, and Torrents, Esperanza, and the remaining sailor on the other.

A whispered prayer from Esperanza drifted on the wind, which then rose and became a mist that wrapped itself around the things, glowing with a gentle light that wouldn't be seen more than a meter away.

Mezk shoved the Kid aside, knocking him to the ground, and spun into action. His own black blade gleamed with a red glow as he sliced into the creatures. They fell under his onslaught, wisps of red energy drifting from their crumbling forms, and were sucked into the weapon in the carrot-top's hand. The two undead figures were dust before they hit the ground.

Edsumar growled in the Kid's head.

Torrents made quick work of the third creature, who now stood, wobbling, with no head on top of its shoulders. It took three steps forward, its hands flailing for a foe, stumbling, collapsed to the ground. It tipped over the edge of the walkway and fell into the darkness below.

Moving around the broken bodies, and leaving the fallen Tillheim behind, the group moved forward, once again in darkness.

The Kid, able to see, didn't miss Mezk leaning down to stab each body—including his own man—as he moved past them, his dirk draining them of their life, or death, force.

"Here," Mezk said after they had moved up a couple more switchbacks, "it's to our right, and we're going to need to scale the cliff face."

"In the dark?" Esperanza's voice quavered.

"Hold on," Mezk said, his voice even and patient.

The thin man leaned down and rolled something along the thin path to their right. A rope lit up with a dull red throb, a ball of light every two meters. The magical hemp hugged the corner of the walkway against the wall.

The path itself was about the width of two men abreast, which would normally be ample room for anyone to walk comfortably. But the added drop off, with jagged rocks, undead soldiers, and black water below, made it feel like it was much thinner than anyone cared to admit.

Mezk took the lead, walking with ease down the trail, the Kid close behind him.

The Kid was sticking close to Mezk quite on purpose.

*As the Godfather once said, 'Keep your friends close, and your enemies closer,'* the Kid thought, *and besides, I want to see what other tricks this guy had picked up from his demon buddies. Not everyone had a soul stealing dagger and nightlight rope in their back pocket.*

The Kid also wondered if anyone could use those things, or if there were strings attached and bad things would come if used. He figured it was better to not risk it.

Mezk reached the sewer gate. It was an archway, about a meter wide, and a meter and a half tall, with an iron gate across it. The lock on the hasp, holding it closed from the inside, looked new.

Arrayed behind the Kid on the walkway were Esperanza, Torrents, and then Jundek. Esperanza hugged the wall, facing it, and panting shallowly. Torrents had one hand between her shoulder blades, perhaps to comfort her, perhaps to keep her from falling over the side, but most likely it was a bit of both.

The gate swung outward into the open air with a high-pitched squeal, and Mezk jumped on it, holding a hand out to assist everyone in getting into the sewer without mishap.

The Kid easily leapt across the space, ignoring the proffered hand, landing cat-like inside and moving forward so the next person could get in.

Esperanza took Mezk's hand, and then grabbed his entire arm, jerking him off balance when she pulled him to her. Mezk wrapped his arm around her torso as Torrents lifted her towards the opening. The gate swung, assisted by Torrents's long reach, and Esperanza was safely deposited inside the tunnel. She rushed forward to the Kid, grabbing at him, panting, and looked away from the opening and the threatening drop that could have led to her death.

Torrents made the transfer easily, followed by the sailor, and then Mezk joined them.

The thin man swung the gate closed—catching it with one hand to make minimal noise—carefully replaced the lock, and clipped it shut. Pulling on the glowing rope with a specific sequence of movements, Mezk reeled it in as the light faded from the magical hemp.

Their guide gestured them forward into the darkness.

"Keep a hand on the right-side wall," Mezk whispered, barely audible, "and when we get to the first intersection, we can use a light."

They moved forward, their feet sloshing through the thick liquid. The smell of waste, human and otherwise, filled their noses. Things squished and wiggled past their feet, and the occasional sound of rushing water echoed through the tunnel. Each time the sound died down to a trickle, and moments later they'd feel a wash of warmer liquid move past their boots.

"Okay," Jundek said, "we're here. You can light a lantern now."

Soft squelching noises came from the sailor as he shuffled his feet and waited.

Esperanza fumbled with her satchel, not wanting to set it in down in the sewers, until she found what she needed. Holding the lantern aloft, she called upon a miniscule trickle of power from her goddess, and an electric spark jumped from her fingers to light the wick of her lantern.

Light flared.

Raising the lantern above her head, she turned to survey the intersection in front of the sailor.

The squelching noises still came from Jundek; held aloft, his throat torn, a half dozen undead creatures fed on his twitching body.

## Chapter 24

The undead creatures looked up, their sunken eyes shifting in their sockets. These weren't the common low undead that the majority of the army consisted of, neither were these like the ones they had faced on the path up from the docks. These seemed much more wild, not mindless, just feral.

Their jaws dropped, unhinging, until the mandible stretched their skin unnaturally and hung to their collar bones. A screeching sound echoed through the tunnels from the unnatural horrors, causing the Kid to throw his hands over his ears.

The things launched themselves towards the remaining four warm bodies, dropping the still twitching sailor.

Torrents caught one by the throat and crushed its windpipe. Reaching up with the other hand, the huge barbarian twisted the neck—reminding him of opening a pickle jar back home. Just a little muscle and twist would do it—and tore the head from the body. A thick liquid, which wasn't quite blood and burned his skin, sprayed across him.

Mezk whirled into motion, spinning through the gathering of undead, striking with his dagger. Two of the creatures, drained of their essence, disintegrated. Dust filtered down to the wet floor of the sewer.

The Kid threw his dagger. The ivory blade pierced a creature's eye, who fell into the runoff with a splash.

The two remaining creatures focused on Esperanza, drawn by the mystical connection between her and Latress.

Esperanza, unfocused after the heights, stumbled backwards and screamed. Lightning shot from her fingertips—reminding Torrents of Emperor Palpatine from Star Wars. The attackers melted into twisted, smoking husks of tight, black flesh and bones, and fell to the ground.

Mezk stabbed each form, dead or undead, with his dagger. Unabashed by the others watching the interaction, he drew in a deep breath as the weapon drew in the energy from within the being.

He smiled at Esperanza—who stared at the man, horrified after seeing the ritual for the first time—and winked at the Kid, who watched him through slitted eyes.

*Why would anyone create beings such as this?* Esperanza thought, as the group, down to four, moved forward. *Nature wouldn't do this, and I don't know why any god would allow this. Does that mean these are of man's creation?*

The four of them moved through the sewers, facing down groups of the undead invaders, and destroying them. It disturbed each of the companions whenever Mezk pulled the soul from a fallen foe, but they needed him, so kept their thoughts to themselves.

Led by the Kid, within an hour of entering the subterranean tunnels, they found their way to an exit near the red-light district along the docks.

Around them, the city burned.

The thick smoke roiled above the parapets and walkways of the city watch. Groups of militia or the different street guilds moved past in clumps, eyes wary and searching for the lurching and shambling forms of the enemy.

Clouds gathered overhead, reflecting the light of the fires within the city walls, casting shadows into the alleys and streets.

Women and children screamed when an undead squad found them, attacked them, tore them limb from limb, devouring them in the middle of the street. Men shouted to one another, trying to come together to create a force that could defend the city, one of the last standing bastions against the demonic hordes in the south.

The group realized that most of the fires had been set by the citizens to hamper or kill the undead army, but it had also created events and situations that just as easily killed civilians.

Chaos reigned.

The Kid scaled a wall, climbing it without effort, his fingers finding nooks and crannies without trying, and ran along the top, looking out across the burning city. He called down to the others, letting them know when they approached a group of the enemy, allowing them to avoid the encounter altogether.

They moved through the city, facing enemies when they had to, and moving towards the Kid's goal, the red-light district.

Mezk bristled at being under the Kid's guidance, unhappy about how the Kid made him the fool, along with an entire crew of Bokk's men. Mezk had no boss, but freelanced with any side that would sign a contract and keep their word. More than one person who'd broken a contract with the demon damned mercenary had been found dead afterwards.

In just under a half hour, the Kid led them to the whoring part of town, and to Jewlnee in particular. The building differed from just a few weeks before.

Iron banded shutters, painted in yellows, pinks, and reds, battened and latched across every door and window. Only the cross shape of the arrow slits showed evidence of people within, and the point of a bolt balanced on a crossbow always accompanied it.

The Kid knew Jewlnee's routine, and two women would be behind any one woman holding the weapon. One would wait to reload the crossbow, and the second was there to pass a loaded weapon to the person staffing the arrow slit, or to replace them if they fell.

With a word and twist of his wrist, Mezk sent his rope up the side of the building, and it wound itself around the spindles in the balcony above, and then knotted itself along its own length to make the climb quicker and easier for those below.

Mezk leapt from the ground to the veranda without effort, but Torrents and Esperanza used the rope.

The Kid leapt from the adjacent building to join the others. Standing with his back to the wall, the Kid knocked on the shutter.

"Hey," the Kid called as the crossbow point pivoted in his direction, "who's in there? Go get Jewlnee for me."

"And who the hell are you?" a young woman's voice answered.

"I'm the Kid," the Kid replied, realizing he only had one name, like Madonna, or Cher, or…he couldn't think of any men that just went by a solo moniker.

"The Kid," the voice grew flustered, "as in, THE Kid? Are you as cute as they say?"

"Oh, by Latress's blustery locks," Esperanza sighed, and then banged on the shutter with her fist, "go get the damned madam and quit your swooning before we all chuzzing die out here. That's the words of Esperanza, priestess of Latress, and destroyer of disease, okay already?"

A squeak came from inside, and they could hear retreating footfalls. Two other young, giggling voices came from inside.

Within a few minutes, the painted and effervescent Jewlnee arrived, opened the shutters, and welcomed the Kid and his friends inside, though she gave a second look and consideration to Mezk. They allowed him in only after the Kid reassured Jewlnee he was on their side and helping.

Shortly after entering, the five of them sat around a table, grapes, cheese, bread, and wine set out in the center. They raised their glasses in a toast, though Mezk looked like an animal that wanted open air rather than being trapped inside.

"To freedom," Jewlnee said, "though most people never realize they have it, don't have it, or the cost of having it."

They raised their glasses, clinking every other glass before drinking to avoid the bad luck of missing one.

After a deep drink, they talked.

"Jewlnee," the Kid said, "I came right to you because I knew you'd have your ear to the ground, and your finger on the pulse of the city. Can you help us find Aku'ji, the necromancer?"

"You're going after her?" Jewlnee asked with a gasp, then laughed, "I should've known you would. You never knew when to quit, and since I last saw you, you seem even more driven, even a little crazy, but with purpose. Like it isn't the same young man I've known for years. Who's in that head now, Kid?"

"Let's just say," the Kid gave the madam a crooked smile, "I'm an old soul, and then a little more on top of that. Can you help us?"

"Yes," the woman said hesitantly, "but she has layers of defense, and she's already calling out for allies within Durgan's Keep. Asking for those that want to survive this occupation to come forward and give her intelligence."

"You mean," the Kid sneered, popping a grape into his mouth, "turn others in."

"Yeah," Jewlnee agreed, "toss them to the wolves. And these people think that they'll come out on top, and when this is all said and done, they'll be holding the cards and have some iota of control within Durgan's Keep."

"Tell us about these layers of defense," Esperanza urged.

"And do some name dropping on these allies, if you would please," said Torrents.

The meeting took hours to play out, Jewlnee calling for maps and informants hidden in the basement below. Between the hours before and after midnight, she brought sausages, hot teas, and other things to keep the group moving and awake. By midmorning, the witching hour, each person was heading out in a different direction with a different task.

Each knew they may not see the others again and were prepared for that.

At the moment of parting, Mezk slipped away from the others without a word, and the three friends that had been through so much together faced one another.

"Be careful out there, Kid," Esperanza smiled at the young man, then turned to Torrents, "you might be a big bad ass, but don't push your luck, a dagger in your ribs kills you as much as anyone."

"Whatever," the barbarian muttered, "your face kills you as much as anyone."

They chuckled together, not because of the humor, but to share the moment.

"Yeah," the Kid sighed, "you kids take of yourself, and I want to hear that call soon, okay Esperanza? You find that bitch, and then you call us to you. We'll answer, if we can."

"Kid?" Torrents said, turning towards the smaller man.

"Yeah, big guy?" The Kid looked up at the barbarian.

Torrents enveloped the Kid in a hug, and pulled the street thief to his chest, holding him close for a few moments.

"You'd have been a great grandma to have," Torrents said as he released the Kid.

"And you're a bidj and pemtie," the Kid's voice was rough as he grabbed the big man's biceps and stared into the other's eyes, "now, go kick some bidj, you big dummy, and let's save the city."

The three moved apart, taking one last glance at the spot they'd stood a moment before, and at one another, and then turned away and moved into the night.

Torrents sought the merchant district, hunting the slave master, Dropsum.

The Kid had learned that Jakdin had switched sides, and his big plan for the city was to throw all the other guild masters under the bus by aligning with the necromancer, and then ruling the underworld once his competition was dead. The Kid hunted Jakdin.

Esperanza called upon her goddess as she moved away from the others, asking for her blessing and guidance in finding the source of the evil in the city.

## Chapter 25

Torrents moved through the streets, staying on the walls and avoiding the center of any avenue. He wasn't a master tactician, but he had enough sense to know that taking out the army one at a time would be the path to a quick death.

To turn this one into a win, they had to take out the head of the snake. And to do that, they needed to cut the legs out from under the snake.

Torrents, ducking behind an overturned cart to avoid being spotted by a squad of undead patrolling the area, realized that snakes didn't have legs, but he knew what he meant.

Moving along the outer wall to the Merchant Quarter, the barbarian crouched in the shadows when he could see the stone archway that led to the shops and businesses. It was guarded, sort of. It had four undead on each side of the opening, and Torrents could see four more on both sides within the entrance.

That made sixteen shambling, lurching, shuffling, mildly dazed, and barely cognizant people lumbering back and forth. The things meandered back and forth, one bumping into a wall, another picking at a lump of moss on a cobblestone, and the others equally engaged and vigilant.

Torrents still didn't think going straight down the middle was the answer. Time to take a page from the Kid's book.

Moving down the street a little, until the archway was out of sight, blocked by buildings, the barbarian looked around to make sure no one was watching or approaching.

He slid his sword into the scabbard on his back, bent at the knees, jumped up, and grabbed the overhang of the porch of a cobbler's shop. Pulling himself up, he moved along the shingled surface, taking his time so he didn't make noise and attract unwanted attention.

The building was built flush to the inner-city wall, and Torrents moved across the roof to the thin parapet behind the shop. Vaulting over it, he landed on another roof. He crept to the edge and looked down into the street.

That's when an idea struck him.

If he could drop the portcullis at each of the entrances to the Merchant Quarters, then it would probably stop most of the undead from getting out, or more from coming in.

This was a genius idea! These things weren't really bright enough to figure how to raise the gate once he'd dropped it, and Torrents didn't see anyone hanging out that looked like they were in charge and could give orders or instructions for such a task.

The barbarian turned back and moved to the parapet he'd crossed, mounted it, and moved along it—bent over and keeping low to remain unseen—towards the archway.

When he came to it, he wondered if he knew enough about such things to drop the gate. He'd seen movies, but was unsure how realistic they'd been. And even if they were historically accurate, it didn't mean that this world would have developed the same technology in the same way.

Scrambling atop the stone crossover, which was about five meters across, he saw the wooden trapdoors in the roof. He opened one, slowly, to keep any noises to a minimum, and saw iron rungs that led down to the small guardroom. And wow, it was small, barely big enough for one man to turn around in. But within it was a wheel with a crank, and it held the chain with a chock to keep the portcullis up.

Moving down the metal ladder, he saw the things outside the small room, owandering back and forth. Two of the undead were nose to nose, trying to go around one another. Each moved in the same direction, mirroring one another as they tried to pass the other.

Torrents watched them move back and forth for almost a full minute before dropping one leg down, and placing his booted foot on the lever that held the chain in place. He extended his leg, moving the lever, and with a series of loud clicks, the chain disengaged, and the portcullis dropped.

The two zombie-like creatures were still moving side to side, trying to go past one another. The outside one was crushed, metal spikes on the bottom of the gate piercing his skull and driving him to the cobblestones. The second looked down, tilted his head at his crushed counterpart, sighed, turned around, and walked to the second portcullis that had dropped into place. Seeing his return way blocked, he turned again, walked back to where the other one had been impaled, sighed, and turned back again. This seemed to be this thing's destiny, as it repeated the actions again and again.

Torrents climbed out of the trapdoor above and moved along the wall to the next guard post for the Merchant's Quarter. He repeated his actions at each of the remaining four entries, then dropped over the wall into the marketplace.

Moving past the tents and stalls, and through the slave market, he made his way towards the Merchant's Guild, where they had thought was the best chance of finding Dropsum.

Seeing the building ahead, Torrents crouched and studied the surrounding movement.

People in chains lined the road outside, and dark, gaunt, humanoid creatures walked along, poking and hissing at them. The prisoners jerked away from the things, trying to stay out of their reach, but unable to do so because of their shackles.

The lead captive, the one closest to the door of the building, had been unchained and was being dragged inside as three other citizens came trudging out. The three leaving were following another undead, who hit their freshly dead and animated flesh with a riding crop, guiding them to a makeshift corral where others like them stood dumbly waiting.

Torrents needed inside, and he needed to get there without having to fight a horde of the things standing guard over the prisoners. He needed a distraction. But he also wanted to free the people.

He needed a plan.

*Well,* the barbarian thought, *squatting in an alley isn't going to free the people, get the guards away from the door, or get me inside. I need to do something.*

Torrents doubled back, giving a wide berth, then crossed the road and crept along the buildings towards the line of captives.

He'd moved past a handful of them before the first one noticed him in the shadows. The woman let out gasp, staring at him. He held his finger to his lips to silence her, moving to the ring set into the stone of the ground to which the prisoners were chained.

Squatting over it and gripping it, he pushed up with his legs. The muscles in his shoulders, arms, back, and legs bunched with the effort.

The woman, seeing what he was doing, turned to the people next to her and whispered something. In almost perfect unison, the prisoners began wailing, shouting, and rattling their chains, clumping together to block out the sight and sound of what was happening behind them.

"Make some noise," a man shouted, "they can chain our bodies, but they can't chain our spirits!"

The line of prisoners came to life, some hesitating and looking around in a daze, but others causing the distraction that the barbarian needed.

The ring tore from the ground. Torrents dropped it, nodded at the captives looking back at him, and moved to the next ring.

The creatures guarding the people beat them with short whips, clubs, and crops, hissing between the cracks of leather hitting flesh.

The second ring freed, Torrents moved to the third and final one.

One guard shouted, a screeching guttural noise, and pointed directly at the barbarian crouching over the last ring.

Other guards turned to look.

The crowd went wild, surging forward over their captors. Torrents pulled, straining to tear the last obstacle free.

He'd expected the people to flee, but they were in a frenzy, falling onto the monsters that held them captive, ripping them apart with their bare hands. Others snatched up fallen weapons, pieces of wood or metal, and joined in.

Five more creatures rushed out of the building to help quell the uprising.

Torrents slipped behind the chaos, through the open double doors, and into the building.

Moving through the foyer, past the benches along the side of the entryway, and around the wall in front of him, he went to the left instead of right. He realized both directions led to the same large, round room as he entered it.

The room was lit with dozens of oil lanterns, showing most of the tables pushed against the outer wall. Two tables had been pulled together in the center of the chamber, and a person lay manacled to its surface.

Dropsum, the slave trader of the Blood Sun Wolf clan, hunched over the person, holding a black orb that glowed with a deep green inner light, chanting.

Torrents crept forward on cat's feet, drawing his two-handed sword from over his shoulder. Raising it above his head, he swung it down towards Dropsum's shoulder where it met the neck.

The man leaning over the table pivoted and threw his hand up, catching the blade and jerking it from the barbarian's grip.

Smirking, the slave master took a step forward and bashed the handle into the warrior's nose.

Blood spurted, and Torrents stumbled backwards, his hands flying to his face.

Dropsum reversed his grip, holding the blade with both hands, and chopped at his attacker with the crossbar.

Torrents backpedaled, tripping over detritus on the floor, and falling to his butt.

"You again," Dropsum said smoothly, smiling, "you've been a thorn in my side long enough. I think it's time to end this and bring you into the fold. Yes, I think you'll make an excellent lieutenant in my little plan."

Torrents grunted, pulling a broken chair leg from underneath him and throwing it at the man. The projectile hit the man in the face, piercing his eye and jutting out. Black blood dribbled from the wound.

"Chuz you," the barbarian said, "you talk too much."

The slave master screamed, reminiscent of the time Torrents had put an arrow through the man's hand, and swung the pommel of the sword at the barbarian's head.

It was the warrior's turn to catch the weapon, and he pulled it with him when he rolled backwards. The sword slid along Dropsum's palms, cutting them to the bone as it came free.

From his back, Torrents kicked out with both feet as the slave master stumbled forward, and bones cracked, the boots crushing the man's chest.

Dropsum sprawled backwards, hitting the table with the small of his back.

Torrents was on his feet in a flash, thrusting the blade in his enemies' guts, then jerking to one side, tearing the flesh, and causing entrails to spill across the floor.

Dropsum pushed off the table and to his feet, meeting the next blow from the barbarian with his hands, which slid off because of the ichor oozing from the cuts in his palm.

Torrents pummeled at the man, cutting and stabbing with his blade. Dropsum kept coming, wounds closing of their own accord.

The slave master swooned, holding his belly, and smiled up at the barbarian.

"You can't kill me," Dropsum laughed, "I can no longer die, can't you see that?"

Torrents looked around the room, searching for some way to bring the final death of the creature in front of him.

His eyes fell on the black orb on the table.

Dropsum followed his gaze, and his smile faltered.

"No," Dropsum growled, "you won't get out of this that easily."

The slave master threw himself at the magical artifact, covering it with his body, as the barbarian thrust at it with his sword.

The weapon slid into the slave master's back, and Dropsum's form muted the tinkling of breaking glass.

Pulling his blade free, Torrents raised it to strike again, and the slave master rolled to face him.

Shards of the artifact littered the man's midsection, jagged pieces of glass sticking out from ripped flesh and torn organs.

Dropsum's eyes were wide as he looked down at his ruined body, green arcs of magic dancing through his belly. The verdant magic swirled, becoming a thick cloud, and enveloped the slave master. It grew outward into a glowing sphere around the man.

The table beneath the man melted.

Torrents took a step back as the magical forces grew, then turned and ran, skidding around the partition wall between him and the outside.

Reaching the foyer, Torrents paused; the building behind him thrummed, and then exploded, throwing the barbarian a dozen meters into the night air.

The barbarian hit the ground, knocking the air out of him.

Rolling onto his back, Torrents raised his sword to ward off any attacks from the creatures waiting outside, as broken shards of wood and chunks of stone rained down around him.

The courtyard was mostly empty. Many of the prisoners and all undead slavers had disappeared into the night. The remaining captives wandered about, making sure nothing moved that wasn't human, and helping the injured.

The big man called out to the remaining townsfolk.

"Hey," he shouted, then quieted to a harsh whisper, "come with me, we have more work to do to free your city."

People began moving towards him, nodding and gathering fallen weapons to arm themselves.

*I found her.* Esperanza's voice whispered on the wind. *Follow my words and come to me. Let us end this.*

# Chapter 26

The Kid smiled as the body crumpled to the ground. He cleaned the viscous black liquid on the tattered remnants of the undead guard at his feet.

He looked up at the urchins crowded in the corner of the ally and nodded at them, then jerked his head to one side, showing that they should run.

The Kid was on the hunt.

This was never his bag, he was more of the trick them and take it type, running scams on the street, or elaborate heists of the corrupt ruling class here in Durgan's Keep. His skill set, between his innate magics and learned abilities, leaned towards stealth rather than wet work.

He was deep into guild territory now, but couldn't pass by as people were being slaughtered by monsters that he felt partially responsible for. The Kid didn't create them, but he was there when a lot of them were being made into the things that now stalked the streets of his city.

He knew where Jakdin's bolt hole was and had already checked there. The man hadn't been in residence, but a quick interrogation of the man's compatriots had told the Kid where to find the thug he sought.

The people the Kid had found hiding at Jakdin's place weren't the same ones whom he'd tricked that night in the Open Door, but others who now hid from the invading army of the dead; they'd been quick to give up the goods on their boss. They'd confirmed what the Kid had already known: Jakdin was in league with the necromancer, and happy to turn on the thieves of the city, causing them to be turned into new undead.

The Kid made his way back to the rooftops, his own private highway. He moved across the buildings where most people would have normally been sleeping, but with the events of the past few days, most had abandoned their homes, hoping to survive, to see another day.

The growing number of walking dead below told the Kid that most of them had failed.

The Kid's mind magic allowed him to do many things, most of them relating to tricking other people into seeing what he wanted them to see, or not see. These abilities didn't seem to work on the dead masses in the street below. But he still dropped his mental blanket over himself, which made most people not even realize he was there.

Making his way through the city, the Kid arrived in the poor section, called the Cheaps. They were so named for the obvious reasons, but also it was the best place in the city to get someone to sing like a bird for just a few coins, or even just a meal or a bottle of crap booze.

Jakdin had set up his base of operations here.

Dropping into a small courtyard in a circle of apartments, the Kid stood up and surveyed his surroundings, using the night vision given to him by Edsumar.

The buildings rose three stories up on each side of him, most doorways covered by a blanket as much as they were an actual door. The place was as quiet as, well, as quiet as a graveyard. Some buildings still smoldered with fires that had been put out or just burned out, and the smell of scorched wood hung thick in the air. There weren't even rats scurrying about like they normally would be at this hour.

The Kid moved towards a doorway, stopping as footfalls echoed behind him. Wrapping himself in anonymity, he stepped into the shadows beside the door he was about to enter and waited.

Three men entered the courtyard from a doorway across from the Kid, and he recognized them as part of the Grey Ash gang, the people who Jakdin worked with.

"I don't believe this," a weasel faced man said, scratching at his neck vigorously. "This whole thing gives me the willies. I mean, we're feeding these things the people who supported us."

"You mean," the bald man with a limp interjected, holding a lantern up to light their way, "people we used to rob."

"Tomato, tomato," weasel face said, and spat on the ground, "they might be the sheep we fleeced, but they were our people."

"Yeah," the third guy, an immense man with stringy, greasy hair, agreed.

"I just don't think it's right," weasel face whined, "we need them, don't we? We shouldn't be giving them to this witch to make things that would eat our faces as soon as look at us, should we?"

"No," baldy agreed, "but what're we supposed to do? It's not like we can beat them, and Jakdin says he's got it under control. We're not gonna be killed or ate, he said so."

"Yeah," the big guy agreed.

"For now," Weasel whined, "but what about tomorrow, or next week? When does good ol' Jakdin turn on us?"

"Yeah," the big guy added sagely.

"Nothing we can do about it," the bald man sighed, and the three entered another doorway, "but we'd best get him these papers before he decides that today is that day."

"Yeah," echoed the voice of the big man, the three disappearing into the hallway.

The Kid slid from the shadows, moving with barely a noise, and followed the receding light and the sound of the men's voices.

The men continued to complain, though now they talked about the lack of whores in town since the undead army showed up.

The Kid shadowed them through a ramshackle apartment, out into another courtyard, and then they descended a set of stairs into a cellar.

The Kid waited for a count of thirty, giving them time to get ahead and out of sight, then entered the basement.

He heard the men debating if the undead would take the place of people in the city, doing the tasks they'd need, when the deep baritone of the big man hushed them. One man knocked on a door, and a muffled voice shouted something. The sound of it closing followed the creaking of the rusty hinges of a door, and the voices became muted.

*Oh great,* the Kid thought, *how am I supposed to get into a closed room without being noticed?*

*You could wait until they come out,* Edsumar suggested in the Kid's head.

The Kid moved to the door, pressed his ear to it, and listened.

The thick wood stopped him from making out the words, but he could hear four voices. He recognized Jakdin's sneer as the man harangued the three who'd just entered. It sounded like it was coming from an antechamber.

The Kid risked it. Crouching low and cloaking himself in his magics, he pulled down on the lever and opened the door a few centimeters.

Looking into the room, he couldn't see anyone in the lamplight that filled the area.

Taking a deep breath, he pushed the door open wide enough to slip inside, duck walked in, turning as he did to close the door.

Turning around, still crouched, the Kid surveyed his surroundings. The big guy and the bald guy stared straight at him with wide eyes.

The Kid's abilities allowed him to go unnoticed, usually. But sometimes, the minds of the people that would normally just gloss over his presence just couldn't accept that something wasn't actually there. Times like when a door opens and closes all on its own. That sort of thing made a person's brain look for a reason.

"Is he a ghost?" the big guy whispered to baldy.

"No," the bald man whispered back, disdain in his voice, "I think that's the Kid. The one who attacked the boss in that bar a few weeks ago."

"He's hard to see," the big guy said, "you sure he isn't a ghost? Maybe the Kid died, and instead of being a dead body, he's a ghost."

The bald man considered this.

The Kid took advantage of this hesitation and reached out with his mind to touch the thugs' thoughts.

*The dead seek revenge on those who hurt the things they loved.* The Kid pushed that thought on the two men. *Jakdin hurt this city, the city the Kid loves.*

It wasn't perfect. The Kid had never tried something like this before, introducing a complex idea to his targets. Usually it was something easy, like he wasn't there, or that a cat is a dog, or that a wagon is on fire. This was much more difficult.

The two men stared at the Kid, considering what to do.

"What the hell are you two yapping about?" Weasel-face said, looking into the room, "I thought we told you to shut it, the boss and I are talking."

"But it's a ghost," the big guy said, pointing at the Kid.

Weasel-face looked in the direction that the thug indicated, squinting as if trying to make something out. His eyes went wide as the Kid slowly became visible to him.

The Kid sighed, stood upright, and threw Edsumar across the room.

The dagger embedded itself into Weasel's throat, and the man stumbled backwards into the room he'd come out of, clutching the weapon in his neck.

The two other men looked from their friend to the Kid.

"Come on, boys," the Kid said, striding towards the door, "we ghosts kill anyone who chuzzes with us. Help me out, and I won't haunt you."

The two men nodded and turned to follow the very real apparition, who strolled past them and into the room beyond. Both saw that the spirit now had its dagger back in its hand, and that the blade was as white as a ghost, too.

"Ghost dagger," baldy whispered, turning to follow the kid, pulling out his own dagger.

"Yeah," the big guy agreed, drawing out a wide buck knife and moving into the room.

Knives flew.

The Kid had already dropped to the floor, rolling to one side and throwing Edsumar at Jakdin. The white weapon missed, sticking into the wood paneling beyond the man standing behind a desk, an array of throwing blades on the wooden surface in front of him. The blades shone wetly.

The big lackey stared down at two blades in his chest, then slipped to his knees, reaching for the knives. He fell forward onto his face, pushing the blades deeper into his torso. One tore through the back of the man's shirt, blood spreading around it.

"Aw," baldy choked back a sob, looking at his fallen friend, "why'd you have to go and do that?"

A dagger appeared in baldy's forehead as Jakdin took advantage of the distraction. The man fell backwards to the ground, empty eyes staring at the ceiling.

"Is that a magical dagger?" Jakdin gestured over his shoulder at the weapon stuck in the wall behind him with a thumb, and turned towards the Kid, who was still prone on the floor. "Too bad I had a protection to guard me from such things. Should also protect me from your damned tricks. But that'll be a nice prize for me to remember you by once you're dead. You know…in about thirty seconds."

Jakdin's hands blurred as he snatched knives from the desk in front of him and threw them at the Kid.

The Kid rolled backwards and to his feet, tearing the poisoned weapon from baldy's forehead as he moved past the dead man.

He couldn't feel Edsumar's thoughts, and the dagger wouldn't return to his hand.

The Kid threw the knife he'd grabbed, and Jakdin leaned to one side, avoiding it, throwing two more at the Kid.

Grabbing the weapons with his mind, the Kid slowed and turned them in a thought, then with a thrust of his hands the two blades shot back at Jakdin.

The thug looked down at the twin blades in his chest, his mouth working as he stumbled into the wall behind him. His hand reached for Edsumar, gripping it and pulling the magical weapon from the wall as he slid down the paneling to the floor.

The Kid's nemesis stared at the weapon in his hand, then slowly turned to look at the Kid with amazement, before gurgling up a bubble of blood.

The light went from the man's eyes as they lost focus and his head dropped to his chest.

Calling to Edsumar, the blade appeared in his hand as his enemy died, his protections gone.

The Kid knew he'd need others to help with the next part.

He moved to the hallway, began banging on doors, shouting that Jakdin was dead, and that everyone needed to defend their homes from this invasion.

People peeked out of doors and listened to his rallying shouts.

*I found her.* Esperanza's voice whispered on the wind. *Follow my words and come to me. Let us end this.*

## Chapter 27

The undead shied away from Esperanza as she strode down the center of the road, a ball of lightning darting off to brighten a dark corner, shooting across the street to illuminate something there, and then zipping around her in an upward spiral to cast a white pool of light around her form.

The priestess moved with purpose and drive, her body language speaking of confidence and poise. Wind whipped around, moving her grey robes, and causing bits of trash to scatter.

The sky overhead responded to the woman's mood and attitude; clouds raced across the firmament above the city, circling inward to a spiral focused directly above her.

A mob of undead, about twenty, lurched into the street from a side alley. They turned slowly, looking for their next quarry. Spotting the lone figure, they staggered into a run and came towards her.

Esperanza never broke stride.

With a wave of her hand, the ball of lightning shot forward and passed directly through the first creature's head, causing it to shatter. As the zombie-like abomination fell to the ground, the electrical sphere repeated the movement another four times on other members of the dead mob.

The remaining fifteen walking dead were within a couple meters of Esperanza, and she raised her arms above her, then jerked them to the ground.

The surrounding winds sharpened and whistled through the wooden porch posts, making business signs wave and creak on their chains. The closest creatures, caught in a half dozen dust devils, lifted into the air, then followed the motion of the woman's hands. Smashing to the ground, their bodies exploded from the impact, and moist bits scattered across the cobblestone road.

The ball of lightning returned to Esperanza's side, and the priestess cupped her hands and blew into them. Her voice started as a whisper and rose to a booming growl, echoing off the stone walls around her.

Throwing her arms wide, then clapping her hands together, she created a thunderous explosion that threw the remaining dead minions backwards. The ones that hit walls stopped moving immediately, the ones that hit wagons or railings tore in half, and still struggled towards her.

"Clean this up," the woman said to her tag-along globe of energy, and the small orb rumbled a bit of thunder of its own, then darted off to obey.

The few monsters still moving were cooked with jagged bolts of lightning as Esperanza turned down the next street, her ball of lightning joining her moments later, dancing a little jig around her.

The priestess called upon the wisdom of Latress, asking for guidance in finding the greatest threat to the city and its people.

The ball of lightning flew around her, stopping for a moment at each cardinal point and pulsing. Zipping to the west, it pulsed purple, and Esperanza turned in that direction.

After traveling another eight blocks, screams made Esperanza turn. A woman and three men backed into an alley, standing in front of and protecting a handful of small children.

Two creatures, human in shape but not in nature, crouched at the mouth of the alley, hissing and lurching forward, preparing to launch themselves at their prey.

Esperanza knew that these kids, if they survived, would never be the same. War changed people and shattered minds in ways others would never fathom.

Calling upon the winds, Esperanza whipped her hand forward like she'd seen a man in the circus do when taming the lion. The air solidified, ten meters away from her, and her wind whip tore into one of the things threatening the people. It turned and hissed at her, then bounded in her direction.

The second leapt at the families in the alley.

Esperanza brought one hand up calmly and clenched her fist. Wagons from each side of the street, caught in the hurricane force gale, flew together and crushed the undead monster in midair.

As the wagons fell to the ground, the priestess's other hand reached forward, and a fist of raging wind plucked the distant foe from the air. The creature was flung upward to a height that the sound of its threatening hiss disappeared, only to come back into range when it plummeted to the ground.

The body hit the cobblestones with a wet thud and stopped moving.

"Go," Esperanza pointed back the way she'd come from, "go with the blessing and protection of Latress. Seek the inn called, The Shooting Breeze, and you'll find safety there. Those of you who can fight, wait for my call, and I'll lead you against these monsters."

The woman turned away from the people without looking to see if they had obeyed, striding towards her pulsing guide as it weaved through the streets towards her goal.

A dark, cloaked form drifted from an alley to block Esperanza's path, its arms held wide, its face hidden in the folds of its fluttering hood.

The being floated a half meter off the ground, cold radiating out from it.

Esperanza's sphere darted forward at her gesture, making a beeline for the thing blocking the way, sparking.

The undead didn't move except to raise its hands, which were incorporeal and glowed with a dim, eerie blue light.

The orb shot at the thing, and faster than Esperanza could follow, the apparition caught her little globe.

Raising its fist, the phantom showed Esperanza the orb in its hand, then squeezed. Electrical sparks rained down on the stones below the specter, and the wind carried away a hollow sound of mocking laughter.

The wraith threw back its cowled face and howled. A banshee scream ripped from the spirit, echoing off the surrounding buildings.

Birds dropped from rooftops and awnings, dead, onto the street. A cluster of rats in the alley to Esperanza's left burst into a violent frenzy, tearing into one another. The glass of the shop closest to the phantom frosted over, cracked, and shattered.

Dozens of distant howls answered the call, screams echoing back to the small street in the dark. There would be more. They were coming, and they'd be here soon.

Esperanza scoffed. She pointed the toe of her right foot at the ground a half meter in front of her and spun in a lazy circle. Moisture gathered at the line she created in the surrounding air.

The priestess narrowed her eyes at the thing floating a meter off the ground in front of her, smiled, then calmly closed her eyes and raised her hands above her—and her voice in prayer to Latress.

The screams and howls of the approaching intangible hunters grew louder, and dogs raised their voices in terror, cats screeched in the night, and horses screamed in their passing.

The spiral of clouds above spun faster, twisting into itself. A funnel descended from the stratus and approached the ground. Mists and fogs roiled from alleys, sewers, and side streets, filling the entire area with thick, humid air.

The phantasm's reinforcements burst into the crossroads, wailing and angry, their sightless eyes turning to face their holy foe. Moisture trailed behind their ethereal forms as they rushed across the square to their enemy.

The twisting clouds from above dropped around the priestess, cocooning her in a furious tornado, creating an impenetrable wall between her and her aggressors.

The specters shot through the wet air, dashing themselves against the wall of weather.

"We may not be able to reach you," breathed the wraith across the road, "but neither can you reach us, or your final goal."

Whispered laughter, that strained sanity, filled the street.

"Wanna bet," Esperanza said, cocking her head and raising one eyebrow, "let's see if I can show you just how wrong you are."

Calling out to her goddess, smiling as she did, the clouds lit up with rolling heat lightning. The bursts of electrical energy followed the conductive moisture, being drawn down from the sky and into the town square. The area lit up, and the undead wraiths within the fog, mists, moisture, and clouds were wreathed and penetrated with the lightning.

The screams from the creatures changed drastically from anger and hunger, to pain and fear.

Within the span of a long breath, the creatures were forever destroyed, and the night fell silent.

The mists parted, and the funnel cloud drew back into the heavens, and the only sound remaining was that of a dog barking in the distance.

Esperanza was on her knees, panting from the exertion. She knew she couldn't show fear to those things; they fed on fear. Only her self-assurance shook their own confidence. That, and a million kilojoules of chuzzing lightning.

Holding a hand out to one side, she called another orb of electricity to her. It popped into existence, then darted away to explore and scout.

After a moment's thought, she called a second one, then a third, and then a fourth ball of lightning. These three circled her in a protective ring that, from a distance, looked a lot like the nuclear power symbol.

The priestess pushed to her feet, leaning over with her hands on her knees to catch her breath and let her head stop spinning.

She focused on the little knife on her belt until her vision cleared.

"That took a little more out of me than I realized," she said to no one in particular, though one ball of energy zipped to her and hovered a half meter in front of her face, as if listening to her. It bobbed when she smiled at it, then darted back to its task of protecting her.

On legs that steadied with each step, the woman moved towards her final target.

Following the pulsing orb for another ten minutes brought the priestess to the aeifain and dasism sanctuary in the northwest quadrant of Durgan's Keep—where the necromancer had taken up residence, claiming it as her personal throne room.

The area was designed and grown using magic, and the beautifully sculpted structures intertwined with trees, bushes, and other natural elements that rose into the air or wove along the ground. Now, the trees were dark and broken, and smelled of rot that burst out from their core. Flowers released fetid stenches that attracted roaches and centipedes instead of butterflies and bees. Topiaries were bent and twisted, knotted into mocking representations of tortures.

Fountains once dotted the parks and gardens here. The pools and basins were now thick with slow-running liquid that resembled the ichor that comes from a running sore. The sprays of water that had once danced above the artistic statuary of the ponds, now dribbled and burbled out of the pipes from below the city, as the putrescence leaked back down into the water supply.

Deer had once prospered within the sanctuary, grazing with safe leisure. Rabbits, squirrels, chipmunks, raccoons, and other animals had scampered through the trees and grass, playing and feeding without threat.

Now, structures built of antlers and bones marked the area, curtained walls and roofs made of hide and fur covering them. The smaller animals scurried frantically through twisting roots and underbrush, attacking one another when they crossed paths.

The entire area was heavy with the fetid miasma of death and rot. It was like the weight of depression and anxiety that Esperanza had battled her whole life had been given form and a home where it could fester and grow.

The darkness inside her pushed up, memories of bottles of pills and alcohol rose to the front of her mind, rearing back and threatening to overwhelm her.

The broken form of the aeifain sanctuary, with decay and deterioration bursting out from under its pretty skin was so similar to what Esperanza had felt for so long, it would be easy to give in to the feelings within her head, heart, and soul.

Or she could fight.

She had the choice; there were two options, and the answer she decided to give wasn't the easy one.

She called to those who'd been trailing a couple of blocks behind her. The few had grown into a small mob.

"Come to me," she said in a raised voice, "we will free Durgan's Keep and destroy these foul monsters!"

She then focused inward, gripping her knife.

*I found her.* Esperanza's voice whispered on the wind. *Follow my words, and come to me. Let us end this.*

# Chapter 28

The three gathered outside of the warped sanctuary. The townspeople they'd gathered surrounded the park, attacking and bringing down any of the undead, human gangs, or anything else that came close.

"Torr, grant me the skill and patience in this battle, guide my blade, and bring the fire and passion to my soul to overcome this challenge," Torrents's hands rested on the pommel on his downward facing sword, his eyes raised towards the sky.

"You're a religious man?" the Kid asked as the barbarian wrapped up his prayer.

"Not really," Torrents shook his head, "but this guy apparently followed a handful of gods. Jonath, Senaria, Chanian, and Torr. Torr's the god of combat, but not battle. It seems there's a very definitive line between the two subjects."

"You know," the Kid tilted his head, "it's really weird watching such a sloped forehead Neanderthal speaking so intelligently. Do you think you could grunt, pick your nose, or scratch yourself once in a while to balance it out?"

"Bite me," Torrents turned away to survey the situation.

"See?" the Kid laughed. "That's more barbarian-like. Now just hunch your shoulders and burp after saying it."

"Are you even paying attention?" Esperanza shot a sour look over her shoulder at the Kid. "Did you hear anything I said?"

"Yeah," the Kid moved up next to the priestess, "this bitch, Aku'ji the Necromancer who is infamously 'Dead and Awake', has taken control, even broken a beautiful park with her evil and her icky minions. The whole place is rigged, and it'll really mess up anyone going in."

"It gets in your head, too," Esperanza said forcefully. "Did you hear that part?"

The Kid nodded, looking across what was now a wasteland, his eyes scanning for anything that might help them or give them a clue what they were facing.

"Gets in your head?" The Kid cocked his head at the priestess. "The place, or Aku'ji gets in your head?"

"I'm not sure," Esperanza looked confused, "I just felt, something, when I went near it."

"Well," the Kid strode towards the wrought-iron gate, "my head is pretty crowded right now, and if she's getting into all three of our heads, she's going to be spread pretty damned thin, and better look out because this is my city, and we don't take kindly to this sort of behavior."

With a shrug, Torrents followed the Kid, lifting his sword to his shoulder.

Esperanza sighed, pulled herself up from her knees, looked at her four crackling orbs of lightning, and then trudged after the other two.


Torrents screamed as the vines, holding him by each limb, pulled outward and stretched him to his limits.

"Some damned overgrown broccoli will NOT draw and quarter me!" the barbarian yelled.

The man tensed his muscles, pulling his hands and feet in closer to him to stop from being ripped apart at the shoulders and hips.

Thin darts shot across the clearing, and thorns dotted the man's neck and chest, the projectiles sinking into his skin. The poison from the plant's spines rushed into the man's veins, and his vision—which was focused on his sword laying below his feet—blurred and swirled.

The barbarian blinked, and the world changed.

He was in a hospital, staring up at the fluorescent lighting above him. Voices spoke to the left of him in hushed tones. They spoke of his accident, and how he wouldn't ever walk again. They were concerned how he'd take it, and how it would change his life now that he couldn't play sports again.

Then a woman's voice asked, too loudly, and it carried clearly to him, if anyone had let him know his father had died in that accident.

The other voices hushed the one who asked, but Torrence's eyes were already blurring as his throat tightened.

The gardens came back into view, a vine now wrapped around the man's thick neck. He'd released his muscles, and was being once more stretched to his limits. The plants pulled, and the world turned into an explosion of color in front of his eyes as the pain burst in his body.

The physical therapist watched his patient as the man held Torrence's knee between both hands.

"You did good," the doctor said, "and from the look on your face, I'd say you felt something there."

The man gently placed Torrence's foot back into the stirrup and stood up.

"Torrence, you've made a lot of progress," the man consulted a tablet on the counter beside him, "and I think you'd be an excellent candidate for that experimental surgery we discussed. With nanotechnology making the advances it is with the help of companies like Jones Industries—and no, they didn't pay me to say that, I just like what they've been doing—you've got a good chance of walking and doing all the things a normal person does."

The doctor looked at Torrence, waiting for a reply.

"You drove here on your own today, right?" The Doctor squatted in front of the wheelchair that Torrence sat in. "First time using the car without someone sitting next to you, right? That's forward movement, Torrence. And you have a girlfriend—okay, you have been talking to a girl, and she knows your situation, and you two even went out, twice—and that could lead to something. You have a lot to live for, a lot to look forward to. You can be the miracle everyone talks about."

Torrence felt the dead weight of his legs, and his arms wouldn't move, and his eyes watered as he struggled for a breath under the pressure of the conversation.

And something else.

"Do you want to go home, Torrence?" the Doctor asked, but it was a woman's voice now; rough, angry, and almost a growl. "Do you want to return to your old life, full of promise and possibility? Or do you want to give up and die?"

Torrence knew this question. He'd asked himself this. The voices in the arena had asked him this same thing. And now, he answered it one last time.

The vines snapped, and the barbarian raised his defiant voice in a battle cry.


The Kid rolled across the ground, small furry creatures clinging to him, biting and gnawing. Any one bite was annoying and a nuisance, but dozens of them at one time caused shooting pain through the Kid's whole body.

It reminded her, *No,* the Kid thought, *I am not her anymore, I am him.*

The sharp pain was everywhere at once as Jen sat up in the wide beige chair; it made that unique sound that only fake leather makes. Her meds sat in a small paper cup on the rolling side tray, beside a Styrofoam cup full of ice chips that were slowly melting.

*Screeck,* Jen thought, *that's the sound that the chair makes.*

"Are you comfortable, Jen?" the nurse asked. "How're your pain levels today?"

"Yes," Jen lied, "I'm fine, they're fine. We're all fine here today."

She didn't feel like having the pity. She didn't want a new nurse asking her if her family was going to visit soon. They weren't; she didn't have any. And that made the new staff members make that face. It was so similar to the face they made when she said her pain was bad, but it was more honest and disapproving. Not of her, but of people abandoning their own family. But her family was dead, or just gone.

The staff were good people, but they were just…young. Even the Doctor, who was over fifty, was still naïve in many ways.

"You sure you're okay?" a hand touched Jen's shoulder, and she winced.

Looking up into the woman's concerned face, which was ringed by flowing red hair, Jen smiled and reached up to pat the woman's hand.

The nurse's hand was icy, dead cold.

Jen's attention was drawn to outside her door as a resident shuffled past, leaning on a walker. The man turned his head, and his rotting flesh waggled when his sightless eyes met hers.

The two nurses behind the nursing station across from her room, giggled. Jen looked at them and saw their faces were the same.

"We all die, you know," the red-haired nurse standing over her said, the hand on Jen's shoulder gripping tighter, "it's the only way to truly end the pain, Jen. Don't you want the pain to go away, Jen?"

Jen tore her eyes from the dead things doing the mundane tasks at the desk across the hall and looked at Nurse Aku'ji.

The short woman smiled, her eyes intense and wide, her hair writhing like a gentle breeze was passing through it.

"You're allowed to give up, Jen," the necromancer said, her voice almost compassionate. "It's okay for you to let go. It's okay for you to move on now. No one will be upset. And you won't have the pain anymore."

*Oh, she's good,* Edsumar said in Jen's head, breaking her out of the dream-like hypnotic state she hadn't realized she was in. *I wish I could eat popcorn, this is an impressive performance. So lifelike, so believable. She even had a little bit of spinach in her teeth from her heart-healthy lunch.*

"How are you here?" Jen asked, her mind fighting with two realities, both of which were causing her a lot of pain, and probably would lead to her death very soon.

"I'm here to help you," Aku'ji smiled, and Jen couldn't help but stare at that little piece of spinach in the woman's teeth.

*I'm always with you now,* Edsumar silently said, *we're connected, usually at the hip when you sheath me. You know, you might want to roll towards that fountain to your left. It might help get rid of these critters all over you.*

Jen leaned left, her ribs catching on the arm of the chair. She tipped over the side, fell to the floor, and began coughing wet coughs, her lungs having that thick feel of mornings and pneumonia.

Nurse Necromancer—that wasn't her name, Jen knew, but the Kid thought it was funny—rushed to her side, trying to pull her upright to clear her lungs.

The Kid looked around, water lilies swirling past his vision. He pushed further down and hit the bottom of the fountain he'd rolled into. The animals were letting go, swimming frantically to the surface. Something shook him. His attention wavered, and the world dimmed.

*I've been down here too long,* Jen thought from her prone position on the floor, *and if I don't get up soon, I'll die.*

The nurse cradled her, try to move her upright, shouting for help at the same time.

But Jen had gone boneless. Between that and the fleshy softness that came after seventy-seven years of life, the lone nurse couldn't bring the woman upright.

"I think I'll go," Jen was hard to understand for the woman, "but not like you offered. I think I'll just change my life to something more like what I always wanted."

Jen's body went limp, her head slowly lolling to the side, and her eyes staring into an infinite distance.

The Kid burst into the air, breaking the water's surface, gasping and crying.

*Welcome back. Kinda like being born again.* Edsumar's voice was teasing, but had a tone of ironic wisdom as well. *Isn't it?*

Esperanza had been fighting for her life since before she'd called to the others. The dark feelings of loneliness, tiredness, and the sense that she just didn't have the energy to even move were seeping into her.

She took one step forward.

The orbs around her dimmed, their movements slowing.

This necromancer controlled much more than just the dead. This woman had discovered more than just rituals of reanimation in those lost catacombs once occupied by Rondarius the Foul. This felt like the black magic that broke the will of those who'd become the living dead, and Esperanza had to believe that she could overcome it.

She moved slowly towards the center of the sanctuary. Two of her orbs fizzled and went out.

She'd stood at the gate as her two friends strode boldly past her.

They hadn't understood what they were walking into.

She saw the Kid go down under dozens of rats, raccoons, squirrels, and other animals driven mad by these magics.

She saw the barbarian entangled by the plants, vines and leaves wrapping and covering every centimeter of the man. She saw his form struggle when the vegetation released toxins and barbs into his flesh.

Esperanza picked up one foot, set it down in front of her, then did the same with the other. Another of the protective orbs winked out of existence.

She knew she had to go on.

She knew she had to go on, but not for her friends. She didn't need to continue to help them, though that was something she wanted to do. She didn't fight for the next step, so she could save the city and help countless lives, though that would certainly be one of the results if she did. She didn't press on, even though she just wanted to lie down and quit, because it would end with the necromancer being stopped, punished, and perhaps removed from the world, though that would be an inevitable result if she continued.

Esperanza moved forward, pushed for one more step, fought for every centimeter, struggled to make the next thing happen, because to not do it was to die.

Aku'ji stood on top of a raised stone gazebo, her dark blue robes draped across her form, her scythe in her hand. An ornate wooden throne, writhing with termites and woodworms, was behind her as the necromancer surveyed her conquests.

Dozens of people of all races, dead and alive, prostrated themselves in front of the red-haired woman, though Esperanza wasn't sure if they did it out of reverence, or because their will to stand had been sucked from them.

Aku'ji the Necromancer turned to watch Esperanza walk towards her. The priestess's shoulders slumped and her eyes lidded, each step ending in a stumble.

"Did you come to finish what you started back in your own world, you pathetic thing?" The necromancer sneered at the holy woman. "Did you come to die, giving up against the struggle of life?"

Esperanza's foot hit the first step, and she fell painfully to her knees, the stone edges of the stairs biting into her shins. Her eyes cleared for a moment.

The final protective orb faded.

"I…can't," Esperanza whispered.

"I know, child," Aku'ji crooned, her smile sadistic, "and it's ok to give up, go home, and let it all be over."

"I can't." Esperanza crawled up two steps.

"Then let go," Aku'ji's voice was rising, anger bubbling up, "like your friends, just stop trying and let it happen."

"I just can't do…" Esperanza reached the top step, falling back onto her feet into a kneeling position in front of the necromancer.

The woman smiled down at her; her lips drawn back in a cruel grin. She reached down to grab the priestess's hair in her fist.

Yanking the daughter of another world's head up, the necromancer brandished her magical scythe in her other hand.

"It will be a pleasure to slit your throat," Aku'ji said, "the moment you give up, give in, and beg for the end to come."

"I just can't do," the priestess repeated, her tired voice gaining an edge of steel with each word, "that!"

Esperanza's hand flashed upward, a small blade barely longer than a finger held in her grip, plunging it into Aku'ji's exposed mid-section.

The necromancer's face contorted with pain and confusion. Her hands loosened, and the scythe fell to the ground with a clatter, while her other hand released the priestess's dark hair.

The barbarian's battle cry rose from behind Esperanza, and the gasping sobbing of the Kid came from one side.

Pulling upward with the knife, Esperanza rose to her feet and stepped forward. She grabbed the necromancer's shoulder, stopping the woman from stepping back, and slid the knife left, then right.

Blood gurgled from the red-haired woman's mouth, and Esperanza moved her own hand from the woman's shoulder to the woman's chest, and gave a small shove.

The necromancer stumbled backwards, her knees hitting the rotting throne, and she dropped into the seat.

The vermin that carpeted the massive chair swarmed over Aku'ji, skittering and crawling into the cross shaped cut in the woman's abdomen and into her open mouth. Within seconds, the necromancer was completely engulfed with insects.

Esperanza turned away.

The kneeling things in front of the gazebo were in motion. The dead that once walked collapsed sideways in motionless heaps. The living that had been sapped of their will and energy slowly stood, and dazedly looked around.

Torrents limped towards her, using his sword as support, leaves and vines dragging from his welted limbs. His whole body was red and swollen from his encounter with the plants.

The Kid sloshed towards them, soaked to the bone. Blood seeped from the hundreds of small bite marks all over his body.

"I hope none of those had rabies," the Kid said, reaching the foot of the steps.

"I'm sure you'll be fine," Esperanza smiled, "though we have to use some vile mixture from PepperGarten…that might help."

"Even if it doesn't," Torrents added as he joined them, "it'll be great to see the look on the Kid's face when he drinks it. Always good for a laugh!"

The big man leaned around Esperanza and looked behind her.

"What happened here?" the barbarian asked.

"I killed her with kindness." Esperanza's smile was proud.

"Kindness did that?" the Kid asked, craning his neck to see.

"I named my knife 'Kindness'," Esperanza held up the small bloody blade, "just in case I ever needed it."

## Chapter 29

The sun rose on Durgan's Keep. The city didn't wake like it normally did. The sounds and smells were familiar, but only to those that had lived through war and tragedy.

The marketplace didn't have vendors hawking their wares, instead; it had armed patrols hunting the remaining undead. They built huge pyres at the base of the exterior walls, and wagons full of corpses made trips to throw bodies over the side to be burned. This was the way things were done, because you didn't want to risk grandma rising from the dead and eating you while you slept.

The aroma of baking bread and roasting meat intermingled with the smell of rotting flesh. Those not included in a patrol brought whatever food they could to those rebuilding businesses or removing the remaining invaders.

No one traveled alone through the stone streets of Durgan's Keep that day, or for the following months.

Except the Kid.

The Kid threw himself off the rooftop, grabbing the flagpole above the cartographer's shop with his mind, and pulled himself to it. He crouched atop the thin metal rod, looking over his city.

The thieves' guild had invited him to a lieutenant's position within it, as did the assassins' guild, and the city council. The Kid had laughed at each of them, probably not the smartest response, but he made it clear that he had things to do. He had no idea what those things were, but he was going to do them all.

The Kid checked on Jewlnee and her house, making sure that she and her girls had everything they needed. The madam assured him that Captain Jaimin was taking care of all the things that were required; and right now, the Raptor Rex was on its way to Red Wind for much needed supplies.

The Open Door had become more literal in use, as its name implied, and had been set up as a command center.

Esperanza coordinated medical teams, sending them throughout the city to help people. The Kid brought the members of the Grey Ash guild to help the priestess, convincing them that the blessing of the goddess of wisdom and weather would benefit them.

Torrents spent his days leading patrols. They hunted down the creatures that hadn't been destroyed when the necromancer died. Many things more dangerous than shambling husks still roamed the dark alleys and byways of the city, and they'd continue to do so for a while to come.

Mezk the Damned showed up, just long enough to claim credit and reward from the city council, before disappearing again. The Kid guessed the demon pact had called the man to other tasks, but couldn't be sure. He'd have to keep an eye out for that one.

The Kid launched himself off the flagpole and into the air. Bouncing off the awning below him and across the road, the Kid landed in an alley. Walking into the street, he changed his appearance using his mind magics. He appeared as a young girl, a street waif, who gives flowers to people hoping to get a few brass sharps to buy a warm meal with.

*What're you doing?* Edsumar asked.

*We're done with what needed to be done,* the Kid silently answered, *so now it's time for me to have a little fun, and also build my brand.*

*We have more things that need to be done,* the dragon spirit said in the Kid's head.

*It'll wait until after winter,* the Kid replied offhandedly. *We also need to help out here, and maybe have some fun, before we worry about the rest of the world. After all, this is my city.*

But today, the Kid wouldn't be accepting coins. Today, he'd give flowers to those that needed them. And maybe pick up a few tidbits of gossip and secrets while he did. And if someone insisted he take coins for a flower, well, then the Kid would have extra drinking money tonight.

## Epilogue

Spring on the hilltop was great for business at the Traveller's Inn, and Jack Tucker whistled as he cleaned a mug with a cloth.

He looked up as the door opened and three people entered, blinking in the shady interior of the common room.

"Hey guys, I'm Jack," Jack waved, "have a seat anywhere, and I'll be right over to help you."

The first of the trio was a huge man in white furs with a giant sword hung diagonally across his back, tan skin and shoulder length black hair showing his native roots. His broad sloping forehead and flat nose told Jack what northern tribe he was likely from.

A woman who didn't stand out at all followed the barbarian. She was of average height, black hair pulled away from tan skin, but that was where the resemblance to the barbarian ended. She was not of his people. And her bland grey traveling clothes didn't stand out either. But the rounded cloud and stars metal placard that represented the goddess Latress peeking from under that cloak, did.

Jack laughed when he saw through the illusion of the third person. The young man—probably not even all the way through puberty yet—smiled quirkily as he looked around the room, taking it all in with a glance. Jack saw a cunning and calculating look as the guest checked out every exit, corner, and customer in the place.

There were five other patrons in residence at that moment.

Nomed hunched over the draughts board at a table in the center of the room, his trademark leather cloak hung over the back of the chair next to him, and his hand-and-a-half sword leaned against the table beside him. Wanderly stood on his knees in the chair across from the handsome man, studying a handful of playing cards in his small hands that had nothing to do with the game between the two.

Hue Blueaxe, towering over the man beside him, leaned back in a booth. The large man held the handle of his legendary double-bladed axe and its head rested on the floor. The gladiator spun it with one hand, like a top, then stopped it, only to do it again and again.

Grenedal Dragonblood leaned in close to Hue, speaking softly and pointing at the sheaf of papers on the table in front of them. The big guy nodded and smiled, agreeing with whatever his secretive friend said.

The only other person in the place was an older man who was badly in need of a shave. Croaker Norge leaned over his tankard of beer, staring at the wall in front of him. But Jack knew that the man had taken in every detail of the newcomers in the mirror above the bar. Jack also knew that the man had swiped more peanuts and filled his mug while Jack was paying attention to the new arrivals, greeting them when they entered.

"Going home?" Jack asked, walking up to the table the three had chosen.

"What?" Esperanza looked up at their host, surprised at his appearance.

The trio had chosen a table under a window near the front door. They'd dropped their satchels and backpacks on the floor at their boots, boots covered with the evidence of many days of travel.

"I asked," Jack smiled and tossed the white cloth across his shoulder, "if you were traveling home today? You are the three from Durgan's Keep, the ones who came from Earth originally, right?"

The three froze. Then Torrents pushed out from the table, his hand on the pommel of his sword over his shoulder. Esperanza gripped her holy symbol, lips pursed as she inspected their host. The Kid leaned back in his chair and smiled at the man.

Chairs behind Jack scraped along the floor as his regulars half rose and reached for weapons. Jack waved a hand behind him—not even turning—to let them know it was okay.

"How do you know about Earth?" Esperanza asked quietly, twisting her holy focus in her hands.

"I'm from there, too," Jack said, "and you don't have to whisper. The rest of these guys have passing knowledge of it also, to say the least."

"Do you know how we got here?" Torrents settled back into his chair, drawing his hand away from his weapon. "I mean, not us in particular, just any of us? How'd we get from there to here?"

"Yeah," Jack said, "but I want you to remain calm. This next part can be hard to hear, okay?"

The three nodded reluctantly.

"I brought you here." Jack said without a flourish.

"What?" Esperanza leaned forward, squinting at the man.

"Why?" Torrents's head tilted, and his face scrunched in confusion.

"Because" Jack pulled out the fourth chair, flipped it around, and sat in it backwards, his arms crossed on the top rung of the ladder-back, "we need heroes, and you three needed something, too. Isn't that right?"

The man looked back and forth between the three, a gentle and patient smile on his face.

"Yeah," the Kid said, a shit-eating grin on his face, "we sure the hell did, and I think we got more than we bargained for. Not that we were ever offered a bargain. What gave you the right to do that to us?"

"Really?" Jack quirked his head to one side. "You're getting self-righteous and upset about this? After what each of you were about to do and go through? I mean, you all remember where you were when you left, right?"

They fell quiet again.

"Okay," the Kid sighed, "fair point. But how d'you do it?"

"That's a story for another day," Jack smiled, tapping the side of his nose and winking at the Kid, "perhaps we should look to the future, rather than the past, eh?"

"What do you mean?" Torrents asked.

"You have a choice," Jack said.

"Yeah," Torrents grunted, "I've heard that before."

"Do you want to stay," Jack ignored the interruption, "or do you want to go back?"

"Back?" the Kid said.

"We can do that?" Torrents asked.

"Yes," Esperanza said, "I want to go back."

Her companions turned and looked at her in surprise.

She held up a hand to stop questions.

"Look, guys," Esperanza said, "we've seen a lot of things in the past six months since we got here. Lots of things that should be impossible, and we can't explain, but we now accept them.

"Here," she continued, "we found an inn on a hilltop, with no towns around it, and no roads or paths anywhere near it."

"Yeah," Wanderly spoke from over his playing cards, "definitely not a trap, right?"

"Shush, Wanderly," Jack said over his shoulder, "go on, Esperanza."

"See guys," the priestess said, motioning from her friends to Jack, "he knows our names, he knows where we're from, and who knows what else this guy knows. If I accepted all the other things we've seen, then I'll accept this, too.

"And I *do* want to go home," Esperanza sighed, a sound that was a mix of wistfulness and frustration, "let me see if I can put this into words, hold on.

"Even though life's complete crap, people are just shit, and it never gets better, just harder," Esperanza said, waving her hands in front of her, "and it seems life doesn't want you to be happy, it wants you to struggle and fight, to become stronger, to face the next thing that shits on you."

Croaker was nodding along with her words and raised his mug to toast that last part.

"It's our job to spit in life's eye," Esperanza continued, "and say, 'Chuz you, I'll be happy if I want to be, and there's nothing you can throw at me that'll change that. There's nothing I can't beat.'

"And that's why I want to," Esperanza hesitated, "I *need* to go back, to go home. I want to bring that back with me, and I want to spit in life's eye. I can't let it win."

The room was quiet again, except for Wanderly's exaggerated slurping from his mug.

Jack turned and shot him a glare.

"What?" Wanderly whispered too loudly, shrugging his shoulders.

"I get it," the Kid said, "I understand why you need to do this. But it doesn't mean I won't miss you. Can you stay for dinner before you go, and is Jack buying?"


The three friends sat around that table for hours, well into the night. They talked, laughed, and cried, exchanging information they had never thought to trade until that night. Places they lived, currently live, and who they knew were among some of the topics.

Jack served them his regular fare, which was more than passable. The regulars came and went, leaving through one door, and returning later, sometimes through the same door, sometimes through a different one.

When the time came, the three hugged and said kind words, and made promises to one another. Then Jack went to a door on the far wall, opened it, and waved Esperanza through it.

She stepped through.

Turning back to the common room, she looked at her friends and waved one last time.

"Pretty cliché, isn't it?" Esperanza said with a smile, "One last look, and then I'm gone."

Jack followed the woman through the doorway and closed it behind them.

Then she was really gone.

Torrents and the Kid stayed up the whole night, Croaker happily sharing bartender duties with Wanderly, as both knew it meant free drinks for them.

When Jack returned, about two hours later, just as the sun crested the eastern horizon, he had a short beard that wasn't there before, and wore different clothing.

"Sorry," Jack said, kicking the dirt from his boots, "got sidetracked. You guys need a room before going? Get some shuteye?"

"Yeah," Torrents said, bleary-eyed, "sure, thanks."

"I have a question first," the Kid said, watching Jack's reaction carefully.

The host nodded and hung his cloak on a peg next to the door.

"Are there more?" the Kid asked. "Are there more like us? People coming here, and doing what we do?"

"Kid," Jack tapped a finger to the side of his nose, and winked, "there's always more."

End of Portals, Book 1

# Book Two: Demons & Daggers

## Dedication

I dedicate this adventure to the minds that explore worlds beyond their own. Minds like yours, my dear reader.

# Prologue

The Traveller's Inn buzzed with the activity of patrons, servers, and a gentle whoosh. *The changing of dimensional pathways,* thought Jack, *like rearranging the furniture of the multiverse.* Lights flashed past windows, odd combinations of colors spinning outside unnoticed by the people within who sat drinking, eating, and chatting at tables.

Jack held up a finger, counting the cycles flashing past that no one else appeared to see. His brow creased in worry, and an old man beside him grinned.

"PepperGarten thinks you are up to your old tricks again," the withered man said. "Are you triggering someone to be shuffled off the old mortal coil, and back on at a different point?"

"Oh," Darome the gnome gasped, "is he bringing a new piece to the game board?"

"Shush," Jack breathed, "both of you. It's not a game. These people are not toys. They're heroes who never knew what they're capable of."

"Why don't they know?" asked Darome.

"PepperGarten knows a bit about that," the old man said, referring to himself in the third person again, "and it's usually because the world beats you down and you're so tied down by your daily responsibilities that you never know how much you change the world around you."

"Yeah," Jack nodded, still counting cycles, "you're very smart, PepperGarten, now shut up."

"Don't shut up, PepperGarten, tell us more!" Darome grinned and jumped from his barstool to the bar, raising his hands to get the attention of the other patrons. "Good people, notice how you cannot notice the changes within and without, for all life is an illusion, something of which I know no small amount about."

The people in the Traveller's Inn quieted, turning to look at the grandstanding gnome atop the bar. Behind him, Cogsley—the bartender—turned to face the little man with no expression, because his head was a transparent bulb with a curlicue wire inside.

"Darome," Cogsley said, drawing out the words with the accent of the affluent, "if you leave muddy tracks upon the buffed and polished surface of my bar again, I shall have you dragged from the premises and beaten with dust mops until you are no longer inclined to leave scuffs and marks where they are not meant to be."

"Durg may have something to say about that," Darome proclaimed, hands on his hips and bottom lip jutting out.

The half-ogre companion of the gnome grunted acquiescence.

"Then, I shall give him a dust mop also, so he does not feel left out, and shall offer a free drink for every wallop he bestows upon your personage." Cogsley's dome flickered with light.

Durg—an immense beast of a man—grunted and smiled, looking between Darome and Cogsley.

"Um, PepperGarten? Care to go on?" Darome asked, gulping and drawing a handkerchief from the pocket of his robe to buff the bar.

"PepperGarten wants to help!" the old man exclaimed, leaping to his feet and dancing in a tight circle. "Can PepperGarten do that thing again? It never sticks, for PepperGarten is eternal as the verdant growth of the Earth! Just ask Kajuun, she saw it more than once."

"Okay, stop," Jack said. It was a quiet statement, but everyone heard his words. "I'm bringing someone new here. He's a good man, but never thought of himself as one. He hides from any confrontation, but I think he has something inside of him—"

"Another zombie, eh?" PepperGarten interrupted. "Bringing another dead person to inhabit the body of someone who died here? You didn't do that with PepperGarten. But you didn't answer PepperGarten, can I do the thing again? PepperGarten just loves the look on the face of people when PepperGarten does that thing!"

"Sure, PepperGarten," Jack said, looking around, distracted.

"Will you match them up with the other two? The Kid and Torrents?" Darome asked.

"Yeah," Jack waved his hand dismissively, "but I'll need to bring them back together. They've…drifted apart. I think those two will do great things together, if they allow it to happen."

"How will you bring them back together?" asked Elementius, an elderly scholar at a table, his younger assistant scribbling notes on parchment.

"I think circumstances will offer an opportunity, and they will do the rest themselves." Jack said.

"And the new guy?" Darome inquired. "How can you bring him into the group if no one trusts one another?"

"Well," Jack looked into the distance, "I guess I'll need to show all three of them that the new guy is a natural hero."

"What if he doesn't want to be a hero?" inquired Elementius, his assistant nodding sagely in agreement.

"Then I'll do what I need to do to make him want to be one," Jack sighed.

"Even if it kills him?" PepperGarten cackled. "PepperGarten knows about that sort of thing!"

# Chapter 1

Nathan tumbled heels over head, falling down the rocky slope, his backpack clanging and clattering, feet going out from underneath him again and again. His double-headed battle axe, torn from his grip, flew to one side as cooking pots scattered to the other. His face hit a rock, his nose popping with the impact. It sent him sideways in a tangle of limbs and straps as the world spun around him, like he was inside the world's largest coin-operated washing machine.

A moment before, he'd been staring down the muzzle of a double-barrel shotgun. Nathan's ears still rung with the echoed retort as the man holding the weapon pulled the trigger and emptied two rounds into his midsection.

It'd been a rough day so far.

Less than three hours ago, Nathan had woken up and got out of bed to the blaring digital scream of his outdated alarm clock. His coffee maker had stopped working after brewing a tepid half cup of Joe. But that was okay, since he could stop at the local Starbucks. Nathan got dressed in his white shirt, striped tie, grey suit jacket, and headed out the door.

Once he'd arrived, he had to work his way through picketers demonstrating for non-dairy milk to be offered. The protestors wouldn't let him into the building, though others pushed their way through. Nathan smiled and told them he understood, and he admired them for standing up for what they believed in.

He made a side trip to a 7-11 to get his coffee instead. The heavy woman behind the counter glared at him when the machine didn't read the swipe strip on his debit card, and sourly informed him she couldn't manually type in a card anymore. It was the slide or nothing.

Nathan offered to pay cash, but only had loose change on him, and had to get a smaller coffee so he could afford it. He apologized and thanked the scowling woman, wishing her a nice day, before heading to the door.

A mother and her three kids were coming in as Nathan left, and he held the door for them automatically. The mother marched by, her nose in her phone, ignoring his jovial good morning. The kids were jumping and screaming, and the middle one hit Nathan's arm, causing his coffee to slam against his chest. The lid popped off, and the coffee scalded his stomach and soaked into his suit jacket.

As the pain subsided, Nathan realized the woman was now screaming at him about touching her child, and how he could've given her poor baby third-degree burns with the coffee. She was threatening to sue him and ignoring his apologies. The sour woman behind the counter was yelling at him to shut the damn door.

He left, still holding his crushed coffee cup.

That was the first hour of his day.

The second hour wasn't much different.

Nathan arrived at a little neighborhood jewelry store—which he owned and had opened thirteen years ago—let in his one employee, Austin, greeting the twenty-something-year-old with a smile. The younger man shuffled sullenly behind the counter and checked his phone while Nathan went to the back to get ready to open. He set up the coffeepot to brew and opened the safe while waiting. Counting down the till, he found the drawer was $17.38 short from the night before.

When Austin came back to fill his coffee cup, Nathan asked him about the shortage. The younger man held the now full mug in one hand and the glass coffeepot in the other.

The twenty-something swung his greasy bangs out of his eyes with a jerk of his head and glared at his boss, looking the older man up and down through slitted eyes.

Austin took three steps forward, raised the coffeepot up to eye-level, and threw it onto the floor. The pot shattered and Austin began yelling at Nathan about accusing him of stealing, and how that shit wasn't cool.

Nathan tried calming the younger man, apologizing and trying to explain he was just asking what happened, but never got to finish as Austin yanked off his clip-on tie, screamed he was quitting, and stormed out of the back room with his still full coffee cup.

The bell out front jingled, and the door slammed shut. It was at that moment Nathan realized the coffee cup in Austin's hand was his, and not the employee's. Now he had no mug, and the coffee pot lay in broken shards in a puddle of coffee. When Austin had thrown it down, it had splashed across Nathan's slacks, staining them to match his shirt and jacket.

Nathan finished opening the shop, cleaned the mess in the back room, changed out of his ruined jacket and shirt, and put on the only other thing he had around; the ugly holiday sweater he'd bought to wear to a friend's party three months ago. He'd won an honorable mention with the sweater, just like everyone else. His friend didn't want to hurt anyone's feelings, so, at Nathan's suggestion, agreed that a participation prize was a good idea.

But the third hour of Nathan's day was, by far, the worst.

Nathan had been open forty-five minutes when three men burst in. Two wore pantyhose over their heads and faces, and both had a handgun in one hand, and a pillowcase in the other. The third man had a ski mask and a double-barreled shotgun. He seemed to be the leader and shouted at Nathan to give them all the money in the register and safe.

Nathan apologized and explained that he'd deposited the money the night before, and only had the hundred dollars in the register, minus the $17.38 it was short.

The man in the ski mask shouted that he hadn't stolen the damned money. That made Nathan pause, look at the robber, then ask, 'Austin?', before turning away at the sound of shattering glass.

The pantyhose guys were breaking glass cases with their guns and snatching rings, watches, necklaces, and other jewelry from the broken displays. The back of the cases was open, but the men still broke the glass instead of just reaching around the case.

Nathan tried to tell them they could just reach in the open door behind the counter, but ski mask jabbed the gun into Nathan's gut to get his attention. That's when both barrels went off.

Nathan had looked down and seen the gaping hole in his sweater—wondering what else he could change into—as the world spun and went dark.

In the blink of an eye, he was outside in the sun, and falling down a rocky slope.

He slid to a stop, laying on his back and staring up into a crisp, clear sky tinged with green. Blinking, Nathan thought his eyes were playing tricks on him. It was like his vision was blurry, but it made the color weird instead of the picture fuzzy. It reminded him of his grandparent's TV when he was a kid, with the corners of the screen losing their color tint and turning a bleary grey.

He worked his jaw, sand grinding between his teeth, and slowly moved each limb to see what condition it was in. To top it all off, he'd caught his beard in his chain mail shirt, forcing his chin to his chest.

That was when Nathan realized he didn't have a beard, or chain mail, or a battle axe a couple of minutes ago. But he had all those things now.

He jerked his hands in front of his face, his shoulders locking in complaint and tangling on the straps of his backpack. The orange dirt of this region of the Crescent Desert coated his thick, callused fingers, and hairy knuckles.

His mind grabbed at the name of the surrounding area, wondering how he could know that, and discarding the fact these weren't the same hands he had a few minutes ago.

A roaring noise blended with a dozen screeches, the former coming from up the hill, and the latter from all around him.

Sitting up, Nathan looked towards the roar.

A creature—a thing was a better way to describe it—stood nearly three-meters tall and lurched towards him. It had the head of a vulture, but jointed and segmented legs like an insect. The monstrosity's chest was a thick leathery barrel, creased with chitinous, overlapping scales, each the size of a dinner plate.

The screeching came from smaller creatures, something that looked like petite lap giraffes—from Sokoblovsky Farms in the Direct TV commercials—blended with the undead cat from Stephen King's Pet Sematary.

These things swarmed towards Nathan. He'd never seen them before, but he knew what they were. The big one was a crigth, and the small ones were jedth, and they were all bullies. Nathan didn't like bullies.

Nathan rolled to his feet and stood his full meter-and-a-half height. Something in his head niggled that this was wrong as well. He should be another half meter taller, and why was he thinking in metric instead of feet and inches?

His new body was already moving as his mind freaked out and questioned everything going on. He had pulled out two hand-axes—these also had double-heads, like his battle-axe—wading into the cat-giraffe things and laying about himself with the weapons.

Each time a swing connected, he kicked the creature away with a thick-booted foot, avoiding the acidic splash of blood that followed.

The enormous monster lumbered down the hill, coming closer.

Nathan looked around for his battle-axe. The weapon, lost in the fall, was far out of reach. The creature was between Nathan and his favorite axe, which he had named Marcid, which in Rokairn meant a female blacksmith.

He wondered, on top of all the other swirls of thought, what's a rokairn?

The knowledge was instantly there, and he knew what it was. It was him, a species of highly organized, skilled, and talented people who favored mountain and cave dwellings, as well as metal and jewel crafting. And they almost always had exceptional beards, even the women.

Nathan tucked his shoulders in and his head down, running towards where Marcid lay without thinking about what he was doing. The monster came towards him on long, lanky legs, listing far to one side and then the other with each step.

Nathan ran between its legs, and stood up when under the beast, throwing his shoulders back and his arms wide, causing the segmented limbs to fly akimbo and the thing lost its footing.

By the time the demon spawn had risen to its feet again, Nathan had Marcid in both hands and was chopping into it.

The creature fell under the attack, Nathan's steel nerves and stone-like muscles making quick work of it.

This monster didn't have the acid-blood thing, but Nathan still avoided the visceral spray, because it smelled really, really terrible, and reminded him of crushed stink bugs.

Some of it got on him anyway, reminding him of the coffee that stained his shirt a couple hours ago, or the spray of blood when the shotgun went off against his belly.

As his body slowed, the deed done, Nathan came back to his mind. He looked across the sandy field of carnage with a double handful of dead demonic things scattered about.

Movement in the east caught his attention, and distant howls reached his ears. The pack was on the move, and the hyena-headed man-beasts that worked with the demonic invaders would be upon him soon, along with the giant hyenas that always followed.

Nathan's stomach lurched, making him bend over and vomit.

## Chapter 2

The Kid threw himself off the building and plummeted towards the cobblestone street below. He released a metal grapple attached to a wire and flung it towards the rooftop he'd just left.

Reaching out with his mind-magics, he grabbed the metal hook and thrust it towards a chimney pipe. It wrapped around the protrusion just in time to catch his falling body, reversing his headlong plunge into a graceful upward arc. He landed on the rooftop across the road.

Crossbow bolts peppered the wood and stucco wall below his feet, missing him by a hair. The Metal Hand Assassin Clan was hot on his trail.

The Kid laughed.

His pursuers took exception to him foiling their job earlier this afternoon. They'd set up the double execution of the new mayor of Durgan's Keep and the high priestess of Promethene, goddess of sound and light. The two public figures had sat lunching together; discussing how to create a new economy by making apprenticeships available to those leaving the religious order's orphanages.

What should've been an easy in-and-out job turned into five assassins dying by their own poisoned darts turned back on them, and the city watch taking four lookouts into custody.

The Kid made it public knowledge he caused the failed missions, exposing and embarrassing the clan at the same time.

The street thief, turned hero of the people, mentally tugged on his grapple and reeled it in, catching the self-coiling metal wire in his hand. His body shimmered and disappeared at a mental command.

The Kid pulled out a dozen newly made throwing stars. They were like shuriken from his world, and it surprised him no one here had made them before. But since no one had, they'd become his calling card.

He dropped them over the side of the building, leaned over the gutter, and took control of their fall with his mind, directing the projectiles towards the people following him and speeding them up as they flew.

The razor-sharp squares sunk into the flesh of throats, chests, and bellies. Men and women from the Metal Hand Assassin Clan fell under the onslaught.

This was what the Kid had been doing since saving the fortified city of Durgan's Keep from an undead invasion last autumn. He'd been harassing and ruining the professional life of the criminal underground—and taking very public credit for it.

Because of his public image, there were multiple contracts out on him, dead or alive. Thankfully, the common people loved him; he was their Robin Hood.

This was such a different life than what the Kid had lived back in his old world—where he was a woman in her late seventies dying of cancer—and he much preferred this new life over the previous one.

The Kid thought back to the people he'd met from his world and who'd helped him save this city. A self-styled time-traveler, Jack Tucker, claimed to have pulled each of them from their dying bodies into bodies in this world, which were also dying at the moment of transfer. From what Jack had said, the energy it took for them to come here also healed whatever body they took possession of. They kept all the skills, memories, and experiences their new bodies had before their arrival. It made for awkward moments in the street when the Kid would meet someone who claimed he owed them money.

Esperanza—priestess of Latress, goddess of weather, wind, and wisdom—had returned to her life in the world they'd come from. She'd been struggling against her faith from Earth, conflicting with her abilities granted by a goddess of this world. After saving the city from undead hordes, they'd escorted Torrents to where he was going, and met Jack Tucker, who opened a portal so Esperanza could return to her original life.

The Kid often wondered what happened to the body the priestess had inhabited here. He also wondered if the transfer back to the other world healed her original body, the way the transfer here had healed their new ones.

Torrents—the barbarian who'd also traveled with them—had gone to Dargaon's Hole, a community of people doing some crazy ass bidj. It was a place in the Wandering Hills where dragons—like real and actual huge reptilian, magic-wielding, intelligent beings—lived and thrived. These powerful creatures once allied with humans who raised livestock to keep them fed in exchange for protection.

Torrents, a massive barbarian, was now playing house with a transposed community of peasants for the past six months, rebuilding an ancient agreement and nurturing a new culture to rise in place of the old.

It was late spring now, and Esperanza had returned to the world that the Kid, Torrents, and the priestess had come from before inhabiting bodies in this world. That was almost six months ago.

*What are you doing now?* Edsumar's voice echoed in the Kid's head.

"I'm playing Batman," the Kid pulled the throwing stars back to his hands, using a secondary thought to wipe the blood from the sharpened blades before they reached him, "and taking out the bad guys so the city will be safe."

*I thought Batman didn't kill people.* The voice questioned. *And it sure looks like you're killing people. So, maybe you're playing Punisher instead?*

The Kid let out a heavy sigh and drew away from the edge of the roof.

"You're harshing my mellow, dude." The Kid rolled his eyes at the magical weapon that couldn't see his face, but knew what he was doing, anyway. "Don't you have some mystical contemplation that involves your thousand-year-old missing belly button, or something else you could be doing besides bothering me?"

*Bothering you is my favorite pastime.* The magical weapon's tone was upbeat. *I don't regret calling to you to recover me from that dank, dark hole I'd been lost in, not for a single moment. You may not have the skills and intelligence I'd hoped for, not to mention the moral compass, but you are by far the most interesting specimen I could've hoped for.*

"You're always so encouraging," the Kid muttered, moving to the other side of the building and crouching to find his egress.

Edsumar was the soul of an ancient dragon, magically imprisoned in a dagger, along with the essences of the five draconian priests who had performed the ritual. When bored, the being offered sage advice and juvenile snark to the Kid.

The weapon had shown some uses beyond stabbing people—allowing the Kid to see in the dark, returning to his hand when thrown, and a couple other things—but mostly exuded attitude at inopportune moments.

The Kid stepped off the rooftop and dropped towards the ground, three-stories below. Without thinking, he threw his cable and grapple over his shoulder and hooked it to the eave above him with his mind-magics.

His mental abilities also tied a loop in the metal cording, and it slithered around his foot. His downward momentum slowed as he touched down on the cobblestone street, the cord winding itself back into a loop with a second thought.

"Can I call you Alfred?" The Kid asked Edsumar out loud, causing people to turn and look, surprised at his sudden appearance.

*Perhaps Microchip would be more appropriate,* Edsumar answered, *as I'm the voice in your ear, not your butler.*

"I don't like the Punisher thing," people drew away at the words as the Kid passed, talking to himself, "I prefer to think I'm making this city safe, instead of just punishing the wicked."

*Isn't it the same thing? By punishing, you make it safe, though you also give back to the community with kindness and coin.* Edsumar's voice wavered. *There is something that requires your immediate attention.*

"What?" He drew the single word out to three syllables contained in a sigh, and the Kid rolled his eyes and turned to look where Edsumar mentally urged.

A stone fist caught the Kid in the midsection, knocking the wind from him, and throwing him backwards into a brick wall.

His vision swam. He pushed to his feet, stumbled to his left, and held up his arms to block any other attacks.

*Drop!* Edsumar said.

The Kid did as the mystical artifact commanded, and debris followed the sound of stone hitting stone, raining down on the prone thief.

"Dafuk!" Anger filled the Kid's shout. "What the hell?"

*Yeah,* Edsumar said, *yelling to attract your foes' attention when you're blinded is always a good idea.*

The Kid pushed to his knees, clenched his fists, and mentally pulled the detritus from around him. Rocks, stones, and pebbles combined into a cluster that, molded by the Kid's mind, took on the forms of weird, mutated crustaceans.

The largest was slightly bigger than a house cat, with eight legs covered in bristling spikes, and a carapace with razor sharp ridges. Two massive claws clacked, the dozens of creatures scuttling forward to defend the blinded rogue. Mirror images of the largest, the smaller ones each acted independently of the others.

The Kid heard screams of terror from around him, as his vision cleared to reveal a golem of stone and stucco standing over him. The illusionary creatures the Kid created swarmed the magical construct. Bricks made up each knuckle of the thing's huge hands, and the Kid followed Edsumar's advice and ducked as the limb swished past his head and shattered the wall behind him.

From his prone position on the ground, the Kid thrust his awareness into the thing in front of him, seeking the kernel of power at its center. The street thief's mind found the tiny pearl of energy at the core of the animated form, and wrapped his power around it, smothering it from the influence of its creator.

The magical energy surged against the Kid's mind-magics, the identity of the being in front of him pushing from the inside, and the control of the person directing it battering at the protective ball from the outside.

The Kid mentally scrambled for a way to win, knowing physical violence wouldn't work. He needed to make the monster stop struggling against him, but stop whatever was commanding this thing from regaining control.

He needed to hide the construct from whatever made it, and at the same time make the golem recognize the Kid as its master.

The illusionary lobster-like things crawling along the golem became starbursts of magical power in the Kid's awareness, which he locked onto. They burrowed into the golem, pushing into its stony hide and underneath the blocks and plaster of the monster's pebbled flesh.

People in the street backed away from the fight, shouting; the towering behemoth growled, a noise like stone grating on rock. The brick-and-mortar monster staggered, tearing at the stony hide covering its wood and iron skeleton, ripping chunks away.

The Kid pushed his magical creatures deeper into the thing attacking him, forcing his pets into the construct's center, seeking the core of power. Once they'd reached it, the Kid didn't have them attack it, instead he had them devour it in reverse, and make themselves become absorbed into the engine that sucked in magic to keep the golem running.

In the Kid's mind's-eye, he saw the ruby-red glow of the pulsing energy take on a blue-ish tint, changing as more of his illusions were sucked into its heart.

The rock monster tore into its chest, grabbing at the wrought iron bars of its rib cage and pulling it open to expose the rune-covered arcane ball at its center. It reached inside and wrapped a massive hand around its heart and squeezed.

The Kid created a shield in front of himself, using his abilities, and covered his face with his arms.

The construct exploded, shards whizzing into the crowd, cutting into flesh with conflicting red and blue pulses.

Stripped of their magic as they passed through his shield, the shards of rock pelted his arms covering his head.

When the dust settled, the Kid rose from his crouch to look around. Covered from head to toe with powder from the explosion, he batted at his hair and shoulders, knocking detritus to the ground and blinking to clear his eyes, trying to see what remained of his attacker.

He focused on the spot where the being had been and stared in disbelief mixed with a growing nervousness.

Where the monster had been was a stony creature, about the height of a medium-sized dog, with a chitinous shell made of layers of shale and brick, eight legs of intricately jointed wrought iron, and two massive stone claws that clicked a complex rhythm that countered the noise of its ticking feet.

*Well, this is something new.* Edsumar's tone dripped sarcasm and amusement. *What the hell did you do?*

"I made a-" the Kid gulped, trying to wet his dust coated throat, then barked out a grating laugh, "I made a rock lobster!"

The creature danced back and forth in front of the Kid like an excited puppy.

## Chapter 3

Torrents growled and swung the huge maul at his target. It missed as the thin, beige, lizard-like creature darted to one side on its two hind feet, its thin forearms flapping at its sides, before falling to all fours and dashing behind the barbarian.

Five more twinglinds—that's what Trinity, the dragon, had called them—moved to flank him, even though he was over three times their size.

Two of the twinglinds darted between Torrents's thick legs, biting at the tender flesh.

The big man yelped and jigged sideways, trying not to crush any of the things under his feet.

The dragons considered the quasi-bipedal creatures good luck, and thus the local human population had adopted the annoying beasts as a sort of mascot for Dargaon's Hole.

If Torrents had his druthers—a word his grandmother had used a lot—he'd crush their little heads and fry them all up in a skillet. The bodies, not the heads. Because the heads would be crushed, and probably wouldn't be good eating, anyway. Not that the barbarian would ever get a chance to test that theory either way, since the creatures were bordering on sacred animals by everyone, and everything, he interacted with.

The barbarian had been here, with the refugees from Hope's Hollow, for months now. He'd had to get away from the Kid, who was just too reckless and carefree for his tastes. He needed to be doing work that meant something, and not harassing local thieves and assassins.

This commune—made up of the humans and the single dragon of Dargaon's Hole—had sounded like a good idea when he'd gotten the letter from the one person who had looked out for him when he had first appeared on this world: Axle.

Axle took the role of patriarch and co-mayor of the small community who had to flee its home after being overrun by undead. He worked closely with the hedge-witch, Rose, the matriarch, and the other half of the mayorship.

The people had survived a tough winter, living off supplies hidden deep in the cavern in the mountains known as the Wandering Hills. There wasn't much, and there was more beer and brandy than beans and rice. Most of the vermin disappeared when the human population was wiped out decades ago, and Trinity had done what she could to keep vermin from the supplies, but a dragon wasn't the best rat hunter.

Trinity also supplemented the community's rations with fresh meat…when she could find it.

Rebuilding had been more difficult than anyone thought it would be. The blend of restoring what was already there—but had fallen into disrepair—versus just building something brand new was always a delicate balance.

Torrents leapt atop a boulder, gaining the advantage of elevation to survey his surroundings, adding to his more than two-meter height. His olive-skin and rippling muscles were covered with a sheen of sweat. He wore a linen tunic, fur boots, and leather pants. His straight shoulder-length hair was plastered to his head in the unseasonably warm spring air.

His body in the other world hadn't been as tall and was much thinner, having lost his high-school jock physique after the accident that had put him in a wheelchair. As a black athlete, he'd dealt with admirers and haters in his sports career, but had a whole new set of problems once his father died in the car accident, changing his life.

Though he had chosen to stay in this world when given the chance to return home, he still questioned that decision.

Esperanza, who he missed, had decided to return. The priestess who traveled with him and the Kid had done what neither he nor the thief could do, returned to face a world and life that had been killing them, but in very different ways.

Torrents still felt lost, but in a way that was unlike what he'd experienced in his previous life. Here, he was needed and was making a difference, but he didn't think he was really living life for himself. Which was the key to life, wasn't it? If you only lived for other people and their purposes, were you even living?

The hiss of a twinglind drew his attention. The creatures scampered away, throwing looks over their shoulders. But they weren't running from him.

Torrents smiled. He'd found what he'd come into the foothills to hunt. Wererats.

They were lycanthropes—from what Rose had told him—similar to werewolves, but with a rat as the root form. The barbarian had laughed at the idea, imagining an angry, humanoid sewer rat that stood about a meter tall, squeaky and shaking a little paw at him. Like Splinter from the Teenage Mutant Ninja Turtles, without the ninjitsu. Axle assured him that wasn't what he should expect.

The wererats had been harassing the settlement, attacking groups of woodsmen during the day, or sneaking in and stealing supplies at night. It was more of a nuisance until they stole a supply of weapons from Dargaon's Hole.

Steel weapons were rare in this day and age, and someone who could craft them was almost impossible to find. The invaders had stolen a dozen short blades, a few swords, and some bows and the arrows to go with them. Without these supplies, Dargaon's Hole couldn't to defend itself, or hunt effectively.

Torrents had volunteered to go find the thieves, recover the items, and convince the wererats to leave the area. They'd either leave on their own, or he and his mallet would convince them.

Turning towards the direction from where that the twinglinds had fled, he saw a grey furry head looking out from behind a rock outcropping. It had matted hair; extended, rounded ears that were laid back against its skull; and a protrusion that was more of a snout than a nose.

The creature's eyes locked onto the barbarian's before it ducked out of sight.

Torrents moved without thinking, his head ringing with the warning of it being a trap, but his body acted on its own. He didn't care if it was a trap. He wanted to feel the burn of his muscles singing as he crushed something that was hurting the people he cared for.

Springing from his perch, the barbarian sprinted towards where the creature had disappeared, his maul held in two hands, his shoulders hunched as he barreled forward.

Reaching the hiding place, Torrents turned, gravel sliding under his feet as they went out from under him.

A woven hemp net dropped over him, and seven small people leapt atop him, jabbing at him with blades. A blow to his head made him stagger and reel.

*Well, this was a bad idea,* Torrents thought, dropping his weapon and covering his head with his meaty arms. Swords and daggers cut into him, but he forced his feet back underneath him and thrust upward.

He launched himself into the air with a roar, grabbing the net in both hands, and pulled it from over him. The wererats piled on top, tangled in the thick weave, and were thrown backwards.

Torrents, net in his fists, turned in a circle, spinning around a handful of times.

One wererat, whose feet tangled in the net, pulled itself free and flew over the side of the hill with a scream. The crunch of bones snapping followed.

Another entangled creature went silent. Its skull crashed against the stone outcropping, crushing its head and scattering flesh, bone, and blood over its companions.

Torrents released the net, and it flew another three paces before falling to the ground.

A blade slid into Torrent's midsection from his left, causing him to double over, grabbing at the weapon.

Three of the beasts leapt on him, stabbing him repeatedly in the back and legs.

Pulling the sword free with his left hand, Torrents reached down and picked up his maul with his right.

The creature holding the sword's handle lost its grip on the weapon as it was yanked off its feet and fell to the ground in front of him.

The barbarian smashed the creature's skull in with the pommel of the sword, still gripping the blade in his bloody hand.

Swinging wildly with the iron and wooden hammer in his right hand, Torrents felt the ribs of a wererat shatter under the blind blow. The creature spun away, flying backwards with the force of the hit, crashing into a second beast. The two crumpled to the ground and lay still.

Torrents swung a few more times, shaking his head to clear it, trying to get his bearings while the three remaining creatures scurried away from him, looking back and forth between one another.

"I'll cripple him," a sharp voice whined. "You two come at him from the side and back."

The barbarian's vision cleared, and he saw the voice had come from a slim ratman, who was drawing the waxed string of a long bow, sighting down the arrow.

The other two wererats moved in opposite directions, circling him, making it impossible for him to keep more than one in sight at a time.

"I'll be damned," Torrents growled, "if I'm going to let my career end because of an arrow to the knee!"

The big man dropped the bloody sword and took the maul in both hands. He crouched to make himself a smaller target and waited.

All four people burst into action when the bowstring twanged.

The barbarian moved the mallet low and leapt into the air towards the ratman, who was dropping the bow and drawing daggers.

The arrow thunked into the handle of the huge wooden weapon, cutting into one of Torrents's fingers, as he crashed into the beast.

Two behind Torrents skidded to a halt—he was no longer where he'd been—and adjusted their courses to attack him.

The ratman in front went down under his bulk, the handle of the hammer thrust sideways into the creature's mouth like a bit for a horse. Its head snapped backwards, its jaws forced open, and cheeks tore where the weapon pushed further in.

Twisting the weapon, Torrents snapped the wererat's mandible, and the fight went out of the creature as it gurgled a scream. The beast writhed under the barbarian, dropping his weapons and clutching at his face.

Pushing down with the handle of the maul, further crushing the leader's jaw, Torrents kicked backwards with a thick leg, and the ribs of the wererat poised to leap upon him collapsed under the big man's booted foot.

The last creature skidded to a halt again, sliding in the gravel and landing on its butt. Scrambling, the wererat backpedaled, turning to flee.

The beast gained its feet, moments before Torrents, and leapt on top of the original outcropping of rock that it had ducked behind to lure the barbarian into the trap.

Rising to one knee, Torrents turned and launched his maul through the air. It spun end over end, the head of the weapon smashing into the back of the ratman, attempting to leap to safety.

Spine and ribs cracked, bone tearing through flesh to glint in the afternoon sunlight. The beast crashed to the ground, twitching.

Panting, Torrents clutched the gaping wound on his side with his bleeding hand.

He smiled.

"Another one bites the dust, mother chuzzers."

Pushing to his feet, he winced as the dozens of minor cuts and wounds made themselves known.

He limped towards his weapon, reluctant to be without it in case any of the creatures survived. He'd have to find their bolt hole; these types always had some hiding place to shelter in.

Bending over to retrieve the maul, the ground shook, making him fall to his knees.

Torrents looked around, confused. He didn't think he was so injured that he should have a problem standing.

Then the ground quaked again.

Looking behind him, to the southeast, a green light expanded across the distant horizon.

"Oh bidj, what happened now?" the barbarian mumbled, turning and falling on his butt. "That's the Demon Front."

## Chapter 4

Nathan was lost. He'd been running west, his short legs covering less ground than a human, but his rokairn stamina and endurance seemed to be endless. Between the two, he may not have moved as fast, but he needed to stop less often than most other people would have. It was the whole tortoise versus the hare thing. And he was traveling alone, which had its benefits.

He ran in something close to a trance, his breath coming in puffs—short, short, long, short, short, long—as he paced himself, letting his mind rest and focusing his awareness to obstacles on the trail in front of him. This must be what people back home called a runner's high.

The body he was in had a mission. It involved something called the Pyridom of Power and blocking the magics that demons used to invade this world.

Thirty years ago, there had been a comet—affectionately known as the Talisman—that had changed the face of the planet with magical radiation, causing summoning and necromantic abilities to increase tenfold. Armies of demons and undead had ravaged the land as a result.

Once the comet had moved on, the creatures and casters that had destroyed society waned and diminished. But three decades later, the world was a different place. That was the world that existed now, the world Nathan appeared in.

Nathan yanked his awareness back, fearing he'd interfered with the workings of the body he now inhabited.

"Sorry about that," the rokairn apologized to himself, "I'll try not to distract you anymore."

His speed slowed, his consciousness taking control instead of his body acting on muscle memory.

Nathan knew whoever he was inside of had just come from Seawall City, a place with a militaristic organization of priests and mages working together in a singular purpose of bringing their goals to fruition.

He was unsure what those goals were, but the body seemed to appreciate the methods employed by the society, similar to a rokairn mindset.

His rokairn brain mulled over the idea of a well-oiled government machine. A magocracy, a theocracy, and a stratocracy, all seamlessly blended to make a balanced council that functions as one.

The enchantments the priests and mages of Seawall City had imbued upon Nathan would only last a week, and his body had intended to go to the Pyridom of Power with these protections and enhancements to shut it down.

Nathan decided running away was a better idea and had been doing just that for the past three days. He'd slept in fits and starts, finding a hiding place—a gap between rocks, a shroud of scrub bushes, or anywhere else he could stop for a few hours—and then moved on.

The Pyridom was to the south, but the road led almost directly west from Seawall City to the city of Red Wind.

When Nathan and this body joined, it had been on the southernmost point of the rocky crags in the center of the Crescent Desert. They'd been heading towards the magical focal point of the cone-like pyramid the demons were swarming over. The creatures were searching for secrets that would allow them to create a foothold, bring in more reinforcements to further their plans, and to overwhelm the societies of this world.

He'd diverted his path away from his southernly direction and instead moved to the northwest and back toward Red Wind. One man, or rokairn, against an army of demons seemed like suicide rather than a good plan of action.

Nathan avoided confrontation whenever he could. Confrontation led to things like a double shotgun blast to the belly, and not to a long, peaceful life.

The hyena men chased him, hounding him in the most literal sense, until he had changed course and headed west again instead of south towards the Pyridom.

These creatures brought to mind the Egyptian jackal-headed god of the dead, Anubis, and Nathan invented the connection of these scavengers to demons as minions and middlemen. He also associated the Pyridom with Egyptian culture, though it was a cone rather than a pyramid. It was like a warped version of the world mythos he knew, and the association allowed him to conclude that running away was the best plan.

His mind wandered over the coincidences and connections of his world mythology and what appeared to be reality here. Could this entire world just be in his mind? Was he actually dying on the floor of his jewelry shop, twin holes torn into his belly? Did his mind make up all this confrontation, hatred, and violence for some reason, to balance out what his life had been?

With a thunderclap, a woman appeared directly in front of him. She had skin that was a green so dark it appeared black, except in the brightness of the cloudless desert day.

She wore a ragged and rusted chain mail tunic that fell to her knees, divided at her waistline by a wide, worn leather belt holding a two-handed blade that dragged in the sands behind her.

Her hair was short and slicked back across her skull, shaded in a midnight blue that wouldn't be apparent in anything but sunlight. Her legs swere bare, but hinted at lines of scales, and her onyx-colored boots rose to her knees. But the one feature that held Nathan's attention was her sea-green eyes that sparked, and orange flecks of energy rained down to the ground around her.

The rokairn slid sideways to a stop in the sand, reaching over his shoulder to grab his double-bladed axe. It came free with a tug. His mind screamed a silent, startled cry, but his body didn't allow it to escape.

"What the heck am I doing?" Nathan panted, not from exertion, but from his quickening heart rate. "I don't want to hurt you!"

He shouted the last words across the space between himself and the new arrival.

"I'm sorry," he said, trying to smile, his hands spinning the axe in a display meant to intimidate, "I meant I don't want to fight, and I'm just trying to get past. If you wouldn't mind, may I go around and leave you to your business?"

"Chuz you, little man," the woman's voice was acid on flesh, and his skin crawled with her words, "you will die because you need to, and I shall devour your remains in celebration of your defeat."

"That's extreme." Nathan's smile warped into a grimace and his left eye twitched. "I just want to get to Red Wind. There's no need for any violence."

The woman moved like quicksilver, not responding to his words, and the weapon at her waist appeared in her right hand, its blade the deep flaky maroon of rusted metal and dried blood.

Her left hand twisted, creating a rounded flame the size of a basketball. It burst forth and flew at him.

Nathan's axe came up when the woman gestured, and the fireball burst into a harmless flash around him.

The magics bestowed upon him disseminated it.

"I don't want to hurt you," Nathan growled, but recovered, surprised by his own words. "I'm sorry, I'm not threatening you. But I think we can settle this by talking. I don't even know who you are."

"You defy the master, and for that, you must die," the woman was now in front of him and swung her enormous sword down at him.

His own axe moved without conscious thought, catching her blade in the underside curve of his and knocking it aside. The sword bit into the ground, a black seething crevasse appearing around the cut in the earth.

She snarled.

"Who are you?" Nathan backpedaled, his weapon turning and slicing across her midsection. "And why are you doing this?"

Purplish tendrils slid from the wound, grabbing the edges of the opening and pulling it back together before disappearing back inside the thin line left on her scaled flesh.

She brought her sword up, twisting it in front of her in a defensive maneuver, readying for her next strike, but keeping the shorter opponent at bay.

"Klendrisia," she muttered, confusion creased her face as she fought against speaking the words, "daughter of the Demon Lord Ghlevid and human woman Delia, and I'm missioned with destroying the one person who could bring the end to our plans. I don't know why you turned away from the Pyridom, but I will not let some trick distract us from the threat you present."

"Demon Lord?" Nathan's axe drooped from its protective stance. "Is that really a thing?"

The woman's sword shot forward, turning away at the last moment as it hit an invisible barrier shielding him.

"The damned mages and priests can't protect you forever," Klendrisia snarled. "I will wear down those defenses until they collapse and then kill you."

"Why, though?" Nathan whined as he backed up, stumbling over his own feet, his axe rising once again. Narrowing his eyes, his voice took on an angered tone. "What did I do to you? I'm sure this is just a misunderstanding, and we can work this out without me destroying you."

The conflicting sides of Nathan showed through, his hands weaving the weapon in front of him with skill and enthusiasm, but his face and body looking afraid and muddled.

"My father commanded it," the woman drew in a deep breath, struggling, trying to hold back the information, and purplish energies coalesced around her, "and I must do as he commands or be destroyed for failure. My future within the legions depends on my success."

Klendrisia's voice was wooden and monotone, her face showing frustration at her confession and sharing deeply personal information.

The energies slid down her body and slithered along the sandy terrain like an oil spill of otherworldly power, creating a ring around the rokairn. Tentacles of the same color erupted from the ground around the short, stout warrior, writhing and stretching towards him.

Sickly yellowish sparks burst forth, centimeters from his flesh, but his magical barrier deflected the attack.

Nathan's mind warred inside of him as his body did on the outside. His nature urged an end to the fight and aggression, and a deep fiery instinct within him warned him of the danger he faced, demanding he respond with deadly force.

It overwhelmed him, and his vision swam.

Raising the axe, he swept it across the eldritch appendages, severing them in a shower of blue sparks that danced in the air before fading from sight.

Nathan roared, a battle cry coming from deep inside. It was an ancient phrase handed down from generations of holy warriors who had kept the peace through battle and diplomacy, and it carried the power of gods and rokairn with it.

"Kaleb triot, den'al venitier!" Nathan shouted and swung his axe in an arc.

His weapon impacted the woman's sword, and her blade shattered in a magical explosion.

Klendrisia stumbled backwards, the confusion on her face replaced with a mix of anger, surprise, and grim determination.

"Please," Nathan imprinted his take on the words over his body's natural phrasing, "what the heck are you?"

"Cambion," the woman screamed, the words torn from her as she leapt backwards onto a dune, and slid sideways, "I'm an abomination to demons and humans, birthed from the unholy union of passion between a dweller of the lower dimensions and this fragile, rich plane you call home!"

The ground rumbled and shook, and the sky lit up with a wash of green energy.

Nathan looked up, turning, seeking the source. To the south, a pulsing column shot into the sky where he assumed the Pyridom of Power sat.

The rokairn's mind screamed at the telltale sign he'd dreaded. The demons had overtaken the monument, breaking into it to release its secret and gifts of magic.

Klendrisia stood and laughed.

"You've failed," she giggled, madness creeping into her voice as she spat the next words with venom, "and now I'm forced back to report to my father. Damn you for failing. I've tasted hope, and it is bitter."

The woman spun to leave and disappeared before she completed her turn.

## Chapter 5

The Kid didn't know what to do, so he went underground, literally.

Hiding in the same basement apartments that once housed Jakdin—the crime-lord who'd betrayed Durgan's Keep to the necromancer who had attempted to conquer it—the Kid stared at the clattering, but cute, creature who followed him.

The rock-lobster—who the Kid had taken to calling Fred in honor of the lead singer of the B-52s and thinking of as a 'he'—had followed him through the city. The thing scaled the walls, clacked along the cobblestones, and even threatened a surprised puppy who had barked at the Kid.

Bringing the construct to life left the Kid mentally exhausted, his magics drained and weakened. He also had a splitting headache.

*This means something,* Edsumar said into the Kid's head, *and I really think you need to do something about it.*

"What does?" The Kid had talked out loud to the dagger, even though no one else could hear it, not caring if a passerby thought he was crazy. "You mean Fred? Or the dip in my powers? I'm sure it's temporary. I just need a good night's rest."

*No,* the dragon's voice contained a sigh in the Kid's brain. *I mean the magical creature that attacked you. That isn't Mezk's style, or in his repertoire. That's straight up holy magics, and someone with the backing of a church created a thing to kill you. And then you not only stopped it from accomplishing its mission, but you also destroyed it, and took its magical essence and made your own immortal minion from it.*

"I could name him Cuddles," the Kid mumbled, "after my Pomeranian, back home."

*If it was a church, which no church has any reason for targeting you, then it was done because someone paid them a lot of coin,* Edsumar said, *like if multiple guilds and clans decided they wanted to get rid of you and your meddling. Make sense? Maybe it's time to leave Durgan's Keep.*

The Kid grunted a noncommittal agreement and stared at the rock lobster.

*Are you even paying attention?* Edsumar's shout in the Kid's head made the street rat clutch his pounding head. *There's something larger going on than one city, and some petty vendettas. Now suck it up, quit hiding in this hole, and this city, and go do something more than messing with some local, small-time, mobsters.*

"You think I'm hiding?" The Kid looked up at the corner of the musty basement he was sitting in, picking at the barrel beside him with a dirty fingernail. "I've been doing things, not just hiding."

*So, at least you admit that you're hiding.* The dagger snickered in the Kid's thoughts, *and all you've been doing is staying out of the way of the world at large. Do you think you were brought here for the limited purpose of saving one city? Don't you even consider that there may be more? A man doesn't drag people from other realities to clean up one town. You do that for epic reasons, like fixing a broken world. And maybe even fixing a broken person in the process.*

"Broken person?" The Kid snorted. "And are you talking about me, or yourself? Are you hoping that Jack is secretly planning on restoring you to your formal draconic glory? Bestow on you some spare dragon body he has hidden in some closet somewhere?"

*Deflect much?* Was the dagger's only reply.

"Me? ME???" The sound of the Kid's voice echoed off the walls, and Fred backed away, nervous, clacking his stone claws. "You think I'm avoiding things?"

The Kid stopped. He moved his gaze from the corner to Fred, then down to the ivory-tooth dagger at his side.

He let out a long breath that spoke of decades of being tired and ready for something to change.

"Fine," the Kid said quietly, "maybe I am avoiding something. I just thought that when I came here, conquered an invading army of thugs and undead monstrosities, and rebuilt the government of a five-hundred-year-old city, I'd get to just relax and have some fun, you know?"

*For a wise old woman trapped in a seventeen-year-old boy's body,* Edsumar's tone was teasing, *you sure can be naïve. I mean, when has life ever gotten easier? If you want to grow, succeed, and accomplish things, then it's a constant uphill battle. Do you think I cherish waking up as a magical artifact? If indeed I even ever slept so I could wake up. I mean, I zone out, and my mind kinda shuts down, but I never really sleep. I don't have the needs of the flesh anymore, but sometimes I swear I still feel the urge to pee. Do you have any idea how frustrating it is to need to pee, when you don't even have a body, and you haven't had anything to drink in millennia? I mean, really, you like to think that having a bit of meat, or a popcorn shell, stuck in your teeth is frustrating? Try wanting to urinate when you don't even have a winky.*

"Did you just call your tallywacker," the Kid stopped picking at the barrel and turned to look at the dagger again, "a winky?"

*Did you just call a Johnson,* Edsumar's tone matched the Kid's, *a tallywhacker?*

"Did you just call a schmeckel," the Kid giggled, and the two continued their penis-name challenge, "a Johnson?"

*You're a pemtie,* Edsumar laughed, a deep-mentally throaty sound that made the Kid rock back on his heels, *but you're okay with me.*

"Ugh," the Kid moaned, "this is like bad 90s TV dialogue. Can we change the subject?"

*Sure,* Edsumar's tone was smug, like the dragon had won some secret battle. *How about changing it to you growing up, putting on your big-girl panties, and doing what needs done?*

"And what exactly," the Kid asked, and Fred scurried forward at the question, moving closer to his master, "needs to be done?"

The rogue paused, waiting for the artifact with the soul of a dragon to answer.

No reply came.

"You want me to answer this question?" The Kid stood and began pacing. "You want me to come to my own conclusions about this life, and what's going on?

"In one world," the Kid gestured with his hands, working through his thoughts, "I'm on hospice care, waiting to die in a sterile hospital room. I didn't even have my own house, or any family left to go to, where I could die in a home surrounded by loved ones. I have a Pomeranian, named Cuddles, who I see every few days. I still think Janice—who always reminds me of that Fleetwood Mac knock-off Muppet in Dr. Teeth's band—has taken my baby home to take care of her, but brings her in to see me. And yes, Cuddles is a her, though I'm also pretty sure I've heard Nurse Janet calling Cuddles Rowlf, and a he.

"Hm," the Kid stopped pacing for a moment, "this definitely has shades of Veterinarian's Hospital to it."

The Kid shook his head to clear it, then continued pacing and talking.

"Here," the Kid smiled, "I'm a free-styling champion of the city. An urban Robin Hood. Hero to the poor and downtrodden. Okay, well, maybe that's a bit of an exaggeration. But I thought, I felt, like I was doing something here. Something good. It didn't feel like I was just hiding and avoiding things, but maybe I was.

"I lived life through TV shows before," the Kid was speaking directly to Fred now, who clacked his stone claws in response to the words, "experiencing it through Alice and Dingbat in Mel's Diner. Happy Days, CHiPs, Hart to Hart, Columbo, Kojak, MASH, Bob Newhart, and others, all showed me it was okay to laugh. How I related to Vera, who always had her head in the clouds, never gave up hope, even when Mel yelled at her. It was like my life at home, except Mel never hit Vera. And if he had, then Jolene would have knifed the bastard behind the restaurant.

"But I didn't have a Jolene," the Kid sighed, and wiggled onto a barrel to sit. "I didn't have anyone, really; I wasn't allowed to have people. Not until he left. And right after he left, my son needed me, right up until he went to college.

"I supported my son through that time, too," the Kid was staring into the distance now, "eight long years, I worked three jobs so my boy could get an education and live a life better than mine.

"You know," she said, "I've never told you his name. He's Dennis. Dennis Michael. I don't like to use his name, because we named him after his father, who was never around since my son was nine years old. And I guess it's easier to think of him as my son, then give him his own identity.

"But here," he said, "I get to be more than I was there. I'm like a superhero and can do things that no one in my other life could ever do. I leap tall buildings, well, sorta. I made a difference to people here.

"I guess I made a difference there, too, but I never felt it. Does that make sense? Do you know what I mean?"

The Kid paused in his introspection, but there was no answer to his questions.

"It makes me question staying here," the Kid jumped down from the barrel and began pacing again, "is it for selfish reasons? I know if I go back to my world, it won't be for long. I'm on the Reaper's short list.

"But you know what?" The Kid cocked his head and put one hand on his hip, very reminiscent of his behavior when he was Jen in the other world. "I *did* make a difference there. I helped others, supported them, and not just my son. I touched a lot of lives, and gave hope to some, and made others laugh. Or maybe I just made them feel better about themselves by them looking down on me and my life. Doesn't matter, I made a difference.

"I should acknowledge that and give myself credit where credit is due."

The Kid smiled, but it was half-hearted.

"But what should I do now?" he asked. "Live selfishly for myself, or help others, or is it something more than either one of those?

"I think it's both," he said, pulling Edsumar from the sheath at his hip and looking at the ivory blade, "and neither. This is a new life, and a new chance, but it would be pemtie to ignore what I've already learned. So, I should take all these things into consideration, enjoy each moment of this second chance at life that I've been given, but still do what I enjoy most, which is helping others.

"Is that what you meant?" the Kid pointedly asked the artifact.

*No,* the Kid could swear that Edsumar's voice had a smirk in it. *I just meant that you should go investigate that magical disturbance.*

"What magical disturbance?" the Kid scoffed. "I didn't sense anything."

The building rumbled and shook, dust and dirt raining down from overhead.

The Kid ran out of the door, bolting down the long hallway, and towards the exit. The newly made minion skittered in his wake.

The thought of being crushed under a falling building made him move faster, but the excitement of seeing what was going on was his real motivation.

He'd found his place and loved the idea of adventure. The Kid knew he'd gotten comfortable with Durgan's Keep, and it was easy to continue doing what he'd been doing here in this city.

But there was more out there, and he took the stairs up to the ground level two at a time. Bursting into the courtyard outside the door, he could see the green tint to the sky outside and to the southeast.

*That...disturbance,* Edsumar sounded smug again.

The Kid harrumphed, his run slackening to a halt, Fred slowing beside him.

*And as a side note,* Edsumar added, *I really hate that creature you made, and can't wait for it to be destroyed.*

"I'm going to need to find Torrents," the Kid sighed, "aren't I?"

*It's likely,* Edsumar answered. *It seems that the two of you, and others like you, are inexorably linked.*

"Others?" The Kid blinked. "Wait, there are more of us?"

## Chapter 6

Torrents limped. He'd applied compresses to his various wounds, binding the ones that wouldn't stop bleeding. He headed west by southwest towards the valley in the Wandering Hills where the people he cared for waited at Dargaon's Hole.

The green light to the southeast still danced on the horizon like a sickly version of the northern lights, with purplish cracks appearing and disappearing throughout it.

Normally, he'd have made the run back to the cavern complex in less than a day, but his injuries slowed him down. The barbarian had been walking for a day and half since he had faced down ratmen and scared off the luck-bringing twinglinds.

"Some luck," Torrents muttered, using a branch he'd cut as a crutch. "Those damn lizard things don't bring anything except salmonella and infection. They remind me of those worm guys from Men in Black, always underfoot and yipping about nothing."

The big man sighed, working his way up a dew-covered hill.

"Great, now I'm talking to myself." He put his wrist against his forehead and nodded after holding it there for a few moments. "Yup, just as I thought, I have a fever. I also really want some coffee after thinking about those worm aliens."

The world jerked sideways, and Torrents wrinkled his brow in confusion. Then something hit him hard in the side, knocking the wind from him.

He lay still, catching his breath, trying to figure out what hit him, and why his side was wet and cold all of a sudden.

"Hmph," he mumbled, turning his head sideways, "I fell over. At least, I think I did. Either that, or the world suddenly flipped vertical."

He pushed himself to an upright sitting position, doing it slow so the world wouldn't spin faster. He picked bits of grass off the side of his face.

"Why is there dew in the middle of the afternoon?" His voice sounded weird in his ears—like it was full of overcooked egg noodles—distracting him. "Did that rhyme? Dew, afternew…oon. Hm, maybe not."

He twisted where he sat, looking around and trying to get his bearings.

"Okay," he pulled the makeshift crutch closer, and set it to help pull himself up, "I think I fell down. Not just down, like to the ground, but down to the bottom of the hill. I'm gonna to have to stand, and I need to walk. If I don't, then no one will find me."

He pushed to his feet, using the crutch as, well, a crutch. Standing, he swayed, closed his eyes, and held onto the thick branch for balance.

"Oh chuz," he shifted his weight for better balance, felt hot pain shoot up his leg and into his gut, then yelped, "oh chuz! That hurt. But I gotta move on, or no one will find me."

He moved forward with a lurch, his backpack sliding and throwing his balance to one side.

"It's like I'm playing the worst game of hide and seek, ever," panting for breath, he shoved the bag with his elbow, and it shifted to the other side, jerking him backwards, "because no one is actually looking for me, and I'm not…really hiding."

Torrents lumbered forward, pushing his breath out with each purposeful step. He made his way up the hill, sloping to one side, making the journey of this hilltop into more of an orbit of it. He went up at an angle, never quite reaching the top, as his satchel's weight pulled him to one side and came down at a similar angle.

He didn't realize that he'd only gone about a quarter of the way around the hill before reaching the bottom again and set off in a direction that led away from his desired destination.

The barbarian couldn't talk anymore, saving his breath for breathing, and moving forward, one step at a time.

His lips moved, his thoughts wandering through and around the concept of stopping, making a fire, and boiling water. It would have to be a defensible spot, because he wouldn't be able to move far for a few days, at least.

That was his intended thought process, but his fevered brain kept roaming in different directions, pulled by the weight of the infection, much in the same way his body was being pulled by the weight of the equipment on his back.

He looked up and saw stars coming out in a dusky sky.

"When'd…that…happen?" each word was a separate gasp for air.

He sighed and shook his head, which almost caused him to topple.

Coughing, slow and light at first, but then catching in his throat, it became harsh and grating.

When he finally stopped, he was panting to catch his breath, and realized he'd fallen to his knees.

"Damn it," his words were little more than a moan, his lips not even coming together in his exhaustion.

Torrents rolled the pack off his back and onto the wet grass.

He crawled around, scraping loose leaves, twigs, and some small brush from the ground, piling it up.

Leaning back and taking his crutch in both hands, one at each end, he put his booted foot in the center. Pulling with his hands, he pushed with his foot. It took three tries before he got the stick to break in half.

He fell back onto the wet grass when it broke, one piece in each hand and his legs stretched out. The effort exhausted him, but he knew he couldn't pass out yet.

Sitting up took all the effort he could muster.

He tossed the two pieces towards the pile of brush and tinder, then pushed them into place with his feet.

Torrents pulled his pack to him, fumbled with the leather ties, and after almost a minute, got it open.

He rummaged through the bag, tossing anything flammable onto his makeshift campfire. Pulling out a metal flask that held oil, he pushed the satchel off his lap and to one side.

The barbarian broke the wax seal around the cork, threw the cork and wax into the unlit fire, and poured the oil on the moist kindling and wood.

Dropping the flask to one side, he fumbled for a bit of flint from a pouch and drew a dagger. Striking the one against the other, causing sparks to fly, he prayed to Torr the fire would light.

With a pop and whoosh, the small pile of flammables went up in a mini inferno, throwing him back in surprise.

"I think I may need to find new eyebrows," Torrents muttered, panting, "but first, I have to get up and get more wood."

Ten minutes later, he lay and watched the flames jump two meters into the air, praying to Torr the fire would last long enough.

He passed out, shivering in the heat, moments later.

Torrents's eyes fluttered open when something cold, wet, and rough touched his armpit. His vision swam as he tried to focus on the figure bending over him.

He jerked away, attempting to sit up.

A firm hand pressed to his chest, holding him in place with almost no effort.

He was as weak as a tissue paper golem in a downpour and crumpled back onto the furs he was lying on.

"Easy, big guy," a man's voice said. "You're okay, you're safe, and you're with friends."

The voice was as familiar as someone shouting through a crowd of cotton dolls during a rave.

Noises pounded against Torrents's skull, and colors swirled into darkness.

His stomach lurched with his attempted movement, but was empty and had nothing to lose.

Torrents closed his eyes and grabbed the wrist attached to the hand that was stroking his chest soothingly.

"Can you stop that, Axle?" he mumbled, wheezing. "This feels awkward."

The hand patted his chest and moved away, replaced with a damp linen washcloth. The cloth scraped against his skin like wet sandpaper.

"Stop cleaning me, too," the barbarian said, his eyes still closed.

"But you stink," Axle's voice was clearer and closer now, "and if someone doesn't clean you, I fear the council will choose to throw you into the wild and let the hyenas have their way with you."

"You should just put him out of his misery," another familiar voice said. "Badass men make the worst patients, even worse than doctors."

Torrents sighed.

"What the hell is he doing here?" the barbarian opened his eyes, searching for the unwanted face that he was pretty sure was looming over him.

The Kid's smile came into focus, holding up one hand and waving his fingers at the warrior in the sickbed.

"Miss me?" the Kid asked.

"Like the plague," Torrents spat, then broke into a fit of coughing, pushing himself to a sitting position with the help of Axle.

"Drink this," Axle said once the coughing fit subsided. "You need fluids."

"Yes," Torrents rasped, "Doctor Mom."

The barbarian accepted the wooden cup held to his lips, and slurped loudly, trying to gulp the offered water.

Axle held the cup at an angle so the big man could only get sips instead of mouthfuls.

"Too much and you'll get sick," Axle said sagely, "and no one wants to clean that up. Speaking of cleaning things up, what the hell did you get in to?"

"Ratmen," Torrents said, holding himself up to look around.

He was in a familiar cavern with a high ceiling and walls that had been worked long in the past. A fire was glowing and crackling in the hearth across the room. He lay on a cot of furs and blankets, a table and chair beside him. The table held jars, pitchers, a large bowl, and a wooden cup. The chair held Axle. On the other side of the bed were his pack and weapons.

People passed through the public space, glancing over at the barbarian and his companions.

The Kid stood at the foot of the cot, arms crossed, and his smug little smile right where it always was.

"Poison?" Axle asked, washing the big man's back now that he was sitting up.

"Maybe," Torrents growled, "or just infection from dirty weapons being stabbed all the way through my abdomen. And stop washing me!"

The barbarian batted uselessly at his friend's efforts to clean the crusted sweat off him.

"Oh, let him do it," the Kid's tone was mocking, "you big baby. This isn't a movie where you can just get up and walk away from the kind of injuries you had."

Axle gave the Kid an odd look, but the two of them had gotten used to such looks when they mentioned things from their home world.

"What are you even doing here?" Torrents gave up on trying to stop Axle from his task and instead glared at the Kid. "How'd you even get here? I thought you were playing cops and robbers at Durgan's Keep."

"Trinity," Axle said, "after she saw your signal fire and brought you back here, she said she heard some sort of dragon god calling to her, and that she had to go. She came back with the Kid."

"How long was I out?" Torrents winced as Axle scrubbed at the healing cuts and bruises on his back.

"Three days," Axle said cheerfully, "since we lugged you in here and tossed you on the cot. You took a hell of a beating, and rightfully should be damned dead right now."

"Well," Torrents pushed Axle away, threw his legs over the side of the cot, and stood up shakily, "I've got to go, something's happened at the Demon Front, and I don't think it can wait."

Torrents, one hand on the side of the bed for support, gathered his pack and slung it over his shoulder. As he bent to pick up his weapons, Axle snickered, and the Kid out right laughed.

"Don't you think," the Kid pointed at Torrents's groin when the big man looked at him, "you should get some pants first?"

# Chapter 7

The bustling city of Red Wind overwhelmed Nathan. A little by the mass of people and the activity, but mostly by the smell. He'd been a proud business owner in Denver, Colorado for over a dozen years, and had visited places like Las Vegas once or twice, so he'd seen crowds of people doing what they do in a city.

But he'd never smelled anything like the people of this city. He wished he were upwind of the whole place.

It was the dirt roads, the animals, the lack of sanitation services, but mostly the unwashed masses.

The whole town was a sprawling mess. It didn't have a building taller than three stories except for the fifteen watchtowers marking the original border, and seven of them were nothing more than dilapidated ruins at this point. Four of the remaining eight were strongholds of powerful cartels within the city, and the government and its meager watch still controlled the other four.

The town comprised mostly brick buildings with some stucco and wood structures, and half of it had been razed and burned to the ground about a dozen years ago. Nathan noted that the smell of wet smolder and mildew still moved through the air when the wind was right.

In the two days he'd been here, he'd learned some of the history of Red Wind and the Red Plains. It was semi-protected by the Lasso River, which snaked around, having been a trading post a hundred years back. When guilds came to the town, it blossomed into a tent city, and later—as it grew, and proper buildings replaced most of the tents—to a merchant run government via a council of money-hungry vultures in human form.

It rose to power as a financial behemoth when the organized crime families took over and opened a booming drug trade. They manufactured the drugs produced from the red flowers that gave the Red Plains their name.

When the war came, following the Talisman, the town fell into chaos, as did most of the continent.

The march of undead armies and demonic hordes scouring the countryside affected criminals and law-abiding citizens alike. Slaughtering them.

The town was now run by several criminal factions who had branched out into protecting its people while trying to build a financial infrastructure from the ruins of their civilization.

Nathan moved through the dusty, crowded street, dodging and weaving around people, wagons, and anything else that pressed past him, ignoring anyone who was in their way.

It was difficult to see where he was going with the reduced height in this new body. It hadn't been an issue when jogging through the plains by himself, but in the swell of stinky residents, it became a challenge.

Dust clotted his nose, blocking some of the smell, but made him cough every time he took a deep breath. He held a kerchief to his mouth and nose, which turned his apologies to barely audible mumbles as he moved out of people's way.

He'd taken up residence in an inn—named Bluster's Boil, a ramshackle establishment that barely passed for a building—and he'd left it that morning on an outing to find a map of the local area. He really, really didn't want to make this his permanent home.

He made a beeline for a jeweler's shop that caught his eye.

Nathan opened the stout door, entered the shadowy shop, and slowed to a stop. He wasn't sure if he'd come in because he was a jeweler himself, or if his rokairn desire for shiny things and craftsmanship combined had called to him.

The small antechamber, which didn't hold any products, had a single curtained doorway catty corner from where Nathan stood looking around.

A man with a bent nose and dark, greasy hair—combed over to cover his balding pate—looked at the rokairn with a squint.

"Whadda you want?" the man leaned on the counter, glaring at him over a dented goblet, and a plate with a hunk of meat as greasy as the man's hair, a lump of cheese, and a chunk of bread.

"Um, sorry to disturb your lunch," Nathan shuffled from foot to foot. "It looks really hunky-dorie."

Nathan smiled.

The man glowered.

"I just came in to look around," the man turned even more sour, and Nathan backpedaled, "no, no, you see I'm a jeweler, too, and just wanted to admire your craftsmanship. I miss it, you know?"

The man's look didn't improve. In fact, he hunched his shoulders further and outright scowled, then jerked a thumb towards the curtain.

Nathan hurried through the cloth and bead partition, keeping his eyes on his feet until he was in the next room. Once inside, he lifted his gaze and looked around.

The room was dark woods and red velvet. Ornate couches with silk cushions were set into alcoves, and alabaster columns accented the areas between the private niches and the main room.

Shorter columns held matched sets of necklaces, rings, bracelets, and other jewelry. They lined every display with black velvet in the center and delicately wrought silver and gold ornamentation along the corners.

A bored looking, broad-shouldered man with his arms crossed stood in one corner, continuously scanning the room.

Two women, draped in diaphanous white silk, lounged on a divan in the center of the room. They rose as Nathan entered, one picking up a silver tray of grapes and cut melons, the other lifting a matching silver carafe and goblet from a marble table. Both slinked towards him with soft smiles and hooded eyes.

An older, effeminate man who was exceedingly thin stood on the other side of the room, his smile a wide slit that ran from ear to ear. The man—also dressed in hanging silks, but his were purple, and reminded Nathan of a Roman toga—clasped his hands together, like he just won a beauty contest.

The man nodded his head in Nathan's direction, and fluttered a hand towards the serving women, indicating the rokairn should enjoy the amenities.

Nathan was stunned, backing away with his hands raised, his jaw trying to push out words his throat wasn't delivering. This place was such a dichotomous change compared to the ramshackle and dusty world outside.

He'd seen upscale establishments in his world, even been to jewelry conventions where the more successful companies would do up their areas like lounges. But he'd never seen anything like this.

The two women didn't speak a word, but offered the platter of fruits, a finely worked chalice of wine, and—by the silent suggestion of twirling fingers through and across the silks that barely covered them—much, much more.

"Talk about high-pressure sales techniques." Nathan waved the women away, flapping both hands like he was trying to shoo a flock of aggressive seagulls away from him on the beach. "No, thank you. I'm just looking. I don't want anything but to look at the craftmanship. I'm sorry, but thank you, I'm sorry, I don't want any of what you're offering. Though, it's lovely, and looks delicious. Not you two, I mean the food and wine. Not that you two aren't lovely, but I'm here for the jewelry, not an escort service."

He moved around the room—keeping his back to the wall and the women always in sight—towards the burly man standing in the corner.

"You here to protect the merchandise?" Nathan asked the big guy without looking up.

The rokairn saw the large man nod out of the corner of his eye.

The older man was sashaying in his direction, leaning down the closer he got to Nathan.

"Oh, you dear, sweet dwarf," the man simpered. "I'm Elequontius, your delighted host. No need to bother that brute. He's simple and can barely put a sentence together, and I shall cater to your every whim and need. If the women bother you, I shall take care of everything myself."

Something inside Nathan snapped. It was more of a click of a deep-seated instinct within the body that he inhabited. Nathan didn't like bullies, and though people might pick on him, he wouldn't stand by and let someone pick on someone else who couldn't defend themselves. He knew being nice wouldn't work with this sort of man, and the proprietor would keep pushing, taking any hesitation as encouragement.

"No," Nathan stood to his full height, his Rokairn accent coming out as he jabbed the thin man in the chest with a thick finger, "first, I'm Rokairn, not a dwarf. Don't talk down to me, and don't be a racist. Second, I don't want a suck up bothering me. I don't want some women throwing themselves at me in hopes that it'll lead to me spending more money. Third, I'll deal with the brute, and the brute only. Am I understood?"

"But, my good dw-rokairn," the man cleared his throat and went on, "this man knows nothing of the goods we sell…"

"Does he stand here each day, watching and observing?" Nathan growled.

"Well, yes," the man took a breath to go on, but Nathan interrupted again.

"I think that's good enough." The rokairn turned towards the guard, ignoring further protests from

Elequontius, "you've been paying attention when you're standing here all day?"

The guard nodded.

"You know enough to show me things and answer simple questions, considering I'm a master jeweler?"

The guard nodded again.

"What's your name?" Nathan asked.

"Nob," he answered, but it sounded like he had a wad of cotton in both cheeks, "and I don't think anyone has ever talked to me in here. But I ain't no pemtie. I can help ya."

"But," Elequontius interrupted, wringing his hands and giving Nathan a sickly smile, "I don't think…"

"And you don't need to. Nob will do the thinking while I'm here. You go polish your…" Nathan pushed past the shopkeeper, Nob trailing after him, "goods. I'll only deal with this man while here."

Nathan drew out a pouch and undid the ties, walking towards a display, pouring an assortment of coins and gems into his palm, displaying them for the older man to see.

"Think this is enough to buy something here, Nob?" Nathan looked up at the big man.

"Yup," Nob smiled as he looked at the currency, "and I know they give you discounts when you pay up front. You lookin' for custom work, or just something to take away today?"

"I'm just looking," Nathan handed the man a red gemstone and a few coins, "but you keep that for yourself since you're going to do such a fine job helping me, and making sure those other people don't bother me, okay?"

"Yup," Nob nodded.

Nathan spent the next twenty minutes inspecting pieces in relative silence, only breaking it to ask simple questions.

He held a platinum and sapphire cuff up to the light, inspecting the settings and cut of the stone, when the far wall shook from some sort of impact.

A scream filtered through the noise-dampening wall coverings, and the sound of steel on steel followed.

Nathan looked towards the noise, his brow furrowing. He thrust the band towards Nob, turned and strode towards the door, unstrapping his double-headed axe from his back.

He pushed through the curtain into the entry chamber, ignored the greasy-haired man behind the counter who stared at him with frightened eyes, and pushed through the door into the street.

Horns cut through the murmur of conversation on the street outside that hung in the air as thick as the dust.

The baying and laughing of the hyenas and their keepers drifted through the streets.

Nathan grunted, turned in the ruckus's direction, set his feet, pulled his shoulders back, hefted his blade, and moved towards it.

# Chapter 8

Standing in the noonday sun, Klendrisia surveyed the city from a small hill on the outskirts, her dark skin glistening a deep green that betrayed her mood.

She hated how her skin betrayed her emotions to anyone bothering to observe her. She fought an inner war, battling herself and her heritage, to overcome her passionate nature and exert control over her mind and reactions.

The demon-spawn watched her gnohls, led by Ghe'hak the Ravager. He was an experienced pack leader, having had the position for almost four and a half months. A full season without being killed.

She remembered when he'd first changed and became a gnohl, and how he'd fought amongst the pack for his place. He was cunning, and chose his rivals with keen ability, taking them out and making his climb to pack leader.

But that wasn't why Klendrisia was fond of him. She liked him because he didn't kill without discretion. The gnohl killed easily and with pleasure that was more than bone deep, but he always did it with a reason rather than delight.

It was the beast's weakness. Someone would exploit it. The keen intelligence that haunted Ghe'hak would be his downfall, and that might come during this battle.

The other gnohls swarmed towards the city walls, now broken and shattered, remnants of a once powerful landmark in this part of the land. The hyena-headed creatures ran forward—some on two legs, others dropping to all fours and bounding over eroded battlements and earthworks.

Packs of snarling hyenas, some as large as a human at their shoulder, wove through their bipedal counterparts.

These animals killed without a thought, devouring any human, rokairn, or aeifain they could find. Their reward for massacring the enemy was the chance they'd evolve into a humanoid and become a gnohl who could better serve their demon masters.

Klendrisia shouted commands that were lost in the dull thunder of hundreds of her minions charging forward, a cloud of dust marking their passage. The orders didn't matter, anyway; these troops weren't assembled for surgical strikes against an enemy. She brought them together as a horde, meant to sweep across the landscape and leave a swath of devastation to bring fear to anyone who saw, or heard of, their passing.

Klendrisia shouted the orders because she enjoyed it. It was part of her nature, to organize what she had to make it more efficient, to help her overcome anything in her way. It was against her demonic side and instead came from her mother's side.

Her mother had been a holy warrior of Jonath—the god of honor, earth, agriculture, and protection—taken prisoner by Klendrisia's father. The woman had been a prized trophy and eventually impregnated. Klendrisia didn't know the details, only that her mother died giving birth to her.

She took after her mother in some ways—or so she understood.

Her sire hated this about her, which was why he'd sent her out with just a single pack of gnohls and hyenas to hunt the rokairn warrior, Nathan.

When she had succeeded in diverting him from his task, two things happened; they tapped into the Pyridom of Power, allowing a new doorway between realities to open and bring in new demons and troops from the Abyss; and Klendrisia had been—reluctantly, by her father—given this new mission.

Hunt down the key to open the gates of the next portal, so her father's armies could spill into this dimension and take it for their own.

Just over a hundred years ago, the first portal had been reopened. It was in the south, on the peninsula named Land's End. Thousands of demons had poured through, but the majority of them were minor beings with no leadership. Heroes rose and fought them back and they made little progress in the way of an invasion. The portal had been shattered, but some remnants remained and allowed more powerful beings to creep through.

The problem with that, though, is the ones with armies backing them wouldn't risk coming through to this world without their armies, and the ones who did come through were rogue elements.

Klendrisia smiled as her forces reached the edge of the city. The meager guard at the border went down in a flurry of carnage, and her troops spread into the city.

She moved forward, drawing her two-handed blade with one hand and raising it above her head. Using her magics to amplify her voice, a simple task, she screamed her fury, so it echoed throughout the town.

Entering the city, the smell of animals and human waste reached her nose. Smells in Gehenna and the Abyss were bad, putrid, and foul, but the human worlds had their special portfolio of reeks, stenches, and fetid aromas that weren't matched in any of the other known dimensions.

The sounds of screams, blending terror and death, reached her ears. She noted screams about death rarely came from the receiver of the gift, rather it came from observers who were too pemtie to run, and instead stood and watched. It was an open invitation to be the next candidate in line to receive the blessings of eternal rest.

Klendrisia didn't have to put effort into the killing. People merely presented themselves for a task she thought of as mundane. She ran her tarnished blade across their bellies, chests, thighs, or whatever was presented as they bolted from her horde. Their enemies fell, leaving a trail of bodies and viscera behind.

She didn't bother to kill them all, just to take them out of the fight. Leaving some alive allowed them to suffer and spread the tale of her and her army crossing the land. It was marketing at its best, in her mind. Eliminating them from the fight, but still being around to spread the word of her conquests.

Ghe'hak had a small group of elite gnohls with him, and striding into the town, she saw him picking out any person who dared make a stand against her and her army.

Heroes fell, dashing themselves against the onslaught of wholesale butchery. Brave men wielding blades of their ancestors died in a split second, ending their legacy and family lines.

Klendrisia smiled. They were pemties, throwing their lives away against an unstoppable force.

The pack leader howled in the fervor of killing, inciting his followers into a blood rage.

The demon half-breed moved through the streets, cutting people down without prejudice. Her actions were almost an afterthought. When she killed a group of five adventurers, her only thought was that they shouldn't have drunk so much that they stumbled when leaving the pub, where they'd been spending their money made in the blood of other creatures.

*Loot, my ass,* she thought.

She strolled through the gore-ridden streets of Red Wind, spotting a familiar figure. A short, stout man stood at a crossroads, wielding his double-headed battle axe, and occasionally pulling out a hand axe and throwing it into a gnohl.

Nathan, the rokairn she'd encountered in the Crescent Desert, stood beside an equally broad-shouldered human with a hand-and-a-half sword.

The two cut down every one of Klendrisia's minions that came within their blades' arcs, and a handful that didn't.

She watched in fascination as the short, bearded man worked his weapon in arcs, figure eights, and wild swings. It was like watching an artiste performing a brutal, ritualistic dance to the gods themselves. The man focused and zeroed in on a target, launched an attack, and then moved to another before the first crumpled to the dusty street in front of him.

But the street wasn't so dusty anymore. It was a gooey pool of blood and grime, a thick, viscous soup of death and determination.

In Klendrisia's eyes, it was a thing of beauty. Every movement was passion incarnate, as this rokairn defended strangers from death.

Of course, it was useless. There was no overcoming the challenge she presented. But if anyone had a chance, it would be this warrior.

She watched his focus break when a gnohl tore a chunk from the big human beside the rokairn. A surprising burst of concern broke Nathan's concentration as the human fell under three of Klendrisia's attacking legion.

The little man was vulnerable. He cared about the creatures dying around him.

The realization surprised the demoness, if she cared to consider herself in that light, and she wondered about it.

How would she feel if Ghe'hak fell? Would she care? Wasn't he just another pawn in this game, a thing to be used and discarded when his usefulness passed?

Why would anyone ever allow themselves to care if someone else died? That was akin to becoming emotionally attached to your sword. It, and they, had their use, but once that expired, why invest any more thought into something no longer useful?

It just felt so…self-destructive and pemtie.

She raised her sword from the dusty street, thinking to step in and end the ignorant rokairn's suffering.

Why should she care if he was in pain? Why did she want to show him mercy and kill him, so he no longer had to face the inevitable distress of watching those he knew die?

This was one of the things she often considered, blaming her human heritage for her weak thoughts. Why would anyone ever care if someone else died or suffered? It was a ridiculous concept, and self-defeating.

Something drew her attention, and she looked away from the dance in the distance. Something called to her, niggling at the edge of her awareness.

A tingle crept along her dark flesh, like a dozen spiders running up her arm. A sharp, but distant, ringing came to her ears.

The key. It was active, and it sung to her.

She reached out with her mind, searching for the artifact that would open the next portal. Her mission goal, once accomplished, would be instrumental in bringing the full might of her father's forces to this realm.

It called to her again.

Like a hound on a scent, she stepped forward without conscious thought, knowing this one thing must come before anything else.

She tore her awareness from the distant, sweet siren call of the magic that would achieve what no one else could and looked one more time at the rokairn.

Nathan was staring at her, the big human, leaning heavily on him as the man's breath clenched in his chest, and he struggled to live another few moments.

Recognition dawned in Nathan's eyes, and Klendrisia could see the man's jaw working, trying to make sounds to ask questions.

They always questioned, these despicable, pathetic mortals, whenever they were cut down like stalks of diseased grain.

You didn't let the weak survive. It made sense to hew the lesser, so the strong may thrive. Why didn't the beings of this place understand that simple rule of nature?

The demoness saluted her foe, smiling with a smug expression.

She would let him live, today at least. Perhaps he'd be challenging and give her some small distraction during the overly simple task of recovering the artifact she sought by killing anyone in the way.

Four humans swarmed around the distracted rokairn warrior, one taking his wounded companion, and another placing a hand his shoulder. The newcomer touching Nathan spoke words Klendrisia couldn't hear. The rokairn turned to look at the hand on his glowing spaulder.

*Priest of Jonath*, Klendrisia thought, *isn't that a quaint coincidence? The very organization that my own dame belonged to, coming to help my nemesis. Oh, I have a nemesis now? Interesting.*

Nathan had turned back to look at her through slitted eyes, but the call of the key was stronger than the unspoken challenge.

Klendrisia buffered her voice with her magics once again.

"Come to me," her screech shook windows in buildings, and the nerves of strong warriors across the town, "kill all in your path, but join me as we seek our goal."

Swinging her sword to her side, she secured it into place with her other hand.

She threw a look over her shoulder at the rokairn, who was running towards her, the four humans behind him shouting in dismay.

She smiled at him, turned away, and moved with inhuman speed towards the northwest, and the song that hung in the air, beckoning to her.

She knew he'd follow. She'd have her chance to kill him soon enough. And hope would die on her blade.

## Chapter 9

"Chuz!" Torrents yelped, collapsing to the ground beside Trinity's foreleg.

The dragon looked down at the tawny-skinned man.

"My apologies?" The dragon said sarcastically. "Perhaps it's my fault you chose to leave the conclave before being well enough to travel?"

The Kid snickered, a bit louder than what would have been considered accidental.

"It's the stitches in my belly," Torrents pushed the words out through clenched teeth, "they might have ripped when I slid off you. And it's not nearly as smooth a ride as I expected on the back of a dragon. I mean, damn it, you jerked up and down with every wing stroke, and any breeze caused you to lurch to one side or the other."

"I can kick you in the knee," the Kid offered, "and that'd help you forget about the pain in your gut."

"Go chuz yourself." Torrents didn't bother looking up from checking his bandages, swearing at the other rider, who was still atop the dragon's back. "Maybe that will distract me enough that I forget the pain in my ass. And by that, I mean you're a pain in my ass."

"Thanks for explaining that one," the Kid slid down the side of the silver-white, winged reptile, landing with a flourish beside Trinity, "otherwise I might've thought you meant your own head being up your ass was causing discomfort."

Fred slid down the dragon's back, following his master.

"Children," Trinity stretched her neck between the two, "I think you'd better consider where you'll be spending the night rather than bickering."

"Children?" The Kid raised an eyebrow. "You realize I'm almost four-score years old in the other world, and in my other body?"

"Yes," Trinity bobbed her head in respect, "forgive my brash, impulsive youthfulness. I am a mere four centuries old. I apologize."

"Whatever," the Kid muttered, walking in a circle around the grassy knoll they'd landed on, "it's quality, not quantity, that counts."

"Oh?" Torrents stood upright, wincing. "So, hiding from life because your kid died and your husband left you is now considered quality?"

"Like you're one to talk," the Kid spat back, his voice turning high-pitched and mocking, "constantly whining how life broke you and took away all your natural gifts, when you killed your own father and put yourself in a wheelchair."

Torrents's turned towards the Kid, his hand reaching over his shoulder for the double-handed pommel of his massive sword.

"Now that Esperanza is gone," Trinity sighed, "you two will kill each other long before any demonic forces can. I brought you as far as I could without attracting unwanted attention. I'll leave the two of you here, at the southern border of the Black Wood, and wish you luck in surviving your own bickering."

The dragon crouched, then launched herself into the air. The down stroke of the wings kicked up a cloud of dust, causing the two below to cough and cover their eyes.

Fred clacked his claws, attempting to snag one of the many leaves that swirled through the air at the dragon's departure.

"I've missed you," the Kid grinned at Torrents, "at least with you I could say anything and get away with it. But I have a splitting headache right now. It's been lingering since I created Fred."

"You're a jerk, and cranky." Torrents sighed, "you know my temper. Why'd you push me? If I was into beating up old ladies, or young punks, I'd have a field day with your face."

"That's what he said?" The Kid raised an eyebrow. "Is that a thing? It started after I was too old to care, but can we do 'he' in that phrase instead of 'she'?"

"Just stick to quoting movies," Torrents bent to pick up his pack and supplies he'd dropped from—what they affectionately called—the luggage rack on the back of Trinity, and winced with the movement, "it'll be easier on all of us."

"Fo-shizzle," the Kid watched the barbarian move around the hilltop, "you should have stayed in bed more than three days, dude. You weren't ready for this, and two more days on and off a dragon didn't help you."

"I'll be fine," Torrents stiffened, trying to hide his discomfort, "and once we get to PepperGarten, I'm sure he'll have something to help me."

"Yeah, I guess," the Kid picked up his small pack, and Fred scurried over to him, allowing him to strap the bag to the construct's back, "but really, who hunts dragons? Can they really be that much of a threat?"

"I'd think…" Torrents began.

"That'd be a refreshing change," the Kid interrupted.

"I'd think," Torrents said with a growl, "that you'd be a bit more cautious of anything a dragon fears. And she explained how her kind has been hunted in the east since the Wizard Wars."

"But that was like a thousand years ago," the Kid scoffed, turning to survey to the south, "you'd think they'd lose interest by now."

The hill they'd landed on was bare except for dew-ridden grass, though it was afternoon. The long-lasting after-effects of the comet Talisman had made weird climate changes that had long-lasting repercussions.

A few trees dotted the hillside below, and a stream trickled to the east, the runoff from the mountains to the north feeding the foothills to the south.

Birds took to wing in the south, an enormous flock of egrets who'd taken to sticking together for the herd-mentality protection.

The Kid pondered for a moment before turning to Torrents.

"Why would a bunch of birds suddenly take off when we're nowhere near them?" the Kid asked.

"Predator?" Torrents stepped around Fred, adjusting the sword on his back and looking in the direction that the Kid was staring.

A cloud of dust appeared in the distance. It was small and faint, but it was a definite indicator of something large. Or of many smaller things moving as a unit.

The laughing bark and howls wafted across the distance.

"What was that?" The Kid fingered his magical dagger without being aware he was doing so.

*Gnohls,* Edsumar's voice answered in the Kid's mind.

"Gnohls?" the Kid echoed.

"What the chuz are gnohls?" Torrents shaded his eyes from the mist-hazed sun above to get a better view of whatever it was in the distance. "Is that cloud headed towards us?"

*Hyena and demon hybrids,* Edsumar mentally informed the Kid, *formed from the broken corpses and spirits of humans they kill. And yes, I do believe they're coming this way.*

"Uh huh, they're bad things, hyena-men with demon heritage," the Kid mumbled. "I have a bad feeling about this."

"Star Wars?" Torrents sighed, reaching over his shoulder to free his weapon. "Really? You're doing that now?"

"Do we run? Hide?" The Kid looked around for cover. "Or do we wait here and hope they're not coming for us?"

"Why would they be coming for us?" Torrents scoffed. "We just got here. They might keep moving past this hill."

The two watched in silence for a few minutes, the cloud turning more in their direction.

"Or not," The Kid drew Edsumar from his sheath. "Looks like someone was waiting for us to arrive. Why do they always have to be looking for us?"

"Because we're awesome," Torrents shrugged, "and know we can kick their ass, and want to take us out for the street cred?"

"So," the Kid sighed, "we're fighting then?"

"Unless you have a better idea," Torrents shrugged again.

The Kid looked around, hoping to see a better idea laying in the calf-high grass. He didn't see anything to help. No cover, no defendable area, no way to take out a large group without getting his hands dirty.

"Maybe they're on our side," the Kid suggested, looking tired, "and are coming here to recruit us to help their worthy cause."

"It's always delightful," Torrents rolled his eyes at the Kid looking up at him, "and wonderfully naïve when you say such things. When have they ever not wanted to kill us? This world is bidj when it comes to good guys, and a chuzzing buffet when it comes to bidjwads wanting to do horrible things."

"Okay then," the Kid sat down on a stone jutting from the ground, "I guess we wait for them to get here, and hope that the high ground is enough advantage to get through this. Can you fight in your condition?"

"Do I have a choice?" Torrents's answer was bitter. "Can I just hang back while you take out something big enough to raise that much dust?"

The two looked into the distance past the approaching danger; they could see where the threat had most likely come from.

The green light to the southeast was getting bigger. It spanned almost a quarter of the horizon in that direction now, with a dark nimbus of greasy smoke ringing it.

Whatever had come through to this world, to the Demon Front, was now burning things and creating a wasteland as they moved further across the continent.

It took almost a half hour for the two to see the forerunners of the horde: a wedge of huge, primitive proto-hyenas burst through the tree line at the bottom of the hill, the shadowy chuckles of the beasts causing the two on the hill to take a deep inhalation of breath.

The phalanx of the creatures surged up the hill, loamy soil churning under their claws, leaving a swath of bare earth behind them. Each beast was almost the height of a man at its shoulder.

Torrents, his lips a grim smile, stepped forward. He chose the stance he'd face the oncoming enemy with a double handed grip in front of him, which would allow him to swing into the bodies of his foes while still blocking their attacks.

The Kid tossed his dagger, Edsumar, into the air, causing it to flip once, then catching the handle again. He did this repeatedly, waiting for the enemy to close the distance.

As the beasts approached the crest of the hill, the Kid stepped behind the barbarian, drew his arm back, and threw Edsumar past the big man.

The dagger cut through the air, its path true, and pierced the eye of the lead hyena. The monster fell to its side, and slid to a stop along the turf, the rest of the creatures darting around it or leaping over their fallen pack member.

Torrents drew his blade up slightly, adjusting for his first strike, and winced at the pulling sensation of the injuries in his abdomen.

The first wave hit the duo, the line of monsters crashing into them.

At waist level, the barbarian swung his weapon in a wide arc. The blade cut across the chest and forelegs of the two lead beasts, severing muscle and sinew from bone. The two went down, but not before one of them locked its teeth onto the warrior's forearm.

Torrents knew fighting a four-legged predator was very different from fighting a man with a weapon. You had to watch out for teeth and claws, rather than blocking or dodging a weapon. Some people fought like their blade was an extension of their body, but most used it as the tool it was, and often that was the way through their defenses.

Animals were different; they reacted in a smooth flow, every movement and reaction connected without separate thought.

The animals the barbarian had struck weren't dead, just injured, and they continued to fight.

Torrents shoved at the one on his right with his booted foot, rolling the beast backwards into its companions and causing them to stumble.

The one on his left locked its jaws around his arm, shook its head, jerking one hand from the barbarian's grip on his sword.

Edsumar appeared in the Kid's hand in the blink of an eye, its innate magic returning it to the rogue.

Fred—the rock-lobster construct the Kid created— waded into the fray. Stone claws tore into thick hide and matted fur, ripping chunks away from the attackers in sprays of blood.

The Kid reached out with his mind, using his magics, and concealed himself in a spray of illusionary mist, ducking under the snapping jaws of the hyena bounding at him.

He came up under the beast, slashing across its belly and spilling entrails onto the wet grass. The creature snaked its head under its front legs to bite at the thief, only to receive a dagger slid across its jowl and along the side of its head, turning the attack away.

Torrents pulled his arm free, blood gushing from the wound, and caved in the hyena's skull with the pommel of his sword.

The barbarian dropped to a knee, returning his second hand to the pommel of his weapon, and thrust it down into the open maw of another of the monsters. Twisting it, he pulled it to the side and jerked it out.

The beast gurgled and stumbled, tumbling down the hill.

The Kid grabbed a handful of gravel from underfoot, held it in his open palm, picked them up with his mind, and shot them forward. The grape-sized stones turned to deadly projectiles, ripping through another beast, made a sharp turn like a tiny, deadly flock of stone birds, and tore through two more.

Fred scurried from one fallen hyena to another, his claws cutting into the beasts' throats and tearing through their jugulars and larynxes, taking them out of the fight as they died in a gout of their own fluids.

As the stones flew from one monster to another, the Kid launched Edsumar at the furthest one, embedding the blade into the creature's ribs where the heart should be. The beast skidded to its side in the grass, fighting for breath and to rise before Fred moved to end its life.

Torrents jumped over the fallen beasts in front of him, bringing his double-handed blade down on the head of one of the three remaining, crushing its skull and spine.

The beast fell, twitching.

Moments later, the last two died, one by dagger and stones, the other by a length of steel through its body.

The two companions looked at one another.

Torrents was panting, his arm a ragged, bloody mess, and held to his injured stomach.

The Kid was rubbing his temples, wincing in pain. He smiled, but it was a shaky smile that lacked his normal bravado.

They nodded to one another, then turned to look in the direction where these things had come from.

Dozens more were flooding from the tree line at the bottom of the hill, accompanied by almost as many gnohls. They all bounded up the hill towards the Kid and Torrents.

"Chuz me sideways," Torrents muttered.

## Chapter 10

The ground rolled and tumbled past Nathan's feet as he glanced down. His dark brown boots blended in the blur of loamy earth below his feet, moving in a constant tattoo to the bellows of his breath.

He'd been following the demoness and her murderous crew for days, sleeping when they rested, ready to move on before they were.

He knew he couldn't take them out alone, but whatever they were up to had to be stopped.

These creatures committed wholesale slaughter on a city just because they were passing close to it. They'd murdered men, women, and children just for the joy of it. They hadn't looted, hadn't taken prisoners, or even destroyed everyone in Red Wind. They'd killed while passing through. Just for fun.

That made no sense.

Why kill at all, let alone without a purpose other than the joy of it? His human mind fought with that, struggling to make sense of a senseless act. He wanted to know the reason, so maybe he could understand the actions of these creatures, though he'd never be able to accept them. His brain tumbled it around, grasping at the slippery ideas like a dog trying to catch a fish flopping in a boat during a hurricane. He just couldn't get it.

Nathan shoved the thought aside, letting his rokairn brain took over. Why worry about something you can't even conceive? That's not how you get things done. If you want answers, but can't get them, then find the next step that will get you closer to them.

That's how you do anything in life, one step at a time. Follow these beasts. Study them, fight them if needed, and find a way to stop them. That was the rokairn way, one step at a time. Take the next hammer stroke, to create the tool you need to do the job that needs to be done. One step at a time. There was never any reason to run in circles, mentally or otherwise, when it wouldn't get you closer to your goal.

The rokairn body soothed his human mind, calming and lulling it in the rhythm of movement and the task at hand—running. All else faded, barring the small thoughts dashing around his head like lightning in a bottle; thoughts of his well-being, his breath, how his legs felt, how his gear bounced, and how to make sure none of those became an issue.

Nathan didn't run fast, but he never stopped. One step at a time. He was the tortoise, and like a force of nature, he would win this battle against an extra-dimensional hare set on destroying a world that he'd been forced into.

He stumbled, physically tripping over an errant stone or root, the thoughts of his human side pummeling the reality of the rokairn side. Memory of the age-old adage, 'A journey of a thousand miles begins with one step,' or the old joke, 'How do you eat an elephant? One bite at a time.'

It all meant the same thing, just keep moving. One step at a time. There was no other way to do anything. People liked to think they can multi-task, but a body can only do one thing at a time. And it's always easier and more efficient to complete one task before starting another. Doing two things at the same time splits your attention—and creates extra work as you adjust your mind, tools, body, or whatever—to switch between doing more than one thing at once.

It wasn't just Nathan's thoughts that had pulled him from his reverie; a scene was unfolding in the distance. The sounds of the laughing barks of the gnohls and their hyena pack was the first thing to catch his attention and was often how he followed the pack without being detected. The second most common way he tracked them was by the damage they left in their wake. Torn earth, broken trees, and dead bodies.

He'd learned to keep a respectful distance after discovering they almost always sent out forward scouts, but sometimes also sent out a rear scout to make sure nothing was following.

That lesson had been a rough day.

He'd been trundling along in his fugue of concentration, not paying attention. A gnohl had appeared in front of him, launching itself from a thicket, screaming as it came at him with a pitted blade. Without a conscious thought, he'd bent under the weapon—the creature aiming poorly because of Nathan's smaller stature—and came up with two hand axes. He'd sliced across the beast's belly, opening twin vents in the thing's guts.

That hadn't stopped it, though; the monster went on, manically laughing as it chopped and hacked clumsily at Nathan.

The rokairn had pivoted, kicking the feet out from under his foe, while cutting a hamstring, and the artery in the bastard's thigh, with two separate cuts. The monster died loudly, and not easily, as Nathan danced in and out, wielding his twin blades as precisely as a surgeon would use scalpels.

The creature died, though, but not before it attracted the attention of two more gnohls and a handful of their proto-hyenas.

Nathan knew he could hunt them. He could kill them. But that would've drawn the attention of the others, and he wasn't ready to face a score and half of these things alone in a place he didn't know well enough to create a reasonable defensive position.

He'd ran, he'd hid. He created false leads and trails, making them run in circles, or just in the wrong direction. This wasn't easy, because the giant hyenas could track by smell. He'd ended up hiding in a stream, in the tangled root system of a fallen tree, to cover his scent and tracks.

They eventually gave up and returned to their war band, but Nathan had learned: keep extra distance. Watch for scouts and stay to one side rather than following the main path they'd left behind.

Now, the band was about a kilometer in front of him, its focus on something on a grassy hilltop.

He broke away without hesitation, circling the hill as he approached. There was a value in coming in behind the group and cutting them down when their focus was elsewhere. But he couldn't risk the chance they'd set out someone to watch for exactly that.

He didn't move to the opposite side of the knoll. Instead—in his mind, the gnohls were at the six o'clock position—he moved to the nine o'clock position of the hill and came in at an angle.

Atop the mound he saw a huge barbarian with a sword taller than the rokairn himself, the man bleeding from his left forearm, his stomach, and other places. Beside the barbarian was a younger man, skinny and wiry, dancing about. The smaller man only had a dagger, but seemed to use some sort of magic.

Dead hyenas and gnohls surrounded them, as well as the rest of the war band, which outnumbered the dead, and the defenders, by a lot.

Nathan's human mind shuddered, drawing the body he now inhabited to a dead stop.

"This is insane," he muttered, trying to talk himself out of what he was about to do. "I should turn west and keep going until there's nothing that wants to kill me within shouting distance."

He'd reached over his shoulder, without conscious thought, and freed his double-headed battle axe. He was spinning it in his hands, a grim smile on his face in anticipation of what came next, even as his voice argued against it.

"Do you want to risk dying to save someone else?" He asked out loud, unsure which part of his mind the question came from. "Or do you want to risk living while making a difference in the world?"

His feet were already carrying him forward, crouched as he moved, making himself less obvious. He didn't have a chance to answer himself; he'd already taken one step and wouldn't stop now.

He could have circled back around to the rear of the war party, but then he'd have to face them all at once. Well, any that weren't directly involved in the battle already.

Instead, a flanking maneuver seemed best, and he moved into a position where he'd be able to see the two men and support them, as well as get support from them.

"Kaleb triot, den'al venitier!" he roared, propelling himself into the side of the attacking force.

It had a chanting quality to it, the rhythm matching the beat of his feet.

Twenty sets of eyes—two from the defenders, the rest from the attackers—turned to look at him in surprise.

His axe was a blur as he spun around the gnohls and their minions. Three fell in as many steps, and another toppled backwards with a shattered knee from the rokairn's boot.

The two men rallied, the big one with the huge sword screaming to the god Torr for blows that strike true, and the smaller one shouting to someone called Fred to take care of the fallen and crippled enemies.

The three pushed the gnohls back, surprising them with their fervor, but the hyenas pushed forward.

The man-height beasts came in low, three snapping at the rokairn's arms. One caught the shaft of the axe in its jaws and tore the weapon away. Another bit into Nathan's wrist, clamping down on the bracer and chain mail covering it. Something popped, and the rokairn wasn't sure if the sound had come from him or the hyena.

Raising the arm with the hyena attached, he punched it in the throat, crushing its larynx. He twisted his wrist, freeing it from the gasping creature's mouth, and grabbed its head in both hands, and spun.

The hyena lifted off the ground as Nathan spun—reminding the rokairn of doing the same thing with his niece years ago, but by her hands, not her head—and when he released his grip, the creature smashed into another hyena, both flying backwards.

The third beast took advantage of this distraction, locking its teeth onto the back of the rokairn's neck, lifting him from the ground, and shaking him like a rag doll.

Small projectiles tore through the hyena, and Nathan saw the smaller man directing the path of the missiles with his hand.

A huge stone lobster clambered across the body of the beast that had released Nathan's neck, and tore out its throat with thick, rocky claws. The smaller creature dropped off the body of the hyena and to the ground with a thunk, skittering to the next fallen enemy to repeat the maneuver.

Nathan bent and retrieved his weapon, noting the damaged shaft that would need replaced. He hefted the axe and took one step, then the next step, towards a foe.

Nathan watched as the smaller man flung a dagger with the hand not guiding the stones, and the weapon flew at a gnohl's head with unerring precision.

A form coalesced in the path of the magical weapon, snatching it out of the air, and wrapping it in thick burgundy material. A shimmer radiated outward from the dagger and the cloth that covered it. A dull boom, barely audible over the combat, echoed across the hilltop.

The person holding the weapon and cloth was the same he'd met in the Crescent Desert and seen in the battle at Red Wind. She smiled at him, winked, raised her head and screamed a cry, then faded from sight.

The sound of the hideous, broken laughter of hyenas filled the air, and the gnohls raised their heads to join the pack in what felt like celebration.

As one, all the enemies turned and bolted to the north, dodging away from the defenders and making their escape from the hilltop.

The demoness appeared a quarter of a kilometer away, at the tree line at the bottom of the hill. Her wave caught Nathan's eye, and then she turned and disappeared into the forest.

The gnohls and hyenas loped down the hillside, following their master, leaving their dead behind.

"Who the chuz are you?" The deep baritone drew Nathan's attention back to the two men.

## Chapter 11

Nathan turned to answer and saw the barbarian with his weapon held high in combat stance.

"Really," the smaller man's voice sounded strained and panicked, "what're you, like fifteen? Like it matters who he is? This guy shows up from nowhere to save us, someone steals Edsumar, and you're worried about him?"

"He's an unknown," the big man growled. "He could be a plant."

"Yeah, genius," the small man said, "he might be a philodendron or a radish. No! He came in on our side, and I've swept his mind. He's one of us, not from here, just like Edsumar said. We're tied together. Chuz Jack Tucker and all his bullbidj."

The rokairn looked from one man to the other, his brow furrowed, lifting his axe defensively. The shaft cracked noisily as it split, the head of the weapon toppling to the ground.

"Nathan," he muttered, looking at the ground where the important part of his weapon lay stuck, blade first, in the soil, between the bodies of dead and dying enemies.

Fred scampered between the gnohls and hyenas, continuing his task of cutting throats, removing the threat of a foe rising again.

The two were staring at the rokairn, waiting for him to say something else.

"I'm sorry, I'm a jeweler?" Nathan mumbled. "And followed that war band to stop them from…"

The rokairn verbally stumbled to a halt, looking back and forth between the two men.

"A jeweler?" The bigger man asked, lowering his sword. "Your shop must be gangsta as chuz."

"That's what you're worried about?" The Kid shrilled. "I just had a priceless magical artifact snatched, and you're asking about some damn guy's store that sells watches, necklaces, and engagement rings to deluded twenty-somethings?"

Nathan and Torrents looked at the Kid.

"You have a magical weapon?" Nathan asked.

The Kid threw up his hands, huffed, and turned in a circle.

"We need to go after them," the Kid shouted.

"No," Torrents said, "we don't."

The Kid spun to face the barbarian, his face pale and incredulous.

"We don't," Torrents continued, "because I'm tore the chuz up. This guy has a broken weapon. And you, you're a mess right now. And how're you even going to fight when the weapon you always use is gone? Right now, we get somewhere that we can regroup."

"And where exactly is that?" the Kid sneered.

"PepperGarten's," Torrents said, "where we were headed, anyway. He'll know things, too; he always seems to know things."

The kid huffed and threw up his hands again.

"Um, I'm sorry," Nathan interrupted meekly as he dug his axe head out of the ground, "do I go with you?"

"I don't care what you do," the Kid sniped. "Follow, go, whatever. But I say we go after these bastards and get Edsumar back."

"We will, but," Torrents's voice was rising now, "I think we need to go to PepperGarten's first."

"If it counts for anything," Nathan said, and the others turned to look at him, "going after them right now would end up getting everyone killed. One step at a time. And if you can't move in the direction you need to go, then move in the direction that will give you what you need, to do what needs done."

Torrents and the Kid stared at Nathan.

"See?" Torrents shrugged. "He agrees with me. I say we keep him. We can always kill him later if he turns out to be a douchebag or something."

"Thanks?" Nathan gulped.

The Kid harrumphed and turned away.

"Whatever, fine," the Kid sulked, "but I can't even hear Edsumar. Whoever that woman was, she's got him blocked somehow."

"Klendrisia," Nathan offered, and the two looked at him, so he continued, "I'm sorry, she's a demon half-breed. Her father is someone named Lord Ghlevid, and her mother was a human named Delia. She's opening portals for demons to come here and take over."

An awkward moment of silence drew out as the two stared at the rokairn.

"How do you even know all that?" the Kid asked.

"She told me," Nathan shrugged, "back in some desert I was in while she was trying to kill me."

"Do people always get so chatty around you when they're trying to off you?" Torrents asked, wrapping his bloody forearm.

"Not sure," Nathan shrugged again, "people never used to try to kill me, not until recently. In the past week, it's happened way more than I'd ever even thought it could. It's like living in an action movie."

"Can we walk and talk?" The Kid moved south across the hilltop, stepping around the dead bodies scattered across the grass, Fred clattering to match his pace. "If we're going to get Edsumar back, we should get going."

"Okay," Torrents nodded, tugging the end of the cloth into the rest of the bandage around his arm, "but you, Nathan, keep talking. I want to know as much about you as we can before we trust you with a watch when we're sleeping."

The barbarian scooped up his pack he dropped during combat—the Kid already picked up everything he needed to carry—and the two began walking down the hill.

Nathan scrambled after them, undoing the leather harness around his chest designed to hold his axe on his back. As he walked, he attempted to lace the head to the holder, leaving the broken shaft on the ground behind, and get it into place on his back.

"Keep talking," Torrents said when he caught up. "The Kid said you're from our world, and came here just like us? Through some magic?"

"I guess," Nathan said. "When I got shot in the belly, suddenly I was here, in this body, falling down a hill."

"Shot in the belly?" the Kid winced.

"Yeah," the rokairn nodded, "double-barrel shotgun from an employee robbing my shop right after he'd stormed out. I guess he quit. He didn't have to. I just asked about the seventeen-dollar shortage from the night before."

"You think you'd fire him," the Kid snickered, then rubbed at his temples, wincing at the pain in his head, "especially after he fired on you."

"Well," Nathan was flustered and hesitated, "it wasn't like that. Not at first."

"Don't pay the Kid any mind," Torrents said, "just keep talking and ignore him. And, by the way, my name is Torrents, like a torrent of water, but with an 's' at the end."

"Um, okay," Nathan glanced up at the big man, then continued, "I came here, and had an urge to go to some pyramid, the Pyridom of Power, and stop someone or something from opening a portal to let demons into the world. It sounds even crazier when I say it out loud instead of just thinking about it. And it was pretty crazy sounding in my head."

The group worked its way up another hill, the land in front of them an endless series of rolling hills, mostly green and grassy, turning to brown and sandy dunes to the east, and to mountains to the west, leaving the forest behind them in the north.

The sky had an ominous green glow to the southeast, and it looked like the rain to the southwest was headed their way.

"Anyway," Nathan went on, "she came at me soon after I came here, and for some reason told me that stuff. I think I had some magical spells on me, because some of her magic spells didn't work on me. That sounds so weird, but they just bounced off me.

"She left when that green explosion happened. I knew I should go stop it, but…"

Nathan stopped, realizing he sounded like a coward.

"I left," he said, stronger. "This wasn't my fight. I don't like to fight. So, I ran away. I ran until I hit a town. I guess it was a city. Somewhere called Red Wind. I was there less than a week when she showed up with a whole lot of those things and killed most of the town."

"Is that why you followed her?" The Kid asked. "I thought you didn't like to fight?"

"Yeah," Nathan nodded, "it was, and I don't fight."

"You did okay back there," Torrents gestured behind them with his head and wobbled on his feet from the effort, feeling the repercussions of his injuries and slowing down.

Fred pushed through the underbrush to one side of the group, peeking out for a moment to check on them before disappearing again.

"Apparently," Nathan sighed, "I can fight, but I never could before. Never really tried. But when I saw hundreds of people being slaughtered for no reason, well, it wasn't about me anymore. I don't like bullies. I can handle being picked on, but I don't like it when others who can't defend themselves are attacked. It just…makes me mad."

Torrents and the Kid nodded in empathy and understanding.

The Kid had given the larger man a shoulder to lean on, helping support him through the difficult terrain.

"I tried to protect people," Nathan shook his head, "but there were so many of those dog-headed things, those gnohls, and they were killing everything around them. Those huge, prehistoric hyenas ran through the streets in packs, tearing through people, not even eating what they'd killed.

"I tried to stop them," the rokairn continued, "but I got stuck in an intersection with them coming at me from all sides. There was a guy with me, he worked in the jeweler's store I'd stopped at, his name was Nob. He stood back-to-back with me, or maybe we were side by side, but he was there, and they got him.

"I watched him," Nathan's voice broke. "He was trying to help, because of me, and I watched him get torn apart, an arm's length away from me. I watched these monsters rip into him, and how they laughed. That damned hyena laugh coming from the men things and the beast things…"

"Hey," the Kid's hand was on Nathan's shoulder, shaking him gently, "it's okay. You did good, man. You did what you could, and that's all any of us can do, okay?"

Nathan realized he'd stopped walking, and the other two had stopped as well. He was shaking, his face contorted as he tried to bring himself under control and failed.

The rokairn cracked, and clenched his jaw, and shut his eyes, a sob ripping from him and tears streaming down his face.

The other two comforted him, Torrents awkwardly patting him, and the Kid hugging Nathan close to his chest and smoothing the rokairn's hair.

"That was a good, ugly cry," the Kid said a few minutes later, when Nathan cried himself out.

"Sorry about that," Nathan mumbled, wiping at his face with the back of his hand, "I haven't done something like that in a long time."

"Sometimes," the Kid held a square of linen cloth out, and the rokairn took it, "that's what we need. We're in a weird world, and it takes time to get used to it. Throw some of the things we see on top of it, and it can break you. But that's why we've got each other. I guess."

"Yeah," Torrents looked away, leaning on a tree and breathing heavily, "what the Kid said."

The Kid laughed and turned to look at the barbarian, a retort ready, but when he saw the big man swaying, he cut it off.

"You ready to go?" the Kid asked Nathan, who nodded. "Good, then help me with him and keep talking. It helps keep his dumb mind off the pain."

Nathan nodded.

The two moved to Torrents, positioning themselves on each side to help him walk.

"What happened after that," Torrents panted, the words coming out one by one, "how'd you get here?"

Nathan took a moment to collect his thoughts.

"As Nob was falling," Nathan gulped, "to the street, four people rushed out to help us. They had magic, too. They did something, and one of their hands glowed, and I felt better. Revived, refreshed."

"Sounds like holy magics," the Kid said, and Torrents nodded.

"That's when I saw Klendrisia again," Nathan steadied the barbarian, "she was watching me, smiling. Then she turned and left, letting out a scream like she did today. All the monsters followed her.

"These people, the holy people," Nathan hesitated, "priests, I guess, carried Nob away. I don't know if he made it, but I sure hope he did."

"They said they were part of the Church of Jonath," Nathan continued, "the holy people who helped us, I mean. They gave me a mission, well, they did after they let me clean up. They also offered to fix up the holes in my chain mail and bang the dents out of my bits of armor that needed it. They did more magic stuff to me, and even gave me a necklace with their little god icon on it."

"That's called a holy symbol. And what mission?" The Kid urged, trying to keep him talking.

"To hunt the demoness," Nathan sighed, "to stop her from hurting more people. Maybe even all the people. They said if I did good, they'd even make me a member of their church or something."

As they crested the next hill, the three saw a massive willow tree, and a tiny, thin man with a white, scruffy beard. The man stared at them, hands on his hips, with a sour look on his face.

# Chapter 12

"So," the wiry man's voice was high-pitched and urgent, "you got rid of the cranky lady, eh?"

Fred pushed forward through the knee-high grass toward the new person, his claws clacking.

"We didn't bump her off," the Kid was supporting Torrents as they moved down the hill, shouting at the old man below them, "if that's what you mean."

"Naw," the man danced from one foot to the other, shaking his hands above his head, "she'da kicked allya asses anyway, so PepperGarten knows that means she got tired of you and bailed on ya."

"It didn't quite happen like that," the Kid rolled his eyes.

"PepperGarten sees you got a replacement, didn't have anything in your size?" the old man cackled, "And what the hell happened to the big dumb guy?"

"Hello PepperGarten," Torrents's words slurred, "I was hoping you'd be out or something so I could come here and die in peace."

"He got in a fight with some ratmen," the Kid sighed, "got poisoned, wouldn't stay in bed to get better, took a two-day flight on dragon-back, fought some gnohls, and then walked for a couple hours to see you."

"Yeah," Torrents breathed, "that last one is the worst part of all that. Can we go inside?"

PepperGarten cackled and jigged in a tight circle.

"No sense of decorum," PepperGarten said, "aren't you going to introduce PepperGarten to the new guy?"

"Yeah, sure," a wide smile crossed the Kid's face. "Nathan, this crazy old coot is PepperGarten. PepperGarten, this is Nathan. Say hello to my little friend!"

Torrents coughed out a laugh, and his knees buckled.

The Kid and Nathan squeezed in tighter to stop the big man from toppling.

"Don't make me laugh," Torrents wheezed.

"Let's get him inside," PepperGarten danced to one side and gestured towards the massive willow tree, "before we end up having to get the shovels. For his grave. To dig it. Because he died. Right here. Before we took him inside."

"Yes, yes," the Kid began helping Torrents forward, "we get it, you don't need to explain it. It's not funny if you have to explain it."

"Maybe to you," PepperGarten giggled, "but to PepperGarten, it's sometimes even funnier when PepperGarten explains it."

Nathan looked around as he helped the Kid walk Torrents in the direction the old man had indicated.

Fred ran around PepperGarten's feet, who let out a squeal.

"What the heckity, heck, hecking, is that thing?" the old man screeched.

"That's Fred," the Kid said over his shoulder. "He's my rock lobster. I made him."

"Interesting." PepperGarten leaned down to inspect the magical construct closer. "PepperGarten sees threads. Fred has threads. Fred threads. He might come in handy one day, but PepperGarten bets you have one hell of a headache. Good job, lad!"

The Kid glanced sideways at the old man and grunted as he guided Torrents forward.

They were on a lawn of sorts. It had the feel of the yard of the old lady Nathan remembered from his childhood. The woman never mowed her lawn or trimmed anything back, making her whole yard one continuous garden.

The rokairn saw vegetables, berry bushes, wildflowers, and a small clearing with stones—large enough to sit on—surrounding a fire pit. Chest high hedges wove their way around the perimeter of the area.

Squirrels and chipmunks darted through the trees and underbrush, and birds chirped and called from all around.

The tree itself was high up on the hillside, its wide, drooping roots and branches hiding the entrance to the earthworks under its boughs.

The four stepped under the tree's protection as rain started falling; a fox darted past them and into the man-sized hole in the mound's side, curtains pushed to one side of the opening.

Torrents collapsed to the hard-packed earth of the floor, and PepperGarten capered past the trio to wooden shelves jammed into the dirt walls.

The Kid flumped onto a grassy tuffet, pulling off his boots, and shaking the loose contents collected on the journey onto the floor.

"Hey!" PepperGarten screamed, and the fox looked up from cleaning her belly, "who do you think has to clean that up?"

"No one," the Kid said without looking up, "it's a dirt floor and you don't own a broom."

"Oh yeah," PepperGarten's face brightened, and he turned back to the shelves and began pulling down herbs, "smart of PepperGarten, wasn't that? Cut off his wrappings, would ya, Nathan?"

Nathan watched the old man plop berries and moss into a large wooden bowl on top of the herbs.

The rokairn squatted down next to Torrents and swung his satchel from his shoulder. He drew out a small knife, unsheathed it, and began cutting away the bandages.

"Do you have any water, please," Nathan asked, "so I can wash his injuries?"

"Yup!" PepperGarten answered with an upbeat tone, then began whistling and humming at the same time, creating an off-key melody that couldn't be followed.

"I'll get it for you," the Kid stood and patted Nathan's shoulder, "PepperGarten can be a bit…difficult to communicate with."

The Kid moved across the cramped space to a hole in the wall that served as a window and picked up an earthenware bowl.

The smell of rain wafted in, acrid and sharp, and birds crowded under the bow of the tree outside. Three groundhogs sat on their hind legs in the doorway, watching everything going on inside with dark, beady eyes.

PepperGarten was adding bits and pieces of the ingredients he'd gathered to a smaller bowl cradled in the crook of his arm. Picking up a mortar, he crushed them into a paste, all the while bouncing from one foot to the other.

The Kid set the bowl down next to Nathan and dropped another linen into it.

Nathan nodded, and began wiping the crusted and caked dirt, blood, and other matter from the wounds.

Fred crept into sight, just outside the door, his rock legs clicking on the steppingstones, then rushed past the groundhogs, causing them to bark and scatter. The fox looked up from her grooming to watch the new animal.

Two ferrets scampered across the floor, coming nose to carapace with Fred. The rock lobster was the size of a medium dog and outsized the two curious creatures many times over.

Fred clacked his pincers, and the two ferrets did a little bouncing, bounding dance that reminded Nathan of how PepperGarten moved.

The Kid moved away from where he'd been standing over Nathan and Torrents, rubbing his temples. He stopped, facing the corner, sighed, and ran his hands through his hair, plastering it to his head and pulling on it.

Releasing his scalp, the Kid turned around, put his back to the wall, slowly slid to the floor, and rested his arms on his knees, dropping his face to stare at the ground between his feet.

PepperGarten glanced at the Kid, slowing his little dance to take in the young man's posture, still mashing the mixture in the ceramic bowl.

"How'd you lose him?" PepperGarten looked back at his mixture, pretending indifference. "He leave you for a troll or something?"

The Kid looked up, startled. His mouth twisted with a retort, then went slack with a long outtake of breath.

"No," the Kid's voice was soft and far away, "I wish. That'd be easier. Some demon-lady took him, but not sure why."

"Klendrisia," Nathan offered, "that's who took him."

"Oh," PepperGarten drew the word out to three syllables, "she's a tough cookie, that's for sure. And since she's already got the Pyridom primed, but we aren't swarming with demons, PepperGarten would guess she's looking to open the network."

"The what?" The Kid tilted his head and squinted up at the bald man.

"Network," PepperGarten cackled, moving around the room and lighting candles in the dim light of the storm outside, "like a computer network, interlinked machines, or maybe networking at a party where you make connections you can call upon for purpose, or maybe like your neural network. You know, millions of interconnecting nodes of information and resources set to trigger specific events within your brain? It's like that, but spans more than just your brain, more than just this solar system, more than the Milky Way, and even more than our one remote universe. In the best terms, it spans the multi-verse."

"Multi-verse?" the Kid asked.

"Like in the X-men," Nathan offered, "or scifi. Parallel universes, or just other realties that can bump into ours and interact on some level."

"Eggs-actly!" PepperGarten beamed at the rokairn like he was a prize-winning heifer. "But the X-Men were just a group of masked kids when PepperGarten last read them in the 70's. Oh, as for the network here, the Pyridom of Power was a doorway to these things. Just like the Highest Spire and the Nine Towers of Magic, though they just tapped the energy of that network. Like a cosmic set of ley lines, and the mages would just syphon off the magic—or so they called it, but it's just energies that humans and others evolved the ability to sense and use—to do bigger and better experiments with. But it can be used to open doorways to other places. Like Hell, Limbo, Gladsheim, Nirvana, Gehenna, the Abyss, the Ethereal Plane, the Astral, and so on."

"What?" the Kid was still confused. "Why? Why would they want to do that?"

"Oh, any number of reasons," PepperGarten added a splash of vinegar to the mix, "to get our resources, take over our world for slave labor or food, or even just make a jumping point to another reality. The troöds have been working on it for almost 70,000 years!"

"Troöds?" the Kid asked.

"Yeah," PepperGarten nodded somberly, "alien, shape-shifting folk, sorta squid-like, but most people think they're reptilian. They waged full war against us about thirty years ago when the Talisman was around. You know, that magical comet that got stuck in orbit and made necromantic and conjuring magic go uber crazy?

"But enough about that," the old man moved to stand over Torrents and shooed Nathan away, "PepperGarten has some healing to do before things go sideways."

The old man knelt by Torrents's side and slathered the mixture into the barbarian's wounds.

Green sprouts pushed their way through the gooey mess, knitting around one another and pulling the injuries tight.

Torrents winced but smiled through gritted teeth.

"Thanks," the barbarian said to the old man with a nod.

"Why're you the one always getting hurt?" PepperGarten asked. "Don't you got enough sense to get out of the way of things trying to kill you?"

"Apparently not," the Kid quipped.

"How about this?" The hermit stood to his full height and stretched. "How about PepperGarten shows you how it's done?"

"And how are you gonna do that, old man?" Torrents asked, smiling despite himself.

"The next murderous bastard to come through the door," PepperGarten cackled, and turned to face the opening as if expecting it happen any moment, "PepperGarten will be their target, and you can see how PepperGarten doesn't get hurt because PepperGarten isn't dumb."

"Great," Torrents sighed, "PepperGarten doesn't mind if Torrents just lays here while we wait, does PepperGarten?"

"Why you talking like that?" PepperGarten shot an annoyed glance over his shoulder at the barbarian. "You sound like a pemtie."

"I'm talking like you do," Torrents grumped.

"No, you're not," the old man turned back to the door, "because when PepperGarten does it, PepperGarten doesn't sound like a pemtie."

The hermit put his hands on his hips, lifted his chin, thrust out his chest, and waited.

The Kid and Nathan exchanged glances, and the Kid smiled and shrugged at the rokairn.

A boom of thunder rattled the room.

The animals in the room went silent, turning towards the door. They stopped moving, licking, scampering, or playing. Even Fred went still.

In a flurry of movement, the creatures in the room bolted for cover, except for Fred, who moved to stand between the Kid and the door.

The doorway darkened with a figure, a glowing red blade in its hand.

## Chapter 13

Lightning flashes and sheets of rain silhouetted the tall, thin form in the doorway, his carrot-orange hair glowing in the afterimage.

Water glistened on the black leather of the man's armor, and a short sword hung at his side.

The Kid gasped and leapt to his feet, his hand reaching for Edsumar, the magical weapon that was no longer there.

Torrents moaned and passed out as the medicine took its toll and worked its healing magic.

"Told you something bad was coming," PepperGarten snickered, raising his chin further, "this guy is bad news."

The man in the door moved forward with inhuman speed, crossing to the old man in a blink, slashing across PepperGarten's midsection with the glowing blade.

It sparked, the red of the dagger blending with green druidic magic in a purplish burst.

In a flurry of movement, the man struck the druid again and again.

Gashes appeared in PepperGarten's chest, belly, and face. Lines of violet eldritch energy appeared, connecting with one another, and becoming a dull green glow.

PepperGarten collapsed to his knees, hooting.

"That's," he gasped, clutching his midsection and cackling, "how you take a hit. Now, do the thing…"

The old man fell face first onto the dirt floor, rolling to one side.

"Avenge," he said, his voice soft, "PepperGarten."

The room grew quiet.

"Where's the Dragon's Dagger, boy?" The newcomer rasped.

"Edsumar?" the Kid said, pulling two daggers from sheaths. "You came here, for Edsumar? Why, Mezk?"

"To add it, and your corpse," Mezk growled, "to my collection."

The intruder moved again, his form blending with the shadows as candles guttered in the wind created from his movement.

The Kid raised his weapons, barely in time, to deflect the soul-sucking blade Mezk wielded.

Metal struck metal, and the Kid cried out, a burst of energy flaring with each strike on his weapons.

One blow struck true, and bit deep into the Kid's shoulder.

"No!" Nathan screamed, running forward, a hand-axe in each hand, slashing at the leather-clad enemy.

Fred charged at the intruder's ankles, his stone claws missing as the tall man danced around the attack, lifting his feet like he was tiptoeing through puddles and not wanting to get his dark boots wet.

The fox screamed its cry and ran at the intruder, snapping at his knees.

The remaining animals scurried for cover, hiding from the fight.

"Don't let PepperGarten die in vain," PepperGarten giggled, rolling into a ball, vines growing from his body and wrapping around him to create a cocoon. "Make it count for something."

The Kid pressed his attack, moving Mezk back across the small chamber in his furious series of strikes.

Mezk drew the short sword from across his body with his left hand, swinging wide and causing the Kid to bend backwards to avoid the slash.

Kneeling as he parried the Kid's blows, Mezk stabbed the magical dagger into PepperGarten's body again and again, draining the druid's soul. The Kid remembered the man doing this in Durgan's Keep, even to his own fallen comrades, taking their spirit to power his demonic weapon.

The red of the blade dimmed each time, and rose in intensity when withdrawn, purple light flashing each time he struck the old man.

Mezk was gritting his teeth and glaring at the Kid.

The Kid focused his magics on the enemy, searching for a mental chink in the man's mind. The dagger stabbing into PepperGarten's body pulsed and brightened.

The Kid felt his attention drawn to the weapon as it called to him, and the mind-mage responded without wanting to. The Kid's concentration zeroed in on the blade, watching the heartbeat-like pulsing that matched his pounding head, and being drawn into it.

A sharp sensation of pain cut across the back of the Kid's head, but inside the skull, just as the dark blade in Mezk's hand burst into a flare.

The Kid felt his mind slip. His eyes rolled into his head, and his body crumpled as his knees went forward, and his shoulders fell backwards.

The Kid hit the floor with a dull thump, his head bouncing twice on the hard-packed dirt before he lay twitching and spasming, thick white froth creeping through his lips.

Nathan was upon the foe, setting his feet wide, and chopping at the carrot-topped attacker.

Mezk weaved to one side, then the other, dodging each blow without effort.

"We don't have that cursed weapon," Nathan shouted. "Did the demon-lady, Klendrisia, send you to get it? It's too late. She already got it."

"You don't have it?" Mezk hesitated, and Nathan's axe sliced into his shoulder.

Mezk grunted and returned to the defensive, standing and swatting Nathan's weapons away.

The man struck out with his dagger and slashed across Nathan's face.

The rokairn screamed and stumbled backwards, dropping his axes to clutch at his cheek.

Pulling his wet fingers from his face, Nathan looked at them, then looked around the room. Torrents was unconscious, the Kid was having some sort of fit, and PepperGarten was a broken and torn mess in the middle of it all.

Nathan hated bullies; he'd dealt with them all of his life. People who pushed others around and took whatever they wanted just because they could. This man, Mezk, with his glowing blade, had shown up here to take something that wasn't his. He'd killed PepperGarten just because the old man was in the way. The intruder wanted to do more than just hurt the Kid and would do so if no one stopped him. And Nathan was the only one left besides a few scared animals.

The fox was still nipping at Mezk, dancing away to stay out of the reach of his weapon.

Nathan felt pressure building up inside of him. His head had a dull thumping at the base of his skull. It matched the pounding of his heart and the intake and release of each breath. But it was peaceful at the same time, like when you accept something that's inevitable.

He pulled all that in with the next breath, held it—not tight inside of himself, but gently, like holding a baby bird in your cupped hands—then he released it, and a wave ushered out and away from him. It wasn't a burst, and there wasn't any physical indication that it happened, other than Mezk stumbling backwards and his dagger dimming for a moment.

Fred darted in, clamoring over the Kid's still spasming body, and latched onto Mezk's ankle and the bone crunched under the stone claw.

The thin man wrenched his leg from the construct's grip and limped backwards. The magical glow of the dagger in his hand intensified, bathing the room in an eerie light. The sound of bone and sinew knitting—a crackling sound like cartilage popping—filled the area, and Mezk sneered and moved towards the door.

"Then I will have to collect the souls from your corpses," the street thug said, "and revel in imprisoning them some other time."

His form bled into the shadows, and he was standing outside in the rain a moment later.

"PepperGarten dies, again," the fallen druid muttered. "Avenge PepperGarten, so PepperGarten may live, again."

The rokairn looked from the dissipating form outside to the form on the floor, encased in writhing vines and branches.

When he looked back at Mezk, the man was gone.

"Ungh," PepperGarten's voice was faint in his cocoon, coming in broken phrases, "so poorly done…PepperGarten…would have beat him up…more better. The…better-est."

The man on the floor sighed and went silent.

The fox ran to PepperGarten, scratching at the wooden carapace and whining. The animals that had hid in corners were creeping out to survey the scene.

Ferrets ran from the corners of the room, leaping onto shelves and knocking wooden cups to the floor. The groundhogs made a beeline for the door, pausing to raise on their hindquarters, sniffing the air, then darted outside into the storm, abandoning the scene within.

Nathan looked around, taking in the scene again, exhaustion coming over him. His weapons lay at his feet, and he moved away slowly until his back hit the wall, sliding down to a sitting position. Dropping his head into his hands, he sighed, his breath catching in his throat.

Nathan never had to take care of anything in his life, and now he had the dead and dying surrounding him. It was overwhelming.

He'd been responsible for mowing the lawn when he was younger. It was a job, of sorts, at his grandmother's house when he was fifteen. She paid him ten dollars every week to show up and mow.

He started out, like any teenager, grudgingly. But with time, he came to like it. It took an hour to do—she had a large lawn, and he'd used her mower that had been his grandfather's—and he'd put on his headset attached to his music player and spent an hour in isolation with nothing troubling his mind. He'd walk back and forth, mowing and getting that time to himself with no other worries in the world. He came to love that solitary time, collecting his thoughts without any other pressures.

The memory was a light touch on his mind, making him smile, and oddly enough, reminding him of his turtle, Sheldon.

Sheldon was a box turtle, nothing special, just a run-of-the-mill turtle. He had (at least Nathan had assumed it was a boy, but it may have been a girl, he never had it checked) raised Sheldon since he was tiny. That turtle, who he'd gotten in sixth grade, was the first creature that had ever relied on Nathan.

He'd found him in a mall parking lot, gingerly moving across blazing hot asphalt, looking like he wouldn't make it to safety.

Nathan picked it up, and showed it to his parents, tears in his eyes, crying about how the poor thing wouldn't survive the cold northern winter. His parents let him take it home but insisted he pay for the ten-gallon tank, and other necessities, from his allowance.

He'd agreed, without argument, wanting to see the little guy survive and be happy. Making trips to the local pet store and library, he searched for books on how to care for Sheldon. He'd bought all the leafy greens the turtle ever needed, shredded carrots, and even had given treats to the turtle.

Later, he learned his parents didn't always take the money from his allowance, but he paid for most of it.

He'd kept Sheldon for almost two decades before passing him on to a reptile preserve when he'd opened his business and couldn't care for him any longer.

It broke his heart to give up his little friend; he was the one being in the entire world who'd ever relied on him for his every need.

And now, two unconscious men, a dead guy, and a bunch of panicked creatures who needed him surrounded Nathan.

Nathan wasn't used to being needed. He was the quiet guy who no one ever expected anything of, but he always liked helping others.

He choked, literally. The pressure overwhelmed him, and a racking sob came out. He had to step up, or everyone he'd met in this world—except for the ones who'd tried to kill him—would end up dead. Most of them lay at his feet at that very moment.

The rokairn sat, sniffling on the outside, but a flood of emotion on the inside. He knew what had to be done. He'd done difficult things before, but it was always for himself. In fact, opening the jewelry shop was a way to push others away from him. It allowed him the perfect excuse for not going to a movie, or dinner with friends, or to see his family. The business always needed him.

Now, someone needed him, and he couldn't run or turn away.

Nathan stood, wiping at his blood-streaked face with the back of his arm. The cut from the magical blade had already closed, cauterized from whatever burst from him had made Mezk leave.

The Kid first; he needed the most help. Torrents passed out in a healing way, or something like that. PepperGarten was dead, so he could wait until last.

Nathan glanced around for a shovel, knowing he'd need that before the day was done. Then he scolded himself, mentally, for the caustic thought that at least PepperGarten came with his own coffin.

## Chapter 14

Klendrisia held the small, burning sphere in her palm, the orange glow matching the setting sun through the broken archway to the west.

Ghe'hak the Ravager barked orders, literally, as the primitive hyenas circled the area on chaotic patrols, their cackles echoing through the hills. Meanwhile, the gnohls built campfires and squabbled amongst themselves.

The demon half-breed stared into the globe of energy above her hand, watching the human with the red soul blade moving through the rainstorm to the south, tracking her and her war band.

She debated killing him, toying with him, or using him. The smart option would be the first or third idea. Her father would say to toy with the mortal. He'd insisted their demonic lives were so long and extended that if you didn't play with your lessers, then you'd die bored when they finally killed you. He'd also point out that if you're involved with their lives, they can never truly sneak up on you. And if they do, then you weren't paying attention, and deserved steel between your shoulder blades.

When her father pushed her, she wondered if she was merely another lesser to be toyed with.

She sighed, knowing she didn't have to wonder; that's exactly what she was to him. She just wanted to be more in his eyes. Someone he'd appreciate, rely on, and even respect. He'd never given her any sort of encouragement, saying she'd done well, or that he was proud of her.

But she didn't care about that stuff, not really. She thought about it, but that didn't mean she cared. It twisted her gut when she thought too long about it, but that was because she couldn't stomach his arrogance at not recognizing her worth. Eventually, she'd make him admit to her value and abilities, even if it meant steel between his shoulder blades.

He'd never see it coming from her. It wasn't that he thought she didn't have it in her; he didn't think that far ahead and never even considered her true potential.

It was the lack of consideration that made her decide to turn her mission from him into her own agenda.

Maybe this other human, the one tracking her, could be a useful tool.

Klendrisia shifted, her dark-green skin tones paling into a deep olive hue, her clothes melting to something the man following would find more appealing. Her rusted chain mail melted away into a high-collared leather corset, crisscrossed lacing knitting down her sternum. Her wide leather belt melted from brown to black and stretched down her legs to form an open-fronted leather skirt attached to the corset with polished silver rings.

The demoness's hair lengthened and spun around itself, become a replica of large horns on her head, beaded tassels looping downward in a decorative fashion popular in the southern continents of this world. A ring appeared in her nose, matching those on her corset, and similar rings popped into existence, lining both ears, as a chain grew along her left cheek to connect the two.

Men were weak in that respect; appearances. They thought they could be the stronger sex by sheer force and muscle, never realizing the value of strengthening their minds as well as bodies. They trusted their eyes instead of their guts, especially when it came to women. Not because they were dumb, but because they never even gave a second thought to the idea that a woman could best them, deceive them, or break them through their own pemtie, limited arrogance.

Klendrisia had done exactly that many times. Sometimes with steel, sometimes with her will, but the result was always the same. She won.

She wasn't prone to losing; it didn't suit her. In fact, she'd claim she'd never lost. Not once. Any time she didn't come out on top, whatever man thought he'd won, lost all ability to think of her as a threat. They wouldn't kill her, didn't imprison her, merely thought they'd beat her down like some dumb bitch of a dog, and that she'd simply be cowed and follow along behind them without complaint.

Most of them had died with a surprised look on their face, but some never even had a chance to do that much. She wasn't pemtie, like men seeking vengeance. Her purpose when killing someone was to remove an obstacle, not feed some pathetic egotistical need to be recognized in that person's last breath. What did it matter if someone knew you were the one who killed them a few seconds before they died? It served no purpose and presented the chance for the enemy to react. Better they only see the floor rising to meet their face before dying. The most they could do then was to put out their hands to break their fall, before feeling the pool of their still hot blood gathering around them.

This man coming for her would be no different. She knew he'd failed to kill the rokairn. There was something different about that warrior; he smelled of foreign magics. No, that wasn't quite right, it wasn't magics he smelled of. It was reality. He wasn't from this place, and she was curious if he could lead her to somewhere else. Somewhere her father and others weren't already competing for. Somewhere the people would never expect a demonic invasion. If such a place existed.

What sort of backwards plane of existence could ever be ignorant of other realities waiting to attack at any moment?


Mezk slogged along the muddy swath left behind the army of creatures who had wounded the Kid and his group.

What happened got to him. He had to run. Not that he hadn't run away from a fight before, that wasn't the issue. It was the fact they were supposed to be weak, and the prize should have been laying there, easy pickings, just waiting for him to snatch it up.

The barbarian—who'd been sitting in a boat beside him, six months ago, as Mezk sized the man up—had been unconscious on the floor. The old man just stood there, waiting to be slaughtered. And the Kid, oh the Kid, he was supposed to be the only one there who mattered, and that was to be his true reward, killing the damn Kid.

Mezk had paid for the golem to be created, its only mission to kill the Kid and recover the Dragon's Dagger. But it had failed, and the Kid had transformed it into the creature that followed him now. The mini construct's magics were not unimpressive, way more powerful than the Kid realized, and were constantly being fueled by the Kid's abilities. It crippled his mind-magics, and Mezk had to wonder if his enemy realized what was happening to him.

That snot-nosed runt had been a thorn in his side for years, pulling the carpet from under his feet way too often. You expected rivalries and competition, but the Kid never even took it seriously. He never cared if he won or lost, just that he'd messed up somebody else's plans.

Six months ago, that'd been stepped up even more. When the Kid saved Durgan's Keep, but when he'd stuck with his new friends instead of gathering the scattered forces of the criminal underground, people had whispered. When the Kid left Durgan's Keep helping his friends, people had talked. Eventually, the Kid returned alone and began disrupting every criminal and illegal act he could find, and the people rejoiced.

After that, no one feared the gangs, the mob bosses, the enforcers, or any other arm of the underground. Well, they did if you were in their face, but once you were out of sight…the public was getting way too ballsy. The Kid was the reason for their newfound self-reliance and needed to be taken out.

The Kid had a bounty on his head, too, and it wasn't anything to sneeze at, either. But that wasn't the real reason Mezk wanted his nemesis dead.

The Kid had a magical dagger, though no one was sure where he'd gotten it from. It did cool tricks, which was enough for most folks, but not for Mezk.

His own dagger—the Demon Seed, a soul stealer—hungered for the other weapon. Mezk's dagger couldn't communicate, besides the urge of base emotions and wants, and it was pushing him to find this other item that housed an intelligence. If the blood dagger could absorb the Dragon's Dagger, it could grow into something much more powerful.

The wielder of such an artifact would be in an extremely unique situation.

Mezk knew what it was like to be powerless. When he was a child, he saw the man—who may or may not have been his father—beat his mother and send Mezk to the streets to bring home coins by begging or stealing. He'd done this, as commanded, hoping the man would become his best friend and give him smiles instead of beatings.

Mezk lost two fingers in his seventh year. One to the constable, who caught him stealing a fish to eat. The other to that man who lived in his apartment and beat him until he could only gasp instead of breathing.

His finger was cut off when he failed to bring the requisite thirteen coppers or more home one night. The big man—breath reeking of rotting and the sour bitters he drank by the quart—held the boy's hand down to the table. The blade used wasn't very intimidating. It hadn't been especially large, and definitely wasn't very sharp. It took nearly three minutes for the large man to saw through the digit, rubbing against the still healing nub of the finger the constable had taken much more swiftly.

The pain was incredible, but it wasn't the worst part. That went to the dull, passionless stare of the broken man doing the deed.

Mezk didn't even remember the man's name, but he remembered the hollow look as the man sawed off his finger, like some sort of automaton. The man didn't even seem to know, or care, what he was doing. It was just something that had to be done, like breathing or bidjing.

Since that moment, Mezk had seen men revel in torture, and glorify the pain they gave to others. That, he could understand. He could respect the passion and high that came with the power and control over others.

But he'd be damned if he'd ever be like the nameless, slack-jawed bastard in his mother's house.

Mezk left that night. Stumbled out into the hallway, dizzy from the loss of blood from a finger that hadn't been cauterized or bound.

The fevers came in a day or two, and the boy had laid in an alley; shivering, vomiting, and bidjing on himself.

An old woman had found him and took him in. At the time he'd thought her old, but now that he'd passed her age, he knew she'd just lived a life that crumples a soul like a scribe with wasted parchment. He'd thought she was kind, and he was lucky.

Until a couple weeks later, when she took him to market, and sold him to a sallow-skinned man who beat the lessons of the street into the boy who thought he'd had it rough before.

In the beginning, he went hungry more often than he ate, having to fight for every scrap. He learned to find food in piles of scraps dumped into alleys, fighting cats and rats to get enough to stay alive, and how to avoid the things that would cause him to lose everything he ate, out of one end or the other.

He learned to wash enough that he could approach a mark, but not so much that his target thought he had a real home. He learned to hear the muted clink of coin in a pouch, and how to tell which leg would collapse easier if he fell in front of someone limping.

And then he learned to kill.

Killing changed everything. In a few months, with a burst of puberty, Mezk went from a starving street rat to teen runner working for a boss. All because of a few stiff bodies.

But there had still been a layer above him, standing on his back, keeping him down. He fought his way up that, too. Only to find there was another level above what he'd thought was the top.

That was when he met Zklypyllik, a demon claiming to wield great power, with the ability to free Mezk from his earthly restraints. They'd made a pact, and Mezk was freed from the bonds of the world he was born into and shackled with the bonds of his agreement and otherworldly restraints.

Now, he sought to break those bonds, to be chained to no one else ever again. Not to the man who'd cut off a child's fingers, not to some back-alley rat herder who used children to fill his beggar's pockets, not to a guild master of assassins, not to some demon, and not to the specter of the Kid who laughed at life.

It wasn't fair that the Kid got to live like that, and never pay the price. So Mezk would steal the Dragon's Dagger, feed it to the Demon Seed—a weapon given to him to use as part of the pact—and then he'd be free. No one would control Mezk ever again.

But until then, the weapon came at a price. It could heal him—as it had done with his missing fingers, and in the druid's burrow when that magical stone lobster had shattered his ankle—but there was a cost. It fed on him—if he didn't give it others to feed on. And right now, it was sick. Feeding on the cocooned druid had done something to the dagger, and waves of urges and illness randomly ebbed and flowed from the extra-planar weapon. It fed on Mezk's mind and soul, seeking something to sustain itself until it could heal.

Mezk slowed to a stop at the apex of a large hill. In the distance, three hillocks away, was a camp writhing with activity. Gnohls and hyenas swarmed around the base and crown of the encampment, barking and yelping. There was a meal worth offering to the Demon Seed.

And a single figure, an orange globe of crackling energy levitating above her hand, waited on the hilltop between him and the camp. He could see her smile in the setting sun as she watched him.

The dagger pulsed, and the urge to move towards the woman overwhelmed him.

## Chapter 15

He'd searched the shed-like lean-to outside for a shovel and dug a grave for the vine-wrapped old man. By the time the other two woke, the next morning, Nathan had buried their host, and built a stone cairn over the grave. He'd pulled rocks from the hillside, the innate senses of his body knowing where to look for them, and how to hammer them to break them to a useable size.

Once he'd built the memorial, a single wooden shaft grew from the rocks within an hour. It rose as high as his shoulder, vines wrapping themselves around the bottom, middle, and top. No branches sprouted, and no leaves grew from it.

When Nathan reached out to touch it, it fell into his hand, and he later swore it was warm to the touch. It had startled him, and he jumped backwards, scared he'd desecrated the grave of the man who'd saved the lives of the two men inside.

As he stared at the short staff, runes glowed amongst the vine wrappings, their familiar script catching his eye. Moving closer to look at them, his mind twisted at the sight. They weren't in the rokairn script, or the common human trading language, they were in English.

"Life grown from stone," the familiar words read, "tended with care, brings together the elements of earth, water, and air. Use it as passion, in the art of war, use the fire, to meld with steel, and to protect evermore."

Nathan hadn't believed in magic, but he'd seen enough since…arriving—if that was the right word—in this world. The memories of his body related stone and earth to the god, Jonath, water to Jonath's daughter, Tarra, air to Jonath's wife, Latress, and passion, war, and fire to Jonath's son, Torr. The idea of protecting people made Nathan's blood sing.

It felt weird.

Nothing in Nathan's life made his blood sing. He hadn't thought of the concept. But when he read the words on the staff, his body—and perhaps even his soul—reacted.

His pulse quickened, not in the cardiac event sort of way, but in a way that made him stand taller, with determination and purpose rising inside him. It called to him, it…sang to him. And the way only music can, it inspired him.

He was chanting in rokairn, and it was solemn, full, and rich. It held generations of meaning and resolve. He lifted the short staff from the ground, and the thought of Marcid—his double-headed war axe that was missing a shaft—flooded his mind.

An hour later, he stood bare-chested in front of a pyre, wood piled taller than he was, and burning to twice his height, even in the constant drizzle. He wasn't sure how he'd gathered the wood, or how he'd gotten it lit. He just knew he was pulling Marcid from the flames, as they were both surrounded by the four elements of these gods, and his beloved weapon was whole again.

Her blade gleamed in the lightning, blessed by Latress. Tarra washed away the soot and cooled the passion of the flames that came from Torr. And the steel and root of the tree had been the gift of Jonath.

Then Nathan felt the need to nap. He was exhausted. His head was muddled and swimming, like he'd been disconnected and in some sort of trance.

Torrents shook Nathan's shoulder and called his name, as the Kid leaned against the wall, watching.

Nathan was curled up to Marcid and had been snoring gently. The rokairn jerked awake, blinking his eyes as he looked around.

"Come on, man, we need to go," Torrents said, turning away and gathering his things.

"Where's PepperGarten?" the Kid asked.

"Um, sorry," Nathan muttered, his eyes turned down and studying his hands. "He didn't make it. I buried him outside."

Ten minutes later, the Kid kneeled over PepperGarten's grave, sobbing openly. Torrents stood quietly, holding his face up to the rain as they both paid their respects.

To one side, Nathan shuffled his feet, looking anywhere except at the two men.

Torrents laid a hand on Nathan's shoulder, drawing his attention up to the man's face. The barbarian gripped the rokairn's shoulder for a few seconds, looking into his eyes, then nodded.

Torrents turned away, and the Kid was standing behind him, wiping at his face.

"That's his way of saying thank you," the Kid snuffled. "I do it a bit differently."

The Kid hugged Nathan, muttering 'thank you' a half dozen times, a sad smile on his boyish face that spoke of years of pain from losing people.

The three gathered food and supplies from the hole under the tree.

That's all it was now. The animals were gone, disappearing into the grey weather. The interior was just a damp, chill hole. The life inside had come from PepperGarten and was gone now.

They left in silence, only the glup-slosh of their footsteps in the mud marking their passage. Within minutes, the slumped willow tree and the paradise beneath were nothing more than a shadowed memory.

Nothing more of interest happened that day, as if the gods themselves were bowing their heads and giving the friends a moment's peace.

Nathan, Torrents, and the Kid walked dejectedly in a line, shoulders hunched against the hail. The rain and balls of ice pattered and pounded on the hoods of their cloaks and the surrounding grass.

The rain started six days ago and hadn't let up. It had been a steady, grey drizzle since PepperGarten died.

Nathan had checked on the Kid's wounds, binding them as best he could. It hadn't been easy; they were deep and probably needed stitches. The rokairn did the best he could, scraping the last remnants of the concoction the druid made into the deep gullies of flesh carved by the glowing red dagger.

He'd even said a prayer—clutching the symbol of the god, Jonath, the priests in Red Wind gave him—asking that the two men who seemed to share his belief of helping others, not die, and maybe even recover.

They camped in gloom, finding what shelter they could, tossing tarps over the low branches of a cluster of trees in the Black Wood.

They made good time, each lost in their thoughts, no one in the mood to talk for the first couple of days.

The Kid remembered people she'd lost in her other life.

Her son, who'd killed himself with poisons you bought over the counter. She had never drunk another drop of alcohol since. She didn't see the need for that loss of control. Life had too much to offer and didn't need to be drowned to be enjoyed or escaped from.

Her husband, who had left when life became too hard, and he thought he couldn't be happy working to support a wife and child who adored him. It was too mundane, too normal, to suffer through. So, he left to find himself.

He found himself with the help of his young secretary, and the used-car empire his wife had financed when they were married.

The Kid, known as Jen in that world, had lived carefully and alone after that. She'd watched her friends die of old age, or self-abuse, but she'd lived on. Until cancer finally got her.

Once she'd come here, she lived differently. She reveled in every moment, delighting in every danger. She laughed whenever she could and said anything that came to mind that might bring a smile to her, or some else's, face. As a bonus, she could also pee standing up now.

It was hard watching people die. Even once she was here and was the Kid—a teenage boy who was a healthy, vibrant, mind-mage—she'd lost people. Esperanza sprung to mind. The young woman, in her twenties, was a powerful priestess of Latress in this world, who chose to return to her life in the other world. And there were others, like the people of Durgan's Keep, who the Kid had fought to protect, many who died in the invasion of undead.

Now he'd lost his magical abilities, too. And Edsumar was gone. He didn't know if the two were related, but he was pretty sure the damned dagger Mezk wielded had done something to him.

The wounds in his gut and shoulder throbbed and felt like they were leaking. But there was no blood, no puss, no discharge of any kind. His headaches were gone, but he could no longer feel of magic within his mind.


Torrents hunted, taking down a fowl or rabbit, as he silently stalked far to one side of his companions. The Kid wouldn't have scared off any quarry, but Nathan trundled along, his axe bumping and scraping his metal armor, making enough noise to warn away a regiment of German tanks.

The barbarian learned he needed to live for himself. Not to please anyone else, and not to merely survive. Since arriving in this world—transported at the moment of his second life-changing car crash—he'd been on the path of realizing the value of choosing your own way.

He'd found self-worth in helping others. First, his friend Axle, then the people of Hope's Hollow. He'd went with Esperanza and the Kid because he thought it was what he was supposed to do. But along the way, as he fought zombies and giants and rotting ghosts that could drain the life-energy from anything living, he'd realized he needed to live for himself.

Once he'd helped save Durgan's Keep, and Esperanza returned to their world, he'd went to Dargaon's Hole to help the refugees of Hope's Hollow survive the winter. Not because it was expected, but because it was for him. It made him feel good, feel useful, and feel whole.

Torrents tried to convince the Kid to come along, to give purpose to both of their lives. But the Kid just wanted to play. He loved messing with other people and making their lives miserable. Sure, it was the crime lords and gangs that the Kid targeted, but that felt petty and hollow to Torrents.

Helping a group of simple people, not just survive, but thrive, in somewhere that the elements alone would have killed them, gave him a sense of belonging and purpose.

He'd left Dargaon's Hole because of the green glow to the southwest, a portent of a danger that would sweep across the land and threaten the very thing Torrents had protected.

His home. His people. His responsibility.

He'd abandoned all the people he cared for, so he could protect the settlement before the danger reached them. That was why he left, and that was why he now moved through this dammed week-long rainstorm with a rokairn he barely knew, and a self-centered brat.

The three traveled northeast, following the swath of destruction left by an army led by a demon half-breed. They found ravaged caravans; the people murdered for sport. They found small villages torn to the ground, brick by brick, timber by timber, and bone by bone. Never any survivors.

One thing united the three: the drive to stop the mindless horde crossing the land and killing for what appeared to them to be no reason at all.

They crested a hill on the morning of the sixth day, and the rain stopped, as if some great being turned off the tap. The sun crept from behind darting clouds, and the humidity began rising from the ground instead of falling to it.

In front of the three companions rose the broken structures of the Nine Towers of Magic. Greasy smoke wound its way into the air from dozens of campfires.

The sound of the gargled laughter of hyenas and gnohls rolled across the hills to meet them.

## Chapter 16

Edsumar couldn't breathe. Not that the spirit of a dragon residing in an enchanted weapon with the souls of five reptilian priests needed to breathe, but that wasn't the point. It felt like he couldn't breathe.

He couldn't reach out with his mind to contact the Kid, or other dragons, or anyone or anything else. Ever since this cambion wrapped him in that cloth, it was like being smothered, something he hadn't ever experienced, even in life. He'd been one of the most powerful creatures on the planet, allied with many of his peers and equals in magical ability and political influence.

He'd worked closely with the mages that built the Nine Towers of Magic, one structure for each 'school'. There weren't nine schools of magic, but the human mages who built the towers categorized them that way, and it was fine, even if they were wrong.

There were five primary types of magic: mind, ley or elemental, alchemical, summoning or conjuring, and holy. Other types of magic came from combining one or more of the five primaries, for example, necromancy combined all five.

They built the Nine Towers as an elite magical school and testing ground, meant to bring the best together in a place where no one would bother them. They constructed them on a nexus of ley lines, feeding magical energies directly into the Towers that acted as conduits for that power. It was one of the five most powerful magical repositories on the planet.

Mistakes were made, hence why the Blue Desert now existed, the sand's color changed by magical runoff and pollution.

The Towers had another purpose, though, to lock away foreign magic and the invaders who sought a foothold in this world. It had done its job well, teaching generations of humans and protecting the realm.

Then the Wizard Wars erupted, and he'd had to go to 'Plan B', which turned out to be a botched attempt to put all his knowledge into an easily transportable item. It finally worked when the Kid came along and finished the ritual.

The mages, sorcerers, wizards, witches, and other magic wielding humans—who all had remarkably brief lives, thus were short-sighted—decided there was a better way. To drain life essences of powerful magical beings and harness (aka steal) their abilities for their own uses. The Wizard Wars.

After the wars, those running the towers fell to infighting, destroying everything they'd worked hundreds of years to build. One group left and went to the coast, founding Seawall City, while the remaining groups scattered, too small and broken to hold the Towers by themselves. The Towers fell into disrepair, though many magics still lingered on, and in, the grounds.

Edsumar could feel the Towers; like a vibration rattling his cloth cage. The muffled sensation gave him the closest thing he'd had to a headache in almost a millennium. He felt it less than a year ago when the Kid and his friends had come here to stop the necromancer that later attacked Durgan's Keep. They'd failed, as shown by the later attack on the walled city.

Edsumar's awareness expanded as someone removed the cloth around him. He could feel the Towers all around him, and the magical shell barrier—invisible to the naked eye, but obvious to anyone with magical senses—that extended to the perimeter surrounding the magical structures.

The Dragon's Dagger pushed his awareness out, trying to pass through the shield, but it came up short. He never could move past it; the well-constructed shell did its job.

Edsumar could feel the cambion as she gripped his leather-wrapped handle and called upon his powers. Her mind was closed to him, and he was unsure if it was due to her nature, a magical protection, or just her raw willpower. As he wrapped himself around her astral form encased in flesh, Edsumar felt his energy slowly sinking into her, like sinking in quicksand.

The dragon spirit calmed himself, knowing struggling would only make it worse. He reached out with his ethereal senses, seeking help, some sort of psychic branch to grab onto, before he disappeared completely.

Dozens of gnohls and their requisite proto-hyenas were moving around the area, their tainted magic emanating through the air like a stench hanging over a swamp or a trash dump. The creatures reeked—or the equivalent of the sense of smell for the magical dagger—of rot, filth, and decay. Their hunger washed over Edsumar, and he experienced the closest thing to nausea he'd felt since he'd had an actual body.

His mind warped and twisted in Klendrisia's grip, feeling himself being harnessed, enslaved, and forced to move his abilities into the closest Tower.

Edsumar knew he was the key. That's how the mages set it up. No single human, or group of humans, could fully access the Nine Towers of Magic without Edsumar opening the pathways for them. When the Wizards attacked, and he'd placed his attendants into stasis, the men failed to get the one thing they needed to access the full powers of the towers. Him.

But Klendrisia had him and was using her magics and the shielded area to force him into unlocking the full potential of the slumbering energies. The mystical dagger would be like a lightning rod, and properly activated, would draw magical energy from across the world to this spot. With that much power in one place, Klendrisia could do almost anything, including opening another gateway so that her father's demon armies could pour through to this world.

Edsumar's mind jerked again, the psychic equivalent of someone grabbing his head and making him look at something. His senses exploded in the awareness of the ley lines, invisible to the naked eye, intersecting above the magical wellspring. Eldritch threads of earth, air, fire, and water burst to overflowing, becoming torrents of energy that blended with the repository below them.

Something else tickled his awareness, something familiar and comforting. It was like catching the movement of someone's walk out of the corner of your eye: you knew a person even though you didn't see them. They had a rhythm to their gait you recognized anywhere.

The Kid's spirit—not her mind, but her energy, her soul—was a pinprick of light on the edge of Edsumar's awareness. The dragon spirit thought of the Kid as both female and male, because that's what they were, depending on the moment and what they were doing. On the outside, he'd seen the changes, too. The masculine exterior was blending with the feminine spirit, and the two were becoming one. The Dasism called it twin or dual spirits, the balance of male and female, completed in one form.

Edsumar reached out, breaking some small part away from what he was doing, and touched the Kid's mind. He felt, more than saw, the Kid look up, gesturing in the dagger's direction and rallying the two men with him to head this way.

Gnohls and hyenas threw themselves in the trio's path. The barbarian Torrents fought with willpower and drive that surpassed any normal mortal. The newcomer, Nathan the rokairn, set his feet and jaw, wading forward, knocking the demon's minions away with each forward step. The Kid was a desperate whirlwind, daggers twirling and spinning, slicing and cutting, surging away from his friends and pushing towards Edsumar.

The Kid's mind felt torn, like scar tissue that grew on a once healthy muscle. The mind mage's psychic powers were blocked after being injured badly.

Edsumar couldn't just watch this happen, a powerless puppet for Klendrisia's game.

The dragon spirit reached upward, drawing power from above, ignoring his instincts that warned which such an action would only quicken the results the cambion desired. Edsumar knew if he could help his friends, and if they could recover him, they'd be able to stop this event that would shake the world.

The magical energies the dragon spirit had deftly wielded when he had a body were now like grasping at steam. It slipped through his grip, burning him when he tried to snatch it and use it for his own needs. The cambion was blocking his ability on top of the limitations that came with being inside of a magical object.

Edsumar redoubled his efforts, and if he still had a head, he would've furrowed his brow in concentration, and his tongue might have even been sticking out from between his lips as he focused.

He linked to a ley line, fire, then tied to another, wind. Lightning flashed, forks coming down across the battlefield. Bodies of gnohls and hyenas exploded upwards, raining back down on the perimeter of the Towers.

He called down bolt after bolt, peppering the area. Something shifted, and drew the lightning to one tower, then another, and another. The Towers were pulling down the power of the ley lines, wresting it from his control. He could no more harness it than he could redirect a river with his bare hands…if he still had hands.

A new body entered Edsumar's awareness, a dark soul stained red with anger, hate, and fear. Those emotions pulsed across the shadow, like ruby red veins of power and destruction.

This shadow person slid through the battle, becoming like smoke, and reappearing to strike with the weapon that possessed him, rather than the other way around.

Edsumar didn't see the way a human, or any other mortal species, saw. He saw in energy, which included magic and emotion. This unknown figure was a ragged bundle of those things, and wasn't wholly in this world, or any other.

The Dragon's Dagger knew the Demon Seed knew he was there, and that it hungered for him.

This new enemy appeared in front of the Kid, and the energies of the two melded as they fought, bleeding into one another, becoming a blur to Edsumar's senses.

Nathan called upon his powers, but it was weak, disconnected. A burst of white energy, turning a muddy maroon as it washed outward, flew from the man and tossed aside the gnohls in its path. But not the hyenas. They surged forward to attack the rokairn.

Torrents stepped beside the rokairn—now that he was free of the gnohls he'd been fighting—his sword cutting into the beasts. The creatures didn't give ground, retreating wasn't in their nature. They killed, or they died. That was their sole purpose.

Edsumar's awareness dimmed as the demon's minions regrouped to attack the three people trying to rescue him.

"Mezk," the sudden sound of the cambion's voice startled Edsumar, "you've done your part, and you now get the agreed upon reward. Take it and follow me. We shall make our escape and live to fight again."

She wrapped Edsumar in the red cloth again, blocking his ability to see the energies and interact with the world around him.

He threw his mind into one last, desperate act. He drew down all the power he could grasp from the ley lines. Fire rained down, joined by lightning, hail, and frozen gusts that cut to the bone.

Gnohls screamed in guttural calls, and hyenas howled in pain. Forms winked out of existence in the downpour of power.

As the last of Edsumar's awareness disappeared, he felt the towers drawing in his power. Sucked deep within them, it erupted upwards.

He saw the Kid, clearly, not surrounded by enemies. The three friends were cutting down the last remaining monsters and moving towards him.

The world went, not dark, but dull. His awareness felt nothing besides the rumble of power from the Nine Towers. Then it felt a new sensation, the dark, pulsating red of the Demon Seed enveloping him.

## Chapter 17

"Let's see what we've got," Torrents put his hand on the Kid's shoulder, surveying the dozens of dead bodies littering the ground around them, "looks a lot like it did when we were here before. Except for all the buildings that were blown up from all the lightning and fireballs. Man, what was that about? We were lucky none of them hit us."

"That was Edsumar, I think," the Kid slumped, his hands on his knees, watching the ground in front of him, panting, "I thought I could feel him reaching out for me, and wanting to protect us. I was trying to get to him, to help him."

Fred moved next to the Kid, resting a stone claw on the rogue's boot.

"We know, we had to run interference as you ignored everything trying to kill you," Torrents patted the Kid, "I think every hair on my body is curled up and singed from all that magic. I just got better, and now I'm bit and cut in a bunch of places from those things."

"They threw them under the bus," Nathan pointed at the place where the demon woman stood moments before. "They were right there. Klendrisia and Mezk just…disappeared. The demoness vanished in a blink. She'd been there one moment, watching me with a crooked smile, and was gone the next.

"I saw Mezk take something wrapped in a red cloth from her just moments before she vanished, then he turned and looked at you," the rokairn pointed at the Kid, "I could see him clearly even though he was a dozen meters away. I saw his lip curl into a sneer, like hate was twisting his features. It's so cliché to say something like that, but that's what it looked like. Then he'd slid sideways and melted into shadow. Like a video of a chocolate Easter bunny left in the sun, then put on fast forward, the man literally melted into shadow, and then was gone."

They stood in the middle of dozens of buildings surrounding five graceful towers, and the one chunky, crystalline black tower sat supported atop the rubble of four other towers. The broken structures looked like stubby legs under the massive black one.

"You guys have been here before?" Nathan turned to see the two nodding. "What was this place?"

"A magic school," the Kid stood, rubbing his face with both hands, "most of the buildings were administrative, barracks, or lecture halls for classes of elite magic wielders. They dedicated the towers to different kinds of magic."

"See the big, fat, black one?" Torrents pointed at the stubby tower that sat on the rubble of the four others, and Nathan nodded.

"That's what she said," the Kid mumbled half-heartedly, and received a glare from Torrents for the effort.

Fred clicked his claws in three rapid beats, a small space between the second and third.

"Cla-clack, clack."

"Did that thing just do a rimshot?" Torrents asked, looking down at the rock lobster in amazement.

"Just a trick I taught him," the Kid shrugged.

"Apparently," Torrents continued with a shrug, "that was some new, upstart god named Onyx, who came into power about a hundred years ago. He dropped one right on top of these to show off, I guess. Those black towers used to give out magic items to anyone who wanted one."

"Really?" Nathan looked at it in wonder. "Did you guys ever get one from it?"

Torrents and the Kid exchanged glances with one another, then looked back to Nathan and shook their heads.

"Why not?" Nathan was looking at the black tower, and the other two could see his mind working.

"I think there were always strings of some sort attached," the Kid shrugged.

"Like what?" Nathan took a step towards the tower. "Like you went crazy and murdered people, or that you suddenly had the urge to go door to door to talk to people about Onyx?"

"Not really sure," Torrents moved closer to Nathan, ready to stop him if needed, "we never found out since we didn't get any."

The ground shook, and the three moved their stance wider to balance themselves.

"Earthquake?" Torrents suggested once it subsided.

"Maybe," the Kid touched the big man's shoulder, turning his attention southwest, "or something worse."

The green light in the sky to the southeast had grown brighter, lines of red, blue, and maroon dancing inside the glow.

"Oh," Torrents said, "what's that?"

"I think that's what they were doing here," the Kid sighed, "and I thought we'd won. I thought we'd killed all the lackeys and chased off the bad guys. But now I think this was just one more step in their bigger plan."

The other two nodded, still staring at the atmospheric show.

"Nathan?" the Kid nudged the rokairn, who looked at him. "Did you say you saw that woman give Mezk something wrapped in a red cloth?"

"Yeah, sorry," Nathan gulped, "I did."

"That would've been Edsumar," the Kid's voice cracked, "she gave him Edsumar."

Torrents put a hand on the Kid's shoulder again.

Fred moved protectively to stand beside the Kid.

"I'm sorry," Nathan said again, looking down and shuffling his feet, "I wish we could've done something."

"We'll get him back for you, Kid," Torrents rubbed the Kid's shoulder, "even if we have to hunt those bastards to the end of the world, this world or another."

"It might just be the end of the world," the Kid sighed, deeper this time, "if we don't find a way to stop them."

"And speaking of that, how come there aren't like dozens of groups like us," Torrents spat on the ground, "even whole armies from different cities, out here hunting these people down before they destroy the whole planet?"

"Probably because they're scared," the Kid's voice was quiet, "they've been through so much here from the stories we've heard. The world already ended once. They're probably tired of fighting, and just want to survive. I'm guessing that just surviving the things they went through during the Downfall makes them a hero."

The group fell quiet, each lost in their thoughts.

"Well," Nathan's voice broke them from their reverie, "sorry to ruin the moment, but do you still think it's a bad idea to get a magic item from Onyx's Tower?"

"Yeah," Torrents's answer was gruff, "I do. I don't trust it. Don't you think if it was a good idea, then others would be doing it? I mean, there were just two very slimy people here, and neither of them even gave it a second look."

"I don't mean to argue," the Kid looked up at the big man.

"Yes, you do," Torrents growled, "but go on anyway. You will, no matter what I say."

"True," the Kid gave a smile reminiscent of his old attitude, "but those two are already dealing with issues where they owe someone. Mezk made a deal with a demon from what the word on the street is, and Nathan said Klendrisia has daddy issues. He sounds pretty controlling, you know, being a demon lord and all."

"Does that mean you think we should go get something from the tower?" Torrents glared at the Kid through squinted eyes.

Nathan looked back and forth between the two as they discussed it.

"Could it hurt at this point?" the Kid shrugged. "We're going to need all the help we can get, and if we fail, we'll be dead, anyway. Even if there are strings attached, if it helps us survive, at least we'll be alive to face the music and deal with it."

Torrents stared down at the Kid, then his face relaxed as he sighed.

"Fine," the barbarian breathed, drawing the word out, and clipped the next word, "whatever. If we're gonna die, I guess we should go ahead and get every advantage we can."

The three gathered their gear, and made their way through the field of carnage, Fred scampering around their feet. Stepping around the burnt and mutilated corpses of the gnohls and hyenas, they picked out a route between the rubble of the shattered buildings along the weed-strewn cobblestone path.

"There are no magical constructs or energies wandering around the complex this time," the Kid noted. "Think whatever they did scared them off?"

"More likely," Torrents shoved a broken door from the pitted road, "whatever they did ate the things. It looked like a lot of magic was being harnessed and slung around."

"Uh huh," Nathan muttered, wanting to add something to the conversation. When the other two looked at him expectantly, he blushed. "Sorry, it's just that I think I could kinda see it. Just like I can see faint lines above us, and below us. It's like when you stare at a light bulb and then look away and you can still see it. Or when you watch a sparkler on the Fourth of July, and you see the trails it leaves."

"You can see the ley lines?" The Kid asked. "I couldn't even see those, and I'm what they call a mind mage. Guess that would make you an elementalist? Or is it because of your connection to the god, Jonath?"

"What?" Nathan looked surprised. "I don't know about any of that. I just know I'm in a dwarf's body, and can use an axe pretty well, and can see things that aren't there. I don't know how, or what any of it means. Is there a reason we're all here? A purpose?"

"Dude," Torrents said over his shoulder, winding his way through a tight cluster of rubble, "you chuzzing rock that axe! And don't call your people dwarves, it's insulting. Rokairn, or sometimes 'the rock people'."

"Stoners?" the Kid asked. "Can we call them stoners, or is that insensitive?"

"Cla-clack, clack," Fred clacked.

Torrents snorted a laugh, then glared at the Kid for good measure.

"And we're here," the Kid said haughtily, "because we were all dying, individually, and Jack Tucker used magic to bring us here to another dying body. And to what end, you may ask. We have no clue. To be heroes? To give us a second chance? Because he could? We don't know. I just know that I'm going to do something with it, even if it kills me. Again."

"That sounds reasonable," Nathan said, "and I'm sorry to ask this, but is it selfish to want to make a difference?"

"I don't think so," the Kid shrugged, "I've always loved helping others. Even when I worked in restaurants, just bringing someone some food they were looking forward to made me feel good."

"Damn straight it's okay," Torrents spat, "it feels good, and gets things done. Too many people go their whole lives only looking out for themselves, even stepping on others or using them to get what they want. Chuz those people, man. They're bidj. Helping others is the way to go, hands down."

"Sorry to ask," Nathan said, "I just don't want to be arrogant, like I'm better than anyone else just because I can do these things. And you think I have some sort of connection with Jonath?"

"I don't think you could be arrogant if you tried, Nathan," the Kid laughed.

"Really, man," Torrents sighed, "you're like humble all the way. And quit apologizing. Every other thing out of your damn mouth is 'sorry', and you ain't even done anything wrong. You'll know when you need to apologize, so chuzzing quit doing it all the time."

Nathan opened his mouth to say something, but the Kid interrupted.

"Don't say you're sorry," the Kid pointed at the rokairn, grinning, "you'll just piss him off, and barbarians are known for ripping the arms off droids, isn't that right, Torrents?"

Nathan snapped his mouth closed.

"Shut the hell up, Kid," Torrents was grinning, too.

"As for your connection to Jonath," the Kid went on, "I think it's obvious if you take a moment to look at it. First, you're on a first name basis with him and keep referring to him like he's an old friend. Second, those priests who gave you the holy symbol saw something in you, and they'd know, wouldn't they? And C, I'm bad at lists, but I'm sure there is something else, too."

Nathan opened his mouth to speak, but the Kid interrupted again.

"Oh yeah," the Kid held up a finger, "I remember now, you've been casting protection magic, and Jonath is a god who specializes in that sort of thing. Those invisible bubbles that were knocking the hyenas and gnohls away from us, and you said you did it back at PepperGarten's, too."

The three fell silent as they crossed into the shadow of the Tower of Onyx and slowed to a stop.

"Clack, clack, cl-cl-clack," Fred clacked ominously.

# Chapter 18

They stood at the foot of the monolith, four crushed towers in ruin beneath, supporting it. Black, crystalline tendrils wrapped around the broken, stubby towers and sunk into the cobblestone courtyard, disappearing into the broken earth.

The ebon megalith rose forty meters into the air, on top of the six meters of the shattered towers that held it up. Though the five remaining towers—lingering in the distance—rose to more than double the height of the Tower of Onyx, all five could have fit into its circumference.

The three companions climbed the mound of rubble underneath to reach the center below the dark behemoth, Fred following. Pieces of the crushed towers shifted underfoot.

"What do we do now?" Nathan asked when they reached the center. "Do we chant something?"

"Say a prayer to Onyx?" Torrents suggested.

"Make a wish," the Kid grinned, "and rub its belly."

The other two looked at the Kid to see if he was serious.

"How the hell would I know?" The Kid threw his hands up. "I'm over here wracking my brain, trying to remember what that crazy necromancer, Aku'ji, Mistress of Death and Wielder of Woe, did when she was getting the Scepter of Necropties from this thing."

"Really?" Torrents looked down at the Kid. "You used the full title and everything? How'd you even remember all that?"

"I'm good at crosswords," the Kid shrugged, "things like that stick in my brain."

"So, then," Torrents rolled his eyes, "what did she do?"

"I've no clue," the Kid shrugged again, "we showed up right after she got it. You rushed in, like you always do, and I had to save you, like I always do."

"Do not," Torrents muttered, "you just provide back up."

"Guys," Nathan interrupted, "sorry, but can we focus here?"

The two turned to look at the rokairn.

"You apologized again," the Kid smirked.

"Sorry, ugh," Nathan threw up his hands, "sorry, it's just that I, oh, no. Never mind. But we really should focus on getting whatever this thing can give us. Anyone know anything about this sort of thing from their previous body's?"

"Oh," Torrents gasped, the other two turning to look at him, "I think I do."

The barbarian reached up, holding his hands above his head, and they shimmered. The effect looked like heat rising off hot asphalt, but they were in the shade, and the ripples in the air were swirling around his hands instead of rising.

Torrents lowered his hands, and the three of them leaned in to look at what he'd received.

Something coalesced in his grip. It shimmered, then solidified.

A long, double-handed, black blade formed from thin air, laying across Torrents's open palms.

The three stared at it for a long moment.

"Wait a second," the Kid broke the silence, "isn't that your sword, but it's black now?"

"No," Torrents glanced over his shoulder, looking for the handle of his sword, but it wasn't there, "um, maybe?"

"It is!" The Kid squealed. "What a rip-off! This thing gave you your own sword, but with a new paint job. It doesn't even have cool racing flames or anything."

"It kills demons," Torrents's voice was low, "I can feel it, like an instruction manual in my head. The bond of a demon's soul is severed, sending it back to where it came from.

"Demons have souls?" the Kid asked.

"It makes sense," Nathan said, and the two looked at him. He swallowed an apology for interrupting, and went on, "the soul would be nothing more than the energy within us that makes up who we are. You know, your mind, emotions, and all the things that aren't your muscles, organs, and all that. That invisible stuff that makes you…well, you."

"Yeah," the Kid tilted his head and pursed his lips, "yeah, I guess that makes sense. Okay, move over, it's my turn!"

Torrents moved to one side, still staring at the ebon blade, while the Kid pushed forward.

The Kid raised his hands above his head, humming a little tune from an old cartoon that lingered in his mind.

Something appeared in the shimmering air around his hands, and a black cloth dropped over his forearms. He lowered his arms, and the three looked at the material.

"T-t-that's all, folks!" the Kid held up a circle of fabric.

"What's it do?" Torrents leaned in to look closer.

"It…" the Kid wrinkled his brow, "makes a hole, it seems. That's weird, it *is* like an instruction book in your head. Maybe that guy on that TV show, Greatest American Hero, should've got his instructions this way."

"Dude," Torrents moaned, "stop talking about old TV shows, and tell us what the hell it does!"

"It makes a hole," the Kid huffed, "just that. I guess I could throw it on a wall and crawl through to the other side. Or drop it on the ground and jump in and it would open another hole somewhere else, like another building nearby. It has to be close, though. I don't think it would let me go much more than ten meters or so."

"What if you dropped it on the floor," Nathan reached out to touch it, stroking the silk-like material, "and had a hole appear above it. Could you keep falling until you hit terminal velocity?"

"I don't know," the Kid's voice wavered high, then low as he did a verbal shrug, "maybe? I guess? But I don't think I'm gonna try it, though."

"Can anyone else go through it?" Nathan released the cloth, wiping his hand on his shirt without realizing it.

"Um," the Kid tilted his head in thought, "they're not supposed to, because it can have unexpected results. Okay, your turn Nathan! Let's see what you get!"

The Kid moved away from the center point of the tower, letting Nathan move forward.

Nathan reached up, stretching onto his tiptoes, and something hit his hand, then tumbled to the rubble below his feet, wedging into a crevasse.

"Oh my god," the Kid squealed again, "don't lose it before you even use it."

"What's with that noise you just made?" Torrents asked the Kid. "That's twice you did it. You never make noises like that."

"I used to," the Kid shrugged, "back home, in my other body. Maybe just more of me is coming out as I get comfortable in this world?"

Nathan pulled a matte black amulet from the rocks below him, holding it up for the others to see. It was in the shape of a small triangular shield, about ten centimeters by fifteen centimeters across. Light disappeared into it, and nothing seemed to reflect off it.

"It absorbs energy," Nathan's voice was subdued with wonder as he turned the artifact over in his hands, "like magic, sunlight, or other things."

"Do you just hold it up for it to work?" Torrents poked it with a finger.

"Well," Nathan pressed it to his chest, and it stuck there, "I think I just wear it."

"Wait," the Kid gawked, "you don't need a chain, or a clip to wear it?"

"No," Nathan shook his head, removing the amulet from his chest and sticking it to the bracer on his right forearm, "it just clings to wherever I put it."

"So, lemme see if I got this right," the Kid grumbled, putting his hands on his hips, the black cloth draping his side, "Torrents got a demon-slaying sword, and you got an amulet that blocks magic, fire, sunlight, and any energy coming at you, and I got a hole? Am I understanding this right?"

"It goes with the one in your head," Torrents grinned, "now you have a matching set."

"Your mom has a matching set," the Kid shot back.

"Cla-clack, clack," Fred clacked.

"Well, yeah," Torrents nodded, "she does. Well, she did, before she died. Thanks for bringing that up, jerk!"

"Oh, no, I'm so sorry for your loss," Nathan said, reaching out to comfort the big man, and saw the smile on his face. "Wait, is she really dead?"

"No idea," Torrents shrugged, "she left when I was a baby. I was raised by my dad. Single parent and all that."

"Oh, you," the Kid rolled his eyes, "the old dead mom comeback. It makes it awkward every time."

Torrents stopped, jerking his head up and looking into the distance.

"We got our presents from this jerk." His voice was low and quiet. "We should get away from the huge magical tower in the middle of everything. I think I just heard one of those dog-men cackle. They might not all be dead. We should get out of here, or at least somewhere more defensible, before they come for us."

The Kid and Nathan nodded. They picked their way down the pile of rubble and onto the street.

Fred scurried ahead of the group, scouting the way.

The afternoon sun was overhead, making the three squint when they left the shadow of the tower. Scavenger birds had circled overhead, and above them was a kettle of wyverns gliding on the higher air currents, both watching for the opportunity to feast. The smell of char and ozone pervaded the area, mixing with the stench of freshly dead bodies in the sun. Low drifts of oily smoke moved through the streets like they had a mind of their own, which was entirely possible in this place.

Rocks tumbled, the sharp clack of stone on stone drifting across the complex. Torrents looked in the noise's direction, raising his hand to shade his eyes, looking for the source of the sound.

A shout from Nathan was the only warning before the small man bowled the barbarian over, a wrist-thick spear cutting through the space where Torrents had been a moment before.

Seven figures boiled over the edge of a stone wall. The muscled, bare-chested men with hyena heads launched more spears at the group. Raising their thick, curved blades high, they charged with the gurgled cackle of their kind. Leaping over obstacles, they ran towards the trio. Four giant hyenas bounded after the gnohls, thick drool stringing from their jowls.

Torrents, catching himself before hitting the ground, saw his new and improved blade already in his hand. He didn't remember reaching over his back to pull the weapon free, but it was in his hand now. Did he even put it away? Had he been carrying it the whole time?

The blade moved through the air even before he finished his thought, ripping through the throat of the first gnohl, and burying itself into the ribs of the next.

The two man-beasts yelped, more like beasts than men, and an orange line appeared around each of their injuries. Their cries cut short as all life left their bodies the moment the blade freed itself. That same orange glow streaked after the blade as it pulled the creatures' souls free from their bodies.

The Kid reached out with his mind, seeking to guide the daggers leaving his hands. A sharp spike of pain thrust itself from the base of his skull, through his head, and ended at his right eye. The street thief screamed, doubling over, his daggers going wide. His abilities weren't just missing, using them now caused backlash. He'd reached for them without thinking, used to relying on them.

A hyena pounced at his curled-up form, and the Kid rolled away. The black cloth he'd been carrying opened underneath him, and he fell into the hole it created.

He dropped a meter, then hit the ground, landing in a crouch, the pain in his head dissipating. The two daggers he'd thrown were at his feet. The Kid snatched up the daggers and threw them in the same motion. Each weapon sunk into a different eye socket of the huge spotted animal as it turned to pounce again.

The creature fell.

The Kid started to pull the daggers back to him with his mind magics, but stopped. Reaching into the black hole on the ground beside him, his hands appeared in front of the Hyaenidae and he pulled the weapons from the creature's skull. Drawing his blades back through the hole, the Kid spun, threw them again, and dropped into the ebon aperture.

Fred ran back and forth, trying to keep up with the Kid as he disappeared and reappeared.

Hyper-aware, Nathan felt the attack before seeing it. The metal symbol of Jonath on his chest pulsed against him, pulling his attention in every direction that there was a threat.

The rokairn set his feet, squared his shoulders, and moved towards a clump of three gnohls. He ducked under the pock-marked blade of one, jammed the top of his double-headed axe into its guts, which tore twin gashes along each of the monster's sides. Intestines slithered free.

Nathan pulled his axe free and swung it to one side, chopping through the sword arm of another, severing it at the elbow.

Kicking out with his boot, the gnohl's knee bent backwards. As the creature fell, Nathan blocked the third creature's downward attack with Marcid.

Sidestepping, he caught the blade in the curve of his axe, and pulled the weapon to the ground, then punched upward with his left hand. The gnohl's face broke, its nose pushing in and up, shoving the shattered bone into its brain. The creature stumbled backwards, dropping its weapon and falling onto its butt.

Torrents stepped over the bodies of his fallen foes, thrusting his sword through the neck of another gnohl, its gurgled scream cutting off as he pulled the weapon free, the orange glow following the blade.

Nathan cut down the remaining gnohl, his axe taking out the creature's knees from behind. He flipped the weapon around and brought it down on the monster's skull, splitting it as the gnohl hit the ground.

The Kid popped up from his hole, now on the ground in a new spot, and sliced across the throat of a hyena, then spun and threw them into the ribs of another beast leaping at him.

The blades buried themselves into the creature's barrel chest as the Kid rolled to the side, avoiding the hyena's clawed feet when it came down where he'd been a moment before.

The proto-hyena spun, blood mixing with the saliva dripping from its jaws. It coughed, and its breath caught, unable to draw air in. It leapt at the unarmed rogue again but met Torrents's weapon mid-air. The ebon blade disemboweled the creature, who landed heavily on its side, gasping as its eyes went wide with pain and the struggle to breathe.

Torrents moved from one fallen gnohl to another, dispatching any still living with the magic of his improved weapon. The orange glow appeared with each cut, severing the creatures' life forces from this realm.

Nathan did the same with the hyenas, but with more effort and less flair, Fred assisted. It was the simple task of cutting throats.

"That went well," the Kid said, pulling his twin daggers from the now-still hyena, "better than I expected. No one even got hurt."

"Well," Torrents was staring at his blade, which didn't have a single drop of blood, or glob of gore on it, "we didn't get hurt. These bunch of gnohls sure did, though."

"What do you call a group of gnohls, anyway?" the Kid asked.

"Same thing you call a bunch of hyenas." Nathan cleaned his axe, wiping it on a corpse, then with a thick cloth, "a cackle, I guess."

"Really? A cackle?" Torrents looked at the rokairn. "You messing with us?"

"Sorry," Nathan met the man's eyes and smiled, "I'm not."

## Chapter 19

The three, and Fred, traveled due south for the rest of the day and set camp shortly before sunset. Grey ash drifted from the sky, an atmospheric anomaly that wasn't as uncommon as it should be.

They found a small copse of trees on the edge of the Blue Desert, where they laid out their bedrolls and made a small campfire.

Once settled, they tended their injuries.

Torrents took most of the damage and changed the bandages on six different cuts from rusty blades. He had dozens of smaller scratches, but nothing worth a bandage.

Nathan only had minor injuries, his armor and magics taking the brunt of the attacks. But he still had the deep gash on his face from the Demon Seed, though the harmful magics dissipated when he used his holy magics.

The Kid's two wounds he received during the fight with Mezk back at PepperGarten's still showed but weren't serious. He spent his evening before bed playing with his gift of Onyx, the magic hole.

He popped in and out of it, practicing throwing his knives. Many weeds died, and he injured many trees during the exercise.

They slept in shifts, and woke early to start again, eating the leftovers from the previous night. Fred had kept watch with each of them, not needing sleep.

They spent the next two weeks in some form of repetition of that first day; traveling, camping, practicing, repeat. It took two days to cross the Blue Desert, then they skirted the western edge of the Upper Swamp while staying in the Red Plains. They hunted and caught what they could along the way. A sense of urgency built as the green lights in the southeastern sky expanded northward.

Whenever they came across a caravan or a small settlement, they bought or traded for what they needed most, and moved on. Villagers were always suspicious of strangers, and even more so since the activity at the Demon Front escalated.

Strange weather became common as they neared Land's End, where the otherworldly beings were. Rains of frogs, ash fall, dry lightning, or even normal rain that burned the skin were a few of the things they had to deal with.

It took two weeks to reach the road that led from Durgan's Keep to Red Wind. The Lasso River surrounding the latter.

As they got closer, they encountered more caravans, people fleeing the area with everything they could carry in fear of what was coming. These people would stare at them, watching their every move, but most refused to talk to them or trade anything, even information. The few that did only told them what they expected: demons appeared with more frequency and people were being taken in the night.

"I still think that we should have gotten some horses," Torrents grumbled. "It would've been faster."

"Not really," the Kid sighed, "we've been over this. They would've cost more than we have, they need more food and water, and they really don't go much faster than we do. We're all young and healthy. We've got this."

The Kid laughed, thoughts of her seventy-seven-year-old body in the Hospice care in the other world sparring with the image of her body now. Or would she be seventy-eight now? Were there cosmic time zones, or did time freeze, or move at a different rate in the two places? Unsure of how the time difference worked, the Kid laughed again and shook his head.

They could see Red Wind in the distance, just a few hours away. A dark cloud of smog hung over the city, which wasn't uncommon in this medieval world. Wood fires, foundries, and other things that used fossil fuels often created that sort of thing. But this cloud was different. It moved, swirling in one direction and then another. Tendrils reached out from it, touching the ground in small twisters, or sometimes going sideways.

Plants grew more withered and sicklier, the closer they got to Land's End; approaching Red Wind, that had become even more common.

Nathan had been quiet for most of the day. Torrents didn't know what to make of the man. The rokairn was a powerful warrior, capable of using holy magic, but was still meek and apologetic in everything he did.

That wasn't normal to the barbarian. Torrents had grown up doing sports, the closest thing he could associate with being a warrior, and had basked in the glory of being a local hero. Since he'd been here, he'd come to understand the value of being humble, but didn't understand saying you're sorry for speaking. It just didn't make sense to him.

The Kid watched the other two, hanging back to keep an eye on anyone or anything that might approach from behind.

The Kid kinda adored Nathan, appreciating his demure attitude, kindness, and concern with upsetting others. That sort of person was rare, but it did get on his nerves after a while.

Watching Torrents, the Kid could see the big man's frustration with the newest addition. Nathan never stood up for himself, always backing down from any confrontation. But when someone else was threatened, Nathan was the first to rise to their defense.

It almost caused an issue with a caravan they'd traded with. When the man they were talking to smacked a pre-teen boy who didn't move fast enough to get what he was sent to retrieve, Nathan had reached for his axe and stepped forward. A gentle hand and shake of the Kid's head kept the rokairn in check.

"That's how this world is," Torrents said later, when they discussed the incident.

Nathan glared at him.

"Look, Nathan," the Kid said, "that child will grow up and overcome these things."

"Kindness is a better way," Nathan argued, one of the rare times he did, "and there's never an excuse to hit someone to make them do what you wanted them to do."

"That's exactly what we're about to do with Klendrisia and Mezk when we catch them." Torrents pointed out.

Nathan shook his head and mumbled, "It shouldn't be that way. There should be another option."

"I want to agree," the Kid said, "but after a lifetime of abuse on both worlds, I don't think there is another way. I wish there was. There are no easy answers when the whole world responded with a fist."

Nathan eyed the horizon, watching Red Wind grow bigger.

"I like you guys," he said, "but neither of you seem to understand that I want to help others without resorting to violence. I've wracked my brain for another way, but I've already seen that the enemy we face won't listen to reason. Though maybe we could bring Klendrisia around. She had said almost as much, complaining that her people—and her father in particular—treated her that way, and she was tired of it. But she acted just like they did, not seeking an alternate solution, and instead doing the same thing they did."

The city crawled with movement, black specks darting around the outside of the crumbled defenses, and spots of fire visible from a distance.

Nathan picked up his pace to a jog, moving ahead of Torrents, his axe in one hand.

"You know," the Kid shouted, he, Fred, and Torrents matching the pace, "running will get us there a little faster, but a lot more tired. We may need to conserve our energy. Even stop for a meal before we get there. I don't think the taverns will be serving dinner, considering the circumstances."

Nathan ignored the comment, and moved at a steady, but faster, pace.

When they got within bowshot of Red Wind, a group of small creatures, about waist high to a human, broke away and came towards them.

"What're those?" Torrents asked, slowing his stride and reaching for his sword.

The weapon was already in his hand. He'd have to get used to that, or risk cutting his head off one day.

"Demons," Nathan's voice was a throaty growl, and he raised Marcid, "they have acid blood, so be careful when you cut them. Or bash and splatter them, whichever."

The creatures came fast, traveling on four legs, their spotted bodies thin and contorted. They resembled pygmy giraffes, if the spots on the animal were scabs and leathery flesh sluffing off every time they moved. Their rounded heads had pointed ears that swiveled all the way around, and large yellow eyes with slitted pupils. The things' mouths were full of needle-teeth in multiple rows.

The three of them had only a moment to see all this before the monsters swarmed. Then they were waist deep in screeching, biting beasts.

Fred launched forward, cutting at any enemy legs within reach.

Torrents's sword swung in wide arcs, tearing through the things easily, the orange glow of the weapon's magic trailing after. The little demons fell by the handful.

The Kid pressed his back to the barbarian, twin daggers in his hands, slashing to protect the big man.

Nathan laid about him with the flat of his axe, swatting two or three of the beasts away at a time. The long thin necks writhed around the shaft of the weapon, grabbing at it like a prehensile snake. Green light burst from the wooden handle of Marcid—PepperGarten's nature magic— destroying the foreign creatures.

Within a minute, the three moved away from dozens of the creatures that lay dead behind them. They brushed at bright red spots on their skin where the blood had splashed and burned them.

Reaching the broken city walls, hundreds of the minor demons ran through the streets, attacking anyone they could find.

Other forms were there, too.

Thin demons, almost as tall as a single-story building, with leathery, plated skin in shades of reddish-brown, moved around on segmented, stilt-like legs. The insectile creatures had four faceted eyes, and short, stubby antennae that resembled goat horns.

The group entered the city, cutting down any monsters that crossed their path. The companions fought their way between the buildings, following Nathan as he moved with purpose, heading deeper into the maze of chaos.

"There," Nathan pointed at a stone structure, short and squat, the symbol of Jonath carved into the triangle of the peak above the steps and doors.

Men and women formed into ranks in front of the broad, oak double doors, the ones in front defending the church with a shield wall, and the ones behind firing arrows into the demonic horde. Through the door, Nathan could see dozens of terrified families inside, every face looking towards the doors, or the hastily shuttered and blockaded windows along the side of the building.

"Kaleb triot, den'al venitier!" Nathan roared his battle cry and charged into the back of the attackers.

Fred crouched low, made a little leap, and scurried into the fight.

Torrents and the Kid exchanged quick glances, the Kid shrugging and Torrents giving a grim smile, before they followed the rokairn into the fray.

## Chapter 20

Klendrisia appeared in the center of the encampment. Men and women dropped to their knees, prostrating themselves face down in the dirt and leaves. She moved through their groveling forms, smiling at their worship and dedication to her.

This was the slave lands. At least that was what she called it in her head. It was in the center of Land's End and the Demon Front, the peninsula in the south-easternmost corner of the continent of Teurone.

This land had once been a center of worship of her father, but the humans and dasism had come and wiped out the loyal followers who'd been working so hard to open portals for the abysmal armies. That was hundreds of years ago.

Just a couple hundred years ago, a foolhardy group of explorers—looters really—had come upon the abandoned keep in the thick of the woods hunting a vampire and whatever treasures it had hidden.

Klendrisia wrapped herself in the darkness again and reappeared outside of the broken structure where it had all started, this plan of hers.

One of the weak-minded fools had triggered the Ruby Door and opened one small portal that let hundreds of soldiers of her father's army through into this land. It also transported one human priestess of Promethene to her father. That woman became the mother of Klendrisia's half-brother, Nomed.

When someone rescued the woman, they stole Klendrisia's half-brother away before his birth. The woman died in childbirth, and an outcast of the church, a male, raised Nomed. The Church of Promethene only allowed female priestesses, and this man was an abomination to the church. But he raised a half-breed demon in the ways of the aeifain.

Nomed had grown to become quite a thorn in the side of Lord Ghlevid and even fought against the demon invasion to the west during the Downfall and the reign of the Talisman. Klendrisia's half-brother had manipulated entire countries to help block the contract between the troöds and the demons, who were working together to overthrow and enslave the people of this world.

Now, Klendrisia was in this ancestral shrine, and the humans here bowed to her and jumped to fill her every whim. Not her brother's, not her father's, but hers. She would succeed where all others had failed.

The people here would all die…or be transformed in the impending ritual. In a few weeks, the month would reach its end. On that new moon, Klendrisia would open a huge portal to this world for her father's armies.

She had manipulated the rokairn, Nathan, who was so hopeful about everything, to bring his friends to help with the sacrifice needed. Dozens of her minions had spilled tainted blood on the holy nexus of the Nine Towers, priming the magical pump so she could open the flood gates and redirect the ley line energies from across the continent to the Pyridom.

She stepped into the fold of the dark again, appearing at the foot of the Pyridom. The conical structure rose into the sky above her. The crigth wobbled past on their insectile legs, followed by clumps of the small, four-legged jedth.

Even now, the fledgling priest of Jonath would be fighting her demons, and then he'd raise an army to try to stop her. That army would bring the anger, hate, and fear she needed to taint the ley lines and turn the largest conductor of magical energy in the world into a beacon portal.

That was a very special sort of portal; it wasn't static, waiting for someone to use it. It called to them, drawing them in, even forcing them to pass through it. Yes, it would draw Lord Ghlevid's armies, but also the armies of the other demon lords, and the Inciter Demons—rogue demon warriors with no master—who sought their place of power as they roamed the realms.

The chaos would allow Klendrisia to gather control and allies to form her army. And the cost was small, just a single world.

The plan had many moving parts, but she'd orchestrated them well. The rokairn warrior-priest, the Dragon's Dagger to open the Nine Towers, the redirection of the ley lines, the demon scouts to draw in the enemy army, her army here waiting to battle, and the last piece she needed.

She called upon the cold void one more time, feeling it caress her, enfolding her in its nothingness, and stepped out into the center of the encampment again.

Mezk was there, sitting on a wooden throne he'd constructed in her absence, human women surrounding him. One fed him withered fruits—his face wrinkling with the bitterness—and two sat at his feet, rubbing on his legs like feral cats in heat.

The Demon Seed lay on the arm of the throne, and his fingers stroked it like a favored pet, or a lover. The red cloth that contained the Dragon's Dagger lay across his lap. The man never let either out of his reach.

Mezk smirked when he saw her watching him.

He inclined his head at her, and Klendrisia kept her expression neutral, knowing any show of emotion—anger, hate, or even a courteous reaction—would make the man feel like he was manipulating her, and that he controlled their relationship. She knew men like him all her life, but in this case, he was the one being manipulated.

Klendrisia raised one hand, motioning for Mezk to come to her. She turned away before he could respond, knowing that if she didn't, he'd gesture for her to come to him. She knew this game.

The cambion walked away slowly, letting the man catch up. When he did, his face was tight.

"When will I get what I've been promised?" Mezk said, falling in beside her and matching her casual pace.

"Soon, Mezk of the Demon Seed," she smirked, "the time will be upon us soon enough. Do you know your part?"

"Of course I do," Mezk growled, a sad attempt to intimidate her.

"Humor me," she purred, "and tell me one more time. I do so love to hear it from your mouth."

"Once the dwarf priest arrives with his army," Mezk's voice sounded forced, "I kill him with the Demon Seed on the steps of the Pyridom, making sure his blood washes the walls."

"Yes," Klendrisia smiled, "very good. Then, and only then, you may kill the two-spirit with the Dragon's Dagger. That should break the bond that keeps Edsumar in this plane, and that will be the time for the Demon Seed to devour his enemy's energies. And that will release you from your pact. Isn't that correct?"

"Yes," Mezk growled, "and then I get to go, a free man, no ties, no pacts, no contracts. Right?"

"Oh, yes," Klendrisia stopped and turned to face Mezk, causing him to draw up short, "except one agreement."

"What?" Mezk's face turned red, ready to explode, "there is no other agreement, that ends it!"

"I just mean the agreement where I make sure you get out of here," Klendrisia smiled again, "safely and unharmed by me and any of my followers. That's all. You do still want that agreement to be fulfilled, right?"

"Yes," Mezk sneered, "of course. But that isn't so much an agreement, as an understanding."

"Oh?" The demoness looked up at the man. "Is that so? Well, I'm so pleased you clarified that. Words make a difference, especially when dealing with my ilk."

"Yeah," Mezk looked worried, wondering if he missed something, or if something had changed because of his words, "just make sure you keep to that understanding. Don't forget that I'll have two magical blades, and even without the consciousness in either of them, they'll still wield power. I'll wield that power."

"Of course," Klendrisia drew out the words, "consider me suitably threatened. And then, never do that again. If I feel I may come to any harm from you, all deals are off, and you may face new challenges that you never would have expected."

The demoness looked at the man, who glared back at her.

"Do we understand one another?" Klendrisia asked.

Mezk nodded.

"No, no, no," she moaned, shaking her head, "you have to say the words. You know that. Otherwise, it isn't clear. Do. We. Understand. One. Another?"

"Yes," Mezk rasped, "we do understand one another. And I'll be free of all this, and I'll live a life with no one holding my leash ever again."

"You and me both, my sweet," Klendrisia's tone was solemn.

Mezk tilted his head, watching the demon-spawn turn and walk away.

The dagger on his hip, the Demon Seed, pushed the urge upon him to stab her now, while she wasn't looking. Kill her before she could set a trap for him.

The cloth wrapped Dragon's Dagger railed against its magical prison. The urges and thoughts from it were muted and blunted, but Mezk could still feel it trying to touch his mind and control him. It wanted out...and it wanted the Kid.

He'd give the dagger what it wanted soon enough, but on his schedule, and on his terms. Once the dwarf was dead, the barbarian broken, and the Kid sobbing at Mezk's feet, then he'd free the Dragon's Dagger and give him the Kid forever.

Once he shattered that blood bond, he'd break the last defense of the ivory blade, and the Demon Seed could devour it. That would break all ties between Mezk and his pact. He'll have fulfilled his part of the deal, freeing the incubating soul trapped within the dagger, and it could go its way to exact revenge on the ones who did this to it.

Mezk wasn't sure where he'd go next. Durgan's Keep sounded good, but he knew that cesspool too well, and wasn't sure if he wanted to bother taking it for his own.

Maybe he'd get a ship and take to the seas. They were dangerous, much more now than they were before the Downfall, but at least he'd be free.

The ends of the world were his only restrictions. He could go to Seawall City or cross the continent and see what lay there.

But another thought niggled at him. Mezk knew he'd be in the center of a huge power play. One well-placed knife, and his biggest rival would be gone. If he killed Klendrisia, everyone else would be a new player in the game. He'd be able to make alliances, form new connections, and perhaps even have them bow to him for a change.

Demons were tricky things, but they weren't infallible. They were so used to having the upper hand over humans, they never considered that the tables could be turned.

If Mezk could kill Klendrisia, he could control the portal annex. He would be the one making the deals and collecting the debts from the demons for a change. They would come to him, ask him for favors and passage.

And with his connections in Red Wind, Durgan's Keep, and the other communities, he could rule this entire part of the continent if he could control the portals to other realms and worlds.

This was food for thought, and the Demon Seed encouraged it. The dagger thought it was a good idea, and that the two of them could work together and bring great things to this world, one deal at a time.

## Chapter 21

The city of Red Wind lay in smoking ruins. The demons had put most of the buildings to the torch, burning out anyone hiding within. When someone came out of a building, they were set upon by hordes of jedth or a crigth and torn apart.

The sooty clouds overhead moved with a mind of their own, dark tendrils reaching down to touch the ground and then pull back into the mass above. Ash fell across the city like a dirty flurry.

The splinter factions of the city had no chance; even if they'd been able to come together, it might not have helped.

Nathan wandered through the streets, helping anyone he could. Parents searching for children—or children searching for parents—were everywhere. The community came together now, but too late.

"The us and them mentally," the Kid said, and Nathan turned to regard him, "they were against each other, and it screwed them when someone else showed up. Now, they draw together, because there's a different *them* to battle their collective *us*."

"Well," Torrents looked over a smoldering pile of wet bodies, trying to puzzle what piece belonged to which corpse, "a little too little, a little too late, they just had their us'es handed to them."

"That's insensitive," Nathan said. "You shouldn't make fun of people who just faced this much death."

"They shouldn't have been pemties," Torrents shrugged, "if they'd been working together instead of trying to beat out the other guy, then more of them might've survived."

"You don't know that!" Nathan spun to face Torrents, jabbing the large man in the belly with a thick finger. "You don't have the right to say things like that. These were human beings, and they murdered them in the street for no reason. You have no right to come in here and insult their memory."

"Hey," the Kid put one hand on Nathan's shoulder, and pulled the poking finger from Torrents's stomach as the big man glared down at the rokairn, "hey, hey. I get what you're saying, but some of us deal with things in different ways, and that's okay, too. We can't expect everyone to be calm and not angry after living through something like this, can we?"

Fred moved between the Kid and the rokairn, lightly clicking his claws.

Nathan sighed, looked down, and shook his head.

"If I hadn't run," Nathan muttered.

"What?" The Kid turned Nathan to face him. "What are you talking about? You fought. You helped protect the church full of people, then you went out into the streets and hunted down dozens of demons, maybe hundreds. What do you mean, 'if you hadn't run'?"

"Not today," Nathan's voice tightened, "not now. When I first got here. I knew what I had to do. I knew I needed to go south. Find Klendrisia, kill her, and stop the demons from coming north. But I ran. I abandoned my responsibility, and because of that…all these people are dead. They're all dead, because of me."

"That's a load of bullbidj," Torrents spat, "you aren't responsible for the whole world. You're one man, or rokairn, and you can't think that you could've stopped a whole army of demons. That's ridiculous."

The Kid held a hand towards Torrents, gesturing for him to stop talking.

"You've done good here, Nathan," the Kid patted the rokairn's shoulder, "you've helped more people in one afternoon than most people help in their whole lives."

"You guys are right," Nathan said.

"I know we are," Torrents shot back.

"Hush," the Kid hissed at the barbarian, then turned back to Nathan, "what do you mean?"

"If I'd stopped her in the very beginning, it would've been different," Nathan looked the Kid in the eye, "even if I'd died fighting demons all alone, it would've been different. Klendrisia would've never come through here the first time, killing good people. She would've never taken your dagger, so that's my fault, too. She would've never gone to the Towers. She wouldn't have opened new portals. All that happened because I was a coward, and because I was a coward, people have died."

"No," the Kid said gently, "they died, because bad people do bad things…"

"I'm not done," Nathan interrupted, "and don't placate me with trite platitudes. They died because I didn't do something. It's that simple. But what I meant when I said you two are right, is that violence is the only way. Talking doesn't help. These people talked to each other, but it didn't help them, it tore them apart. Talking to Klendrisia won't help. The only thing this damned, pemtie world understands is blade and blood."

"Whoa," the Kid leaned away from Nathan, "such strong language. Did you just say the word 'damn'? Shouldn't you have said darn, or shucks, or golly gee whiz? Such a potty mouth, and from you Nathan. I expected better."

Nathan didn't laugh.

"Look," the Kid leaned back towards him, "we can't change the past, right? We can only do something different the next time. And what can we do right now?"

"We can go kill the demon bitch who caused all this," Nathan said through gritted teeth.

"You ain't gonna go alone," a deep, slow voice said from behind Nathan.

Nathan turned to look and behind him was a big man with a dull look on his face, a conical helmet on his head, and a shirt of chain mail.

"Nob?" Nathan breathed. "You're alive?"

"Yah," Nob nodded, "thanks to you. So, stop talking dumb. You can only help when you do things. Not after it happens. Okay?"

"Yah," Torrents's tone mimicked, "what he said, dork."

All three of the others looked at Torrents.

"Him," Torrents pointed at Nathan, "he's the dork, not you, Nob. You seem cool. He's a pemtie though."

"Yah," Nob nodded again, "but don't pick on him. It ain't easy being like that. I feel bad for him."

The Kid snickered and held his hand out to Nob.

"I'm the Kid," the Kid said, "and the other dummy behind me is Torrents."

Nob shook the Kid's hand.

"Whose kid are you?" Nob asked. "You don't look rokairn, or whatever Torrents is."

"No," the Kid laughed, "that's what they call me. I'm the Kid, no other name."

"Yah," Nob nodded at the Kid, and turned to the rokairn, "poor people can't afford fancy names like Nathan. Oh, and the priests at the temple want to see you, Nathan."

The Kid called Fred back to his side—the rock lobster had been diligently snapping the throats of any demons they came across, the acid blood not affecting his stony hide—and the group moved through the streets, taking time to help people they passed. It took almost an hour to travel the six blocks, and when they arrived, they had a group of twenty people with them.

The priests met them on the steps, taking the townsfolk into their care.

A thin, grey-haired man with a neatly trimmed beard stepped up to the group.

"This is Pelese," Nathan said to his friends. "He's the high priest here."

Each gave their greeting, introducing themselves.

"You folk," the priest's voice was full and rich, "have done a lot to help Red Wind, and I wanted to thank each of you."

Pelese held up his hand to forego any interruptions.

"I understand you've decided to go further into the storm," Pelese continued, "seeking the heart of this attack?"

"Yeah," the Kid's forehead wrinkled in confusion, "but we just decided that. How'd you hear about it already?"

"My son," the priest smiled, "Jonath protects, and he whispers to others to help when we can. And that's what I want to do."

"What does that mean?" Torrents asked.

"It means he wants to help," Nob grunted.

"It means," Pelese cut them off, "that I want to tend your wounds, give you supplies, offer the blessings of Jonath, and send as many able-bodied people with you as will volunteer to go."

"Like me," Nob smiled and nodded.

Torrents, Nathan, and the Kid exchanged looks.

"No," Nathan said, "no one needs to go with us. They've suffered enough, and too many have died."

"Hey," the Kid rested a hand on Nathan's arm, "this is their town, their world, and they're allowed to help defend it if they want."

"The child speaks wisely," Pelese said, earning him a sharp glare from the Kid, "and though you may seek the heart to destroy it, others can handle the arms of a many limbed foe."

"Ugh," Torrents muttered, "all the fancy talk. Is he reading poetry or something?"

"All things in life are poetry," Pelese smiled, "if you take the time to listen. Some are dark, some are hopeful, and all should be shared. Allow these people to share this burden, and the glory of the sagas that will be written and sung to recount the brave deeds, the lives lost, and the future that will come from it."

"How can we say no to that?" the Kid raised an eyebrow.

"No," Nathan said.

"That's how," Torrents muttered.

"This is my responsibility," Nathan ignored the barbarian's comment. "I can't ask anyone else to go with me!"

"My son," Pelese said, interrupting the Kid, who had opened his mouth to say something, "you aren't asking. They are going with you, or without you, to protect their homes and families. The ones who would not go are either unable to rise and hold sword and spear or have fled in hopes of not falling to the inevitable. Would you brand every man and woman a coward, and deny them the right to defend their loved ones?"

Nathan sighed and looked away.

"Then it is done," the priest smiled, "come inside so our chirurgeons may tend to your injuries. A hot meal and a warm bed also await."

The sun rose, breaking through the thick clouds in single rays, on two score of armed townsfolk. Others lined the streets. Any not gathered could not get out of bed or were tending to the injured.

It was a motley army, some barely old enough to fight, others much too old to wear a sword anymore, but they were prepared to face something that couldn't be beaten.

The crowd cheered, a ragged sound, grim along with hopeful, as the columns of people on horseback and a few supply wagons moved away and down the broken street.

Nathan rode a pony at the head of the procession, bracketed by Torrents and the Kid. The barbarian rode on a roan mare who pranced excitedly, and the Kid had a dapple who kept nuzzling him for treats. Fred scampered along on one side, making horses whiney and shy away. Nob rode behind Nathan, spear in a stirrup and sword on his side.

The temple gave each of them what healing they could spare and patched or replaced their equipment.

They'd travel east, across the Red Plains and the western portion of the Crescent Desert. When they hit the crag wasteland in the center of the desert, they'd veer southeast towards the Pyridom. The trip would take three weeks with the wagons and extra people.

It was on the tenth day of the journey, and the third day into the heat-blown sands, when the deserters left in the middle of the night, taking most of the supplies with them.

# Chapter 22

"They took all the water," Nob's voice cut through the chill, desert, night air, "and the horses!"

"Stop yelling," Torrents hissed. "You'll bring them all down on us."

Nob quieted, looking around. Seeing Torrents crouched beside the wagon a few meters away, the burly man moved over to the barbarian and crouched as well.

"What're we gonna do?" Nob whispered, much too loud.

"The Kid is checking it out," Torrents reassured him. "We don't know what happened yet."

"Yes, we do," Nathan's bitter voice came from on top of the wagon. "They stole all the supplies and left us to die in the middle of the desert."

"Let's just wait until the Kid gets back," Torrents directed his voice to Nob to reassure him, "before we jump to conclusions, okay?"

Nob nodded.

"The only conclusion is," Nathan growled, "people are bidj."

The Kid hunched, moving along, keeping low so he wouldn't be seen over a dune from a distance. He wasn't sure if it was necessary. He wasn't worried about the deserters seeing him—they'd already be long gone since they were on horseback and had adequate light—but there were other things that hunted at night.

Fred was three paces behind him, shuffling along with natural ease in the desert. The Kid had thought that odd, considering lobsters were not especially graceful on land. Then again, he didn't know a lot about this magical construct he'd created by accident. The rock lobster seemed to be in his element in the sands. Literally.

It was a waning moon, almost down to a quarter, just ten days until the new moon. Not that the moonlight mattered, the green glow of the demon-lights—which is what they'd begun calling the atmospheric effect in this area that resembled the northern lights, except in color—lit the night sky, making the moon a blurred smear, sickly yellow beyond the dancing swirls of demonic energy.

The Kid still didn't understand how the deserters snuck out of camp without waking anyone. Leading that many horses away without making noise was an impossible task. And how did they pack everything with no one noticing?

Could they have used magic to silence themselves, or to keep everyone asleep?

The Kid didn't think magical skills were so common that anyone among the townsfolk would have the ability. There were the priests, but they had left the three of them behind with the camp. They also worshiped the god of protection, and that meant guard-duty was in their repertoire. Jonath often gifted his priests with extra abilities, including heightened awareness and perception. No one should have been able to sneak past them, let alone a bunch of people with fully loaded horses.

Besides the priests, the only people left behind had been the older men and women. That meant the deserters consisted of the young. Did that mean anything? Perhaps they were prone to rebellion, or easier to sway? And why would they leave now, anyway?

There was no way these people slipped away in a well-lit night, on a flat desert landscape, without help.

Or something taking them. But how did you snatch up two dozen people and forty horses without raising an alarm?

And Fred didn't sleep, and he knew to wake the Kid if something was happening. But Fred hadn't noticed anything, either.

When the Kid was woken—by Nob—the street thief had begun a search. The Kid had checked around the camp, easily finding the tracks of the horses leading into the night. But they'd ended less than twenty paces away.

The sands had been blowing, partially covering the tracks, but it hadn't blown enough to conceal them completely.

It made no sense.

Without the food, water, and supplies that were taken, people were going to die. Too many had died already, and now the people who'd come with them would likely be next. The old didn't travel well on foot through a desert with no water.

The Kid was sick and tired of losing people. Not in the way he lost the deserters when he was tracking them, but losing them to death. Death was the natural conclusion to life. Everyone had to take that irrevocable step sometime. But to see so many killed before their time was taking its toll on him.

Hope's Hollow, Durgan's Keep, Red Wind, and now they were taking a journey down the River Styx and into the belly of the beast. No one making this trip was likely to survive it, and there was a good chance the rest of the world wouldn't survive it, either.

It was exhausting, always having to deal with death.

Something caressed the Kid's mind, breaking him away from his thoughts, and he froze like a mouse hearing the cry of a hawk.

Fred, feeling something wrong with his creator, scurried over to the Kid and clacked his claws in a display meant to frighten a foe.

"You can still feel my mind," the Kid patted Fred, "can't you, boy? I wish I still had my other abilities, too, but at least we're still connected."

The Kid's lost his mind mage abilities when Mezk stabbed him with the cursed dagger. If something had touched his mind, and even Fred sensed it, that meant it could connect with any mind: mind mage, normal, or magical. What sort of thing could do that?

Something tickled at the back of the Kid's thoughts, like when doing a crossword, and couldn't remember the clue needed to fill in seven-down, thirteen letters. A being that could do those things, it could hunt anyone, and wouldn't leave a trace or raise an alarm.

"I'm a fool's pemtie," the Kid muttered, shaking his head as he rose.

He ran as fast as he could back towards the camp.

Time flew faster than the Kid's feet and he was within the circle of the encampment's abandoned wagons before he knew it. Fred, still beside him, reached up with a claw and pinched the Kid's inner thigh.

"Ow!" The Kid slapped at his thigh, glaring down at the construct. "What the hell was that for? And where is everyone? You see anyone, Fred?"

Fred danced left and right and turned in a circle.

"Yeah," the Kid looked around as he spoke, craning his neck to check the top of wagons, "I don't see anyone either."

He moved to where he'd left Torrents and Nathan, inspecting the sands beside the wagon. It showed an imprint where the barbarian had been kneeling, a thin line of his blade beside it.

Climbing atop the wagon, sand scattered across the canvas covered crates, showing where Nathan stood when the Kid saw him.

He turned, preparing to jump off the side to the sands below, and tripped over Fred. The thief stumbled, wind milling his arms as he swayed at the edge of the wagon. He regained his balance and dropped back on his heels.

"Fred!" the Kid growled, looking at the rock lobster. "What's gotten into you? And how'd you even get up here? Been practicing your jumps, or did you learn to levitate?"

The Kid turned back to the edge, preparing again to jump down, and stopped when he noticed the swirling patterns in the sand below.

"I swear I heard him," Torrents said, trailing a dagger in a spiral pattern in front of him, "like he was shouting at that damn crab. It didn't sound like it was far away, but it was faint."

"That makes no sense," Nathan said, still scanning the horizon, "but there's something else here, even if it's not the Kid."

"Perhaps," Nob said, "the two of you should go out into the night and find your friend. I can wait here; in case he returns."

"You might be right," Torrents stood, shoved his dagger back into its sheath, and brought his ebon blade up, resting the flat on his shoulder, "he's been gone too long."

"How long has he been gone?" Nathan was studying the clouds moving overhead, his voice serious and focused. "I mean, really Torrents, how much time has passed since we've been waiting?"

"I don't know," Torrents wrinkled his brow, "I really…don't know. That's odd."

"What's odd?" Nathan's voice was expectant, like he was looking for a specific answer. "What exactly are you finding odd at this moment?"

"It doesn't matter," Nob said, "you should find your friend. Perhaps one of you could go one direction, and the other can go the opposite direction. It would be quicker if you separated."

"I'm not sure." Each word was a separate sentence as Torrents spoke them. "I can't put my finger on it exactly, but it's like…like this is just a single moment. I know the Kid's been gone for a while, but it feels like he just left."

"Go on," Nathan prodded, nodding, but still watching the sky, "how could that be, Torrents?"

"We've had an entire conversation, right?" The barbarian looked up at him and went on when he saw Nathan nod. "Maybe more than one, but it's like no time passed. And, the wind is blowing, but the sand isn't moving. That's not really normal, is it?"

"You should go," Nob's voice was a command, "find your friend, leave here and go seek him."

"Not really," Nathan said, "and the wind isn't blowing up here, a meter off the ground, but the clouds are moving. And when did Nob start speaking in complete sentences?"

Torrents turned to look at the burly mercenary, but only glimpsed the deep green shadow surging towards him before screaming.

The shadow launched itself at the barbarian, enveloping him as he tumbled backwards onto the sands, bringing his sword to bear.

The weapon was no longer in his hands.

Torrents screamed.

Fred pinched the Kid again, harder this time, causing him to squeal.

"Fred!" the Kid sputtered through clenched teeth. "What's gotten into you?"

The lobster ran to the Kid. He didn't grab the man's clothes and pull himself up. He just ran up him, settled onto his chest, and seized the Kid's ears in his massive claws.

"Ow!" the Kid jerked away, but found his back flat against the ground, his elbow digging into the sand for a moment before he reached to grab Fred's pincers, "Wait, what just...how am I laying down, Fred?"

The canopy of the canvas tent above the Kid flapped in the wind.

Holding Fred's claws in place, the Kid sat up and looked around without turning his head, thus avoiding having the rock lobster tear his ears off.

"I'm…" the Kid enunciated slowly, "I'm in my bedroll, in my tent? How'd that happen? Where'd the cart go?"

Fred released the Kid's ears, scrambled backwards down his chest and sideways onto the sand beside him.

The Kid put both hands under him, pushed up, and stood, ducking in the enclosed space. He walked, while bent, to the door flap, and pushed out into the night air.

The dark, oily cloud he'd seen over Red Wind hung low in the sky above the camp, dirty tendrils quivering as they touched tents and guards on duty.

Each person the Kid could see stared straight ahead, their bodies relaxed, even if standing.

"Night hunters, Fred," the Kid said to the rock lobster who'd moved forward and pressed against his ankle, "dream hunters. Invisible, ethereal demons who devour hope and fear. That's what's here, but you can't see them when awake. They're like the…psychic assassins for the really, dark, slimy folks. And I'm pretty sure we have an infestation."

Fred clacked what the Kid assumed was an agreement.

"I think…" the Kid moved forward, one step at a time, "your bond with me, and maybe because you were touching me, allowed you to interact with me when I was, wherever I was. It could be because of my mind-mage abilities, but they don't seem to be around anymore."

The two moved through the camp, looking into tents where the cloud tentacles reached down and touched people, and at the comatose guards still standing and staring into the distance, taking stock of the situation.

The Kid saw the horses, in a tight group, about twenty meters away from the camp on a dune. The animals were whinnying and stamping nervously, shaking their heads and rolling their eyes.

Passing a wagon, the Kid spotted Nob standing on the other side, a tendril from above obscuring his head.

Moving closer, the rogue heard noises from underneath. Drawing two daggers, he bent to look beneath the buckboard.

Torrents and Nathan lay underneath, back to back, curled in their bedrolls, both twitching in their sleep.

The barbarian's ebon blade lay an arm's length from the man, and the rokairn clutched his axe, but his magical amulet was half buried in the sand at his feet.

The Kid stooped under the wagon, duck-walking forward. He slid the blade to Torrents's hand with his foot, while reaching out to retrieve the amulet and set it on Nathan's bare chest.

## Chapter 23

Torrents fell backwards, screaming in surprise. It turned into a cry of rage, as he somersaulted heels over head and came up on his feet.

The shadow spirit was on him, a mouthful of black mist teeth stretching the creature's features until nothing more than a maw trying to devour Torrents's face was where its head had been.

The barbarian shoved both fists forward, attempting to hold the thing away from him, but his hands slipped into the mist, going numb and falling to his sides.

Then Nathan was there, swinging his axe at the ephemeral body of the spirit. The blade passed through harmlessly, but when the shaft touched the being's form, it shot a spray of green flashes resembling fireworks.

The creature spun towards the rokairn, a hiss that sounded like a distant teakettle issuing from above it. A wispy image of a tendril flashed into existence, extending from the sky.

Nathan flipped his axe and stabbed the vine wrapped handle at the thing as it pulsed towards him. The spirit flowed to the left, moving around the shaft. The rokairn swept the weapon's handle sideways, cutting through the ethereal demon.

Green fireworks burst around the creature and the hissing noise filled the air, the tentacle of smoke appearing above it again.

Torrents stepped backwards, looking around for something to use as a weapon, when he noticed his sword was now in his grip and his hands were no longer numb. He raised the blade, staring at it in surprise.

With a shrug, the barbarian brought the sword to bear in a double handed hold, angling it diagonally across his chest in a full body defensive posture.

The thing surged towards Nathan again and crashed against an invisible bubble surrounding him.

Looking down in surprise, Nathan saw his black shield amulet resting against his breastbone.

An ebon blade slashed across the specter, and the thing melted into tattered wisps of smoke with a sigh.

The Kid was crouched beside Torrents when the barbarian's eyes fluttered open. Beside him, Nathan moaned and sat up from his bedroll.

Fred danced back and forth anxiously.

"Good morning, sleepyheads," the Kid smiled, "when you clear the cobwebs from your head, I need some help to wake the others."

"What was that?" Nathan twisted to look over his shoulder at the other two, blinking in the chilly night. "Were we dreaming?"

"Sorta," the Kid duck-walked backwards to get out from under the wagon, Fred scurrying to one side, "I think you were facing a Night Hunter, it's a demon spirit, and probably working with the folks we're going after."

"How many are there?" Torrents asked, crawling out from under the shelter.

"Not sure," the Kid held out one hand to help the big man to his feet, pointing towards the sky with his other hand, "but I think that ominous cloud is a nest of them. Some sort of hive mind, or something where they all gather. See the tendrils, like what we saw back in Red Wind?"

Nathan emerged from the other side of the wagon, looking up, and holding his chain mail shirt in one hand, his axe in the other. The black amulet still clung to his hairy chest.

"Do you know how to stop it?" Nathan asked, pulling his pack to him and strapping on various pieces of his armor.

"I think you guys can do that," the Kid pointed at Nob, who was standing a meter from Nathan, an even-more blank look than usual on his face. "I think your trinket blocks them, and Torrents bigger, blacker…sword can send them back to where they come from."

"Then let's do this." Torrents raised his blade.

"You want pants first?" the Kid laughed, pointing at the barbarian's minimal night clothes.

"Nope," Torrents said over his shoulder and strode around the wagon.

By the time the barbarian got around the wagon, Nathan had removed his amulet, slid his gambeson over his head, followed by his chain mail shirt, and pressed the magical shield to the center of his chest.

Torrents looked Nob up and down, the burly man staring slack-jawed into the distance, a streamer of oily smoke wrapped around his head.

The barbarian raised his sword and swung it with one hand through the tendril, splitting it. The tentacle jerked upward and away like a living thing, retreating into the swirling mass above.

Nob gasped and fell to his hands and knees, the big man's conical helm tumbling from his head to the sand. The guard vomited between his splayed hands.

Nathan put a hand on Nob's shoulder, steadying him.

"You go," Nathan looked up at Torrents's worried face, and the Kid behind him. "I'll stay with him for a moment. Everyone may react differently, so we'll need to get the ones who aren't too bad to stay with the ones who are."

Torrents nodded and turned away, striding towards the closest grey tentacle.

"You sure?" the Kid asked. "Are you okay?"

"Yeah," Nathan grunted, rubbing Nob's shoulder, "go on, I'm fine, and I'll make sure that Nob's doing okay, then I'll be right there to help."

The Kid took a step backwards, then turned and jogged after Torrents who was already severing the next tendril.

He caught up in time to check on the young guardsman who'd just been freed from the demon's grasp.

Torrents had already moved on to the next person.

They continued this pattern, Nathan, Nob, and others joining as they freed more people.

When they had a dozen people released, the Kid and a handful of others went to retrieve the horses and bring them back to the camp.

Within fifteen minutes, every person who could be woken and freed from the grip of the spirit cloud had been. The camp was a flurry of activity as friends checked on one another.

"Fourteen dead," Nathan reported, his arms held behind his back as he stared at his feet, "and seven others who probably won't ever be right again. They're sick, confused, and dazed. Like that thing took part of them. No one wants to go back to sleep, they're afraid."

"That's what it fed on," the Kid was leaning against a wagon wheel, Fred running in circles around his feet, pausing every few seconds to look for danger, "that and hope. It seems like people who were touching others were less…damaged. But this thing is attracted to strong emotion, and the people who were the most positive or negative were the ones to get the worst of it. It focused on the young more than the old, too; I guess because young people have more intense emotional reactions."

"How do you know so much about these things?" Torrents asked from where he squatted in front of a fire, poking at the burning dung with his dagger.

"It's part of being a mind-mage," the Kid shrugged. "These things hunt active minds, and abilities like that can draw them to you. I suspect if I hadn't lost my powers, I would've been quite a treat for them."

"I hated them," Nathan interrupted.

"What?" Torrents looked up from the fire.

"These people," Nathan waved an arm towards the people huddled in small groups, and the pile of canvas wrapped corpses at the edge of the encampment, "in that…dream, or whatever it was, I thought that a bunch of them had taken the horses and water, and just abandoned the rest of us."

"Yeah," the Kid nodded, "I did too. So? That's what the things were feeding us to create fear."

"But…I hated these people," Nathan said again. "I didn't care if they lived or died. That's not true. I wanted them to die, and even suffer for what they'd done."

"Okay," Torrents said, "I was right there with you, in the dream, and in that sort of mindset, too. It was just part of what was going on. It's no big deal."

"It is a big deal," Nathan hissed. "I don't hate anyone. I don't want to see people hurt. But everything you guys had said, you know, about violence being the answer, I really felt that way about these people. And now, half of them are dead or…broken."

"You didn't do that to them, though," the Kid said.

"Doesn't matter." Nathan shook his head.

"Get over it," Torrents stared straight at the rokairn, and everyone turned to look at the barbarian, "this isn't all about you. Look, I know you're Mister Sensitive and all that, and you're all about being nice, and that's fine. But this isn't all about you. You're whining and crying about pemtie bidj that doesn't matter. You didn't do this, and you're allowed to feel angry once in a while. Suck it up, we have a job to do. And we can't do it if you're all emo and bidj. You'll become the burden, the one who's abandoning us, even though you're right beside us."

Nathan stared at Torrents with slitted eyes, chewing on his lip, and fingering the haft of his axe.

Torrents stared back, his face tight.

"Wow," the Kid said, "there's some thick tension right now. How about we all just hug it out and be friends again?"

Nathan turned on heel and walked away.

The Kid moved to follow.

"Let him go," Torrents said, his tone short, "this is something he has to work out. Words aren't gonna fix this one. You should know that. We've all gone through some bidj, but in the end we all had to figure it out for ourselves."

The Kid watched Nathan walk away, Nob trailing after him.

"You know," the Kid muttered, "you're a real asshole, and I want to say you're wrong. But I can't find a good way to prove that right now. But I don't have to hang around you either way. I think I'll go find someone that I can help. Have a good night, Torrents the barbarian."

The Kid turned and walked towards the opposite side of camp from where Nathan went.


No one slept again that night, and they were on the move an hour before daylight, leaving behind a pyre of sixteen bodies. Though only fourteen died in the attack, two more had taken their life before the night was done.

Three others escorted the seven people who couldn't function anymore back west, including a priest of Jonath to provide extra protection, heading to Red Wind. They took the wagons, which meant they needed fewer horses to carry the same amount of people. They distributed the remaining supplies between the horses going the other direction.

The Kid, Torrents, Nathan, Nob, and the ten people from Red Wind that could still ride and fight, turned their horses and wagons to the east, heading for the rocky crags that dominated the center of the Crescent Desert.

The people of Red Wind spoke of the monsters of the crags, horrible creatures that hunted any who entered the rocky area.

The townsfolk had gained a new respect for the three men who had been nothing more than strangers to them when this all started.

Ichaelson—the higher ranked of the two remaining clerics of Jonath—took the lead, guiding the meandering line of horses across the dunes. The older man with the gap in his teeth knew the sands and called upon the guidance of his patron deity, who ruled over the element of earth, to help him find a true path.

The second, Vindalai, was a solid woman who always carried her signature weapon, a meter-long shafted handle with a steel head shaped like a brick—halfway between a maul and war hammer—with the symbol of Jonath stamped on the side. She took up the rear, always on the watch for signs of anything approaching.

The two clerics gravitated to Nathan, and one or the other would call to the rokairn, waving him over whenever they saw him looking in their direction. When he went over, the priests would instruct him about the ways of their god, telling him tales or lessons from their religion. But they also sought to learn from him, asking him questions of faith and encouraging stories of willpower and determination. The rokairn brushed them both off, remaining surly and withdrawn.

Three of the younger men—Dodd, Shad, and Tradler—imitated Torrents, shedding armor in favor of less cumbersome furs.

"What the hell are you wearing?" Torrents sneered, scrunching his face up as they rode up beside him. "You're gonna get yourselves killed, dressed like that. If the heat of the desert doesn't get you, then the first demon you come across will cut you open in a split second. You're all pemties."

"But," Tradler's eyes were wide with a panicked look, "you never need armor."

"And I get really cool scars because I don't wear any, pemtie," Torrents sighed. "You trained using armor. I didn't. I was raised using agility and getting the hell out of the way."

"We could learn to do that," Shad chimed in, "you can teach us."

"Really?" Torrents leaned back, wiping a hand across his brow. "Whew! I was worried that we could face a horde of demons any time now! I didn't realize we had years, or at least months, to teach you three a whole new fighting style!

"Look, geniuses," Torrents slowed his horse and turned in the saddle to look at the three, "you don't change your strategy in the fourth quarter unless you have to, okay?"

"Uh, I don't know what that means," Dodd sounded whiney every time he spoke, but Torrents thought he sounded spoiled and entitled, "but I find it easier without the armor."

"It means," Torrents stared down the greasy-haired teen, "get your damned armor and put it on. Did you ever stop to think why I use this gigantic sword? It keeps things further away from me. You boys are using short blades. Anything attacking you will be right up on you if you want a chance to hit it. By not wearing your armor, especially with that type of weapon, you're inviting something in close enough to do more damage than you could handle. Is that clear enough? Get your chuzzing armor back on, you pemtie bidjs."

The Kid kept the remaining half entertained with wild stories—some from this omnild, others from TV sitcoms—and the antics of Fred.

The rock lobster would act out any story the Kid told, though its limited actions often made no sense in relation to the tale. Varina and Dinwiddie—a couple who'd lost their three children in the battle at Red Wind—always clapped and talked about how their kids would have loved the performance.

Mecklen was sour about the little stories and shows, complaining that they should be 'saving their spit' to help survive the desert heat. He was an older man, a veteran of the Demon Front who constantly grumped about things, his words drawled as he chewed on the thick pinch of tobacco in his right cheek.

The last two didn't speak much. The young woman, Ablemarle, was polite and to the point. But the slim man traveling with her never spoke, and the Kid didn't think anyone even knew his name.

By the afternoon of the second day after leaving the nightmare camp, as they came to call it—the younger men had dubbed it 'the Battle of the Nightmare Camp'—the crags were visible as small, jutting shapes in the distance.

Everyone took to riding with the hoods of their cloaks up to protect them from the brutal sun, and anyone without a cloak fashioned some sort of head covering from whatever cloth they could find.

They traveled from sunrise to about noon, then set up shade tarps to shelter from the most intense part of the day. Ichaelson, who had some elementalist gifts in addition to the holy magics of Jonath, combined the two things to help find water whenever he could. A few hours before sunset, they'd mount up and move again, until they set camp for the night a few hours after the sunset.

It tinted the sands green from the energies blanketing the land to the south. The light of the Demon Front had been intensifying as they drew nearer to it, and closer to the new moon.

Vindalai, a veteran of many years and battles on the Demon Front, told the others that she'd never seen it like this. The desert was barren most times, but now there was no sign of life creeping across it or flying above it. Even the cacti had withered and dried to husks.

The sun was most of the way across the sky, with just a couple hours of daylight remaining, the sands transitioning to rock under the hooves of their mounts.

More than one of them sighed audibly, relieved to have something besides the hot shifting sands under their horse's hooves.

They rode in silence, each wrapped in their own thoughts, approaching the elevated crags in the center of the desert. Their shadows grew long in front of them as the sun moved further west behind them.

Sand erupted in plumes and sprayed around the riders. Figures burst from the gullies along the side of the road, throwing off canvas cloaks that blended with the sands and raising crossbows at the group. Other forms dropped dun-colored tarps and moved from recesses in the surrounding rocks.

A score of stout men and women surrounded the haggard group. Spears, javelins, crossbows, and bows pointed at the group.

The riders bunched together, their horses bumping against one another, making the animals whicker and shy away from the edges, pushing to the center.

Ichaelson's head snapped to the side, a stone ricocheting off his head. The priest slid backwards in his saddle and then toppled to the ground.

Vindalai slid from her roan mare to land near her fellow priest, pushing horses' rumps and bridles, trying to stop her friend from being trampled.

Shad's horse reared, as he jerked hard on his reins, and fell to the ground in reward for his efforts.

Dodd was spinning in circles, struggling to pull his sword from its sheath, his horse jerking its head back and forth, trying to free itself from the control of its rider.

"Kreelon ghrust!" Nathan commanded in a strange language with his rumbling baritone, then repeated, "Stay still!"

"Troj?" A gruff figure pushed forward from the crags, pointing at Nathan over his crossbow, "Trojet Bellstamp? Is that you? We thought you were dead!"

## Chapter 24

"Gretna," the short, stout man shouted, "watch the hills! Dandron and Galax, you two take the sands, one to north, one to south, eyes on the sky and your feet. Let's not have a repeat of last month when we lost track of this dimwit. Troj, where the hell have you been?"

The rokairn that surrounded them broke into organized groups. The three the leader tasked moved to lookout positions, the other sixteen set up a perimeter around the horses.

"It's me, Grundy," the rokairn who had spoken moved towards Nathan, his head tilted. "Grundy Stonegap, your squad commander and friend of fifty years. Maybe you recall some of that?"

Nathan looked between the Kid, Torrents, and Nob, shrugging, then slid out of the saddle and dropped to the ground. The wind whistled through the rocks surrounding them and a small dust devil danced across the trail ahead.

"Sorry, Grundy Stonegap? Trojet Bellstamp, that's me?" Nathan asked, shaking his head.

Something chewed at his mind, a familiar ring to the names he repeated. They were right, they fit. Memories swelled, and Nathan stumbled as the weight of it came over him.

This man, this rokairn, walking towards him, was someone he had known. He'd known him for most of the life that belonged to his rokairn body. Recollections of Grundy gaining a squad leader position ten years before Nathan—or Trojet—was allowed to go on patrol rose in his mind. His past from this world filled his mind, washing over him and overwhelming him.

Nathan knew he'd accepted his first position assigned by the Crescent Crag Clan under this man, and images of the rokairn warrens under the desert flooded back to him. His people lived here, hidden from the heat and dangers under the sands.

He'd saved Grundy's hide, and some of the others, many times, and they'd done the same for him, usually when fighting demons or undead from the south.

A hand on his shoulder brought him back to the present.

"You alright, khaudarn?" Grundy steadied Nathan. "You don't look too good. You're pale. Did you see a ghost?"

"Sorry, it's complicated," Nathan mumbled. "I've gone through a lot since we last patrolled together. I'm not the same rokairn you knew."

"Really?" Grundy laughed. "How is that? Did these pemtie humans do something to you? Last I knew, you went off on some crazy quest to Seawall City, thinking you could take on the whole Demon Front by yourself."

Grundy put his hands on Nathan's shoulders and turned him to face him. Growing serious, he searched Nathan's face.

"It's alright," the patrol leader shook Nathan, "the council will overlook it, maybe give you a mild reprimand, but they'll let you come back."

"No," Nathan's voice firmed, "I can't go back. Not now, maybe not at all."

"What?" Grundy smiled. "Of course you can. It'll be alright. You're an excellent warrior, you're just going through something."

The Kid traded looks with Torrents.

The barbarian shrugged, and moved his horse closer to Dodd, grabbing the bridle of the man's mount to calm it. Shad and Tradler moved to each side of their friend.

"Control your horses," Torrents called out. "Nathan'll work this out, then we can be on our way."

Vindalai helped Ichaelson to his feet, as the older priest rubbed his head.

The Kid moved closer to Varina and Dinwiddie, who were helping Ablemarle and her friend calm their mounts.

The Kid threw a glance at Nathan, understanding what he was going through. The Kid had gone through a similar thing when he'd met people who knew him before…before he'd been in this body. It was easier for the Kid, though, because the Kid had eagerly thrown himself into this world and embraced the change, going with it.

Nathan struggled, confused by the duality of his mind and his body, and the memories he could access when needed, but usually suppressed.

"Nathan?" Grundy watched Torrents, then looked back to the other rokairn in front of him. "Is that some sort of human name they gave you?"

"It's hard to explain." Nathan squared his shoulders, visibly calming, as he focused on the patrol leader. "I think I've had a calling from Jonath. The god. The one of protection."

"Yes, Troj," Grundy smiled, speaking like he was addressing a child, "I know who Jonath is. What is this calling, though?"

"I've had…" Nathan hesitated, "a vision, and given knowledge from beyond. There is another spirit within me. I did die, but this other soul saved me, and now we're bonded. Sorry, I know that doesn't make much sense.

"Before you say anything," Nathan continued, moving Grundy's hands from his shoulders, "you need to understand that I'm going south to the Demon Front. You've seen the lights, and probably noticed that there are more demons than ever before. Things are coming to a head, and I need to go do whatever I can to stop what's causing this. I have to do this."

Grundy took a step back, looking Nathan up and down, squinting, his face moving from concerned to determined.

"Yes," Grundy nodded, "I see that you've changed, but I don't like the idea of you running into the mouth of hell with a bunch of grassland humans. They'll run; you know. These people aren't known for their dedication. They're short-lived, and don't understand our ways, and how we focus and achieve what others cannot."

"The demons attacked Red Wind," Nathan gestured at the people behind him, "and these people came with me from there to fight, in any way we can. Our people, the Crescent Clan, will be next. We will not remain untouched; the demons will come."

"They can't reach us," Grundy scoffed. "We can collapse the tunnels and stay underground for a century without blinking. Their problems are not ours."

"Yes," Nathan nodded slowly, "but in a century, when we reemerge, the enemy will still be here. It won't be our world anymore. It's time to fight, to defend our world. And I'm going to do that, with humans, rokairn, and anyone else who will stand with me. I'd rather die than let my world be taken by these creatures who want nothing but destruction. We rokairn are built to create and protect, not hide and let others destroy. If we hide now, we won't have the chance to recover."

"Are you trying to convince me?" Grundy turned away, crossed his arms, and looked to the green glow in the southern sky. "I hear you, brother. But I don't know that the council would agree. They think to choose this fight would be akin to choosing to die. I feel your words though, and they…have passion, but I'm not sure of the wisdom of them."

"Will you stop us?" Nathan asked, and Grundy turned his gaze back. "I know we cannot fight you and the demons. I would ask that you allow us to pass in peace if you will not join us. But I plead for you to call the clan and march with us."

"No," Grundy said flatly. "I will not stop you, but I will not dedicate the clan to your cause. It is not my place to do so."

The wind rose, and sand scattered across the group. A hawk called in the distance, its hunting cry echoing off the rocks.

Grundy seemed to consider something, looking towards the sound.

"A sign, the call to hunt. We will give you what we can," the patrol leader gestured to the rokairn who'd created the perimeter, "water, food, and some weapons if you need them. Then I must return to the tunnels and let the council know what we've found."

"I understand," Nathan sighed, "and thank you for the safe passage."

Grundy recalled his lookouts while the humans mounted their horses. The two groups exchanged introductions and goods, and within an hour moved deeper into the Crescent Crags and parted ways.

The humans and Nathan set camp, as the other rokairn disappeared into the broken landscape.

After two days, they reached the southern edge of the crags, another two days brought them to the northern edge of Tull's Swamp.

They moved along the western edge of the swamp, curving to the southeast. The Pyridom once stood in the center of the swamp, but the magics and demon incursion caused the wetlands to wither and recede, creating an alcove of desert in the center of what once was home to thriving life.

The northern arm of the swamp turned fetid, reeking of stagnant pools and dead or dying life.

In the distance, the sky changed from green to an emerald canopy overhead, reaching from horizon to horizon.

Packs of jedth roamed the desert to the south, and the group veered into the marsh to avoid them. They saw crigth also, usually solitary, but now appearing in threes, hunting for sport.

The group from Red Wind grew more nervous. Even Shad, Tradler, and Dodd lost their bravado, growing quiet as they came closer to their final destination.

The priests, Ichaelson and Vindalai, called upon the blessing of Jonath frequently to help the group pass unnoticed.

Mecklen sharpened his sword as they rode, rarely putting it away, and the others took no comfort in the war-grizzled veteran's actions.

"What's the plan?" The Kid asked once they could see the Pyridom in the distance, indicating they were less than a day from their destination, "Do we even have one? Or are we just charging in and hoping to find a huge power outlet that we can pull the plug from?"

The Pyridom was an inverted cone in the distance, standing alone on the plain of sand. Lightning lanced down, curling around the tall spire. The once reddish stone had a sickly, glazed look and had taken on an orange tint, contrasting with the green clouds around it.

"We go in," Torrents's tone was grim, "find the leaders, and cut off the head of the snake. Maybe if we do that, the rest will fall into chaos, and we'll have a chance of surviving."

"Surviving?" The Kid scoffed. "I was hoping we'd win, not just survive."

Torrents didn't answer, not looking over. He stared ahead, studying their destination.

"We'll camp," Nathan brought his horse up beside the other two, Nob trailing behind him, "at least for this evening. I don't want to go in and have night follow us. I think a morning attack will be best."

"Attack?" It was Torrents's turn to scoff, though his was harsher than the Kid's. "We're lucky we got this far without running into some of these things. It's almost like they were avoiding us. We can hope to make a surgical strike and do some good, but I wouldn't think of it as an attack. The Kid doesn't have his powers. We lost half our force to the nightmare demons. The rokairn turned their backs on the whole situation. We don't have the numbers to do anything but charge in and pray we find the one person, or creature, we need to find to stop this mess. If we make it to the Pyridom without getting killed first, and if we find that person, and if we can kill them before they kill us, then maybe we can stop this. But I think it'll be like kicking a hornet's nest from the inside, and making it back out will be…"

The barbarian trailed off.

"We can do this," Nathan's voice was quiet, but firm, "we were brought here for a reason, and it wasn't to fail. And we were all dying when we came here, so maybe we can do one last bit of good before that time comes. I won't give up, not now, and not even with my last breath."

"Give up?" Torrents turned in the saddle to look at the rokairn, a grim smile on his face. "I didn't say bidj about giving up. I'm gonna go in and give 'em hell, shove their own hell right back down their damned throats. I'm never giving up again."

"That's my boy," the Kid murmured. "We got this, even if it gets us before we're done."

## Chapter 25

The sun rose on thirteen humans and one rokairn riding across the sands from the edge of Tull's Swamp towards the Pyridom of Power.

Dark green clouds roiled, purple lightning arcing through them, the smell of ozone and decay hanging in a warm humid miasma below them.

The sands at the base of the Pyridom mimicked the movement of the clouds above, alive with thousands of jedth and hundreds of gnohls and crigth. Winged creatures circled the pinnacle of the structure, their screeches rolling across the sands, making the horses dance and nicker.

Bright blue orbs dotted the bottom of the ancient structure, showing the seeds to the portals that would open. One sphere, ten times larger than the others, acted as a beacon at the top of a flight of stairs for the group to follow.

Torrents led the group, his sword that severed demon ties to this plane in his hand.

Nathan rode beside him, his amulet glistening and sparking as they drew closer, repelling the demonic energies in the air. The rokairn held Marcid in his hands, the vine-wrapped handle glowing a vibrant shade of green.

The Kid dropped from his horse, handing his reins to Varina. He took his place beside the others, twin daggers in his hands. Fred scurried along beside him.

The townsfolk clumped together in two groups, except Mecklen, who rode a short distance apart, to have room to swing his sword.

Shad, Dodd, and Tradler rode in a wedge of their own, as the remaining four followed closely behind the priests.

The gnohl and demon horde parted as the group approached, clearing a path to the bottom of the Pyridom, and the steps and raised platform on which it stood.

The structure was old, constructed before modern people inhabited the land. Built by ancient peoples for long forgotten purposes, by the time modern civilization arrived, time and weather scoured the runes and hieroglyphs from the structure.

"That's odd…" the Kid watched the mass of demons extended along each side of them, "they're just letting us through."

"Do you think it's the magical things we got from the Tower of Onyx?" Nathan asked, turning in his saddle to crane his neck and see the wall of creatures close behind them.

"I have a bad feeling about this," Torrents said, his voice barely audible over the chattering and screeches of the mob surrounding them.

"Really? You're pulling that line out now?" The Kid said without humor. "Just don't shout 'It's a trap!' and order all fighters to protect the cruisers."

"Lando said that last part," Nathan murmured without enthusiasm.

The enemy ranks parted, and the group could see the base of the Pyridom, a single figure silhouetted in front of the large portal seed.

Klendrisia stood waiting, the smile on her face turning to a frown.

The group—except for the Kid, who was already on foot—slid from their saddles, readying weapons.

"Is this all you brought?" the demoness demanded as the group drew closer. "Where's the armies?"

"At least we have our target," the Kid mumbled, then raised his voice to address the cambion. "We're all you get, unless you'd like to go home and come back in a couple years so we can raise an army for you."

The woman sneered.

"Why?" Nathan called to her. "Why did you want us to bring armies? Why did you let us get this close?"

"Because," Klendrisia answered conversationally, her voice carrying across the distance, "I needed a sacrifice to open the gates. I guess your pitiful group will have to do. It won't let as many pass through, but it'll be a start."

"It's a trap," Nob nodded.

"It always is," the Kid sighed, "isn't it?"

"At least," Nathan hefted his axe, "she won't get everything she wanted."

Torrents nodded along with Nob, raising his double-handed sword.

"Get her…" Torrents's shout cut off.

Horns wailed from the west, and all heads turned in that direction. A cloud of dust rose in the distance, raised by men on horseback charging towards the demonic horde.

The sickly rays of sun that cut through the clouds glinted off steel weapons held high.

"There's got to be a couple hundred riders," Torrents gasped. "Where did they all come from?"

"I sent for them," Klendrisia's voice was smug, "weeks ago, I sent messengers to Durgan's Keep, and beyond, even to Diaz City and Runsk. Made sure they knew they had to be here for the battle on the new moon."

The ground rumbled, and Nathan pointed to the north.

"There's more," the rokairn sounded grim, "the Crescent Clan is coming, too."

"Are they riding…" the Kid squinted, his voice filling with wonder, "waves of sand?"

"They brought their priests of Jonath." Ichaelson's tone was awestruck. "Our human priests haven't been able to do that for generations!"

They watched the humans reach the edge of the otherworldly force to the west, and the rokairn crashed into the wall of creatures behind the group.

"Now," Klendrisia smirked, "this is a party. Thank you for convincing the rokairn to attend. It'll make the perfect invitation to all my people. They won't miss this for the world. Which, by the way, will be mine when this is over."

"Kaleb triot, den'al venitier!" Nathan roared, raised his axe, and rushed Klendrisia.

Nob followed his friend.

Torrents followed suit, gripping his blade in two hands.

The Kid ushered the small group past him as he guarded their backs.

The demons and gnohls between the group and their mistress pressed backwards, scattering.

Nathan took the steps two at a time.

"Now my pets," the demoness purred, "kill them all, but leave these three for Mezk!"

She swirled her fingers at Torrents, the Kid, and Nathan.

"Oh, Mezk, my sweet, you're on," Klendrisia trilled, turning and disappearing into a fold in the air.

The tall, thin dark-clad form with carrot-orange hair burst from the space where Klendrisia had been a moment before.

As Nathan reached the top step, Mezk thrust Demon Seed into the warrior-priest's chest.

The rokairn's momentum carried him forward, and Mezk sidestepped, thrusting a foot across Nathan's path.

The warrior-priest went down, face-first, onto the stone platform.

"Your blood shall wash these steps," Mezk growled, grinning as the demonic dagger pulsed black with red veins in his right hand, the velvet-wrapped blade of the Dragon's Dagger gripped in his left, "you damn dirty dwarf!"

The assassin dropped into a crouch and spun to face the oncoming rush of the barbarian.

Torrents slowed to a stop before reaching the top step, Nob beside him.

"Too afraid to face your own death after watching your friend die?" Mezk sneered.

"Nuh uh," Nob shook his head.

"You missed something." Torrents pointed behind the thief with his blade. "It might be important."

Mezk opened his mouth to say something, stopping as he heard a metallic rustle of chain mail behind him.

He shot a look over his shoulder.

Nathan stood behind him, feet shoulder-width apart, Marcid held in both hands across his body. The magical amulet on his chest shone black, a scratch marring its surface.

"Guess your dagger counts as a demon," Nathan shrugged, and raised his axe. "My turn."

The rokairn took two quick steps forward, lifting his axe overhead and chopping downward.

Torrents took two steps forward, thrusting with his sword at the same time.

The two weapons tore into Mezk's black form and clashed into one another, the assassin melting into the shadows to slide away.

Mezk rose from a pool of shade behind Nob—still coming up the steps—the assassin's black blade swiping across the man's lower back.

Nob screamed and tumbled forward, smoke rising from the bone-deep gash.

Demon Seed pulsed as it fed, Mezk breathing in deeply through his nose, as if experiencing the rush of feeding on a soul.

The mass of monsters at the foot of the steps swept over the people of Red Wind and Fred, who disappeared amongst the feet of the gnohls and demons, his claws clacking.

Gnohls, hyenas, and demons frenzied and attacked, horses torn apart as they backed away, screaming.

Varina shrieked, claws and teeth tearing into her. Dinwiddie leapt from his horse towards her. The man never reached his lover, wife, and partner, as one of the flying creatures snatched him. Dragged upward, high into the air, three of the creatures pulled on his body, tearing limbs loose, blood raining down on the mob of demons below, feeding its frenzy.

The abominations had the look of sleek hunting cats crossbred with vipers. They were the size of racing hounds, slim and muscled with leathery wings covered in a fine down of fur. The colors of that fur spread across the spectrum, giving them a beauty that belayed their deadliness.

Vindalai, the priestess, stood back-to-back with Mecklen, Ablemarle and her companion doing the same a few steps from them. The four fought valiantly. Mecklen used decades of combat experience to place precise blows, taking down the small jedth with ease.

The priestess screamed war cries between blows; her face red, her breath coming in forced puffs. Her massive maul crushed the cat-snake beasts diving from above, knocking them into the swirling mass of demons trying to claw their way to the group.

Ablemarle and her partner moved like oil over a hot skillet, sliding from one place to another, separating, then coming back together. They never left each other's sight but moved to strike, then to cross with the other.

Ichaelson prayed, loudly chanting words lost in the battle's tumult. He called to Jonath, beseeching the god's protection for his companions. Dodd, Shad, and Tradler stood in a loose triangle formation around the older man, shielding him as he prayed for their safety.

Shad shouted in surprise, his feet going out from under him. Dodd turned to look, moving towards his friend, only to see him dragged into the breaking tide of monsters that surrounded them.

Shad's shout stretched into a scream, as Dodd saw his friend's arm stop moving. The rest of the body disappeared, but that one arm lay where it had fallen, severed, spurting blood onto the sand-coated steps of the Pyridom.

Voices wafted past the young man, like scents of dinner burning on the wind, a memory from his childhood, each moving past him, barely noticed. Tradler yelled a warning. Dodd never saw the segmented claws of the crigth reaching over the others and enclosing his head in a scaly hand, twisting. Flesh and sinew creaked and tore. Dodd's body fell under a wave of smaller jedth, the larger demon popping the man's head into its maw like some sort of macabre candy. The creature made slurping noises, followed by a throaty 'yummy' sound.

The remaining friend, Tradler, felt his mind stretch, the world around him distorting, and then snap back into place. Almost audible to the young man, he physically felt it in the back of his skull. His eyes blurred, and he screamed as he raised his sword and plunged into the surrounding mob.

It crushed him to the ground and held him down.

"…won't do any good," a familiar voice was shouting at him, "damn it, Tradler, stop fighting me. You can't save them now!"

Ichaelson had one foot on Tradler's back, standing over the young man, fighting the demons with two tonfa— short staves, each the length of his forearms with a handle jutting perpendicular to the shaft—knocking the monsters away in rapid strikes.

Mezk raised the dagger and stabbed it down into Nob again, draining him of any remnants of the energies that made him who he was.

A sharp scream came from below the assassin, and a form shot up the steps.

The Kid leapt at his nemesis, a dagger held in each hand, blades pointed down.

Torrents moved towards Mezk, thrusting forward with his enormous blade.

Nathan ran to Nob's side, fell to his knees, and checked on his friend. He turned the body over, and Nob's eyes rolled in his head, sightless and lifeless.

Mezk moved, side-stepping the attacks, shifting in the sight of the others. The Demon Seed sparked, blocking the demon-slaying sword of the barbarian, and the assassin's left hand flashed with an ivory blade toward the Kid.

Mezk ran his shorter blade down Torrents's longer weapon, catching the sword's cross guard, then twisted his wrist to deflect the barbarian's great sword, causing it to miss and strike the ground a hair's breadth to his right. The assassin continued the movement, running the demon blade along the back of Torrents's hand.

The barbarian screamed and jerked backwards. His arm went numb to the shoulder as he felt the pull of the Demon Seed and the buffering protection of his weapon.

The Kid looked down, following the path of the assassin's second attack aimed at him. Mezk buried the white blade of Edsumar to its hilt in the Kid's chest.

# Chapter 26

Falling to his knees, the Kid saw it all.

To his right, on the steps, Nathan knelt over Nob, tears blinding the rokairn, his axe abandoned beside him. Torrents clutched his arm, the gash along his hand and forearm red with blood and demonic energy. The mass of demons at the bottom of the stairs swarmed over the small group of people who'd come from Red Wind. Fred had disappeared into the mass shortly after the fray began and hadn't been seen since.

The armies clashing with the demons and gnohls in the distance were lost in flashing lightning, green roiling mists, and dust clouds of sand.

The blue, glowing portal seeds pulsed and expanded, Klendrisia's sacrifices feeding them.

Mezk pulled Edsumar from the wound in the Kid's chest and lifted the blade to plunge it in again.

The Kid's head pounded, white light expanding to cover his vision.

*There you are*, a voice said in the Kid's head. *Ah, this feels so much better. You been doing okay?*

The Kid blinked, but internally. He was inside his head, the outside world receding.

"Edsumar?" The Kid laughed. "Yeah, I guess I'm alright, though I'm in a bit of a tough spot right now. Maybe things just look worse than they are. What about you?"

*Been stuck in the dark with no one to talk to. It was boring, and I hate to say, a little lonely. You think I'd be used to it, after spending all those years in the temple until you showed up. I've gotten used to chatting with you.*

"Yeah," the Kid smiled, "you're just an old softy. So, what's the plan?"

*No plan. Mezk still has control over me, so I get to just hang out and see what happens.*

"If only I had my powers," the Kid sighed, "this would turn out totally different."

*You do have them.* Edsumar's voice sounded amused to the Kid. *You never lost them. You just…invested them.*

"What's that mean? Invested them? Is there a brain trust somewhere I wasn't aware of?"

*Oh, you got jokes now!* Edsumar teased. *No, you did that thing, made Fred, and most of your abilities are tied up in him. When the Demon Seed pricked you back at PepperGarten's, your remaining abilities went dormant as it blocked the dagger from pulling your soul from you.*

"Fred?" the Kid asked. "Fred has my abilities?"

The Kid was on his knees, the real world coming back into focus with a jolt that pulled him back to the here and now. The stone edge of the steps bit into his shins, and a hot breeze swirled around him.

Mezk stood above him, a maniacal grin on his face as he brought Edsumar down for the killing stroke.

A grey streak, accompanied by a clattering stone on stone sound, rushed towards the Kid from the side of the stairs. Something hit him like a boulder, and the Kid fell as the ivory dagger came down.

Fred, now standing on the prone form of his master, clacked his claws at the oncoming weapon.

"Cla-clack, clack," came the familiar tattoo of sound.

The blade bit into the stone-hide of the construct, sinking between the plates.

Mezk hissed and pulled on the weapon, trying to free it to strike again. It didn't budge.

The dagger sunk further into the massive rock lobster, and Fred scrambled away from Mezk. The little protector scampered off the steps, into the flowing mass of demons, and disappeared, the dagger embedded in his carapace.

The Kid had felt Fred. He felt the rock lobster coming when he'd thought of him while talking to Edsumar. He felt the little protector knock him over and Edsumar bite into the stony creature, the connection with Edsumar's mind interrupted when it happened, and so had the link to Fred.

As those were severed, the Kid's mind flooded with awareness. It was like waking up to realize you'd been sleeping on your arm, and it was numb. When you move, it tingled, then became pins and needles as feeling returned to it.

The mind-mage abilities, once closeted away, rushed back into the Kid's mental grasp. His brain made connections it hadn't before, knowledge of how to use his gifts in ways he hadn't used before.

Was this from the time that the magics held Fred together? Or from the brush with demonic powers? It reminded him of when he'd first come to this world and done things with his powers that the original soul who inhabited the body never thought to do.

His mind probed his body, knitting muscle and tying nerve endings back together. He did it in a blink of an eye, a single moment where tissue and organs sealed, pushing blood and bone back into their accustomed places, and it was excruciating!

The Kid screamed, clutching his chest, awareness of his surroundings rushing back to him.

Mezk stood over him, staring toward where Fred disappeared into the crowd. The scream brought the assassin's attention back to him.

Demon Seed flashed, the ebony blade slashed towards the Kid…and reflected off an invisible barrier.

The Kid thrust his hand forward, and Mezk flew backwards. The mind mage picked up his daggers, which he had dropped on the steps, and rose to his feet. He threw them underhand, one at a time, taking control of their flight with his mind.

The blades flew in wide curving arcs, weaving around Mezk, cutting the assassin again and again.

Clenching his fists, the Kid raised them, and the daggers mimicked his actions, rising above the black-clad enemy. The mind mage brought his hands down, then crossed them in front of himself.

The twin blades plummeted, embedding into the flesh between Mezk's collarbone and neck, cutting across the man's throat.

Mezk's mouth moved, trying to cry out. Blood poured from his severed neck instead, and red bubbles of the viscous liquid frothed on his lips.

The demon dagger in the assassin's hand pulsed with red veins, siphoning off his life essence.

The Kid's daggers flew around his nemesis, slicing into his forearms—leaving deep cuts from wrist to elbow, severing tendons—and causing the demon blade to clatter to the stone parapet as Mezk's hands lost the ability to grip.

The weapons spun in the air and darted behind the assassin, sliding across his calves, opening the meaty muscle and cutting the Achille's tendon.

Mezk fell forward on top of the Demon Seed. Convulsing, his body withered and shriveled as the dagger fed on the man who'd been its master.

The Kid looked around—his daggers spinning in the air and blood flying from the blades, leaving them clean before returning to his hands—and took stock of his surroundings.

Nathan knelt beside Nob, cradling the dead man's head. Torrents was on his knees—his sword on the ground next to him—clutching his injured hand, the muscles in his neck standing out. Fred was nowhere to be seen.

"Nathan!" the Kid barked, "Torrents needs you; can you do something about that soul sucking thing?"

The rokairn looked up at the Kid, his eyes lost in grief, then looked at Torrents. He looked at the Kid again, nodded, and eased Nob's head to the stone floor before standing.

Nathan moved to Torrents, touching the barbarian's injured arm, his lips moving in prayer. A mist of red rose from the limb, and the Kid thought it was blood before realizing it wasn't liquid. The pulsing energy darted in one direction, then another, then flew at Mezk and slammed into the body, causing it to jerk.

The Kid looked down the steps.

Tradler lay on the stair, Ichaelson standing over him, with Vindalai standing next to the senior priest. Mecklen, Ablemarle, and her silent companion held off the horde on the other side.

Injured, they all looked close to falling under the onslaught of demons around them.

The rokairn and human armies had fought their way closer, and though diminished, it looked like they were beating the demon army.

The portal seeds had stopped pulsing and were blossoming in spasms of sparks and color.

"You've done well," Klendrisia's voice came from above, "you've made the ultimate sacrifice. One of a dark soul, tainted with desperation, their blood shed by someone of purity."

The demoness, floating in the air above the battlefield, gestured to the portals.

"My gateways open," Klendrisia's throaty voice was ecstatic as she threw her arms wide, "and all who come through shall be under my contract!"

The portals opened, forms coming out in a trickle at first, then a stream, then a flood. Like a dam bursting, the blue portals became cracks in reality, then spread to become fissures before finally tearing a rift between worlds. Creatures of all sizes and shapes poured from the extra-dimensional doors.

The large glowing gateway at the top of the steps pulsed, a final doorway waiting to open. Then it winked out of existence.

Mezk's body jerked, his flesh rippling and expanding. His leather armor tore, splitting at the seams. Leathery wings erupted from his back, and an extra set of arms burst from his ribcage. The body pushed up from the ground from where it had lain and rose to one knee.

It stood, metamorphosing.

"I have a host," a deep voice intoned from Mezk's husk as skin sloughed from the bone carapace growing from his body, "I am free of the dagger that was my prison. I am Zklypyllik and I shall take my vengeance on the…"

A two-handed blade sliding through their abdomen interrupted the newly formed demon. Torrents stood behind them, holding the pommel of the weapon.

"Vengeance this, bitch," the barbarian growled.

A throaty chuckle came from the form as they continued to grow, now the height of two men. The demon reached behind them and pulled the sword from their back, dropping the weapon onto the stone platform.

"That petty toy will not banish me in this form," the figure boomed. "I cultivated the seed in the dagger on this plane. I am native to this world, and you cannot send me away. You shall all become my first feast as I conquer this realm."

"Within the constraints of our contract," Klendrisia said, "you are bound by our agreement. I didn't think I'd need to remind you of that, Inciter Demon."

The rokairn and human armies reached the Pyridom as the portals opened, and the flood of demons swarmed across them, attacking and feeding.

The priests of Jonath called upon the gifts of the element of earth to defend the land, causing rock and sand to burst upward. Spears of stone launched into the air, piercing demons, and dust devils swirled across the landscape, enveloping the invaders.

"Chuz this," Torrents shouted, snatching up his sword and swinging at the gigantic demon in front of him. "Maybe I can't banish you, but I can kill you."

Nathan planted his feet at shoulder width, gripped his double-headed battle axe in both hands, hoisted the weapon, and took a step forward to attack.

The Kid watched the small group at the bottom of the stairs retreat upward, fighting their way up the steps and closer to the still-growing demon.

The overwhelmed armies were being torn apart by the hordes of thousands of demons swarming across the desert. Klendrisia hovered over the scene, a victorious smile on her face.

The Kid sighed.

He had his powers back but didn't have Edsumar or Fred. A demon, which appeared to have finally stopped growing, that couldn't be banished, was towering above him. Oh, and they were conjuring a flaming sword into existence, how Voltron of them. Huge, curled horns spiraled from their head, and their face contorted, so a bear-like snout—complete with a triple set of fangs—jutted out.

The demon grasped the fiery weapon with all four hands, and when they pulled them apart again, the being held four blades of fire. Flames erupted along their bone carapace, and something resembling lava dripped from the red veins pulsing on their surface.

Nathan hacked at the giant demon, his axe cutting deep into the being's calf, green sprouts appearing in the wound.

A flaming sword bashed the rokairn, but did nothing more than knock him sprawling, the amulet on his chest absorbing the demonic energy of the weapon.

The rokairn heard Klendrisia laugh and clap from above. The cambion alternately shouted orders to the chaotic battlefield—her magic projecting her voice across the massacre from her vantage point—and spoke in a foreign language, seemingly to herself. Each time she did the latter, another demon group came through one of the portals lining the base of the Pyridom.

"Kid!" Nathan shouted, standing up and stepping in front of the street thief, "you got your hole?"

"What?" the Kid's attention snapped back to his surroundings. "Not since I got this body!"

"What?" Nathan said, then shook his head. "No, your magic hole. Do you have it?"

"Like I said," the Kid's eyes widened, "oh, yeah, yeah. Why?"

"Give it to me," Nathan shouted over the sounds of battle. "I have an idea!"

"Don't use it," the Kid fumbled the magical artifact from a pouch, and handed it over, "remember, it can have weird results."

"I'm counting on it." The rokairn pointed at the Demon Seed laying on the ground between the giant demon's feet. "Can you get that dagger for me?"

Before the Kid could answer, Nathan turned to Torrents. The street thief grabbed at the blade with his mind—the tainted magics of the weapon making him queasy—and pulled it to his hand.

"Torrents!" the warrior-priest shouted, and the barbarian gave him a quick glance as he parried flaming swords from the demon. "Trade me!"

The rokairn threw his axe to the barbarian, and the barbarian tossed his sword to the warrior-priest without hesitation or question, his face tight with the pressure of combat. Torrents knew his ebony blade wasn't doing much good, even with its enchantments. Maybe the priest's nature-blessed blade would be more effective. Both caught the other's weapon at the same time.

"Now," Nathan turned back to the Kid, reaching for the dagger the thief held, "hand me that."

## Chapter 27

Nathan took the Demon Seed dagger from the Kid. Made of some dense, unknown metal, it felt heavy and cold in his hand.

The rokairn pulled the amulet from his chest and attached it to Torrents's sword and lifted the magical black material of the hole with his other hand.

"Klendrisia," Nathan shouted up at the demoness, "you control all the portals, right? They do as you will, is that right?"

The half-demon looked down at him, her face scrunching up in confusion.

"I do control them," she sneered, "and the beings who use them. I shall control this entire world!"

"Remember when you said you tasted hope because of me," Nathan fumbled with the hole in one hand, the demon dagger in the same hand, and the two-handed blade in the other, "and it was bitter?"

"What are you babbling about, dwarf?" Klendrisia snapped.

"Well, sorry about this," Nathan dropped the magical hole on the ground at his feet, "but I hope you're getting used to that bitter taste."

A dark round circle opened behind the hovering woman, who turned to look behind her at the rift in the air.

Nathan took the sword in both hands, still fumbling to keep the ebony dagger in his grip at the same time and stabbed it downward into the hole.

The blade disappeared into the blue-black darkness, reappearing out of the hole in the sky. Piercing the levitating demoness's breastbone, Nathan jerked the sword back.

Klendrisia's body folded almost in half as she was pulled into the magical rift.

The top part of her body emerged from the hole at Nathan's feet, and he jammed the cold, dark dagger into Klendrisia's eye socket. The woman screamed, and her legs—still dangling in the air—kicked.

Nathan watched as many things happened at once. The banishing magic of the two-handed sword pulled at Klendrisia's essence; the shield-amulet blocked her control and commands of the portals and demon army; the empty prison known as the Demon Seed activated, seeking to fill the void inside it with Klendrisia's soul; and the magical hole on the ground wavered.

Nathan shoved the sword forward again, back into the hole.

Klendrisia scrambled at the edge of the aperture, clawing at the sand covered platform, nails digging gouges into the stone, causing both to crack and split. With nothing to grip, she slipped further into the midnight orifice. Above, her legs were drawn into the hole.

Her scream cut off as she disappeared into the dark. The hole folded behind her, drawing closed as if something in another world pulled at the center of the cloth and drew it through a knothole in time and space.

It disappeared without a sound.

The ground shook, sand dancing along the stone walkway as the earth rumbled. A glossy sheen crept up the Pyridom, coating the sloped walls of the structure. The stone's sickly orange color deepened, becoming black and smooth in blotchy patches—like some sort of time lapse fungus—claiming the shady side of the structure until the whole magical landmark was a midnight hue.

The portals lining the base of the Pyridom flared and blossomed outward, disintegrating the closest demons.

The massive demon in front of Torrents hesitated, their forked tongue tasting the air.

The barbarian, the warrior-priest, and the street thief looked out across the land.

On the battlefield, screeching fiends and demons scrambled away from the Pyridom. Lifted by an invisible force—a mystical wind catching them in its power—they flew towards the blue gateways. Without Klendrisia to control the magic, Nathan watched the creatures sucked into the portals.

Overhead, the flying cat-snake demons crumpled into balls under the crushing force and plummeted at downward angles into the closest.

In less than ninety seconds, only a few gnohls and proto-hyenas remained of the enemy forces.

The green clouds broke apart, the purple lightning fading, and sunbeams shone through like spotlights.

Less than a hundred humans and a few dozen rokairn, scattered across a mostly empty battlefield, looked around. With a shout, they raised their weapons and attacked the remaining enemies.

"The contract," the demon boomed, and the Kid, Torrents, and Nathan looked up at them, surprised that they was still here, "has been broken. I am free of it, and the bonds that the demon bitch used to restrain me!"

"Aw, damn it," the Kid muttered, "they left the worst one behind."

"It's all good," Torrents smiled and pointed with Nathan's axe. "He's lost his hellfire stuff. I don't think he's got it all going on anymore. I'll take care of this. But, just in case, feel free to help out."

The massive demon swung two swords at the barbarian. The blades no longer guttered flame, instead resembling cooling volcanic rock.

Torrents stepped back and swept the battle axe sideways, catching both swords in the weapon's arc and guiding them to where he'd stood a moment before.

Vibrant green light sparked where the weapons touched. Vines erupted from the demon's swords, flowers bursting into full bloom. The blades crumpled to the ground with a noise like wet snow falling from an eave. Where they landed, a dark, rich soil was all that remained.

The demon screamed, slashing with their remaining two weapons. Torrents rolled under the swords and between the giant's legs, slashing, severing a leg at the knee.

Nathan drew hand axes from his belt and charged forward.

The Kid telekinetically lifted his blades, bee-lining them to the demon's head.

The three danced the tango of combat with the giant foe. Marcid's magic claimed the demon's last two blades. The demon went on the defensive from a kneeling position due to the missing half of one of their legs.

Vindalai and Ichaelson joined the group, followed by Ablemarle. Mecklen trailed behind with Ablemarle's silent friend, both injured and leaning on one another for support.

The rest of the rokairn army joined the fray. From the sands at the feet of the Pyridom, stone spears flew over the heads of the group and pierced the monster's chest. A giant hand of sand, almost as large as the enemy, rose from the desert and grabbed the invader and dragged them down the steps, weaving between the combatants still attacking the massive invader, and onto the desert floor.

Nathan, Torrents, and the Kid lost sight of the demon as humans and rokairn from both armies swarmed the monster.

Looking across the desolate landscape, the Kid saw outriders chasing down the stragglers of the enemy army, and others checking the dead and making sure they wouldn't get back up again.

The Kid put a hand up to shade his eyes, searching the sands for Fred.

"That's a good sign," Nathan said, pointing at the Kid. When the Kid looked confused, the rokairn explained, "You, shading your eyes. That means the sun is out. Been a while since we've seen that."

Ichaelson looked up from where he was binding Mecklen's knee. The limb looked shattered, bending backwards at an unnatural angle, and the grizzled warrior grimaced as the priest set it.

"Nathan," Ichaelson's voice was somber, "would you like me to say the parting prayer over your friend Nob, or would you like to do it?"

Nathan looked over at Nob's body. The demon had stepped on him, crushing him during the fight. Most of the guard's body was a broken and twisted heap, withered and drained.

"No," Nathan said slowly, not moving, "I'll take care of him. I'll return him to the earth, as is Jonath's way. From ash and dirt, we grow, and so we shall return, renewing the land."

Ichaelson nodded, then called to Ablemarle, asking how Tradler was doing. The younger man was in a state of shock, and though his body would heal, his mind might never recover.

Vindalai stood next to the silent man who'd never spoken a word, and both—already bandaged—watched over the battlefield for any threats.

"Do you think we should go look for Varina, Dinwiddie, Dodd, and Shad?" Vindalai asked the man next to her. "Try to recover their bodies, or whatever we can find of them?"

The slim man shook his head, pointing at small groups that had broken from the armies of both races.

Parties of a half dozen soldiers roamed the battlefield, already stacking bodies to be burned, before they could scatter the ashes. They took the boots, weapons, and any useful items from the dead, piling them separately. In a land where the dead walked, only a body burned to ashes couldn't rise again.

"You seen Fred?" the Kid looked at Torrents.

"Nuh uh," the barbarian grunted, "can't you just call him, or think to him, or something?"

"Not anymore," the Kid shook his head, "that stopped working when he was stabbed with Edsumar."

"Edsumar?" Torrents's face brightened. "You got him back?"

"Nope," the Kid sighed. "He was embedded in Fred when Fred ran off."

"Need help finding them?" Torrents offered.

"Naw," the Kid hooked his thumbs—hands resting on the dagger hilts—through his belt, "I think the walk alone will do me good. Thanks though."

"Yeah," Torrents watched the Kid, shoulders slumped, turn away and move down the stairs.

"Hey Kid," Torrents said.

The Kid stopped and turned to look at him, squinting in the sun.

"You okay?" Torrents asked.

"Just exhausted," the Kid said, and Torrents nodded, "not just my body, but everything. So much death. I'm just so tired of it, you know? Just so tired of it all."

The Kid turned away and moved down the steps to the desert floor. He moved in a zig-zag pattern, widening each pass as he went further from the Pyridom, which was now a sleek, black pillar on a smooth black base. It looked cleaner, but more ominous at the same time. A looming mystery for some other time.

The Kid meandered back and forth, turning the idea of life and death over and over in his mind, searching for Fred or Edsumar.

Something moved. The Kid turned towards it, shading his eyes.

A large, flat, grey stone—about a pace wide, by two paces long—shifted in the sand. It rose at an angle, silt sliding down its uneven surface to collect on the ground. The stone shifted again, a crack forming down the middle as the single rock face became two, then spread apart.

A rocky, reptilian neck and head extended from the top edge, and a long tail emerged from the sands, twitching.

"What the hell?" the Kid murmured, drawing his blades and crouching, ready to attack.

The draconic head swiveled towards him, grey, sandy eyelids blinking over faceted stone eyes.

"Kid?" The voice sounded like chalk screeching on a slate chalkboard. "Is that you?"

"You know me?" The Kid asked, still ready to defend himself. "Do I know you?"

"Yes," the screeching changed, shifting to the sound of a rock scratching a sidewalk to make a hopscotch board on a hot summer day, "we know you. We've been with you a short while, though maybe long in your terms. It's very confusing for us right now, and we can't be sure."

"We? Us?" The Kid stood up, cocking his head, the wheels in his mind turning.

The rock monster stood, sand sliding from its body, which was about the size of a horse, if horses had wings. Which they might here. The Kid wasn't sure. But this was a dragon, a small stone dragon.

*Yes. We, us. We know you,* a familiar voice said in his head, though it had an odd echo, like someone added reverb to it before broadcasting it into the Kid's brain.

## Chapter 28

Red Wind was bustling in ways it hadn't in decades. It was a building boom; the city was experiencing growth in more than one way.

Most of the buildings were damaged, and more than half destroyed. The city was rebuilding but doing it a little better since the Church of Jonath had a controlling factor.

Before the invasion, crime syndicates controlled the community. Since the invasion, those same groups fled before the final battle, were killed, or were too scattered to wrest control from the priests.

The people loved the church and the priests, because they were the ones helping rebuild everyone's homes and businesses. They brought in food, supplies, and protected the people while the city had no walls or militia.

It had some sort of law, though. After the Battle of the Pyridom, they awarded Mecklen the office of Reeve. He immediately complained about it, and then deputized Ablemarle and her silent partner, who the Kid had nicknamed Teller.

Ichaelson and Vindalai were local heroes, and their presence brought more people—especially the younger folk—to church services than anything else.

Tradler was a lost soul, though. The young man wandered the streets in the dawn and dusk hours, shuffling through the dusty lanes, like he was haunting the town. During the day, he would sit in whatever tavern, pub, or drinking hole he could find, pickling himself with a mug or glass of anything he could wrap a shaking hand around. Anything to not remember, not think, not care. At night, he slept wherever he fell, sometimes at a bar, other times on the side of the street.

Logs were being brought down the Lasso River, cut into planks at the sawmill on the banks, and hauled across the plains and fields to the city.

The rokairn opened trade talks with Red Wind, and in a show of good faith sent priests of Jonath to the city to teach the human priests how to work stone in ways only one with the blessing of Jonath could.

With these resources, they rebuilt the outer wall of the city, parts of it raised from the stones of the ground itself.

"It's only a matter of time," Nathan said, "like you guys told me, people are poo."

"I don't think we said it quite like that, though," Torrents laughed, "but we get the idea."

"You're telling us," the Kid leaned on double-width planks set on two barrels to create a makeshift table, "that they offered you the jeweler's shop, and the old owner is dead, and you could just have it?"

"Yes," Nathan nodded, "they consider it fair payment for what I did for Red Wind."

"And you said no," the Kid continued, flapping his hand at Nathan, "because you think that one day, crime will return here and ruin it all."

"Something like that," Nathan nodded again, "it always does. Might not be now, or even soon, but it'll come."

"But…" the Kid started again, and Torrents elbowed him.

"Maybe, Kid," the barbarian leaned down, his breath reeking of ale, and looked at the Kid pointedly, "maybe Nathan doesn't want the jewelry store because he'd have to run it alone."

"He could hire people to help him," the Kid's voice went shrill as he continued to wave his hands, "I mean, gee-willikers! It can't be that hard!"

"Maybe," a voice that sounded like gravel falling downhill said, "he misses his friend Nob, and doesn't want to be reminded of him every day in the shop where they met."

The three looked at the stone-hide dragon who lay curled on the ground at the foot of the table, head raised to look over the edge of the planks.

"Fredsumar," the Kid wobbled, turning to look at his friend, "egg-cellent point!"

"Fredsumar?" the dragon rumbled. "When did we get that name?"

"It fits," the Kid picked up a chunk of cheese and popped it in his mouth, talking between chewing, "You were Edsumar, then Fred absorbed you, my psychic magics bonding the two of you, and so Fred and Ed-sumar, becomes; Fredsumar!"

"Hmmm," the dragon lowered his head again to his fore-claws, "we'll talk about that later, when you're a bit more sober."

The dragon had grown since the last new moon, when they'd left the Pyridom of Power, its sleek, black structure looking suspiciously like a Tower of Onyx.

When the Kid first found him, Fredsumar had been the size of a horse. In the past four weeks, he grew to the size of an ox, or maybe a buffalo. He was now twice as wide as a horse, his body one and half times as long, and that much again in length with his neck and tail. His wingspan was the most impressive part though: snout to tail Fredsumar was about the length of two pickup trucks, but his wings from tip to tip wider than eight pickup trucks end to end when he spread them to full length.

"So, Nathan," Torrents broke the uncomfortable silence, "if you aren't setting up shop here, what will you do?"

Nathan considered, chewing on a strip of jerky.

"I think I'll go east," the rokairn nodded, "I have previous memories of the Seawall City, and it sounds like something straight out of a fairy tale. It has mages, priests, wizards, sorcerers, and a fine-tuned, organized military. I think I'd like to see this firsthand again."

"Can we go?" The Kid leaned over the table, his chin in his palm, elbow resting on the stained planks, squinting and smiling. "Or is this a private thing where we're not allowed to join you, even though it's not like it's your city and you have any authority to stop us? Why would you want to, anyway? That's just being silly, Nathan. You aren't the boss of me…"

"Yes," Nathan interrupted.

The Kid tried to focus on the rokairn, blinking and swaying.

"Yes?" The Kid asked. "Yes, what?"

"Of course you can come." Nathan took a long pull from his ale, wrinkling his nose at the bitter taste. "I can't believe rokairn are legendary for loving this stuff, it's horrible. It's so bitter. It's like liquid Torrents."

"What did you just say?" The barbarian cocked his head downward towards Nathan. "Did you just say what I think you said? Did you just say…a joke? And without apologizing before it? And after it?"

The three laughed together, Fredsumar snorting a small dust cloud on their feet.

"And during it," the Kid added, "and ten minutes after it."

"Yeah," Torrents dropped a hand onto the Kid's shoulder, "we get it, Kid. Drop it, you've gone too far with it now. It's no longer funny."

"But," the rogue tried to move the hand from his shoulder, but missed the barbarian's arm, "why was it funny when you said it then?"

"Because," Torrents moved his hand, and the Kid almost fell over without its support, "I said it. You know, Kid, you really lose all sense of comedic timing when you drink. I mean, you're like anti-funny."

Nathan and Torrents laughed again.

"Your face is anti-funny," the Kid said, then burst into exaggerated laughter.

"So, let me get this straight," Torrents said slowly, "if my face is anti-funny, then it's not funny looking at all? Maybe even handsome? Is that right?"

"I didn't say all that," the Kid cocked his head and furrowed his brow, "did I? I just meant, your face isn't a laughing thing, it's not funny. That means your mouth, too. Like all the things that come of it, isn't funny. Your words are anti-funny. And yes, maybe you're a little handsome. But you're not funny looking. Maybe a little funny looking, in a handsome way."

"Okay, Kid," Torrents sighed, "stop now, you did it again. You over explained and took the joke too far. Just stop…talking."

"Oops," the Kid hiccupped, "I did it again."

Torrents facepalmed with one hand, and gently shoved the Kid with the other. The thief slid sideways and fell to the floor.

Laughter bubbled up from under the table.

"I've fallen," the Kid's giggling voice said, "and I can't get up."

# Epilogue

The canvas walls of the pavilion flapped and popped in the wind. The sun in the west cast long shadows across the oasis, the lines of palms duplicated along the sands, stretching for the east like they were searching for the sunrise.

The cloth building had three poles, the center one slightly higher than the other two. It was oval, nestled in the sparse grass and the tall, slim trees of the watering hole.

The smell of roasting mutton came and went with the wind, the greasy smudge of smoke ripped away from the vent hole as soon as it drifted out.

"That's odd," Torrents said, "I don't recall there being sanctuary at this oasis."

"What do we know?" The Kid shrugged. "Things change so quickly in the desert. And it's a tent. How hard could it be to set it up and take it down? It could be anywhere tomorrow."

"But we just left the rokairn lands in the crags." Torrents shifted the weight of the new sword on his back. "And we're on the border of the Seawall City territory. And there's no pack animals or wagons to transport it. Plus, the grass is still fresh around it, not worn, so it hasn't been here long. Don't you think anyone setting up here is just asking for trouble?"

"I know that smell," Fredsumar rumbled as he trundled along behind the trio.

"Lamb?" Nathan asked, looking over his shoulder. "I do too. My grannie used to make it. Super simple and basic, but it was wonderful. Always reminds me of Chanukah, and the sounds of family bickering and judging you."

"Ah," the Kid sighed, "the good old days. Shall we go in?"

The two humans and the rokairn moved to enter, reaching for the tied flap of a door.

"What about us?" Fredsumar tilted his head to look at the tent as it swayed in the wind.

The others turned back to look at the stone dragon.

"It won't be a problem," a new voice said, making all three jump, and Nathan to let out a loud squeak, "I'll roll up the side for you, old friend."

A man stood in the doorway, holding the flap open and to one side. He was human, between thirty and fifty years old, of medium height, and wore a turban-style head wrap over his pale face.

"Torrents, Kid," the man nodded at them, "it's good to see you again."

"Jack?" The Kid's voice rose with surprise. "Jack Tucker?"

"What the hell are you doing here?" Torrents laughed and clapped the shorter man on the shoulder.

"Welcome to the Traveller's Inn. Come inside," Jack stepped out of their way, and gestured to the interior with a wave of his hand, "and we'll talk once you each have eaten have a plate of mutton, hot potatoes, and some green vegetable thing I picked up. They're like Brussels sprouts, but the size of a racquetball."

The three filed in, their eyes adjusting to the dim light. Behind them, the wall was lit with the setting sun, and the wall across from them was the mellow blue of shadow.

The tent was spacious for a tent. The ground, covered with overlapping rugs, had six rough wooden plank tables scattered around, with no obvious organization.

A third of the interior space—from the pole to the right, to the far wall—created a separate room with a curtain. Tapestries and banners hung from the ropes along the top of the cloth walls.

A table—littered with pitchers, bottles, carafes, glasses, mugs, cups, and a small keg—in front of the opening to the private room created a makeshift bar.

On the left, between the center pole and the support pole, stood a spit—two metal 'y-shaped' poles standing on each side, with a cross-pole supported between them—over an oval rock-framed firepit.

A thin old man stared at the three and slowly turned the handle, roasting a goat over the fire.

"You?" The Kid froze, staring at the man, eyes wide.

"Oh, damn!" Torrents stumbled, catching himself on a table before he fell. "Really? You're here? I'm gonna need a drink."

Nathan pushed past the other two, trying to see who they were talking to and about.

"Yeah," a voice cackled, "PepperGarten is here. Did you expect somebody else? Mother Teresa, maybe? The Pope? Gandhi? Gloria Steinem?"

"You didn't die," Nathan whispered, "but I buried you. And built a cairn. A big one. With lots of rocks. They were heavy, too. My back hurt for three days after that. How are you here?"

"PepperGarten got better!" The old man giggled. "It's hard to keep a good man down, and it's good to keep a hard man down. Or is it down to hard a good man? Well, whatever, something like that."

"Gentleman, and Kid," Jack said from across the tent, "I have a table here for you. Why don't you get some food, and then we'll talk."

Jack stood at a table beside a rolled up and tied panel of the tent to the far left. Fredsumar sat on his haunches outside, his head on the edge of the table closest to the wall.

"Fredsumar," Jack addressed the dragon, "I have an extra goat or two if you're hungry."

Their host scrunched up his face and tilted his head, eying the dragon.

"Do you eat?" the innkeeper asked.

"You bet he does," Torrents interrupted, moving to the table, but making a wide berth of PepperGarten. "He's grown a bunch since he…"

The barbarian trailed off.

"What do we call it?" Torrents asked. "Since you were born? Metamorphosed? Well, since he got this way, instead of being a knife and silly rock crab."

"Fred was a rock lobster," the Kid moved past the old man, but watched him the whole time, "and now that we're talking about it, I haven't seen Fredsumar eat at all. Do you eat?"

"We were a dagger, thank you very much," Fredsumar grumbled, "and we take sustenance, but not like others. Not like we did when we were an actual dragon."

Nathan walked to PepperGarten and looked him in the eye. The withered old man wasn't much taller than the rokairn, but Nathan still had to look up.

The rokairn thrust out his hand, and PepperGarten looked down at it, a grin splitting his face.

"Welcome back, PepperGarten," Nathan said. "I'm pleased to see you have returned from…wherever you were."

PepperGarten grabbed the rokairn's meaty hand in both of his and pumped it up and down.

"PepperGarten is pleased, too!" The old man's voice was shrill and excited. "Oh, the things PepperGarten has seen and done since coming here. PepperGarten remembers when Jack first brought PepperGarten here…"

"Wait," the Kid cut the man off, stopping halfway to a seated position, "Jack brought you here also?"

"He was the first one," Jack's voice was wistful and warm, like he was remembering something fondly, "and he's proven his worth many times over."

"Was he always this weird?" Torrents asked, sitting on the bench seat furthest from the old man and keeping a wary eye on him.

"Oh, yes," Jack laughed, "always. PepperGarten lived for years on the streets of New York City before coming here. But man, he took to the nature magics with a passion!"

The Kid dropped onto the bench across from Torrents, sitting as close to Fredsumar as possible.

PepperGarten was still pumping Nathan's hand, and the rokairn gripped the man's wrist with his other hand and tugged his trapped hand free.

The four new arrivals settled around the table, as Jack served them plates piled with food, and mugs full of mead, wine, beer, or spirits; each as they requested.

The evening passed into night, and the group told of the events since they'd last seen Jack. They also filled Nathan in on who Jack was, and how the man could bring people from their world to this one.

When the meal was done, the six settled around a table beside the firepit with mugs of hot tea, or small glasses of digestifs. The conversation lulled into comfortable silence.

"Okay," Jack said, slapping his thighs and standing up, "I guess it's time to get to it."

"Get to what?" Nathan asked, smiling.

"Oh," the Kid said quietly, looking down, "you're going to ask, aren't you?"

"Yes," Jack nodded, "I am. But it's still your choice, as always."

"Ask what?" Nathan urged.

"Do any of you want to go home?" Jack looked at each of the three in turn, pausing to gauge their reactions.

"Nope," Torrents said, leaning back on the bench, belching, and rubbing his stomach. "I'm good. I think I'll stick around. Thanks for asking, though!"

"PepperGarten wants to stay!" the old man said, his voice solemn and serious for once. "PepperGarten likes it here, better than New York. This is home now, and PepperGarten never wants to go back to that other place. And PepperGarten would appreciate it if you quit asking."

"Nathan?" Jack looked at the rokairn. "What about you?"

"We have a choice?" Nathan asked. "I mean, is it like Wizard of Oz where we click our heels together and say, 'There's no place like home,' and we shoot back to where we were before?"

"Not quite," Jack laughed, "but something like that."

"Well," Nathan took a deep breath, and let it out slowly, "I think I'd like to stay, for a while at least. I need to find out what happened to me in Seawall City before I came here. Well, what happened to Trojet Bellstamp before I took over his body."

Jack nodded, then turned to look at the Kid, who was still staring down, wringing his hands in his lap.

"Kid?" Jack spoke softly. "Do you want to go, or would you like to stay?"

"I don't want to go," the Kid spoke slowly, "but I don't want to keep doing this. This stuff, these things, we've been doing. There's been so much death, and I don't think I want to handle it anymore. I just want to live and enjoy life. Is that an option? I don't want to go back, because I'm dying there. Esperanza had a chance of living when she went back. Torrence or Nathan could survive what happened to them. Me? I'm a dead person if I return to that other world. Can I stay, but not have to do…all these things anymore?"

"Yeah," Jack nodded, "any of you can walk away anytime. I mean, you're drawn to each other because of the connection of your home…reality. But, yeah, you can go anywhere you choose to go. You don't have to stay."

"Really?" the Kid's voice flooded with relief. "It's okay to just…leave?"

"Yeah," Jack smiled and nodded, "I'll even pack you a bagged lunch of leftovers to take with you."

"We'll go with you," the gravel-rumble of Fredsumar filled the room. "We should be able to fly soon, and we can take you anywhere we choose to go."

"It's settled then," PepperGarten cackled and clapped his hands, "PepperGarten agrees to join the two of you, and help you on your journey to somewhere that isn't here!"

Fredsumar and the Kid exchanged looks, then the Kid shrugged, and the dragon nodded once.

"Okay," the Kid smiled, "you can go with us, PepperGarten."

"PepperGarten knows PepperGarten can go," the old man huffed. "That's why PepperGarten said that PepperGarten would go with you. You're welcome."

The group settled around the table with their drinks and conversation and talked late into the night. They discussed their world and the things they missed, which mostly were certain foods; the differences in this world, and the beauty of both worlds; the fact that they had magic items and lost them; and the night ended with talk of how to save this world and make it…less apocalyptic.

They bedded down on the carpets, moving the tables to cloth walls, and fell asleep to the crickets and night birds of the oasis.

In the morning, Nathan and Torrents woke to find that the Kid, PepperGarten, and Fredsumar were gone.

Jack sat in the only chair in the tent, leaning back on two legs. The man puffed on a pipe—a huge wooden pipe, deep brown in color, with swirls of grain along the bowl, and long bent stem—and blew smoke rings, sorta. The rings wobbled and broke apart with the slightest breeze.

"They're gone," Torrents said, stating a fact, not asking a question, as he stood and stretched.

"Uh huh," Jack grunted, pulling on his pipe again.

"Where'd they go?" Nathan asked, sitting up.

"Dunno," Jack mumbled around the stem of his pipe.

"Will we see them again?" Nathan rubbed at his neck.

"Maybe," Jack shrugged, "if you need to, or they need to see you. Never know with these things."

"What do we do now?" Nathan asked.

"Same thing we do every day, Natie," Torrents said in a snide, stiff accent. "Try and save the world."


End of Portals, Book 2

# Book Three: Mystics & Monoliths

Dedication

To people who do more than endure change, this book is
for those that challenge it, overcome it, and thrive from it.

# Prologue

The Traveller's Inn was in a lull. Jack sat at a table, chin in his hands, and a picked-over plate of assorted veggies and cheese forgotten in front of him. He let out a sigh, picked up his ceramic mug of water, brought it to his lips, then set it down without taking a drink. He sighed again.

"What's going on Jack?" asked Croaker from the bar.

Jack looked at the older man, taking in the long brown coat, matching frayed fedora, tattered vest, and dungarees. Croaker had a concerned look on his weathered face, his mouth pulled tight amidst his stubbled cheeks and drooping jowls. The man's eyes were sharp over the dark bags under them.

"Nothing," Jack sighed again, "just trying to figure out how I'm going to…"

Jack looked away, his eyes moving to the door.

A tapping noise on the pewter plate drew Croaker's attention. He looked at the raven on the bar beside his plate, and the bird cocked a beady eye at the abandoned crusts of bread scattered among scraps of ham. Croaker reached down and picked up a crust, waving it at the bird.

The raven hopped twice, eyeing the man and the bread in turn. It opened its beak and cawed.

"Do not tease the local fauna," said Cogsley, the automaton bartender. He ran his white-gloved hands down his tuxedo coat and tilted his bulbous glass dome of a head at the raven. "He is new here, and getting settled in."

"Who is?" asked Wanderly, his squeaky voice proceeding him out of the kitchen. He entered the common room carrying a trencher piled with steaming brisket, rolls, and fried potatoes. He lifted it above his head, slid it onto the bar, climbed up a stool, and plopped down. "Cogsley, my good man, your finest lager, please. Nothing washes down a light snack like a good lager, wouldn't you agree, Croaker?"

"That's a light snack?" the older man rolled his eyes. "How can you be half my height and eat twice as much as me?"

"It's a gift of my people," Wanderly grinned, breaking a roll in half and piling dripping beef on it. "What's up with Jack? Is he stuck again?"

Cogsley set down a pint of lager in front of the wee man, and the three looked over at the master of the house.

Jack glanced towards them, his eyes distant, then coming into focus as he saw them staring.

"What?" Jack asked with a shake of his head. "Did I miss something?"

"Out with it, big guy," Wanderly chided. "We're all friends here, and you just bought me lunch, so the least I can do is offer you free advice chock full of wisdom!"

"Calling your advice wisdom, it like calling a copper flek a fortune," muttered Croaker.

"With a single penny," Wanderly said, pulling his shoulders back and puffing out his chest, "you can make a wise investment to create a fortune. Or offer a sucker bet to some clueless schlep. Either way, step three is always profit. See? Wisdom!"

The three looked back at Jack and waited. Jack sighed again.

"He has been doing that overly much," Cogsley drawled in his exaggerated enunciation, "perhaps he is in need of a tonic for whatever it is souring his temperament."

"Damn it, Cogsley, why do you always use twenty words when a handful will do?" asked Croaker.

"I do it in hopes you will understand a handful and take my meaning." Cogsley turned towards the codger. "In your old age and lacking education, you often miss my meaning. And I am surprised that you know anything of a handful, for the ladies claim you do not even have that much where it counts."

"Oh, burn!" Wanderly squealed through a mouthful of potatoes. "I didn't know you had it in you!"

"That is precisely what she uttered after a midnight rendezvous with Croaker," Cogsley said.

The raven bounced up and down, cawing, moving an ebony eye from the bartender to Croaker.

"Shut up. That didn't even make sense," Croaker said, tossing another crust to the bird.

"You ready to talk yet, Jack?" Wanderly asked. "Or do we need to continue with the banter?"

"I need to bring someone over again," Jack said. "The Kid has moved on to other things, but I need someone to complete the triad. Torrents and Nathan won't be able to handle what's coming without a third, and the new person needs to be a heavyweight."

"How's that different from the last time?" Croaker asked. "And do you get to pick what sort of things they get to do once you bring them from Earth to Aetheria?"

"Sort of," Jack said, standing. He wiped his hands on his thighs, then stretched backwards, arching his back. "I can choose guidelines, then I can pick someone who fits them. I have my eye on a young lady. She's strong willed, passionate, protective, and driven. And I know what body the new person will get, but…"

"But what?" Wanderly asked. "She sounds perfect. Why the hesitation?"

Jack rolled his head from side to side, shrugged his shoulders, and looked at Wanderly.

"She's hard to get along with," he explained. "When she sets her mind, she's like a bull in a China shop. Lots of people find that hard to deal with."

"What's a China shop?" Wanderly asked.

"Delicate crockery," Croaker snapped, "now, hush. Jack, why is it important that anyone likes her? If she gets the job done, isn't that what matters?"

"Yeah," Wanderly snickered, "look at Croaker. No one likes him, but he's effective."

"Shut up, runt," Croaker muttered, tossing a bit of ham to the raven. "Jack, just send someone with her that can help guide her. Someone that others like, so they put up with her. Kinda like my partner, Phoebus, was for me. He was a buffer between me and people, so I could do the work while they adored his annoying prattle and charm."

"I can't send a fourth," Jack sighed, throwing up his hands. "It has to be three."

"The Kid had the Dragon's Dagger," Wanderly pointed out, "and he was intelligent. Why didn't he break your rules?"

"Edsumar wasn't a person," Jack said, "not in the strictest sense. And they picked him up later, found him, rescued him. I don't have someone like that available."

The raven croaked and ruffled his feathers, eyeing Jack.

"What?" Jack said, looking at the bird. "No, I don't think…but, maybe. Would you be willing to go?"

The bird twisted his head behind him and began cleaning his tail feathers, one eye still on Jack.

"Is the avian speaking to you, Jack?" Cogsley asked.

"No," Jack scoffed, "no, don't be silly. I can't speak to animals. I just understand them sometimes when they're in the Inn."

"Does he understand you?" Croaker eyed the bird.

"Ravens are smart," Wanderly chimed in. "They know things. Look into any mythology and you'll see. They remember things, also."

"Maybe," Jack said absently, not talking to the men, "but is a single raven able to handle being the caretaker and guide for someone that can level a city if they really want to?"

"Level a city, Jack?" Croaker said. "You sure you want to bring in that kind of firepower?"

"It's needed for what's coming," Jack sighed.

"There he goes again," muttered Cogsley.

"But if the Inn brought you," Jack said to the raven, "then I guess you're the option I have at my disposal."

# Chapter 1

Torrents the barbarian threw his arms around the stone pillar, hauling himself up the corner of a building on the northern side of the city square. He wanted a better view of the hanging that was about to take place.

He swung his muscled leg over the wide railing and pulled himself over and onto the stone balcony. The crowd backed up a step. The newcomer shouldered his way through the throng of figures, most of them politicians and robed councilors, and claimed a space at the opposite edge of the railing overlooking the common area below.

People moved aside for the broad-shouldered figure with two swords on his back. The weapons had replaced his usual double-handed sword that was lost a few months ago at the Demon Front, battling otherworldly invaders. A long dirk was inside of each of the large man's knee-high boots, and a cudgel swung from his wide leather belt.

The man blew a strand of his black hair from his eyes, and it fell back across his face. He reached up and pulled his shoulder length hair into a ponytail and tied it back with a leather cord.

"Torrents the Barbarian," someone behind him uttered his name in quiet awe. The young councilman leaned over to a woman, explaining who the warrior was in a conspiratorial whisper, "Hero of Durgan's Keep when it was invaded by a necromancer and her undead army. Defender of portals at Land's End when the demonic horde burst through it and into this world."

The barbarian ignored them and raised his hands to smooth the furs that he traditionally wore. His hands dropped awkwardly as he realized they weren't there.

Torrents had traded his usual grey furs for pale leathers. The outfit was still warm to wear but was better protection. It was worth sweating a little to avoid getting a blade in the gut.

Autumn was setting in but wasn't like back home on Earth. It was muggier, and the humidity lent itself to sweating profusely, short tempers, and fighting. He could spot at least three different squabbles below him. His hand dropped to the cudgel on his belt without him thinking about it.

He scanned the crowd for his partner, Nathan, the rokairn priest. Torrents couldn't help to think 'dwarf' in place of the word rokairn, because that's what his friend's people looked like to him. The term dwarf was hurtful in this world, just as was calling an aeifain or a dasism an elf was rude. It was an ethnic slur and using the term could cause trouble.

Torrents spotted Nathan pushing his way through the mob of people. Almost everyone was a head-and-shoulders taller than the rokairn, and the priest squeezed past clumps and groups of humans who didn't bother to acknowledge the polite apologies of the smaller man.

Torrents could see the head of the double-bladed axe on the rokairn's back, its wooden handle wrapped with living vines and leaves. Nathan stood out for more reasons than his height, his thick, braided beard, and the massive weapon. The priest had taken to adapting Earth fashions to this world.

The rokairn wore a doublet with lapels, in a checked pattern in brown shades, and loose pants that matched in color, but was the style worn by sailors. All of Nathan's accessories—from his belt and leather wrist cuffs to his hat and boots—were black, though he had a bright green feather that bobbed on the wide-brimmed hat that made Torrents think of pirate movies.

The rokairn, who was a jeweler back home on Earth, had a variety of rings, necklaces, bracelets, and earrings on him. All were excellent quality, though few were flashy, and most were just simple works of art.

Nathan had a bead on their target, tracking the new person down like a fat kid who smelled popcorn, using the abilities given upon him by his god.

There were gods in this world, real ones that did things. As in, deities who interacted with and affected their faithful. Torrents was still wrapping his head around that, even though he'd hung around with a priest or priestess since he'd arrived in this reality. People could pray to the gods, and they answered, giving help, causing miracles, and answering requests of their followers and worshipers. It was a weird concept after seeing so many evangelists, social media posts, and politicians talking about praying to help others and getting no measurable results.

But Nathan got results from his god, Jonath. Jonath was a god of many talents, or as Nathan said, areas of influence. It meant magical realms, skill sets, and a few other things. Jonath was the master of the element of earth, agriculture, protection, guards, and of all things…perception. Torrents didn't know how it all related but thought of it in the same way that big business diversified. Sometimes, you got ahold of something by association rather than intent.

The crowd was cheering and jeering, excited about the impending hanging. They jostled for a better view of the wooden platform and noose, as street vendors wove their way through the throng, shouting out their wares and prices that couldn't be beaten.

People were people, and this—in Torrents's mind— was no different from a sporting event back home. They came to see a spectacle, and there was a chance they'd go overboard and even riot. It didn't matter if their team won or lost, emotions ran high, and people rode that wave. Families came—children held in the protective circle of adults—and they shouted and booed along with drunken louts, city officials, and famous or infamous figures in the crowd.

Those individuals would each give commentary in their own specific arena after the event. Some in the city square with the body swinging lifelessly behind them, some in bars and taverns with the drunks singing lively behind them, and others in shadowed rooms, whispers slithering around them.

Gambling was common and scattered throughout the crowd—usually near the food and souvenir vendors—were people collecting bets. Taking down names, gathering money, and scribbling on a chalkboard or a wax tablet, these people fed off the crowd the same way a remora would feed off a shark—or a drug dealer off people looking for an escape. Bottom feeders, welcomed by the population, who had the delusion of pulling one over on the inevitable odds. It happened occasionally, but more often they paid the price in gold or flesh.

Seawall City was different from any other city that Torrents had seen since he'd come to this world. It was built almost exclusively with stone, and most of the roofs made of baked ceramic tiles that reminded him of the Spanish roofs of the southwest United States.

The city lorded over an angry sea to its east. Stone docks jutting out into the ocean, incessant waves breaking against the pylons. They'd constructed higher docks since the Downfall, when everything in the world had changed as the comet that orbited the planet altered all the rules of magic and might. Now, the waters raged like a living beast, trying to tear down the stone that mere humans had constructed.

There were three tiers of docks used. They used the lowest in the winter; they were the thickest, and the most reinforced, to avoid being destroyed by violently tossed ice floes. The middle ones were for the spring and autumn, though it was the seasons of storms. The highest was for the summer, when ice melted, and the seas rose to the halfway mark on the hundred-meter-tall walls that the city perched atop.

They'd built the metropolis with the combined force of magic, and the blood and sweat of men. They'd laid it according to a grand plan; the streets in orderly grids and spokes that resembled a wagon wheel, the farmlands outside the walls and sheltered with rock formations grown from the bones of the land.

The outer wall of the city was a wonder. It was thick enough that two wagons could pass one another when on top, and most entrances that led into the building-thick wall were wide to allow a single wagon entry. The wall was a castle unto itself, built to shelter most of the city's populace if needed.

Seawall City had its own currency, a rare thing in an age struggling to survive in a time after this world's apocalypse. They traded in gold, silver, copper, and brass, whereas the other cities that Torrents had visited mostly bartered and traded in goods and services. Commerce was returning, but it wasn't where it had been before society collapsed.

The barbarian scanned the crowd again, spotting Nathan, who was nervously fiddling with his beard with one hand and clutching the symbol of his god with the other. The rokairn's mouth moved, and Torrents could almost hear his companion apologizing to each person he brushed against as he passed.

The priest followed his holy symbol the way a woodsman would follow a compass, glancing down at it, looking around, then turning and moving in a new direction.

Shouts from the crowd erupted.

A group of eight men-at-arms surrounding a figure appeared in the portcullised entrance from the thick stone outer wall of the city. A wizard—or a mage, sorcerer, or something, Torrents never knew which was which, or which witch was which—led the procession.

In the center of the group was a pale, thin woman. At least, Torrents thought it was a woman; it could have been a lithe and delicate man. But any way you looked at them, this person was beaten and broken under the lash, and possibly other tortures. It could have even been magic; after all, magic-using elitists—spellslingers to uneducated masses like the barbarian—controlled the city.

With an intake of breath, Torrents realized that the person about to be hung was an elf. *Aeifain*, the word echoed through his mind. They were their own species, though thought to be related to the Dasism, who roamed the wild, open spaces of the world.

Out of curiosity, Torrents focused on the figure—knowing it couldn't be the one they'd come here to find—his sharp eyes picking out details. Looking closely, he could see the aeifain was female. She held her head high and haughty, ignoring most of the crowd, and looking down on the few she did glance at, though she was a half head shorter than most of the adults.

He'd never met an aeifain but heard they were an arrogant bunch who treated everyone else like they were ghetto-trash. Torrents dealt with that sort of attitude often enough before he'd come to this world. As a black high-school student and athlete, he'd seen how people would look down on others.

Torrents shrugged off thoughts about the woman who was about to be hung and scanned the crowd for Nathan again.

He saw the rokairn moving through the mass of people, a valley in the waves of humanity, the crests rolling in to fill the space he'd occupied only a moment before.

Nathan stopped, looking from his holy symbol to the gibbet, where the aeifain was being led to the noose.

Torrents scanned the guards, then looked closely at the mage (or wizard, or whatever) who led the procession, wondering he'd be the one they'd need to contact and bring into their little group.

Looking back at Nathan, the rokairn was gesticulating wildly, pointing towards the raised platform.

The barbarian looked at the group surrounding the prisoner again. When he and Nathan came into this world from their own, they'd inhabited a body that had just died. The energy transfer of their souls had healed the physical wounds of the body they'd taken over and allowed them to have a second chance at life.

Torrents studied the group. It'd be nice to have another sword-swinging warrior beside him, muscle to back him up. Nathan kinda filled that role, but was much too meek to offer any real intimidation factor. He did okay when it came down to brass tacks, but not so much when he was trying to not get into a fight. The best way to do that was by flexing before your enemy got enough balls to draw and throw down; Nathan did it wrong and came off as a wimp for it.

Then again, maybe it'd be the spellslinger. Torrents had hung out with priests, and the Kid (who had travelled north and west a few months ago), and they all had some magical abilities, but each was prone to rely on a weapon rather than magic. Someone who could just whip out a fireball to clear the way through the fodder before Torrents got there to take out the mastermind with his sword might be a nice change of pace.

Torrents had been all-state football and basketball—and had even run some track and field—before his car accident severed his spinal column, paralyzed him from the waist down, and confined him to a wheelchair. He knew that sort of thinking wasn't PC, and people told him he shouldn't think of himself as restricted and limited. They didn't know what it was like, but he did, and he'd look at it however he felt like looking at it. Screw those hopeful wusses that preached that the world was all chuzzing puppies and rainbows.

He just wanted his life to mean something. It wasn't in his nature to be selfish and self-centered. He'd learned that the hard way. But life had to mean something, and that meant doing big things that others considered worthwhile, right? Or did it? Could he live his life for himself, doing what he wanted while helping others? His thoughts wandered to the Kid, and what he was doing right now.

The Kid had been his opposite but had also become his best friend. He'd never told him, because that wasn't manly, and would be ridiculed. Wouldn't it?

The barbarian pulled his mind from the bitter tar pit of his thoughts, focusing on his original idea, building their team. He liked teams. And it was always three of them brought together to face some problem, or army, or world-threatening event for some reason.

He'd faced an undead horde and things that put zombies and vampires to shame. He'd fought back an invading force of demons from another dimension, all to save a world he'd never asked to be a part of. But here he was, facing things down and being a hero, when in the real world, he rode the aluminum rails of a chair.

But he'd liked Esperanza, the priestess of Latress, (who apparently was a goddess married to Jonath) before she'd returned to their world where she'd just attempted suicide. He missed the Kid, though he'd never say it out loud. The Kid had been a cancer-riddled old lady in the body of a street-thief boy who had magical powers that let him make illusions and jump around like he had trampolines on his feet.

Now it was just him and Nathan. He liked the guy, but in the real-world Nathan owned a jewelry shop, and been—to put it bluntly—a wimp. The man had no spine, no guts, and no backbone. He'd apologize for breathing. Not that he didn't have some skills, but he'd never admit to them.

That annoyed Torrents.

The lead guard assisted the aeifain in stepping up on a bench so he could drape the noose around her neck. The man tightened the rope so it was snug around the woman's throat.

The barbarian looked back to the rokairn, trying to decipher which person was destined to join them. He knew it wasn't the prisoner, but couldn't figure out which of the seven other people the priest meant.

He also wondered how that person would die. Would the crowd riot? Would the aeifain lash out, knocking one of them to the ground?

The spellslinger in charge of the death-squad rested his hand on the lever that opened the trapdoor under the prisoner. He shouted something to the crowd, lost in the excited shouts and screams of the bloodthirsty mob, then pulled the control.

The floor dropped away, and the body fell, jerking. The crowd went quiet with a gasp, and the crack of the bones and sinew in the aeifain's neck was heard in that moment of silence.

Then the crowd cheered, drowning out all other noises.

Torrents looked back at Nathan, raising his hands in confusion, indicating he didn't know which one was their new companion.

The rokairn pointed at the spasming body hanging under the wooden platform as her death throes waned and she stilled.

Torrents looked at the prisoner in confusion and saw her eyes open and focus on the crowd.

Then terror crossed her face, and she let out a strangled scream.

## Chapter 2

Nathan watched Torrents swing his leg over the balcony of the city building and shook his head at the man's boldness. The barbarian was fearless and would take on a pack of wild dogs before breakfast, a city council before lunch, and overthrow a warlord before dinner if he could. Not that there was much call for it here.

Seawall City was a strict place of rules and organization. Patrols policed the flagstone streets, four soldiers accompanied by a single elementalist, mind mage, sorcerer, alchemist, or some sort of priest.

Magic ruled here, in name and in power. The strong backs supported the mageocracy blended with theocracy. A council made all the decisions for the city, and it was the only safe haven within a two week walk. Law and order were top priority and anyone entering Seawall City was vetted and cleared by a subcommittee.

Every merchant, farmer, and visitor required written permission to enter. There were barracks outside the manned fortifications of the metropolis, holding pens for caravans, and if you didn't have permission and clearance, you were turned away.

Not too long ago, as Nathan and Torrents were waiting to enter—in a holding pattern as their diplomatic papers from the Crescent Rokairn Clan waited approval—they'd stayed in those lodgings outside the walls. They'd seen a group of merchants begging entrance, promising good behavior and valuable trinkets for the population. Rejected, the traders were turned away, and told to leave before they paid the price of disobedience. The leader of the group refused. An hour later, the remaining people in the wagon train left, the still-smoldering corpse of their leader lying in the road as an example.

The woman—possibly the wife or maybe the concubine—who'd rushed to the fallen man received a different treatment.

Statues lined the last stretch of the road that led to the city. At first, Nathan thought they were incredible works of art, but once he'd seen the woman turned to stone—and later moved to the roadside—he'd realized that those, too, were examples set by the powers-that-be, a permanent warning to others who decided to not follow the very strict rules and laws of Seawall City.

The outer wall had tenets carved into them in meter tall letters. Eight rules surpassed all others. It kept it clear, kept it simple, but was absolute with no leeway for individual cases.

The entire city was an armed encampment, built with magic that withstood man and nature. The walls towered thirty meters above the ground, and a hundred meters over the sea in low tide seasons, less in high tide seasons.

There were two entrances into the city—besides the docks—one on the main road to the west, and a second that allowed entrance from the road to the north that followed the coast. Every entry point had a barbican with portcullis on each side, a squad of eight sentries directed by a magic-using commander attending it. One group stood guard in the entryway, and the other kept watch from atop the fortification. Less than a score of men could easily defend the entrance until reinforcements arrived from within the city.

Nathan threaded his way through the crowd, concentrating on the symbol of Jonath in his hands. The disk was an engraved image of a trident made into the scales of justice, rising from a mountain. The priest had a gut feeling, almost a premonition, that the third person who would join them would be somewhere in the square today.

He looked up from the religious relic in his hands, searching faces and wondering who it would be. He had to trust Torrents that there would be a third person, and the subtle feelings he received from somewhere—maybe his god—told him he needed to be in this precise place to find whoever it was.

A portcullis in the stone wall opened, and the noise of the crowd rose in excitement. Guards and a mage led a prisoner from the opening and made their way through the mob to the raised wooden scaffolding erected for the hanging.

Nathan caught a glimpse of the procession passing in front of him. The prisoner was a woman of rare magnificence. Her blonde hair was so pale he compared it to white gold, small braids trailing down to her shoulders at each temple, and her skin matched her hair though a shade or two darker. Her slanted eyes were larger than a human's and her ears came to a point, breaking through the straight locks to peek out on each side of her head. They'd dressed her in an off-white robe and bound her hands tightly with a silver cord.

Nathan couldn't take his eyes off her. Her presence filled his awareness, drawing his attention until nothing else distracted him. He saw her flexing her fingers, trying desperately to bring circulation back to the numb appendages. Slightly shorter than the other women in the courtyard, she looked around the crowd, her wide eyes searching for someone—anyone—who might help her. She shuffled her feet along the flagstones, as if in a daze or drugged. Either was possible.

"Lynch the witch!" a man shouted, and the crowd shouted its approval.

Practicing magic within the walls of the city was only allowed with the proper paperwork. Even Nathan had restrictions; any magic he used with any outward effects would be considered a breach, and he'd be subject to repercussions and punishment.

Seawall City preferred a monopoly when it came to the use of magics.

According to rumors, Aeifain were innately magical, and could do a variety of magic. There were five types of magic: alchemy, mind magic, elemental, holy, and the summoning of items or living beings. None of these were allowed within the walls without proper documentation and permission.

A man jostled Nathan. The rokairn turned to apologize and lost sight of the execution procession.

"Wanna place a wager?" the man drew Nathan's attention with the words. "A silver gets you five, if you can guess how long the witch dances for, or if she messes herself. Or if you're really daring, you can bet on her lashing out with forbidden sorcery and killing a guard. If you're right on that one, you'll get a hundred-to-one odds."

Nathan shooed the man away, shuddering at the human bottom-feeder. The rokairn despised people who took advantage of others, and what could be worse than profiting on another living being's last moments?

*Bullies came in many forms,* Nathan thought, moving into the mass of bodies, away from the bookie. *Taking advantage of anyone, in any way, or their circumstances, is a form of bullying.*

Nathan had dealt with it in his old life more than he'd ever realized.

He wondered about his jewelry shop in that other world that seemed so far away, and pondered if his body had died from the double-barreled shotgun that went off in his belly.

Nathan had been alone there, his family distant from him geographically and emotionally. He'd lived his life for his business, a small jewelry store in a not-so-good part of town. He missed it occasionally. It was easy and familiar. If he'd kept his eyes down, almost no one would bother him.

Here, in this world, people seemed to appear from nowhere, asking for his help, his advice, and his guidance.

Nathan liked law; he liked rules. He wanted a society that protected its people, and Seawall City appeared to do that at first glance. But there was something rotten in the state of Denmark, to quote the Bard, or at least paraphrase him.

On a deeper inspection, Seawall City had a stranglehold on its people. Nathan allowed that might be necessary with the current state of affairs, but then again, perhaps it was just an excuse to tighten the chokehold. He also allowed that he didn't know the entire story. But he had a hard time conceiving of what happened to make it so the government controlled the people's actions, and possibly dictated their thoughts.

Nathan's stomach twisted as the crowd shouted, jeered, or spit on the aeifain being led to the gallows. A few threw clods of dirt or manure.

No one threw food though, and Nathan wondered at that for a moment before realizing anyone who did would likely join the woman on the executioner's block. Food was scarce, and though Seawall City didn't appear to suffer from a lack of resources, they practiced rationing.

A tater-tot sized lump of poo hit the side of a guard's head. He turned, growling, his sword glinting in the sun. The blade slid effortlessly through the neck of the man who'd thrown the feces.

The severed head smacked on the flagstones and rolled wetly. A wife screamed, and three children began wailing, crowding around their mother. A headless body accordioned to the ground, ankles folding, knees bending, waist twisting, shoulders slumping, and the entire form collapsed like a slinky forming into its solidified state, wrinkling to the flagstones.

The head bounced twice, rolled three times, its eyes open and blinking as dirt filled them, the mouth working with no lungs and air to voice the scream the face mimicked.

The mage leading the prisoner's procession laughed. But it wasn't even a hearty or cruel laugh. It was an off-handed gesture, an afterthought.

Nathan twitched. He'd never been a twitcher. He hesitated, he stuttered, he hemmed, he hawed, and he'd occasionally stumble verbally. But the twitch was something new.

He understood people couldn't attack the authorities willy-nilly without repercussions. But this wasn't a repercussion, as much as a knee-jerk reaction that was barely even acknowledged.

This person—this human being, this life with a family—was snuffed with no more of a reaction or thought than most people would give to swatting a mosquito.

Nathan twitched again.

He felt a drive, countered by a pull, and that meant a choice. Jonath called for judgment. Who would come? Who would die?

Nathan knew in the olden days—three decades ago, before the world went to crap—priests of Jonath were called upon during each new moon to make judgments on criminals and the damned. Towns and villages held wrong doers until that day, waiting for a traveling judge to arrive and do their duty. They hadn't gotten a priest showing up every month, except in large cities where they had magistrates year-round, but most had seen a justice at least three or four times a year.

The rokairn's god now called upon him to do his duty. Who would die today?

But Nathan also knew whoever died would be reborn with a soul from his world and would join him and Torrents to face whatever horrible thing came next.

The decision stopped Nathan in his tracks. He stared at the aeifain criminal, who may have been here merely for being what she was. Was it right to condemn her? And wasn't the guard who killed the civilian on a whim and the lead mage more deserving of death?

The rokairn was allowed within Seawall City's walls only because they had an agreement with the clan of rokairns who made their home in the craggy wasteland a day or two travel to the west. But they'd treated him like a second-class citizen.

People shoved in front of him at the deli, ignored him when he flashed coin to buy something, or even jostled him off the road so his boots sunk in manure scraped to the side.

Was the aeifain so different? Would they have led Nathan to the gallows if he hadn't had papers that pointed to a military power just a day-or-so march from the city walls?

Nathan twitched again, felt the pressure of the weight of his decision overlapping the impact of seeing this woman shoved by the city guards.

The priest looked from his holy symbol to the gibbet, then turned to Torrents and gesticulated towards where the aeifain was being led to the noose.

The barbarian looked confused, raising his hands in a shrug.

The sound of the floor of the hangman's platform opening cracked across the stone courtyard. The crowd gasped and then went silent.

Nathan's head snapped to the dancing and dangling woman, her broken neck causing her head to bounce grotesquely. She was a parody of a marionette, her legs dancing on air, her bound hands flailing outward at the elbows, and her tongue forced from her mouth, below bulging eyes.

Nathan felt—no, he saw—the spirit launch from the form at the end of the noose, dashing with a silver-gold light, into the sky. It was like a magical bolt from a mystical bow (the thought of Hank the Ranger from the old Dungeons & Dragons cartoon came to his mind) being shot into the heavens.

The priest knew he could choose anyone in the crowd, and they would die, their spirit released into the next realm, and someone would then take over their body. He was now the executioner, but also the life-bringer, all in one package.

His breath came in short, contorted pants. He had to choose. The wizard who guided the escort? One of the guards, maybe the one who slew an innocent moments ago? Or maybe someone from a crowd?

How could he choose who would die?

The woman at the end of the noose twitched, and Nathan's body mirrored the movement.

His decision made; Nathan mentally called to Jonath. As was his duty as a priest of justice, summoned retribution for the deserving.

The aeifain's eyes flew open, and she began gurgling and struggling.

Chapter 3

Aiyana Riandell woke with a jerk, her body spasming and her throat clutching at her gasps for breath. She reached up, trying to feel at her neck to pull away whatever was constricting her airway, but her hands were bound together, and connected to her waist. She gagged and sputtered, kicking out with her feet, tightening her shoulders and neck enough to draw in a breath.

The realization that the crowd around her was cheering, yelling, screaming, and shouting hateful things at her wasn't surprising. That's exactly what they'd been doing moments ago as she marched through the streets of Chicago during the protest. She remembered the brick flying at her, then the sharp pain in her head. She remembered falling, but was confused at how she seemed to hang in the air.

She opened her eyes.

The buildings of downtown Chicago were gone, and instead of brownstones, shops, and apartments, there were structures of whitewashed.

The crowd was different, too. They weren't businessmen, and black folk dressed in hats and sweater vests. Instead, there were hundreds of people dressed like hippies. The women wore peasant blouses and skirts, and the men dressed similarly, but in trousers.

There were no Fords, Chryslers, or Buicks lining the curbs. She saw horse-drawn wagons through the mob.

Five soldiers rushed forward, surrounding her. One reached for her with one hand, a sword held in the other.

She screamed, and the men jerked back.

The bright sunlight bled away, clouds roiled across the blue sky, turning the air from a crisp, cheery autumn day to a shady omen of things to come. Thunder rumbled overhead; two banks of clouds collided, and lightning jerked in a jagged streak through the sky. A bolt touched down nearby, a loud crack echoing off the stones as dust tumbled from the building across the street.

Wind tore at Aiyana's robes, and she wondered when she'd changed clothes from her pleated wool skirt and white button up shirt.

The wind lifted her, allowing her to suck in fresh air, filling her lungs as panic overtook her. Aiyana pulled at her bonds and felt her wrists heat with the effort. She tilted her head down to look at the knots and see if she could free herself, and instead saw blue flame dancing across the ropes.

She screamed again, and the flame raced up her arms, seemingly in response to her panic. Her loose garments caught fire, and she struggled against the bonds. The ties fell away in ash, and Aiyana clutched at her throat.

There was a noose around her neck.

The fear she'd felt melted with the heat of the flames, and anger seeped into her awareness.

How dare they do this? How dare they string her up for marching against oppression and trying to free other human beings from society's prejudices and discrimination?

They would pay.

Her body lifted higher, back arching and legs stretching their full length. She threw her head back and her pale hair spread around her in a halo, and she burst into flame.

Aiyana fell to the ground, landing on her hands and knees, scraping them. Her head was bent between her arms, and the ashes of her clothes swirled around her; lightning struck again and again in the courtyard, white-hot light blocking out everything else.

Men-at-arms backed away, swords held defensively in front of them. They spun as explosions sounded around them, detritus raining down.

Sheets of rain erupted from the sky, washing across the people who'd come to witness death. The crowd screamed, but for very different reasons than a few minutes ago. They stampeded for shelter, separating into clumps of people, pushing down streets and alleys to escape the square.

The world turned grey, split by purple-white streaks of energy. Explosions sounded from across the city, fires breaking out in the housing and business districts closest to the square.

The woman, who'd been dangling at the end of a rope and her life, now stood. She rose, unfolding into a pose that artists would have shuddered at in inspiration for their next statue or painting. The ground beneath her feet trembled, and small gouts of rock and dirt plumed up around her as she stood with clenched fists, the same purple-white light of the storm in her eyes.

A small, hairy man appeared from the grey mist of the downpour, holding a cape or cloak of some sort towards Aiyana.

"Miss?" the strange little man said, "put this on, then we should get you out of here. The city guard will regroup, with mages, and be back soon."

She eyed the bearded man. He wasn't quite a midget, being only a head shorter than she was, but he wasn't what she would think of as full-sized, though proportioned like anyone else.

"I know," the man continued to speak to her as he came forward, "it's strange when you first get here from Earth, and I'll go over all of that soon, but we must go. Otherwise, the people who did this to you will come and do worse. Can you run?"

She looked over his head and watched the last of the crowd disappear into the rain, through doorways, or down alleys.

Looking behind her, she saw the wreckage of some sort of wooden platform. The body of a man twisted in the rubble. The robed man blinked at her, trying to focus his eyes. A triangle of bloodied oak stuck an arm's length out of his midsection.

He worked his fingers in an intricate pattern and then blew across his shaking palm.

Aiyana felt something settle across her mind, like a net tightening around her thoughts.

She defensively flicked a hand towards him, and the plank slid deeper into the wizard's body, ending his life.

A vaguely familiar man charged at her, a bloody sword held high. This was the guard who'd abused her and led her here. Another flick of her fingers and he flew backwards. He slammed into a man who was counting money and cackling about bets and suckers. The guard's back snapped as he hit the wall, and his sword flew into the air, coming down into the skull of the second man. They both slumped to the ground.

"Justice has been done," a deep voice came from behind her.

She turned to see a short, bearded man in bright clothing looking pointedly into her eyes. She felt a spark of a connection with him and shuddered.

"Miss?" he said.

She looked down at the man, who still held out the poncho-like wrap.

"My name is Nathan," he continued, "and I came here from the same place as you. I'm here to help, but we must go. You need to cover yourself, though. We're going to attract enough attention without you, well, being like you are."

He adverted his eyes, and she looked down to see she was naked. Her clothes had burned away along with the ropes that bound her. Her body was as foreign as this place.

She was slim, and her breasts were smaller than they'd been since she'd hit puberty. Her skin was light and almost hairless, nothing like what she expected or was used to. Her hands rose to her face, tracing the fine features they found there, along her pointed ears, and ended on her hair, pulling a lock forward to look at it. It was fine, straight, and pale, unlike her thick, dark curls that spoke of her Italian heritage.

The man, Nathan, stepped close enough she could reach out and take the clothing he offered. She snatched it and wrapped it around herself.

"It's…upside down," Nathan gestured at the hood trailing on the wet stone below her feet, "turn it around, there's a clasp at the neck to keep it around you, and holes you can put your arms through."

The small man mimed turning the garment over and fastening it around her neck.

She followed the instructions, looking from the cloak to the man, to her surroundings. The moment she'd pushed the knotted cord of the clasp through the frog epaulet, Nathan grabbed her hand and pulled her forward.

"Wait," she commanded, and tore her hand from his.

He turned to look at her; she drew her arms into the cloak and pushed them back out the slits on the sides. She wrapped one hand around her waist to keep the cloth from opening and gestured with the other hand towards her guide.

"Fine," her voice was cold, and she felt herself looking down her nose at the man trying to help her. She sighed at his hurt expression, and softened her tone. "You don't need to hold my hand. I don't know you, and I'm perfectly capable of moving without you dragging me around."

Nathan's eyes met hers. They hardened, but not in anger or offense, and a small smile of approval played across his lips.

He nodded and started away.

She followed, her head turning to look at everything in this new place.

Memories bubbled to the surface. She'd come here—but no, it wasn't her, it was another her—to bring warnings to Seawall City about her people being destroyed, killed wantonly by…something. It wasn't clear. She didn't know if she didn't see what did it, or if trauma blocked it. She only knew she'd barely escaped.

She'd been to Runsk, Dioneze City, Rumay Bay, Durgan's Keep, Red Wind, and every small village between her ravaged homeland—Icon Hall in the Grey Forest—and this place. She'd received similar welcomes at each. Distrust at best, anger, and open hostility at most.

The other races were jealous of her people, the Aeifain, because her people were superior in every way. They lived longer, stayed healthier, and magic came to them easily. The lesser races may be stronger of muscle and sinew, but they were slower of movement in mind and body.

She remembered Seawall City—again, not her, but the other her, her mind wrestled with that concept—and that they'd allowed her in. When she'd been to the Council of Elders—users of magics, every one of them—they'd listened to her portents that magic would unbalance, the Demon Front ripped asunder, and the Monolith of Onyx birthed in its place.

They'd laughed at her, spoke down to her like she was a child who was too airheaded, inexperienced, and ignorant to understand how the world truly worked.

But they were the children, and she told them so, warning them that their carelessness and lust for power would bring their downfall.

They didn't laugh at that. They had her clapped into chains and irons and dragged her below where they spent weeks interrogating her.

At first it had been gentle, and almost friendly. They fed her well, and spoke to her kindly across a table, but they still housed her behind bars when they weren't talking to her.

They dampened her magics, three mind mages in a constant triangle around her whether she was being questioned, sleeping, eating, or even just moving her bowels.

She'd been patient with them, knowing they were like children and needed to have their lessons and lectures repeated more than once before they sunk through their thick skulls. She pointed out their mistakes, using that slow and persistent tone that her people always used with humans.

Then they tired of the talking and decided they didn't believe her. Shackles again, and hot irons, and questions about her people and their magic. They dug into her flesh, searing into her bones, demanding that she tell them secrets passed down for thousands of years.

She couldn't recall if she'd told them. She wanted to think she hadn't, but her mind and memories had holes. She didn't know if they'd drawn things from her that her people would exile her for telling the lesser races.

Exploring these memories, she felt the casting her jailor had sent upon her mind as he lay dying in the rain and rubble of the gibbet. It was her leash, and if she allowed herself to know who she'd been, and all that secret knowledge she hoped she hadn't shared, then the wizards of Seawall City could track and find her.

The thoughts washed away, like the tide on a shore rushing back to the infinite sea to hide in the dark places where light fled, and monsters hid.

Aiyana stumbled, drawing up short in the alley Nathan jogged down, a few paces in front of her. They moved through the city, staying in alleys and smaller avenues, avoiding people whenever they could. They ducked behind carts to avoid city patrols that may or may not have known to look for them. Scampering across streets, they slid between buildings whenever they could.

They moved into the lower section of the city.

Seawall City didn't really have a poor or bad part of town, but it had a section a bit more crowded with people who had less money, influence, and power, and packed tighter than the affluent areas.

They entered this part of town now, and Nathan led Aiyana down a backstreet barely wide enough for a wagon from the trash, discarded crates, and refuse littering the lane.

A large man stepped into the alley between her and the rokairn—Nathan was a rokairn, she knew that now, though her head swum with all the thoughts that had disappeared with a flash of insight a short while before—swords bristling and muscles flexing. Dark hair pulled back into a ponytail, loose strands plastered his face in the rain.

Everything spun down into slow motion. The intruder looked at Nathan's back, then at Aiyana.

Aiyana called upon the elements, reaching out to the strong currents of the ley lines they'd built Seawall City upon. Close to the wall they were just a few blocks from, the ocean pulsed with power. Under her feet, the land pulsed with tectonic plates pressed against one another, fire pulsing along the same line as volcanic activity that lay dormant a kilometer underground. The winds swirled with power as the lines overhead bled magical energy.

The elementalist's magics burst from her hands, balls of flames dancing across her palms. The rain split away from her, and the winds whipped her hair, drying it and her cloak in moments, as the ground trembled under her feet.

"Whoa," the intruder muttered, stumbling backwards and throwing his hands up submissively. "I ain't gonna hurt ya, babe."

"Oh, sorry," Nathan spun to face the two, holding up his own hands in a cautionary warning. "Don't do that, um, lady. That's Torrents, he's with us. He's here to help. He's been trailing us from…the rooftops? Well, I know he's been watching, and he's okay. Don't bring down the city watch by, um, doing what you're doing."

The rumbling slowed then stopped, the wind died, and the rain folded back across Aiyana like a curtain closing. But the flames still danced on her hands.

"Where are you taking me?" She glanced between the rokairn and the burly human, not trusting either by some deep, embedded instinct that spoke of centuries of distrust of her people and theirs.

"Right here," Nathan gestured to a door to his left, "it's an inn called The Fiddle. It's not the best, but we won't attract attention, and we have friends here."

"It's not a good inn," Torrents said.

"Don't…" Nathan glared at the large man, "don't say it. I know you love to, but really, now's not the time for this."

"It's a rundown place, a hive of scum and villainy," Torrents went on, his face wrinkling with amusement, "The Fiddle…is a vile inn."

Nathan sighed and raised a hand to rub his temple.

Aiyana laughed, and the two men shared a startled glance.

"Okay," the aeifain smiled, "o-pun the door then, and let's get out of the rain."

## Chapter 4

The three sat in a booth, Nathan and Torrents with their backs to the room, and Aiyana across from them, dividing her attention between the two men and the rest of the inn.

The aeifain had pulled the hood of the cloak up and shifted uncomfortably on the wooden bench. She was constantly reminded of her lack of clothing by the rubbing of the rough material.

She stared at the rokairn for a moment, taking in his beard, dripping doublet, and the holy symbol hanging from the chain around his neck. Nathan fiddled with the charm—a trident balancing the scales of justice on the center tine—and kept glancing at her, opening his mouth to say something, then shutting it and dropping his eyes.

She shifted her gaze to the barbarian.

The big man smiled at her, leaning back into the corner of the booth, one arm along the back of the seat, and the other turning his pewter mug around on the table. He had one leg folded on the bench between him and the priest, the other stretched out under the table so his foot stuck out of the end. He nodded at her each time she looked at him and gave a little wave.

Looking around the tavern part of the inn, Aiyana took in The Fiddle's atmosphere. It was what she thought she should expect from a medieval pub: dark wood paneling on the walls; thick wooden posts with wrought iron coat hooks jutting from them for hats, cloaks, and sword belts; a layer of hay across the floor to soak up drinks or other fluids that might spill during an evening of drinking; a short bar along the far wall with a fat guy in a stained apron serving up drinks and conversation; and three barmaids running food and drinks from the kitchen and the bar, respectively.

Every time the door opened, she inspected whoever entered. The flare of muted daylight behind them—the storm having cleared—left the new arrival in shadow until the door closed. Then the ominous silhouette would coalesce into a non-threatening form of a laborer, shopkeeper, or a trader looking for a room, a meal, and a few drinks.

There were openings where windows would have been in more advanced civilizations that let in light and whatever breeze was passed. Light-colored waxed canvas was rolled down to cover them when autumn brought cooler temperatures. Shutters hinged on the outside allowed further protection from the elements.

To her left between the bar and the stairs that led to the rooms above, was the open-air kitchen. It had three walls and a roof, and the fourth wall was a half wall with heavy tarps, rolled up to let the wind take away the heat of the ovens and the smoke of the grills. On chilly nights, or winter days, they lowered the canvas walls, and the kitchen provided part of the heat for the common room.

Aiyana looked up as a figure blocked her view of the kitchen. The aeifain, lost in her thoughts, hadn't noticed the large woman come out of the room she'd been staring into.

"You okay, honey?" The large lady stood between the table and the kitchen, holding a wide wooden platter stacked with steaming food, pewter plates, and more.

The woman sported a stained apron. Browns and yellows of gravy and meat juices blended with deep purples and russet reds of wines. Bits of dried greens were stuck next to tidbits of raw meat that had turned a grey on the protective cloth.

Looking up into the woman's face, Aiyana judged the rest of her. She was stout, not fat. She was thick and solid, like she had an extra portion because she worked in a kitchen, but also had muscle below that layer of soft flesh. Her tousled brown hair, tied into a bun atop her head, had a bright green ribbon with baby's breath flowers tucked into it and held the mound into place.

"Tugas," the woman's voice was gruff, with mood or years of smoking, it was hard to guess, "that's my name, lass. And I'm the one who's feeding you, so be nice and wipe that damned aeifain glare you got on yer face, okey-pokie?"

Tugas thrust the wide wooden trencher onto the table, right under Aiyana's nose. The aeifain had to lean back or get hit with her dinner.

"Here ya go, sweetie," Tugas smiled at Nathan, showing a missing tooth in front and center of that flirtatious expression, "I made my meat extra juicy just for you, dear heart. I wanna see ya lick yer platter clean, ya got me?"

Nathan mumbled something as Tugas dropped a metal plate in front of him and slapped a bloody red roast onto it. She used her fingers, and followed with a plump tomato, a steaming potato—that she broke open by shoving a finger into it, then splitting it by pushing the ends together—three rolls, and small leg that probably once belonged to some sort of fowl.

She smiled down at the priest, slowly licking each one of her fingers that had touched his food, then sucking on the thumb for a moment without breaking eye contact with him.

"I even brought ya some salt, ya hairy wee warrior of love," she said, setting down two small, covered wooden bowls, "and the butter. I know you like the butter. And later, if you wanna come in my back room and judge, I'll be there. I'll even have some sweet cream as desert for the two of us."

Tugas winked, then turned and sashayed away, her wide hips knocking a patron to one side. He laughed and looked back at the table.

"Someone's getting lucky tonight." Torrents pulled one of the pewter platters from the wooden board and set it in front of him, turning to put both feet on the floor, "and it ain't me."

Aiyana sniffed and blew out a small breath, reaching for the last plate. Using the double tonged fork, she daintily served herself a portion of seasoned greens, a potato, and a single roll. She looked around the table, searching for something, her hand resting on the bread.

"Here," Torrents's hand reached under the table and came back up with a dagger, and he set it on the table with its point facing him and slid it towards the woman, "I'm betting you wanted something to cut your potato and butter your buns. You can keep it, if you like. We'll get you a belt and sheath tomorrow."

"And clothing?" Aiyana's her voice tinged with bitterness. "Can we get me something to wear besides a wrap that comes to my knees?"

"Oh," Nathan's embarrassed response came out as a gasp, "I'm so sorry, hold on, I'll take care of that right now."

The rokairn slid off the bench and dropped to the floor. He half jogged towards the kitchen, stopping at the open doorway to take a deep breath before entering Tugas's domain.

"So, naked, huh?" Torrents smiled. "How's that working out for you? I expect it should help you get attention when you want it."

"You're a…" Aiyana swallowed the word barbarian, "pig. I didn't choose to not have clothes."

"You were the one that burned them off after they hung you and you came back to life," Torrents stabbed a piece of beef with another dagger that he'd brought out from under the table, raising the dripping meat to his mouth, turning his head sideways, and biting off a piece.

Chewing, he added, "Remember when you had a magical hissy fit and blew up most of the courtyard?"

"That wasn't me!" Aiyana spat, then drew a deep breath to calm herself. "That wasn't me. Those things are impossible. It was a freak storm, nothing more."

"And the fire on your hands, the winds lifting you, and all the other things? Were they just another freak coincidence? Face it, lady, you're in a new world where magic works. Deal with it and handle your bidj."

Aiyana ignored him.

She looked down, her chin raised, and sawed at her food. She swiped butter from the small dish, slapping it onto her potato. She chopped her roll in half, mashing it, then tearing it apart. She added butter to it also with the tip of the blade. Reaching her fingers into the bowl of salt, she took a pinch and sprinkled it across the greens and tuber.

"What gives you the right?" She looked at the barbarian, her face drawn tight. "Why would you even think that you can speak in such a manner? Who are you, and why should I even sit here with you?"

"I'm the guy who helped save your ass after you came back to life from being hung by a city that hates anything that's different, and especially anyone that can do magic that threatens their control over it."

Torrents's voice was tight, a hint of bitterness that bordered on empathy leaking through.

Aiyana was staring at him, her lips drawn into a line, and Torrents stared back, matching the expression.

Nathan walked back up to the table, put one hand on it, and prepared to bounce back onto the bench when he noticed the locked stares of the two.

"Oh, no," he sighed, and pulled himself into the booth, "so, you're both doing your best to be charming and make new friends, I see."

The two broke their staring contest, their glares turning to the rokairn.

He nodded at Torrents, then turned and smiled at Aiyana.

"Good," he pulled a small knife from his belt and began cutting his food into small, bite-sized pieces, "now that I have the attention of you both, and your spiteful glares, I think we should talk. Though it might be better to do this with full bellies, I don't think it's going to wait until after we eat."

Nathan popped a bite of potato topped with a bit of roast into his mouth and chewed while turning to look at each of them pointedly.

"Eat," he gestured at their plates with his knife. "I'll talk. And eat, just don't interrupt while I'm chewing. To start: Aiyana, you came from Earth and arrived here at the moment your body and soul were teetering on death. You inhabited another body, in this case an aeifain, who was also dying at that very moment."

Nathan took a bite, allowing the woman to digest the information as he chewed.

"I have clothes coming for you," the rokairn said, "and don't ask what Tugas wanted in exchange, because I don't want to talk about it."

Torrents snorted while chewing and slapped the smaller man on the shoulder.

Nathan's knife pivoted towards the barbarian.

"You," the priest thrust the knife in Torrents's direction, "need to stop provoking her just because you're impatient. We all took some time to adjust to this thing we're in."

Aiyana made a noise, nodding once, and opened her mouth to say something, but Nathan interrupted her.

"You," he thrust the tip of his blade in her direction, "need to listen, and stop turning your nose up at everything around you."

Torrents nodded with a smile, and then looked back down at his food when Nathan shot him a glance and frown.

"Do what you need to do to mentally accept where you are," Nathan looked at the aeifain. "Think of this as a dream, a second chance, a delusion, a miracle, or whatever. But realize you *are* here, and you're not leaving by waking up."

Nathan, setting down the knife, gripped a rough spoon with his other hand, scooped some greens onto his roll, set down the spoon, and took a bite. Juices dribbled down his beard, and he thrust his chin out, pulled a napkin from under the table, and wiped at his chin before the liquid hit his doublet.

He looked between the two, daring them to interrupt or say something.

"Biting off more than you can chew?" Aiyana said with an air of innocence.

"Yeah," Nathan said around the mouthful, pausing to finish chewing before continuing. "In more ways than one. I want to give you the lowdown, the bottom line, the nitty gritty."

"What about the 411, and all the things?" Torrents asked. "You gonna drop that, too?

"Lay it on me," Aiyana said. "I can dig it."

Nathan sighed and slumped before looking back at the two, then took a drink from his pewter goblet of deep red wine.

"Ugh," he grimaced, "never much liked wines, so bitter. Anyway, look, we've got a thing to do. But we don't know what it is. Torrents has met two other people from our world, and each time they faced…a thing."

"A thing?" Aiyana tilted her head, her own goblet pausing in front of her mouth. "That's a bit vague."

"Yeah, sorry," Nathan shrugged, "it is. Do you know anything, from *other* memories that aren't yours, but you have in your head?"

"And where are you from?" Torrents interjected. "What happened that brought you here? How'd you die?"

Aiyana blanched at the questions.

"I think we should stick to the more immediate questions," Nathan caught Torrents's eyes with his, and tilted his head for emphasis, "and focus on what we *need* to know right now. Agreed?"

Torrents looked at the smaller man, then sighed, nodded, and shoved a huge bite of potato into his mouth with his fingers.

Nathan looked at Aiyana with a gentle smile, coaxing her to answer.

"I do have memories," she hesitated, "about Icon Hall in the Grey Wood, the homeland of my people. It lays in smoking ruin now, and I think it's directly related to the events of the Demon Front and the Monolith of Onyx."

She paused. After taking a deep drink of her wine she went on in a rush. The story spilled from her over the next half hour.

The two men's reactions were very different. Torrents turned grim, and his eyes kept moving to his swords that hung from a hook on a nearby post. Nathan looked worried and anxious, and his hands moved towards the aeifain and then drew back more than once.

The conversation trailed off when Tugas delivered a linen-wrapped bundle of clothes to the table. She patted Aiyana's hand and assured the woman the clothes would fit.

The stout kitchen mistress turned away, then said over her shoulder, almost as an afterthought, "You got nothing to worry with either of these men. They're good people."

The three left the table after the conversation and meal without planning or discussing what came next. Nathan said they should sleep on it.

They went upstairs, each exhausted after the day's events, but each in a very different way.

Aiyana had her room, rented by Nathan, and the rokairn and barbarian were to share one. The last words said before they parted ways were Torrents complaining about Nathan's snoring.

The two men woke, hours later, by a banging on their door and Tugas swearing.

"Hey, sexy man," her gruff voice muted through the thick door, "ya better get going. Someone is coming, and they're looking for ya and yer new girlfriend."

## Chapter 5

Administrator Khizhane cleared his throat and rose to his full height; he still had to look up to meet the bounty hunter's eyes.

The gnohl grinned, his jowls peeling back from his teeth, revealing yellowed canines.

"You," Ghe'hak the Ravager breathed, "want them dead, or brought back to you alive?"

"Alive, if possible," Khizhane cleared his throat again, and moved to the trolley with the crystal decanters without breaking eye contact. "But it's the device that is the most important thing. I'll update you with the 'script-messenger' I've given you."

Ghe'hak licked his lips and turned away so Khizhane wouldn't see his amusement at the man's nervousness. The small magical scroll was in the creature's pouch, and Ghe'hak had learned to read and write enough of the human's language to use the quill and parchment, but it was likely to be a way to keep track of him, as well. The alchemist may not trust the gnohl, but the feeling was mutual, and the man's endgame wasn't the same as the demon hybrid's.

The gnohl was used to people fearing him, as well as hiding that same fear. But the smell of it was obvious to his keen senses. The acrid taint was distinctive to his nose, though humans would never smell it. It was the tinge of a storm on the horizon, mixed with the urge to run or hide, and it twisted into a unique scent that he knew well since his change.

When he was just a hyena, he'd smell fear every time he'd encountered creatures. He'd been an apex predator, but when the demonic energy had transformed him to this humanoid form, the nuances of different kinds of fear had blossomed, becoming subtle variations on the theme.

People were pemtie and superstitious things who thought they'd overcome fear by logic, by willing it away.

They were wrong. Fear was something much more primal than that, and you couldn't shed your bones, only change your skin.

Ghe'hak looked around the room again. It was decadent, and smelled of the biting, pungent odor of alcohol and the musk of sex. He'd interrupted Khizhane, having come in through the window unheard, and had watched the pale, skinny man coupling with a thick, buxom woman for a few minutes before they'd noticed him.

A stout beam of Valenwood, a rare lumber from the forests of the Aeifain a thousand kilometers to the east, split the mahogany paneling on the walls at regular intervals. The once-plush maroon carpeting underfoot was threadbare with the wear of foot traffic and showed signs of scorching and chemical spills. Ghe'hak could smell traces of the latter.

Shelves lined three of the walls—the fourth wall housed windows with silver-gilt framework and colorful stained-glass panes—were filled with books and scattered with trinkets and antiques from the time before the Downfall.

It was how the gnohl entered without being noticed.

Some glowed with the aura of magic, and Ghe'hak saw that shine with his altered eyes, though most never knew it was a gift bestowed upon him at his changing.

The gnohl didn't know if others of his kind had the same talents as he, perhaps he was special. But he was smart enough to consider the beings who transformed him wanted him to think that, like all the others probably did, too.

He'd been at the Demon Front for the last battle, watched Klendrisia fall to the people he now hunted, and he'd slunk away. He was unsure if it had been cowardice or wisdom. But the voice—the voice that whispered in his head—told him to hide. To creep away as the rokairn and humans scoured the battlefield for survivors and ruthlessly cut throats.

He'd admired their decision. You don't let an enemy survive; they'd only come back to attack you later.

It had taken three sunsets for the armies to depart. He'd killed scouts left behind, feasting on their flesh, as well as the rotting corpses of his brethren once fresh meat was no longer available.

Then he'd gone to the Monolith of Onyx, following the shadowy whispers of temptation to its source. The god had been speaking to him.

He rarely thought about the voice in his head. After a wonderful fight where he'd attacked and slain a caravan crossing the sandy wastes of the Crescent Desert, glutted on flesh, booze, and battle, he'd allowed himself to think, to ponder, to consider. The voice could be the other side of his thinking, the smart side that went beyond instinct and obeyance. It could be what came after survival. Or it could have been the demon lords beyond this world, whispering ideas and suggestions to make him their puppet. Or perhaps a god.

Ghe'hak decided it was a god, making him special. That made it worth listening to, considering, and following.

At the foot of the towering structure that was as black as midnight and painted with ink, he'd prostrated himself, and was given the gifts of a god.

He fingered the hilt of one of those divine favors—a black bladed khopesh, its long blade ending in a sickle-like curve—and he knew it would serve him well before he was cut down in battle.

That he'd be slain in combat was a given. He savored that moment and gazed longingly to his release from this world when he'd be brought to the feet of the one who made him who he was.

Ghe'hak's mind swam, wondering who that was. Was it Senaria, the goddess of nature who created him as a powerful proto-hyena? Was it the demon lord who tasked him with assisting Klendrisia? Or was it Onyx who had taken him in after his cowardly reaction to hundreds of kin being slain?

The voice in his head told him to stop thinking, to watch and listen, and to learn the ways of his enemies.

Khizhane watched the filthy gnohl stroll around his office like the beast owned it. He called upon the powers within him and knew which parts of this creature would make potions, ointments, or tonics that would cause bloodlust, lend strength, or allow someone to track like a bloodhound.

Ghe'hak was a dangerous ally, and a deadly adversary. But Onyx whispered to Khizhane, telling him to use this creature for his task.

The gnohl had faced two of the enemies of the state, and knew their scent, their ways, and their fears. This foul-tempered being was the best tool at hand, the best compound to blend with the mixture to create the reaction the alchemist wanted. Seawall City was another tool.

Seawall City was on the verge of an awakening, on the precipice of an event that would allow them to sweep across the continent and claim the discarded, lost, and forgotten treasures of the mages who died in the Downfall. But the council was hesitant, weak, and fell to infighting much too easily. This would be the catalyst to Khizhane taking power…of becoming the agent of a god.

The alchemist scented the air like a beast and smiled. He watched the bounty hunter turn back to look at him, the man-beast's brow wrinkling in curiosity.

"Perhaps," Khizhane cleared his throat, "you aren't up to the task? I know you failed to kill them many times before…"

"Three times!" Ghe'hak snarled. "Once before they met PepperGarten the Druid, again at the Nine Towers of Magic, then in the last battle at the Demon Front. But two of those were my Mistress's failures, not mine. And the last was a moment of clarity where I chose not to die in a flurry of rage and hopeless aggression.

"You should know," the gnohl growled, "I'm not like the other bastards of my ilk and spawn. I'm smarter, faster, and less driven by sheer instinct. I think instead of reacting. I plan, and that's how I rose to power over the others who fought for scraps and place in the pack. That's how I survived when they died."

The administrator cleared his throat again.

"Yes, well," he swallowed, "that's why I chose you to help, that and the gifts of Onyx that have been bestowed upon you. With the two of us working together, we shall both rise in power to heights we've not even dreamed of."

"Maybe you dream too much," Ghe'hak turned and strode towards the politician, and the man flinched, taking a step backwards. "Maybe you should worry more about now than what is coming after. And you should worry about helping me do what I need to do, because I can smell the betrayal on you. You only wait until I turn my back to sink your teeth into my neck or flank. Don't cripple me, whelp, or we'll both die."

Khizhane cleared his throat again.

"Of course," he saw the creature's eyes widen at his comment, "of course not. I'll do everything in my power to see you succeed. Then I'll be the one to reward you, to shower you with gifts, women, power, and title…once I'm head of the Council of Mages in Seawall City. But if I fail, you will be hunted, captured, tortured, and interrogated until they decide to kill you. Then you'll die in shame and shackles. So, we understand that we both succeed, or we both fail?"

Ghe'hak's lips pulled back over his teeth, but Khizhane wasn't sure if it was a snarl or smile.

"Yeer," the gnohl growled, "we understand us."

"You have their scent?" Khizhane asked.

"I never forget spoor," the gnohl's voice may have been prideful or angry, the administrator couldn't decide which. "Two of them, I can track on a moonless night in a storm. The third, I will know soon enough."

"You can't go into the square until nightfall," Khizhane sliced the air with his hand to stress his words, "and even then, you can't kill anyone. If any of the council thought there was a threat, we would lose all as they act."

"Perk yeer ears, pup," that smile from Ghe'hak again that might have been agreement or a sneer, "I'll follow them away from here, track them, and take them apart. I'll cripple them, then drag their broken bodies back to you to be presented to yeer whimpering council of magical, sniveling bastards."

"Yes," Khizhane coughed into a kerchief, years of fumes causing irritation over the lengthy conversation, "very good."

"And my payment?" Ghe'hak stepped closer, looming over the smaller man.

His payment? Khizhane didn't know what the beast meant. They hadn't discussed payment, but the administrator cursed himself thrice the fool for not considering the cur wouldn't want something in return besides the prize that came with the long game.

"Your p-payment?" Khizhane leaned back, the words sputtering in his throat as he held back another cough. "What more is it you want, besides the glory and power that would come from this?"

"A sacrifice," Ghe'hak's teeth drew back again, showing more teeth than before.

Khizhane knew it was a grin this time and shuddered.

"S-sacrifice?" the administrator stammered. "Of course, that makes sense, considering what you came from. What sort of sacrifice do you require?"

"A blood sacrifice, of course," the gnohl turned away and paced the room, "to make your potions. I need something to protect me from the sight of Jonath, and the magics of the elementalist. A single assassin, no matter how skilled, is no match for the power of a god and the might of the fires, winds, waters, and very earth itself. You will give me those before I even begin tracking my prey. And you will let them get out of the city before I begin my hunt."

"Out of the city?" Khizhane swallowed. "Of course, I'll begin that right away."

Ghe'hak nodded, "And I'll return before morning."

"Now, I need you to leave," the administrator's mind was awhirl with plans that leapt into his mind, the alchemical lore, and processes for what needed to be done washing over him. His voice became decisive and commanding, the tone of a man who knew what needed to be done and who didn't want to waste time talking. "I have a lot to do, I need to…you know, it doesn't matter what I need to do. But I cannot do it with you here."

"Oh, I know," Ghe'hak growled, and strode across the room, shoving open the same stained-glass window he'd entered through, "I'll return before the sun rises. Have everything in order, or I'll hunt you tomorrow night instead of this trio. Are we in agreement?"

Khizhane waved absently at the gnohl, dismissing him.

Ghe'hak's lips curled over his teeth, and he leapt out the window.

The night breeze cut through the room, tousling the politician's hair.

*Yes,* Khizhane thought, *I've a lot to before the sunrise.*

*First, I must reroute the guards that are closing the net on the three fugitives. Then I need to find innocents, flay them for their fat to make the protective ointment for the gnohl, and drain them of blood to create the tonic that will hide him from the sight of a god.*

Khizhane moved from behind his desk to a pull-cord on the wall and tugged on the thick braid of golden rope.

He paced while waiting, mentally planning the night. Stopping, he turned and moved to his desk, sliding a piece of parchment from a wooden tray and dipping a quill into the inkwell. He began scribbling, jotting down a list of details that would be easy to forget or overlook, creating an indented list by the time a sleepy-eyed assistant pushed open the door minutes later.

"Get me Tymere," Khizhane commanded, then paused and cleared his throat, collecting his wits with a long push of breath. Drawing in again, calming his nerves and readying for the exhalation of instructions. "Then I want you to gather the hag from the food kitchen and her young son. Also, bring me the priestess of Promethene that's always asking for more food for the orphanage. Take them to the lower level, under Tymere's guard. This must be done within the hour. The future of the city depends on it. Do this, and you will be a rewarded, fail and you and your family will pay the price. Do you understand?"

The man, barely more than a boy, nodded, turned, and rushed from the room.

Three deaths would bring great rewards. It was a sacrifice like what Khizhane's sire had done so many years ago.

The boy who rose to the powerful, yet disdained, position of chief alchemist of Seawall City, remembered his father leaving him, his mother, and his twin siblings to die so he could defend the city. But Khizhane had lived when his father had died on the walls under the barrage of an army of demons. His family didn't make it, but Khizhane survived.

He remembered his father's last words to him.

"Protect your mother and the twins," the words echoed, a sickly sour thought that had a taste of bitter oranges turning in his memory, "then maybe you'll be something like a man."

He never wanted to be like his father. A failure dragged down in disgrace. Overrun and torn to pieces by wave after wave of insects that sheeted the plains and walls like a dark rain of chitinous fury.

And now, this was Khizhane's chance to surpass the man who raised him, beat him, and told him he'd never amount to anything more than a petty clerk. The man who'd said phrases and study were for the weak, the man who'd died to bugs.

Bugs. Just bugs.

It was those same insects that had been Khizhane's first breakthrough in alchemy.

Alone in the world, though the orphanage run by priestesses of Promethene had taken him in, he'd gathered the husks of the beetles, roaches, silverfish and other hexapoda and crushed them to a powder, instincts of his magical ability guiding him. The first dust he'd created—and blown into the faces of the sisters of Promethene—was his first step towards greatness. It showed him how to refine his skills to changing, and controlling, the minds of others.

Khizhane would become chief of all councilors, a lord among petty, squabbling politicians. He'd make this city great again, and hell would rain down on any who stood in his way, just as those beautiful, shining bugs had rained down on his father.

Clearing his throat, Khizhane pulled his shoulders back, and left the room to prepare the chamber where he'd formulate his future.

## Chapter 6

Torrents pushed out the door into the chill night air, back in his leather and fur armor that he wore to protect him from weapons and weather. Half of the clothes in his wardrobe were on his back, the other half jammed into the satchel slung over his shoulder. One sword was in the 'X' of scabbards on his back, and the other was in his hand as he leaned around the doorframe to check the back alley.

He stepped into a low ground mist crawling across the night cobblestones, moving like the fog, slowly and carefully.

Aiyana followed him, her new outfit of black brocade trimmed in silver along the wide, flowing white cuffs that fell to her knees, rippling with each step. Tugas had also brought the aeifain hair ties, a pair of doe-skin knee boots, a comb, and various other necessities. The purchases were in the white suede bag that bounced on the woman's hip, opposite of the dirk Torrents had given her.

Nathan came out last, his chain-mail tinkling like a metallic stream with each step, his thick boots thudding, and his eyes everywhere that Torrents wasn't looking. He held Marcid, his double-headed axe, in his hands. The druidic magics caressed his leather gloves and tickled his awareness. The breeze rustled the magical vines intertwined on the stout shaft. The gift of extended perception given to him by Jonath allowed him to see onto the rooftops in the night above, behind him in the trailing fog, and around corners they passed.

Nathan left space between them. Though he had no combat training in his world, his body did. Torrents followed the rokairn's example without discussion.

Torrents picked up the habit from sports, but he'd also learned the lesson from his training here. You never wanted to be close enough to the other person that you couldn't make a sudden stop, swing a sword, or risk both people being taken down by a single assailant.

At the end of the alley, Torrents poked his head around the corner, jerked back, and waved the others to wait.

Aiyana and Nathan pressed against the stone wall of The Fiddle.

A patrol marched past, a person without armor centered in the protective box of eight men-at-arms.

As the squad moved away, Torrents waved the others forward and stepped into the street. Metal poles, standing slightly taller than a man, had globes that glowed dully on top of them; an alchemical compound within dimly lighting the avenue. Torrents knew the magical orbs drew energy from the sun, then reflected that stored energy back at night—like solar panels, but he'd heard this was done with a fungus or an algae mixture.

They moved along a northwest-southeast spoke of the city's blocks, staying to the alleys when they could. The moon was a waning crescent, and the light from the celestial body seemed to mimic, or perhaps mock, the alchemical lights along the road.

The dim lighting wasn't an issue for the rokairn, whose people were born and bred to live their lives in dark tunnels. Nathan could sense the stone, see the cold and the heat emanating from objects, and could slowly find his way in the dark if he had to.

He knew the aeifain species was known for excellent sight and hearing, with their larger eyes able to see in dim light like it was lit by candles or lanterns—they could even read by moonlight—though they couldn't see in complete darkness.

The barbarian had no such gifts, but he had training and instincts. Nathan suggested months ago that in situations like this the barbarian should take the lead, because then the rokairn could keep watch from behind, and they could move as fast as the slowest of the group without unintentionally losing someone.

Besides, Torrents wasn't helpless. He just relied more on his training than on the natural abilities of his species.

The barbarian considered why he was doing this. Not the saving someone part, or escaping from the city in the night, but…all of this. The whole idea of hanging around for the next adventure, like he took a number at the deli of fate and was waiting his turn to pick up whatever order the big man behind the counter served him, wasn't something he'd ever pictured himself doing.

He wondered if this was where he belonged, if this was what he was meant to be doing. Torrents bounced from activity to activity when he was younger. Taekwondo, little league, and later softball, then track and football in high school. He'd never really felt like he belonged.

That wasn't quite true, though. It was almost like he belonged too well, that he performed to fit in and even excel past what others could do. He loved sports, but it never drew him in. It was just what everyone expected.

When his life had gone to bidj—his father dead, and his legs unable to move—he'd decided he didn't want to do what others wanted him to do. In hindsight, that was probably the one time he should've done what others expected: physical therapy, socializing, talking to a mental health specialist. But he'd brushed it all away.

And now he was in a mystical world where magic worked, in the body of swordsman better built than most action movie stars.

But was this what he wanted to do? Run around, fighting for a cause he didn't even know existed until it was thrust upon him, he tripped over it, or someone shoved it into his lap?

The patrols thinned as the three moved further from the docks and closer to the outer wall. Torrents led them towards the North Gate closer to The Fiddle, but as the protective barrier of the city came into view, guard posts and patrols became more frequent.

Soldiers manning the walls focused on people trying to get in, not people trying to get out. News of the fugitives may not have reached here yet, but the guards would stop and question three people leaving the city in the middle of the night, no matter what direction they came from.

The three crept past another guard post, four blocks from the gate and their escape to the freedom outside of Seawall City. Shops crowded the street, wagons that normally held fruit, vegetables, shoes, bolts of cloth, or other goods emptied for the night. They slid through shadows cast by awnings and overhangs, slipping past closed doors of businesses where families slept on the upper floors.

Torrents indicated a stop by holding up a clenched fist beside his head. Aiyana and Nathan sidled up to him.

Nathan's divided his attention between the barbarian, the gate, the guard post they'd just passed, and the rooftops. His gaze kept going back to the rooftops, as if he'd glimpsed something and couldn't quite put his finger on what it was, or what had been up there.

"We've got two more blocks of shops," Torrents said under his breath, avoiding the sibilant whisper that would cut through the silence and draw attention, "then an open area between the last building and the wall."

"Are we going through the stone tower things?" Aiyana whispered, the sharp 's' standing out. "Or do you think we can climb the wall, or maybe there's a way around it?"

"We could cause some kind of distraction," Nathan suggested, scanning the top of the buildings across the street again, "but I don't know what sort or how to do it."

"I think I could start a fire," Aiyana offered, twisting her fingers in her hair, looking back the way they'd come.

"We don't want to set the city ablaze, and risk killing innocent people who are sleeping in their beds," Nathan leaned into the street to look back the way they came, following the aeifain's example, "you sound as bad as Torrents."

"I'm not that bad," the barbarian murmured, turning to glare at the rokairn, and noticed the smaller man searching the night in the other direction. "Something out there, bro?"

"What?" Nathan glanced back at Torrents. "I don't know, but I feel something. Like we're being followed, or watched, or stalked. It's not like the guards, though. Some of them were looking for us, I'm sure, but they weren't hunting us. Just keeping an eye out. But I feel...something else. But I can't see it, like it's keeping its distance, or it's just behind a wall, or something indiscernible in a thick fog."

"Well," Torrents dropped a hand on his friend's shoulder, pulling the rokairn's attention away from the mist-laden street behind them, "let's worry about that when we need to. I need your eyes on the ball, and your head in the game. Your eyes are better than mine at night, so look over there and give me your opinion."

Nathan nodded, moved past Torrents to the corner of the building, and knelt. He scanned up and down the wall, starting on the left, his head slowly moving to the right.

Torrent's watched his friend take in the details: two men leaning on a merlon, spears on their shoulders, chatting quietly without concern; the soldier atop the wall-walk who marched a dozen steps, turned to look into the city streets for a dozen seconds, then retraced his steps to the outer wall and repeated the ritual; the three men hunkered down inside the archway under the battlement and tossing coins against the wall, the one getting his closest winning all three; the spellslingers, the upper one and the lower gate one, who stood together and chatted while glaring at the men under their command with the disdain of men who knew they were better than those that surrounded them.

"Hold on," Nathan's voice was almost inaudible, "I want to see if I can tell what flavor of magic those spellslingers are using tonight. They usually post mind mages, but if they're some other kind, it might make it easier for us. Elementalists and alchemists make lousy guards. Holy casters do okay if they're linked to the right god, but mind mages do the best, and we're screwed, if that's what's out there. The fifth type, summoners, aren't really welcome in Seawall City, so we probably don't have to worry about them."

"Are you about to pray?" Torrents sighed.

"Yes," Nathan's voice sounded irritated as he pulled his symbol from inside his chain-mail shirt, "it's how I connect with Jonath to get extra information, you know that."

"It's always just so," Torrents searched for the word, his mouth quirking, "awkward. You look like a little-person rabbi with your beard, and I can't understand the words. I feel like I should drop some coins in the collection plate. Do you have a collection plate, Aiyana?"

"He's Jewish?" Aiyana wrinkled her nose.

"Jeweler, yes," Nathan bowed his head, "but not Jewish. I had an aunt who was, and a grandmother on my father's side, but it never stuck for me. The former married into it, and the latter married out of it. Catholic for Nana Janie, and I was raised…loose on the religion."

"Baptist here," Torrents said, "but it never really stuck for me, either. When I graduated in 2018, society wasn't really big on faith-based identity, and 2020 changed everything."

"2020?" Nathan's head jerked up. "You mean the year 2020?"

Torrents nodded, "Yeah, why? What year did you think I came from?"

"1997," Nathan said.

"1966," Aiyana said at the same time.

"What?" Torrents shook his head and took a step back and into the street. "It was January 15th, 2023, when I had my second accident. Are you telling me we're all from different years?"

Nathan grabbed the barbarian by his wide leather belt and pulled him back into the sheltering shadows of the building.

"Don't get us busted," Torrents said to himself, allowing the rokairn to draw him back into the protective cover, then said to Nathan, "but we'll talk about this later."

"2023?" Aiyana breathing heavily, in short gasps as she stepped away from the two men. "You two are from the future?"

"Really?" Torrents rolled his eyes. "You're okay with being in a world and throwing around fireballs, but being from different times is going to freak you out? He's a dwarf, you're an elf, and it disgusted you when you heard he might be Jewish? You gonna freak out when you hear I was Black back in the other world, too?"

"You're a colored?" Aiyana's face lit up, and she took a step forward, one hand coming up as if she were going to touch Torrents. "Oh, no. That's where I was when I got hit in the head, then woke up here. I was marching in a protest near Marquette Park in Chicago with Martin Luther King Jr. supporting equal rights for coloreds. That was August 5th, 1966."

She stared at Torrents expectantly.

"Oh, sista," he laughed, "thanks, but calm the hell down. It still ain't right when I was coming up; I guess it's better, but it ain't right. But hold on, you're okay with Black people, but you got issues with Jews? That ain't right."

"No," her voiced rose, "I don't mind the Jews. I was just surprised. Besides, he isn't one, is he? He was just related to some."

"Sounds like you got issues," Torrents snorted and turned away.

"Do you two mind?" Nathan hissed through gritted teeth. "I'm sorry, but I'm trying to connect with a higher power to get us help in getting out of here."

"Naw," Torrents said, "you do you, man."

Nathan, on his knees, prayed. Muttered words of a foreign language rose from him in a quiet, steady chant. His presence was palpable to the two onlookers, and a feeling of warmth and calm exuded from him.

"Hey," a gruff voice called, "you two, what are you doing out here at this hour?"

Torrents whipped around, surprised.

A city guard walked towards them, others of his patrol lingering behind and talking among themselves.

Torrents reached out, grabbed Aiyana, and pushed her against the wall. Putting a hand on each side of her head, his sword clinking against the building, he leaned down towards her.

His warm breath brushed her cheek and neck as he whispered, "Go with me on this."

Torrents looked up and away from the aeifain, glancing over his shoulder towards the guard.

"Hey, man," the barbarian tried to sound casual, but his voice cracked, "I'm just making out with my girl, you know? Her daddy don't like it when we're out late, and we're just saying goodbye."

"I'm a father, too," the man moved closer, "and I can't say I blame her da."

The patrolman hesitated, squinting into the shadows.

"If you're out for fun," the guard said slowly, raising his voice so the others on patrol could hear, "what's with the swords? And the one in your hand? You sure she wants to be here?"

"Aw, bidj," Torrents muttered.

"Yes," Aiyana called, peeking out from under Torrents's arm, "I want to be here. Everything is just fine, officer. Thank you for checking on me, but I assure you, everything is well. You may go. I'm not in need of any assistance."

The man stopped, nodding. Then he leaned forward, squinting into the darkness again.

"Hey," he grunted, "is she…an aeifain? Is that the one that killed all those people in the square during the hanging?"

The guard was backing away, his hand on his sword, and his buddies moving forward.

"Aw, chuz," Torrents muttered.

"You shouldn't use such language," Aiyana reprimanded him with a gasp.

"Really?" Torrents rolled away from her, pushing the aeifain behind him with his free hand and raising his sword. "You're gonna do that now?"

Nathan rose, wiping his eyes and coming into view of the patrol.

"And isn't that the rokairn who helped the witch?" One of the other patrolmen pointed at Nathan.

"Fudge," Nathan sighed. "Mind mages, and I feel a summoner close by. Also, we're being watched from above by someone or something."

"He didn't find it necessary to swear," Aiyana pointed at the priest.

A sharp whistle pierced the night as a patrolman sounded the alarm.

## Chapter 7

Nathan's head jerked towards the noise, taking stock of the situation at a glance.

The night watch was smaller than during the day. Four guardsmen approached with swords drawn; the spellslinger accompanying them hanging back, chanting and moving his hands in ritualistic gesturing.

The soldiers on the gates, mages and men-at-arms alike, were on their feet, looking in the direction of the other patrol.

A ballista bolt ripped through the air, appearing in front of the guards, and embedded in the wall over Aiyana's shoulder.

"There's our summoner," Nathan shouted.

Raising his axe, squaring his feet, and lowering his shoulders, he stepped into the street.

"He's called a sorcerer." Aiyana said through gritted teeth, twin orbs of flame appearing over her open palms.

"Don't kill them!" Nathan darted towards her, shifting his weapon to one hand, and slapping her hands down with the other.

"Fine," the wizardess spat, and the flames changed, transforming to cool blue, crystalline globes. "I won't kill them, but I'll be damned if I'm going to get hung again."

Two balls of ice shot forward, tripling in size in the space of the breath it took them to hit their targets. One struck the ground in the center of the patrol, coating the cobblestones with a layer of ice. The second hit, right after the first, and ice encased the men's boots, freezing them in place mid-step.

Guards shouted in surprise, and three fell forward as their momentum continued. Ice around their feet and ankles cracked and broke, and they slipped and slid, trying to regain their footing.

The fourth tore his foot free, the limb shattering at the ankle. Lifting the stump, he left his boot behind with his foot inside of it. The guard didn't seem to notice until he set the bloody appendage down to take the next step. His leg dropped lower than he expected, and he looked like someone who forget there wasn't another step on the stairs.

He pitched forward, his sword flying from his hand, screaming, and clutching at his broken leg.

"Surprise charge!" Torrents yelled, pulled his second sword from the scabbard on his back, and ran towards the gate.

"Stick together," Nathan shouted at the barbarian's back, "darn it all, we'll be torn to shreds if we separate!"

Nathan froze, looking around, trying to find something to help, indecision falling over him.

The summoner called upon his mystical powers again, chanting and gesturing from behind the four incapacitated guards.

Aiyana was behind the rokairn, calling upon the ley lines and the magical energies.

Torrents was charging eight armed men and two mind mages. Nathan knew one had illusionary powers, and the other had abilities that enhanced the mage's body.

Nathan was torn, unsure if he should help Aiyana so she didn't lash out and kill the guards. He knew the effect that could have on a person's mind. He remembered recoiling from the idea of killing Klendrisia, a woman who was half demon. He'd been sick for days after his first battle in this world, after killing for the first time, even though it hadn't been human. He'd never forget how it felt to wish someone dead, just because they pissed him off. None of it had felt good, and most of it twisted his guts so he could barely eat or sleep.

He watched his friend charge into battle and knew the man was outnumbered and outgunned. The barbarian was a very capable warrior and had faced worse odds than this. But he hadn't faced two mind mages with the power of the law behind them. There would be repercussions if they killed, or even injured, any of the city watch. The rokairn doubted Torrents cared about that, probably hadn't even thought about it.

Nathan couldn't decide who to help. It was a simple decision, but one he couldn't make. He was as frozen in place as the guards in front of him.

He wished for his simple life. A life doing the books, counting down a register, and smiling politely at people who looked down on him, because he was selling the jewelry, but they had the money to buy it.

In his old life, Nathan never had to make a single life or death decision. It never came up. A really bad day meant he had to wonder if he'd be able to afford the rent that month. A rough day just meant he forgot his umbrella when it rained, or they declined his credit card when he tried to buy his lunch.

A grinding noise brought Nathan's attention back to the moment.

The mage on top of the wall drew his arm back and brought it down. A huge, clawed hand rose over the parapet behind him and fell to the walkway, mirroring his movements. A triangular, reptilian head on a long, sinewy neck rose over the fortification. The dragon scanned the area, scaley lips drawing back over its teeth.

The second mind mage ran forward from the wall, leaping out into the air and landing in front of the tunnel that led under the outer wall. He moved to meet the charging barbarian, the spellslinger's height and bulk increasing two-fold until he was almost twice the man's height and double his previous bulk. The man hunched as he ran forward, his oversized knuckles grazing the ground to propel himself forward faster at a slightly sideways lope.

Ice exploded in front of Nathan.

Behind him, Aiyana hurled another frozen projectile at the wizard in the street. The ice globe shattered when it met another summoned spear.

The ballista bolt, ammunition of a siege weapon, embedded itself into the street in front of the rokairn, blasted off its intended course.

This broke his indecision. Nathan raised Marcid and grabbed the shaft behind the head with his free hand. He set his feet at shoulder width, squared his shoulders, and whispered to his battle-axe. A faint green glow flickered along the haft and blade of the enchanted weapon.

Calling upon the powers granted to him by Jonath that connected the priest to the earth and soil under the stones. Seeds, hidden within the cracks of the cobblestones under the feet of the approaching mage, responded. Encouraged by the druidic magics within Marcid, ropey vines burst upward. They thickened in a grotesque mockery of old time-lapse shows of plant life that Nathan remembered from the nature documentaries he used to watch after getting home after a long day.

The plants wrapped around the mage's legs, entangling them, and the man pitched forward. He landed in a bed of blossoms; the blooms growing until they engulfed him.

Torrents leapt over the fallen caster and his twin swords rang out, striking the spellslingers' weapon.

"Aiyana, go help Torrents," Nathan turned and waved the aeifain towards the battle at the gate. "I can handle these guys."

The woman shook herself, as if coming out of a trance, and looked around, the lines in her face softening. She saw the dragon, and the lines returned, accompanied by a tight-lipped grin of excited determination.

She focused on the dragon climbing onto the parapet, its maw opening in a silent roar. It towered above the stone battlement, wings spreading to block out the soft light of the moon in the west.

Shards of ice flew from the woman's hands, pelting the great beast across its wide chest and spread wings. The attack had no effect.

Aiyana wrinkled her brow in concentration, her awareness diving deep into the earth. Kilometers below, her mind sought the scalding river of energy that sang of the ley line of fire. It was undulating and pulsing, pushing forward to writhe in its corridor of strata; and it was searching for a way to the surface. Aiyana smiled and gave it what it wanted.

The twin-towered gate rumbled, the surrounding ground rippling like a pond disturbed by a stone thrown into its center. Cracks ran along the ground, growing wider under the portcullises' passage, growing longer, and extending into the city and countryside. Steam burst upward, followed by guttural liquid.

Then the earth vomited.

Stone burst upward, the sound waves knocking the soldiers forward, their arms flailing to keep their balance.

Aiyana focused on the ley line, drawing it upward towards the dragon. Jets of lava spurted into the air and rained down all around. The magma spattered across three city blocks, the stone where it landed softening from the heat. A geyser of glowing red shot into the air, coating the ceiling of the tunnel and melting the stone above. It flooded outward, as well as into the city, creating a network of lave rivulets and stone islands along the way out of the city, the three's escape route.

The structure exploded, the wall above the passage shattering upward. Fiery stones rained down like a localized meteor shower, and the walls melted to a smooth, black surface.

The dragon didn't seem to notice that its perch had disappeared and exploded all around it. It remained hovering in the air as if the building was still underneath it.

The mage at the dragon's feet had run along the wall, fleeing the volcanic eruption. As the wall broke into flaming projectiles, the man flew into the air, screaming, lava spattering him, and he spun and tumbled through the night and fell to the street below with a wet crunch.

The dragon's eyes went blank, its movements jittering before stilling. The huge form shimmered, then faded from existence.

Torrents stood surrounded by eight guards and the mind mage that had come from the gate moments before. All ten men faced the destruction, dodging the magma that spattered around them.

As the rain of hellfire slowed, then stopped, they looked around. Silence fell. The group noticed the barbarian in their midst, and every single city soldier took a step back in surprise. Torrents shrugged, his twin blades bobbing with the gesture, and smiled.

The men's voices rose in a battle cry as they charged forward at the barbarian as a unit.

Torrents spun and twirled on the defensive, his blades a blur, batting away weapons.

Aiyana saw Nathan take advantage of the distraction. Calling upon his abilities, he focused on the remaining spellslinger.

Vines burst from the cobblestones around the mind mage, wriggling up his legs, roots digging into the man's flesh, seeking sustenance and liquid. Blood welled around the holes of the thorny vines, burrowing between his ribs, and climbing the man's body. Green tendrils writhed across his torso, pulling his arms to his sides. Leaves unfolded, and flowers bloomed, pushing into the man's open mouth, surrounding his face, and seeking nourishment in the moisture of his eyes.

He swayed, bound by his floral prison, then leaned to one side and fell to the soft padding of the growth around his feet, coughing and gagging. He went stiff, then limp, and lay still.

The wizardess saw Nathan turn towards motion beside him.

Aiyana drew her attention back to the moment, and spread her arms, the wind whipping her hair, her eyes unfocused, staring into the distance. She rose to her tiptoes, rising off the ground, floating an arm's length in the air. Her lips tightened into a line, and she moved forward, gusts gliding her towards the battle.

The men-at-arms surrounding Torrents, glanced her way as they moved towards the barbarian, then stopped and stepped back, their swords shifting to defensive stances. The group backed away as one, splitting around their target and breaking the circle. Once they'd disengaged and Torrents didn't move forward to continue the fight, they turned and ran down the street that separated the outer wall from the businesses.

"Holy volcanos, Batman," Torrents laughed, "that was hot!"

"Guess I rocked their world, didn't I?" Aiyana shouted over the winds that swirled around her and she settled back to the cobblestones.

"You cut off our way out, though," Nathan's voice was gruff, his words sharp, "how are we supposed to get across a collapsed building with lava flows?"

"Carefully?" Torrents suggested with a shrug.

"This is one time we don't want to go with the flow," Aiyana giggled, her feet touching down on the ground as she dismissed the magically controlled air currents.

She collapsed to her knees, her legs buckling as they took her full weight. She knelt, her hair falling across her face, gasping.

"You okay?" Torrents rushed to her side.

The barbarian guided his first sword into its scabbard on his back, his other hand still gripping the second.

Reaching down, he slid his free arm under Aiyana's arms and around her back, lifting her to her feet.

Nathan moved beside them and looked around at the area.

"The two other spellslingers are indisposed for the moment," the rokairn said, "but it won't be for long before the magics fade, or they find a way to release themselves. And those guards will bring back others in a couple minutes. We need to find a way through this mess."

"I didn't mean to do all this," Aiyana wobbled in Torrents's helpful grip, "I was just so angry, and had all that…power."

"Not now," Nathan brushed off her comment, "we need to move."

The rokairn put action to his words and moved towards the fallen gatehouse, stepping with care around steaming pools of lava and smoldering stone.

Torrents followed, helping Aiyana, and glancing over his shoulder every few steps.

The sound of combat echoed off the stone walls from the direction that the guards had fled, followed by shouts.

Guttural growls bit through the night, punctuated by screams of men fighting for their lives, and failing.

"What the hell is that?" Torrents's head jerked in towards the noise.

"If I had to guess, I'd say that was our stalker," Nathan said flatly. "We need to get out of here."

Aiyana's legs buckled, and she would have fallen if Torrents hadn't pulled her against him. Her eyes rolled, and she turned her head and tried to focus on the big man.

"She's not gonna be much help to us like this," Torrents muttered.

"You take care of her." Nathan scanned the rubble for a path. "Follow me and I'll try to get us out of here."

"I'm okay," Aiyana mumbled, her voice groggy. "Just need to rest a moment."

"Well, girl," Torrents awkwardly put his second sword away, jostling the woman in his free arm, "I think those tricks you did took more out of you than you know."

The barbarian scooped the aeifain off her feet and into his arms.

"Lead the way, boss," Torrents took a step, leaning forward to look over the woman, and checked his footing.

"Boss," Nathan harrumphed, leaping to a large stone outcropping, "the last guy that called me that shot me in the gut with a double-barreled shotgun."

"That's because you're so gangsta," Torrents said vaguely, following the shorter man's leap once the rokairn moved to the next stone.

"Guess you didn't always have the stomach for violence," Aiyana laughed weakly, "or didn't have the stomach for doing shots. Either one works, but I don't think either is very good."

"She's making a lot of puns. Is she delirious?" Torrents made a small jump over lava that was blackening as it cooled.

"Sounds like it," Nathan's reply was distracted; he stopped and cocked his head. "Hear that?"

Torrents also stopped and turned his head one way and then the other, listening.

"No," the big man shook his head, "hear what?"

"Exactly," the rokairn murmured, "it's quiet, the fight is done. Our stalker may be coming for us now."

"Gotcha," Torrents hiked Aiyana up, getting a better grip on her, "enough talking, more walking."

The rokairn picked up the pace, moving quicker but stopping more often to tell Torrents where to put his feet since the human couldn't see as well in the dark, even with the extra light from the lava and the moon.

They reached the other side of the collapsed structure as whistles and klaxon bells rang out in the city behind them.

"Sounds like someone found the bodies," Nathan said, picking up the pace and moving into a jog. "We should put some distance between us and this wall before they get here."

"What about our friend?" Torrents moved beside the rokairn, easily keeping pace now that they were on open and level ground, Aiyana bouncing in his arms.

"Either it's coming for us, or it's not," the rokairn said in rhythm to his footfalls, "either way, no need to worry about it until we need to worry about it. I'll keep an eye behind us, just get us to some cover."

Torrents nodded.

They moved along the road, passing the silent stone guardians of transformed people who'd broken the eight tenants of the city. The statues were eerie caricatures in the setting moonlight, like a line of dancing figures that paused at an awkward moment. Some were bent in a contorted rictus of pain, forever frozen in their last moment, and others looked as if they had stopped to look around. Aiyana couldn't decide which was more unsettling as she watched for pursuit over the barbarian's shoulder.

"Then where do we go?" Torrents asked a few minutes later.

"I have no idea," Nathan said, "but we'll know when we get there."

## Chapter 8

They watched the sunrise over the eastern ocean while huddled in a rock outcropping on the shore.

The three had traveled until the sky changed from a moonlit glow on the path to the speckled black that came with the setting of the moon and the midnight lit by stars.

When the eastern sky hinted at sunrise, shifting to the indigo that preceded the morning, they turned off the road and into the weeds, following a game track to get out of sight of any caravans and local traffic that would begin lining up to get into Seawall City.

They'd passed farmhouses during their trek—long barrack-like structures operated by the city—and watched for the lights of early risers.

Torrents carried Aiyana for more than an hour before she recovered enough to walk. Which was fine for the barbarian and the priest, who'd needed to slow their pace because of the lack of moonlight and being tired after being roused from their beds, fighting, then running.

They didn't want to be seen by anyone, not this close to the city they'd so recently assaulted by destroying the entrance most of the food and supplies came through. Even without a magical fugitive and the two of them being so memorable, they were still being hunted for what they'd done.

"At least there won't be any witnesses to describe us," Torrents said, hours later, rigging a lean-to to shelter the exhausted wizardess in their midst.

"That's cold and uncalled for," Nathan looked at the larger man with a confused look of disgust, "people died, and I'd rather them live and be able to finger us in a lineup than they lose their lives."

"We didn't kill them," Torrents said offhandedly.

"Even if we didn't do it," Nathan's voice rose, "they died because of us."

"Hey, chill out, man," Torrents said over his shoulder with a casual shrug, "I know they died, and I didn't want that, either. But whatever is hunting us wanted it. We may as well count the few blessings we have, right?"

"They'll know it was us," Nathan held a small shovel, intending to go dig a latrine. "I bet whoever, or whatever, is hunting us will make sure the city guard thinks we did it."

"What do you mean, 'whoever or whatever is hunting us'?" Aiyana leaned against the rock wall of the overhang, near Torrents.

"I mean, I sensed something, but it wasn't human." Nathan sighed, "I'm sorry. I don't mean to alarm you, but it's the truth."

"Are you going to start apologizing all the time again?" Torrents hammered in wooden stakes, struggling with the canvas that kept trying to pull away in the ocean breeze.

The wind coming off the ocean had the crisp biting feel of an autumn storm, and the eastern horizon was lined with dark clouds that lit up in sparks and bunches.

"I'm sorry, but it's just who I am," Nathan turned and walked away, his remaining words growing faint in the breeze, "you're just going to have to deal with it."

Torrents smiled to himself, hammering in the third stake.

"Why do you give him such a hard time?" Aiyana asked, pushing to her feet and looking around.

"What do you mean?" Torrents hammered in the final stake. "And shouldn't you be resting?"

"Well," the woman bent and picked up a few pieces of driftwood, "I can't just lie around while you guys do all the work. And I mean, you obviously like the man. Why do you constantly cajole and antagonize him?"

"It's good for him," Torrents stretched, pushing his fists against his lower back, "and it's what's friends do. We make fun of one another. Toughens us up and lets the other know we care."

"I somehow doubt your words are having the effect you're hoping they have," Aiyana moved in a slow circle, picking up twigs and branches, "maybe you should consider being nicer to him?"

"Naw," Torrents laughed, "it'd make it too easy for him. I'll toughen the old man up, so he doesn't cry when the kids talk smack to him."

"I'm not sure what that means," she dropped the pile of wood near the canvas wall, "but I think I get the gist of your jive talk."

"Jive talk?" Torrents laughed and bent to organize the wood into sizes. "Man, you are from the old days, ain't cha?"

"It means your BS," Nathan came around the curve of the rock, carrying the shovel, "and the latrine is dug, about six or seven paces around the corner."

"Latrine?" Aiyana arched her eyebrows.

"Yeah," Torrents's mouth quirked up on one side, "we gotta go somewhere, and they don't have indoor plumbing in the wild. They barely have it at all in this world; even royalty uses a hole in a board more often than not."

"Ew," Aiyana wrinkled her nose.

"It's that," Nathan huffed, "or undress from the waist down and walk into the ocean, but I'm not sure how safe that would be."

"Are there…" the aeifain glanced at the water, "monsters in the sea?"

"Probably," Torrents built a pyramid of branches, breaking the larger ones into more manageable pieces, "but there could also be riptides and undertows, and they'd grab you and sweep you out to where you couldn't get back. I'll risk a snake or a bug while balancing over a hole with three branches for a seat."

Nathan stared out at the morning fishing fleets at the southeast and shook his head.

"I don't know how their catch will be today," the rokairn muttered, "the storm might push schools in, but they're risking their lives going out there."

"Not sure they have a choice," Torrents finished the fire, tossing kindling under the triangle of branches. "Seawall City can be pretty unforgiving if you don't do your job."

"They're forced to work in dangerous conditions?" Aiyana's attention shifted from the waves to the fleet of boats that were specks in the distance.

"Oh no," Torrents laughed, "looks like the lady may want to introduce unions to the city. That'd go over great, wouldn't it?"

"They have enough reason to kill us already," Nathan dug in his pack, pulling out a ball of twine and a fishing hook. "Why not add one more to the list?"

"I see your sense of humor decided to make an appearance. Good. A little food and you'll be back to your normal grouchy self instead of your extra-grouchy self. I'll go find us a pole," Torrents trudged up the dune to the grassy plain beyond it and looked at the trees in the distance to the north, "all the branches look too gnarly down here, I'll be careful not to be seen. Be back soon. Anyone need anything?"

"Get her a walking staff," Nathan raised his voice so the barbarian could hear him, "she'll need it if she's not used to walking a lot."

Torrents grunted and waved over his shoulder in acknowledgment and disappeared over the rise.

"I did walk thousands of kilometers to get here," Aiyana sounded defensive, "I think I'll survive."

"Probably," Nathan smiled, "but I bet you had one on your way here. Besides, it works as a defensive weapon, too, in a pinch. You seem to have misplaced all your gear, so we'd better start getting you some new stuff."

"I also use my staff, once properly treated, as a focus for my magics," Aiyana stopped, looking surprised at her own words. "How did I know that? And I could see the runes and ritual to purify and dedicate the staff to my casting."

"Yup," Nathan breathed out a long sigh, "It's like that. You are you, the person who came through from our world, but you're also the other person. The one who lived here for years. My body is sixty-three years old."

"Mine is two hundred and sixteen, and I was young among my people." the aeifain gasped, "I'm how old?"

Nathan laughed.

"It's like that here," Nathan smiled up at her, "and you look great for having two plus centuries on you."

"You look wonderful for your age," Aiyana complimented without thinking, "I wouldn't have put you much past thirty or thirty-five."

"Thanks," Nathan shook his head, "one boy, or woman, we traveled with was about sixteen or seventeen, but in our world, she was about seventy-seven. She had cancer, and that's what brought her here."

"Oh my," Aiyana's hand rose to her mouth, "she has the cancer?"

"Well, she did there," Nathan nodded, "but not here. And she may not have it if she returns home. We can't be sure unless she decides to return."

"We can go back?" the wizardess looked hopeful, but then darkened, "but I'm dying there. I don't think I survived."

"Torrents and I have discussed that," Nathan's eyes focused on the horizon, "and the same way us coming here healed the body we inhabit now, it might heal our bodies on our return. We don't know for sure though, and there's only one way to find out. One woman, Esperanza, did go back, and I pray that she made it okay. I just don't know if I should pray to her god there, or her god here."

The two fell into a comfortable silence as they organized their camp and prepared for the day. Aiyana moved slow and careful, still not recovered from her casting.

The storm was moving towards them at a slow but steady pace and would be upon them in an hour or two. The shelter wouldn't be perfect, and Nathan assured Aiyana that they'd get wet no matter what, but it'd be better than nothing.

Torrents returned with two branches, almost as tall as he was. He handed the thicker one to the aeifain, who moved away and sat on a grassy tuffet to inspect it.

She slid her hands across it, rolling it in her grasp. Drawing out the dagger Torrents gave her, she whittled off the knobs and bumps where smaller branches had once been.

Torrents rigged a fishing pole with the other, using Nathan's twine, fishhook, and a bit of jerky for bait. The barbarian took off his boots and stepped into the tide until it reached his knees, then began casting the line as far out as it would go. He watched the line as the tide brought it in, then he'd pull it in and toss it out again, replacing the bait when needed.

"Can't you ask Jonath where the fish are?" Torrents called over to Nathan.

"Can't you use your barbarian survival wits to guess where they are?" Nathan retorted and saw the big man sigh. "You kids, always wanting everything right away, never wanting to work for anything. It's sad. I had to work for everything I had, from the time I was just a lad."

"Okay boomer," Torrents laughed, "I get it. But couldn't Aiyana use her water thing to pull the ocean away and we could just pick up all the fish flopping around?"

"No," came the aeifain's voice, cold and distant, almost trance-like, "it would tire me needlessly, and if they're any other elementalists monitoring the ley lines, there's a chance they'd detect me doing it. Doing small things, like lighting the campfire, will go unnoticed. Draining a dozen square meters of the ocean would not."

Torrents sighed, and then whooped as his pole bent from a bite.

"So, we're going to Red Wind?" Torrents asked around a mouthful of fish. "Won't they expect that, since you have friends there and kinda came from there?"

The three sat inside the lean-to, the rain pelting the tarp and making it flap and sing. They'd cooked the fish Torrents had caught in a small covered cast-iron pot with the lid on, adding seasonings from the barbarian's stash and green onions they'd found in the plains.

"Probably," Nathan looked up from his tin plate, "but we have to go somewhere, and we have to do something. When you guys met me, what I was doing turned out to be key to what needed to be done. Perhaps this will follow the same pattern as Aiyana?"

"But you said that you chose her," Torrents pointed at the rokairn with his fork, "and that you could have chosen anyone."

"Wait," Aiyana looked up, her eyes narrowing, "you chose me? What's that mean?"

"The point is moot." Nathan held up a hand. "She was the corpse around, and I didn't have an option of choosing the beheaded peasant."

"Only corpse around?" the aeifain sounded distressed and held a hand to her stomach. "I'm right here, and it's…disturbing to hear you talk that way."

"Sorry about that," Nathan blushed, "I guess I'm losing some of my couth and manners the longer I stay here."

"It's a hard world, princess," Torrents took a bit of hard, dark bread and tore a chunk off, "and we gotta play the cards we're dealt."

"How worldly of you," Aiyana glared at the barbarian, "to put it so succinctly. And I'm not a princess, and don't recommend you addressing me as such again."

"My humblest apologies," Torrents said with a mock bow from his sitting position, "your highness. Please forgive this humble pemtie for his horrible words and stuff."

"Does he rub everyone wrong on purpose?" Aiyana asked Nathan.

"It's his defense mechanism, so no one gets too close to him," Nathan explained, sounding tired. "He's lost people, and it wears on you. He makes fun of people, and if they stick around, he thinks it means they like him."

"I resemble that remark," Torrents smiled around the bread he was chewing, "but really, what are we going to do?"

"If the spellslingers are trying to take over," Nathan leaned back, bumped the tarp, and jerked forward as a trickle of water ran down his collar, "then we're kinda responsible, and need to do something to stop them."

"Didn't you say something similar about the demon invasion?" Torrents tilted his head to look at the priest.

"Yeah," Nathan sighed, "it feels like a big domino effect, and we're only making it worse. Like we can't do any good, no matter how hard we try."

"You can't think like that," Aiyana's voice was commanding, "you stopped a demon army, more than just that if you what you say is true, from conquering this land, this whole world. Just because someone else took advantage and twisted what you did, doesn't mean you didn't do something good.

"I think," she went on, "if my opinion counts for anything in this conversation, that we move forward with the plan. Sitting here, or hiding somewhere else, is still choosing to do something, even if it's doing nothing. And if that path leads to a worse future, then let's cut it off at the pass, Kemosabe."

A cackling howl cut through the conversation, and the three stared out of the makeshift tent into the grey rain.

"Then there's that," Nathan pointed outside with his fork, "we're being hunted."

"You think it's the same thing that attacked the guards while we ran away?" Aiyana asked.

"Yup," Torrents nodded, "it's a gnohl. I'd know that sound anywhere. We heard enough of them a few months ago."

"What was a gnohl doing in Seawall City?" Nathan muttered, more to himself than the others. "They tend to hunt in packs, and this thing sounded like it's alone."

"How do we avoid it," Torrents didn't look away from where the sound echoed, "while traveling across the countryside? Magic?"

"No," Nathan and Aiyana said at the same time.

Torrents looked from one to the other, waiting for an explanation.

"I can't hide us," Nathan shook his head, "my god helps me see things, be more perceptive, and deal a little with earth ley lines, and druidic magics of growing. But not concealment."

"Mine is," Aiyana hesitated, looking up to find the words, "much more proactive, and more offensive based. I can make a fog to hide us from someone nearby, but I can't hide our scent from hounds, or the sounds of our footsteps, but I can't magically hide us. That's more of a mind-mage thing."

The woman shook her head, dislodging the knowledge and memory that threatened to release itself in a flood. She knew it would be dangerous for some reason, something to do with what the mages in the city did to her. They'd marked her, and that knowledge was the key to them finding her.

"I have so much information in my head about magic," the aeifain put her hands to her temples and rubbed. "I think whoever this person was before me studied magic for decades."

Aiyana sprung to an upright sitting position, gasping. The two men jerked in surprise at her sudden movement.

"Are you alright?" Nathan touched her forearm, and she turned to look at him.

"I…know…where to go," Aiyana said, the words breaking into multiple sentences. "It's what this person was doing. She wasn't just talking to people about the Towers of Onyx, she was collecting something. No, that's not quite it. She was growing something at every major or minor ley line nexus she crossed. That's why we need to go back to the same cities, and that's why I have the urge to prepare this staff."

"We should go," Nathan said. "You can tell us more as we travel, but we need to get away from whatever is following us, and we need to do it now."

"The rain'll hide us," Torrents was tense and staring outside again. "We should finish. We need to pack up and go. It's harder to find scents and prints when your prey is moving through a torrential downpour."

"I see what you did there," Aiyana smirked, then grimaced at her own humor, "but nice pun anyway."

"Let's get moving then." Nathan shoveled the last few bites into his mouth.

## Chapter 9

"I wish I had more time," Aiyana said.

"To do what?" The rain ran in rivulets down Torrents's cloak, and he hunched his shoulders to deflect the bulk of the downpour from his face.

"To work on my staff," the aeifain wasn't as wet as the others, though she didn't appear to be doing anything in particular to cause that, the rain just didn't hit her as much, "to prepare it as a focus for my spells. That's part of the reason I was so exhausted before. The staff acts as a grounding rod for elemental magics."

The three trod along a trail off the thoroughfare, making their travel slower, but safer. They could see wagons and people walking along the road to the east. The trio would cross the trade route every few hours when there weren't people on it—so no one could identify them—hoping to confuse their scent further from whatever it was following them.

"You can do a little every night," Nathan suggested, "we've got weeks ahead of us before we reach Red Wind. You'll have time."

"If we live that long," Torrents muttered, and the rokairn shot him a glance. Torrents raised his voice, faking cheeriness, "but I'm sure we will. Though we might regret it."

The last part was muttered again.

"You know aeifain have excellent hearing," Aiyana informed the barbarian.

"Oh my, Grandma," Torrents snickered, "what big ears you have."

"Very funny," the aeifain rolled her eyes, "even I understood that reference."

"Good," Torrents smiled, "at least you get some of the references. So, we're just following the road north and taking the merchant's route?"

"We have little choice." Nathan drew his shoulders back, causing water to run down his hood and into his collar. He bent over again. "We can't just cut across the desert with as little supplies as we have. We can take the northern trade route across the desert, instead of going all the way north to around it, but we couldn't cut straight across like we did when we came to Seawall City."

"We should get a pack mule, or something." Torrents suggested.

"Good idea," Nathan said, surprising Torrents, "we'll need something to carry the extra water and supplies we'll need for that part of the trip. It's too bad we had to sell our horses in Seawall City when we got there."

"You're the one who said we'd need the money to live in the city," Torrents mumbled.

"And we did need it," Nathan countered. "It was the right move."

They fell into silence, reserving their energy for the journey instead of arguing.

Aiyana's mind wandered. She felt the memory of what the person who'd owned the body before her had been doing, but knew she couldn't dig into the memories because of whatever the mages had done.

*What had they done?* She wondered.

They'd placed a marker of some sort inside of her, tied to her mind. She thought it was to warn them if she picked up where the previous inhabitant of her body left off.

She pushed the idea aside and thought her predicament. She always wanted to change the world, to help make things better. That was back in her world, though. Could she do it here, instead?

If the mages of Seawall City wanted to control the flow of magic, then maybe she could instead. That thought, the first part at least, surprised her. She shoved it aside, avoiding lingering on the idea of stopping them, and instead turned to the idea of helping others.

She watched Nathan, wondering about the rokairn and why he seemed to be bitter and upset. It didn't seem to be his nature from what she'd seen of him and what the barbarian said about him.

Torrents was pretty easy to read. She didn't feel threatened by either of the men, but she'd been around enough to keep people at arm's length until she knew them better.

After all, she'd trusted Tony when he'd smiled and said sweet things back in college last year. And he'd only wanted one thing, just like her mother had warned. And Professor Ridley had seemed helpful in the beginning until his intentions became clear.

But none of that really mattered anymore. This was a new world, a new place, and seemed more dangerous. No, that wasn't right. After all, she'd died in the other world by walking down a street with a bunch of other people who wanted equal rights, pay, treatment, and opportunity.

In this world, though, the threat of violence was immediate and obvious, and perhaps that would make it easier to avoid. And she could help people, she knew it, but it would be going into the lion's den.

But here she had magic.

It took three days before Nathan felt it was safe to stop at a village along the trade route to buy a pack animal. The beast—a mule with a white stripe on her nose—cost them most of the currency they had remaining from Seawall City. Torrents pointed out the coins would be almost useless the further they got from the city, and it also told people where they'd come from.

They'd sent the barbarian into the settlement alone; a rokairn and an aeifain were too noticeable to show their faces, let alone the two of them together. That would've been a dead giveaway to anyone looking for the three travelers, but a single northern barbarian didn't stand out too much.

Torrents presented a wanted poster with rough sketches of the three of them when he'd returned with Millie, the mule. There was a reward for them for murdering a dozen guards, and a handful of spellslingers.

News had traveled faster than they could, perhaps just word of mouth, but it was also possible that Seawall City used magic to send information to all the outlying towns.

They avoided crowds on the road for the first week. Once they'd traveled far enough on the Northern Desert Road, they stopped caravans heading in the opposite direction to trade goods and information.

It took two weeks to reach the Red Plains, and another week to reach the newly rebuilt city of Red Wind itself.

An arc spanned the road into the city—announcing its name—decorated with autumnal wreaths and colors. Caravans and wagons formed a line entering, filled with crops from the harvest and goods from the surrounding area.

Woodcarvers and furniture makers had wares piled into their wagons, and farmers had crops overflowing in theirs. It had been a good summer since they'd eliminated the threat and decay of the Demon Front.

The trio moved along the side of the road, passing people hoping to find space in the open-air marketplace erected in the center of town.

The town smelled different from when Torrents and Nathan had last visited. The odor of charred buildings and bodies was replaced with the wood smoke of chimneys, spices, and that subtle musty smell of the changing of the seasons that brought cheer with the end of the work of summer, and the beginning of preparing for the colder months.

People shouted greetings to old friends and strangers alike. The feel of the place was so different than it had been a few months before that Torrents was taken aback, but Nathan smiled with pride.

"It feels like we did something good here," the rokairn rubbed at his nose and eyes.

"Are you getting teary, old man?" Torrents chided.

"Sorry, seasonal allergies," Nathan mumbled, "and shut up, jerk."

"You two really have to work on this," Aiyana was walking beside Millie, her back straight and stiff, taking in the scene, "you mean such kind things, but say them in such a…derogatory manner."

"Deal with it," Torrents shrugged, but he was smiling contently.

It had a been long time since the barbarian had people he could joke with in the way he'd teased his friends when he was in high school. It warmed like hot chocolate warmed most other people.

"Let's start at the Church of Jonath," Nathan gave the direction like a suggestion rather than a command, "they can probably offer us a place to sleep tonight that's dry and clean, and definitely catch us up on the latest happenings in the city."

"Okay, fine," Torrents said with a shrug, "this is your town, you lead the way."

"I hope they can offer a bath," Aiyana sighed, "I know I want one, and both of you need one, to be sure."

Aiyana studied Torrents and realized that both of her companions seemed much more relaxed and comfortable than they'd been since she's met them.

Red Wind was being built, but it was less of new structures and more of a rebuilding. Broken shells of foundations showed, but new wood and stone rose above the charred cornerstones of the old structures.

They moved past a dozen buildings before someone shouted Nathan's name, immediately followed by someone shouting Torrents's. Within minutes, they had a small crowd of excited people around them, shaking their hands and clapping them on the back.

The line of merchants and farmers stared at the trio as the townsfolk welcomed them back as returned heroes. Aiyana, on Nathan's suggestion, had pulled her hood up to minimize the chance that someone would recognize her as an aeifain, but she still carried herself in a way that spoke of privilege and confidence.

By the time the three reached the church, they had an escort of two dozen people.

Father Pelese was waiting at the top of the stone steps, as if he'd been expecting them long before they'd arrived.

Arrayed behind him were four other clerics, each holding a bundle in their arms. Fruit basket, fine linens, and other similar items held in front of smiling faces.

Pelese made a brief speech, telling the gathering of the deeds of the guests, welcoming them back and their new friend—the aeifain, Aiyana—then ushered the three inside and away from the forming throng of people.

It surprised and concerned Aiyana that the older priest had recognized her as an aeifain, but the people seemed to accept it since the announcement came from the respected elder of the town.

Pelese showed the trio the church, touring them through the new addition added on as the congregation grew. A school room was added, as well as a mediation chamber.

After that, he guided them to a private room that functioned as his office. The three sat in cushioned chairs across from the priest, who remained standing. A large oak table served as a desk, and stout oaken shelves lined three of the four walls, only broken by a single stained-glass window.

"I'm so extremely proud of this artistic interpretation of Jonath at Silver Keep," the priest stood beside the window, gesturing like Vanna White showing off a prize for contestants, "it was a gift from the artisans of Durgan's Keep, welcoming Red Wind back into the brotherhood of cities that are growing with Land's End after the war."

"Great." Torrents drew out the word to three syllables, showing his lack of interest. "And why are we in a dank back room of the church?"

"What my friend means to say," Nathan interjected, "is that you must have another reason to bring us away from prying eyes."

"Yeah," Torrents rolled his eyes, "that's exactly what I was saying."

"Yes, of course," the priest issued a polite laugh, "and he is correct. I did bring you here for an ulterior motive. There has been an uprising recently, a social obstruction, people from the past who want to see the old order restored, rather than the new one that we are leading where every man has a chance to thrive."

"Oh, come on, already," Torrents sighed. "Get to the point."

"Shush," Aiyana shushed, "let the man get to it in his own way, show some respect."

Torrents turned towards the wizardess, his eyes wide, and Nathan patted his arm.

"Yes, well," the priest continued, "alacrity may be of essence."

Pelese paused, pondering for a moment.

"The drug cartels are returning," the man ran a hand through his salt and pepper hair, "and frankly, Blanding House is threatening everything we've built since you left. They recovered some artifact, an item of power and magic, that seems to be somehow tied to a newly formed monolith to the east."

"A crystal," Aiyana sat forward in her seat, "pale blue, and when close, it smells of sea, tides, and shores?"

"Well, yes," the older holy man seemed surprised, "but how could you know of this…"

"Damn it," Aiyana stood as she cursed, pushing past Torrents and pacing behind the three chairs, "that's what I planted when I spoke to you last."

"Ah," the priest sighed.

"Spoke to you last?" Nathan repeated.

"Ha!" Torrents threw his hands up. "You said you were here, but you said you were talking to people. What's this planting thing? And how the hell do you plant a crystal?"

"You don't," the aeifain scowled at the barbarian as if he were a special child in a class of slow learners, "I tied certain energies to the water and earthen ley lines that intersect here."

"Stop it, you two!" Nathan snapped, holding up a hand towards them. "Go on, Father Pelese. How did they get this crystal, and what exactly have they been doing with it?"

Pelese walked to the door, leaned out and spoke to the waiting acolyte there.

"Fetch Ichealson and Vindalai," he said to the young man, "and warn Reeve Mecklen and his deputies to stay clear of Carter's Lane later tonight."

He turned back and returned to his desk.

The older man settled into his broad-backed chair, steepled his fingers, and began telling the tale of how Red Wind backslid into the shadowy world of drug lords and gang wars.

# Chapter 10

"Shh," Nathan hissed, waving his hand behind him.

"He was never this bossy until you showed up," Torrents whispered to Aiyana, the two crouching in the dark alley behind the rokairn, across the street from Blanding House, "he used to always apologize and ask what everyone else thought, now he just tells people to be quiet and do what they're told."

"Some people need to be told what to do," the aeifain gave him a pointed look.

"That's cause Imma bad boy," Torrents grinned, "and you like it."

The two fell silent; the sound of a high, soft whistle COMING from the rooftop across Carter's Lane.

They'd been keeping watch from the alley for almost three hours, since shortly after nightfall. They weren't being stealthy; but weren't trying to be obvious either. No one had paid them much attention, except for a mangy grey tabby, who kept meowing, purring, and rubbing along the fur at the top of Torrents's boots.

Three men exited the two-story building. They didn't speak to one another; just walked out, clunked across the wood plank porch, stepped into the road, and looked around. After a moment's pause, two of the men looked at the third, who nodded, turned, and all three men walked away under the quarter waxing moon, moving down the street in the opposite direction.

"The lookout on the roof is going in. Five more should be leaving the back door in a minute," Nathan's harsh whisper made Aiyana jump, "and that's when we go in the cellar door around the side."

"And why didn't we each watch a separate door?" Torrents asked, loosening his swords in the scabbards on his back.

"Because I didn't want you playing cowboy and kicking down a door when you got bored," Nathan stood and brushed off the knees of his trousers before recovering Marcid from where she leaned against the wall, and strapping the axe to his back, "and I didn't want Aiyana getting lost or overwhelmed on our first outing. We need her with us to identify the object."

"Thanks for the vote of confidence, dwarf," Aiyana said coldly.

"You're welcome for me caring, elf," Nathan replied, stepping into the street and shouldering his weapon.

"H-he," Aiyana sputtered, "called me an elf, and that's upsetting. And I don't even know why it bothers me."

"Echoes of your other self," Torrents shrugged, took the woman by the elbow, and guided her forward, "guess if one word pissed you off, maybe he coulda been right about not letting you go off on your own? Besides, you called him a dwarf, so technically, you started it."

They moved across the street, Nathan a few steps ahead of the bickering barbarian and wizardess, looking in one direction, then the other.

They reached the alley between the Blanding House and its neighbor. Torrents steered Aiyana in front of him and turned to look in each direction down the street to make sure they weren't seen. There were people out, coming and going from the alehouse a few blocks down, but no one was close by and no one was paying attention to them.

Once in place next to the building, Torrents sighed.

"You two are the worst ever at sneaking," the barbarian muttered, joining them squatting in the shadows. "I miss the Kid. He knew how to sneak."

"Quit your belly-aching," Nathan hissed, "just hush and wait for the signal."

They hunkered in the building's silhouette for what felt like hours but was actually less than a half of one. The alley was littered with discarded materials from the two buildings that stood sentry on either side. Rats explored the impromptu mazes of trash, causing Aiyana to twitch and jerk with each scratch or rattle of movement.

The sound of horse hooves and the call of a driver echoed off the buildings outside the alleyway, the clatter of wagon wheels growing louder by the moment. Angry shouts and surprised screams tracked the progress of the too-rapidly approaching buckboard.

"There's Ichealson and Vindalai," Nathan spoke a little louder, making sure they could hear him over the ruckus from the street. "Get ready."

Torrents moved to one cellar door and Nathan to the other. Each man bent over in the cool night air to grasp the handle of the door they straddled, both looking at the massive padlock holding the doors closed.

The noise of the wagon rushed closer, then exploded with sound as it crashed into the porch of the building that the three hid beside. The Blanding House shook, and shingles swooped and fluttered down from the high rooftop, slapping and clattering to the surrounding ground.

The two men jerked upright; the arched iron grips of the cellar's doors held in tight fists. The doors chunked to a sudden stop. With a pop, the brackets holding the lock tore free, sending the solid security device flying over Aiyana's head. It clattered into the trash behind her, rats squealing and scurrying in all directions at the unexpected assault.

The cellar door swung wide, like an alien maw that opened from side to side rather than up and down. Pungent odors of molding vegetation and sharp spices eddied around the three intruders.

The sound of a night bird called from somewhere nearby. The feral cry cut through the racket from the front porch as people poured from the house to find a toppled wagon, broken posts that supported the veranda above, and leaking casks of lamp oil scattered across the wooden planks from one side of the house to the other, and from the door to the street.

Angry voices filled the night from around the corner; shouts from other buildings joined in as people who'd seen the whole thing ran to tell their story and accuse or defend one side of the other.

The wood splintered from Torrents's and Nathan's rough handling, and now Aiyana stood centered at the shallow, stones steps that led down into the urban cave below the den of thieves. The two men stepped onto the stairs and descended into the inky depths. In a staggered formation, the rokairn first with a throwing axe balanced in each hand, followed by the barbarian who had two short blades held at a downward angle in front of himself.

The large room they entered, which covered the size of the entire building above it, looked recently deserted. Four long tables were in the center of the area, large bales of red leaves stacked to the right, long shelves to the left that held the crisscrossed boards of a wine cellar—dusty bottles filling more than half the space—a square, stone strong room directly ahead, and in the far right corner a narrow stairway led up. Tallow candles stood in holders with polished tin backing on each side of the half dozen support beams in the basement.

Torrents moved toward the wine racks, and Nathan grabbed the man's sleeve.

"Sorry, upstairs," Nathan muttered. "We don't have time to browse the wine list tonight."

Torrents grumbled but moved across the room towards the only way to the ground floor.

Nathan took the lead again, each step on the wooden staircase thumping and drawing a creaking groan from the grey, aged wood planks. Though the rokairn only came up to the barbarian's chest, they both weighed about the same.

Torrents's booted feet found every creak that Nathan's missed, and the little noise Aiyana made as she followed was pure silence in comparison.

Nathan pushed the door at the top of the stairs open a crack and looked out. He could see straight into the kitchen where serving maids, or women of some sort, were cleaning a stack of stoneware and a pile of mugs. The aromas of braised meat and baked bread rolled across the hall.

The priest shoved the door open all the way and moved to the right, towards the foyer where the front door stood ajar. Movement and voices could be seen and heard from the outside. The three darted for the stairs directly above the door they'd just come through and across from the front door.

Entering the foyer, they could see the dining room—where the evening meal had been interrupted—in a disarray of dishes and overturned chairs, through a wide-open archway to their left. A parlor, through an identical archway, was to the right. The rokairn led the trek upward and away from the main floor.

Nathan was almost to the second landing, and Aiyana was just stepping onto the stairway when the front swung open. All three jerked to a halt and turned to look at who was entering.

"Alright, alright," the annoyed voice shouted, the man waving his hands; he turned away and back towards the scene outside, "I just want to get something."

An angry voice sneered something at the lanky man in the doorway. If he had looked inside, he'd have seen the three of them.

Nathan bolted upstairs, taking them two at a time. Torrents followed, taking the steps three at a time. Aiyana turned at the noise they were making, and with a jump and squeak, shot up the stairs after them.

The door slammed, and the three heard the man stomping into the parlor below, muttering about how he was always having to do everything.

The second floor had a railing that went all the way around the foyer, and anyone looking up would see the three intruders.

Nathan looked at the two doors on the far left wall, across at the three, and ended at the two on the right wall. An oil lamp was mounted between each door, but only every other one was lit.

"Which one is it?" he wondered in a whisper.

"That one," Aiyana pointed at the door directly opposite of where they stood. She breathed in deeply, like she smelled something comforting and familiar. "I can feel it in there, and it's grown. It's truly become the Eye of Agnew, and I can sense the power of the ley lines feeding into it."

"Not now," Torrents muttered, put a hand on the aeifain's lower back, and pushed her forward to follow Nathan, who was already moving towards the door.

She squeaked again; her feet forced to follow her body.

By the time the wizardess and barbarian reached the door, Nathan was on his knees inspecting the frame.

"There's something here, guys," the rokairn pointed and traced a line in the air about two fingers-width from the doorframe. He started at the bottom of the left side, moved up to about shoulder height, swung his hand in a repeating up and down arc three times until it pointed at the right-hand side of the doorframe, and then traced the line back down to the ground.

"It's a…" Nathan paused and looked at Torrents, who raised his eyebrows in anticipation of the coming words and smirked, "it's a tripwire."

Torrents let out a disappointed sigh.

"I don't see anything," Aiyana leaned in to look, and Nathan's hand stopped her from getting too close. "What's it made of?"

"Magic and metal, as best I can tell," Nathan wrinkled his forehead, peering at the squinting woman above his shoulder, "I don't know if it's my rokairn blood, or the gifts of Jonath, but I see it like most people would see a spiderweb in the morning dew and first rays of sunlight."

"Oh," Aiyana's face brightened, "that I can take care of."

Her hand flared blue, and the two men leaned away from the sudden, intense heat—Nathan patting frantically at his shriveling eyebrows—she ran her hand around the area that the priest indicated.

Bringing both hands to her mouth, she whispered into her cupped hands, opened them, and blew gently across their palms.

Silver dust glittered where Nathan had indicated the tripwire was and floated to the floor.

"That was nifty," Torrents clapped Aiyana on the back, making her lurch forward and bump her head on the door.

"Yeah," she glared at the big man, rubbing her forehead, "silly alchemists always think their magic can match real magic. But it never does."

"Quit quibbling." Nathan palmed the handle, pushed downward on it to lift the latch inside, and pushed the door open. With his other hand, he swept Aiyana inside, then followed her.

Torrents came inside, stepping on the hem of the woman's robe, and knocking into the rokairn as the big man twisted to close the door behind them. Darkness fell over the room as it clicked closed and the latch fell into place.

Gentle silver moonlight streamed through the shutters of the two windows in the room, leaving a thin sliced sliver moonbeam on the knotted rug that covered the floor.

A silhouette rose in front of the shutters to the right, its shoulder flaring out like a man using his arms under a cloak to make himself appear larger.

"Stand and deliver!" a shrill voice croaked in the darkness.

## Chapter 11

Nathan's eyes were adjusting to the dark when light blinded him, golden orbs flaring to life over Aiyana's palms. Torrents threw an arm up to block the sudden brightness, and even Aiyana winced.

"Ack!" the voice screeched. "Moonless night, fly on the moonless night!"

"Damn it, lady!" Torrents grunted. "Turn it down before you announce to everyone on the street and in the hall that there's someone in this room!"

"But," Aiyana's voice was panicked, "there's someone in this room."

"No," Nathan's gentle hands groped for her arms, lowering them and the light, "it's not a someone, it's a something. A bird."

"You can see already?" Torrents rubbed at his eyes and turned away from the flares.

One orb disappeared, and the other faded to less than a candle's glow, mimicking the moonlight outside.

As their eyes adjusted, they each took stock of their surroundings. All the furniture—two beds, a table, three chairs, and two footlockers—were pushed against the walls.

In front of the shuttered window to the right was a t-frame stand, a huge raven perched atop it. The bird ruffled its feathers, pulled its outstretched wings tight against its body, and glared at the group with one eye from its turned head.

A stand was in the center of the room, a blue gem—which ebbed and flowed in darker than lighter shades—with brown flecks hovering over it. A cage made of bones from long-fingered inhuman hands arched over it, topped with a huge fanged humanoid skull was missing its lower jaw. The encasement stood knee height, and two hand-spans wide.

"That's morbid." Nathan said, leaning in to look closer at the protective enclosure.

The rokairn let out a short, shrill scream and danced backwards as the skull looked at him, the hands tapping and turning with spider-like movements to direct the thing's gaze.

"That thing's alive?" Aiyana squeaked, stumbling backwards.

"Naw," Torrents's voice was casual, "not in any way is that alive. What's the matter with you two? It's like you've never fought the living dead before."

"We haven't," Nathan regained his composure, "so why don't you take care of this?"

"Sure thing," Torrents laughed, flipping his sword and catching the blade. "I'll just bash it into little itty, bitty pieces."

Aiyana moved across the room, straightening her robe, and approached the raven. The bird cocked its head to look at her, and she mimicked the movement.

Torrents brought his sword up and swung downward towards the undead cage. The thing crouched and sprung straight at the barbarian's face, the jewel shifting to the back of the skull with the momentum and glittering like a poisonous sac.

"Oh bidj," Torrents yelped, falling to the floor, trying to dodge the creature in his surprise. "It's a goddamned face-hugger!"

The thing missed, landed, and skittered across the room and under a bed, its digits clicking like an enormous insect.

Torrents leapt after the thing, upturning the bed to see the abomination scamper under the chairs along the wall.

The bed clattered, the metal frame slamming against the wall, and the thin straw mattress folded over itself and slid to the floor.

Nathan ran to intercept the skull-crab, leaning down to look under the chairs and chop at the animated creature with one of his hand axes.

It launched itself at the rokairn, its boney finger-legs digging into and clinging to the priest's face. It lurched forward, the fangs turning outward and stabbing into Nathan's forehead.

The rokairn danced backwards, dropping his two hand axes, and batting at the boney opponent with both hands.

"I'll get it!" Torrents raised one of his reversed swords to bash the thing from his friend's face.

"No, no," Nathan shouted, spinning and falling backwards onto a chair, shattering the wooden legs and back, "you're going to hit me!"

"Can you burn it off?" Torrents held his weapon ready, turning to Aiyana. She still stood by the bird, who was ducking and bobbing, excited at the commotion.

"Not without risking burning off part of his nose or something," the wizardess said, backing up to a wall.

The rokairn screamed and pulled the creature from his face, ten deep scratches appearing along his neck and cheeks.

Nathan threw the magical construct across the room. It turned in midair to land on its feet, then scurried up and over the footlockers, up the wall, and across the ceiling.

"Now I can get it," Aiyana said through gritted teeth, and thrust her hand holding the golden light towards the monster.

The globe burst forward, growing in intensity, from yellow to blue, before striking.

Fire washed across the ceiling, enveloping the wooden beams and the planks above them.

"Oh bidj," Torrents muttered.

Nathan snatched his hand axes from where they'd fallen, stood, and threw them hard and underhanded at the creature.

One struck, slicing off three bone-fingered legs before falling to the floor, the other stuck into the large dome of the skull.

The undead creation fell from the ceiling, landing on what would be its back, and turning over to its finger-feet with the help of the hand axe embedded in it.

Torrents leapt forward, bashing the thing with the pommel of his short sword.

The creature slammed to the floor, another leg spinning away.

The barbarian hit it again and again, pieces breaking off and shooting across the room with each blow.

Moments later, the thing lay still, and three companions stood in a loose circle around it, panting.

"I got it," Torrents smiled.

"Yeah," Nathan muttered, recovering his axes. "Good job. Now, let's get the crystal and get out of here."

"Yes," Aiyana stooped and fished the gem from the broken, twitching remains of the animated monstrosity and tucked the jewel into her pouch, "and quickly, the ceiling is on fire."

She spoke calmly enough that it took a moment for the words to register for Nathan and Torrents. The two men looked up and saw the spreading blaze.

"The roof, the roof," Torrents muttered rhythmically, "the roof is on fire. We don't need no water, let the mother-chuzzer burn."

A moment later, they heard shouting voices, the front door slamming open, and heavy footfalls on the stairs in the hall outside.

"Plan B?" Nathan looked at Torrents.

"Yeah, sure," the barbarian shrugged, "let's do that. But what's Plan B?"

"No clue." It was Nathan's turn to shrug.

"Step aside, boys," Aiyana said with a grand sweeping gesture, "I got this."

She stepped to the window beside the raven, swept the bird up on her forearm and hustled it to her shoulder, unlatched the shutters, flung them open, and hurled another glowing globe downward.

The flame arced over the railing of the veranda outside the window, spun in a ninety-degree turn and shot towards the ground.

The night exploded.

The oil-soaked ground and front porch outside of the building ignited, flames billowing upward and out. Screams came from below, and the footfalls and shouts in the hall reversed direction.

By the time Aiyana turned back to the two men, they'd already opened the door and were moving into the hall.

She lifted the hem of her robes awkwardly with her staff in one hand, ducked to avoid the growing fire overhead, and beat feet for the door.

The raven squawked and hunkered down, leaning against her cheek for balance.

Torrents led this time, his two swords held properly now. Men burst out of the door closest to the stairway, and the barbarian swung his dual weapons, making them dodge back into the room and slam the door.

Nathan waved for Aiyana to hurry, pushing her in front of him when she caught up so he could take up the rear, leaving her protected between the two men, but also allowing her to use her magics without risking taking a sword to her belly.

Aiyana spun when they reached the top of the stairs, and with a wave of her hands, the rugs lining the hall crystalized and wrinkled with the frozen moisture of ice. She did this in both directions and added a layer of permafrost to the door where the men had come out through moments before.

The door jerked, the ruffians behind it trying to come out again, but it was frozen shut. The door opposite opened, and a half dozen, half-dressed men burst out. They lost their footing on the ice, and arms flailing and legs kicking, they went down in a heap.

The trio took the stairs down two at a time, Aiyana stumbling and only keeping her balance with a steadying hand from Nathan behind her.

Reaching the foyer, they saw the inferno out front; the blaze consuming the dried planks of the porch below and on the veranda above.

"Not going that way," Torrents breathed, using one hand on the banister to spin himself back in the kitchen's direction and the basement they'd come from.

He charged down the hall, and three men stepped into the hallway from the kitchen. With a roar, the barbarian barreled into them, knocking them backwards and toppling them onto one another.

"Go," Torrents shouted, "get into the basement. I'm right behind you."

Aiyana turned sideways to squeeze past the large man, who was slapping at the fallen thugs with the flat of his blades, knocking their weapons across the floor. Nathan followed her example, grabbing the barbarian's belt in passing and jerking his friend backwards and towards their escape route.

The hall was filling with thick smoke that burned their throats and stung their eyes. Combined with the greasy, splintered planks lining the floors and ceilings of the Blanding House with decades of history, the fish oil flamed high and hot, and smoked more than most other combustibles.

Nathan barreled down the slim stairwell, bouncing off the wall as the steps turned, and continued down. Aiyana lightly stepped down each riser, dropping with a dainty movement, the bird on her shoulder bouncing up and down. Torrents slammed the door across from the kitchen closed, banged the bolt into place, then jammed one of his short swords into the crack between the door and the frame.

The big man turned and pounded down to the basement, only to draw up when he reached the bottom.

"You pemties," Aiyana spoke quietly through tight lips, "you left the doors open."

Nathan and the aeifain were standing at the bottom of the steps, staring out the open double cellar doors at the three men milling about outside in the night, each covered with soot, armed with a Billy club, and looking extremely upset and in search of someone to take it out on.

"We can't lock it," Nathan's voice was harsh from the smoke above, "we broke that off."

"Doesn't matter," Torrents waded past the other two, his height allowing him to lift his arms above their heads on the narrow staircase, "it was on the outside, anyway."

"Move aside, boys," Aiyana echoed her words from the second floor, "I got this, again."

"You gonna burn them?" Torrents asked as the woman pushed him and Nathan apart to pass between them.

"No, sir," Aiyana's voice was light and confident, and she almost seemed to sashay past the rokairn and barbarian, "that upsets Nathan, and doesn't do me much good, either. I've a better way."

The aeifain stopped in the center of the floor, put a hand on a cocked hip, the staff leaning against her shoulder, and stroked the raven on her shoulder with the other. She looked around the room, as if sizing it up for new furniture, and then nodded decisively.

Aiyana swung her arms in a wide curve, from her hips to above her head. Her wrists crossed, her fingers moving, then she leaned to her left, like in some dance from a bygone era. She bent at the hips until the arc of her arms pointed towards the solid stone of the strong room.

"Hey," one man squealed from outside the cellar door, "you don't belong in there!"

Aiyana's eyes twitched towards the doors, and a smile tugged on her lips.

With a spasmodic jerk, she leaned over a little more, the staff falling to the floor, dropped her arms—still crossed—in the direction of the stone walls of the protected room to her left, and pulled like she was a mime with an invisible rope.

The walls of the strongroom melted from solid stone to liquid mud and flowed across the room towards the cellar door.

The two men barreled down towards the three. At the bottom step, their boots met the warm, gooey flow of the viscous earth. They threw their arms out to help maintain their balance, but the gelatinous goo moved up the stairs, carrying the men backwards.

The thugs toppled over as the slow-moving mud rolled inexorably up the steps. Their arms became stuck in the travelling quicksand, creeping upwards along the framework, outlining the steps that led outside. It formed a circle around the opening, continuously thickening and closing. The men rose with the mud wall, one turning sideways, and the other erected upside down as the circular hole closed to form a wall covering the entire exit.

The center opening in the newly formed wall grew smaller and then closed completely. One man's arms stuck through to the interior, and the knee and toes of a boot of the other man could be seen. The wall solidified into stone again, wet gray earth becoming lighter as it dried within moments.

"Wow," Nathan breathed, "that's a neat trick."

"Yeah," Torrents's voice was muffled and bottles clink from behind the rokairn and aeifain, "sure is."

The two turned to see the barbarian pulling wine down from the racks and sliding the bottles into his satchel

"You're doing that now?" Nathan asked.

"Yeah," Torrents shrugged, "why not? They probably stole it anyway."

The big man stopped, staring with wide eyes over the rokairn's shoulder into the shadowy recesses where the strongroom had been moments before.

Nathan spun to look behind him, worried about what terror or foe could have been hiding in the room.

The light from the tallow candles flickered and glinted off steel, copper, silver, and gold. The tables standing within the protective walls were lined with small coffers and chests. A center table held scales and weights. The solid earth wall that made up the fourth upright of the room housed a rack holding a variety of weapons.

Torrents pushed past Nathan, moving the priest to one side as the barbarian slid a fifth bottle of wine into his satchel with the other.

The younger man stepped forward as if in a daze, stumbling on the dried mud trail underfoot because he was squinting at the wall.

The rack of weapons held a simple long sword of common design but extraordinary craftsmanship, a scimitar, and a falchion from the western sands of the Great Desert people, three small throwing spears made of a sleek black metal, a recurve bow made of yew, and a huge blade with a hand and a half grip.

The barbarian fingered the weapons, his mouth hanging open, fingertips tracing along their trim lengths.

Pounding sounded from the door above, followed by the thudding noises of bodies hitting the door, trying to force it open.

Torrents snatched down the bastard sword. He shoved it into the scabbard leaning against the rack, and strapped it to his back, removing the empty scabbard of the sword he'd used to block the door upstairs. He followed suit with the bow and spears, bundling them together and tying them along the large sword's sheath. Picking up a quiver of arrows, he belted it around his waist, tying the trailing laces on the bottom around his thigh.

"What?" He smiled at Aiyana, who watched him grabbing a handful of coins and dropping them into his satchel. "We're gonna need them if we're going to fight our way out of here."

"Are we going to need the money for the fight, too?" Aiyana arched an eyebrow at the smirking barbarian as the man shoved more coins into his bag, reaching up to stroke the raven, who leaned towards the coins with interest.

The barbarian shrugged, and the elementalist turned away.

Aiyana fished the gem they'd recovered from the room upstairs from her pouch, drew it out and held it in front of her between two fingers, studying it.

Chanting quietly to herself, the wizardess leaned her staff against the wine racks.

"Do we have time for that?" Nathan asked, glancing at the noises coming from the top of the stairs.

Aiyana made a hissing, hushing noise, moved her hand under the raven so he stepped on her wrist, and reached towards the priest. The bird transferred to the rokairn's shoulder, and the two stared at one another, unsure of what had just happened.

Splinters of stone rose from the ground, gathering around the gemstone. Aiyana released the stone, and it hovered in the air in front of her; the threads of earth and water coalesced in a globe around the artifact. Brown and blue energies, a green glow enveloping it, solidified into a sphere in front of the elementalist as she bonded the artifact to her.

"Hand me my staff," Aiyana's voice was breathy, and she held a hand towards her arcane focus leaning against the wine racks.

Torrents snatched the staff from where it stood and handed it to the wizardess.

Once she touched the enchanted wood—still whispering words—the earth, salt, and water shell that encased the gem fell away in a sprinkle of dust and sand.

The gemstone floated to the staff and hovered over the top of it.

Aiyana breathed out with a rush, and the room went still as she regained her composure.

The sound of splintering wood from above made the aeifain look over her shoulder at the stairs.

"We won't need any of those weapons where we're going," Nathan said, pointing at a blank dirt wall. "My little eye spies…"

"What?" The wizardess looked at the wall, then cocked her head at the priest. "I don't think I can do the stone to mud trick again, not without a good night's sleep."

The rokairn stepped to the wall, dropping his hand axes into the loops on his hips, and pressed his thick, callused fingers to the stones. Moving his hands in an arcing, sweeping motion, he inspected the stonework.

Something thunked, and the wall swung away from Nathan, revealing a bolt hole common in criminal hideouts with a history. Cobwebs danced and dust swirled, a dry, musty smell of long disuse drifting into the basement.

"Shall we?" Nathan drew out his hand axes again, and swirled them among the dangling webs, collecting them in a way that made him think of the most disgusting cotton candy ever served.

He stepped into the passage, Aiyana following. Torrents grabbed another double fist of coins, shoved them into his satchel, and ducked into the ancient passage to follow.

When he closed the hidden door behind him, everything went black.

"Yo, guys," he whispered into the dark, "I can't see bidj."

"Here," a cool, delicate hand took his and laid it on a dainty shoulder, "we can see, you just follow and try not to take me down with you if you fall. Okay?"

The three moved into the dark, the noises of men breaking into the basement faded into the distance, and soon enough, they felt the cool night air on their faces.

## Chapter 12

The gnohl darted between the gouts of flame and dripping oil that fed the fire inside of the Blanding House on Carter's Street. He slid his razor sharp khopesh along the midsection of a man running past. The jutting curve at the end of the blade disemboweling the panicked human.

The smoke was thick, most of it billowing out the windows and spiraling into the night sky in a swirl. It didn't bother the gnohl as much as it did the blinded and coughing men running from the building. Flames hissed and scalding steam rose as the bucket brigade threw pail after pail of water through the ground-floor windows, hoping to stop the spread of the blaze throughout the whole town of Red Wind.

The hunter cackled his gurgled laugh as the unskilled piece of bidj dropped his weapon and clutched at his spilling guts.

Ghe'hak was in his element within the fiery husk of the Blanding House. Men fell to his blade, screaming at the horror erupting from the shadowy corners of their burning home, not ending their lives, but wounding them so the pain of the fire could take them instead of the swift edge of a blade.

The gnohl fought for two reasons, two purposes, and both compulsions were strong. But only one of the urges was his own.

One reason was to make sure his quarry escaped. He needed the aeifain, rokairn, and human to complete their mission so he could reap the fruits of their labors. The final magical artifact created from their endeavors would allow the gnohl to open the dimensional gates between this world and the others, drawing through the waiting armies of demons, devils, and otherworldly beings.

The second reason was because he loved killing the weaker prey species. He craved the chase, the pursuit, and the feeling of warmth spilling from his quarry when he cornered it. The carnal surge totally overwhelming his opponent, again and again. Sensing their desperation, smelling their fear, and seeing their scrambling attempts to escape what he knew was inevitable. It was a rush that couldn't compare to anything else.

These were lesser beings, put into creation by the gods for the stronger to destroy and devour.

The staff came back into his awareness when he drew his bloody dirk from the chest of a man on the ground, bracing one foot on his torso to pull the blade from where it had wedged between two ribs.

The staff was a magical artifact centuries in the making. Well, the staff was being created now. The events that allowed it to come into existence had been what had taken time.

His master—using the term loosely—Khizhane, wanted it so he could command respect from the other humans in Seawall City. But, Ghe'hak knew, if you couldn't get respect by battle and might, then you didn't deserve it.

The staff pushed back into the gnohl's mind, forcing his instinctual thoughts aside. The staff would change everything. Khizhane, who fancied himself Ghe'hak's master, was a fool who thought to use the eldritch relic to beg respect from other fat, fleshy, weak men who relied on magic and deception for their power.

Ghe'hak eviscerated another thug, tearing the man's liver from his falling body with his teeth in frustration over the thought of the weak creatures begging for respect as a way of life.

The gnohl threw back his head, tossing the sweetmeat into the air and catching it between his jowls, flipping it up again to chomp down and slurp it between the jaws of death.

Ghe'hak had to have the staff. These pathetic pieces of prey must be slain quickly, no time for enjoying the kill. Ghe'hak needed to stay on the trail of his primary quarry, to return the staff to his master, Khizhane.

He moved, looking into the kitchen longingly at the women huddled together in the corner, avoiding the flames. He wanted to slaughter them also but pushed away the urge of the bloodlust—that incessant call of the kill—and moved towards the door in the room that led to his true quarry, the aeifain and the two men who had avoided his blade too many times.

Bursting into the night, he ran, ignoring the sparks that smoldered in his fur. He had to find them, knowing only then would his purpose come to the grand goal he truly wanted. Slaying Khizhane and becoming the Lord of the land.

The alchemist stewed, leaning down, and glaring into the brazier of vision. The image of the gnohl withdrew, sliding into a mental distance and withdrawing from the awareness of the man.

Khizhane stood, stretched, and leaned backwards, his fists jammed into his lower back. Bones and cartilage popped audibly, echoing from the walls of the chamber he secretly etched out of stone in the basements of the council hall.

Seventeen men, women, and children had died during the excavation, but none of them mattered. Their blood and bones mixed in the mortar that strengthened the walls forced the souls to answer Khizhane's commands to watch the other councilors who would oppose him.

The gnohls still pursued the three criminals who'd attacked the city. Assisted by Ghe'hak, directed by

Khizhane himself, it was only a matter of time until they brought down their prey.

Thinking of the demonic man-beast, the alchemist snickered. The gnohl still believed all his plans and intentions were his alone. Clueless, the monster didn't know doses of potions guided his drive and decisions. The protective salves, given to the gnohl by Khizhane, hid him from the prying eyes of the rokairn priest of Jonath, but were a second line of control.

Three councilors had already fallen to Khizhane, though no one attached the wizard's, mind mages, and sorcerer's fate to his plan. Lylianne, Chritijua, and Shulleeta were each removed from power, two of the three executed.

Shulleeta, the only one who'd survived, had come to Khizhane, begging his help in regaining her position in the group of people that controlled all political, economic, and other decisions for the most powerful city on the continent, maybe in the world. Now she worked to further his goals, thinking she'd seduced him with her wiles when he'd bedded her.

The alchemist turned back to his laboratory. Three alcoves showed at the far end of the long room, each dedicated to a specific type of research that would soon come into play.

The first used a chemical combination to create pulses of energy along copper wiring, allowing many results. Khizhane had toyed with light sources, enclosing them with gas, and using the energy to create a constant spark that was amplified by the gaseous composition within the globe.

The second used alchemic magics to track a device over a long distance. This was a tentative magic, and often rock or metal could interfere with the results. It was how he followed the gnohl, one device hidden within the communication contraption he'd given the creature.

The third alcove held his latest experiment; a mixture of powders bought from the rokairn outside of the city, which when sudden force and flame were applied could propel a metal, explosive projectile a long distance.

The back wall hosted the tables and tools required for harvesting the components to achieve specific alchemic reactions. This was the area where he'd stripped the fat and flesh from the priestess, kitchen worker, and the latter's young son.

The vision brazier was in one of the three alcoves nearest the wall he walked away from.

In the center of the room were a half dozen tables holding tubes, burners, and distilling equipment used to refine materials to their most effective components.

This was where he'd made the potions he'd given the gnohl, Ghe'hak. It was also the equipment he'd used to distill the poison that he'd given more than one person who opposed him.

The Council of Thirteen was weak, and fought amongst itself, unable to move forward or make quick decisions. Once he'd removed them, or at least enough of them, they would vote him in as…what title did he want? Chief Councilor? No, too thin of a phrase. Maybe Emperor someday, but it was too soon to consider that now.

Perhaps High Minister would be an appropriate term to suggest. He'd heard the phrase in a tavern years ago, and it had stuck in his head.

It didn't matter, not really. Once he was done, and his plans had come to fruition, the council would disband by their own hand. Small portions of the city will be doled out to the loyal, who will and serve as advisors and representatives.

High Minister had a nice ring. But that would wait. Khizhane had work to do before worrying about the icing on the alchemical cake he was crafting.

He had heard the reports from the men who'd interrogated the aeifain when she was their prisoner. Her people had seen a future where the few ruled all, and where magic controlled the land.

Khizhane moved to the vision brazier again, adding a liquid containing traces of her blood. The alchemist focused on the aeifain, narrowing in on her thoughts, hoping to trigger more clues that would lead him to victory, and using her knowledge against her.

# Chapter 13

Nathan, Torrents, and Aiyana met with Pelese outside of Red Wind, a day after leaving the Blanding House, and gave the man a bottle of wine and some gold. They carried a letter from the priest addressed to any priest of Jonath to give them aid if requested.

The journey from Red Wind, down the Stream River, to the Lasso River, and crossing the Inner Bay took just over a week. Once they'd reached the Stream River, they'd booked passage on a barge dragged along the sluggish canal by a team of horses that walked along the side of the waterway. The Lasso River, thankfully, flowed faster, speeding along their progress.

At the Inner Bay, they hired a ship to take them across. When they arrived in Durgan's Keep—the city atop the rock wall that overlooked the western portion of the Inner Bay—they made their way up the winding path that twisted back on itself as it ascended the cliff face above the docks.

Torrents led the others to the only place he knew would be safe, The Pheasant Plucker's Inn, a popular brothel and house of pleasure near the shipyard.

They sat at a small, round table, facing one another. The raven pattered across the surface, picking at leftover bits of food on the plates in front of them.

Perfume wafted through the room, accompanied by the sounds of moans and giggles from the other chambers that lined the hall outside the curtained doorway.

The room was just large enough for the table, a sideboard holding a variety of drinks and glasses, a couple extra chairs, and a small chest where they kept linens.

The travelers bathed and stored their bags, armor, and weapons in the rooms in the basement set aside for them.

They wore borrowed casual outfits, while the few clothes they carried were cleaned, courtesy of the house's madam, Jewlnee.

"Is it cannibalism if your raven keeps eating that chicken you didn't finish?" Torrents pointed at Aiyana's plate.

"My people don't eat much meat," the aeifain dodged the question with an airy tone, "and when we do, it's almost always fish, or occasionally fowl. We avoid the heavier meats, such as beef, mutton, or pork. And we always avoid shellfish, which is more akin to insects than fish. Good on protein, but they're scavengers and rarely carry healthy results."

"We didn't need a nutrition breakdown of all the foods, you know?" Torrents sipped at his wine. "Speaking of food, why'd you keep the bird?"

"He's a raven," Aiyana raised her chin and looked down her nose, which wasn't easy considering how much taller Torrents was than she, even sitting down, "and I couldn't leave Captain Farrell to die in the fire."

"I still like Nevermore," Nathan said from around a rib, his fingers greasy and smeared with a thick, dark sauce, "but you do you."

"I like Heckle and Jeckle," Torrents smiled, "after you explained how offensive it was to me."

"It isn't right," the aeifain sighed, picking up a small bunch of grapes, "and to the point of the question, I like Captain Farrell. He's smart."

"He could be a spy." Nathan wiped his fingers on the cloth napkin tucked into the collar of his doublet. "As we discussed on the barge, he probably came from someone in Seawall City with information or instructions about us."

"Or that could be arrogance and paranoia," Torrents began his standard argument again, but stopped when Jewlnee entered the room.

The madam of the brothel was smiling, her mass of red curls pinned to the top of her head, her emerald eyes bright under the rainbow swath of eye makeup.

Two young women shadowed her, sliding past the large woman and clearing the table.

"Stand and deliver!" Captain Farrell croaked as he pattered back and forth across the table, pecking at the disappearing food or the women's fingers, causing the ladies to jerk away.

They cleared plates, bowls, utensils, and other items from the table.

Jewlnee carried a tray of warm honeyed pastries in one hand, and a cloth in the other. She wiped the table with the latter, then set down the former to oohs and ahhs of the three companions watching.

"Now," the madam pulled a chair from the corner and settled between the priest and the barbarian, "enjoy the deserts, but it's time to talk. What brought you back here? Have you heard from the Kid?"

"We haven't," Torrents lifted a confectionary, a string of honey trailing behind, "but we've heard that he went northwest, past the Wandering Hills. I bet he's doing just fine, though, and having a great time while he's at it."

"I hope so," Jewlnee muttered, then brightened with a forced smile and looked at Nathan and Aiyana, "and what curse forced the two of you to travel with this uncouth mess of a man?"

"Divine providence and punishment often look alike," Nathan said piously, raising his symbol of Jonath in one hand and his wine goblet in the other, "but Torrents has his uses. At times."

Aiyana just smiled a tight-lipped smile, her stiff posture speaking volumes.

"Don't be such a prude," Torrents jostled the wizardess with an elbow, "and don't pretend that you haven't been in a whorehouse before."

"I beg your pardon," the madam settled her bulk on the remaining chair and sat, her tone indignant, "this is a house of fine repute. 'The Pheasant Plucker's Inn, pluck your favorite bird!' That's our motto, and we only offer a clean and safe entertainment."

"My apologies," Aiyana said, "it's just…different from what I'm used to."

"Well," Nathan dropped his holy icon back under his napkin and patted the aeifain's hand, "it's a different world. Now Aiyana, why don't you explain to our hostess what we're doing here. And remember, I trust this woman, Torrents trusts this woman, and most importantly, the Kid only said good things about Jewlnee, and he was—erm, is— a great judge of character."

"Yeah," Torrents grunted, his mouth full of pastry, "we've heard all this before, but we could use a refresher. Tell her the whole story. She knows this town and the people, and the more she knows about what we're doing, the more she'll be able to help us."

Aiyana took a deep breath, held it for a few seconds, then let it out in a rush.

"Of course," the aeifain's smile was genuine this time, looking at Jewlnee, "I appreciate all you've done."

"Think nothing of it," the madam grinned, "the boys will pay for everything, one way or another. Those bottles of wine were a fine start. I know just the customers to impress with them. Just tell me what's going on, and I'll see how I can help."

Aiyana looked to Nathan, who nodded, then at Torrents, who was too busy refilling his wine goblet while juggling three pastries in his other hand to notice. She stroked Captain Farrell, took another deep breath, then began talking.

"Before I came here," her words came slowly, falteringly, "to this world, I mean. Before I came here, this person, this body, who knew magic in a way I don't believe I'll ever be able to match…set a plan in motion. She'd left her home. Icon Hall is the impression I get of the name, and I'm not sure why she left it, but I get the feeling that something terrible happened there, and she wanted to fix it.

"She went to different cities; Runsk, Dioneze City, Rumay Bay, here, Red Wind, and, finally, Seawall City. In each, she went to whoever ruled and told them that magic was out of balance."

Aiyana stopped, her forehead wrinkling.

"It's okay, sweetie," Jewlnee patted the girl's hand again, "take your time. The Kid told me how confusing it can be, trying to understand how this whole world works."

The aeifain nodded with a nervous twitch of her lips.

"I'm not actually sure about all this," Aiyana shrugged, and Nathan slid her goblet closer to her hand, "the memory is…foggy."

Captain Farrell rose to his full height and peered into the goblet with one beady eye.

"I don't know if she actually talked to rulers, or just people in positions of power," Aiyana sighed. "She may have been talking to people like you, or criminals.

"Oh!" the wizardess gasped, her hand jerking to her mouth. "I'm so sorry. I didn't mean people like you. I just meant common folk, like you."

"Honey," Jewlnee laughed, "if I didn't know you were born aeifain, I'd never be able to tell the difference. You have enough condescending confidence to be the queen of the aeifain. But I understand, and I promise not to get offended when you say pemtie things like you just did. You just tell your story. Now, go on."

"I still apologize, sometimes things just seem to come over me, bypassing my own thoughts," Aiyana nodded, waved Captain Farrell away from her drink, picked it up, and took a long, deep draught.

Sputtering, she set the wine down.

No one spoke, but all eyes were on her.

"Right," Aiyana breathed in, summoned her confidence, and went on. "Five cities, five intersections of ley lines. This woman I am now laid the magical weavings, using artifacts of her own people as seeds, and she planted…something. I don't know.

"And I want to find the link to here," she rushed on, looking at Jewlnee, "drop a magical connection to this space, a token of myself and power, so I can find this place again. You feel like a friend, and my instincts say I can trust you, and I don't have anyone else in this world besides these two…men, that I can say that about."

Jewlnee nodded.

Aiyana threw herself back in her chair, sighed, and dropped her hands to her sides. She closed her eyes, and the others could see her eyelids moving like someone in REM sleep.

"You're doing fine," Nathan's voice was warm and comforting, and the wine was settling across the aeifain's mind like a cozy blanket, "keep going, get it out."

Aiyana paused for a long time, then she opened her eyes, leaned forward, set her elbows on the table, and picked up her goblet. She took another long swig, draining it, and began again.

"Five magical rites will create five new magical items that are attuned to specific frequencies of the ley lines." She took a quick breath and went on. "These items had to…ferment, to be given time to marinate to get their abilities. They should be ready. The Eye of Agnew. The Finger of Yender. Takoven's Rib. And the Spine of Japria. The final item cannot be made until the other four are brought together."

She stopped talking, falling back as if exhausted.

No one spoke.

"And what are all these things for?" Nathan said after more than a minute of silence.

"I don't know!" Aiyana's voice cracked, and she threw up her hands. "I don't have that information. I can't find it. I know the Eye of Agnew, the gem we stole in Red Wind, is like a compass to find the others, and later will be used with the other things to do something…bigger."

"What was the woman's original purpose?" Jewlnee asked. "Why was she speaking to powerful people in each city?"

Aiyana stared at the woman, her eyes tracing the voluminous waves of silk material wrapped around her.

"Magic was off balance," the aeifain nodded at Torrents as he refilled her wine, "it was clogged before, but when the Demon Front was routed and the Pyridom of Power changed, it was like a bent hose being unkinked. Magic rushed back, but it didn't come out even like it should have. It's…being pulled…"

Aiyana's forehead creased, and her face told the others that something was on the tip of her tongue. Any interruption could wash away the thought or idea and make it unrecoverable.

"East!" Aiyana shouted triumphantly, sitting up, "To Seawall City!"

The small group stared at her, unsure if there was more. They waited as Aiyana's lips silently moved and she stared up into the corner of the room.

"They're taking the energies," the aeifain's voice was full of soft realization, "they want a monopoly. They're hording it."

She looked around the room at the others, as if she expected them to understand the import of her words.

"Don't you understand how dangerous this is?" Aiyana leaned forward, her voice intense. "Don't they? They should! They're spellslingers, by the gods! They must be pemties to think they can just have it all!"

"What's it mean?" Torrents asked.

"Fly on the moonless night!" Captain Farrell croaked.

"It means, that if what Aiyana says is true," Nathan stood, pushing his chair back and holding his goblet in a white knuckled grip, "we probably need to collect these artifacts, and then use them to release the pressure, or risk that it explodes and devastate half of the eastern seaboard."

# Chapter 14

"I had a simple life," Nathan muttered, talking to himself. "I had a simple jewelry shop, and went to work six or seven days a week, depending if I had an employee that was worth anything. Was it enough for me? Yes, it was enough. I lived simply, worked simply, and sold stuff to people who had dreams in their eyes, or looking for forgiveness, or just wanted something to make them feel better about their own problems."

"You okay there, buddy?" Torrents laid a hand on the rokairn's shoulder but pulled it back when Nathan jerked away.

"I ate bran in the mornings." The priest looked up at the buildings that had once been artistically carved stone, interwoven with living trees as they moved through what was once the aeifain district of Durgan's Keep. "I think I was developing diabetes, or hypertension, or something. I hit that age where people started taking pills every day and complained to their friends about their latest doctor visit. I never wanted to do all that. I wanted a simple life."

Aiyana and Torrents exchanged glances, the barbarian smirking at the wizardess, who gave him a look of mixed unsureness and concern.

The priest had gone on like this since they'd left The Pheasant Plucker's Inn, repeating the concepts in a dozen different ways, and headed towards the part of the city where the ley line intersection was the most powerful: the Aeifain District.

They made the docks for humans and were all clunky corners and simple concepts. The Rokairn District—which they hadn't been to—was said to contain glorious statues, stonework, and a marvel of artistic construction.

This District was a dead place at its core, but life and business carried on as if no one noticed. The once thriving gardens now lay like graveyards fallen into disuse, looming shadows of things past, with broken stones jutting from the earth like shattered teeth of the giants of history.

After the Downfall, people turned on the beautiful and graceful race of the aeifain. In the best of situations, they asked the elegant and haughty people to leave, but with swords, glares, and often scared looks. In the worst, common citizens razed entire sections of cities and burned hundreds of what was supposed to be an almost-immortal folk, so they'd never come back.

The Aeifain vanished from Durgan's Keep. They hadn't left town one by one, or in small groups. People didn't force them out en masse. They'd simply disappeared. The fair folk locked gates to the district one day, and the following day, no one could see anyone moving inside.

It took months, which was a relatively short period of time considering the events of that era, before the city broke down the gates.

The place had been empty. Nothing was gone except the residents. Shops had all their wares lying on the shelves or tables under a layer of dust. All the homes of the aeifain still had every article of clothing in the wardrobes, food rotting in cabinets, and valuables hidden in all the usual places. Even the livestock were gone.

No one knew where the mystical people had gone to, and no one really cared. The world had been in the midst of an apocalypse, and the only memorial held was riotous looting.

Now, over thirty years later, people populated the abandoned section of the city again. Shops flourished, merchants hawked their wares, smithies smithed, and people went about their lives as they lived in the space that had once belonged to others.

Since the necromancer invaded Durgan's Keep, undead had been popping up now and then, wandering the streets in small groups. No one knew where they came from, but rumors hinted the sewers were full of the things, shuffling about and eating anything they found that moved. The rat population in the city had a surge right after the attack, and since had dwindled to suspicious levels. Stray cats, dogs, and street vagrants had similar swings in numbers, and people whispered they were snacks for the living dead that roamed the warrens below the streets.

"I lived a simple life," Nathan repeated, not looking up at the beauty that had turned grey and muted, "and now I'm looking for the magical finger of a Troll Lord. A Troll Lord!"

The rokairn laughed deep in his throat, but it wasn't joyous, and instead brought up a thick wad of phlegm he spat on the intricately carved cobblestones beneath his feet.

"Aeifain were once…" Aiyana hesitated, knowing the history was an embarrassment to her people, though she didn't quite understand why, "more than they are now."

"Yes." Nathan waved a hand over his shoulder at the woman, dismissing the explanation he'd heard just an hour before. "I know, about six thousand years ago, your people got power hungry and magically tried to remove the impurities. It made trolls, who were strong, pemtie, and almost impossible to kill, and it made you guys. And this is proof why what these people in Seawall City are doing is dangerous."

"Wait," Aiyana stopped in her tracks, "I seeded it here, or somewhere very close to here."

The two men stopped, turning back to the woman, who turned in a slow circle, looking around. They were in a square, next to a large well wide enough that someone couldn't reach across and touch the hands of anyone reaching from the opposite side. The buildings surrounding them formed a cul-de-sac, rising higher than most of the buildings in the city, if you counted the petrified branches that loomed overhead, leaning out from the top of the structures.

Rats scurried in the dusk, light filtering through scattered clouds, and lightning flashed from far away, tense moments passing before thunder tumbled in the distance.

"Seeded?" Torrents laughed, covering his nervousness. "Sounds like you planted a tree or something."

"I did, sort of," Aiyana was bent over—staff tucked under one arm, Captain Farrell dancing to her hunched shoulders—moving around the well, searching the ground with a furrowed brow, "I found the intersection of the water and fire ley lines to be strongest here.

"I dug up a cobblestone," she dropped to her knees, holding her hands over the stones, "and buried the knucklebone of Yender underneath it, tying the elements to it."

"A simple life," Nathan ran his fingers through his sweaty hair, causing his chain-mail shirt to jingle, "that's all I wanted, and now I'm here. Why am I here?"

"I think he's losing it," Torrents tugged on his short sword, pulling it a handsbreadth from the scabbard and slamming it back into place.

"It's…" Aiyana muttered, her high voice blending in an eerie song with the rokairn's, "not here, but far below us. We need to go down."

"That's what she said?" Torrents laughed, but it didn't have any humor or force to the words.

"Down," Nathan leaned over the side of the well, "so, this magical knuckle dug into the bowels of the earth to find fertile ground?"

"Maybe?" Aiyana looked around, as if waking from a trance, and looked up at the surrounding buildings. "The wind speaks, it hunts again."

"What hunts again?" Torrents asked, following her gaze. "The wind?"

"No," Aiyana's voice was a whisper, "the hunter. Maybe the thing that's following us, maybe something else. Something down in the well."

"Then we go down," Nathan dropped a rope into the well, and secured it to the wooden arch of intertwined branches that served as the well winch, "so we can find this relic."

The rokairn pulled himself up onto the low wall of the well, swung his legs over the edge, grabbed the rope, and dropped.

Torrents looked over the lip of the well, watching the priest descend into the darkness, hand over hand on the rope, moving quickly.

The barbarian looked at the wizardess, who shrugged.

With a sigh, the big man put his belly on the wall, lifted his legs and spun his body until his legs dropped over the side, grabbed the rope, and followed his friend.

Looking up, Torrents saw the aeifain standing on the rim of the well, the raven on her left shoulder, and her staff leaning against her right. She stepped off the wall, and the barbarian let out a shout.

The woman wafted down.

Like a dropped feather, she swayed from one side to the other, lazily drifting on a breeze that pressed past the big man on the rope.

She floated past him, the raven taking flight to circle downward after the woman.

"Damn spellslingers will be the death of me," the barbarian muttered, wrapping the rope around one thigh, then around his waist, rappelling downward.


"Sewers," Torrents growled, "are the worst place ever, and I'll be so glad to be the hell out of them."

The three were standing at a crumbled wall on a small walkway that ran along the fetid runnel of feces and waste that dropped from a broken city above them.

They moved along the fresh water, following Aiyana's innate sense, aided by the Eye of Agnew, to track the magical artifact that had moved of its own volition. They followed her in a winding path, dropping lower to the sewers, backtracking underneath where the well was, and finding the broken wall that led to clean water that fed the well system under the city.

They spent hours with Aiyana holding the Eye of Agnew out in front of her at each intersection, using its compass-like nature and her attenuation to the elements to narrow their search for the next artifact.

They stumbled across remnants of the undead that had attacked Durgan's Keep almost a year ago. They performed the 'slash and burn' routine—as Torrents called it—hacking the rotting flesh and scarred bone figures until they writhed on the ground in pieces. Then applied fire to destroy the remains and broke the magics that animated the dead and rotting corpses.

The three peered into a perpendicular tunnel, the stones placed so cunningly, and with such precision and skilled flair, the walls appeared smooth except on close inspection. Runes of the rokairn language graced the archway that was the portal to another layer of construction buried deep below the city.

"Why not?" Nathan muttered, and then read the language of his people aloud for the others, "'Trappings of light bring justice to craftsmanship, caged luminescence filter art to the eyes of the unwary.'"

"Deep." Aiyana smiled. "See what I did there?"

Nathan shook his head and moved forward, the other two following close behind.

"What are these tunnels?" Torrents asked, trailing his fingers along the cool stone.

"I think rokairn built the city," Nathan said.

"Yeah," Torrents interrupted, "that's what the Kid said when we were here last."

"They built these tunnels after," Nathan pointed at another stone archway covered by the carvings of language, "and the runes are mocking those people who would never think to look below their feet."

"My people," Aiyana tapped the stone floor for emphasis, "say the same thing about humans, but that they never look up. If you ever want to kill a human, just find a place above their eyeline and they'll never see the arrow until it takes their eye."

"You guys are making me nervous," Torrents said from behind them, the shadows on his face from the small ball of fire in Aiyana's palm making him appear skeletal, "so can we stop talking about how to kill people like me?"

"Oh no," Aiyana turned, raising a hand to her lips, "we're not talking about killing your people, just humans in general."

"Hold on," Torrents stopped, "are you saying my people aren't even good enough to be considered humans?"

"Depends," Nathan stopped and turned, making the aeifain do the same, "on which world we're talking about. Northern barbarians are little better than animals. They worship animal spirits, fear the weather gods, live in little more than huts, and dress in the skins of their kills. So, maybe they are a bit less than human."

"Dude," Torrents moved forward, his hand curling into a fist, then he stopped. "Wait, you just chuzzing with me?"

Nathan smiled, then turned away and began walking again.

"He was chuzzing with me," Torrents's voice rose in pitch, "he was totally chuzzing me. I didn't think he had it in him."

"Stop," Aiyana said softly, tucking her staff into the crook of her arm, Captain Farrell croaking and pecking at the shining crystal on top.

"Stop what?" Torrents asked. "Swearing? Does it bother you, princess?"

"No," her voice was commanding, "stop. It's here."

"Stand and deliver!" Captain Farrell croaked.

Nathan turned to see the aeifain pointing at a wall.

Etched into the wall was a relief carving of a circle of fire and water, curling around each other. Colored paint flaked and peeled. The stone itself looked as if something had been eating away at it, softening the lines, and removing the details. The border of the relief told a pictograph story of the twin gods. Torr, god of fire, passion, and skill in combat, and his sister, Tarra, goddess of water, healing, and calm reflection, as they traveled the plains of existence to fight in the light and in the darkness. The twins were a balance who worked in unity to hold reality together, not against one another to break it.

The rokairn moved in front of the others, sliding his hands across the stone. Pebbles fell to the ground with a tak-tak-tak, and sand crumbled away in a cascade.

Something clicked, a sharp noise muffled by the thickness of the stone.

Nathan put both palms to the wall and pushed. The wall slid forward, then shifted to the right, sliding to one side under Nathan's guidance to reveal the room beyond.

## Chapter 15

Eight rokairn-sized creatures of baked clay and steel lurched towards the trio. The orange hue of their armor mottled to a brown, bringing images of floating feces in the sewers to mind. Eroded surfaces, like the relief carving on the door, showed pockmarked craters across their carved skin.

The room was octagonal, each wall showing an alcove housing a guardian. More relief carvings decorated each recess, and myriad ornate weapons hung between the niches.

A thick powder coated the floor. It would cover a shoe to the toe if someone moved through it, as shown by the ruts in the dust left by the lurching statues approaching the door.

A pedestal in the center of the room emitted a stark light that cycled from blue to white to yellow to red to purple, then repeated.

Captain Farrell took wing, launching himself at an automaton.

Torrents reached over his shoulder and pulled his new bastard sword from its scabbard, moving forward, without ever putting one foot in front of the other.

The orb of fire hovering over Aiyana's pale palm burst to life, flaring to triple its original size. She moved her hand forward and the globe burst outward, expanding as it went. The fireball encompassed the approaching constructs, but the blaze wavered; the creatures absorbing it.

Steel rods showed between the plates of armor on the figures, but as the flames disappeared, the gaps closed The clay warriors healed, the dust on the floor congealing into wiry ropes of sinew. Braids of powdered clay wound their way up the bodies of the automatons and knitted around itself to form muscle that thickened into hardened skin on the constructs.

"Hold!" Nathan shouted in rokairn, and the statues slowed and stopped, weapons held high and ready to attack; his companions doing the same.

"We are the children," Nathan intoned, saying the words in rokairn then repeating in the drab language of humans, "of the elements. Water and earth make our bodies, fire and air make our minds and souls. We are bound and call upon the guardians of the Twin Gods to hear our request."

"What?" Torrents turned, his weapon held above him, an animated statue quivering within striking range. "Where'd you get that, and how'd you know what to say to stop these things?"

"It's an ancient script of my people," Nathan said solemnly, then pointed at the pedestal, "and it's carved into that thing in the middle of the room."

Nathan stood, feet apart, shoulders squared, battle-axe held in both hands, his breath coming in sharp puffs. Aiyana's hands whirled with small balls of icy shards, her shadowed face confused.

The scene froze, the figures unmoving except for the trembling of their stone muscles, and the trio all in ready stances that spoke of coming violence.

Dust drifted down from over of the pedestal in the center of the room holding a globe of flame and liquid that swirled around one another, reminding Nathan of the symbol on the door, and Torrents of the yin-yang symbol from the dojo he went to in his teens. It moved like it was breathing.

In the center of the globe, something writhed. It wasn't fluid enough to be tentacular, and it wasn't long enough to be considered serpentine. It weaved and twisted within the primeval soup of elements, glimpses of bone white segments breaking the surface, then fading into shadowy portends of shape as it submerged into the magical globule.

"What…now?" Torrents said through gritted teeth, glancing away from the thing in the center of the room to look at Nathan.

The rokairn sighed and dropped his arms to waist level, his grip on the axe going limp.

Shuffling—a staccato of footfalls muffled within—came from the corridor that led deeper under the city. It wasn't the sound of one set of feet, but dozens. Wet sucking noises—like a baby at the teat, or an old person with bread pudding—grew noticeable as a mass of figures appeared within the light spilling out of the door and into the passage.

Aiyana turned and looked back down the hallway in surprise at the sudden noise, moving away from the door. She stumbled to one side as she turned, bumping one of the guardians, and backed up so the stone construct was between her and the hallway.

Dozens of undead forms rushed past, but not with any speed. A mix of rotting people with layers of greyish-yellow skin sloughing off, meandered past the opening in mockery of a mob rushing from some threat in a panic. Yellowed bone broke the storm-dull coloring of the throng pressing past the room that held the powerful magical artifact, older and desiccated bodies pressing through the shuffling crowd. Thin, vellum-like skin enveloped the bony remains that fled, like a skeleton had been shrink-wrapped with ancient tissue paper.

A few of these monstrosities were jostled into the room. They looked around, not even noticing the three living beings, their eyes focusing on the pillar in the center with the glowing artifact wrapped in a bubble of elements, and then turned and fled, forcing their way back into the stream of decaying bodies outside of the door.

The animated stone statues rushed forward, hacking with axes and bastard swords. All the weapons wielded by the magical constructs were immense to almost ridiculous proportions, requiring two hands to manipulate.

Torrents thought the statues fighting the living dead looked like it belonged in an anime series from the 2010s, and a small, surprised laugh burst outward from the huge warrior.

The undead didn't defend themselves. They fell under the onslaught or pushed back into the press of inhumanity and moved away.

"What the hell…" Torrents stepped towards the doorway, "is so chuzzing terrifying that the goddamned undead run from it?"

"Do we really want to find out?" Nathan put a restraining hand on the barbarian's arm. "Or do we want to just get this thing we came for and get out of here?"

Aiyana moved across the chamber and thrust her hand into the elemental globe.

Captain Farrell, recently landed on the wizardess, took to wing, cawing.

The wizardess stiffened, her eyes going wide as her hand disappeared into the magical vortex that swirled and sparked. Flashes of fire and steam burst from the sphere, her wrist vanishing into the arcane energies, her forearm reddening.

The aeifain braced her feet and pulled back, grabbing her elbow with her other hand as she leaned away from the globe, trying to free the writhing thing within. She gritted her teeth, her jaw tight, and a high-pitched keen came from her as her face tightened.

Torrents was at her side in two strides, grabbing her arm, his body language mimicking the woman's reaction.

Nathan turned to the two. Dropping his axe, squaring his shoulders, and setting his feet, he lowered his head, and charged towards them.

The rokairn hit them at a running speed, knocking the two away from the globule.

The three hit the ground in a tangle, another three creatures standing in the doorway before spinning back to the flow of bodies in the hall behind them. One fell under the attack of a stone guardian as the other two moved out of the chamber.

The raven landed on Aiyana's side as she lay prone, and Nathan and Torrents disentangled themselves.

The bird cocked his head, a small noise that sounded like concern coming from him.

"I'm alright," Aiyana stoked the raven with one hand, the other clutching a jointed bone, the length of her forearm, "let me get…"

She stopped talking, the hand petting her familiar reaching to retrieve her staff that had fallen to the floor in front of her.

The aeifain pushed herself to a sitting position. She stared at the thing in her hands that whipped back and forth, a finger with fifteen joints seeking something just out of reach.

Aiyana set the tip of it to the crystal, and the Eye flared with light, the first three joints of the Finger of Yender curling around it to create a setting before stiffening and becoming a straight line that held the sister artifact in its singular grasp.

Magical energies flared, then dimmed. The items bonded and joined, the Finger twisting its base around the top of the staff.

"Now what?" Nathan recovered his axe, and strode to stand near the passage, where the stream of inhumanity had slowed to a trickle. "Can we go now?"

The guardians within the room returned to their niches, taking up places that had housed them for unknown years.

"I hunger," dust stirred in the hallway outside, a deep breathy whisper echoing through the chamber, a hissing, sibilant murmur that ground against the trio's nerves. "I am coming, and I shall feed."

"I think that'd be a good idea," Torrents nodded, securing his long sword, and drawing the short blade from his back, "we should definitely go before whatever that thing is arrives. I make it a habit to not hang out to meet something that the dead would run from."

"Okay," Aiyana swept Captain Farrell from her hip onto her forearm, still red like a bad sunburn. She winced and pushed to her feet. "Let's get out of here. I'm guessing that whatever's coming was drawn to the magical energies once we opened this room."

"I'll guard the rear." Nathan waved the two ahead of him. "I see best down here, and Torrents, you need to guard her. Go, I'm right behind you."

Torrents put a hand on Aiyana's shoulder—Captain Farrell flapping his wings to keep balance and using his beak to pull himself to her shoulder—and followed her towards the door. She turned right and followed the exodus of undead somewhere ahead of them in the dark.

The surrounding air crackled with static electricity, and something huge lunged at them from the darkness behind.

"Kaleb triot, den'al venitier!" Nathan shouted and spun, brandishing his axe, and bringing it down to slash along a snout larger than he was.

Ghe'hak the Ravager followed the wyrm, staring at its receding bony exoskeleton as the monster hunted the gnohl's quarry. Ghe'hak held his weapon at the ready—a khopesh, a blade that curved, sickle-like, and the tip curved on the backside—in front of him. He didn't want to rely on his teeth and his claws with the creature in front of him.

In most situations, those were fine, but now he was looking at the thick hide of an ancient, dangerous monster. Steel felt like the better option over his natural weapons.

The thing in the hall in front of Ghe'hak lunged forward, a flare of fire around its thick body, vague sounds of the rokairn's battle cry coming from beyond it.

The gnohl checked the straps on his eclectic armor—piecemeal remnants of leather and steel, covering his limbs and chest—and sprinted towards the enemy of his enemy.

These people knew where to go to find the magical artifacts that would be the tool he needed. He'd bring back the hordes of hell, which would raise him to the position he deserved, a prince of the armies of the Abyss.

But he had to make sure they reached his goals, the purpose he'd set them in motion to do. He'd followed the aeifain since she'd arrived in Durgan's Keep the first time, defending her from brigands on the road, and other more dangerous things.

He also followed her this time, but not by the river and boat route she took. He'd used the alchemist's device to contact another scrying bowl within Durgan's Keep. The mystic trio who'd answered him, hungry for the scraps of power he'd promised, had summoned him here. It allowed him to wait for the aeifain and rokairn and damnable human to arrive at the docks.

He'd destroyed the magical focus of the miniature monolith empowered by Onyx a century before, hidden in a livery on the northern portion of the city. The three witches—who preferred the term mystics—bathed in their blood as he slew them before toppling the point of focused magic. The gnohl hoped it also disrupted the lines of power that fed that bastard Khizhane, who held his influence above Ghe'hak like a child teasing a pup with some tantalizing tidbit of a treat.

The gnohl pulled his focus back to what was in front of him; a beast that slept longer than any predator should. It spoke of complacency that led to indolence, a confidence that could easily lead to a downfall from the belief there wasn't anyone or anything that could harm you. The gnohl knew he was the one to prove this ancient predator could die.

Silence wasn't important. This creature wasn't even aware of the gnohl following him. The man-monster cut down the remnants of the dead humans that wandered these corridors, the dregs the monster in front of him hadn't crushed against the walls or devoured in passing.

The thing in front of him paused, then shot forward down the hall, its long body undulating, snake-like, to reach something ahead.

Leaping forward, Ghe'hak slid along a sheet of ice on the floor, attacking the hind end of the creature. He jammed the khopesh between large, overlapping scales and twisted the blade. A chunk of flesh pulled free from beneath the scales as the gnohl ripped the weapon free.

The wyrm spasmed, trying to turn its body in the tight quarters to get to whatever was attacking it from behind.

Wasting no time, Ghe'hak attacked the massive form again and again, blood and gore flying, spattering the dark walls around him.

The tail lashed out, and the hunter dove under it, coming up close to the body, slashing forward at the cloaca visible underneath the gargantuan form.

Ghe'hak cut into the slit-like opening, slicing it to the bone and running his blade along the scales of the beast's underbelly to the closest appendage. One of the monster's legs went limp, the body collapsing on top of it.

The gnohl threw himself backward to avoid being caught under the behemoth, rolling to his feet, and looking for an opening to continue his attack.

The beast surged forward, moving away from the gnohl. It would seek a place to escape, or to turn around and face him head on. The gnohl didn't want to give up his advantage of attacking the flank of the monster.

The Ravager got his name for a reason, and his jowls slid back in a toothy grin. He pressed his advantage, the adrenaline of the fight filling his body as he lost himself to the rage.

The beautiful, savage delight of letting go and being swept along with the instinct and savagery that even his kind didn't understand was heady. It was a dance of skill and predisposition beyond any understanding of any being that clutched to the concept of being civilized.

The gnohl relished the sensation, his cackling barks of battle lost to the three people running from the other side of the ancient wyrm.

## Chapter 16

The mighty ship known as the Raptor Rex bounced, the sea monster shooting underneath it and making its escape towards deeper water.

The sailors raised a cry, the sound a blend of panicked relief and exhausted jubilance. It had been a hell of a battle, won by the deft maneuvers of the helmsman, the cunning commands of Captain Jaiman Rabbit, and the magical bombardment of Aiyana.

Nathan, Torrents, and Aiyana booked passage on the ship hours after escaping the draconic wyrm hybrid in the sewers attracted to the magics of the rokairn chamber.

A running firefight, literally, within the tight walls of the sewers led them to two choices, and neither was a good one. The passage split; the left showing the open night, water pouring in a cascade off the cliff side to the dark below, and the right holding a dead end with a glimmering portal of magical energies that crackled and hummed.

If they'd followed the passage to the left and jumped down the cascade, the fall would have meant certain death for multiple reasons.

Aiyana could call upon the winds to carry her but weakened by her assault on the wyrm, she wasn't sure she had the strength remaining to lower herself. But she did know that trying to carry all three of them to safety would end up with three corpses in the rocky churn below.

The portal was an unknown.

The three had argued, debating if it would just kill them, send them to come unknown place—perhaps in this world, perhaps in another—or if it would lead to safety.

They chose the uncertain fate and plunged through the portal, the exhausted wizardess supported by the barbarian.

It had led to a dark chamber that had five other portals. The chamber of broken stone with an abused and shattered monolith in the center, didn't have a mundane exit. They'd camped, using the term loosely, in that chamber. Aiyana had slept to recover from the fatigue of the magics she'd wielded while Nathan studied the six portals.

Each had a broken archway overhead, and the one they'd come through showed sigils and pictograms that appeared to relate to Durgan's Keep. The other five also had similar markings, but nothing that looked familiar. After hours of inspection, Nathan thought he'd figured out which one probably led to Seawall City but wasn't sure.

Torrents had prepared a small fire, which clogged the chamber with smoke, then put it out and settled on soaking dried beef and seasonings in a pot for a makeshift meal. After hours of staring at the shifting scintillating energies of the magical doors, Torrents had fallen asleep.

When the other two awoke, Nathan filled them in on the shifting colors, and how he thought the different colors would lead back to a different place within the different locations.

The doorway they'd come through cycled from silver, to blue, to green every three hours or so. He theorized that the silver was the sewers, and the green or blue would be somewhere else in the city. They walked through the same portal they'd come out of when it was green and stepped out into the bright sunlight of high noon in the Aeifain quarter of Durgan's Keep.

They'd appeared in a quiet garden cul-de-sac, overgrown with years that spoke of disuse and not being attending with the loving care of a tender.

They'd made their way to The Pheasant Plucker and Jewlnee gave them food, drink, and a place to rest. The next day, they'd booked passage with Captain Jaimin Rabbit on the Raptor Rex and set sail down the Ruled River to the Broken Sea.

For two weeks they'd been on board the three-masted carrack and were within a day of making port in Rumay Bay.

Torrents had taken to sailing like a…well, like a fish to water. After the couple of weeks, he'd climbed the rigging to adjust the set of sail like a man who'd sailed for years, had a steady hand for the wheel, and an eye for the sextant, compass, and stars when the first two weren't close at hand.

The barbarian fell in with the crew with unexpected ease, sharing their coarse humor and juvenile jests. He even taught the sailors a few new curses and swears before they sighted their port.

Nathan, on the other hand, didn't fare as well. He stayed underdeck and kept a bucket close. The rocking of the ship and the spray of the salt air made him greener than his natural ruddy complexion.

Aiyana was somewhere in between. She stayed on the forecastle any time she was awake and often was seen with her arms widespread, as if greeting the winds and sea spray. Captain Farrell was never far from her side and stayed either on her shoulder or in the rigging nearby. She called to the winds and water, gently nudging the elements to aid their speed on the trip, and hardly tired from the effort.

She spent hours working on her staff, whittling, and carving arcane symbols into its wood. She bored out a hole in the top and embedded the Finger of Yender—still wrapped around the Eye of Agnew—in the magically enhanced talisman of her power.

Captain Jaiman was a rotund and jolly man until he wasn't. Most times, you could hear him laughing and telling tall tales when someone would listen. But when trouble loomed, he turned dark and intense, his short beard bristling with beads of ocean tears, as he called them.

"You did well, lass," Jaiman beamed at the aeifain, "It's been a long time since I've sailed with a water witch, but I don't recall ever having one as skilled as yerself on me ship."

"Thank you, Captain," Aiyana raised an eyebrow, "but I'll thank you to recall that I'm also more than a hundred years your elder, and perhaps lass isn't the term to use for someone such as myself."

"Of course," Jaiman raised his hands in front of him in surrender, "I dinna mean no harm. Just an affectation of my career when I see a beautiful young woman who can calm a sea or sing to the winds to make the Old Rex dance across an angry swell."

Torrents watched the woman—young yet ancient at the same time—put her curled fists on her hips as she turned to correct the mariner on terminology. The barbarian smiled to himself.

The time on the ship had made him feel the pull of wanderlust. He wanted to travel and see all the amazing things in the world.

In the other world, he'd been able to get in a car, on a plane, or even a bus or a train, and in hours or a couple days, see mountains, seashores, endless plains, or giant forests. But he'd never done that. He'd almost never traveled, except on a couple of family outings to visit extended family.

He'd been a Boy Scout and done some camping, but always within a short drive of civilization. Hikes through state parks, picnics with neatly mowed fields of grass, and one vacation to the shores of the Great Lakes were about all he'd ever done there. He'd spent most of his life in suburbia or in cities.

Here in this world, his body was raised on the cold northern tundra and staying alive had always been the priority. Hunting the migratory herds of deer and moose, or the flocks of geese and ducks, had been a way of life and survival. It was never a pleasure trip when leaving his tribe in their buckskin tents to do these things.

Since he'd been in this world, in this body, anytime he'd traveled had been to face some danger, or to run from one.

Now he felt the joy of doing something for the sake of doing it...and he wanted more. Simple adventures of discovering new places he hadn't been before, without an army of undead, or demons, or whatever was waiting at the end of his trip.

The longing pulled at him, and it was a taste of excitement in his throat that made him look at the dark outline of land to the north with anticipation. He wondered what was past all that and thought how much he wanted to find out.

His attention came back to the Captain and Aiyana.

"It's at that broken-down castle," the aeifain was stabbing her finger towards the shoreline. "It's not past it, and we need to go there, not up that river thing."

"Can see the Rumay Ruins from here?" Jaiman squinted towards the land. "Doesn't matter, we're not going to the Ruins, we're heading for the settlement on the northern part of that isle, at the mouth of the Forked Tributary."

"You might be going there," Aiyana didn't look like a young woman as she looked down her nose at the man who stood a half a head taller than her, but rather like an empress giving a command, "but we're going to those Ruins seated on the blue bluffs overlooking the wind and waters. My gut, my magics, and my staff say that's where we'll find Takoven's Rib."

"Don't get all dramatic with me, girl," Jaiman lost his flirtatious demeanor, trading it in for indignant bluster. "I'm Captain on this here vessel, and don't take orders from some elf witch…"

"Oh my god," Torrents moved between the two, who were almost nose to nose, pushing them both a step back with a hand on the captain's and the wizardess's chest, "get a room, you two."

Aiyana met the barbarian's eyes with a glare, and pointedly looked down at his massive hand nestled between her breasts, then slowly back to his face.

"Oh, sorry," Torrents jerked his hand back and Aiyana stumbled forward from the sudden movement, "Didn't mean anything, just trying to make sure you don't blow up the whole ship in a fit of anger."

Jaiman put both his hands on Torrents's hand that was still on his sternum.

"It feels like yer interested in checking out my chest, m'boy," the captain smiled up at the barbarian, "but I don't know if the aft deck is the place for such a tryst."

Torrents jerked his other hand back, and stepped backwards from between the two, wringing his own hands in a mix of nervousness and embarrassment.

"C-captain," Torrents took a deep breath, let it out, and started again, attempting composure. "Let's humor the lady. Drop us at the Ruins, take us to shore in a longboat, and once we're done, we can hike overland and meet you at Rumay City."

"You," Jaiman raised his eyebrows, "want to be let off at a haunted castle, find a relic of power, then cross three dozen kilometers of land and enter a pirate city from the landward side, to find what they'll call a landlocked ship?"

"Uh," Torrents shrugged, "yes?"

"Oh ho," Jaiman clapped his hands, "if you can do all that, and make it to the Tributary Docks, then I'll commission a bard to write a song about each of these adventures, so the land will know what you've done. But I'll take the completion of my payment now, before I turn the prow towards land."

"Why?" Aiyana took a small step forward. "Why do you need the money now? I thought you trusted Torrents?"

"Because," a thick voice said from behind them, "he doesn't expect us to live long enough to pay him."

The three turned to see a pale, shaky Nathan, clutching the railing of the seven steps from midship to the aft castle, stepping onto the raised deck.

"Jonath has warned me," Nathan continued, using his battle-axe like a cane, "that he has little power at the Ruins, and that three wailing princesses control the earth and other elements within those walls."

"Wait," Torrents turned, stepping away from the aeifain wizardess and human captain, to face the rokairn priest, "princesses?"

"Something more akin to banshees," Jaiman nodded, "or some soulless spirits that have sung sailors to their rocky deaths for generations. And the Talisman only seemed to strengthen them when it was in the sky."

Nathan nodded.

"Good," Aiyana smiled, "then it's settled. Torrents, pay the man. We've a boat to catch."

"Fly on the moonless night," Captain Farrell croaked, "stand and deliver!"

## Chapter 17

Torrents, Nathan, and Aiyana stood in front of the moldy walls of a castle. Sheer grey-green stones of fuzzy moss rose to heights that made the trio crane their necks towards the sky.

The building reminded Torrents of a really old cartoon, He-Man and the Masters of the Universe. It had even been a cheesy movie in the century and millennium before he'd been born. It didn't have the skull mouth across a moat with portcullis as teeth Castle Grayskull had sported, but it was still ominous and suggestive of a bad day.

Nathan took up a flanking position behind the barbarian, his feet set at a shoulder width, and his axe held in both hands. The magical vines growing on the haft of the weapon writhed under his fingers. The rokairn looked more fit and ready for action, now that he wasn't on the ship, though he scowled and shook his head at what lie in front of them.

Aiyana stood, staff held to one side, with the raven, Captain Farrell, on the opposite shoulder. The woman breathed in deeply, as if sucking in the essence of the tainted building in front of them.

Carrion birds circled overhead—reminding Torrents of the wyvern that had once circled the Nine Towers of Magic months ago—and the wind made a sound that spoke of paper cuts in the soul. There was a murky moat with floating dark-green vegetation, and a rot-ridden drawbridge between where they stood and the looming entrance that looked like a yawning mouth, long starved and dead from lack of nutrition.

The smell in the air was of decay and of long stagnant water and plants; it crept in and out of the trio's awareness as the three moved forward with caution.

Torrents looked back towards the Broken Sea. The longboat that brought them to the stone wharf had reached the Raptor Rex, and the ship was raising sail and moving away even as the smaller craft was winched upward. Captain Jaiman really, really wanted to be far away from here before anything happened that could threaten his ship and crew.

With a nod, Torrents pulled his two-handed blade from the scabbard on his back, shoved his satchel behind him, and stepped forward.

The other two followed, no one speaking.

They moved around time-rotted holes in the thick wooden planks of the drawbridge, their feet muffled on the spongy growth of moss underfoot.

The air grew chill as they stepped onto solid ground again and moved through the gaping hole of the outer wall.

The courtyard ahead was littered with thorny, flowerless weeds. Though it was still early autumn, the wind bit like the season had turned the calendar forward three months, and spoke in whispers that threatened their thoughts, hinting at a thousand ways to hurt them.

The inner walls of the courtyard held broken-down buildings. An open-air smithy showed a huge, rusted anvil, and tools littered the weed-choked cobblestones that had melted with age and humidity. The collapsed stables looked to have once housed dozens of mounts. A horse skeleton glared through empty eye sockets from under the broken roof.

The castle itself was a stereotype of concept. Four towers—one at each corner—rose three stories high; square stone walls with evenly spaced arrow slits along the ground level, held stained glass on the second story lining the face of the building. The windows, once vibrant and bright, now reminded Torrents of headlights that had gone foggy and muted, showed a dim memory of light that had once shone true.

Rats the size of cats sidled out of massive cracks in the walls of the castle ahead of them. Three dozen formed a rough semi-circle around the structure. They rose to their hindquarters as one and hissed a broken screech.

A faint, shrill scream echoed off the walls. The three exchanged glances, unsure if it was the wind or something more.

The stout double doors to the castle crashed open, flying outward to slam against the walls of the small alcove they were in. A ragged, torn form—long and thin, trailing streamers of mist behind it—flew from the opening, rising above the trio. Two others followed, each heading to opposite walls to flank the intruders.

The ground under their feet writhed.

Torrents looked down to see hundreds of huge wriggling centipedes, fast-moving shiny cockroaches, dark iridescent beetles, and fat glistening flies erupting from the moss-filled cracks between the cobblestones.

The cold stones underfoot warmed, the green fungus turning brown and smoldering as red lines of heat appeared between the flagstones.

Torrents and Nathan began an odd dance, raising their feet high, then dropping one and lifting the other. Each step brought the crunch and squish of the chitinous vermin under their boots as they tried to stop the things from swarming up their legs and under their armor. The smell of the crushed creatures rose to their noses, causing them to cough and gag from the bitter, caustic stench.

Aiyana raised her staff and slammed the butt on the ground, with a dull boom. Water splashed around her, becoming ice in an instant, crackling and crinkling, coating the stones beneath their feet with a hiss. The insects shriveled and popped with the sudden temperature change.

The rokairn and human took a step closer to her, entering the circle of protection her magics offered from the attack of thousands of carrion-eating attackers that now swarmed the courtyard.

"This is just messed up," Torrents raised his voice to be heard over the hum of white noise from the insects, the screech of the rats, and the shrill scream of the three spirits overhead, "how do we even fight this?"

"Dead zone for me," Nathan growled, looking around frantically. "I can't feel the touch of Jonath; it's like he's locked out of the walls of this cursed place."

"Use your axe, priest," Aiyana's voice was calm, and filled the area to muffle the sounds around the three, "call upon the druidic power of nature within Marcid."

"Okay, I'll give that a try," Nathan nodded, gripping his axe tighter and hunching his shoulders over the weapon. "Come on, Marcid, old girl, let's mess these things up."

Seeds caught and smothered by the moss covering the ground within the walls responded to the call of Marcid, and tendrils of stalks pushed their way into the wane sunlight, blossoming into flowers, then transforming into hungry pods of Venus flytraps, sundews, and pitcher plants. Flowers threw off seeds in puffs and wherever they landed, more of the carnivorous flowers sprouted.

Leafy minions snapped closed when the insects overran them, the plants bending under the weight of the sheer numbers of the enemy.

The screeching spirits above darted through the air. As one, they turned and speared towards the intruders. The wispy faces of cowled women came into sharp focus, their jaws unhinging and dropping wide enough to swallow the head of a person.

The rats dropped back to all fours and charged forward, scampering in a zig-zag path towards the circle that protected the three companions.

"Good work, Nathan." Aiyana raised her staff in one hand, and Captain Farrell danced on the opposite shoulder, the surrounding air exploding outward, knocking the spirits from their trajectory. "Torrents, keep those rats at bay. I shall handle the ladies of the mist."

Torrents stepped to the edge of the frozen ground, dropping to one knee—bug carapaces crunching—and swung his massive blade across the path of the overgrown rodents. Steel met bone and won the contest. Rats burst with the impact, and the barbarian swept three to one side as their bodies exploded.

Aiyana began chanting and the Eye of Agnew burst into a blue-white glow, the Finger of Yender bending to point the crystal towards the doors flung open moments ago.

The wizardess stepped forward, the icy circle around her extending, becoming an oval, then an elongated pathway.

The screaming spirits recovered, and swirled around one another, then split into three again and rushed towards the aeifain and her charges.

Molten earth bubbled up from the cracks between the stones underfoot, spilling over onto the icy path and melting it.

"Oh chuz." Torrents rose to his feet again, stepping forward to keep ahead of Aiyana's slow but steady advance, sweeping his blade at the rats who threw themselves in front of them. "The ground is, literally, lava. This game isn't as fun as I imagined as a kid."

"You're still a kid, kid." Nathan faced the rear and walked backwards, his fingers red and his knuckles white from the tight grip on Marcid, keeping the bloom of plants continuous to neutralize the insect threat. "Now, less talking, more…um, death and destruction?"

"Can I…add that…to a…resume later?" Torrents's words came one or two at a time, spaced between sword swings.

Aiyana stopped and looked up at the ghostly apparitions above, knowing she wouldn't be able to follow the path that led inside to Takoven's Rib without dealing with them first.

Wind swirled around her, moving the hem of her black robes, ruffling the silver and white cuffs. Frost formed in the surrounding air, and a light snow drifted to the ground, hissing on the glowing red cobblestones and the lava that rose between them.

This was a matter of saving the world. At least Aiyana believed it to be so. The five artifacts were created—birthed, if you will—to bring balance and throw off the oppressive yoke of magical tyrants who wanted the magic all for themselves. If she failed, then this land, and all the people of it, would become slaves to people who horded the power and wealth of magic and all the ills and woes of being oppressed by a selfish master.

The aeifain knew she could make a difference but wasn't sure if she would. The magics drained her, pulling the energy from her whenever she used herself as a conduit. If she failed, countless people would die or suffer because of her weakness.

She steadied herself and pressed on.

The ground rumbled, the stones around the trio rising higher, elevating the insect swarm to knee level, then thigh height. The lava poured into the frozen circle created by Aiyana, coming closer, shrinking their protective circle.

Nathan couldn't call upon his god here, the lord and master of the element of earth. Aiyana couldn't touch the tainted ley lines of the elements of earth or fire, because the elementalist spirits of three sisters who'd died to become immortal and rulers of this enclosed realm they'd created a thousand years before Durgan's Keep was conceived had claimed them.

Aiyana felt that connection, the one created by the bond of blood and soul of three women who overthrew the patricidal line to create a haven from the world. But it was tainted, as only spilling innocent blood could do. The thing these women hated, is what they'd become.

The wizardess sighed, and tears brimmed her eyes. The three spirits that now defended their corrupted dream couldn't see how it had failed, how they'd changed what they'd meant to be pure into a dark mirror of what they'd fought against. She mourned the sisters and reached out with the elements she could touch.

Wind tore at the screeching forms, ripping away their ethereal essence, shredding the protective figures that had become tyrants. The incorporeal bodies stretching across the space above the aeifain were surrounded by water particulates—coating and solidifying them for the first time in over three score generations—and became chained by gravity. They fell towards the stones below them.

Hitting the ground, the beings shattered, the spiritual energy within their icy cocoons flying in all directions to release the souls.

Howling winds and the screeches of the women became a sigh on the breeze. The swarm of insects burned from the heat of the ground; the protection of their enslaving mistresses lost. The remaining bugs scattered in the growing light. Raised cobblestones fell back to the ground in a widening circle, and the courtyard once again became level.

The handful of rats that hadn't died to the blade of the barbarian ran off, frantically searching for a place to hide.

"Stand and deliver," Captain Farrell croaked from Aiyana's shoulder as she strode forward, moving through the doorway to the inner keep.

Nathan and Torrents followed the aeifain into the dim interior. Doors and passageways lined the stout hall, disappearing from their perception as they kept pace with the wizardess.

The staff in Aiyana's hand glowed and the Finger of Yender pointed the Eye of Agnew, clenched in its knuckles, deeper into the building.

Dust rose in small clouds with each step forward, and a thick musty smell filled their nostrils. Empty guardian suits of armor lined the hallway, the coppery taste of aged blood and metal filled their mouths.

Their skin crawled with the feeling of being watched by something ancient and curious. Small arcs of static electricity danced in the upper corners of the tall ceiling, revealing faded tapestries showing scenes of battles and men kneeling to receive the blessings of kings and priests.

A large, round chamber appeared in the grey shadows of the interior, lit by slanting muted sunlight from the slits of windows above.

In the center of the room, a large, curved bone—flat and rectangular on its sides—floated the height of a tall man off the ground. A hole in the flagstones of the floor was below it, and a dark cloud riddled with flares of lightning hovered above it.

"Takoven's Rib," Aiyana breathed, "has been reborn. The archmagi has sent his contribution in answer to the seed I planted on this isle."

Her voice was quiet, reverent, and she stepped forward, lifting her staff towards the artifact.

The staff rose from her grip when she opened her hand. The Finger of Yender—still twisted around the Eye of Agnew—slid from the protective sleeve of the wooden vessel and drifted towards the curved skeletal icon. A frenzy of ice and precipitation swirled around the items, and the bottom joints of the Finger curled around the scepter of the rib, becoming one before sliding back into the staff. The newly reformed artifact slowly drifted back to Aiyana's waiting hand.

The three stared at the event, silent as their thoughts soaked up the moment.

A large stone fell from the domed ceiling, causing the building to rumbled and shift. Another crashed down, then another. Light burst through the new openings above, streaking down into pools of dancing dust above the floor.

The wizardess stared at the staff in her hand, familiar with her arcane carvings, but now something totally new.

"Fly on the moonless night!" Captain Farrell shouted, and took wing, flapping back the way they'd come.

"Oh no," Nathan grabbed Aiyana's forearm and jerked her around towards the exit, "we should go, now!"

"Is it me," Torrents spun on a heel, sword in one hand and the other wrapping around the mesmerized aeifain's waist, "or is the chuzzing sky falling?"

Torrents swept up the wizardess, her toes dragging along the ground, and the priest her arm.

Nathan set his feet, squared his shoulders, hunkered down, and ran. The barbarian followed the rokairn towards the double doors that led to the outside.

Stones the size of a man's chest fell around them, exploding on impact with the floor. The light of the opening seemed further away than they'd traveled to get to the antechamber that had held the magical artifact.

Torrents scooped up the rokairn priest in the crook of his other arm—the one that held his sword—carrying both of his friends and lengthening his long strides even more.

They burst into the courtyard, the hall collapsing into rubble behind them, dust and detritus billowing out all around the hunched barbarian, his two companions protected in the shelter of his larger form.

The ground outside buckled and lurched, stones popping up like a deadly game of whack-a-mole.

"Keep going!" Torrents yelled.

He set Nathan down and shoved him forward, swinging Aiyana over his shoulder in a fireman's carry, her staff hitting him in the side of his head, as it was pinned under her body and lay against his shoulder.

They ran across the courtyard, dodging the flagstones that leapt in the air, and sped through the yawning maw of the gate and onto the drawbridge.

Crossing the planks of the aged defensive door that spanned the murky moat, now half gone from the earthquake that was the cause, or the result of, the collapsing castle.

The three turned, Aiyana coming to her senses when Torrents set her down, and watched the structure fall into itself, dust rising above it.

## Chapter 18

Torrents stared at the wall that surrounded Rumay Bay. It wasn't much more than sharpened stakes and reeds, encircling the pirate city that was the jewel of the northern side of the isle. But it was a huge contrast to the bleak castle they'd left yesterday.

Using the term 'city' was generous. It was a collection of shanties, huts, and structures made of wooden beams and thatch roofs. The larger structures had wooden plank walls, but most were cob, set with straw, sand, and mud loaves.

The wide inlet from the Broken Sea allowed ships to dock, but most vessels were sleek and small, with only the most experienced captains daring to bring a larger ship to harbor.

The locals dressed in loose clothing: knee breeches, sleeved blouses, vests, and long socks or knee boots. Hats were the custom here, keeping the sun off in the summer and insulating the head in the colder weather.

"Rumay Bay," Captain Jaiman pronounced it Roo-may, "is an old town, named for the rum it ran in the old days, supplied by sugar cane plantations across the delta. The hurricanes of the Talisman flattened the stone buildings that originally stood here, and no one saw fit to rebuild them afterwards. Easier to rebuild wood and straw than stone."

"When can we go north to Dioneze City?" Aiyana pressed, anxiety and deadlines implied in her tone.

"What's your rush, girl?" Jaiman laughed. "It's hard country to the north, and I've put the right bribes and sent messages to the right people to get us through, but it takes time. And we've only just unloaded our cargo; we still need time to load the bales and crates we'll take north for trade in Dioneze City."

"I'm sorry," Nathan wiped at the sweat on his brow, even though it was autumn, "she seems to have picked up a sense of urgency as we move further into this whole thing."

"Grog or ale?" Torrents's question made the whole table stare at him. "I know they don't mix, but they both sound good, and I'm not sure which one to pick."

"Ale," Jaiman nodded, "you can drink longer with it, get less drunk, and save the grog to help you sleep before bed."

"Good thinking," Torrents smiled, "glad I asked someone with experience with this."

The four were standing around a tall table that came to just above Torrents's waist, chest height on Aiyana, and up to Nathan's nose.

"And it's best to wait for the tide," Jaiman turned back to Aiyana, who was chewing on her lip, "and move upriver with two teams of horses. Coming back down is much easier because it goes with the current."

"Until then," Torrents waved at the buxom woman carrying a tray of drinks, "I'll buy the drinks."

Aiyana picked at her meal of crabs, shrimp, and seaweed salad, lost in thought.

The next step in the chain of artifacts was the Spine of Japria. She'd planted it in the brutal settlement of Dioneze City, a place ruled by might and cruelty. She had a vague recollection of the time spent there by her previous self.

The wisps of shadowy memory were of her hiding and disguising herself, usually comprising of a raised hood and downcast eyes, shifting through the populace that would as soon sell you to the gladiator ring as slipping a blade between your ribs. Either way, they got your boots, belt, cloak, and other possessions.

The rough and uncouth people of Rumay Bay seemed kind and cosmopolitan compared to the vague understanding Aiyana had of the place to the north. At least here, most people were laughing, and content to keep to themselves or their small groups made up of their clan, family, or clique.

She spooned a thick sauce, spiced with peppers, over boiled potatoes, considering the trail she'd laid out before she was even here. The last stop had been her first, the Eye of Agnew. It had belonged to a powerful Mind Mage nearly a millennium ago and saw beyond what mortal eyes could perceive.

The Finger of Yender was an ancient relic of one of the Troll Lords, a being that had been of the race that both trolls and aeifain had branched from. The elemental magics within this single digit—of a long dead being that walked the realm seven thousand years ago—could focus and blend other magics.

Takoven's Rib was steeped in the holy conduit that led to the trickle-down magic of gods, though not just any god, but the Changing Wheel, who was the one god that all other gods bowed to. Legend said that Takoven, the priest whom it had belonged to, had been instrumental in turning away the comet called Talisman that changed the face of the planet during the Downfall, and every moment afterwards.

It was rumored that the Spine of Japria blended earth and air, made of magical metal from the Talisman itself, and thus steeped in alchemical magic.

The last artifact, though…that relic was lost in Aiyana's memory. She couldn't put her finger on what it was supposed to be. Her former self had planted it somewhere in Runsk, and she could feel the echoes of its voice. She didn't know if it came from her memory or from the perception of the collection of magical items that now incubated in her staff.

The last item was linked to the elements of earth and fire, as well as summoning magic that allowed someone to call beings from other places. It was also supposed to allow the holder to be called to other places in this world, or another world altogether. She didn't know what form it was supposed to take, but thought teleportation was high on the list of probabilities.

Her other self knew, but had buried the knowledge deep, hiding it. Aiyana wondered if this was to protect the information from others, or so she herself could still come back for it, not realizing the consequences it would carry.

It was night and Aiyana wondered when that had happened. Tiki torches lit the sandy pathways between buildings, and sailors caroused and sang bawdy tunes of sex, monsters, death, boobs, drinking, lovely lasses, and hidden treasures waiting to be found. The wizardess felt a tinge of prophecy in more than one of those themes.

She returned to the Raptor Rex, preferring to sleep on board so she could do whatever she could to make sure they left at the first thing in the morning.

Nathan, Aiyana, and Torrents had been in Dioneze City for a week before a city patrol took them to the slave pits.

It had taken six days to travel up Dioneze River to the trading post that had grown at the border of the city. The horse team on the walking path next to the waterway pulled them northward by day, and they'd anchored so the team could rest at night. It was necessary to set watch after dark to keep an eye out for brigands and marauders. They'd only been attacked twice, and both times Torrents and Nathan had been on shore to turn them back.

The rokairn had insisted on staying on shore with the teamsters who worked the horses, preferring it to the constant rocking of the ship. Torrents had joined the smaller man, but Aiyana stayed on board, alternating between basking in the elements and 'fine-tuning' her newly upgraded staff.

They left the company of Captain Jaiman Rabbit and the crew of the Raptor Rex at the trading post and traveled north, across the slave-dug trench that had widened into a stream over the following decades, and later swelled to a full-blown river from storms during the Downfall.

The overland journey from the trade post to the city had taken two days, and patrols from the city had often stopped the three friends on the road to check papers and wring bribes from travelers. The documentation Jaiman provided covered the first part. The remaining gold from their stockpile from Seawall City, supplemented by gems from Nathan's pouches, covered the last.

The patrols weren't in unified colors and outfits like Seawall City. They didn't even have standard issue gear like the watch in Durgan's Keep. The men and women who stopped them on the road weren't much different from the roving bandits who assaulted them on their trip upriver.

Piecemeal armor would be a kind way to describe their gear. Most had spears and clubs, with the strongest—usually the leader—carrying a rust-pocked sword, and maybe a steel chest plate or a shield. Most had bits of leather armor strapped on that didn't fit well, scavenged from whoever they'd killed who couldn't pay the 'tax'.

Aiyana's urgency had infected both Nathan and Torrents, though the rokairn showed it more than the barbarian.

The priest had fallen into a dour mood and spoke little. When he did, it was usually in short, clipped answers, without apologies tacked on.

The city itself, when they'd gotten close enough to see it, was like the patrols they'd met on the road.

The wall surrounding Dioneze City was constructed of timbers, sharpened at the top, with a walkway behind it that men in conical steel helmets patrolled. Thin watch towers of wood coated with something that dully reflected the sunlight were set at every fifty paces.

Five gates allowed entrance to the city, each with groups of men of various numbers guarding it, and people trickled in and out. Few of the hunched merchants and travelers at the gates, beaten down by the world, looked up or made eye contact.

Aiyana kept her hood up, the memory of the prejudice of her people firm in her mind. The only human city closer to the territory the aeifain had once inhabited was Runsk, and the discrimination against her kind was almost as prevalent here as there.

They did not view rokairns with the same level of disdain, though they didn't accept them as equals to humans, and Nathan stood out more than someone of his physical stature should.

Torrents purchased lodging at a rundown inn at the edge of the city, close to the wooden parapet that passed for a wall. The wine and ale were watered down, the spirits served were harsh and biting, and meals were more watery liquid and potatoes than meat. The rooms were squalid, a curtain separating their space from the hall, and they'd taken to sleeping in shifts to make sure no one came in.

Their weapons and armor—not to mention Aiyana's staff—drew more attention than it was worth. On their second day they hid them in a hole they dug outside of the city; except Aiyana's staff, which they covered the top with a burlap sack, and the shaft with cloth strips.

Roaming the streets during the day, they searched for the Spine of Japria. The rokairn and barbarian followed Aiyana, who appeared to be rich woman trailed by her two bodyguards.

The wizardess led them back and forth through the city streets, searching for the magical emanations that would indicate the relic was close by. Something was interfering, making them backtrack and double back, but never quite leading them to their quarry.

By a process of elimination, they'd decided it had to be somewhere near the arena in the center of the city.

It was their fourth day in the city when the street cleared, as if by an unheard and immediate command, and three patrols surrounded them. A sling whirred, and with a sharp crack, a stone hit Aiyana on the side of her head, dropping her to the ground unconscious.

Captain Farrell took to wing, stones whizzing past him as he disappeared above the rooftops.

The dozen men were upon them before Torrents could draw the short sword he carried, or Nathan could pull the hand axe from his belt.

In less than a minute, surrounded by spears and swords, they disarmed, bound, and led the two men away into slavery. They gagged, bound, and tossed the wizardess into the back of a wagon.

## Chapter 19

The wide, shallow basin churned as Khizhane poured the mercurial compound into the alcohol solution resting on the tripod over the blue, focused flame.

The liquid swirled, bubbled rapidly, then fell into a flat mirror-like surface. Moments later, a rough, unshaven face sporting an eyepatch appeared on the surface like he was leaning over and looking up from below.

"Khizhane," Manalo Maqsher, Lord of the Pit, and Slave Master of Dioneze City sneered, "so good to see you again."

The man's tone spoke volumes of disdain, and his twisted smile made the master alchemist cringe.

Khizhane pulled himself together with effort; he was supposed to be the one in control of this relationship. He'd reached out and found this man, paying him in power. He was the one pulling the strings, not the other way around.

The administrator had known guys like this, they'd bullied him his whole life. Once, not so long ago, he'd have reacted to the man's tone, feeding into it by demanding respect. But Khizhane had learned demands meant the other person had control. If you let them dictate your reactions, you weren't the one in charge.

Khizhane cleared his throat, let a small smile play across his lips, then relaxed his face into a complacent curiosity. He waited, cocking his head slightly, looking down into his viewing dish. He knew the man on the other side was a powerful thug in his world, but nothing more than a tool and a hyperactive insect in Khizhane's, and the man feared him. That's why the man poured on the bravado, to ease his worry.

Manalo was holding a device created by Khizhane, a magical item that allowed them to speak across thousands of kilometers as if in the same room, barring any storms that might interfere. This wasn't the kind of thing most people ever even dreamed of hearing tales about, let alone holding in one's hand.

"Lord Khizhane," Manalo's smile slipped a moment as he corrected to adjust for his patron's title, "forgive me. I've been dealing with many things. The good news is that one of those things was the three people you're hunting."

"I shall overlook your insolence," Khizhane waved his hand in dismissal, "but do remember the potions I gave you to see magical energy and gather power can also sour at my whim. They'll do more than cause you to have the runs and vomit a bit. They'll eat away at your insides, taking control of you until you are nothing more than a squalid sack of..."

Khizhane stopped, waving his hand again with a bored sigh.

"You know this already, Lord Maqsher," Khizhane's face lit up as if remembering something, "but wait, you're not a lord, yet. You're just some keeper of a pit. A simple slave master, waiting for things to happen so you can take the title you so desperately desire. But I don't need to remind you of these things. You know well enough to not forget, even after you gain that title from my support and blessing."

He delivered the last sentence deadpan, a dark threat in it.

"Uh, of course," Manalo swallowed, straightened up, and pulled himself together. "Of course, Lord Khizhane. I'm grateful for your patronage and support. I am but your loyal servant."

The face looking up at Khizhane bent closer to the surface of the basin, as the man bowed to him from a quarter of the continent away.

"Since I've lost contact with the whelp Ghe'hak, I must rely on you for now. Tell me about the aeifain and her lackeys." Khizhane smiled, in part to the man's reaction, and in part because of the news. "Did you recover all of the artifacts?"

"Yes," Manalo's words spilled out in a tumble, eager to move past the awkward moment, "we have her staff. It has the crystal, the rib, and a really weird, huge finger stuck in the top of it."

"That's it?" Khizhane frowned, cleared his throat, and furrowed his brow, staring into the bowl. "That's not what I wanted to hear."

Manalo's jaw worked, and he locked his lips as he searched for words to remove the look of concern on the Councilor's face.

"They're in chains," the petty lord glanced behind him, possibly looking at the prisoners. "I can have them on a ship tomorrow and heading to you."

"No," Khizhane cleared his throat, "just the staff is fine. Use the Nexus Room in the catacombs below the city. Break one of the ley line generators I sent you. It should create enough power to open a portal to me."


Ghe'hak the Ravager watched the scene, growling quietly, low, and deep in his throat. The gnohl was a shadow, nothing more than a passing thought in the corner, his quarry chained to a wall, and Manalo bent over the scrying pool in the center of the room. He saw and heard everything in the chamber, his mind struggled with wanting to serve the voice coming from the bowl, and rebelling against it.

The pitiful human bowing and scraping made the gnohl's stomach to churn. After he'd finished sucking up to a man thousands of kilometers away, Manalo turned from the scrying device, wiping his brow, and fingering his eyepatch.

Khizhane held a loose thread of control that only existed in Manalo's imagination, but it was enough. The slaver didn't know what could happen, what the alchemist could truly do, which was a powerful motivator in making Manalo do what Khizhane wanted. The man on the other side of the scrying bowl was a master manipulator.

Disgusted by Manalo's weakness, the gnohl's jowl drew back, baring his canines.

Ghe'hak needed the three prisoners free, but without Khizhane knowing they were still alive and working against his plans. They had to continue their mission if he was going to complete his.

After following the wizardess and the two men through the sewers of Durgan's Keep and facing the dragon, he'd hid around the corner from the nexus chamber. When they passed through, he hadn't seen which gateway they'd used, and leapt into one of the six portals.

He'd come out in Runsk, a day's travel to the west of Dioneze City, and couldn't smell his quarry anywhere. Using the magic given to him by Khizhane, the gnohl realized he wasn't even in the same city as his targets. He'd killed dozens of people in a savage rage, and once he felt better, he headed east to find them.

He'd been in Dioneze City for a few days, lurking in alleys and on rooftops, before catching their scent. It was fresh, and he'd tracked them to a poorly defended building of weak and inebriated humans who preferred drinking to killing.

He'd never understood that. Feeling broken in your mind by brewed drinks made no sense to him. Why would anyone decide to taint their senses with concoctions that veiled the world, instead of acting with a clear head? It was a sickness that humans cherished.

He'd found the wizardess and her guards as they'd buried their armor and weapons in a stand of trees an hour's walk from the city. Then the pemties were captured and imprisoned by Manalo, the inferior male who quivered at veiled threats, instead of killing the bastard who made them.

Now, crouched in a corner, the gnohl looked from the sweating man who'd spoken to Khizhane through magics to the three people he needed to complete their quest to create a magical artifact that would open the door between worlds.

Did he kill the man and free the people? Or did he take the lesser artifact and hope it could do what he needed?

He growled louder, frustration and anger bubbling up and boiling over, and the man—Manalo Maqsher—turned to squint into the darkness where the gnohl hid.

That was enough, he made up his mind.

Ghe'hak leapt forward, claws and teeth bared.

The man went down, blood spraying from claw marks down his face, tearing the eyepatch away. Identical marks ran down the man's chest and belly. Manalo's head bounced on the stone floor, his good eye glazing, then sliding closed.

The aeifain woman stirred as the gnohl crouched over Manalo. Knowing they couldn't see him, that they couldn't know he hunted them, he had to hide again.

Ghe'hak snatched up the magical staff leaning against the table holding the bowl the man had spoken into, then darted back into the shadows. The wizardess blinked, trying to focus through the haze of her muddled perception.

He climbed, fingers digging between the fitted stones of the basement wall and squeezed into the space between two of the rafters overhead. Now, he was just another vague shadow in the dancing light of the oil lamps and the dim glow of charcoal braziers. He wedged the staff crossways between the rafters above him.

The gnohl watched the woman try to call upon the element of wind, her hands jerking in the manacles and mumbled words spilling out around the gag in her mouth. The two men, similarly restrained, jerked as an unseen force slapped them.

The barbarian jerked his head back, which thudded against the wall. The big man swore, the words undecipherable behind his gag. The rokairn shook his head to clear it and winced from the movement.

They'd been drugged. Even if Ghe'hak hadn't seen the viscous liquid poured down their throats, he smelled the acrid scent on them.

The woman wrinkled her brow in concentration, and the keys on Manalo's belt jingled and danced, the jailor's blood-soaked shirt flapping in the unnatural breeze.

The man moaned and rolled to his side, vomiting. His hand moved to his midsection, and he flinched as he touched the open wounds on his belly.

The witch looked around, looking for some other way to escape. Her eyes fell on the small item that Maqsher had dropped. She mumbled something, turning to look at the big human chained beside her. Lifting her foot to point, while pointing as best she could with her hands. The item flew into the air and towards the large human's hand. The barbarian jerked to the side, snatching the small leather pouch from the air as it bounced off the wall above his arm and fell. He closed his hand around it, hiding it in his grip.

The sound of boots and voices came from the hall beyond the heavy closed wooden door, and a bearded face appeared at the opening framed with iron bars, his bloodshot eyes darting around the interior.

The three prisoners feigned unconsciousness, their heads lolling, and their chains jangling as they went limp.

"Get in here, you damned pemtie fools!" Manalo's voice was pained as he pushed to his knees, still clutching his guts. "Fetch a chirurgeon; these bastards did something to me."

The door flew open, and four men pushed inside, a fifth taking up guard outside, and a sixth moving back the way they'd come to find the surgeon.

"Help me up," Manalo waved his free hand at the two men, "and someone let the Arena Master know that we'll be having a special show at sunset. I want traps on the walls, beasts in the pit, and archers in the stands to make sure these bastards get what's coming to them!"

Another man turned and left the room, rushing to do as Manalo commanded. One man moved towards the slave master to help him up.

The remaining two moved towards the prisoners, unshackling them from the walls one at a time. They started with the rokairn, his heavy form dropping to the ground. The guards connected the manacles between the priest's feet, so a short length of chain allowed shuffling movements.

They shook Nathan, then slapped him hard. The rokairn's eyes fluttered open, his glare of anger causing the men to step away.

They repeated the process with the barbarian, then the wizardess, checking her gag as well. They took extra time to cover her hands with rough sacks, forcing her fingers into fists so she couldn't make the somatic gestures required for casting, before locking her wrists behind her back.

The chirurgeon and a dozen guards arrived as the prisoners were forced to their feet. The female surgeon went to work on cleaning and binding Manalo's chest and belly wounds.

Four men held each prisoner. A fifth pinched the captive's nose closed, pulled the gag free, and with his other hand—which held a glass vial of dark liquid—held poised at the lips of the restrained person. When each of them finally gasped for breath, he forced the potion into their mouth and poured it inside. The man administering the dose jammed his hand under the prisoner's jaw, forcing their mouth closed, making them swallow.

They led the prisoners away, Manalo in the lead, walking slowly and clutching his guts. The guards formed a living wall on all sides of the rokairn, human, and aeifain, with the surgeon trailing behind.

Ghe'hak watched the procession leave the room, Manalo looking around with worry, trying to spot either the thing he'd dropped, the staff, or both.

The gnohl wanted to kill the barbarian and priest because of what they'd done to him, his pack, and his mistress. But it was because of them he was now able to become his own master. And besides, the elf witch would need them again if she was going to find the remaining artifacts and build the relic the gnohl would use to open a portal for armies of demons.

Once the sounds of the procession disappeared down the hall and up the stairs at the end that led to the arena the gnohl dropped to the floor.

He had the staff but needed to get to the arena in case he had to help them escape. The three prisoners were capable but the same flaw that many of their races had: compassion. They might not kill when they should.

If pursued, Ghe'hak would be the one killing their hunters, and would enjoy it. Every throat cut, or torn out, every life taken would be something he looked forward to.

## Chapter 20

People carrying skins of wine and shouting to friends and vendors filled the arena. The structure took up four city blocks and was one of the few stone and mortar buildings that was taller than a single story.

The outer walls of the arena rose higher than any other building in Dioneze City, and the inner walls were higher than most of the eaves of the structures surrounding it.

Guards swaggered through the crowd, pushing people to one side as they walked along the stair-step like benches, or moved up and down the ramps between seating areas. People moved out of the way, avoiding looking at the protectors of the city, knowing the rough men were just as likely to rob them, legally, as protect them.

Most of the crowd wore rough, woven linen in greys, browns, and the occasional red or yellow made from dyes of the binaple bushes that were plentiful in this part of the world. Woman wore face coverings, wrapped loosely around their heads to hide the chance that their beauty, or youth, would attract attention.

Most people had a weapon at their side, usually the thick, short dagger blade that were bought and sold in the city. It was a slightly curved design, recognizable as Dionezen. The stunted cross guard often held markings of their family, the maker, or favored gladiators they cheered for in the arena.

The smell of the gathering was the tangy, salty mix of sweat from unwashed bodies soaked into clothing, and dung that clung to them from the clumps of horse manure many used for nightly fires. It blended with the sharp bite of the cheeses—liberally mixed with peppers—popular in this region, and the overhanging waft of garlic and onions that often accompanied the peppers.

The sun hung heavy in the western sky, a thick miasma of grey clouds striping the horizon in a shadow that foretold cold weather. Night birds called; their high-pitched songs interrupted by the callous call of a raven somewhere in the jutting wooden beams the walls of the arena.

The crowd rose to its feet, the throng jeering as three people were shoved onto the sands of the fighting pit. Sharpened wooden spikes slid from holes in the walls, and winches cranked back willowy branches that would snap forward when touched by anyone within the ring of blood.

Swaggering guards, tasked with making certain no combatant escaped, took places in the front row, leaning quivers of arrows or bundles of short spears on the knee-high wall that ringed the spectacle. They strung bows and stretched muscles. Every soldier wanted the extra coins for stopping someone trying to escape, but were afraid of punishment for acting before the time was right.

Nathan shook his head, his knotted beard scraping his bare chest, trying to clear the chemical cobwebs of whatever they'd forced down his throat from his mind. It burned, his larynx raw and ragged. He stared at his feet covered in a thin layer of piss-yellow sand, wondering where his boots were, and why he wasn't wearing them.

Blood came to his mind, but he didn't know why. Sound pressed down on him, as if a thousand people were screaming a warning of his death. Or perhaps cheering for it, he couldn't tell.

"Jonath," he groaned, his lips stiff from dehydration, and his head pounding, "I think I need you."

The rokairn looked around, realizing he'd fallen to his knees.

The roar of the crowd beyond his blurred vision crackled with laughter. The mocking sounds reminded him of the bullies on the playground who'd so often pushed him off the spinning metal merry-go-round in his childhood. It had caused many scraped knees.

He shook his head again, shoving the memory away, and pain bumped inside his skull. It wasn't sharp, but it was like think, moist cotton filled the inside of his head and the motion jabbed against blunted nerves.

"Jonath," he mumbled again, his hands curling their fingers into one another. The sensation muted and he looked down to see two fingers between two others and wondered why there wasn't one finger from one hand, then another from the other.

He lost track of the thought, though the skin between his fingers itched with the wrongness of his grip.

"I," he burbled, his voice slacking off to nothingness as he grasped at the thought, "I, need help. I don't have fire to burn the fog."

He wondered what he was talking about, and shook his head slowly, so the pain didn't jostle his thoughts.

"I need to think, Jonath," he hadn't realized his hands were unshackled until they he'd tangled them in his matted hair as he ran them across his scalp, nails digging into the desensitized flesh, "and I know you don't do fire, but you protect your own. Help me. Help. Me."

The crowd was singing, almost. It was rhythmic and carried the suggestion of a tune, but it wasn't singing.

"Let me," tears cut paths down the priest's dirty cheeks, "think. Please, grant me this boon. Let my body, no, mind free from the…thing, shackles, chains, prison that holds it, please."

The rokairn fell face down into the sands, his hands spasmodically gripping the grainy texture of the floor of the arena.

The priest's awareness cleared.

It wasn't like clouds parting, like the stories say, or light dawning. His thoughts crumbled like an avalanche, rocks of awareness tumbling into a pile that cleared the path ahead.

He raised his gaze, and saw the rounded walls, the crowd on their feet on top, double fists in the air, chanting for blood and pain and death.

His mind opened, though his body was sluggish. He knew where he was, but not how he got here. It didn't matter, only what he did next would matter.

Dark apertures opened in the walls, smooth forms darting in for the kill. Others slinked out, hugging the walls, seeking a better position to attack.

Nathan stared at the apex predators with pointed snouts and thick, scaly bodies with triple-beveled ridges down their backs. Long tongues writhed from the elongated mouths, short cilium-like tendrils on the mutant appendages jutting from their maws—that appeared prehensile—waving in the air, as four smooth tendrils on each side of the beast's heads writhed in anticipation.

They made him think of crocodiles—if crossbred with Dobermans—but the size of wolves. They displayed pack tactics, a few moving to attack and the others circling to flank. Their jaws looked capable of crushing skulls, their wiry muscles corded and powerful.

"Croco-wolves?" He cocked his head, then pulled his awareness away from the distant concept of defining his enemy and focused on protecting himself and his friends from the creatures.

Nathan looked around, taking the scene in with a glance.

The crowd cheered with the bloodlust of someone who'd never faced death themselves. The guard's faces showed greed and hunger. Nobles sat in a canopy of entitlement at the prime vantage point of the circle of the arena, raised above the crowd by an arms-length.

His friends stared blankly as death lunged towards them.

"Torrents, look alive!" he shouted at the barbarian, the warrior lost in a drug stupor.

Jonath may have cleared his head, but it hadn't extended to the others. Torrents was slack-jawed and staring at the attackers without comprehending the danger.

"Jonath's stony fist," the priest swore, and reached for his friend, shaking the man, gripping the barbarian's shoulders, "get a chuzzing weapon, you simple-minded pemtie!"

Torrents didn't respond.

Nathan slapped the young man, making the barbarian's head jerk backwards.

A fist sent Nathan tumbling heels over head, blood bursting down his chin, the wet coppery taste of the liquid mixing with the sharp, spinning starburst of pain as he rolled to his feet to see Torrents coming for him.

"Not me!" Nathan shouted, pointing at the creatures gliding towards them. "Get them, kill them, defend us!"

The big man looked around, not understanding. Then a creature leapt on Torrents, its clawed feet gouging the man's shoulders and its tongue slid across his face, leaving a glittering trail.

Instinct took over. The barbarian grabbed the thing's jaws and forced them wider, the bottom mandible ripping free under his powerful grip. The tongue wrapped around the man's forearm and Torrents screamed in rage and pain, the tentacular appendage digging into his flesh.

The man ripped the lower jaw loose, flipped it in his hand, and slammed it down on the monster's eyes.

The beast's face ruptured.

The barbarian gritted his teeth and shoved the beast to its side in the sand, the body spasming and thrashing.

Torrents dropped the jaw and launched himself forward, lowering his shoulders into a defensive position that reminded Nathan of a lineman in football, knocking back the charging monsters like the offensive line trying to get to a quarterback.

The rokairn saw Torrents break through the line of attackers and sprint for the wall of the arena. The big man slid sideways in the sand, coming to a stop at the wooden spikes jutting from the uneven surface of the wall. Three beasts shot towards the barbarian; the man grabbed a sharpened spine and broke it off.

The look in Torrents's eyes was feral and unthinking, only instinct and aggression showing on the face that was normally considering and thoughtful.

He thrust the makeshift spear forward, tearing along the throat and side of the first croco-wolf (as Nathan had dubbed them), and the barbarian followed through, swinging the wooden shaft like a club to bash in the skull of the second creature.

The third slid to a halt, its legs splaying open in front of it, lowering its head. Torrents drove the spike downward, skewering the monster's skull at the base of its neck.

The barbarian didn't pause, bloodlust and rage contorting his face in the joy of killing. He pulled his weapon free and ran forward to attack the next beast.

Nathan turned towards Aiyana, only seconds having passed since he'd rose to feet after his head had cleared. His body was still lethargic and sluggish, but his mind was sharp.

"Aiyana," he shouted into her face, grabbing her shoulders, "fight it, come back to us, help us!"

Their captors unshackled the companions moments before they shoved them into the arena, but the woman still stood slouched and limp in the same spot where she'd stumbled to after entering the fighting ring.

Nathan didn't want to slap her, but it worked for Torrents, sort of. He decided against it and instead shook the wizardess. Her head flopped back and forth, her platinum hair sticking to a line of saliva that dribbling from her open mouth.

"Dammit," the rokairn swore, uncharacteristically, "sorry about this…"

Then he slapped her, and her eyes snapped to his, her jaw tightening before her gaze went soft again. He slapped her again, backhanded, and harder this time.

A line of blood appeared at the corner of her mouth, and she looked at him, her face growing hard.

Nathan wasn't sure how much of her was in there, and if she even knew him, but he had to try.

"Call the elements," he screamed, panic rising in his voice, "do something, anything. Help me and save yourself. Save Torrents. Do something!"

Nathan knew he was bordering on hysteria and needed to get a grip on himself. He demanded the others do things but wasn't trying to do more than get them into action.

Shoving the woman away—she stumbled backwards, trying to stay upright—he turned to face the enemy, but was too late.

A croco-wolf leapt at him, its jaws wide and the tentacles on the side of the beast's head reaching for him, its tongue with dozens of tiny feelers leading the way of countless pointed teeth.

## Chapter 21

Nathan threw his arm across his face to protect it from the attack, just as the wind rose and sand flew in a spiral around him, biting into his skin and face.

A gasp came from behind him, Aiyana's voice increasing like the crescendo of a gospel soloist, rising to the heavens in a note that was pure, thick, and heavy but carried the weight of need and desperation.

The sandy breeze became a whirlwind. The whirlwind became a dust devil that rained down hell on the sleek predators.

The beasts' flesh wore thin, the deep black color with green undertones fading to moss color, replaced with shreds of red tinged with pink, then bone white with the liquid maroon of open wounds.

Small tornados of sand and spite weaved and danced across the arena, snatching unwilling partners into their grasp, before discarding them and turning to the circling crowd for the next available person. Screams replaced the chorus as the chanting audience became a part of the show they'd only wanted to see, and never imagined they'd become a part of.

"Where's the Spine?" Nathan dropped his arm from his face, which was reddened under the assault of the earth. "Where's the treasure of Japria?"

Aiyana's eyes shifted, becoming unfocused then snapping to the canvas-covered stage that housed the ruler of Dioneze City from the elements, Ballingturn the Bold, Master of the Dark Arts, and Lord of Pain.

The man was beautiful, muscles glistening with an oiled sheen, matching his hair that gleamed a dark black that appeared purple in the light of the magical globes under his pavilion.

His face contorted in a scream of drug-hazed passion, the left half painted with red streaks, and the right covered by a ceramic mask of forest green. He held a metal rod of curved segmented bone in his grip, the artifact the length of his muscular arm.

His harem of young men and women pawed and cooed over him, fawning in competition to gain his favor.

The man, still shy of three decades, but powerfully built, rose as the whirlwinds towering twice the height of the arena spun towards him, colliding with one another, and combining to become three, then two, then one final massive force of nature.

The raging winds tearing him to pieces drowned his scream, accompanied by the choir of his harlots and slaves. The metal spine flew over the fighting ring, the man's hand still clutching it. The relic fell onto the sandy floor and rolled, the bloody appendage flying free.

"There," Aiyana's words came with a breath, like someone who spoke while expelling a drunken belch, "there's the thing that you want."

"The Spine of Japria," Nathan spoke as if he was having a casual conversation over coffee, but his muscles tensed, locking and freezing him to the spot where he stood, "It's the next…"

He went down under two of the reptilian hounds, bowling him over from behind. Short claws on wide feet tore at the rokairn's shoulder, digging grooves into the priest's flesh. The creature's finger-thick tentacles that hung down, four on each side of the head, trailed along the man's face, tingles and pops of the chemical electricity biting at his cheeks and eyes.

The second beast's fleshy, feathered tongue writhed across Nathan's shoulders and chest, the cilia-like protrusions wiggling into the claw marks that had gouged his chest. The tongue swabbed back and forth, the smaller feelers lapping at the priest's life blood.

Curling his knees to his belly and bringing his arms in to protect his chest, Nathan planted his feet and fists under one of the croco-wolf's stomach and thrust upward with all his might, flipping the beast over his head and onto its back. The tongue searching the wound on the rokairn's shoulder lost half of the probing protrusions that were latched into the man's flesh.

The rokairn grabbed the other beast's foreleg and twisted towards himself, the bone snapping. Punching out, the man's fist ruptured the animal's closest eye. The lizard-hound scrambled backwards, making a noise somewhere between a hiss and a growl.

Nathan pushed to his feet, setting them firm, then squared his shoulders and looked around the arena.

Torrents was at the edge with a scatter of bodies at his feet, a mix of the mutant animals, and people from the stands the whirlwinds had snatched and discarded within the round walls of the fighting pit. A crazed smile split the barbarian's face as he clubbed animals and onlookers alike, chasing down and leaping on any that moved. He was in a mindless killing rage, blood decorating his bare chest and arms with spatters and streaks.

Aiyana collapsed to her knees, the tornado dissipating. The aeifain stared at her hands in her lap, palms up, the fingers spasming open and closed. Her body rocked and shuddered, her shoulders twitching. The woman's hair hung across her face, hiding it so Nathan couldn't tell if she was crying, laughing, or talking.

"Kaleb triot, den'al venitier," the rokairn shouted the ancient battle cry of his people, throwing his hands up to the sky. Columns of rock burst from underfoot, creating a wall that rose on each side of Nathan and Aiyana, extending behind him to trap Torrents within, and extending forward to create a path that led to where the Spine lay in the sand.

The walls formed a trench of sorts, and the proto-wolves threw themselves against the outside, scrambling upward, using stony protrusion to get over the structure and to their prey within.

Guards leapt from the stands to the top of the wall, running forward with spears ready, or nocking an arrow to the string of their bow.

Nathan slumped. His eyes slid from Torrents to the croco-wolf heads cresting the trench wall, to the magical artifact, to Aiyana, and finally to the men running towards him.

He'd killed enough and didn't want to kill more. He was tired, and just wanted to get away from here. He didn't even care about Aiyana's mission anymore. They couldn't do anything if they were dead.

With a tired gesture from Nathan, stone spikes shot outward along the top of the wall, piercing the animals laying siege as they reached the apex of the defensive barrier. They skewered the men running along the top, stone ripping through their armor and flesh alike.

"Jonath," the rokairn rasped a prayer to his deity, "grant my friends the perception and awareness needed to complete their task. I humbly beg of you to lend your help at the moment of my most dire need."

Nathan reached across the empty air, one arm extending towards the raging barbarian, and the other towards the catatonic wizardess. He felt for their consciousness with his mind and sensed their awareness slip and stutter. It made him think of the lawnmower he'd once used to cut his grandmother's lawn, pulling on the threadbare grey cord, the engine would try to catch and turn over, but would pop and jump, and then fail. He pulled hard, yanking on their spirits, trying to jump-start them with his.

The barbarian's eyes jerked to him, and the big man thrust his chest forward, pulled his arms back, and raised his head to howl into the twilight. Torrents hunched forward, a feral grin on his face, stalking towards the rokairn, the bloody makeshift club dragging in the sand beside his feet.

The aeifain had raised her head, matted strands of platinum hair hanging in a ragged sheet across her eyes. They were hollow, haunted, and broken. But the woman slowly rose, pushing up with her hands, bending at the waist to stand, then tottering upright.

"Good enough," Nathan grunted, reaching out and taking the woman by her wrist and dragging her forward. "Torrents, take the point."

Nathan moved towards the Spine of Japria, bending to scoop it up as he came to it. Torrents loped past him, towards the raised stage that had held the ruler of this place a couple of minutes before, now just a platter of carnage.

Calling upon the powers of Jonath again, the priest formed stones stairs that led up to the platform above. They rose grudgingly, slowly forming until they spanned the distance from the arena floor to the top of the outer wall.

Torrents took the steps two at a time, pieces of stone crumbling and tumbling away at each leap.

Nathan followed behind, leading Aiyana by her wrist. When the priest moved upward, the steps shifted, melting back into the component sand the priest had made it from. He quickened his steps, jumping the last bit to land on solid wood, the last of the stone falling away under his feet.

His arm jerked as Aiyana fell, thumping against the wall below. Nathan still gripped her wrist.

The priest looked down, preparing to tell the woman to climb until he saw her. She hung limply, swinging in a small circle below him. She looked at her feet, not reacting to her situation.

Nathan knelt, set the Spine of Japria beside him, and reached down to grab her arm with both hands. He dragged her upward and over the edge until she lay on the blood-soaked wooden planks beside him.

Rising to his feet, Nathan picked up the artifact with one hand and pulled Aiyana to a standing position with his other, taking stock of their situation.

The arena was emptying, the once cheering crowd disappearing through the exit ramps leading to the streets outside.

A familiar face was on the opposite side of the fighting pit, surrounded by a dozen guards. Manalo Maqsher smiled at him from across the distance. The guards around him broke into two groups, each circling in opposite directions to move around the arena to reach the three friends.

"We have to go," Nathan spoke mostly to himself, knowing the other two probably didn't understand his words, "now."

Torrents looked at him, a tiredness washing over his feral grin.

"There," Nathan pointed at the closest ramp out of the arena, and Torrents looked to where he pointed. "Go that way. We need to get out of the city."

The barbarian stalked towards the passage the rokairn indicated, his bloody club leading the way. The priest stumbled along behind, forcing his feet to move, and pulling the aeifain along with him.

A dark form winged overhead: a raven. It flew from rooftop to rooftop, watching and following them.

They reached the street without meeting any resistance. The city was in chaos and people panicked in the area, shouting about the arena monsters roaming the streets, the invisible spellslingers killing people in their homes, and the murderous man-wolf hunting in the alleys.

Looters charged into business, beating merchants in their stores or booths for an armful of cloth or a basket of fruit. City guards attacked the looters, taking the goods for themselves after they cowed or killed the townsfolk.

The three stayed in the shadows to avoid notice in the twilight. When someone threatened the group, Torrents growled and raised his bloody weapon, which was enough to turn away most. The few that were desperate—or stupid enough—to attack the group, were quickly defeated by the rage-drunk barbarian. It never ended well for the other concerned party.

Leaning around a corner, Torrents looked down the main road through town. Pulling back into the alley, he turned to Nathan and Aiyana.

"Gate's just down there," he mumbled, jerking a thumb over his shoulder in the direction he'd just looked. "I think we're going to have to be out in the open for this last bit. Should be ok, the street's crazy and no one is paying any attention to anyone else. They're just trying to get anywhere but here."

"Got it," Nathan nodded, gesturing for Torrents to lead, "and I'm glad you're back with me."

He followed the barbarian, pulling Aiyana along behind him.

The gate, and freedom, was just a few blocks away. They limped towards it, struggling to move as fast as they could without drawing unwanted attention.

A man stepped into the street, blocking their way. His face was shadowed, but they could see the eyepatch and scratches on one side, and a smirk on the other. Manalo Maqsher stopped a short distance away.

A ragged gang filtered into the street, coming from shop doors and alleys—a few dropping from porch roofs—and surrounded the trio. They held clubs or long daggers. They looked like starved wolves in human form.

"Did you think you could escape me?" Manalo sneered. "I would've hunted you down, no matter where you went. Instead, you will die now."

Nathan looked up at Aiyana. She rocked back and forth; her eyes vacant. Glancing at Torrents, he saw the barbarian take a firm grip on the spear-like spike of wood. The big man swayed too, unsteady on his feet, and Nathan wasn't much better. They were in no shape for a fight. The priest shut his eyes to mutter a final prayer.

"Extra silver to the man who brings them down," Manalo shouted at the tuffs around the trio, "and a position in my personal guard!"

Rough laughter came from the men, who stepped forward, raising their weapons.

A snarl echoed from an alley, and Nathan's eyes snapped open. A dark, hunched form shot from the side street. It was man shaped, but it ran hunched and its large head way dog-like. The telltale cackled laugh of the gnohl echoed off the buildings.

The beast tore into the street gang, a curved blade in one hand, and swiping with bloodied claws with the other. Two men screamed and went down under the monster's attack.

Manalo took two large steps back, looking around. He faded back, moved onto a porch, and into a doorway, disappearing.

Their attackers were occupied by the gnohl, and Nathan jerked Aiyana forward with one hand, and pushed Torrents towards the gate with the other. They ran as fast as Aiyana's stupor allowed, Nathan having to call Torrents to his side to stop the big man from joining the fight.

They reached the city gate and passed through without anyone trying to stop them. The guards had either headed for safety or were out looting the city.

"We're on the wrong side of the city," Nathan muttered, stopping to look around once they'd moved far enough away from the fortifications. "We buried our gear on the opposite side."

Torrents sighed, slumping, his eyes tracing the wall.

"I guess we better get started then," the barbarian said, his voice strained and quiet.

"No," Nathan shook his head, looking at a stand of scrub bushes not too far away. He pointed at them. "We'll go there. We're too tired and broken to risk trying to travel that far, maybe get into a fight, and then find the place and dig it up in the dark. Our lives are more valuable than our armor and weapons."

The rokairn took the lead, the legendary stamina of his people showing through. Torrents was stumbling, two blood stained short swords in his hands, and Nathan wondered when the barbarian had picked those up. He hoped it meant the big man was coming back to himself, his mind returning.

An hour later, the three collapsed in a copse of trees to the north of the road. They'd passed the river surrounding the city and were outside the range of most of the patrols.

Captain Farrell lighted on a branch overhead, looking at the group with a beady eye, his head cocked to one side.

Torrents lay with his back against a thick trunk, his arms resting on his knees, the two swords discarded on each side of him.

Aiyana folded to the ground in a cross-legged position, then leaned backwards until she was lying on her back. Her eyes fluttered, she sighed, and a sound broke in her throat with a sob. She curled into a tight ball and rolled onto her side.

The priest looked around, searching the dappled moonlit ground for a spot to stand watch while the others slept. He was exhausted but couldn't sleep yet. He'd guard them as long as he could, then wake Torrents when he could do no more.

Nathan laughed, looking up at the raven. "What do you think, Captain Farrell? Maybe you could keep watch over us for a while?"

## Chapter 22

"The other relics aren't any good without the Spine of Japria," Aiyana waved her hands in the air, her voice rising, "just as the Spine of Japria isn't any good without them. I need my staff. It has the Eye of Agnew, the Finger of Yender, and Takoven's Rib embedded in it."

"Stop saying it," Torrents spat on the ground. "We know that already. It didn't help all the other times you said it, it isn't going to help by saying it fifty million more times."

"But Runsk has the last relic, right?" Nathan leaned on a rock, rubbing his temples with his fingers. "Sorry, but you still haven't clarified that if we get it, if we can use it and the Spine to do something."

"She doesn't even remember what *it* is that we're looking for in Runsk, Nathan," Torrents's voice was almost a shout, "and asking her that again and again isn't helping, either. So, stop, both of you, just stop."

Aiyana opened her mouth to say something, but Nathan interrupted, holding up a hand.

"He's right," the rokairn sighed.

"He is?" Aiyana's voice was scornful and sarcastic.

"I am?" Torrents sounded surprised.

"He is, you are," Nathan nodded. "We're chasing our tails, having the same conversation again and again. It's not fixing anything, and we need to regroup."

"Fade back and punt," Torrents mumbled, "or go for a hail Mary pass."

"Fine," Aiyana's reply was curt, "but this isn't a college football game. We need to figure out what your metaphors look like in our circumstances."

"High school." Torrents saw the question in the aeifain's face. "High school, I never made it to college level. I was paralyzed before I could get that far."

They'd traveled for over two weeks since leaving Dioneze City, the days were chilly, and the nights were cold. The forest to the north—Diaz Wood that blended into the Grey Wood north of Runsk—was bright golds, reds, oranges, and yellows as autumn turned, hinting at the desolation of the coming winter.

They'd left Dioneze City with just the clothes on their backs, and the two short swords Torrents salvaged from some blurry encounter hidden behind the haze of being drugged and the exhaustion of their escape.

The town had been a wasp nest of activity, and they'd agreed it was much too dangerous to go back for their gear. Manalo was still out there, and probably hunting them.

Shoes, food, waterskins, cloaks, and all the other essentials things were lost.

Torrents woke without a shirt, belt, and boots. The furs that had protected him from the elements and weapons gone.

Nathan no longer had the holy focus of his god's symbol. He didn't have his backpack of food and the dozen items he used to cook, or make a fire. They didn't have any of the luxuries of the road that were completely invisible in the day-to-day life of cross-country travel, assimilated in everyday activities, and taken for granted.

Aiyana's silk and satin robes were tatters, showing wear and tear, and displaying the ravages of her experiences and the journey. Oddly enough, she was the one that retained most of the tools of her trade, the magics being within her. But she was crippled, the staff that she'd been lovingly carving with instinct and skill was gone. She felt the loss keenly, like a part of her she'd spent so much time and energy cultivating, had been ripped from her.

Captain Farrell was the only one not affected. He led them to muddy pools of water to drink, to various bushes that held berries and the hope of living one more day. The gastrointestinal repercussions of partaking of both those things set aside, that simple animal saved their lives more than once.

They'd met travelers on the road and had almost begged for anything to help them. People were people, though. Some shared a simple soup in the dark night, others chased them away with threats or weapons. A few offered castoffs; a threadbare shirt, a blanket that could be used as a cloak or cover from the elements, a patched pot to boil dug up roots or tubers, or herbs plucked from wild areas that hadn't yet fallen to autumn's grip.

The three were ragtag, tired, and less than optimistic about their chances on the road. Smiles and jokes were infrequent, and the idea of the greater good was overshadowed by merely surviving.

They camped northeast of the city of Runsk, in a small circle of firelight as the sun set, within a ring of stones that jutted from the earth, a broken remnant of an empire lost to history and memory.

The rivers that ringed Runsk, Dioneze City, and Red Wind were forgotten monuments of defense and reminders of lost power. What did it take for someone to command a force large enough to create a border of water around an area that took days to travel from one side to the other? The answer to that was lost but hinted at greatness that had once controlled a corner of the continent in millennia past.

"Whiskey before women," Captain Farrell croaked, earning a glare from Aiyana and a smile from Torrents.

A shadow outside of the firelight's circle moved, coalescing into a humanoid form larger than Torrents. The throaty growl approached the circle of light, and the barbarian grabbed his sword, and rose to his feet.

Nathan stood, the second blade in his hand.

The hyena head came into the circle of light, its slavering jowls dripping a thick strand of saliva hung below yellowed teeth and the stunted, furry muzzle that twisted the face.

Ghe'hak pulled himself to his full height and towered over them. His tongue lolled out of one side of his mouth in an appearance of casual friendliness, but the bared teeth and narrowed eyes showed a belligerence that could have been caution or aggression.

Short, dark spotted fur covered the man-beast's chest and shoulders. Leather breeches covered his bottom half.

A curved blade, a khopesh, hung from one hip, and a long, thick dagger nestled in a sheath on the other.

The creature swung a satchel off his shoulder, and slowly reached into it, exaggerating his actions so the people could see each movement.

His clawed hand came into view, a thick piece of mutton in his grip. He tossed it forward, and it landed in the dirt beside the stone ring around the crackling fire.

"Food," the gnohl growled, pulling a skin from the same satchel, and tossing it beside the meat, "wine. I come to talk, not to fight. You cook this, drink this, I share this. Until it is done, we don't fight. And maybe not have to fight after. Peace, that's the word that makes you people not think I want to kill, right? Let's do the peace."

No one looked at anything except the gnohl, not daring to turn away from the familiar form that had killed the gang who attacked them as they fled Dioneze City.

"I am Ghe'hak, the Ravager," the visitor growled, reaching over his shoulder to something that jutted above his back but hard to see in the light of the fire, "and I have an offering to prove I come to you without threat."

He pulled a long, thin item from behind him, a blue stone glimmering in the firelight. He tossed the staff to the ground beside the meat.

Aiyana lunged for the staff before it could bounce a second time and caught it. She clutched it to her breast, with an animalistic noise.

"My staff," the aeifain breathed, holding it like mother would her child, "you had my staff."

Nathan risked a glance at the woman, but Torrents never stopped looking at the intruder.

"Why?" Nathan turned back to the monster. "Why would you bring this to us?"

"I help you lots," Ghe'hak's lolling tongue was back in his mouth, his face twisted into a sneer. "In the sewers, who attacked the wyrm, drawing it from you? In Seawall, who killed the guards that would kill you? In Dioneze, who came to save you when you could barely walk to run away from a fight? Me, that's who did that. It was Ghe'hak the Ravager who saved you many times."

"What do you want?" Torrents spat the words, emphasizing each with quick jabs of the blade he held.

"Good question," Aiyana added. "Why show yourself now? And why would you give us the staff?"

All the arguments between the trio were forgotten or laid aside.

"It is yours," the gnohl's language became clearer, and Nathan wondered if the intruder had been exaggerating by using broken speech, "and one man wants this magical stick to take the power of the Monolith in the east, the tower of Onyx that has many magics coming to it. He wants it to control all magic, taking all the power."

"You're a damn liar," Torrents interrupted. "You're one of the dog men that Klendrisia made to bring demons here."

"Yes," Ghe'hak shrunk in on himself, his shoulders bowing, "I was just an animal, a hyena, and she ensorcelled me to kill for her…changing me from what I was to the thing I am now. This is my world, too, and I don't want things from other places ruling it."

Silence fell, the three considering his words.

Nathan saw Torrents wasn't buying it, and the man gritted his teeth, as if he were trying to find the lie in words, the ulterior motive that lay hidden in the thing that stood at the edge of the firelight.

Aiyana clutched the staff, not paying attention to the gnohl's explanation.

Nathan shifted, missing Marcid in his hands, wondering at the double-edged parallel of his lost blade and the visitor's explanation.

"Whatever this thing," Aiyana paused, biting back her words, "whatever Ghe'hak wants, it doesn't matter. We have the staff, we have the missing artifacts, and I need to bind the Spine of Japria to it. I have to do this. I can't explain it, but I'm going to do it."

The aeifain looked at the rokairn, catching his eyes.

"But Nathan," she continued, "my memory tells me that your god, Jonath, has created more than one artifact that changed the course of history. The Trident of Jonath and Jonath's Battlemachine are two that come to mind. The latter breaking the forces against him so he could clear the way to make the Silver Castle that changed the course of the battle that led to banishing the Talisman and freeing the land from its alien magics."

The priest nodded, the movement slow and considering, the truth of the tales filtering into his mind from the memories of the body he inhabited.

"You can help," Aiyana went on, "call upon your god, bring his magic to help me create something that will protect the land. Bind his power to the Walking God and open the pathways."

The wizardess shook her head, unsure what that meant, but knowing it was important.

Nathan knew it, too. The gods were intertwined, and Jonath was bound to the Walking God, a best friend of sorts according to myth.

Jonath had once captured the essence of chaos, in the form of Quixe, and offered the imprisoned being to his friend when they both still walked the lands with mortals. Before the Walking God became more than the blend of aeifain and human, before he'd ascended to the concept of the god of travel, legend, myth, stories, and magic hidden deep within each and every person.

Accepting the gift, the Walking God then freed Quixe. The god of chaos thanked him, laughed at him, mocked him, and loved him. The Walking God explained it to the force of nature known as Chaos, telling the being that chaos focused on a prison would lead to breaking reality. But freed to do as it will, chaos would balance those who sought to control the world and realties that surrounded it.

A cosmic triumvirate of justice, chaos, and the magic that came from belief was born that day.

Jonath went on to marry Latress, Goddess of the element of air and mistress of wisdom. The two had twins, Torr, god of the element of fire and skill in battle, and his sister, Tarra, goddess of the element of water, and mistress of healing.

The Walking God wed Promethene, goddess of sound and light. Their offspring were Senaria, a goddess who ruled over another sort of honor, the honor that came from within, the code of nature, seas, forest, and beasts. Their second child was the god who ruled over secrets, and speed in travel, and thieves and cutthroats worshiped him, though he also held sway over healing in the night and sleep. Chanian was often overlooked, but he rode his steed—the lightning falcon—and moved in ways and places no one else could.

Aiyana called to the Walking God, turning away from the one god that challenged her deity, Onyx, the new god who rose to power when the world was in upheaval in the decades before the Talisman. When Verl'zen-luk came from the crypts of the Great Desert and Onyx shattered the hierarchy of powers, tearing his power from the grasp of the then-existing gods.

Nathan stepped forward, Torrents and Ghe'hak fading from his awareness, the immensity and impact of what the wizardess washing over him.

He reached for the staff the aeifain held out to him, his grip wrapping around the thick shaft, his awareness and connection to his god enveloping him and bleeding into the artifact in front of him.

The Spine of Japria was in his other hand, the sword he had held gone, and he brought it forward to touch the staff Aiyana had lovingly carved and enchanted over the past months.

Ghe'hak growled, stepping backwards out of the circle of firelight, and stumbling further in retreat as the white-hot light of magics burst outward and upward, lighting the sky above them.

It mesmerized Torrents as he stared at the event before him. Everything else stopped, and this boy who was barely a man in his world witnessed something no person alive had ever seen.

The creation of an artifact that wasn't just the energy within a world, but the energy of the planes of reality and existence that spanned the multiverse, wasn't something that happened on Earth. It wasn't something that had happened in Aetheria in nearly a thousand years.

But here it was, and Torrents fell to his knees. The reaction of his mind and body was better than his favorite underdog football team winning the Superbowl. It surpassed his first time with a girl. It ruptured his awareness, and his hands reached for the light as his mind screamed that it would envelop and devour him.

But he didn't care. This was something nothing else could compare to.

He watched the aeifain in a nimbus of glowing power, raise the staff above her head and call upon its power, summoning something from the nether. A dark photo-negative of space flared, dampening the blaze of beautiful light, and a mass of reality superimposed itself over what wasn't there.

Torrents saw his swords, the rokairn's double-bladed axe, armor, and other items buried in a shallow hole over two weeks ago, appear between the wizardess and the priest.

Then it was over.

The light receded, and his friends—who'd been wiped from his awareness in the moment—came back into his reality. A frail, beautiful woman fell forward, and a thick-bodied, bearded man crumbled to the ground beside her.

The staff, still an imprint of light on his vision, hovered above the earth, energies swirling and being drawn into it as it hummed, not with sound but with the vibration of creation. Then it fell, the top-heavy crystal teetering in the air. The white gold knuckle of the finger bone shone, and the spine that had been bound with the polished wooden shaft dimmed to bearable levels.

This priceless and powerful talisman of magic fell into the dirt.

Torrents stared, stunned and unable to move at the horrific thought that such an item would lie in mere dust and the soot of ashes of the firepit, now merely glowing coals under the weapon of might.

A form sailed across his vision, and he wrinkled his forehead, trying to decipher what it was.

It was the gnohl, the man-beast bending to retrieve the god-blessed relic, snatching it and bolting into the night.

A small, dark form darted down toward the gnohl—Torrents only now realizing the form had a name, in fact, both shapes had a name, and identity—as Captain Farrell tried to stop Ghe'hak from stealing the priceless artifact.

Torrents burst into action, leaping to his feet, and launching himself across the embers of the firepit towards the inhuman thing running into the deepening night.

The barbarian threw himself at the thief, a flying tackle to stop the game-ending move of the opponent. In a flash of light, the gnohl disappeared, and Torrents rolled across the wet grass where Ghe'hak had been a moment before.

"Stand and deliver!" Captain Farrell croaked as he circled overhead.

# Chapter 23

"I'm sorry," the barbarian sat on the ground, his head in his hands, "it's all my fault."

"We know, but you're only human," Aiyana's voice was condescending, "I must expect such things from your kind."

"Don't do that," Nathan paced around the renewed campfire, but looked at the wizardess, adding weight to his words. "Don't be so…aeifain."

"I'm sure I don't know what you mean." She did a poor job of concealing her arrogant tone. "I'm only saying that humans often fall short when they're needed most. They have no fortitude when it comes to once in a lifetime events."

"You're being a bitch." Nathan stopped pacing and turned to face her. "Don't forget that you're human also, and you're only driving an aeifain body because some mystic called Jack pulled you from Death's grasp and put you into it. So, don't get uppity."

"She's right, though," Torrents still held his head in his hands, "I chuzzed up."

"Just because she's right," Nathan's tone turned lecturing, "doesn't mean she has to say it out loud. You tried, and that counts for something. After all, she and I weren't even able to realize what was happening, so we were of no help."

"That's because we were channeling the power of two gods, and various realities, into a magical construct that took months to create," Aiyana said with a careless shrug, "but he was just dazzled by pretty lights and the thought that he got to see something special. Yeah, it's about the same. Good point, dwarf boy."

"Which way does the wind blow?" Captain Farrell muttered, cocking his head from atop the rock beside the camp, "Whiskey before women."

"That's new." Torrents raised his head from his hands. "Well, the first part at least. I always thought the damn bird was being sexist when he said that last part."

"He's smarter than you think," Aiyana reached out and stroked the raven.

"I could say that about Torrents, too," Nathan muttered.

"Oh, zing!" Torrents smiled. "Good job, ding me and defend me in the same breath. Double points!"

"Which," Aiyana paused, each word a separate sentence, "way...does...the...wind...blow? Whiskey before women. Do you guys think...?"

It was a question, but she left it unfinished.

"Yeah, no," Torrents shook his head. "I'm not smart enough to be a mind reader. What the hell do you mean? I don't know what you're asking."

"Which way does the wind blow is a reference to what direction is the easiest to go? Where should you head that makes the most sense?" Aiyana spoke faster, her words coming quicker in her excitement. "And whiskey before women suggests you should prioritize what you want. Do you think that Captain Farrell is trying to tell us what to do next?"

"Nope," Torrents shook his head again, "I think you're reading a bit too much into something that some pemtie bird said."

"What can it hurt?" Nathan shrugged.

"What?" The barbarian looked at the priest. "You're buying into this? Listening to the awesome advice of crow?"

"He's a raven!" Aiyana said defensively.

"First," Nathan interrupted, holding up a finger between the two, "he is a raven, and they're smarter than crows. Second, an enemy sent him from what we know, so he may know something. Third, and most importantly, we need to do something, so why not do this?"

"This?" Torrents cocked an eyebrow and tilted his head in confusion. "What is this? Can either of you say something that makes sense?"

"I can feel my staff," Aiyana's eyes were closed, and she spoke over the barbarian, "it's far away but I can feel it. It's to the east, probably in the city where I first entered this world."

"That's not the way the wind is blowing," Nathan popped his fingertip into his mouth, and pulling it out held it up to the chill autumn night air, nodding. "I think we should prioritize finding the staff over anything else, but it looks like we head west to Runsk."

"Oh…my…god," Torrents muttered to himself, "these two have a religious experience and they think dumb animals are telling them how to save the world."

The three left camp, traveling into the night. A few hours later, they moved along the ridge that Runsk was built on. It was only the height of two men, but it gave the city the advantage of the high ground needed if someone attacked.

The city was a monument of ego. The rock outer wall atop the ridge was barely taller than a man, but wide enough for two men to pass abreast. A thin battlement held crenels to stab a spear through and a merlon to protect any defender atop the parapet.

Wood and stone buildings stood on the other side, baked clay shingles on the roofs that bordered the outer wall. The inner buildings had slate or wood shingles covering the structures.

A patrol of two bored men walked the parapet, who did not bother to glance away from the city. Their actions told Aiyana they were confident that they were impossible to attack. She felt it was more from arrogance than any superior protection.

The witching hour had crept up on the three as they'd approached the city, the moon sinking towards the western horizon and the wind rising to sing the songs of the night. The leaves scattered and danced around their feet in the autumn's darkness.

"Son of a bitch," Torrents muttered, his shadow fading and reappearing behind him as clouds slid across the moon.

Captain Farrell shook himself on Aiyana's shoulder.

"Shut up," Nathan hissed, "there are guards, and they will hear us."

"Shh," Aiyana's sound was a brief command.

"You sure you know where you're going?" Torrents whispered.

"No," again the aeifain's voice was curt, "and you constantly asking doesn't help. Narrowing in on a cave leading to the magical emanations of portals isn't like looking over a crowd to find the deli on the corner. Now, hush."

They all fell silent.

The wizardess led the way, her keen vision seeing the landscape—and the guards on the short, stout, stone wall atop the ridge—as she tracked a vague feeling that whispered of magic that smelled like foreign spices.

The closest comparison that she made of following the faint impression of magic was the scent of an exotic food she didn't know well, but knew she liked, hanging on the wind. If the wind was in her mind, and the ginger and garlic aroma were potent magic that folded time and space. It was close enough of a comparison for her to go with it.


Nathan watched Aiyana move forward and knew the woman was feigning confidence. She was so young, but he recognized the pressure of proving herself made her hold her head high and speak like she knew what she was doing.

That was a skill the young usually never had, except in rare or extreme cases. Older people—CEOs, police, and anyone else the public looked to for direction—learned the value of faking it, and people bought it. Or maybe they didn't; maybe, people faked believing them because the other option of the blind leading the blind was unthinkable. Or uncomfortable, at least.

They'd discussed, as they walked the three hours to the city, whether they should go inside Runsk to look for the portals.

*That was jumping ahead though*, Nathan thought. *Aiyana suggested the portals existed from out of the blue, her only data point being that Durgan's Keep had a cavern underneath it with the same thing. Well, it had a portal, and that portal led to a room of six portals, counting the one we'd come through.*

The aeifain conjectured each ley line nexus had such a portal, and that room with other magical doorways was the same one. Depending on where you entered, the other five portals would lead to the five closest ley line nexuses. Nexi? They'd argued over that term, bringing up octopi, or octopuses, and platytpi, or platypuses.

Didn't matter, what mattered was they went the quickest route with the least resistance.

The entrance was little more than a crack, forcing Torrents—who was in between Aiyana and Nathan because of his human lack of vision in the dark—to turn sideways and suck in his stomach to pass through. The aeifain slipped through with no problem, the human squeezed himself past the narrow opening, and Nathan wondered if his thick, rokairn build could even get by.

He eyed the crack, turned his head sideways for a new perspective, then nodded and straightened.

Moving towards the passage, he crouched and duck-walked into the deeper darkness of the catacombs below the city.

Moisture coated the walls of the caverns under the city, which doubled as sewers. The three waded through the ankle-deep muck of waste. Nathan was extremely glad they'd recovered their gear before the gnohl had stolen the staff. But he was pretty sure he'd need a new pair of boots, unless he wanted everyone to wonder what smelled like poo whenever he walked past.

Minutes passed, dragging on because everything looked the same. The aeifain led them through a maze of natural corridors until they came upon the thin shimmering gateway that called to her.

When they moved through it—the energy rippling through their bodies felt like a sensation between being torn apart and tickled—they arrived in a small chamber that could have been the same one they saw under Durgan's Keep, or at least its twin.

"Which doorway, Nathan?" Aiyana looked at the priest.

The rokairn shook his head, unsure if the gesture was meant to answer the most powerful spellslinger he'd ever seen, or if it was in wonder of her newfound confidence in him.

The ritual—which had been a 'rousing success' in Aiyana's words, even though they'd lost the end result—seemed to create a respect for the rokairn in the aeifain because he'd been a part of the same ritual.

But Nathan hadn't known what he was doing, only acting on the instinct of his faith and relying on the guidance of the god who granted him the abilities that were the boon of favored priests.

"Which one do we go through?" Aiyana rephrased her question, turning with her arm outstretched to take in the other five magical doorways with her gesture.

"Calm down," Torrents sounded exasperated to Nathan, "give him a minute to think about it."

"It took me hours last time." Nathan rubbed at his eyes, dragged his hands down his cheeks, then combed his fingers through his beard. "I had all night to study them while you two slept."

"You mean," Aiyana leaned forward with her fists on her hips, though Nathan didn't think she even knew she was doing it, "this might take you hours to figure out which doorway we need to go through?"

"Yeah, sorry," the rokairn rubbed his temples again, "it might take me hours. Or I might not figure it out at all if you're both staring at me and bickering every couple of seconds."

"Okay," Torrents nodded, pulled his satchel across the sword on his back to in front of him, and opened it to pull out a blanket, "sounds like the perfect time to get a nap. Wake me up when you figure it out."

The barbarian laid down on the blanket, shifting his satchel to under his head like a pillow, then pulled the woolen material over him.

"Are you really going to go to sleep right now?" Aiyana huffed and a gentle snore answered her. "He can't really be asleep already. He's just being a jerk and ignoring me."

"Aiyana," Nathan drew the woman's name out, "no one could ignore you while they're awake. And he really is asleep. He has a gift in that area. You should get some sleep as well. I have a puzzle to decipher. I need to find the facet that shows what I seek."

# Chapter 24

The morning sun blinded them when they stepped out of the portal. The side they'd left had been a dark, dank cavern, and the other was a rough-hewn hollow in the side of a cliff face overlooking the eastern ocean and the sunrise cresting the horizon.

Nathan had been busy for a long time after Aiyana and Torrents fell asleep. The rokairn had sat studying the subtle shifts in the shades of color, the density of the rippling air, and even the gentle changes in the vibration's hum from the magical doorways that wouldn't have been heard if anyone had been awake and talking.

The energy of the portals had a rolling pattern. The vibrational rate at one extreme felt like it was very distant. The vibrational rate on the other end of the energy cycle felt larger and more intense, with subtle shifts between the two extremes.

Nathan thought the largest portal might lead to places that were like a nexus of nexus. That one also took the longest to cycle, and had the most differentials, which made the priest believe it led to the most places when compared to the other doors.

Directly across the chamber from what Nathan had thought of as Portal Prime was what he'd nicknamed the Sub-portal. That was the one they'd came through to get here, and it didn't flicker through frequencies, but it shifted colors. It was just a doorway to the closest exit. It seemed to fade, like the other side was closed or obstructed, or it may have been shifting to different locations in the city.

The remaining four doorways were more of a challenge to puzzle out. They seemed to cycle slower than the sub-portal, but faster than the Prime. The gateway closest to the large doorway pulsed slightly faster than the largest door, and the ones furthest away that sat beside the sub-portal cycled faster still, though not as fast as the smallest gateway.

That was all easy to figure out because the pattern matched the other cavern they'd discovered under Durgan's Keep. Using his rokairn instincts and the gifts of Jonath, Nathan matched each of the four remaining portals to a cardinal direction, debated if seasons were part of the shifting rotation, then added in the possibility of ley lines influencing the direction and distance that each might lead. He even considered if the four gods of the elements— Jonath, Latress, Torr, and Tarra—might tie into the equation.

Hours later, Nathan stood with his hand on his chin, considering, his elbow resting in the palm of his other hand. He was pretty sure that he'd figured it out, and in less time than it had taken in the cavern under Durgan's Keep. He felt more confident than he had the last time. There was still a margin of error, but he was willing to risk it.

Waking the others, he told them with absolute faith that the fourth doorway was the one they wanted to pass through to get to Seawall City, or at least close to it.

Now they all stood in a cavern seven paces wide, four paces deep, with a sheer drop below them to the rocky base of the cliff that overlooked the eastern ocean. Above wasn't much better, but Torrents was pretty sure he could make out the grey stone of Seawall City's wall above them. They weren't on the dock side, with the winding stairs that led to the various levels, so they wouldn't have an easy trip getting to the top.

"We should camp here," Nathan nodded in agreement with himself.

"We just slept," Torrents leaned over the edge of the opening, one hand gripping the rock as he tried to find something familiar or helpful. "We should just go."

"Look before you leap," Aiyana yawned and stretched, basking in the morning rays of the sun, appearing to be happy to be out of the damp cold of the cavern, "but yes, I agree. I'm ready to go as soon as we figure out how to scale the wall, up or down."

Captain Farrell hopped across the stone floor, pecking at a snail.

"I can't swim in this armor, and I'm not giving it up again. I get the feeling we'll need it," Nathan stripped off the armor, "and you two just rested while I stayed awake to figure out how to get here. Now, you do the next part while I get a couple of hours sleep. And I wouldn't mind some breakfast when I wake up."

The rokairn yawned, arranging his cloak as a blanket over the bedroll he'd laid out.

"Wake up," Aiyana was shaking him, "we have to go, now!"

Distant horns echoed, trumpets, the kind that called large groups of people to action.

Nathan sat up, rubbing his face with both hands.

Torrents hung over the edge of the lip of the cave. His fingers dug into a fissure in the rock so he could lean out. He swung gently back and forth, looking up with a look of concerned urgency.

"What's going on?" Nathan stood, stretched with his fingers interlocked, raising his arms over his head, and standing on his tippytoes.

The rokairn let out a slow moan of contentment as a series of pops sounded from his back.

Bending down, he picked up his shirt of chain, slid it over head, pulled his beard free from the interwoven links, and patted it down against his chest.

Pulling his greaves and bracers to him, he stopped and looked at the aeifain expectantly.

"Well?" he urged.

"Magic," Aiyana turned her head upward, as if trying to see through the tons of rock over their heads. Her eyes grew distant and unfocused.

Captain Farrell flew over and landed on her shoulder, turning his head, and leaning forward to look into her face with a beady eye.

"Lots of it," she continued, "something big, and I think it has to do with my staff and the ley lines."

"Okay," Nathan buckled a steel bracer to his forearm, "and have you figured out how to get out of here?"

"I can feel my staff," she cocked her head, as if not hearing the rokairn's words, and instead was listening to some distant noise, "and I should be able to. After all, I made it. I think I can attach myself to it and use the magics within it to draw me to it. With this much ley line power around us, I should be able to bring the two of you along, as well."

"Aiyana," Nathan looked up from buckling on his belt, the hand axes hanging from it slapping on his thighs, "you're not a summoner. I don't know as much about how magic works in this world as you do, but I know that it's summoners, or their opposites, that can reverse a conjuration and move themselves to another place. Or sometimes, a mind mage might have some limited ability in it. My point is, if you try this, will it have a chance of killing you?"

"Or us?" Torrents added over his shoulder. "Since you're going to try and bring us with you, is there a chance that we could all die? Coming to this world was a second chance for all of us, and I'd hate to throw that away if we can avoid it."

"Oh?" Nathan turned to the barbarian. "Did you find a different way out then? Is there another option that we hadn't considered? Perhaps you could toss me up to the top of the cliff?"

"No one tosses a dwarf," Torrents muttered with a smirk.

"No, I think it'll work," the wizardess stepped between the two men, breaking their eye contact with one another and making them focus on her, "though everything you both said makes sense, and I hear you. But listen to me and let me tell you why I think this will work.

"I needed the fifth piece, the final artifact, and I thought it was in Runsk," she turned and began pacing the length of the cave, her hands held behind her back while she looked down at her feet, "it felt like it was, but that might have just been my mind playing tricks on me. When my people disappeared, and I wandered, lost and unsure where to go, my path ended at Runsk. But it had begun at Icon Hall, the ancestral home of the aeifain within the Grey Wood. I'd laid a trail, like plowing a five-hundred-kilometer furrow to plant in, or to bury the magical wire of the ley lines."

"You can bury a ley line?" Torrents turned his back to the ocean and stared at the woman.

"No," she shook head, then nodded, "but, yes. Ley lines follow the energies of the planet, the world, the society, currents in the air, water, mountain ranges, and tectonic plates. They can be in the air, water, land, and so on. They sometimes intersect and even run the same course as one of the other elements. This often happens where humans, aeifains, or rokairns build a city. Sometimes they instinctively build on such a nexus or energy freeway, but other times, the ley lines seek the energy generated."

She looked back and forth between the two men, making sure they were following. Each nodded, showing they were keeping up so far.

"Mages, wizards, sorcerers, priests, and alchemists learned these intersections and interactions of energies could be focal points that could be built on to strengthen their magics. The Talisman flared these lines, but dampened portions of them, like they clogged under the pressure of the surge of power. A bottleneck in magic.

"But I digress, back to what I did, what the thirteen spellslingers of my people did. They linked it to me, the energies. They tied them to me, and I ran with it, the line of magic reeling out behind me, and ending at Runsk. Does that even make sense? Can you understand the concept of how incredibly insane something like that is?"

Nathan looked at her with his head cocked but nodded slowly.

When she turned to Torrents, the barbarian shrugged and waved one hand in a rolling motion, indicating she should go on.

"The fifth thing, the final thing," Aiyana turned towards the sun that was well above the horizon, twisting a strand of hair between her fingers, her face washed in a golden light, "wasn't missing. It wasn't waiting to be found. It was the seed inside of me, the thing that I'd been creating the whole time. It was the staff that I'd been carving, enchanting, and putting my blood, sweat, and soul into. I'm connected to it.

"That staff that I bound the Spine of Japria, Takoven's Rib, the Finger of Yender, and the Eye of Agnew to, is a part of me, an extension of who I am, and the magics that come from within me. You, Torrents gave that staff to me, you found it. You chose the vessel that I'd fill. I poured myself into it over the last couple of months. Then when I transformed it into the relic, the Staff of Aiyana, using the power of two gods, and Nathan as an anchoring conduit, it changed everything. Nathan, you were—in a very literal sense—my rock. I suspect it tied both of you to it, because of those very reasons."

She stared at the barbarian, realizing he stood on the edge of a precipice, and thought it was as much figurative as literal. Turning to look at Nathan, the rokairn nodded for her to go on. Aiyana smiled a little, looking down before continuing.

"So," she sighed and stroked the raven on her shoulder, "yes, I think it will work."

"Then we should do it," Torrents said from behind her. "Get busy with the magic, sista."

"Yeah," Nathan smiled at her, "we trust you. How can we help?"

The army of Seawall City was on the move. High Minister Khizhane stood atop the city's wall and looked out over the plains at a thousand soldiers marching in formation. Small clusters of spellslingers wove between the larger groups of fighting men and women. Though it didn't match the massive force the demons brought into the world a few months ago, it was still an impressive sight.

Khizhane had broken the council, dissecting the ruling body into its component parts of people who wanted social power, and those who wanted magical power. He'd offered them exactly what they wanted, and they'd supported him and raised him to Chief Councilor, Lord of the Board, and the one man who could direct the unified city.

Once he'd disbanded the council, restructuring it to be more diversified and specialized—but in truth bringing more control and power into his hands—he'd taken the title of High Minister. No one objected. Perhaps they'd not even noticed what he'd done. He thought that was naïve and blind of them, but most people avoid seeing problems if things are going well.

The alchemist held the Staff of Aiyana, though he would never call it that. He considered other names for the artifact, making lists, meditating, and even taking polls among his staff. Laughing as the puns drifted into his awareness, and he thought of how Aiyana had enjoyed the low form of humor.

Could the staff be influencing him? That would be ridiculous, but he might investigate the possibility after he'd finished the today's task.

As High Minister, Khizhane called upon the people of Seawall City to answer the clarion call of his ambitions. To come, outfitted and armed, ready to take commands and follow. To join him in a march upon the Monolith of Onyx, to draw its power to the city and create something that hadn't existed in thousands of years. An empire with the power of magic and steel to control the lands.

People answered the call. A week ago, there was only a few dozen. Three days ago, he had hundreds camping in the fields beyond the city's defenses. Last night, when his lieutenants had come back with a count of well over a thousand, he'd decided it was time to prepare his advance. And in doing so, Khizhane would show them what an alchemist—once considered the lowest of the magic-using spellslingers—could do.

Alchemy was about planning, thinking, and being prepared ahead of time for every contingency, anything that could possibly go wrong. The strength of mind and self-discipline was far superior to the other schools of magic. It didn't rely on a god to dole out petty rewards, or allow someone to dip into its magical stream in the way ley lines allowed wizards to do, like someone drawing a bucket of water from a stream. It didn't beg help from otherworldly creatures, like sorcerers. And it definitely didn't work like mind mages and their pitiful and exhausting method of magic. Alchemy was ritual and study, brains, and stamina over instinct and knee-jerk reactions.

Khizhane pulled his shoulders back and breathed in deeply, drinking in this moment before they achieved his ultimate goals. He gazed across the field with his army upon it and then looked at those arrayed around him.

Ghe'hak stood behind and to one side of him, a bodyguard, and a lieutenant whom the others feared and respected. The remnant of the demonic forces that had been overthrown and ejected from this world. The gnohl showed the other councilors that Khizhane, and the alchemist alone, could control anything left from that dark stain of their past.

The other councilors were arrayed behind the two who stood at the edge of the city wall. The most powerful men and women of Seawall City, all waiting for Khizhane's command. The High Minister of Seawall City would bring the Monolith of Onyx under his control and, with that, the focused power of the ley lines which spanned the continent.

Lord Khizhane smiled and raised the Alchemist's Artifact—no, that felt contrived in his mind—and the assembly noticed the movement, a hush falling over the crowd, then voices rose in a thunderous cheer. The alchemist held the most powerful magical relic known in the lands aloft, and the sound and adoration of more than a thousand people raising their voices in his honor washed over him.

With a swift motion, he brought the Staff of Power— no, that name wouldn't do, too simple, and kind of pemtie—down, the butt thudding against the stone walkway atop the wall with a hollow boom reverberating across the valley. The air shimmered, a wave of power rippling outward, washing across the bumper crop of warriors in the field in front of the alchemist, and to the stone quarry of the city behind him he'd mined for all its resources.

The cloudless morning, the sky a gentle pale blue. As the magical emanations reached the firmament above, the air scattered into component parts and fell downward in a scattered rain of blue light. As the precipitation of energy fell over Khizhane and the others, and it coated them with an ethereal shroud, as if the sky itself were pouring over the assembled. Each and every person faded and disappeared from where they stood a moment before.

The stone wall that the High Minister stood on faded from his perception, becoming a blurred observation, reality melting in a relaxed sigh of the surrounding universe. The grassland in front of him shimmered and wavered in his sight, and pulled away from his awareness, disappearing.

He blinked his vision clear, seeing the military formations of squads, patrols, and platoons of soldiers wavering in front of him. It took him a moment to realize it was as much from the people recovering their equilibrium as him recovering his.

He'd successfully moved his army across the land using his magic.

The fighting force was arranged on a sandy flatland, the gentle rolling green grasses that surrounded Seawall City gone, replaced with scrub grasses scattered around the feet of the army.

Khizhane looked down, seeing the stone steps under his feet. They weren't the grey flagstones of his city, but worn, pockmarked, and a dull dun color. He turned in a circle, taking in his surroundings. A light layer of gritty, yellow sand covered stairs that led up to a wide platform that extended a hundred meters in each direction. Looking at the dark, shining surface of the structure atop the platform, Khizhane raised his eyes to take in the black tower that rose into the sky, the noon sun behind him.

The Monolith of Onyx loomed over everything.

Ghe'hak growled from beside him, crouching with his hand on his weapon as he spun, trying to get his bearings.

The council gasped in wonder; the effects of magic that not seen in the land for hundreds of years settling into reality. The people who'd mocked the alchemist for years now stood in awe of what just happened.

Khizhane had done it. He had teleported a thousand living creatures thousands of kilometers. They stood at the foot of the font of magical energies that ripped the ley lines from their ancient pathways to this place.

The High Minister smiled, settling the butt of the Staff of the Ages—no, that didn't work either, it was too new, and sounded trite—pulled himself upright to stop the quavering of his body, and resisted the urge to fall to his knees. It wouldn't be the thing to do in front of the people that would worship him and cower at his might after this show of power.

Khizhane turned towards the magical structure, and the surrounding council parted, pulling back into two rows to stand behind him. The army at his back raised a tattered cheer that grew in strength, the sound and power of their adoration filling him with energy he'd never dreamed of possessing.

The alchemist raised the Artifact of Portals—that wasn't any good either, too limiting—and raised his voice in a ritualistic chant. He pulled components from a pouch at his side, scattering herbs and powdered metals that would transform the conduit of a god to do his bidding.

## Chapter 25

Nathan was down on one knee, short, tough grass beneath him, chanting. That grass was sand the last time he'd been here…and demons had been everywhere.

The army was in front of them, spellslingers dotting the countryside where demons had once been, and the power-mad man stood where a demoness had been on the rokairn's last excursion to this place. The man shouted with raised arms—Aiyana's staff held high in one hand—invoking an incantation to bring magical energies under his control.

The priest called upon the protections of his god, Jonath, asking the deity to hide them, knowing that it wasn't something his god usually allowed. Jonath was about guarding, not hiding. Boldness, not stealth.

Torrents stood with his hands on his knees, losing what food was in his belly. The journey through the chilling aether that lingered between reality and other worlds caused the big man's body to purge itself.

Aiyana was on her knees, her head bowed between them, gasping for air. Her head swam from the magical feat she'd just performed. She'd broken down the molecules of herself, her raven, and the two men, and moved them— within the magical slipstream created by the leader of the army in front of them—along ley lines in the form of energy. Then she'd reconstructed each one of them, drawing the power from the combination of magics that her staff tapped into.

She raised her head. Her eyes watered as she blinked in the afternoon sun and glared at the man who held the artifact she'd created.

The air around the group shimmered, the effect so like heat rising from the ground above an asphalt highway, or a desert, that Aiyana thought nothing of it until Nathan grunted and pushed to his feet.

The rokairn wobbled where he stood, his hand fumbling for Marcid. He pulled the axe from its harness across his back.

Torrents pulled his waterskin from his satchel, popped the stopper, and held it above him. He squirted the clear liquid into his mouth, swished it around, and spat on the ground in front of him.

The wizardess shook off her concern for the men, and looked back to the gleaming, crystalline structure that towered over the countryside.

The Monolith of Onyx, the god of magic who was tied to ritual. Alchemy was the definition of that, though each type of magic had some sort of ritual to it, even if it was just a wave of a hand. Conjuring or summoning things was the second most ritualistic type of magic, often requiring a sacrifice, incense, or another offering.

Movement caught the aeifain's attention and her head snapped towards the neat, organized squares of the squads, platoons, and battalions of soldiers. The spellslingers undulated in weird, jerking movements, their heads tilting back unnaturally, their bodies twisting and contorting. The people glowed with the energies of magic, and the wizardess was pretty sure she was the only one of the three companions who could see it. There was a faint swirl of silver light that resembled steam coming from a kettle just before it boiled, and the energy swirled together above the assembled mass, intertwining before bending towards the monolith.

Aiyana saw all this through the shimmering field around her small group and was grateful for whatever Nathan had done. She felt the pull of the ritual tugging on her connection to the ley lines, trying to drain her of her power as it was doing to the others.

Screams began, first one, then another, and then dozens. The sounds bled together, becoming—in Aiyana's mind—like a screaming teapot, her mind tying the noise to her earlier comparison.

The silvery energy wove around itself. A loose braid of magic wound above the writhing spellslingers, drawn towards Khizhane. The alchemist called upon the power of an interloper god who had wrested power from a long-standing pantheon.

The font of drained souls and power slammed into the High Minister, and the man stumbled forward before recovering.

Ghe'hak hunched and licked his jowls, clawed fingers spasmodically opening and closing, the creature tensing, waiting for something.

"What's he waiting for?" Aiyana mumbled.

"What?" Torrents stepped beside her, his hand steadying her, though she hadn't realized she'd been swaying.

"Okay boss," Nathan was on her other side, "what're we doing? Need us to wait, or do we move forward?"

"Wait." Aiyana's voice was a whisper.

Captain Farrell crouched on her shoulder, then launched himself into the air. The bird flapped frantically, gaining altitude to get above whatever was happening on the field.

Aiyana's eyes went wide, then narrowed, her pupils expanding before a white haze swept across her cornea and her body relaxed as her mind went somewhere else.

She flew.

Her mind was one with the raven's, connecting on a level beyond reason and realization, past emotion and feeling. It just was. The bird and the woman became one, each knowing what the other was experiencing. Later, she would tell the men that she saw through Captain Farrell's eyes, but it was more. It was a joining, something of two souls sharing two bodies.

The aeifain saw the orderly groups of warriors from above. The magic that affected the spellslingers bled over to the soldiers, drawing on the very essence that made them who they were. That spiritual energy—their souls—were being drawn from them, sucked from their bodies to power a ritual that would redirect a machine made to control the magic of a world.

A hand shook Aiyana and tore her awareness from her familiar, forcing her mind back into her own body. The sudden shift was disorienting, and she felt emptier than the moment before, but more herself.

Torrents's long, tanned arm pointed towards the platform, and her gaze followed his finger.

The gnohl, Ghe'hak the Ravager, was tearing thick chunks of flesh from the High Minister's midsection, the alchemist falling backwards under the assault.

The hyena-headed man-beast tore the staff from the alchemist's weakening grip and raised it above his head with a cackling laugh.

Aiyana looked across the battlefield, death and carnage decimating the army, though there wasn't an enemy around to attack them. Bodies withered, becoming drained husks, flesh puckering and twisting around bones.

The small groups of spellslingers were still jerking, dancing on invisible strings, the magics who had once inhabited their bodies turning inward and animating them as the living dead. Hurky-jerky movements of unnatural contortions made them turn towards the three intruders, the hunger of the dead drawing to the warm, pulsating minds and bodies of the living.

It released the hundreds of warrior soldiers to death, their souls passing from this world to the next, and their bodies—without that kernel of magic—dropping to the ground.

The phalanx of spellslingers who crowded around the Lord Councilor—fawning for attention and competing for favor—rushed away from the man.

Aiyana realized they did this for two reasons.

The first was the mystical power wedging its way into their minds and souls, drawing out the magical connection within them.

The second reason was that the most powerful man they'd ever known had been disemboweled a few steps from where they'd been standing, and the slavering monster who had done it was looking around for something else to do.

The once-council of spellslingers came to their end in different methods.

Three burst into flame, two were ash before they could even open their mouths to scream, but the third screamed for far too long.

Five melted, their faces sliding down the front of their finery and silks, exposing their skulls, which moments later followed suit. Another moment passed and their body shattered into a swirling silver mist that was sucked into the staff held high by the gnohl.

Another exploded and rained down bits and chunks across the platform. The last of the councilors turned to stone, their body hardening, cracking audibly as flesh became rock, then hissing as their form became a fine grit and slid to the ground like sand in an hourglass.

The magical artifact drew power from each person. Aiyana's Staff glowed, then flared, and when the light cleared, Khizhane was back on his feet, lurching towards Ghe'hak.

The gnohl had turned to the Monolith of Onyx, pumping the fist that held the staff in the air and calling to his demonic masters.

Pinpoints of blue light flashed into existence, each one a dozen paces apart, and circling the deep umber colored base of the structure. The portals that would allow the demons and devils of the hells and the dark gulfs of other dimensions ruptured the air in the world, like a cancerous malignance finding a foothold when everyone thought it was gone.

The alchemist pulled a potion from a pouch, uncorked it, and drank it down in one gulp. While doing so, he drew a square of gauze from a different pouch and slapped it onto the gaping wound below his ribs. The effect was palpable and immediate; flesh twisted and knitted around itself, blood drew back into his body, and in moments, only a scar the size of a man's hand remained, a visible swirl of puckered flesh.

The gnohl didn't notice the human rising, and neither did he notice the wizardess, priest, and barbarian running across the stunted grasses towards the stairs leading to the monolith. The three wove around corpses, and both Nathan and Torrents slashed at the withered, undead husks of what remained of the various spellslingers.

Khizhane cleared his throat and drew a long tube from a holster on his hip and thigh. Snapping the wand-like item into a bracer on the underside of his right arm, he pointed it at the gnohl's back. The alchemist slammed the palm of his other hand onto the butt of the wand. A sharp crack of noise, a puff of acrid smoke, and a flash of fire burst from it.

The gnohl jerked, his side exploding, and the creature twisted to look down in surprise. Most weapons barely cut into Ghe'hak, but this one was a magic the world hadn't seen in over 30,000 years. The alchemical compound of an explosive powder in a lead casing and the pressure of the explosion tore through his tough flesh.

Ghe'hak still stared down at his side in wonder while two more explosions ripped through him. The gnohl's head jerked up to see Khizhane's grim face, the alchemist moving towards him in slow, measured steps.

The Lord Councilor had a different wand that clicked into place on the bracer on his left forearm, jutting out over his hand, a long thin copper rod, with a coiled wire strapped to his arm and stretched to a metal box on his belt.

Ghe'hak lunged for the High Minister, the staff falling to the ground, discarded by the gnohl in feral rage.

Khizhane's eyes followed the artifact to the ground, and he stepped sideways. It wasn't to move out of the path of the attacking demon-spawned beast in front of him, but to circle closer to the newly awakened relic.

The Staff of Aiyana was a magical device birthed by the power of two gods, the soul of one of the powerful wizards in modern memory, and then baptized in the blood of a hundred spellslingers. The series of trials that created—then enhanced—the artifact was the perfect storm, a unique combination of events that could never be recreated.

The Lord Councilor moved, closing the distance between the man and the clawed hands that sought him. Aiyana saw the alchemist didn't have to hit the gnohl with any precision or power, but merely touch any part of the creature with the copper wand.

The jolt of electricity that came from the alchemical device when the tip touched the gnohl was enough to throw the monster backwards. The creature landed hard, sliding along the sandy stone the last half of the distance. The holes caused by the explosions in his side and back moments ago caught the pockmarked stone of the ground and were torn wider.

The blue portals no larger than a flower in full bloom, flared, growing to the size of a barrel hoop. Hands, tentacles, claws, and other limbs burst through the ethereal openings, then were cut off when the apertures snapped back down to the size of a pinhole. Extremities thumped to the stone below the portals.

The staff lay between the High Minister and the demonic hybrid, forgotten and ignored. The alchemist stalked towards the gnohl, moving past the relic, a grim smile on his face.

Khizhane never enjoyed having an audience. He never craved the attention; he just wanted the power and the benefits that came with it. He was pleased to have traded all the watching eyes of the council and the army below for the power the Staff of Souls had absorbed—maybe that name would be okay, but he wasn't sold on it, either.

The alchemist knew Ghe'hak wanted the praise, though his very nature fought against it; his masters had built it into him. The gnohl was a broken effigy of servitude that hated himself for wanting to follow a master's commands. He wanted to be free, to be the pack leader, and give the commands instead of craving them.

Movement caught Khizhane's eye as he stepped over the prone gnohl who betrayed him. The alchemist's eyes widened in surprise when he turned.

An aeifain, a rokairn, and a human rushed up the stone stairs and onto the platform.

The Lord Councilor's mind turned the information over in his head. It settled on the thought that the gnohl had betrayed him again; the beast had failed to kill the three people who had made the Staff of Magics—hadn't he already discarded that name?

The alchemist thrust his right arm in the gnohl's direction, his free hand opening a gauge on the device on his belt. Gasses released from three thin, oblong canisters on the man's back. A nozzle housed on the metal bracer on his wrist hissed and sputtered as the alchemist bent his gloved hand down to avoid getting any of the liquid or gas on it.

Moving his hand from the valve on his belt to the bracer holding the tubes, he flipped a switch, and a spark jumped in front of the nozzles with a click. Flame jumped forward, rolling across the gnohl, engulfing him.

The alchemist closed the value with the dial on his belt and turned from the burning monster to give his attention to the interlopers. He cleared his throat, studying the three who should have been dead, corpses laying in the dirt thousands of kilometers to the west.

## Chapter 26

The burst of flame cut off the path in front of Aiyana, blocking her way to the staff she'd created. It was the life work of her people; their power, hopes, and dreams all lay within that one item. It was the key to her helping the world, to bringing a balance that would ensure all people would have access to magic.

Nathan shouted a prayer and a curved crystalline surface appeared in front of them, and the flame swept sideways.

Aiyana knew Jonath was a protector, a guardian, and a shield was something that went with that role. She watched the rokairn's surprised look, and guessed that he'd felt the power of his deity. She wondered if he'd been selling his benefactor short with his expectations, if the priest had limited his god by ignoring the passive gifts within his grasp.

Captain Farrell shot into the sky, flapping to get height and find a safe place away from the danger. The raven found an air current and circled overhead.

"Your god isn't stronger than my magics, you arrogant rokairn." Khizhane smiled. "You shall be one more pemtie who underestimated alchemy."

"Um," Torrents crouched, keeping under the ongoing flame coming from the High Minister's device, "what's he talking about?"

"Madmen," Nathan grunted, keeping the protective barrier up as the flame buffeted the shield, "babble."

"Madman?" The Lord Councilor laughed, the sound rolling off the stone tower behind him, amplified by the magic of the structure reverberating the seed of mysticism within the man. "Alchemy is the penultimate power. It comes from the mind and study, the long-earned ritual of someone who is so passionate…"

"Is he gonna monolog?" Torrents interrupted, raising his voice to drown out Khizhane. "This feels like a monolog, and it sounds like a boring one. Can we pop out and have lunch while he talks about himself and his plans?"

"Planning over ability," Khizhane spat, "training over talent, and that's what will make the difference."

"Who is this guy, anyway?" Torrents continued as if the alchemist hadn't spoken. "I've never seen him. Either of you know this guy? He seems to think he's someone important."

The alchemist's face twisted with obvious anger, and the hand resting upon the device on his belt twitched. He twisted the dial to eleven, slapped the second button on the bullet launcher wand, causing a rapid fire of six shots in sequence. He thrust his left hand forward and activated the electrical conduit.

The cloud of napalm that coated the magical protective barrier between him and the upstart interlopers rippled with streaks of lightning, then burst into a series of explosions.

The shield shattered, dissipating in a cloud of disappointment.

"Bitch," Aiyana rose to a standing position, holding the staff she'd created in her hand, "I've studied longer than your grandparents have been alive. I surpass you in study, talent, and passion. Not to mention, you're a dick."

Aiyana was an elementalist, known as a wizard or wizardess, a conduit for the powerful lines of magic and energy that follow the natural currents of the world, currents most people can't see. She knew an arcane focus, such as a carefully carved staff with magical relics and artifacts bonded to it, is another sort of focus. She also knew that a giant tower of black crystal that usurps and redirects all magical flows and energies on an entire continent is a focus that can shake the bones of the world.

Aiyana, at that moment, linked to all three things. Her mind connected with the staff she'd created, linking with it, her power reserves swelling. The ley lines lit up in her mind, showing the paths of fire, air, earth, and water as each was bent to be pulled into the tower.

And lastly, she connected with the tower.

The Monolith of Onyx was exactly as advertised, but it had a few extra bullet points and features that weren't marketed. It was a hyper-focus of energies, and could turn that power into a physical object that contained magical abilities afterwards, or to cause various other events or effects that needed substantial amounts of arcane energy.

Strands of static electricity arced from the smooth black planes of the tower behind her and touched the woman on her shoulders, knees, ankles, and other joints, connecting her with the landmark, joining her with the inanimate icon that was the direct adversary of her god, the Traveller, the Walking God.

The staff Aiyana created over the last three months shone, a dark streak running its length, and the smooth polished wood took on a darker sheen. It assumed the texture of the tower behind the aeifain, and the wizardess wasn't sure if the structure was forcing its appearance on the relic, or if the artifact was draining the texture from the monolith.

Perhaps a bit of both.

Pulling on the warm feeling coursing through her, Aiyana called upon the aura of two clashing gods, drinking in the essence to her core, and launching it forward in the same instant the priest's shield collapsed.

The arcane force shot into the alchemist, and he burst apart. Not in a bloody explosion, but into clean, precise, and neat components. Each limb, every joint, and even smaller sections of organs, blood vessels, and nerves cleanly separated from the rest of the man's form, showing him broken down to his most basic elements.

Even those items, after hanging in the air for a moment, broke down further to their next smaller level of structure. This continued, exponentially, tearing the man's existence to smaller forms and pieces, until only a blurred cloud showed the molecules being dissected into component atoms, then electrons, protons, and neutrons. Beyond that, the human eye couldn't track the dissemination of his essence.

Aiyana collapsed, falling to her knees, then to her elbows, the staff underneath her.

Nathan and Torrents rushed to her side, the rokairn looking exhausted from his own efforts in defending the three, but nothing close to what the aeifain experienced.

Only Torrents looked unaffected, and he stood over the other two while Nathan helped the aeifain to an upright position.

Steel glinted, and a large dark form darted in, the edge of a khopesh slicing across Torrents's midsection.

The barbarian danced sideways, more from instinct than intent, and spun to face the threat. His blade appeared in his hand, without him drawing it, and his over-the-shoulder scabbard fell to the ground behind him.

Gentle static danced along the superior steel of the human's weapon, small spiderweb strands connecting the weapon to the tower beyond.

"Hope this doesn't mean there're strings attached," Torrents's eyes followed the blue-white arcs back to the monolith, then he shrugged, "but, whatever. I'll deal with that bidj later."

The gnohl hunched in a feral, maddened pose in front of the barbarian. Torrents stood in a defensive stance, his blade held above his head and angled down across his face and chest, his other hand held in front and to one side, ready to slap away a blade.

Ghe'hak was blackened. Scorch marks where flesh had melted away revealed dark, chiseled scales beneath. Proof of the demonic influence on a creature that prayed to dark powers. The bond of his pack was transferred to beings beyond this realm, creating a bridge of power that spanned realities and dimensions to give his masters a path to this world.

Aiyana could barely lift her head after her effort, and Nathan called upon the protective magics of his god to shelter her.

"Finally," Torrents smiled, "something I can do. Beat down a mother-chuzzer with a sword."

His words stopped when the gnohl lunged forward, the beast's dark, carbon-scored weapon weaving a series of attacks. The big man's blade snaked in and down, then up, knocking back each attack.

The two warriors moved with instinct and skill; blades clacking off one another. Each parried blow would have killed a lesser skilled weapon master. Strength fell to dexterity, and movement became a blurred dance that tricked the eye into a frenzy of movement.

The two turned and spun, Torrents drawing the enemy further from his friends, teasing him along the walkway that circled the monolith, luring him away from the two people crouched in exhaustion.

The barbarian fell back and Ghe'hak exploded in a frenzy of aggressive attacks, pressing the advantage as the big man frantically defended. Torrents's back pressed to the smooth wall of the monolith behind him, and his two-handed great sword flared with a gentle blue light.

The big man launched into a series of counter attacks, pushing the gnohl back. Swinging in strong overhead blows, the barbarian drove his foe to his knees.

The gnohl's clawed hand shot out, tearing through Torrents's calf, making the large man fell to one knee. Ghe'hak leapt to his feet, lifting his curved blade overhead and swinging it down.

The barbarian slapped the blade to the side with his left hand. The weapon cut into the stone a finger-width to the warrior's left. Torrents thrust his large blade into the throat of the gnohl, impaling the creature. The blade broke through the spine and flesh of its neck, an arm's length of steel showing on the other side.

The man-beast pulled back, trying to twist away from the sword in his gullet. Torrents pushed to his one good leg, then turned the blade, and jerked the weapon left and right, tearing the wound further.

Ghe'hak stumbled back, the sword in his throat sliding out of the hole that poured out a black liquid that was once blood. The creature's head wobbled on his shattered neck, like a macabre mockery of a bobble head.

Torrents swung his weapon again, slicing lines into the chest and midsection of the gnohl. The barbarian limped forward, pressing his advantage, and continued to chop and hack at the beast.

His adversary stumbled backwards, weakly batting at the attacks and failing to stop them. The gnohl reached the edge of the platform and teetered.

The barbarian thrust his sword straight ahead, the gnohl trying to knock the blow aside with his shorter, thicker weapon and failing. The magical, glowing blade of Torrents the barbarian slid into the creature's chest, where the heart should have beat.

Ghe'hak dropped his khopesh, grabbed the blade in his chest with both hands, and tumbled backwards, his clawed hands slicing open, fileted to the bone. The gnohl's last breath escaped his one unpunctured lung, and he flipped heels over head into the open air beyond the platform. The body turned twice before crunching on the rocks below, landing on its neck and shoulders. It crumpled into a twisted ball, laying still.

Torrents turned back to his friends, glancing at his great sword crackling with energy, burning off the tainted liquids of the gnohl's blood and innards.

Aiyana was standing, leaning on her staff, with her other hand steadying herself on Nathan's shoulder. The aeifain was staring up at the Monolith of Onyx, the tower's magical energies sparking outwards. The pinhole portals expanded with each burst, growing larger each time they fed from the mystical power.

The silvery mist that had drained the army of soldiers in the field now surged outward, seeking more life and magic to feed the tower.

"They," Aiyana breathed, her words broken as she tried to get her breath, "started something. The monolith is hungry and tries to open the portals at the same time. One action will lead to the other purpose, coming to fruition."

"I'll do what I can," the priest disentangled himself from the wizardess, and looked at the structure, "maybe I can shield it, or something."

"No," Aiyana shook her head, "I don't think that's the way to go. I got this one."

"But," Nathan started to argue, but the aeifain's hand slid across his face and stopped his comment.

"I got this," she sighed, her voice tired.

Her eyes focused on the tower like she was listening to an echo on the wind, her attention consumed by the monument. She raised the staff, whispering to the artifact as her free hand gently stroked it.

The wind ruffled their hair, and a gentle spray of moisture hit their faces. The ground underfoot warmed, and heat rose from it, the smell of sulphur making them wrinkle their noses.

"I call upon the ley lines," the wizardess intoned, "demand and beg, plead and bargain, for the highways of blood that rule the world to draw in the power closest to them…"

"No," Torrents shouted, limping to a run and was beside the other two within a moment and a few steps.

"Wait." Nathan held his hands up and stepped between the big man and the woman.

"The power that was once yours, guided by this staff, call it home," the aeifain continued, "and turn that to the portals."

The mists that shot and twisted across the landscape jerked to a halt, turned in a tight loop, and curled back to the tower. When they reached the structure, they slid along its surface, then melted into it.

Silver rays of power burst from the base of the monolith, each one piercing a portal, and the blue apertures flared and jerked wider.

"Now, turn the portals back to the ways, to the lines, to the currents of the world." Aiyana's voice slipped from the common trade tongue to aeifain and back again, what sounded like words she might say anytime, becoming a holy ritual to change the course of history. "Feed the portals and use them to feed the ley lines to guard this world, and open the ways again so they may be traveled by those that would protect this realm and reality."

Her staff flared, the Eye of Agnew growing into a starburst, the Finger of Yender releasing the stone it held and swirling around—making Torrents think they were being mocked, because it looked like the 'whoopdie-doo' hand gesture—the crystal it held a moment before. Takoven's Rib bursting into a beveled lava appearance, and the Spine of Japria clicked as the links twisted and rearranged like puzzle pieces falling into place. The shaft of the relic, the staff that had been carved and engraved by a woman from another time and place, who'd come here and joined the dead body of an aeifain who had fought to her last breath to save a doomed world, shimmered.

The black shining surface of the staff wavered and shimmered. The wood that had changed to the shade of onyx to match the monolith of the tower changed. It began in waves, like a ripple across the staff's surface. The ring of repercussive effects like a stone in a pond. The silver color expanded, washed over the artifact, and the five separate relics fused, bonded together, and became one.

The jointed bones of the Troll Lord wrapped around the gem, linked and melded into the rib, the spine curled around the others on one end, and then burrowed into the wood of the staff on the other. A polished shine of silver crept across them, infusing itself, blossoming across each until they were one.

A single silver ring often represented the Walking God, sometimes accompanied by three magical bolts that traveled in a triangle around it. Jonath was known to have an affinity for silver, his weapons and his castle being a testament to this. The two forged a world six thousand five hundred years ago when the Walking God took on a mortal form, found Jonath, and the two together ascended to godhood.

The staff found by a northern barbarian, held by the aeifain who followed the Walking God, and blessed by the priest of Jonath reaffirmed that bond, that friendship, that love that had saved a world so long ago, and it reached out to do it again.

Aiyana raised the weapon and leaned to her left. The tip—just the tip—gently pressed against the midnight black monolith beside her, and the spot where it touched the tower shimmered.

A ripple, like a stone in a pond, traveled outward, each ring changing the tower, the black swelling and wrinkling, a silver sheen replacing it. It moved upward and outward, replacing the luster of Onyx with the shine of the friendship of two other gods.

When the ripples reached the top of the monolith, energy exploded outward. A visible wave reverberated across the land, the blue flares at the base of the tower shooting towards the skyline, and exploded, landing on the other side of the horizon, or disappearing beyond awareness.

The Staff of Aiyana hummed, then slowed, and the starburst of the crystal atop it faded, becoming dim and calm.

"It is done," Aiyana muttered, and leaned on the transformed staff. Captain Farrell landed on her shoulder, cocked his head, and looked at her lips as she spoke. "This is no longer my staff. Instead, it is now a key to the portals, to the network of doorways that span this continent and beyond. It is the Key of Aiyana, and shall protect the passages that protect this world."

## Epilogue

The winter was difficult. It came early, and it came hard. The new growth of Land's End, Tull's Swamp, and the Crescent Desert was amazing, but wouldn't be seen until spring.

The desert had creeping crabgrass that slowly found a foothold in its sands as the moisture of Tull's Swamp edged northward. When spring finally blossomed, the Pyridom of Power, renamed the Monolith of Onyx, renamed the Tower of the Paths, was surrounded by yellow-green grasses that dug deep into the sandy soil and refused to die.

Tull's Swamp migrated north, bringing grass to the Tower, and to the Crescent Desert. Within three years, the Crescent Desert would be known as the Crescent Plains, and within a dozen years a small forest would take root.

The swamp proper became a tree-strewn landscape, joining the blighted woods of Land's End as they healed and changed into a massive forest, and grew into a thriving woodland long before the desert transformed to a grassland.

Seawall City became a chaotic place, different factions vying for power, and foreign invaders attacked either to take their riches, or to make sure they never rose under the power of mages and priests again.

Even though a wizard and a priest had been key in saving the land from a new apocalypse and invasion, people didn't listen, care, or hear those facts. Rumors and suggestive reasoning were much easier to believe, and the idea that all magic was evil was easier to accept.

Years before the trees grew, and the grass crept, and months after they renamed the monolith the Tower of the Paths, three friends sat in a small inn a few blocks from Jewlnee's The Pheasant Plucker. It was a place that locals ignored, like it was outside of their awareness, and didn't exist for most.

It looked like the other structures in Durgan's Keep, in a vague way, if anyone bothered to compare it to the neighboring buildings that abutted it. It had a shingle hung that displayed a hunched man in a robe, leaning on a staff, in front of a two-story inn. The words 'The Traveller's Inn' were printed underneath the carved and painted image.

"Why did we decide this was the place we wanted to come to?" Aiyana asked, looking around at the dregs of society, who had wandered in.

"Because," Torrents's face was excited with expectation, "it wasn't here before."

"What's that mean?" The wizardess wrinkled her nose, displeased, though it was likely that anything in this place would be unable to please her since she'd already made up her mind about it. "Is it a new place, and that's why you wanted to try it?"

"No," Nathan drew the word out; his voice spoke of expectation, though in a different tone than the one the barbarian had. "It's Tucker's place. He's why we're here."

"What's that even mean?" Aiyana huffed, her shoulders bouncing as she glared around the room.

The fifteen people in the room were scattered, and looked unhappy, like they didn't know why they'd come in, and weren't sure why they hadn't left yet.

The exception was a table of three who laughed raucously. An old man coughed into his hand, his face red with amusement and gasping for breath. A short man, smaller than any adult woman, threw his hands up and his head back and howled in amusement. The third, a devilishly handsome man with dark hair and sparking eyes, smiled, though he didn't laugh out loud.

"Glad you finally made it," a voice said from between Torrents and Nathan, making Aiyana jump, and Captain Farrell shifted on her shoulder, "did the snows hold you up?

They came early, and I could see why you hadn't stopped in sooner."

"It's not like this place was here a week ago, anyway," Torrents said, looking up at the man.

The barbarian stood and wrapped his arms around the man beside the table, hugging him with an enthusiasm that made little sense to Aiyana.

"But it's good to see you, Jack," Torrents pushed the man away to look at him, still holding the man's shoulders, "you been okay, man?"

"It's Jack," Nathan leaned close to Aiyana, as if that explained anything, "this is what we've been waiting for."

"Been okay, Torrence," the pronunciation of the barbarian's name was subtly different, "but before you ask; yes, I will be asking before the night is through. I think you have a different answer for me this time, don't you?"

"Yeah," the big man said slowly, sinking back into his chair, "but…can it wait until later? I kinda just want to enjoy the night. I like Nathan and Aiyana, and really just want to relax and spend this last bit of time with them. You okay with that?"

"Of course," the man named Jack patted the furs on the barbarian's shoulder, then ran his hand back and forth in a comforting motion, "Torrence, you can spend as much time as you like with your friends. That's what life is about, or at least, what makes it worth living. Now, how about drinks? Or maybe a meal. I promise we can do more than last time. Mutton, beef, chicken, we got it all in this location."

The three ordered food and drinks; beef and beer for the barbarian, lamb and mead for the priest, and chicken and wine for wizardess. Each dined on potatoes with butter and parsley, fresh-baked buttered rolls, and split peas with ginger. Small tarts were presented for dessert. The entire night was a procession of food and a non-stop waterfall of drinks.

They ate, drank, laughed, and talked for hours. It was well past midnight when the conversation slowed, and they looked around as if realizing there were others in the building.

The place had emptied, except for the three men who laughed at the table earlier. The strangers had adjourned to the bar, and two of the three enjoyed cigars and brandy.

Torrents took the lead, and ordered the same, though he'd put down the cigar before there was two fingers-width of ash, and just enjoyed the brandy.

Nathan, on the other hand, appeared to be relishing the experience, blowing rings above him, and punctuating them with squirrel tails of smoke.

"It's been years," the rokairn sighed, "brandy and a cigar were two things that my ol' grandda used to love. He'd sit on the front porch in a tank top in the summer, or in his flannel hunting jacket in the winter, just loving the quiet peace of a good smoke and a drink. Of course, crickets and frogs were the quiet in the summer, and the gentle crunch of snowfall was what I heard in the winter. But it all made him smile. He was so relaxed in those times, and this…moment, brings me back to him, and makes me miss home."

"So," the sound of Jack's voice broke the three out of their individual reveries, "does that mean you're ready to go home?"

"Hm," Nathan sighed with a smile, looking at Aiyana, "no, not yet. But maybe soon. I had a simple life there, and I think I'd like to go back to it sometime. But there's an…allure in this world. I don't know if it's the bond of the priesthood, or the wonder of the adventure within a new world. But I think I want to stay, just a little bit longer. The trials here build character, and I think I've needed that for a long time. I've been too complacent in my other life and need this to truly appreciate what I have there."

"What about everyone else?" Jack looked at Torrents and Aiyana.

"What?" The aeifain looked confused.

Captain Farrell, who was on the table, took that moment to snatch up a bit of cheese and gobble it down.

"Do you want to go home?" Jack spaced each word with a pause for emphasis.

"Not yet," Nathan leaned back on two legs of his chair and drew on the cigar.

"No," Aiyana's voice was filled with confusion, "this world is filled with so much possibility, so many opportunities, and it has magic! I can, and already have, helped people in so many ways. Why would I ever want to leave?"

"Yes, I want to leave," Torrents's single utterance brought silence to the entire room, "but not the world. I like it here, and frankly, I miss the Kid. He got me. He understood me, and he chuzzed with me. Not in the literal sense, 'cause that would be icky. Not because he was a dude, mind you, not that I'm into dudes, but because he was an old lady. That's just weird."

Jack laughed, and it was deep and honest.

"I'd like to go find him, or her, or whatever," Torrents said over his brandy snifter. "I just want to go have some fun, and some adventures, without the world hanging in the balance of what I do. Is that okay, or do I need to punch you until you say yes?"

The three men at the bar fell silent. The muscular one without a shirt reached for his double-handed blade, that leaned against the bar, beside him. The older, grizzled man threw back a shot of whiskey using the same hand that held a cigar, then grimaced, and shot a measuring glance in the table's direction. The shortest man looked oblivious, and he flicked a peanut across the bar at the mirror behind it.

"You do you, man," Jack sighed, "but I assume you want the rest of the night with your friends and me to help you along in a few hours?"

"Nope," the barbarian swallowed the rest of his brandy, "I'll go now, and they can move forward as they like. I'll just begin moving north and west, and I'll find the Kid soon enough."

"Then say your goodbyes," Jack waved at the others who stared at the barbarian, "and I'll see you to the door."

"Bye," was all Torrents said. Standing up, he slung his sword onto his back over his cloak and tossed his satchel over his shoulder. "Let's go. I'm ready."

"This way," Jack gestured towards the back of the inn.

"I don't think so," Torrents shook his head, "I'll be going out the front, not that I don't trust you, but I don't trust you."

"Of course, understandable," Jack was all smiles, and gestured to the front door, "this way then."

Torrents moved across the floor, put his hand on the handle of the door, and pulled it open as he turned back to his friends.

"Good luck guys," Nathan and Aiyana stared in wide-eyed amazement at the open door behind the barbarian, and the big man looked confused. "What's the matter?"

"They're just surprised by what's outside the door." Jack gripped the big man's shoulder, spun him, and shoved him outside into a snow-covered tundra. "Good luck, but I don't have time to be subtle."

The unremarkable man turned back, and the door slammed closed with an artic gust of wind.

A broken smattering of applause from the three men at the bar was the only noise in the room.

"Things are about to change," Jack said, "and not for the easier. I need to know you two are ready for it, or if I should go recruit three more people."

The inn proprietor stared at the wizardess and priest with expectant eyes, and his lip quirked into a smile.

The small man at the bar giggled.

"You think I should join them?" Wanderly asked.

"You should mind your own business," Croaker Norge muttered.

"But, I could…" Wanderly pressed.

"Minding your own business is what you could do." Nomed turned back to the bar, put a hand on the smaller man and turned him, too. "This is their adventure. Let them have it without your meddling."

"Well," Aiyana shooed Captain Farrell from her wine, and looked back at Nathan, "I think we should go to Icon Hall and find out what happened to my people. Sound good?"

"Whatever," the rokairn leaned back and pulled on his cigar again, "right now, though, I'm just going to enjoy my cigar and brandy. I'll worry about the rest tomorrow."

End of Portals, Book 3

Sneak Peek of Portals, Book 4, Sigils & Satyrs

## Chapter 1

Aiyana stood on a thin rock column above the murky water of the courtyard. She glanced at Nathan, who was watching the swirling movement causing bubbles to rise to the top while swatting at the swarm of gnats clustered around him.

"Think it's something alive?" he asked.

"Dreardon Castle is rumored to be home to many things," she sighed, "all of them horrible and dangerous. I think we should assume everything wants to kill us here. That's why I asked you to make this pedestal for me."

Nathan stood on the steps leading from the gatehouse into the long-deserted ruins, the rotted doors bracketing him. He grunted, his hands gripping Marcid, his magical battle axe.

The courtyard was large enough to fit a small village, and sculptures of people going about everyday tasks stood in waist deep water. The statues were weatherworn, but the detail and care of the craftsmanship was apparent even in their deteriorated state.

Movement drew their attention. An elongated, algae-green form broke the surface, then disappeared a moment later.

"What was that?" Nathan asked. "A branch? A snake?"

"Not sure." Aiyana shrugged.

"Who builds a castle in a swamp, anyway? And then makes a sunken courtyard?" Nathan shook his head. "It was bound to get flooded, they had to know that."

"It wasn't always a swamp," Aiyana said. "When this place was the seat of power in this area, it was grasslands. But over time, the lowlands flooded and became what it is today."

"You're sure the book you need is in this place?" he asked.

"According to my research, it is." Aiyana nodded.

"And you really need this particular book? It's absolutely necessary?"

"Yes," Aiyana sighed again, "it should help me find where the Aeifain once lived. When we opened the portal network—"

The water erupted, a dozen tentacles shooting from the depths and towering above the two friends. They slammed down on the steps, writhing towards the axe-wielding rokairn.

"Okay," he grumbled, lifting his weapon, "here we go!"

Nathan swung the axe, striking one of the rubbery appendages, and the blade turned sideways, sliding along the length of the tentacle.

More of the alien arms burst from the fetid water at the base of the column Aiyana stood on, ringing her. They fell inward, collapsing around the wizardess.

Flame erupted from her crystal topped staff, and a circle of fire rose in an upward spiral.

The attacking arms twisted away and fell back into the dark waters with a splash.

Nathan backpedaled to the broken doors, stepping over fallen timbers and ducking behind the rusted portcullis that leaned against the wall.

The tentacles followed, snaking along the damp flagstones, seeking its prey.

"A swamp squid?" Nathan shouted, batting away the limbs with the flat of his axe. "Swamp octopus? A swamptopus?"

"It just wants a snack," Aiyana laughed, "and you're snack sized!"

"Fun sized, dammit!" Nathan retorted. "And I don't want anything this disgusting touching me!"

"I'll take care of it," the wizardess said, raising her staff again.

Calling out to the elements, Aiyana drew upon the ley lines of air and water, pulling in the power of nature from around her.

A chill wind cut through the cloying humidity and swept across the flooded area inside the castle walls. A thin layer of frost formed on top of the water, crackling outward from the woman.

The tentacles flailed against the ice forming around them, breaking it, and pulling back under the dark surface.

Nathan stomped from his hiding place, glaring at the retreating limbs.

"Is that going to kill it?" he asked.

"I don't think so," Aiyana shrugged. "I bet this place freezes over in the winter, and whatever that was probably hibernates or something."

"Swamptopus," Nathan said firmly. "It was a swamptopus. I've decided that's what it should be called."

"Whatever it is," Aiyana dropped from the pedestal Nathan had made for her, "it'll come back out when this ice thaws. So, we better be gone before then. On the bright side, now we can walk to the front doors of the castle without having to wade through the water."

They moved across the slick surface, Nathan using slow, solid steps to keep his balance, and Aiyana using her staff.

Nathan, always an admirer of craftsmanship, paused at a statue of a woman carrying a small child. He leaned in, inspecting the detail.

"These are amazing," he called to Aiyana, "so much fine work, right down to individual hairs in the eyebrows.

They're so lifelike that it wouldn't surprise me if they started walking around."

"That's unlikely," she called over her shoulder. "As much as they look like living people, they're just statues now."

"Now?" Nathan turned and shuffled along the ice to catch up. "What does that mean?"

"It means they're not going anywhere," Aiyana climbed the steps of the castle, "and we're here. We can discuss them later."

The castle stood open to the elements, the interior foyer littered with leaves, debris, and animal droppings. Moldy tapestries hung in tatters on the high walls, and the few pieces of remaining furniture were in similar condition.

The crystal atop Aiyana's staff flared into a blue light, casting a flickering, otherworldly glow in all directions.

More sculptures stood in the hall and the adjoining rooms, each appearing to be in the middle of some mundane task.

"We see just fine in dim light," Nathan grumbled. "That will only attract attention."

"Or keep the curious away," Aiyana shrugged. "Rats and other vermin will avoid the light. And we can handle anything that shows up."

"But we can't handle roaches and rats?"

"Nathan," Aiyana stopped and looked at the man, "we can't read in this light, and I am looking for something specific, and will need to be able to make out details to find it. Okay?"

"Yeah, fine," Nathan mumbled. "But now I can see the faces on the statues in here. They're creepy. And why does that one look terrified?"

Nathan pointed at a statue posed with one hand held in front of his face, and a sword in the other.

"It's nothing we need to worry about," Aiyana reassured him. "Let's just find this book and get back to The Citadel."

The two searched rooms until they found the library, a vast two-story room with shelves of books that filled the walls from the floor to the ceiling. Padded chairs with the stuffing torn out sat next to gnawed tables.

A podium stood in the center of the room, a dusty glass dome covering whatever was on it.

"There," Aiyana whispered reverently, "that's got to be it."

She hurried to the pedestal and wiped at the caked on grim on the glass with her sleeve. Peeking through the clean spot, she gasped.

"It's here!" she said. "The Tome of Lost Souls."

"Did you ever doubt it?" Nathan asked, watching the door, his back to her.

"Well, there was the chance that someone could have taken it."

Aiyana leaned her staff against a wood column. Moving to the podium, she held her hands above it, closing her eyes.

"Wards," she mumbled, "but nothing too bad. I should be able to disarm them."

"Great," Nathan shifted his grip on his axe, "I'm getting creeped out, and really want to get out of here."

"A powerful priest of Jonath, like you, getting scared of things that go bump in the dark? Aw, that's cute." She teased.

Mumbled arcane words cut off any reply from Nathan.

Aiyana drew upon the mind magics of her people, very different from the elemental magic she used earlier, and traced the unseen lines of protection of the enchantment surrounding the dome.

"And…" she said quietly, "here we go."

Blue sparks showered around her, and she pressed her hands through the glass. Drawing back, she pulled the thick leather and brass bound book from the encasement.

She gazed at the volume, turning it over in her hands.

"It was written by the Lost One," she said, "and they were documenting all the missing races. Not just ones that died out in wars, but the peoples who disappeared without a trace."

*Hello, child,* a voice in Aiyana's head said, *I feel your desires to find the lost aeifain city, Icon Hall. You want to open their city for the knowledge and expand the portals further.*

Unsure if she'd imagined the voice, or if it was real, Aiyana shook her head to clear it.

"Yeah, yeah," Nathan was grumbling, "I know. You've told me. And this will lead you to your people, the wondrous aeifain, because you can't remember where they lived. Can we go now?"

Aiyana turned, smiling, and pushed the massive tome into her robe. The book slid into the pocket, disappearing into a cloth cavity smaller than it.

"What was that?" Nathan whispered, going stiff. "Did you hear it?"

"I'm sure it was nothing," Aiyana whispered, moving up next to her friend, "but we can go now, anyway."

"If it was nothing," he cocked his head to look up at her, "then why are you whispering?"

"Let's just get to the standing stones so we can portal back to The Citadel," Aiyana said in a conversational volume, moving towards the door they'd come in.

A hissing, slithering noise came from the hall.

"There!" Nathan whispered. "There it is again! You had to hear it."

Aiyana stopped in her tracks.

"Did I mention the cursed queen?" Aiyana whispered.

"Cursed queen?" Nathan sputtered. "No, and don't you think you should've said something *before* we came here?"

"It's just a legend," Aiyana said defensively. "Dreardon Castle was ruled by a queen. No one remembers her name. But she wanted to be a wizardess and control the elements. In her greed for power, she slew all the priests of Jonath, sacrificing them to gain their power over stone. Same for Latress's chosen, for wind, Tarra's for water, and Torr's for fire."

"All the priests of Jonath?" Nathan gaped at her. "I'm a priest of Jonath!"

"Anyway," Aiyana continued, "she collected tomes of magic, and slew whole sects of priesthoods. The gods cursed her, sinking her lands into water and making it so anyone she looked upon turned to stone."

"The sculptures," Nathan mumbled, "that's why you said they were just statues now. They were her people before. And that's why you thought someone may have taken the book!"

"We really should go now," Aiyana stood straight and took a step forward, "if it is her, legend says she can't leave the castle. We'll be safe once we cross the threshold. As long as we don't look back."

"Looking back is what I do!" Nathan hurried to catch up to her. "Fine, but we're going to talk about this habit of yours of forgetting to tell me things later!"

The priest moved in front of the wizardess, Marcid held across his body. He leaned forward to peek into the hall outside the library.

Aiyana put a hand on his shoulder, stopping him.

"Um," she hesitated, "if it is her, maybe looking to see if it is her isn't the best idea?"

She felt him tense under her grip, his muscles hardening, becoming as hard as stone.

"She can't turn something to stone if it's already stone." Nathan said firmly.

Aiyana saw his ruddy skin shift to a pale, pebbled shade of rock.

*The gifts of Jonath,* she thought, *he can make his skin like stone.*

*Let him handle this,* the voice in her head said, *keep heading for the portal stones. That is what is important. The priest is not important compared to what you must do.*

Nathan squared his shoulders, set his feet at shoulder width, and took a step forward into the hall.

A dark shape shot from the shadows, bowling him over, and the rokairn tumbled out of sight. A snake tail as thick as a man's body, and the length of three, slithered past.

*I can't leave him*, she mentally shouted. *He's my friend!*

*Then help him, and the world, by doing what needs done*, the voice sneered. *Haven't you failed, and let enough people die? Can't you see how important your mission is? Isn't the fate of an entire race more important than one rokairn? Don't let his sacrifice be for nothing.*

Aiyana rushed into the hall, looking to the right towards where Nathan had disappeared, then left towards the exit. The dull glow of daylight seemed further than they'd traveled to get to the library.

Looking into the darkness to the right, she raised her staff, and the blue light filled the hallway.

Nathan was rolling to his feet, pushing a scaley feminine figure from atop him. The woman's lower half was reptilian, and its sinewy length was wrapping around the warrior.

Looking past his foe, Nathan saw Aiyana.

"Run!" he shouted. "Get out! I've got this. I'll be right behind you!"

Aiyana hesitated, going through what she could do to help without hurting her friend.

*Nothing*, the voice said, *you will only hasten his demise by launching fireballs, or slow his attacks if you use ice. Run, as he told you to.*

She turned and ran for the front door, calling upon the winds to move her faster.

Reaching the threshold, she turned and looked behind her.

"Kaleb triot, denal venitier!" came Nathan's rokairn battle cry from the gloomy depth of the castle.

Aiyana turned and looked at the gate in the outer wall. The summer heat had already turned the ice to slush, and tentacles were tentatively exploring the broken surface.

With a rush of anger, the wizardess pushed the power of wind and water she held and thrust it across the courtyard. The water rippled in knee-height waves, solidifying as the wind ripped across its surface. Tentacles severed, flopping and writing on the muddy ice.

She ran, her footing supported by the textured surface of the frozen swamp.

Reaching the gatehouse, she turned back to look for Nathan.

The rokairn burst through the open doors of the castle, his beard flapping and Marcid bobbing as his pumping arms matched his feet.

Aiyana thrust her arms forward, and wind rushed past her towards her friend. She spread her arms just before the gust hit him, parting the gale, and brought them back together.

Nathan ran past the wall of weather, but the creature behind him took the full brunt of the hurricane force wind, tossing the cursed queen back into the building. The wind rebounded, catching the rokairn and lifting him into the air.

Lifting the elemental power, Aiyana pulled the air current back to her, carrying Nathan with it.

The rokairn hit the steps, still running, and bolted past Aiyana and out of the gatehouse. He slid to a stop twenty paces outside of the castle wall and bent to put his hands on his knees.

Panting, he looked up at her as she sauntered towards him.

"I," he breathed, "thought I told you to run."

"I'm not very good at being bossed around," she said with a sniff, walking past him. "We should get to the standing stones."

"Why'd you stick around?" he asked, trotting to catch up.

"Thought you needed help." She smiled. "I'll always be there to lend you a hand when yours aren't enough."

"You know I can make hands of stone if I need an extra, right?" he teased.

"Doesn't matter," she shrugged, "I'll be right beside you, helping scoop up clay for you to make them with. Just deal with it."

Ten minutes later, they arrived at the standing stones, and Aiyana used her staff to open the magical doorway.

They stepped through and appeared on the grassy plain of another ring of stones.

"Another hour of walking and we'll be back at The Citadel," Aiyana said, stretching with her face held up to the sun.

"Yay," Nathan pushed a fist into his lower back, grinning as it popped, "more walking."

An arrow shaft clacked off his stony skin, followed by a dozen more that struck the surrounding ground.

"What the hell?" Nathan looked around, bewildered.

"Does this day never end?" Aiyana sighed, waving her staff in front of her and calling the wind to knock another dozen arrows from the air. "Looks like we've got an army attacking us?"

She pointed, and Nathan followed her gesture.

Dozens of humans stood in a loose cluster in a clump of trees a football field length away. They had swords and bows and were charging towards them. small siege equipment.

Two men stood apart beside a piece of small siege equipment.

"That's a ballista, right?" Aiyana asked.

"I guess," Nathan shrugged, "but I think it looks more like a trebuchet. Hold on, they're using it. Let's see if it shoots something, or slings something."

The device jerked, and a flaming ball flew in their direction. It jerked again, the top beam sliding back, then forward again, launching a second fiery projectile.

"You got the last thing," Aiyana smiled. "I'll get this one."

She raised her staff, and the wind picked up, gusting past them. Dirt flew into the oncoming men, and the flaming missiles fell downward.

The pitch and flames exploded on the ground in the midst of the soldiers, scattering them and the fire across the field.

She called upon the element of fire and water, spreading the flames, and making smoke to roil across the attacking force, providing a smoke screen.

Gesturing again, she used her mind magics to blanket herself and her companion.

"And now we're invisible to them," she said. "Should we finish them?"

"I think we've done enough for today," Nathan grunted. "Besides, between you and me, I am pretty sure we're unbeatable. We can let this one go."

## Calendar

The basic calendar is a lunar calendar. There are thirteen months in each year. There are twenty-eight days in each month. There is a new moon on the first day of every month. The first day of spring is on the Equinox.

| **Seasons** | **Months** | **Days** | |
|---|---|---|---|
| Spring | Loen | 1. | Ginof |
| | Hapok | 2. | Bestuf |
| | Axara | 3. | Midā |
| | | 4. | Therin |
| Summer | Surem | 5. | Uthr |
| | Santara | 6. | Dunwith |
| | Xaco | 7. | Lasin |
| Autumn | Harton | | |
| | Thon | | |
| | Ault | | |
| Winter | Witen | | |
| | Maleo | | |
| | Frear | | |
| Thaw | Milwen | | |

# Glossary

Aborgas: Small hamlet near Red City.

Aeifain: Willowy race of beings with almond eyes, pale skin, and slightly pointed ears. Often more advanced in arts, culture, and magic than the lesser races.

Akar Lake: Body of water near Ruger Whitley Estates.

Ault: Ninth month of the year, and the third month of the autumn season.

Axara: Third month of the year, and the spring season.

Bestuf: Second day of the week.

Bidj: A swear word meaning waste or offal.

Binaple: a fruit that grows on binaple bushes used for make red, orange, and yellow dyes.

Changing Wheel, The: The god of cyclical change who all the other gods bow to.

Chuz: A harsh swear word.

Dangrazio: Subterranean metropolis and trading post.

Dasism: A race who follow the path of elements and nature. Physically, they are slighter than humans, with olive skin, pointed ears, and almond eyes.

Dioneze City: A broken city on the eastern part of the continent run by slavers. Known for its gladiatorial ring.

Dragon Estates: An ancient castle rumored to have a dragon residing in the caverns below it.

Dargaon's Hole: Ancestral home of dragons in the Wandering Hills.

Dunwith: Sixth day of the week.

Durgan's Keep: A city-state in the far east that was founded by a rokairn and his adventuring companions.

Edgewater: Medium port town on the coast of the Sea of Seron.

Everyway: Largest city on the continent of Teurone.

Ez'rainia-fromton: City of the dead located in the Great Desert. Was the city in which Verl'zen-luk had been imprisoned before his rise to godhood.

Fate's Run: Dockside gambling hall in Tarnish. Run by a woman named Fate.

Frear: Twelfth month of the year, and the third month of the winter season.

Ginof: First day of the week.

Glass Valley: A valley made of glass in the slim desert that was formed when a stone dragon fell from the heavens.

Gray Lands: Home of the Aeifain.

Great Desert: A large desert east of the southern Rolling Mountains, which is home to Rogen the Plague and the Great Desert Empire.

Great Desert Empire: A civilization built by Rogen the Plague and his nation slaves, located in the Great Desert.

Hapok: Second month of the year, and of the spring season.

Harton: Seventh month of the year, and the first month of the autumn season.

Highest Spire: A structure that is fifty kilometers at the base and spirals upward. Doors that lead to other places in time and space are spaced every six meters. The height of this tower in unmeasured.

Hope's Hollow: A small village on the on the borders of the Black Wood and the Wandering Hills.

Humbrey: A Kingdom of thirteen houses that embodies nobility and honor.

Icon Hall: Aeifain home on the eastern portion of Teurone.

Jonath: God of justice, protection, strength, and earth. His symbol is a trident and balanced scales.

Kez'et-dual: A demon enslaved by the Troöds.

Khelikian: God of Insects.

Kord: A twisted gold wire that is the standard currency.

Land's End: A demon-ridden peninsula on the south-eastern most portion of the continent.

Lasin: Seventh day of the week.

Ley lines: Elemental energy currents, invisible to the naked eye, from which wizards can draw energy.

Loen: First month of the year, and of the spring season. It begins on the spring equinox.

Mage, Mind: Practitioner of the art of psychic magics such as body alteration, telekinesis, telepathy, etc.

Maleo: Eleventh month of the year, and the second month of the winter season.

Malvor: Duchy in the Kingdom of Trysteria, south of the Kingdom of Humbrey. Run by Duke Malvornick.

Mida: Third day of the week.

Milwen: The thirteenth month of the year, and the transition month between winter and spring.

Nine Towers of Magic: Abandoned during the Wizard Wars, this secluded and elite university was dedicated to teaching magic. Located east of the Black Wood.

Nomed: A demon-human-aeifain hybrid.

Northwood Community: The largest city in Northwood, founded by humans, dasism, and other races.

Obsidian/Onyx: God of Magic who came to power when the Talisman appeared in the sky.

Obsidian/Onyx Towers: Black towers raised by the God of Magic to distribute magical tools, goods, and weapons.

Ocean Wood: Lands reclaimed by the Dasism from humans under Kala the Black.

Olde Kingdom: A fallen Kingdom in the southern portion of the Everyway Plains.

Oracle Plain: Grasslands north of the Common Wood, east of the Slim Desert, and west of the Rolling Mountains. Home of the mystical order of the Oracle.

Pantageas: City run by mages and wizards in the northern Everyway Plains, just south of the Kingdom of Humbrey.

Paradise Island: An island created by a dead volcano. Now a refuge for pirates and seagoing folk. Run by small governments and individuals, known for its waterfalls.

Parsay Gevies: God of Luck, Chance, and Dreams. Referred to as Parsay by adults, who pray to him for luck, and as Mister Gevies by children, who pray to him for dreams to come true.

Pek: A silver coin, worth one-tenth of a gold kord.

Pemtie: A moron, ignorant, or stupid person, idea, or event.

Phaz, Day of: A day that happens once every four years. Shrouded with myth and superstition.

Promethene: Goddess of Song and Light. Her clergy is almost always women. Wife of the Walking God, Mother of Chanian and Senaria.

Pyridom of Power: A landmark on the east coast of the continent that focuses magical energies.

Red City: Run down city once plagued by lycanthropes and undead. Located on the coast of the

Red Wind: Located in the Red Plains, this city is known for its crime lords and drug trade.

Rock Crag Wastes: a rocky area geographically located west of the Great Desert and east of the southern Rolling Mountains.

Rogen the Plague: Rokairn slave master and lord of The Great Desert Empire.

Rokairn: The Stone Folk. A short, stout race known for their attention to detail, organization, and dedication to fine craftsmanship. Both sexes are known to have beards.

Rolling Mountains: An immense mountain range east of the Oracle Plain, and west of the Northwood.

Rondarius the Foul: Insane Necromancer

Royale Bay: A bay north of the Sea of Seron and east of the Everyway Plains.

Rugber Whitley Estates: A small community known for the mind mages born there.

Rumay Bay: A shanty town on the shores of the Broken Sea that was once a hub of trade before The Downfall.

Runsk: A warlord-controlled city nestled between the Grey Forest and Diaz Wood.

Santara: Fifth month of the year, and the second month of the summer season.

Sea of the Great Plague: A body of water south of the Great Desert.

Sea of Seron: A body of water south of the Everyway Plains.

Seawall City: A fortified city run by spellslingers in a military fashion, located on the east coast of Teurone on the Eastern Ocean.

Senaria: Goddess of nature, innate honor, and woodlands. Daughter of The Walking God and Promethene.

Sharp: A brass coin, with one one-hundredth of a gold kord.

Shuglak (shug-lak): Horse-sized herd creature with large round ears, a single nose horn on a flat hog-like snout, and two tusks jutting from the bottom jaw of males.

Shulyar City: Dasism name for Silver City.

Silver Castle: One-time home of the god, Jonath, who built it.

Silver City: Also known as Shulyar City, a city built by the god Jonath.

Sinking Swamp: A swamp that hides the Library of time, west of Trysteria and north of the Everyway Plains.

Slim Desert: A thin desert between Everyway Plains and Oracle Plain.

Spellslinger: A generalized term for a wielder of one of the five types of magic; alchemy, mind magic, holy, conjuring, and elemental.

Stadia Isle: A pirate island in the Sea of Seron.

Surem: Fourth month of the year, and the first month of the summer season.

Talisman: A comet that returns on a regular basis, but now is in orbit around the planet.

Tarnish: Run-down desert city on the coast of the Sea of the Great Plague.

Tarra: Goddess of water and healing. Twin of Torr.

Teurone: Continent detailed in this book.

Therin: Fourth day of the week.

Thon: Eighth month of the year, and the second month of the autumn season.

Torgoth: God of Trade and Commerce.

Torr: God of fire and combat. Twin of Tarra.

Transvartius: A wise and benevolent man sometimes known as the Traveller, the Hidden Diplomat, and disciple of the Walking God.

Traveling God, The: God of innate magic, such as mind mages and wizards. Also known as the Walking God.

Troöd: A race from another dimension, that are reptilian in features. They have two distinct species, greys and greens. The former deal in summoning magics, and the latter are chameleon like soldiers.

Trysteria: Kingdom in the northern portion of the Everyway Plains.

Uthr: Fifth day of the week.

Vallenwood: a wood harvested from Vallenwood trees that is strong and beautiful.

Velentian Brandy: A strong alcohol drink.

Verl'zen-luk: God of ritual Magic.

Witen: Tenth month of the year, and the first month of the winter season.

Wizard: Practitioner of elemental magics which tap into the energy of ley lines.

Xaco: Sixth month of the year, and the third month of the summer season.

# About the Author

Travis I. Sivart is a prolific author of Fantasy, Science Fiction, Social DIY, and more. He's created The Traverse Reality, a shared universe that connects his cyberpunk, fantasy, and steampunk worlds, with characters his readers love.

Travis I. Sivart has been writing and telling stories since he was a young child. Perhaps it was inevitable that he would call grappling with words and language a career—and loving every moment. He is privileged to share his work with a large and welcoming audience. Get in touch to discover more about his work, writing process, and future endeavors.

You can sometimes find him live-streaming the writing and editing of his latest project from his home in Central Virginia, surrounded by too many cats.

You can get a free book, and discover Travis's other series, podcasts, live-streams, social media, and more at www.TravisSivart.com.

**If you enjoyed this book…**

Please let others know by reviewing it on Amazon or Goodreads, and let others know your thoughts!

**Other series by Travis I. Sivart**

The Steampunk Cycle

An anthology of automatons and airships, bustles and beasts, corsets and curses, dandies and dastardly deeds awaits you as you explore tales of terror, mystery, and adventure.

**Portals**

Three people, drawn from our world and forced into new bodies, face dark forces in a shattered land of demons, undead, and magic. Can they overcome their own demons and save two worlds?

**Journal of a Stranger**

Time traveler Jack Tucker shares his thoughts, ideas, philosophies, and inspirations and experiences across 70,000 years of the past, present, and future in the form of his private diary..

**The Downfall**

The magical emanations of the comet, the Talisman, brought insectile horrors from the bowels of the earth, increased the powers of an insane necromancer and a shape-shifting, demon-summoning race. Can five people forced together by fate survive knowing the world is ending, and still fight to save it?

Travis I. Sivart